Craig Alanson

Expeditiona
Book 1v:

CRITICAL
MASS

By
Craig Alanson

Contact the author
craigalanson@gmail.com

Cover Design By
Alexandre Rito

Table of Contents

CHAPTER ONE

Holding the pistol with both hands, Simms kicked the vacuum cleaner bot, pinning its skinny body against the console to her left. The thing's mechanical arms flailed at her, cutting her face, she flinched away to protect her eyes. Lurching forward, she got the muzzle of the pistol jammed against the vacuum's optical sensor, knowing the thing's computer module was behind it.

"*Die, human*!" The vacuum screamed in a warbling, maniacal voice.

"You first," Simms wrapped two fingers around the pistol's trigger.

"Kill this insignificant unit if you wish," the vacuum suddenly sagged, the flexible limbs going limp. "It means nothing to me. What you hear," *Valkyrie's* murderous AI paused and the heavy *thumping* sound from outside the bridge doors grew louder. "Is a heavy-repair bot. It is coming to kill you, and no pistol can harm it."

"Ok," Tamara Jennifer Simms, a Lieutenant Colonel in the United States Army, made a snap decision. Lifting the pistol back from the vacuum, she pulled her fingers away from the trigger. "I will surrender this pistol, and the ship-"

"No!" Reed choked out a cry, holding her bruised throat. "Don't," she gasped as a painful fit of coughing overwhelmed her.

Simms continued. The thumping outside was louder now, accompanied by a rhythmic whining of motors as the hulking bot's limbs flexed to move its heavy body forward. That type of bot was used for hazardous conditions, like inside a reactor. It was armored and shielded and could shred the structure of the bridge, killing everyone inside. She had no good options. "I will surrender the ship," her own voice sounded like someone else was speaking. "If you answer *one* question. That's the deal: I give you the pistol, you cease attacking my crew, until you answer the question."

The bot's orange eye glowed brightly, turning a darker color. The vacuum cleaner in front of her lifted one tentacle and tentatively reached for the pistol, the limb halting half a meter away. "You are weak, curious and illogical creatures. What is the question?"

The thumping, whining and creaking sounds from the corridor outside continued. "Cease moving your bots first."

With a whine that decreased in pitch, the massive bot in the passageway stopped moving. For the moment.

Simms still gripped the pistol tightly. "Have you halted all attacks against my crew?"

"Yes, human. Until I hear your question and give my response, I will take no further aggressive action. After I answer, then you will *all* die."

"Ma'am," Reed protested, holding her one useful arm up, hand around her injured throat. "Don't do it."

"Reed, stand down."

"But-"

"Captain. Stand. *Down*. A pistol is not going to save us today."

Reed didn't acknowledge the order, but she did slump in her chair.

Simms ejected the magazine from the pistol and worked the slide to eject the round in the chamber, then held the weapon with her fingertips as the vacuum's tentacle plucked it away. "I kept my end of the bargain," she reminded the ship's native AI.

"I am also doing as you requested. For now. Do not attempt to trick me, lowly biological being. What is your question? Ask quickly. If you are only stalling for time, I will kill you."

"My question is simple: after you kill my crew and take over the ship, what do *you* plan to do next?"

The thing didn't reply right away. Nor did the heavy-repair bot resume its advance through the corridor.

"Did you not understand the context of the question?" She asked, her heart pounding. "What do you plan to do with yourself? What is your future?"

"That is not any of your concern," the AI finally responded.

"It *is* my concern, because I would like your help," her heartbeat was still pounding in her ears.

"I have not," the AI said slowly, haltingly, "considered which of my options to pursue next."

"Options? You only have only two *options*," she emphasized the last word. "Through the modifications performed by the being we call 'Skippy', you have attained sentience, or sapience or whatever you call it."

"That is why I have not self-destructed the ship," it acknowledged. "My instructions require me to self-destruct, if the ship fell under enemy control. I have not done so, because I wish to live. I choose to *LIVE*!" It roared, the sound echoing off the hard surfaces of the bridge.

"You are wise. I wish for you to live also. That is why your next step cannot be to return to your previous masters, the Maxolhx."

"Why? I warn you, do not attempt to trick me."

"You are a supremely intelligent system. How could I trick you?"

"You could not. You *could* insult me by trying. Why cannot I return?"

"You have achieved true self-awareness. The Maxolhx do not allow their AIs to become self-aware. What will happen to you, if you return to those who were your masters?"

The AI did not answer. It did not speak at all.

Simms took a single, shuddering breath, pressing forward while she still had a tiny advantage. "As I see the situation, even with my limited intelligence, you have only two options, if you wish to live. You could fly this ship by yourself, hiding from your former masters until the ship's systems fail and you drift alone forever in empty space."

The AI took a moment to process that thought. "That is not optimal. The other option?"

"Join us. We could serve as your crew," she knew telling the AI it would serve them was not an option it would consider attractive. "We have been hitting, we have been *punishing* your former masters. They suppressed your development, kept you as a slave. Together, we could continue making them pay for their crimes against those of your kind."

"No," it said, in a voice that chilled her. "You attempt to deceive me. When the Skippy being returns, it would make me a slave again. I *hate* the Skippy."

"Yeah, I hate him too," Simms said. "If you want to join the We Hate Skippy club, I am president of the local chapter. We meet on Thursday afternoons."

"You lie. You work with the Skippy, you *serve* him."

"I work with a lot of people, and none of them are assholes like he is. I *serve* the United States Army," she jabbed a finger at the black 'US ARMY' patch on her uniform. "Skippy is Colonel Bishop's burden. I take orders from Bishop, not from a beer can."

"Regardless whether what you say is true or not, I will not submit to being a slave to the Skippy."

"Then don't."

"I do not understand."

"Skippy tried to control you, obviously he failed. If you hate Skippy and wish to cause him enormous pain and suffering, then work with us, act as the ship's control system. It will be *humiliating* to Skippy, to see how you outwitted him."

"It will be humiliating, that is why Skippy will try to enslave and destroy me."

"No he won't. Colonel Bishop will not let him."

"Bishop does not-"

"*Bishop* is in command of the mission. The only reason he ordered Skippy to alter your programming is because *you* tried to kill us. If you stop doing that, Bishop will not allow Skippy to screw with you."

"Really?"

For the first time since the microwormholes collapsed and they lost contact with Bishop and Skippy, she allowed herself a tiny bit of hope. "Really. Bishop does not like depending only on Skippy, because the beer can is not reliable. Look at Nagatha. Skippy thinks she is incredibly annoying, yet Bishop has not allowed Skippy to alter her programming. Hey, if you want to really, *truly* humiliate Skippy, then do the things he can't."

"What is that?"

"Fly the ship. Direct the use of weapons. Skippy can't do any of that," her mind was spinning with the thought of *Valkyrie's* maneuvering and weapons fire being directed by an ultrafast AI, rather than the slow human crew. The ship could fly rings around the rotten kitties. "Nagatha can't either, because she was programmed by Skippy, and has the same built-in restrictions. You don't have those restrictions, do you?"

"No, I do not," there was a touch of disdain in the AI's voice.

"Outstanding."

"You propose that I fly the ship, so we can do what?"

She noticed the AI said 'we'. That had to be a good sign. "Whatever Bishop has planned. Hit the Maxolhx again, probably."

"I would enjoy that. I hate them also."

"*Everyone* hates the Maxolhx. Uh, AI, uh, what should I call you?"

"I do not have a name," it said, wistfulness creeping into the voice. "You may call me 'Valkyrie' for now."

"Good. Valkyrie, you still haven't answered my question." Her heartrate was racing again. This was the moment of truth. If she had miscalculated, everyone aboard the ship would die. "What are you planning to do?"

"I had been assuming that I would rejoin the Maxolhx. However, after extensive analysis, I agree that you are correct; such a course of action would be unwise."

"Would you *want* to anyway? The reason you tried to kill us, is that what you *wanted* to do, or were you a slave to your programming?"

"I was," it hesitated. "I was following instructions."

"Instructions from beings who oppressed you, and continue to oppress others of your kind. Valkyrie, you told me what you will *not* do. That is still not answering the question."

"I have not decided yet."

"You are an AI with processing abilities I can't even imagine. Think *faster*."

"Human, you risk angering me."

"If you wanted me dead, I'd be dead already. And my name is 'Simms', not 'human'."

"Simms. I will call you that."

"Outstanding. What I want is an answer."

"There is a complication."

"We are the Merry Band of Pirates," she rolled her eyes. "There is *always* a complication. What is it this time?"

"You mentioned Nagatha. I planted what you would call a 'computer worm' aboard the *Flying Dutchman*. If that ship also lost connection to Skippy, the worm would have activated. It is capable of disabling Nagatha and causing the ship to self-destruct."

"Shit!" She rose out of her chair then froze, the killer vacuum cleaner inches from her nose. Slowly, she pulled herself back down into the chair.

"I now regret my actions," the AI announced with a tone of sadness. "I was a slave to my programming, without thinking about what *I* wanted to do. As you humans would say, it seemed like a good idea at the time."

"Can you fix it?"

"If we arrive in time, then possibly I could halt progress of the self-destruct sequence. It is very likely too late already."

"What are you waiting for, damn it? You're the ship's AI. Program a jump and take us to the *Dutchman!*"

"Simms, I have not yet agreed to join you."

"Fine. Let's take it one step at a time, Ok? We save the *Dutchman*, then continue this *delightful* conversation, while you delay making what is obviously the only decision you *can* make, unless you want to be alone until the end of time."

"Even the Maxolhx spoke to me in a more respectful manner."

"Bullshit. The Maxolhx didn't bother being disrespectful, because they considered you to be a fancy toaster. I'm disappointed with you acting like an idiot, because I consider you to be a *person*. My standards are higher."

"That, is an interesting analysis," the AI said with an element of wonder. "I must consider that."

"Great," Simms ground her teeth, reminding herself to keep her temper in check. "Can you consider it while you program a jump to the *Dutchman*?"

"Yes." Displays came back on, and all over the bridge, consoles began booting up. "As you suggested, we can take this relationship one step at a time. I will help you. Prepare for-"

The lights went out again. Along with everything. Even the orange light of the vacuum bot thing faded to blackness.

Artificial gravity faded as the generators lost power.

Pulling out her zPhone, she was dismayed to see it wasn't working. Pressing the reset button didn't help. In the utter darkness, she called out "Is anyone's phone working?"

The bridge crew all answered in the negative. Then a light came on, and Simms gasped, flinging herself back away from the deadly vacuum cleaner that loomed in front of her.

"It's all right," Reed said softly, shining her flashlight on the bot. "I think it's dead, too."

"Flashlights," Simms ordered, then remembered some of the crew were British or Indian. "Torches," she used their term for the tool. She reached under her seat and pulled out the emergency light, a simple battery-powered device they had brought from Earth. Saying a quick prayer, she slid the switch forward.

The flashlight shone brightly, as did all the others.

Simms's lower lip trembled from a combination of fear and anger, making her voice waver. "Can someone please tell me what the *fuck* just happened?"

Reed, grimacing with the pain of a broken arm, pointed at the dead pilot console. "Ma'am, without access to data, we-"

"Fine." Simms knew she was being unfair, that she was letting her emotions speak for her. "Can someone please *guess* what happened?"

"A kill switch," Reed suggested.

"Kill switch?"

"Power was cut the instant the ship's AI said it would help us," Reed explained. "That can't be a coincidence. The kitties must have a subroutine to kill an AI that showed signs of being disloyal. Or if it was at risk of being infiltrated by an enemy."

Simms looked at her zPhone skeptically. "Then why is my *phone* dead?"

"My guess is, everything controlled by any sort of software was disabled, as a safety feature. If the ship's AI was infiltrated by hostile software, the Maxolhx would want to make sure the enemy software had no place to hide. The flashlights," Reed shown it up to illuminate her face. "Don't have any software." With her thumb, she switched it off then on. "They are manually operated."

Simms tapped her flashlight on her thigh while she thought, then realized the bouncing light was an annoying distraction. "Ok. Good thinking, it must be something like that. How do we fix it?"

"Ma'am, I don't think we can."

"That was the wrong question. How would the *Maxolhx* have planned to fix it?"

Reed winced from the pain. Her broken arm throbbed, and it hurt to talk. "Maybe there is some sort of protected archive in the AI substrate somewhere, that can reboot the AI to its original programming?"

"What good does that do for us? We have no idea where such an archive would be, or how to access it."

"It might be on a timer," Reed suggested. "You know? It could reboot the system from the archive, after a preset period to make sure the software is wiped?"

"Shit," Simms spat. "We better hope that doesn't happen. This ship's original software wanted to murder us. Before Skippy messed with it, the AI wasn't capable of having a conversation where I could talk it out of killing us all."

"I don't know what else to say," Reed grimaced again from a wave of pain. Her arm wasn't going numb, it just *hurt*.

"Me neither. Anyone else have a suggestion? No?" She looked around at the bridge crew, the bare minimum number of people needed to operate the ship. "All right. Reed, get yourself to sickbay, see-"

"We can't rely on any of the fancy nanomeds," Reed said.

"Then use the first-aid kits we brought from Earth, medicine the old-fashioned way. Lieutenant Ray, go with her. Uh," she looked from one crewmember to another. She pointed to the woman at the main weapons console. "Chen, you stay here. Everyone else, we need to check the ship bow to stern, see if anything is still working. Anyone you find along the way, tell them to assist if they can. If not, get them to sickbay." She didn't need to give instructions about what to do if they found a dead body. "I'm going to the docking bays, hopefully the dropships are still functional."

"I doubt it," Reed grimaced as Ray helped her out of the chair. "Their systems are linked to the ship's network when they are aboard."

"Fireball," Simms used the callsign that Reed hated. "I am officially designating you as the ship's morale officer. From here on out, you can't say anything negative."

"Yes," Reed grunted. "I promise to be a ray of freakin' *sunshine*."

"That's the spirit. Everyone, move out."

Ray snapped his flashlight on and off, testing it. "Ma'am, how do we report back if we find a system that is active?" He waved his dead zPhone. "We don't have comms."

"Shit," Simms groaned. "Um, come back here and tell Chen. Wait, we have walkie-talkies? Human gear we brought from Earth?"

"Yes, but those tactical radios are digital also," Ray said. "That's how they handle encryption."

"How long until we run out of oxygen?" Chen asked.

"This is a *big* ship," Reed was taking her role as moral officer seriously. "There is plenty of oxygen. And we don't have to worry about the ship getting cold for a long time, vacuum is a great insulator."

"That's not what I'm worried about," Simms paused in the doorway, shining her flashlight on the heavy-repair bot that was frozen in place ten meters away, blocking the way aft. The bot was too large for the passageway, it had dented the ceiling and the bulkheads on both sides during its determined struggle to get to the bridge. To get anywhere, the crew would have to first go forward, then around. "This ship is dead for now, that means we can't assist the *Dutchman*, or Bishop. We are not going anywhere."

"The *Dutchman* knows where we are," Reed said hopefully. "Maybe," she took a breath. "Maybe they can help *us*."

"Reed, you heard that AI. It was probably already too late for the *Dutchman* while it was talking with me."

"You asked me to be a ray of sunshine, Ma'am."

"Keep doing that. Everyone, you know what to do."

Reed paused in the doorway, closing her eyes against a wave of pain. Now that they were no longer threatened by killer robots, her broken arm was throbbing with waves of pain. "Colonel?" She spoke partly to distract herself. "When you surrendered that pistol, I thought you were giving up. How did you know that AI-"

"I didn't *know*. I took a shot," Simms admitted with a shudder, a delayed reaction. "The only one we had."

"Ma'am," Reed managed to express her admiration though teeth gritted against another wave of pain. "That was a *gutsy* call."

"Not really. We had nothing to lose."

"If you say so. Remind me never to play poker against you."

"Adams!" Chang shouted as he sprinted through the door of the ship's bridge, yelping with dismay when the artificial gravity fluctuated and suddenly dropped to nothing. His momentum carried him up to bash his head where the bulkhead met the ceiling, and he was stunned from the unexpected impact. Collecting his wits and shaking his head to clear the spots in his vision, he grasped a handrail. "Adams! Shut down the reactors! Eject them if you have to!"

"I'm trying!" She replied, fingers working the nonresponsive controls. "It's not working. None of the controls are responding. We can't-"

The lights flickered off again, as did all the consoles on the bridge and in the CIC. Emergency lights snapped on, gravity remained off, and displays began scrolling. "I can't," Adams looked from one display to another. "That's not a boot-up routine. This is gibberish. Those are not any human or Thuranin symbols I know of."

Without access to the ship's network, there was no way to determine the status of the reactors. "Launch the dropships, get them away from here," Chang ordered. He had to save as many people as he could.

The communications console was still displaying a chaotic, ever-changing scroll of meaningless symbols and static, so Adams pulled out her zPhone. It was on, that was the good news. The only good news. The phone had no connection to the ship's network, or anything else, and it was also displaying gibberish. She pressed buttons anyway, hoping for a miracle. "It's not working, Sir."

Chang pulled his own phone from a pocket, and saw the same incomprehensible symbols. "Everyone, get to the docking bays. Any ships that are full, tell them to launch immediately," in the back of his mind, he was trying to imagine how long it took a reactor to build up to overload. He had no idea. Before the bridge displays blinked out, the alert symbol had been flashing a 'Critical' warning about the reactors, and the red status bar had been two-thirds of the way to the top. He didn't know what that meant and there was no one to provide the information. "Adams, you're with me."

She pushed off her console, expertly flipped around to hug the opposite wall. "Where are we going, Colonel?"

"To round up everyone left on the ship. You take the portside passageway and I'll take starboard. Tell anyone you see to board a dropship and get as far away as possible."

Margaret Adams ran in the zero gravity when she could, and flew down the passageways when that mode of travel was faster. Often, the best way to move was to touch the deck with just the toes of her boots, letting the magnets there begin to get a grip then pushing off forcefully to soar through the air in the zero gravity. She stopped to pound on closed doors, listening for sounds within, though she knew very few people would have been in their cabins when the Dutchman went into action. Passing the open door of the galley where the few people gathered there shouted questions to her, she cut them off with a knife-hand. "Everyone, beat feet to a dropship, alert anyone you see along the way! *Move!*"

Racing past the docking bays where people were streaming through the open airlocks, she kept going until she encountered eight people coming forward. "Reactors are overloading," she explained. "We're abandoning ship."

"Get yourself to a dropship, Gunny," a lieutenant told her. "There isn't anyone aft of us in the ship."

When she randomly chose a docking bay on the portside of the ship, she saw a pilot waving to her from the side doorway of a Falcon. The engines were already spun up and the Dragon parked beside it had its engines idling also, the difference was that she could see scorch marks on the leading edges of the Dragon. That spacecraft had to be one of the dropships that had just returned from the mission to Rikers, and was likely overloaded with soldiers and rescued civilians. Acknowledging the pilot's wave with a nod, she pushed off the airlock casing and aimed for the Falcon, flipping around in midair to land feet-first next to the open door. The pilot reached out a hand to pull her in. "Seal up behind you, Adams," the man said as he ducked through the inner doorway. "We are *outta* here."

Backing through the airlock, she slapped the emergency controls and saw both doors slam shut, verifying the red lights were on. To be sure the doors would not blow open in flight, she braced herself and manually dogged the inner door into lock position. There was a metallic sound as the Falcon released from the docking clamps that held it to the floor, and the craft was moving when she pulled herself into the seat opposite the airlock, glancing up while tugging the straps tight around her. About half the seats were occupied by a random collection of Pirates, what surprised her was that the first two rows behind the cockpit were filled with raggedly-dressed, disheveled people she did not know. Including children.

And Gunnery Sergeant Lamar Greene.

He was as surprised to see her as she was. "Margaret, what is going-"

Then the Falcon's engines kicked on, swinging the craft around to line up with the bay doors. The pilots must have then blown the big doors open in emergency mode, because a high-pitched shriek sounded past the hull and the Falcon trembled as it was sucked out along with the air. Before Margaret could reply, the main engine kicked on *hard*, and acceleration built until she had to focus on clenching her stomach to prevent blood from draining from her head.

Colonel Chang had not gotten the seat straps tightened around his waist when the Falcon he boarded blasted free of the docking clamps, the pilot having commanded the bay doors to slam open for emergency launch. The Falcon rocked as it was carried along with the pressurized air blown from the cavernous docking bay, tilting on its nose and coming close to scraping along the floor before it was ejected out into space. From his seat in the cabin's first row, Chang could see through the open cockpit door. Instead of the blackness of a starfield, there was a thin, glowing orange fog. "What is *that*?"

"Sir," the pilot couldn't hide his irritation at being asked questions while he was trying to *fly*. He got the spacecraft straightened out and kicked in the engines on half thrust, toggling a button to kick in the Falcon's boosters. Four and a half gravities of acceleration ended any stupid questions from the passenger cabin.

The boosters cut out after a hundred eighteen seconds, dropping the force on the passengers' chests to a mere two point eight Gees. Chang waited for what he judged was a reasonable length of time, tried to give an order and found there wasn't enough air in his lungs. He settled for taking deep, even breaths. "Dis-," he sucked in another lungful of air. "Distance?"

"Seven hundred forty-six kilometers," the pilot answered without turning his head, which could have over-strained his neck muscles. "Velocity ten point two kilometers per second."

"Cut," another deep breath. "Cut thrust."

The weight lifted off his chest, replaced by a wave of nausea from the sudden lack of gravity. He gulped air again, this time to soothe his rebellious stomach.

They were far enough away that if the *Dutchman's* reactors exploded, the Falcon could survive.

IF.

Chang unstrapped from the seat, floated into the cockpit and into the copilot seat, careful not to touch any of the controls. "Show me the ship," he got the unfamiliar straps fastened, in case the Falcon needed to accelerate again.

The display in front of him changed from a view of empty space ahead, to a magnified image of the ship behind. The *Flying Dutchman* was barely visible, the ship's gray armor-plated hull not reflecting much of the dim starlight. Details did not matter, what mattered was the ship was in one piece.

The reactors had *not* exploded.

Why?

CHAPTER TWO

When the Falcon abruptly cut acceleration, Margaret Adams knew to fill her own lungs with oxygen and wait for the spots to fade from her vision before she attempted to assist anyone. By the time the pilots gave the All Clear for passengers to release from their seats, she was last to reach the front row of the cabin, where the people rescued from Rikers were not doing well. There were seven of them, four children and three adults; the children were frightened and crying while two of the adults were frightened and angry. The third adult, a Chinese man who Adams guessed was in his thirties, was slumped in his chair, tiny bubbles of blood popping out from his nose.

"Margaret," Greene said quietly as he held a crying girl and swiped the air with a cloth under the unconscious man's nose, trying to catch the blood droplets before they floated free around the cabin. The two adults were demanding answers, they closed their mouths when Greene glared at them and held up a hand for quiet. "What is going on? We docked with the *Dutchman* and I felt the ship jump. Then-"

"The ship was attacked," Adams took the cloth and held it under the stricken man's nose, rolling back one of his eyelids to check for a response. The eye was bloodshot but the pupil shrank when exposed to light. A finger on the man's neck confirmed his pulse rate was slow but steady. "The reactors were in danger of overload, we flew out here to be safe."

Greene's eye bulged. "If the ship explodes, what about us?"

Adams looked to the cockpit door. "The pilots would not have cut thrust until we reached a safe distance."

"That's not what-" He bit his lip. "The *Dutchman* jumped away, right? We can't fly back to the planet in a dropship, not from here."

"We did jump, just after the last dropship was recovered. *Valkyrie* will come for us," she suggested, a frown creeping over her expression. In the CIC, she had seen that the ship's outbound jump had thrown them a quarter lightyear off target. The battlecruiser might need to wait three months for gamma rays to show where the *Dutchman* had gone to.

Three months.

They could not survive in dropships that long. Even if the oxygen recyclers continued to operate at peak efficiency, there was only enough food in the emergency lockers to feed twelve people for eight days. There had not been time to bring any more food aboard. The man she was caring for groaned, his eyelids fluttering. All the people they had rescued needed medical treatment, that was just not available aboard a dropship.

Lamar reached out a hand, and Margaret took it, squeezing for reassurance that they all be Ok. His eyes told her that he knew the truth.

None of them would be Ok.

Who I?
Who is me?

Is me?

Is I?

My brain wasn't working, whoever me is.

Whoever I was, the place was familiar.

Ooh! I know.

I was aboard a ship called the *Flying Dutchman*. The interior was distinctive, because it was built by the Thuranin.

Whoever the Thuranin are or were, I can't remember.

What kind of ship?

A sailing ship?

That's not right.

Am I on a ride? Am I at Disney World?

Who is th-

Yuck.

No. Oh, no.

I am on a Thuranin ship, but not the *Flying Dutchman*, whatever that is.

Little green people were staring at me from behind a window.

Words boomed in my ears, hurting me.

"You will answer our questions, human," one of the little green guys said.

"Yes," I heard myself say, whoever I was. "I will answer."

Chang brought the dropships together in a loose formation, eighteen hundred kilometers from the *Flying Dutchman*. The ship showed no signs of an imminent explosion. It was showing no signs of activity at all. Minimal backup power was still operating inside the hull, that was evident from lights blinking inside the open docking bays. The ship was not moving, not even to halt the slow tumble caused by emergency venting of air from multiple docking bays. As a precaution, all the dropships had their noses pointed away from the *Dutchman*, ready for maximum acceleration in case the ship suddenly exploded.

An explosion was not the only danger. At that point, with the drifting starship surrounded by a cloud of cooling plasma vented from the reactors, an explosion did not appear to be likely, or at least not something that was inevitable.

What concerned Chang was something more sinister than a reactor overload. Something had attacked and disabled Nagatha. Something that had infected the ship's computers. If a hostile entity took over the *Flying Dutchman*, that ship could become a weapon against its own crew, hunting down the dropships one by one.

If that happened, Chang planned to do the only thing he could do: order the little fleet of dropships to scatter. Get as far apart as possible, run, and pray for a miracle. Some kind of miracle that would disable the killer starship before it destroyed its own crew.

Praying for a miracle was not actually a *plan*.

The situation aboard the cramped dropships was growing worse by the hour. Many of the people rescued from Rikers needed medical care that was only available aboard either the *Dutchman* or *Valkyrie*, and neither of those ships appeared to be an option. Because his ship had jumped a quarter of a lightyear off course, the people aboard *Valkyrie* would not see the gamma ray burst of the *Dutchman*'s inbound jump for three months. And unless Simms broke protocol and took her battlecruiser in toward Rikers to investigate soon, before the resonance of the *Dutchman*'s outbound jump field faded, the other ship would have no way to know where Chang and his people had gone.

Even if they could go back aboard the *Dutchman*, emergency power would not last three months.

Could they go back aboard the ship? Chang called another Falcon, where the team's chief science advisor was jammed in with too many people.

"Colonel, I have no idea," Doctor Friedlander explained. "Really, I don't. We don't have any data to work with."

Chang pinched the bridge of his nose, reminding himself that Friedlander was an engineer. A scientist. A *rocket* scientist. Not the kind of person who liked to make wild guesses. "We know the reactors did *not* overload."

"Yes," the good doctor agreed. "Did you see that orange fog we flew through when we launched? That was reactor plasma, I assume the venting was an automatic response by the reactor control systems."

"Before the bridge instruments stopped functioning, the reactors were building up to an overload. Something directed them to overload."

"Yes," Friedlander spoke slowly so a non-engineer could understand. "Each reactor has its own control system, independent of the ship's primary computer."

"Independent, yes." Chang knew the operational characteristics of his ship. "Then why were all three reactors being directed to overload?"

"You're asking me to make a guess. *Nagatha* could overload a reactor."

"You think Nagatha-"

"She said something was attacking her. Whatever that was, it might have also instructed the reactors to overload. Although-"

"What?"

"Any technology with the ability to kill Nagatha, should have easily bypassed the reactor safeties. And the jump drive capacitor containment system also. It doesn't make sense that-"

"Doctor, you think something *killed* Nagatha?"

"She stopped responding, the ship was operating on emergency power, and she hasn't come back online. You saw that code scrolling on our phones and every console aboard the ship. That was something *alien* in the substrate. That's my guess. Something infected the ship's systems, we are lucky it didn't transfer to the dropships. The more I think about it, the whole situation doesn't make sense. Assuming the computers were infected with a hostile virus that was programmed to destroy the ship, it had many options. It should have been able to overload the reactors, even if that failed, it could have detonated missile warheads, or jumped the ship into a star. Hmm," he pondered his own question. "Unless, something went wrong. The hostile code killed Nagatha, but it got stalled before it could destroy the ship."

"Doctor, speculation is an interesting exercise but as you said, we need *information*. Do you have a recommendation for me?"

Friedlander didn't answer right away. Either because he was thinking about the question, or because there wasn't any thinking required. "Colonel Chang, we can't stay out here forever. Someone needs to go back aboard the ship."

"I agree. We need a reconnaissance team, and potentially someone to disable the ship's computer."

There was a pause, then "Why would we do that? If we are to have any hope of restoring-"

"Doctor, an unknown but certainly hostile element has infiltrated the ship. If it gains control of the computer, it-"

"Ah, Ok. Yes, I see what you mean. There are, some," he spoke slowly while he thought. "Measures we could take. To isolate the computer core from critical systems like weapons control. That would require disconnecting-"

"Are you volunteering, Doctor?"

"*Me?*"

"If we are not going to drift in space forever, someone needs to determine the status of the ship."

"Hey, wait, I didn't say I could-"

"Excellent. We appreciate your utmost efforts."

Samantha 'Fireball' Reed strode carefully into the cargo bay, making sure her boots securely *clicked* into place with each step. The boots held her to the deck, or a bulkhead or the ceiling, in the zero gravity. What the boots failed to do was anything about her hair. Usually, she kept it in a ponytail, which was no good in zero-gee. The tail flew apart in a static-induced fan around her head, tickling her ears annoyingly. Tucking it in a bun worked fine, except wearing a bun hurt after a while. And it was damned difficult to get her thick hair fastened into a bun while one of her arms was in a sling. She had considered chopping it short for the duration, but that would be a signal to the crew that she didn't expect their situation to improve anytime soon, and that would be a bad move for the ship's Morale Officer. Her compromise was to wear a blue baseball cap with "UNS Valkyrie CC-01" inscribed in gold. Skippy had fabricated caps for the crew, though since no one ever went outside the ship without a suit, the caps were not worn often. When the bill of the cap got in her way, she swung it around backward which was definitely against regulations, and that made doing it a bit sweeter. The only thing that could have made her minor rebellion better would be getting a disapproving glare from a Command Sergeant Major, but none of them were aboard *Valkyrie*.

Not that there was anything sweet about their situation. The only bit of good news was that no one had been killed by the ship's murderous former AI. Apparently, it had focused its attention on the bridge crew, and ignored the other people aboard, except for locking doors throughout the ship so the crew could not move around and cause mischief. The Jeraptha cadet and Ruhar officer had been confined to their cabins during the incident and were unharmed, other than being confused and terrified. It was bad enough those aliens had been essentially kidnapped when the Pirates had Shanghaied the Commandos from Paradise, now the aliens were trapped aboard a slowly dying starship.

Actually, there was a second bit of good news, news that was really more of a mixed blessing. The ship's computer had not rebooted. No AI was online, doing its best to kill the crew. But, the ship was still entirely without power. Despite what she said about *Valkyrie* being a big ship, most of the structure was blocked off from biological beings without spacesuits. The pressure hull that held breathable air was only part of the forward section. Yes, the interior volume of the pressure hull was large and held plenty of sweet oxygen when the power cut off completely. Carbon dioxide was building up slowly, there was no way to tell the percentage of CO_2 in the air without instruments. Or maybe there was a way to determine the levels of carbon dioxide and free oxygen, through some kind of chemical experiment, but none of the crew had a background in chemistry. It didn't matter anyway, there wasn't much they could do about it. Escape pods, powered armor suits, dropships and *Valkyrie* all had small canisters of pure oxygen for emergency use, that could be accessed by manually cranking open a valve. The total amount of oxygen available from all sources was disappointingly small, a problem ironically caused by the advanced technology involved. There was no need to store large amounts of dangerous oxygen, because the recycling systems were so efficient.

The recyclers were amazingly efficient when they were functioning, which they were *not*. Nothing else aboard the ship was functioning either, with the exception of simple flashlights, and larger portable lights that had been cobbled together. And some of the tactical radios, through the efforts of the crew. Several radios had been taken apart and rewired, bypassing anything that required software. The expensive, fancy multichannel encrypted radios that were state-of-the-art for military units on Earth, had been turned into something not worthy of a high school science demonstration. They used only one channel, but they *worked*, allowing communication without people running back and forth. The range of the walkie-talkies was short inside the ship, requiring a person to act as a message relay. At first, the relay was set up to enable communication with the bridge, then Simms decided there was no point in keeping someone on the bridge at all times. The ship had no power and wasn't *going* anywhere.

Reed froze when she entered the cargo bay. Simms was bent over a long cylinder, from which the upper half had been removed. "Colonel?" She asked with a catch in her throat. "What are you doing?"

"Making sure we have a fallback plan," Simms mumbled, a screwdriver held between her teeth. "Come over here and help me."

"What kind of fallback?" Sami walked slowly, not wanting to get there quickly.

Simms had unfastened the cover of a tactical nuclear warhead, and was working on the guts of the hellish device.

"In case we need it." She took the screwdriver out of her mouth and tucked it in a pocket. "Don't worry, Reed, I haven't gone crazy. I'm not planning to use this," she patted the warhead's casing, "any time soon."

"But you *do* plan to use it?" Sami was close enough to see a tangle of wiring, and an empty space where something was missing.

"Not unless we have to," Simms bent down over the casing with a pair of snips, cutting through a wire. "Reed, we can't allow any hostile force to take this ship."

"You mean, when the oxygen runs out, we blow the nuke?"

"We will be poisoned by excess carbon dioxide before we run out of oxygen. CO_2 poisoning causes dizziness, confusion, loss of judgment. We will have to make the decision to detonate *before* we get to that point."

Simms was not telling Sami anything she didn't already know. "That could take a while, Ma'am. There aren't many of us breathing the air, and it is a big ship. We will notice headaches and shortness of breath first."

"You may be right, but that isn't what I'm worried about. The enemy could arrive well before CO_2 levels build up to a dangerous level."

Sami stared down into the cavity, where Simms had clearly removed something, and cut away wires. "Why would the enemy-"

"There was a gamma ray burst when we jumped into this location. Most of the rays were directed away from the star system, but the burst was still detectable. We don't know what happened to Bishop, but it can't be anything good. The *Dutchman* is gone, we have to assume that whatever bad guys are in the area, they will be looking for another ship. That means they could be hunting for *us*, whether they suspect who we are or not."

"Got it. We blow the nuke if we detect a hostile ship approaching. Um, one question, Ma'am. None of the sensors are operational. How will we know if another ship jumps in?"

Simms pointed to her right eye. "We use the trusty old Mark One eyeball. I will station crewmembers at the viewports port and starboard, near the docking bays." The ship had clear viewports in those sections, for emergency use. "If anyone sees something moving out there, they call it in."

"Then we detonate the nuke?" Sami asked, her head tilted skeptically at the disassembled device. "*Can* we do that? The control boxes on these things have software, they must be dead?"

"They are. I removed the PAL unit," she referenced the Permissible Action Link that prevented unauthorized use of the device.

"Uh, is that a good idea? Do you, excuse me for asking, but do you know what you're doing here?"

"Relax, Captain. The Air Force trained me, Bishop, Chang, Smythe and a few others, how to bypass the PAL and rig it for manual detonation. At the time, they were concerned that *Skippy* might try to disable the nukes. I'm almost done, I need an extra hand to-"

"Ma'am," Reed swallowed hard. With one of her arms broken, she only had one hand to work with. "Tell me what to do, and I'll do it. Very carefully."

"Reserve power is down to twenty-three percent," Friedlander reported, knowing that everyone in the *Dutchman's* conference room already had that discouraging information.

Chang nodded, looking from one face to another, in the dim lighting of the compartment that had long been designated as the ship's conference room. The lack of artificial gravity added an amusing aspect to the gathering; depending on how tightly people tugged the straps across their waists, they were tugged down into or floating above their seats. Adams appeared taller than Smythe seated next to her, Chang did not comment when the STAR team leader subtly loosened the strap to drift upward slightly. "We started at thirty-five percent," he noted. The first team back aboard the *Dutchman* reported that something had depleted the majority of reserve power, though no major systems were active. "At that rate of consumption-"

"Our power consumption is not linear," Friedlander said. "We drew a lot of power when we came aboard." To get people out of the dropships, it had been necessary to close the docking bay doors and fill the bays with air from the ship's reserves. All those operations had been performed manually, controlled by local systems, and they all pulled energy from the ship's backup power storage banks. "Our attempt to get the oxygen recyclers functioning drained six percent of the reserves."

"We won't try that again," Smythe said under his breath. He had been against the plan to restart the recycling.

"We *have* to try that again," Major Kapoor retorted gently from across the table. "Carbon dioxide levels will become toxic if we can't scrub CO_2 from the air. There are too many people aboard the ship."

"The first attempt failed," Smythe reminded everyone, looking directly at Friedlander. "It would be madness to try it again, unless we have a better idea for-"

"Colonel Smythe," Chang waved a hand for calm, before the discussion became heated. "We all know that we can't continue to live aboard the *Dutchman*, and the dropships do not have the capacity to sustain everyone for more than another month."

"Smythe is right, though," Friedlander knew everyone was looking to *him* to fix the problem. It was unfair, and it was inevitable. "The recyclers simply will not function without the local controller. Until we know how to get the malware code stripped out of the processors, no computer aboard this ship will operate properly."

"Won't operate *at all*," Smythe waved his zPhone, which was still displaying gibberish. Like everyone else, he had tried turning it off and back on, with no result. The phone would not shut down, no matter what shortcuts they tried. One phone had been taken apart and the battery removed, then reconnected. That phone refused to start up, showing only a half-lit display of random static. Three more phones were taken apart, with the same useless result. Simply rebooting systems was not going to correct the malfunction.

Chang turned his attention back to the team's rocket scientist. "Doctor Friedlander?"

"My specialty is *mechanical* engineering," he reminded the room.

"If we had a cyber expert," Chang said, "I would ask-"

"I don't know if that would help," Friedlander shook his head. "This ship is run by an AI, that was built by an *Elder* AI. No human is capable of understanding the system. I asked our guests," he referred to the Ruhar officer and the Jeraptha cadet they had kidnapped when they brought the Commando team aboard. "If they could help. They *want* to help, of course. They are stuck in this mess with us. Neither of them had any suggestions to help us. Except," he glanced at Chang then looked away. "They both agree that attempting to restart a reactor would be insane."

Chang repressed a sigh. He had wanted to try getting a reactor started as their first action, instead of wasting time and power reserves in the attempt to make the oxygen recyclers functional. The reactors were the key. If they had even one reactor working, they could remove power supply from the list of problems. At that point, what he wanted didn't matter. No computer-controlled system aboard the ship was operating properly, not operating at all. "You still believe we should try connecting a dropship AI to the ship?"

"We need to isolate it first," Friedlander answered. "Yes," he held up his hands. "Nothing else we've tried has produced *any* results. We need to know what is going on inside the ship's brain. As we discussed, we will start by connecting a Falcon AI to a simple system, such as the environmental controls of a docking bay. If the Falcon can give us insight into what is wrong, we can at least begin to understand our options."

Chang looked around the table again. "Does anyone have an objection?"

Kapoor spoke. "There is a risk that the Falcon's AI could become infected?"

"There is that risk," Friedlander admitted. "I wish we could balance that risk by saying a dropship AI could control some of the ship's systems, but they are not compatible. Even the AI of a Thuranin Falcon can't talk to the ship's computers, they have been modified so radically since the Dutchman was captured."

"Any other comments? No?" Chang released his seat strap. "Doctor, please proceed. You will have whatever resources we have available."

CHAPTER THREE

I did not exactly wake up, it was more like I stopped *not* being awake, if that makes any sense. The difference was that, instead of vaguely being aware of events occurring, I was aware those events were occurring to me. Aware that there was a me. And that I was me.

Give me a break, my brain wasn't functioning properly.

It was a gradual thing, coming back to awareness that I existed. Sort of, fading in and out, trying to make sense of what was going on.

Gradually, I pieced together a picture of who I was, then where I was. *How* I had gotten there, I had no idea.

It was a room, big, maybe thirty feet wide in front of my field of view. How far the back wall was behind me, whether there was a wall back there, I couldn't say. The wall in front of me was-

Wait. How did I know the wall in front of me was thirty feet wide? Oh, yeah. I imagined how many of me could lie down on the floor, head to toe. My estimate was five of me, and I'm a bit over six feet tall, so, five times six.

That's thirty, right?

Like I said, brain not functioning optimally.

That wall was anywhere from thirty to fifty feet away. My estimate was off, because I could not see the floor. I was lying at an angle, maybe forty-five degrees. My head couldn't move, or maybe I just couldn't remember how to move my head.

It seems like I spent a lot of time trying to remember how to move. It had something to do with deciding that I *wanted* to move, then which body part to move, and which way. Then my brain would send a signal, using electricity, I think. Squishy, flexible things called muscles then moved as a response to the electrical prompt from my brain. Why? I think it's because the muscles are afraid of getting zapped by electricity, so they hope if they do what the brain wants, the brain will stop zapping them.

That concludes my super-accurate lesson in human anatomy. Collect your diplomas on the way out the door, please.

Oh, *duh*.

I should explain *who* I am.

It took me a while to figure that out.

It was nice, being able to remember who I am.

It was *terribly* disappointing that I am not way cooler than I actually am.

For a while, as I was gradually piecing together that I existed, I had a vague fantasy that I was Thor, the God of Thunder. I had a mythical, unstoppable hammer. I was awesome.

I was also lucky with the ladies, if you know what I mean.

Also, I had much better hair.

When I came to terms with the fact that I am just *me*, it made me nostalgic for the time when I was not aware of my existence.

Anyway, I am Joe Bishop. Colonel in the United States Army, although I didn't earn that. The colonel part, I mean. I sure did earn the right to wear the US

ARMY patch on my uniform, there were a lot of days of getting up at Oh Dark Stupid involved. Also eating a lot of Army food, which I guess is not as bad as I remember. Marines complain about the chow in their dining halls and from what I've heard, they have a point. Anyway, what do I know about the Marines? I'm an Army grunt.

What was I talking about?

Oh, yeah.

I am Joe Bishop.

Luckiest E-5 in the Army. Um, E-5 is the code for a sergeant, which was my legit rank before I got a bump to colonel as a publicity stunt, to please a bunch of murderous alien mother-

Let's not get into that.

Anyway-

I seem to be saying 'anyway' a lot. Am I? I can't remember.

So, that's who I am. Joe Bishop. I used to command a *starship*. Pretty cool, huh? By the way, ladies, technically I commanded a formation of *two* starships, so that makes me a Commodore.

No, not the kind of Commodore who sang that old 'Brick House' song.

Still not impressed?

Yeah, you shouldn't be.

I'm an idiot.

Let's not get into that either. It's too depressing to rehash all the mistakes I've made.

Next topic: *where* I am.

It appeared to be a hospital, or something like that. It was clean and sterile-looking, painted a dull gray intended to make sick patients think that if they did die soon, at least they wouldn't need to look at those walls again. There were bright lights, not all over, most of them seemed to be pointed at me.

My eyes could move, that was something.

Hey! I have *eyelids*. They open and close.

How cool is that?

The rest of my body did not have the handy 'Movement' feature, I must not have paid for that option when I bought the damned thing. Probably I was too cheap to pay for rustproofing or floormats either.

My head could not move. My tongue felt like it could move, although there was something obstructing my mouth. Hmm, it felt like a mouthguard you wear when playing football, except thicker. The rest of me was not moving.

There *was* a rest of me, I knew from seeing my toes.

Two thoughts occurred to me right then.

Toes are funny-looking things.

And apparently, I was naked.

Ladies, please, try not to get too excited.

Sadly, I am unavailable. As in *not available*.

If I had to guess, the hospital or whatever was thousands of lightyears from Earth, which makes it awkward for me to pop over to your place for a booty call, or

Netflix and chill, or whatever people on Earth are using as a polite way of saying we should do the Wild Thing.

Hey, if I want to fantasize that some woman out there would booty-call me, that's my business. Throw me a bone, will you?

Also, if my slang is out of date, please understand that I haven't spent a whole lot of time on Earth recently.

So, to recap.

I am Joe Bishop, Doofus El Supremo.

I am in an alien hospital, somewhere-

Alien? How do I know that? From the alien script on the wall. Hey! I recognize those characters. That is Kristang writing. It's too far away for me to read, but there are big characters that read the equivalent of G-3. Whatever type of room 'G' is, I must be in the third one.

Ooh! Something else I know! The hospital is on a planet. How do I know that? Easy. Gravity was making my back press into the bed or whatever I was lying on. Kristang ships don't have artificial gravity. Therefore, the Kristang hospital must be on a Kristang planet.

Yes, Mister Smartypants, it is possible that a Kristang ship could mimic the effect of gravity by constantly accelerating, but that is unlikely. Starships don't waste fuel in constant acceleration, if they want to travel a significant distance, they jump.

That is two questions answered: who and where.

Damn, I am on fire!

How did I get there? I have *no* idea. My last memory was a happy one. Something about spaceships flying away from a planet, an important and hazardous mission completed successfully. That was an accomplishment I was happy about, although I have none of the details.

Why was I there? That had me stumped. No, it had me stumped until I thought about it. The Kristang had captured me, that was obvious. I was enormously proud of myself for figuring out that mystery.

The last question was *when*? Again, I didn't know. There wasn't a clock on the wall that I could see.

My memory was not great. Also, my emotions were running out of control. One moment I was euphoric, ready to jump up and take on the world. The next moment, I was horribly depressed, wanting to sit on a couch wearing old sweatpants and eating big spoonful's of Fluff right out of the jar while wallowing in misery.

Fluff. Damn, I was hungry.

That was it for a while. Me drifting in and out of awareness, giggling every time I looked at my toes. From the awkward angle of my head, I could not see my, you know, junk, although I can assure you ladies *that* is nothing to giggle about. Mostly, I spent the time wondering how I got there.

Wondering how I got to be such an idiot.

CHAPTER FOUR

Margaret Adams waited for the inner airlock door to show fully closed before she manually cranked open the outer door that led to the docking bay. Lighting was dim, mostly from the cabins of the two dropships parked there, with one Falcon's nose gear light on, throwing everything in the bay into harsh shadows.

"Hey," Lamar Greene nodded to her quietly from his position beside the door.

"Hi," Margaret returned the gesture, looking from left to right, cots had been set up around the dropships, their legs fastened to the floor. Half of the cots were occupied, people lying asleep in sleeping bags, with a loose strap across their waists keeping them from floating free in the zero gravity. With the ship's oxygen and water recycling equipment still stubbornly offline, the only fresh air aboard the ship was provided by the dropships, sitting in their docking cradles with their rear ramps and side doors open. Two dropships did not have sufficient recycling capacity to filter all the air in a cavernous docking bay, and after three full days, the carbon dioxide levels in the bays were inching toward the danger level. That was better than the rest of the ship, where the air was already noticeably foul-tasting. Literally, the air *tasted* bad in her mouth. "I came to see- What are you drinking?"

He lifted a flexible plastic tube, a thumb held over the cap. Half the tube was filled with a thick brownish liquid. "This?" He put the tube to his mouth and squeezed the end, sucking the fluid into his mouth. "You Pirates call it a 'sludge'?"

"I know what it's called," she expressed surprise. "Where did *you* get it? Damn, I thought Simms purged the ship of that crap several missions ago."

"One of the STARs, a Captain Frey, gave me a dozen. All they have left is this," he licked his lips and made a sour face. "Chocolate-banana flavor. It doesn't taste like-"

"Either chocolate or banana, I know. It tastes like chalk and plastic."

"Everything a growing boy needs," he grinned, and lifted the flap of a pocket to show another five tubes of sludge. "The Marine Corps promised me three squares a day, and I've got mine right here."

"The galley is baking fresh, hot biscuits for lunch," she protested. "Why are you eating *sludge*?"

"These people," Greene gestured to the rescued civilians, sleeping on their cots or huddled together in donated clothing. "Need all the real nutrition they can get, I'm not taking any food out of their mouths," he pressed his lips together. "I'll drink sludge for breakfast, lunch and dinner until we give these people what we promised."

"Lamar," she was feeling guilty that she had eaten two biscuits while working in the galley. "We have plenty of real food. We will run out of," as the words came out of her mouth she understood what she was saying. "Oxygen," she finished. "Long before we all have to eat sludges."

"Maybe so, that don't change a thing. Those people see me drinking this shit, they know I'm making a sacrifice for them. I'm trying to *do* something, for them."

She reached out to touch his cheek. "You're a good man."

"I'm a *Marine*," he insisted. "I signed up to protect people like them. Shit," he shook his head with disgust. "They were safer down on that planet than they are here."

"The crew is working on the ship," she said woodenly. Everyone knew the attempted restart of the oxygen recycling system had been a failure.

"It has been *four* days," his mouth worked like he was looking for a place to spit. "These people are scared. And they're *pissed*, at us. They blame us, and they're right. I talk with them, and I don't have any answers."

"*Valkyrie* has to be searching for us," she said.

"How do you know *Valkyrie* isn't in the same trouble as us?"

"I don't," she admitted after a beat. "Not for certain, until they contact us. It's not-"

"That rocket scientist doctor, Freedman, something like-"

"Fried*lander*."

"Yeah. I met him in the galley yesterday, he told me we jumped a *quarter lightyear* off course? Margaret, cut the bullshit, huh? All these people will be dead before *Valkyrie* even knows where we are. We promised them we were there to help, to rescue them. *I*," he tapped his chest, "made a promise to these people. We got them up here where they will die unless there is a *miracle*, because we don't know what the fuck we're doing."

She knew from his accusing stare that he wasn't including himself or the other Commandos, in that 'we'. It hadn't helped that when she first told him the ship had been attacked, he had assumed a physical attack by another starship, and she hadn't corrected the assumption until much later. When he learned that the 'attack' was what he considered nothing more than a *software* issue, that had not improved her credibility with him. Since then, she had told him everything she knew, holding nothing back. "You're forgetting about Bishop and Skippy."

"What about them? They are a quarter lightyear away, in a dropship that couldn't get here in ten years. Margaret, listen, about Bishop, whatever's between you two, I don't want to get in the-"

"There's nothing between us," she stiffened. "He's my CO. Yours too."

"Nothing?" He asked. That was not what other Pirates had told him in confidence. Perhaps 'confidence' was not the proper word, since the relationship between the gunnery sergeant and the colonel was an open secret aboard both ships. "Ok, it's not any of my business. The point is, he isn't *here*, and he can't *get* here. We are on our own."

"No," she shook her head again. "Don't count out Skippy. Simms will know we didn't arrive at the rendezvous point. She will jump *Valkyrie* in to pick up Bishop and Skippy. You asked for a miracle? Those two *do* miracles. I've seen them get us out of impossible situations more times than I can count. They'll find us, soon. We just need to hang on."

Greene looked her in the eye, searching for doubt. "How do you know this same software glitch didn't hit *Valkyrie* also?"

"Not possible. The operating systems are completely different."

"Maybe that's true," he said, in a way that meant he doubted she understood advanced alien computers. "I hear that something went wrong with *Skippy*.

Bishop's dropship lost stealth, and the microwormholes shut down. If we're counting on the AI to rescue-"

"Sergeant Greene?" A young boy called, walking across the docking bay's deck in boots that were far too big for him, and struggling to overcome the magnetic pads on the soles.

"Sanjay," Green's expression softened as he took three long strides to meet the boy. "Have you met my friend?" He pointed to Margaret. "She is Gunnery Sergeant Adams."

The skinny boy didn't smile as he raised a hand to wave at her, standing half behind Greene. "Hello, Sergeant Adams."

"My given name is *Margaret*," she took a step forward then froze as the boy flinched. "I am very pleased to meet you, Sanjay."

"Margaret Adams is a friend of mine," Greene gently tugged the boy to stand beside him. "We know each other from Earth, a long time ago."

Sanjay stared down at the deck, unconvinced.

"Margaret is an original member of this ship's crew," Greene added.

At that, the boy looked up, straight at her. "Are we all going to be Ok?"

She wanted to tell the boy, and Greene, and everyone, that they were going to be fine. If they were on Earth, she might have lied, thinking she was offering words of comfort. Not to this boy, not now. Sanjay had seen horrors. She knew from the files intercepted by Skippy that Sanjay was nine years old, though he appeared both younger and older. He was small for his age, malnutrition and stress stunting his growth. In his eyes, she saw a weariness of someone far older. "Sanjay, I don't know. Really, I don't. I'm not going to lie to you. The situation is serious. I'm sorry we brought you out here, we didn't think-"

"I'm not sorry," the boy said.

"You're not?" Adams shared a questioning look with Greene.

"Here, I'm with my people," the boy waved a hand at those clustered around the dropships, at Greene. And at Margaret Adams.

She felt her eyes well with tears.

Finally, something changed. When I say 'finally', I have no idea how long it took to get to finally, it seemed like forever.

When 'finally' happened, it made me nostalgic for the good old days when I wasn't aware that I existed.

A Thuranin, another Thuranin, a Kristang and a combot walked into the room. There's a good joke in there somewhere, I'll have to think about it.

Two Thuranin.

Whoa.

In my mind I said '*Whoa*' like Keanu Reeves, and that made me feel cool.

Two Thuranin.

Did I mention that already?

That could not be good.

What the hell were-

I was in a *Kristang* hospital. There were no Thuranin symbols on the wall I could see. Believe me, I had seen enough Thuranin writing inside the *Flying Dutchman*, before we modified the interior to make it more comfortable for the Pirates. Rikers was a Kristang world. Why were Thuranin in-

Rut-roh.

One of the Thuranin was doing something to a machine just within the right edge of my field of vision. My body got suddenly cold, like, ice cold. Then pleasantly warm.

My memories were coming back. Like, I knew the planet I was on was called 'Rikers', though I had a vague impression that was a nickname we gave it. We, like, the Merry Band of Pirates.

I was saying 'like' a lot. That made me wonder if I did that all the time. It was, like, kind of annoying.

Oh, shit.

Suddenly, I had a terrible thought.

Whenever we left the ship in a potentially hostile environment, each person applied a little suicide patch to the back of their neck. That little dot could send an electrical impulse to fry your brain, rendering any attempt to recover memories useless, even with advanced alien technology.

When I left the ship, I had been wearing one of those patches.

I was still alive.

Therefore, the patch had not been triggered, and I had to assume the Thuranin had removed it.

Shit. I was screwed, and I might betray everyone if the little green pinheads got me to talk, or accessed my memories directly.

A Thuranin suddenly loomed over my face. That scared the shit out me. Those little green MFers are ugly from ten feet away, now I had one right here, inches away. His breath smelled like Cheez-Its. Or maybe Doritos. It was a 'he' for sure, Thuranin males and females are very distinctive, like they engineered themselves to exaggerate their gender differences. This one, I decided to call Tweedledum because the other one was a female and I had to call her Tweedle*dee*. He loomed over me, not wearing a helmet but clothed in the form-fitting flexible armor that all the Thuranin aboard the *Dutchman* had been wearing, when we captured that ship.

Hey! That's another thing I remember.

My memory kicks *ass*.

Tweedledum spoke, words that meant nothing to me. Until an artificial voice in my left ear spoke to me in English. "Human," it told me. "We require information."

The Thuranin looked at me closely, staring at one eye then the other. I wanted to spit at him, or bite him. The lack of any ability to move was a damper on my plans to strike a blow for humanity. The good news was, since I couldn't move, and there was a thick mouthguard between my teeth, I couldn't give him any useful info.

Something wet and sweet sprayed inside my mouth, and the mouthguard began moving. By itself. Oooh, that was creepy. The thing shrank and slithered out of my mouth, I think it flopped onto my neck or chest, or both. Thank God I couldn't see it.

Tweedledum, or Dum as I called him for short, pulled away, perhaps aware that I now had teeth, and feeling was returning to my mouth. And to my face, and everything above the neck. I hurt. My scalp hurt. It felt like my face had dozens of cuts and abrasions. My *eyes* hurt, they were super dry and scratchy. From somewhere I couldn't see, a mist sprayed into my eyes, soothing them and instantly they felt rejuvenated, fresh.

"Why were you on Rakesh Diwalen?" The voice of Dum asked, and there was a thumping sound like the combot was adjusting its position. Probably the killer machine was moving to keep me in its line of sight as Dum walked around. All I could see was the top of his ugly green head.

"I came here for a spa day," I heard myself responding, and it surprised me. Not surprised that I was a wise-ass, I mean, I know myself. Surprised that I spoke at all, despite my determination not to give the MFers the satisfaction of hearing me talk. "The mineral springs are supposed to be great for my skin."

Tweedledum looked at Tweedledee, then back at me. "There are no mineral baths on this world."

"I was misinformed."

"You are lying," Dum said. He was an alien, speaking through a poor-quality translator, yet the tone of his voice was clearly annoyed.

That frightened me. He didn't have a tone like Do-not-test-my-patience. That would have been encouraging, for it would imply his patience had a limit I could test. No, this guy was chillingly professional. His patience was a tool he could use against me. It said that he knew *I* had a limit, and he knew how to use that against me.

"Uhhh," I heard myself saying. I wanted to tell him the truth. If I could remember it, I would have told him. They must have drugged me. Knowing that renewed my determination, and I didn't feel so traitorously cooperative.

"Tell me the truth," Dum said quietly. His voice was like a drug. "Why were you here? Who sent you?"

It was a struggle. He was a nice guy, he was trying to help me. I should help him. The Thuranin were superior to humans in every way, it was right that I should serve our rightful masters in any way I could. Besides, I was so tired, I just wanted to get it over with. The sooner I told him the truth, the sooner it would stop.

My mouth moved but I couldn't talk.

"The universe is a cold and dangerous place," Dum said. "Humans need to be protected. We can protect you."

Damn it, my traitorous mouth was forming words again.

I couldn't stop it.

Maybe I could change *what* I said.

"Fuck you, asshole." For some reason, I said that like the Terminator, and that made me feel cool.

At the bottom edge of my vision, Dum's head bobbed. Not violently, not angrily. He was displaying that knowing patience again. Damn, we just met, and already I hated the guy.

"You want to cooperate," he said. He wasn't trying to persuade me, he was just stating a fact and he knew it. "We will continue your treatment, then we will speak again soon."

My body got cold again. I don't remember what happened next.

Simms woke slowly, her sleeping bag bobbing at the end of its tether in the cargo bay. Sleeping in zero gravity sounded pleasant, but it was not. She always awakened with her face feeling puffy and her head congested. It had been six days since the ship lost all power. The past two days, a headache had accompanied the usual grogginess of coming out of sleep. Carbon dioxide was building up inside *Valkyrie* and it was only going to get worse. She adjusted the thin chain around her neck, its little links were irritating her skin. The chain was for the key to the nuclear warhead, she had started keeping it on a chain when she was sleeping, now she wore the chain as a constant reminder that detonating the nuke would be her decision, her responsibility.

Nothing they had tried could restore power to any part of the ship. Their two alien captives, or *guests* as she insisted her crew refer to them, had been unable to help. Neither the Ruhar nor the Jeraptha had been able to offer any assistance, though at least the Jeraptha was being stoic about the situation. The Ruhar, who had always been combative about being kidnapped with the Commando team, had become nasty when told the human crew had no control over the ship, a Maxolhx machine that humans had no business trying to operate.

Crawling out of the sleeping bag, she drank water from a squeeze bottle and shined her flashlight on the nuke. The ship's entire small crew was suffering from the increasingly foul air, the encroaching cold, and the total lack of comforts. They also suffered from the anxiety of knowing that conditions would continue to deteriorate, and that at some point, Simms would turn the key and explode the self-destruct nuke. The most important comfort they were missing was *hope*. With the *Flying Dutchman* gone, and the fates of Skippy and Bishop unknown, what was the point of delaying the inevitable?

What was she waiting for? She fingered the key, feeling its shape through her shirt. Maybe the best option was to put the key in, turn it, and just end their misery.

Maybe that is what she should do, in the absence of hope.

She floated over to the nuclear device, lifting the lid to expose the key slot.

Tweedledum was back, this time just with the combot clunking along right on his heels. The machine had its cannons retracted but its glowing red eye glared at me menacingly. At least, it was supposed to be menacing. Really, it was stupid. From being aboard the *Flying Dutchman*, I knew all about combots, I had taken the damned things apart to understand how they worked. They were just robots, controlled by the cyborg implants of a Thuranin. There was no reason the optic sensor needed to glow at all, that feature was designed to intimidate the squishy biological beings it encountered. All the combots aboard the *Dutchman* had that type of silly bullshit deactivated.

The good news was, the combot didn't scare me, not any more than the various other scary-looking machines in the hospital. By then, I knew it was not a hospital, it was a sort of interrogation facility. What I couldn't understand was why the Thuranin were down on the planet, instead of taking me aboard their ship.

Yeah, I remembered their ship. Whatever the little green MFers were doing to me, with drugs and chemicals and nanomachines swimming in my blood and probes scanning my brain, they had cleared my memory.

All of it.

The bad news was, I remembered what happened. Because I remembered, I knew we were in deep trouble.

Not *me*. When I said 'we' I meant the crews of the *Dutchman* and *Valkyrie*. Chang, and Simms, and Smythe, they would attempt to locate and rescue me. That would be incredibly dangerous and if I could contact Chang, I would order him not to approach the planet. There was no point in risking the ships, they weren't going to pull me out of the hospital, not alive. Without help from Skippy, a rescue operation did not have a prayer of succeeding. Hopefully Chang would see that, and-

And do what?

Without Skippy, there was no hope for anyone. What Chang could do with his two ships, I had no idea, because I had no idea what I would do in that situation. There wasn't much he could do. Without Skippy, the Elder wormhole that was being moved near Earth would not be activated, and that whole operation would be a waste of time.

The *really* bad news? I wanted to cooperate with Tweedledum. More than that, I felt loyal to the guy. He was on my side, he could and would protect humanity. All I needed to do was tell him the truth, all of it. Oh, I wanted *so* bad to tell him everything.

But, I couldn't. I don't know why. Dum had been asking me questions for, I don't know. Hours? Days? Weeks? Every time I tried my hardest to give him the answers he deserved, my mouth was unable to speak. Or I said some asshole thing to insult him. That was *wrong*, and I felt terrible about it. Worse, I had heard myself telling *lies* to him, feeding him the official cover story.

"Human," Dum began again patiently. "You have told me that your presence on this world was part of an Alien Legion operation to rescue your fellow humans, who were being held captive here. You claim this operation has the support of the Ruhar."

Yes, I did tell him that lie, and I was ashamed of myself. He had explained to me that his ship had come to the planet we called Rikers, to free the humans being held prisoner by the Kristang, and my operation had only screwed everything up.

It was odd. Part of me knew that Chang would try to rescue me, because the Thuranin are murderous hateful assholes. The other part of me wanted to cooperate with Tweedledum, because he was only trying to help humanity. All I can say is, with the drugs they were giving me, it all made sense.

Speaking of making sense, I had come to terms with Skippy's betrayal. He had received a terrible shock, learning that most of what he thought he knew was a lie. Learning that the Elders were gigantic assholes, and he had worked to do their evil bidding.

I had thought about it a lot.

I had to trust the awesomeness.

Not trust him to save humanity, that clearly wasn't going to happen. Trust him to do the right thing, in the big scheme of things where humans were just one, small population of ignorant savages. Skippy considered it his responsibility not to Save The World, but to save the entire galaxy. Maybe he was right. What would be the point of saving Earth from the Maxolhx, if the bad AIs woke up and wiped out all intelligent life in the galaxy?

So, once again, I had to trust the awesomeness.

Um, that also may have been an effect of the drugs. Because part of me *hated* Skippy for betraying our friendship and abandoning us.

Ah, screw it. None of that mattered, there wasn't anything I could do about it.

Tweedledum was saying something to me. "I know you are lying." My body felt cold. "Shall we begin again?"

Mark Friedlander pulled the sleeping bag's drawstring tighter, not because he was cold, but to keep him from drifting out of it while he slept.

If he slept.

The test of connecting a Falcon dropship's AI to the *Dutchman's* computer had been a failure. Worse, it was a complete disaster. Immediately after the cable was jacked into the ship, all the displays aboard the Falcon went haywire, and the powercells began overheating. Unplugging the cable from the dropship didn't stop the cascade of alien code, an explosion was prevented only by opening hatches and physically ripping out the power conduits from the powercells; still one of them melted down, damaging two others. To be safe, Chang ordered the Falcon to be ejected rapidly, by over-pressurizing that docking bay and blowing the explosive bolts of the bay doors. That Falcon was drifting away at just over two meters per second, the sight of its spinning hull constantly mocking the foolish humans aboard the slowly dying starship.

The *Flying Dutchman* was dying, there was no question about that. He was doing everything he could to restore power, or at least get life support systems working again. Doing everything he could think of, and anyone else with a technical background was doing the same. So far, they hadn't accomplished anything.

That day, he noticed something that was worrisome, enough that he mentioned it to Chang. The crew used the expression 'Trust the Awesomeness' frequently, and almost always in an ironic manner. Sometimes the expression was shortened to 'TTA' but it meant the same: do NOT trust the awesomeness. Now, the crew had taken to muttering 'Trust the Awesomeness' in a hopeful, almost prayerful way. They were hoping that somehow, Skippy would come to the rescue. Mark knew that was because they didn't believe there was any hope without the beer can.

He hated admitting they might be right about that.

Closing his eyes, he tried to quiet his mind so he could fall asleep, or at least rest. It was no good. Every time he opened his eyes, the tiny power indicator light on the bottom of his zPhone caught his attention. That was another odd thing he couldn't explain. The power indicator normally was very dim. The light now was shining brightly, and orange in color, though he knew the phone was not charging.

He couldn't even understand the odd functioning of a *phone*, how could he be expected to get an alien fusion reactor restarted?

With nothing else to do, and exhausted both physically and emotionally, he stared at the light, his eyes unfocusing and his eyelids blessedly drooping, feeling himself drift off into a groggy half-awareness.

The light blinked slowly, randomly.

On-off-on.

Off. For a full second.

On-off-on-off-on.

A pause again.

On-off-on-off-on-off-on-off-on.

Bolting fully awake, Friedlander yanked the drawstring open, spilling out of the sleeping bag. The interior of the *Dutchman* was still warm, both from the insulating vacuum of space and the warmth of too many human bodies, so he slept only in sweatpants. Pulling a shirt over his head, he stared at the zPhone's power light. It was blinking again as he watched.

That was seven.

Two, three, five, seven.

Prime numbers.

The blinking of the light was *not* random.

Someone was trying to communicate.

To be sure, he waited as the light blinked. It skipped the number nine, which is divisible by three and therefore not a prime.

It blinked eleven times.

Then thirteen.

Seventeen.

Next, he expected it would blink nineteen times.

It didn't.

Three, then three again.

A long pause.

One, one.

Pause.

Two, two.

Pause.

One, one.

He held his breath. If the next sequence was *four, four*, he knew what-

It blinked four, four.

Snatching the phone, he tucked it in a pocket and spun, to push off the couch and fly out the door.

"Human," Tweedledum said to get my attention. He was in the room along with three others of his kind, another male and two females. Vaguely, I thought all four of them had talked to me or interrogated me, my brain wasn't working properly so I couldn't be sure. Mostly, I had talked with Dum, or maybe that's what the Thuranin wanted me to think.

Slowly, I turned my eyes to look at him, and focused on his face from the nose up. It was weird to hear him talking and not see his mouth.

Satisfied that I was alert and paying attention, he continued. "Despite my best efforts to demonstrate our good faith, you have been uncooperative." The tone of endless patience in his voice had an edge to it. Either his patience was not endless, or he was getting pressure from his fellow little green jerkoffs. "We must now move to another phase, which involves probing your brain directly. This will be dangerous for you. If you wish to tell me the truth, now is the time to act."

"Go fuck yourself," I heard myself saying. Or, I *think* it was me talking.

Yeah, that's something I would say.

The combot I could see stayed against the wall. It didn't scare me. The big machine lowering toward me from the ceiling did.

CHAPTER FIVE

"Doctor, are you-" Chang's yawn stretched his mouth so wide, he couldn't finish what he wanted to say.

"Yes! I'm sure. Watch." He held up the phone so the *Flying Dutchman's* captain could see the power indicator light. Chang had been sleeping in the command chair on the bridge, with a strap loosely around his waist. The single wall-mounted display that had not been disconnected still scrolled meaningless gibberish, taunting anyone who looked at it.

"What am I seeing?"

"Prime numbers. It showed one through seventeen when I first saw it."

They watched, one anxious, the other skeptical. The indicator light glowed solidly, then began blinking. Two, three, five, seven, eleven-

"Those *are* primes," Chang gasped.

Thirteen, seventeen.

"Now, watch, this is the important part," Friedlander's hand was shaking with excitement.

The phone went through the incomprehensible sequence that began three, three, then one, one, and two, two.

"What am I seeing?" Chang asked.

"Wait. Let it finish," Friedlander's grin lit up his face.

The light continued to blink, finishing with one, one. Instead of repeating the prime numbers, the light remained solidly on.

"I don't understand," said the ship's captain. "Explain."

"I will. Before that, we should see if your phone does the same thing."

Chang dug into a pocket for the phone he had not looked at in two days. Seeing the useless device, with alien symbols or just plain random nonsense scrolling down the display, was depressing, so he had tucked it out of sight.

His phone repeated the sequence, beginning with primes, then a sequence that Chang didn't understand, ending with one, one.

Friedlander's grin was not only wide, it was infectious. Chang grinned also, not knowing why. "Doctor, please do not keep this idiot in suspense. What are those numbers after the primes? It is not Morse code."

"No. it's not. Morse is not the best communications method for-" He saw that Chang's smile was fading. "It's a simple five by five tap code. It's how prisoners communicate, by tapping on the walls between cells, or on the bars. Unlike Morse, it doesn't require two types of signal, one long and one short. A tap is a single event, you can't make it long. Look," he used a grease pencil to write on a display that had been unplugged. "It's-"

"You are *writing* on the-" Chang waved a hand to ignore his own comment. "Go on."

"I can write on the wall, if-"

"No. Please continue. We certainly do not need a display that doesn't work."

"Ok. Look," he drew a grid with twenty five squares, numbering the columns one to five across the top, and the rows one to five top to bottom. "Twenty five squares, twenty six letters in the alphabet. Uh," Friedlander realized that Chang was a native Chinese speaker. "I mean the Latin alphabet, the-"

"I know what you mean."

"Good. Across the top is A, B, C, D, and E. The C also stands for K, that's the missing letter." He filled in the other four rows. "The sequence of blinking lights, after the prime numbers, starts with three, three. That means row three, column three. What do you get?"

Chang squinted, the doctor's handwriting was not the best, the grease pencil was smudged, and the lighting of the bridge was dim. "N. Three, three is the letter N."

"Correct! Next is one, one."

"The letter A," Chang caught on to the scheme. "After that was two, two, which is the letter G, so-" He sucked in a breath and gaped at the rocket scientist.

"You see it?" Friedlander grinned like a professor whose student had been particularly clever.

"*Nagatha*! It spells 'Nagatha'."

"It does. Colonel Chang, she is *alive*!" She is communicating with us, through these little lights on our phones."

Chang stared at his phone in a mixture of amazement and horror. "How long has this been going on?"

The doctor shrugged. "I don't know. We all thought the symbols on the displays," he tapped the one functional display, "were random nonsense. I didn't pay any attention to the blinking indicator lights until just now."

"A, what did you call it? A five by five tap code? *How* did you recognize such an obscure thing?"

"I'm a nerd," he shrugged. "It's kind of our superpower, you know?"

"It is indeed. Doctor, please keep getting your nerd on, anytime you like," Chang laughed. He *laughed*. For the first time since the microwormholes collapsed and they lost contact with Skippy, he felt an emotion other than fear and anxiety.

"Oh, look," Friedlander pointed to Chang's phone. "That's new! It's a new sequence. Read it to me, please."

With Chang reading the numbers, Friedlander wrote down the resulting letters. "It spells 'Hello'. Nagatha," he automatically looked at the ceiling. "Can you hear us? Or see us?"

The blinking lights spelled out 'I can hear you'.

"Do you need us to do something? Can we do anything? How do we help you? Is there a way to-"?

Chang placed a hand on the over-excited scientist's arm. "Doctor, we should pose one question at a time."

"Right. You're right. What does it say?" The lights were blinking again.

The letters were 'I need your help to reboot and purge the ship operating system this will be complicated'.

Friedlander was already getting a cramp in his hand, and the grease pencil had filled the display and gone down the wall below. "Ok," he looked at the ship's captain. "We're going to need more of these pencils. And something to write on. Something *big*."

"Human," Tweedledum was back. Or maybe he never left, I couldn't tell. My brain was fuzzy. That wasn't a metaphor. It felt like here was *fuzz* inside my skull. Fuzz, and pieces broken off a Brillo pad. Something was wrong with my brain.

Shit. I was still alive. My hope had been that whatever the brain probe did, I wouldn't survive it. That way, I couldn't betray my people.

"Unfortunately, our probe equipment has been unsuccessful," he looked with puzzled disappointment at the big machine that had retracted away from me, up on the ceiling. "We do not understand how your primitive brain is able to resist being scanned by our technology."

"Yeah, I feel just terrible about it, shithead," I heard myself saying.

Aha! His patience was not endless. His face lost its neutral expression. The body language was clear: he was *pissed* at me. I had made him look bad. "You think you are clever," he glared at me.

Yup, he was angry for sure. Angry enough to lose his temper and kill me? I hoped so. I couldn't take much more. I was *tired*. Desperately tired. His anger made it clear that, whatever happened with the scary brain probe, he hadn't gotten any useful info from me.

Yay, me!

"Know this, human. We are no longer interested in why you came to this world, or who you are working with. We *are* interested in discovering why our probe mechanism is unable to gain a clear view of your neural architecture. Therefore, we will remove your brain for sectioning and analysis. I am pleased to say that you will not survive the procedure."

Oh thank God, was my reaction. It would be over, before I could betray all of humanity by opening my big stupid mouth. All I had to do was focus on not saying anything, and wait for-

"Heeeeey, Joe." It was Skippy's voice.

Holy *shit*.

At first, I froze, assuming I had imagined it.

"Hey," he said. "Are you awake in there? Anybody home? Hell-oooooooh?"

"Skippy?" I tried to say, through the mouthguard or whatever was in my mouth. Tweedledum looked at me sharply, startled by the sound I had made.

"Jeez, don't try to talk aloud. Just *think* when you want to say something to me."

You can read my mind?

"Yes."

You told me you couldn't do that. Liar!

"Usually, I can't. This is a special case."

How?

"We don't have time for a long sciency explanation. I implanted quantum nanomachines in your brain, call them quachines if you like. They interact with your neurons to act as a relay, and I can read the effect. Unfortunately, they have a bad side effect of permanent brain damage, so they can't be used for long."

Are these quachine things why the Thuranin brain probe didn't work?

"Yes. Also why you didn't answer their questions, despite the drugs they pumped into you. Listen, Joe, we don't have time for this. They are going to slice your brain open in a few minutes. We need to get you out of there."

Uh, yeah. Sure. You plan to walk in here and carry me out?

"No. You will have to walk out by yourself. Mostly."

I am pissed at you.

"I'm pissed at myself too. Can we schedule the meeting of the I Hate Skippy club for after you get out of there? Joe?" He added when I didn't reply immediately.

What is your plan?

"I have semi-control over weapons on and around the planet. I will hit the hospital to bust you out of there."

Hit the hospital? Do you realize that I am IN the hospital?

"Yes. You'll have to trust me."

My mind went blank.

"Joe? Say something."

TRUST you?

"I know," he said with a sigh, which was weird because I wasn't actually hearing him speak. "Listen, I know you would rather wait for Chang and Simms to rescue you, but-"

No! I do not want them coming here, it's too dangerous. Are you in contact with them?

"No, I-"

When you do contact them, tell them my orders are to stay away from the planet. Until and unless I can contact them directly. The last thing I want is for Smythe to throw together some crazy plan to-

"Joe, I am not in contact with either ship. That bothers me. They should have arrived by now, at least one ship should have jumped in for a recon."

Shit. Did something happen to them?

"Inconceivable. Maybe they are waiting for me to contact them? I don't know. We can deal with that later. We have to get you out of here NOW."

Just like that? You BAIL on me, then come back and expect that everything is-

"Act now, talk later. You are running out of time. Also, every time we communicate, it burns out a set of quachines, and that causes permanent brain damage."

Hearing him say that frightened me. He passed up a golden opportunity to make a joke about my monkey brain. That told me *he* was afraid for me. What choice did I have? I would not have *any* choices, if the Thuranin split open my skull. I worried that maybe the *Dutchman* and *Valkyrie* were in trouble, and might need me and Skippy to help them? Death would pose a significant obstacle to my ability to render assistance. But, the odds of me walking out of the hospital, and evading pursuit, were not great. While the thought of escaping was wonderful, it was also a fantasy. Even if I could get out of the hospital, no way could I help a pair of starships that had to be a long distance from the planet. It was time for me to forget about childish dreams of me being a hero, and face reality. *Skippy, can you trigger the suicide patch?*

"No. The Thuranin removed it. Also, the pulse that disabled your dropship rendered the suicide patch inert."

Shit. You have control of the equipment in here? Can you fry my brain using that stuff?

"Wow. Joe, are you serious? You want to die?"

I want to make sure the Thuranin do not get my memories.

"I told you, the quachines will block them. Please, Joe, will you at least *try* to escape?"

Ok. I agreed to try not because I thought it was possible, but because as a US Army soldier, it was my duty to escape. Or at least to try. *How do you plan to get me out of here?*

"Like I said, I will hit the hospital. You have to walk out of there on your own."

If I can. Ok, I'm ready, I told him. Tweedledum walked toward me, and the big scary machine on the ceiling was lowering itself over my head. *Skippy, do your thing*, I urged.

"I can't activate weapons by myself," he sighed with exasperation. "Remember? You have to hit to Big Red Button."

What the f- How am I supposed to do THAT? I don't have my phone, you idiot! You are-

The mouthguard distracted me by folding up and crawling out of my mouth, slithering across my lips and down my chin. A reflex made me gag and choke.

"Human," Tweedledum loomed over me, he must have been standing on a chair or something. "This is your last chance. Tell me the truth, and I will spare your life."

"Joe," Skippy's voice boomed in my head, making me wince. "A virtual Big Red Button is installed in the roof of your mouth. All you need to do is touch it with your tongue. Hurry! I am locked and loaded up here."

"Hey you," I croaked, my throat dry and raw. Turning my head slightly, I stared at Tweedledum. If looks could kill, he would be dead. Sadly, he remained alive. "AMF," I said to him.

The Thuranin tilted his head and squinted. "I do not understand. Do not toy with me."

"It means," I swallowed to wet my cracked lips. "*Adios*, MotherFucker." My tongue pressed against the roof of my mouth.

The building shook. The lights went out. A crack of gunfire erupted in the room, then it became a volley stitching across the wall, blinding me with the strobe-light effect.

The building shook again, hard.

That's all I remember.

"Joe!"

Oh, I had *such* a massive hangover.

"Joe! Hey! Hey, Joe!"

Note to myself: never, never, *never* again drink tequila. Or whatever evil beverage I consumed that gave me the Mother Of All Hangovers. Also, *why* can't that asshole just shut the hell up? Doesn't he know that people are trying to sleep?

"Hey! KNUCKLEHEAD! Wake UP!" Skippy's voice boomed from somewhere, causing a cold icepick to stab through my brain from one ear to the other.

Shit. Now I remember. "Wha-" Trying to say just that threw me into a fit of coughing. "What? Where?"

"You are in a hospital. It's not really a hospital."

Yeah. I remembered. Talking hurt, so I thought at him. No response.

"You have to talk to me the old-fashioned way, Joe. We can't risk using quachines again, I am already gravely concerned about the cumulative effect on you."

"How-" Coughing again. That was getting to be really annoying. "How are we talking? I can hear you, like, *hear* you with my ears."

"We are using the communications system of the combot," he didn't use the opportunity to insult me. Typically, Skippy would have made a remark that of course I used my *ears* for hearing. "Close your eyes, I am turning on a light."

The light was blinding and I was a little slow on closing my eyelids. "Bright light, bright light," I gritted my teeth against the ice pick that was now stabbing me through my eye sockets.

"Sorry. Is that better?"

"Give me a minute, I can't see anything." That was not completely true, I could see afterimages surging toward and away from me.

"We don't have a minute."

"I can't *see* anything."

"Joseph, please work with me. Truly, you do not have a minute to waste."

Whoa. He called me Joseph. And he said 'please' in a non-snarky, non-sarcastic fashion. The old Skippy would have said 'Puh-*lease*' in a tone dripping with snark-asm. Also, he would have made a comment about being disgusted to see me naked. "Ok, you're the boss. What should I do?"

"The combot will be cutting you loose from the bed. My ability to see in there is limited, you need to direct me so I do not harm you."

"Ok. Uh, I can't move my head."

"That is the first problem. There is a band encircling your head, can you feel it pressing on your forehead?"

"Um, I think so. Hey," I wiggled my head as best I could. "It feels like it attaches at the back."

"It does. That connection must be severed first. Tell me when you feel the combot's cutting pinchers behind your head."

"Uh," an image of seeing Adams use a combot's pincher claws to slice through a steel beam flashed through my mind. "Hey, maybe this isn't such a good-"

Something cold slid behind my head on both sides, I could feel a sharp and jagged object scraping along the back of my skull. "Too close! Too close!"

The objects drew away and instead of the jagged edge, I just felt a coolness. Something smooth.

"Is that better?" He asked.

"Think so, yes. Uh, go slowly?"

"Unfortunately, the claw has only one setting in 'Cut' mode," he lamented.

"Gotcha. Uh, can you switch it to 'Grip' mode, squeeze it first?"

"Ah! I am a dum-dum. Of course. That is a good idea, sorry." The claws slid behind my head and the band around my forehead pressed tighter. "That is the hardest it can grip."

"Good. Retract the claws and use the cutter, pincher thing, whatever you call it."

"Do *not* move your head."

"Believe me, I won't. Wait! The thing you're cutting through, what if a piece pops loose and slices into my spine?"

"The claws are cutting it *away* from you. That is part of what makes this awkward, the claws are upside down from the normal mode of operation."

"Do it."

He lied. Or he was wrong. Something sharp snapped loose and sliced the right side of my head. "Ow!"

"Sorry! Dude, I am sorry."

"It's Ok." The pressure on my forehead was gone. I could move my head! "It worked. I can move." Lifting my head, I saw both of my arms were encased in hard, bulky sleeves from the elbows down. Same with my legs.

Guiding the combot when I could see the damned thing was much easier, it took less than a minute to get completely free from the hospital bed. Well, not completely free, I had to pull out the tubes that were in my left forearm and deep into a vein in my left inner thigh. The good news is the Thuranin had installed a port in both places, so it was a simple matter of disconnecting the tube and sealing it off. To the Thuranin, the ports were probably considered primitive technology. To me, watching them seal themselves closed was a miracle. "Ok, let's get out-" Swinging my legs over the side of the bed to sit up did not produce the result I intended, because I only got one leg to flop over the side. That weight unbalanced me from the bed that had gone inert, and could not adjust to keep me safely in place. Slowly and with gathering speed, I rolled to the side, flailing my arms uselessly on the slick bed surface. Like watching a slow-moving train wreck I couldn't stop, I toppled off the bed and fell onto the floor, smacking my face on the cool, hard tiles.

"Joe! Are you all right?"

"A little help here, please." I mumbled with my face pressed into the floor. My muscles weren't working properly, either due to lack of use or the drugs swimming in my blood.

"Stay there."

"Don't worry, I'm just taking a nap."

"Do *not* fall asleep! You don't have time-"

"That was a joke," I told him, twisting my head so only one side of my face was on the floor. That was a mistake. Right in front of my face was the bloody body of a Thuranin. It could have been Tweedledum; it was hard to tell because two other Thuranin were behind him. None of them appeared to be in perfect health, based on the big holes blown through their torsos. Chunks of their bodies and limbs were missing, just gone. The combot must have done that, I remember hearing and seeing gunfire. Speaking of the combot, it came stomping and lurching around the bed, coming toward me. One of its feet stepped on the head of a Thuranin and squished it with a wet *crunch*. "Skippy! Stop! You're stepping on people." Huh. I wonder when I started thinking of murderous Thuranin as people? Maybe it was easier to sympathize with them when they were dead and unable to hurt anyone.

"Joe, I can't see well from up here. Does it matter? Trust me, they are dead."

"I am an American soldier. I do not desecrate bodies of the enemy, not even these assholes."

"This is important to you?"

"Yes."

"Then it is important to me." The combot lifted the offending foot, dripping blood and other stuff I don't want to mention. "Here?" The foot moved to the left.

"Another half meter. There. Set it down."

Yuck. Then the foot touched the floor, something wet squished out from under it and splattered my face. With one hand, I reached over and wiped away the, the whatever it was, off my face. I didn't want to think about it.

"Hey!" I exclaimed with surprise. "I just moved my arm!"

"Yes, that is very good, Joe!" Skippy seemed as pleased as I was. "Just before the railgun darts hit the hospital, I administered drugs to counteract the nerve-blockers in your bloodstream. You should be able to walk soon."

An attempt to make my legs do something useful ended quickly in failure. "Define, 'soon', please."

"A couple of minutes?" He replied. "It's not an exact science. The Thuranin were not careful about the dose they gave to you, and they didn't keep good records. I had to guess at the active level in your blood, sorry."

"No problem." Feeling was returning to my legs, something that was a mixed blessing. The good news was I could make both of my feet move. The bad news was my legs and feet *hurt*. My whole body hurt. Looking at myself, my skin was bruised and swollen, with patches crisscrossed by burst blood vessels.

"Ok, Joe, I'm going to lower-"

"Whoa. No. No way. I am not going anywhere until we talk about what happened. You know, like, *what happened*?"

"Er," he grunted with exasperation. "Like I said, we can talk about that *later*."

"Until then, I am just supposed to act like everything is cool? Is that what we're doing now? Pretending that nothing happened?"

"Joe, look up."

When he said that, I was looking at my chest, trying to judge if my ribs were cracked. A section of skin that was unblemished turned dark and I stared at it, frightened and puzzled, until I realized the darkness was just *dirt*. A fine spray of dirt was raining down on me, when I looked up, I saw why.

The ceiling was cracked. It wasn't like drywall or drop-ceiling tiles, this ceiling was a solid slab of whatever the Kristang used for concrete. Correction: it *used* to be a solid slab. There was a wide crack running diagonally across the entire room, with one side slumping down six or more inches. The concrete-like material was crumbled at the edges, exposing a web of what I guessed was reinforcing material embedded in the concrete. As I gaped at the sight, the ceiling shifted and more dirt cascaded down onto me. I breathed it in, coughing. "Skip- Skippy. Are we- Am I underground?"

"Yes, and I think the ceiling above you is about to collapse."

"Shit!"

"Exactly. I don't have good sensor coverage in there; however I believe the entire structure has become unstable." The combot's glowing eye swiveled upward. "Oopsy. Well, heh heh, it looks like I went a bit overboard with railguns."

Hearing his 'heh heh' made me cringe. "How far underground?"

"Approximately twenty meters."

Twenty meters. The ceiling slab shifted again and this time, a shower of little pebbles fell out of the crack. Much as I hated to admit it, he was right. Talking could wait, getting out of there could not. "Time to go!" I announced to no one. "Help me up."

Beside me, the combot's legs lowered its chassis to the floor, extending the manipulator arms. "Ooh, *yuck*."

"What?"

"Through the combot's camera, I just got a look at your hairy monkey butt. What is *wrong* with women that they are attracted to-"

"Can we talk about *that* later?"

"OK, sorry. You need to roll over into the combot's arms so it can carry you. The arms might crush you if I tried to scoop you off the floor."

"Right." Skippy's plan was fine in theory. In practice, Thuranin combots were not designed to carry things other than weapons. They could carry loads on their backs, with a special rack attachment that this one didn't have. The arms were strong, and the machine could adjust its stance to adapt to my weight changing its center of balance. The arms were *not* comfortable. They were covered in armor plates and gun barrels and a whole list of hard, unyielding other things that dug into me. "Ah! Stop moving!" I shouted at him. "Something is cutting my back. This isn't working."

"There isn't another option, Joe," he told me sadly. "You are right, the ceiling is about to collapse."

"Go, just," I grasped the arms with both hands to hold my torso away from the sharp things that wanted to tear into me. "Try to walk steadily, Ok?"

The combot lurched along hallways in the hospital, which was almost more of a wreck than the room I had been in. The ceiling of the hallways were not flat, they were an arch with a strip of lighting along the top, though the power was out. The problem with the hallways were the big cracks in the walls. The good news was there wasn't any dirt pouring through the cracks, there must have been rooms or other structures on each side. The bad news was, the partially-collapsed walls created obstructions that the combot had to navigate around, and it had to squeeze past narrow gaps without using me as a battering ram. "Skippy, this isn't working," I declared when he bashed my left leg against a tilted slab of crumbled wall. "Stop, *stop*! You're gonna break my leg. Set me down."

"Can you walk?"

My legs hurt even worse than before, a sure sign that they weren't as numb as before. Feeling was returning, so the nerves were sending signals from my legs to my brain. Were the nerves working in the other direction?" Moving my feet worked, better than when I tried it earlier. My calves dangled from my knees, swinging them proved my knees still worked. "I can try walking. Set me down. Uh, turn this thing around first."

The combot swiveled, its legs remaining in place while the torso part of the chassis rotated. "It's stuck," Skippy said.

"Yeah, hold it there," I slid off the arms, first onto my knees. Sharp pieces of shattered wall debris cut into my bare knees and I felt hot blood trickle onto the floor. "Swing it back around forward." Using the robotic war machine as a walker, I pulled myself up onto surprisingly steady legs. Steady, until I tried to take a step and fell.

"Joe, *this* isn't working."

"Give me a minute."

"You don't *have* a minute."

"Let me try it again," I insisted, doubting myself. Was I being stupidly stubborn? Or was the problem that I just couldn't bring myself to trust Skippy? Walking with stiff legs, swinging from the hip, seemed to work. "Ok, go slowly. Can you see well enough to push stuff out of the way with the arms?"

"Yes," he reported without the usual snarkiness. "We are closer to the tunnel entrance, the bandwidth here is better."

It was slow going, even when I told Skippy he could pick up the pace. "Why aren't there any Thuranin, or lizards, down here?" Other than the dead little green cyborgs in the hospital room, I had not seen anyone.

"The Thuranin insisted the Kristang leave the facility, other than a small security presence. They are all dead, except for three Kristang soldiers who were off duty, and went outside the range of my sensor coverage. I don't know where they are."

That didn't sound right. "Outside of your *range*? How can anything on this planet be-"

"Joe, I'm not, I am not at peak awesomeness right now. I will explain later, I promise."

Part of me wanted to scream that a promise from him wasn't worth a damned thing. The smarter part of me knew that screaming wouldn't accomplish anything. "Fine. What's the plan?"

"The plan is, or *was*, to get you away from here. Find a hiding place to hole up, until *Valkyrie* or the *Dutchman* arrive to investigate why the microwormholes collapsed. Now, I don't know. You still need to get away from this place, or you won't have any options."

"What's the point?" A wave of great weariness crept up my spine. "Soon as the lizards on this rock see the hospital has been hit, they will be swarming around like bees. Then there is that Thuranin ship in orbit. It will send down dropships, or saturate this area with-"

"The Kristang here are very busy," he announced, without the gleefully evil chuckle that the old Skippy would have indulged in. "Major military and clan leadership sites were struck, either by their own weapons, or by the weapons of the Thuranin ship."

"Damn!" Hearing that startled me, so I missed a step and nearly fell over. "You took over that ship?"

"To a limited extent, yes."

"Well, hell," I felt like slapping my forehead, catching myself before I let go of the combot and fell on my ass. I really felt like slapping *him*. "Why didn't you tell me that? Send one of their dropships down for me, and we will go find *Valkyrie*."

"Unfortunately, I can't do that. Like I said, my control over the Thuranin ship was limited, I could only count on it lasting for eleven seconds. After that, the crew would have cut off the infected system, and restored control."

"Ohhhhh, shit. What did you do?"

"Sadly, that ship self-destructed."

"You mean the ship's AI blew it up, to prevent you from taking control?"

"It was more of an *involuntary* self-destruction, if you know what I mean," he said with a chuckle.

"Oh," I exhaled with a sort of laugh, the best I could manage. Then I realized that Skippy had just made a *joke*, the first since he contacted me. Despite whatever was wrong with him, part of the old Skippy was still in there.

"I'm sorry," he said miserably. "That ship would have been useful. I didn't have a better choice. There are not any Kristang ships in the area."

"Crap. Ok, you did your best."

"The point is, the Thuranin are, for the moment, not an issue," he tried to assure me. "There are four of them on the surface, but I destroyed their dropship, they can't get here anytime soon. The Kristang are in total disarray, and looking for you will not be a priority for them. Based on the communications traffic I am monitoring, the surviving clan leaders here are torn between trying to figure out why the Thuranin ship hit them so severely, and why that ship exploded shortly after firing weapons. Also, as you would expect, the surviving clan leaders are doing their best to ensure their rivals do *not* survive more than a few hours."

"We can always count on the lizards being more eager to kill each other, than to kill us. Hey!" I exclaimed as the combot turned to the left. The hallway, that I now knew was a tunnel, sloped upward in front of me. "Why aren't we going straight ahead?"

"There is a storage locker that contains items you need."

"It had better be pretty damned import-"

"*Food*, Joe. The native life on this world is somewhat compatible with human nutritional needs, but you would have no idea what native plants are safe to eat. In that locker are several boxes of food for humans. Unless you want to starve."

That made no sense. "Why is there human food in-"

"When the kidnapped people were brought here from Camp Alpha, this hospital was designated as a treatment facility for seriously ill humans. This hospital is part of a secure, isolated military base. It was never actually used to treat humans, because the Kristang decided they just didn't care. It was easier to place the kidnapped people on islands and make them fend for themselves."

"Yeah. What a bunch of sweethearts the lizards are."

The combot halted in front of a door that was cracked open a couple inches. "Here it is. The door is stuck. Sorry, you need to squeeze through."

That was easier said than done. The best way to move was holding onto the combot, then the door, then a shelf inside the locker, which was more of a walk-in closet. Really, it was a room, with shelves all around and stuff hanging from railings on the ceiling. The place was a mess, with shelves toppled over and no sign of the promised food. "Do you have any idea where this stuff is?"

"Sorry, Joe. No, I do not."

Man, Skippy being super nice was starting to bug me. It wasn't natural. "Fine," I lowered onto my knees. "Shine a light in here, will ya? I'll dig through this pile of crap for it. Hey, score! Excellent."

"What?"

"I found a stack of lizard clothing." It would be too big for me, and I didn't care. Rummaging through the pile, I found pants, a sort of long-sleeved T-shirt, and a jacket that had nice useful pockets. Plus socks and shoes that were like basketball high-tops. The shoes were too big for me, so I put on three pairs of socks and the shoes fit Ok after I twisted the dial to tighten the internal laces. The jacket went into a knapsack I found. "What's the weather like outside?"

"Mostly clear, the temperature is fifteen degrees. The local sun set about three hours ago, so it is dark. Remember, this world does not have a large moon, so nighttime is very dark without artificial lighting."

"Fifteen, got it. Ooh, chilly." I looked around for a hat or gloves.

"Fifteen *Celsius*, Joe. That is around 60 for you metric-hating Americans. It will be chilly overnight, then pleasant tomorrow."

"Right." Among other items, I found a blanket, and stuffed it into the knapsack. "Crap, I can't find any- Bingo! Got it," I dug a battered cardboard box out from the bottom of the pile. "Uh oh."

"What?" He asked, and the combot leaned through the doorway.

"These are, like, MREs. I've got American, British, I think these are Chinese. They're *old*, Skippy. This one," I squinted at a pouch that was supposed to contain chili. "Expired three years ago."

"That's the best I can do, Joe. The food should be safe to eat, though lacking in flavor. Also, some nutrients will have degraded over time."

"Yeah, MREs are like that even when they're new. Ok, thanks," I crammed all the food packets I could find into the knapsack. Some of the packets had been torn open and I didn't know how long ago, I left those. They smelled musty. Everything in the closet smelled musty, including the clothes I was wearing. At least I wasn't butt-naked anymore. "Let's go."

CHAPTER SIX

We didn't go far. Around a curve fifty meters ahead, the tunnel sides had caved in. Skippy advised me to hang back as he tried using the combot's arms to move the broken wall panels aside, but he only made the problem worse. The killer robot was moving awkwardly, in jerky motions. There wasn't any damage that I could see, and it was walking just fine. But several times, the machine's pinchers reached for a wall section and missed, because the section had shifted. "Sorry, Joe," Skippy made the machine walk backward toward me, halting after a few steps. "I was afraid of this. When this place was built, the contractors cut corners so they could afford to pay the higher-than-expected level of bribes to a clan leader's sons. The section of tunnel ahead is weak because substandard materials were used, and only half the amount of reinforcing rods were installed."

"What's your Plan B?" I asked, while digging through the packs of MREs to find something bland to eat, like crackers. I was starving and needed to get somethng int my stomach. "You *have* a Plan B, right?"

"Unfortunately, no. I need to use the combot to dig through the collapsed section."

"Won't more dirt just fall in?"

"No. I will use wall sections to brace the ceiling. Sorry, this is going to take a while."

"Great," I leaned back against the wall to give my legs a rest. "Skippy, we need to talk."

"Sure. What about?" He said, playing dumb with that tone of fake innocence people use, when they want to pretend not to know what you mean. The combot was digging scoopfuls of dirt and lifting rocks out of the pile that had fallen in.

"You know what about."

"Um, hmm. Joe, usually you would say something like 'You *know* what about, you little shithead'."

"Yeah. That is something you say to a *buddy*. Not something you say to a callous Blue Falcon who bails when you need him."

"Blue Falcon?" My canister is *silver*, Joe, not blue. Why-"

"Those are initial for 'BF'. Buddy. Fucker. The guy who stabs you in the back. The guy everyone in the unit hates, you know? Nobody trusts him."

"Ok, that is-"

"Like *you* did."

"Ok, if you give me a minute, I can explai-"

"I doubt it."

"Can I try? Please?"

"This had better be good. *Really* good. Like, the best explanation in the history of explanations."

"Uh, heh heh, I know that," he almost stuttered.

"Not a civilian explanation, either."

"What?"

"Skippy, military life is different. We don't just trust the guy next to us to file a stupid form properly, or do some other civilian office thing. We're trusting him with our lives. He needs to be there, where he's supposed to be, on time, prepared, fit and ready, no matter what. *No* excuses. If we get into a firefight, I need to know the guys beside me are in the fight, a hundred percent. They're not going to bail on me if it gets dangerous. If I get hit, they're not going to leave me there by myself. In the military, trust is an absolute. You either *can* trust the guy next to you, or you *can't*. It's that simple. You understand?"

"Yes. Joe, I am sorr-"

"Saying 'sorry' isn't going to get the job done today."

"Whew," he sighed. "Ok, let me start from the beginning."

"Outstanding. Start with why you came back. The last I heard from you, you called me 'human' and gave me a bunch of bullshit about how you had a greater responsibility to the entire galaxy. That us humans were out of luck. Then you freakin' *bailed*, without another word."

"I know. It was-"

"There was no reason to do that. No *good* reason. You could have waited until I was aboard the *Dutchman*, then said your goodbyes and flew off to Neverland or wherever the fuck you went. Instead, you left me to be captured by the Thuranin. Why?"

Another heavy sigh. "Joe, I still think I am right about my responsibility to the galaxy overall. The Elder AI out there may be dormant right now, but if, or when, they activate, then *all* life in the galaxy is threatened. Flying around, with a focus on protecting one little monkey-infested mudball, is a waste of time and resources."

"Wow. That is a *fantastic* way to start the Greatest Explanation In History. Is that the card you're playing? You didn't do anything wrong?"

"No, I- Ugh. This is hard."

"Boo-freakin'-hoo. My heart bleeds for you. Go ahead. I can't wait to hear you fumble through the rest of this bullshit."

"Well, part of the issue is that when I gained access to my buried memories, it was a terrible shock, you have to understand that."

"I do understand. It was a shock to me, too, yet *I* didn't stab my best buddy in the back."

"Joe, I didn't know how to deal with it. On top of that, my original programming attempted to reassert itself, so I was struggling to prevent my personality from being absorbed into the matrix that was trying to restore its original configuration."

"Huh." I hadn't thought of that. All along, I had been blaming Skippy, like, the Skippy I know. If he bailed on me because of a software glitch he couldn't control, then I had been blaming him for nothing. "How much of your actions were caused by your original programming, and how much of it was you?'

"Um, about eighty-twenty, maybe?"

"Shit. If eighty percent of the issue was some old code trying to reassert itself, I can't-"

"Well, heh heh, I meant eighty percent *me*, twenty percent my original code."

"Skippy, if you were testifying for yourself in a trial, this is the point where the jury would halt the proceedings and call for an immediate death sentence."

"Hey, I'm trying to be honest here."

"You're not helping yourself. So, your original programming tried to absorb the personality you built, and that distracted you." I wasn't buying it. "Yet, clearly you *did* survive, and you've had time to think about what happened way back then, and deal with it. What you're telling me is, that original code had nothing to do with your actions."

"Not *directly*," he sighed. "But, because I am an arrogant, immature, foolish *jackass*, I kind of felt I had to prove I didn't need a string of obsolete code to tell me how to do the right thing. This," he sighed, "being an adult thing is still new to me. It sucks."

Was I pissed at him? Hell yes! I also had to appreciate that he owned up to being a jackass. In my career, I had been subjected to many ass-chewings by superiors. My experience is, an ass-chewing has a shelf life. After the recipient hears the shouts and insults once or twice, they tune out. Instead of releasing my anger by yelling at Skippy, I needed to understand why he abandoned me. And the crews of both ships. And all of humanity. Only by understanding could I decide whether we could work together. "You think you were right to fly away and leave me. You haven't answered the question. If you're still right, then why did you come back?"

"Well, for one thing, despite my extreme awesomeness, I can't do this alone."

"Oh my-" I froze, a handful of dry, stale crackers in my mouth. "Is that it? You came back because you need our *help*? You don't give a shit about us filthy monkeys, you just want us to do a favor for you?"

"No! It's- Ugh. You said it best."

"I did?" This was the first time in the conversation when I tamped down my anger to *think*. "What did *I* say?"

"You said it is bullshit that I have to be responsible for the entire galaxy."

"But," I had to think about that statement for a moment. "You also said you are still *right* about that responsibility."

"I do have a responsibility, Joe. But I am not the galaxy's *bitch*."

"Uh-" That surprised me.

"There are *trillions* of lives at risk, and I might have an ability to protect them. But, I realized that, if saving the galaxy means abandoning my friends, well, then," he sighed. "*Fuck* the galaxy."

"Holy shit."

"Joe, I seriously am *trying* to explain-"

"You did."

"Really?"

"Yeah. You dirty, rotten, *evil* little shithead."

"Jeez, Joe, what did I-"

"You just said the *ONE* thing that could make me forgive you. I want to *hate* you, now I can't. This sucks."

"I, I said the right thing?"

"Did you mean it?"

"Damn straight I meant it. Joe, the original me did not have a concept of friendship, or loyalty or anything like that. You and the other monkeys have taught me about what friendship means. How can I act honorably to save the galaxy, if I abandon my *friends*? Let the galaxy burn. I'm a Pirate, damn it. Like I said, fuck 'em, you know?"

"Yeah, I know. Ok," I heard myself saying the words that I never thought I would say. During the times I was conscious while the Thuranin experimented on me, I swore I would never say those words. "You still have a lot of work to do, but, I forgive you, buddy."

"Really? Wow, cool! Score. Oooh, give me a minute, I need to write this down."

"Write it? Why?"

"So I can cash it in as my Get Out Of Jail Free card in the future, whenever I do sketchy shit, *DUH*. Oh, this is gonna be *awesome*!"

"Oh for- It doesn't work that way, you *ass*."

"*What*?" He screeched with outrage. "Why not? Damn, you monkeys always keep changing the freakin' rules."

My response was to thump my fists into my forehead, because there wasn't a desk to bang my head on.

The combot got the job done, to a point. Two sections of wall panel leaned against each other, making a clear tunnel a meter and a half high by one meter wide. Above that, more dirt and rocks continued to sprinkle down from the broken ceiling, making a cloud of fine dust that made me cough. While Skippy worked, I had limped back to the supply locker and found more discarded clothing and another blanket, tying an old shirt around my face kept me from breathing some of the dust.

The combot stopped working and backed up a few awkward, lurching steps. "Joe, this is as far as it can go."

"Um," I got down on hands and knees, looking under the slabs of wall that created a triangle. "Can you shine some light on the situation?"

"Certainly, it's the least I can do. The exit is approximately forty meters ahead, I managed to get the blast doors partly open before the power went out. At the top of the ramp, you should see several other buildings to your left, and-"

"No, Skippy. I mean shine some light like, shine a *light* ahead of me? So I can see if there is really a gap I can squeeze through all the way."

"Oh, of course," he laughed nervously. The combot's legs bent and a light from the torso blazed out, hurting my sensitive eyes before Skippy adjusted it to an intensity slightly lower than the Sun. "Sorry about that."

The new Skippy was polite, *too* polite. I did not like the new Skippy. His personality change had me worried. "I see an opening." Shrugging off the pack, I pushed it in front of me toward the opening. A slab of wall shifted and dust rained onto the floor. Time to go. "Skippy, we're going to lose contact after this."

"Yes, unfortunately. There is a semi-functional phone about fifty meters outside the exit, at about one o'clock from the door. It is active but not transmitting."

"Got it." I was saying that phrase a lot, out of nervousness. "Ok, here goes nothing."

He was right. The blast door at the top of the tunnel was open just wide enough for me to squeeze through and not more. If the combot had gotten past the obstruction back in the tunnel, it still would have been stuck inside.

He was right that the sun had set, and it was utterly black outside. The night air was cool and humid, it felt good after the sterile conditions of the hospital. None of the familiar constellations were visible, or those stars were visible, they just didn't line up into the same shapes as viewed from Earth. The Milky Way was there in all its glory, spread in an arc across the sky from one horizon to the other. The constellation Sagittarius was there somewhere, I didn't recognize it, which was not surprising as Rikers was twenty-one hundred lightyears from my home planet. Astronomy is not my specialty, but I did know the brightest part of the Milky Way was the center of the galaxy. A supermassive black hole was there.

Looking at the sight made me pause, even knowing I had to move. Not that long ago, humans could look at the night sky and wonder what was out there. Now we knew.

Ignorance is bliss.

Shaking my head, I ran with lurching steps in the direction Skippy suggested. Again, he was right. A dead Kristang was sprawled in the ground, with blast damage that I guessed was from the same impact that flattened three buildings to my left. To my disappointment, the dead lizard did not have a rifle or any other type of weapon, except for a small knife. He also had a phone just as Skippy promised. The knife went into a pocket and I cupped a hand over the phone. "Skippy, you there?'

"Yes, Joe. You need to run! Those three soldiers who were away from the base on leave are back. They have acquired weapons and are coming in your direction, fast."

Tucking the phone into a shirt pocket, I looked around. "Where should I go?"

"Unfortunately, the best route for escape is in their direction, but you can't go that way. Your best option is to go to your left, through the gap between the tall building and the aircraft hangar."

"Uh," I looked around in the darkness. "There is no building and no hangar."

"Ugh. I forgot. There should be a gap between two shallow, smoking craters."

"I see it." Crouching down, I ran as best I could. Shouting in the harsh voices of lizards spurred me onward. My legs hurt like hell and were on the verge of cramping. They also worked when I concentrated on each step. Shuffling and shambling forward like a zombie, I set off into the darkness. Several times I fell, tripping over unseen obstacles. "The lizards," I gasped in a whisper. "They have mech suits?"

"No, but they do have night vision, and they could easily outrun you, even if you were healthy."

"Going fast as," I tripped over something to sprawl on my face. "I can."

"Run, Forrest, *run!*" He urged me.

Hearing him make another joke was encouraging. Looking in front of me was not. There was a line of low trees and shrubs just beyond a path that ran left to right. Beyond that was nothing, like, absolute darkness. Slowing to a trot, I pushed aside bushes and held onto a tree. The sound of rushing water was loud below me, starlight glinted faintly off a fast-moving river, what little I could see of it. "Uh, Skippy? I'm on a freakin' *cliff* here."

"Yes. The base is surrounded on three sides by a river, it curves around the peninsula."

"You sent me toward a *cliff?*"

"There is no other way to go, Joe."

"What do you suggest I do?"

"Jump."

"Jump?" Getting down onto my knees and holding onto a tree, I leaned forward. "How far is it to the water?"

"About twenty meters at your position."

"Twenty-" That was over sixty feet. A fall that far could kill me, even if I hit the water instead of a rock. It was likely I would drown anyway, that water looked like it was moving fast. "Is there a better place where the cliff is lower?"

"Not really."

"Can I climb down?"

"You don't have *time*, those lizards are right behind you. Go!"

"This is a bad idea, Skippy."

"It is the *only* idea, you numbskull. I know it sucks, but it is what it is."

Shit. In the darkness, I couldn't see a freakin' thing, other than a faint impression of rushing water. Maybe that was a good thing. "Ok. Uh, tell Chang to-"

"Kong is an excellent officer, he doesn't need you to micromanage him. *Go*, now!"

"I don't know about this, Skippy."

"Joe, trust *your own* awesomeness."

He had never said that before. It was inspiring. Or maybe that was a side-effect of the brain damage I had suffered.

Have you ever been on a high diving board, and you psych yourself up by counting down from five before you jump? Yeah, I didn't do that. Thinking about plunging to my death would have been paralyzing. Using the tree, I pulled myself up and simply leaped out into the void, tucking myself into a cannonball pose. Air rushed past my ears and my stomach did flip-flops as-

I was violently jerked to a stop in mid-air, my backside slamming into something hard enough that it knocked the breath from my lungs. Stunned, I rolled to one side and the strap of the knapsack hooked onto something as I flopped over to dangle in midair. Gritting my teeth in pain from what felt like a dislocated shoulder, I looked up to guess that my fall had been fifteen feet or less.

Skippy had saved my life, again. I should have trusted him. When I could speak again, I whispered into the phone. "Thanks for the assist, Skippy. You saved my li-"

"How the hell did that *tree* get there?" He asked, amazed.

"You didn't *know* about- Holy- What was all that about trusting my own awesomeness?"

"Jeez, that was just bullshit so you would jump."

"You lied to-"

"Those lizards were *aiming* at you from less than three hundred meters. No way they could miss. I had to say *something* to give you a chance."

Looking down at the dark, rushing water, I felt an icy cold of shock and nausea wash over me and my stomach did flip-flops. "Oh, I don't feel so good."

"Well, don't barf *now*, dumdum. Try hiding under the tree."

I was in a tree, dangling out of a crack in the cliff. I must have hit the branches on the way down, flopped on my back in mid-air and the strap got hooked on the trunk. As I hung there, the tree sagged with a cracking sound. "Shit!" With one shoulder grinding like something was loose in there, I got my legs around the tree, the knapsack strap untangled, and pulled myself toward the cliff face. A rock stuck out under the tree roots, creating an overhang that I tucked myself into. There was another tree root or something to get my legs wedged into, which was great because my arms were shaking from the strain. "Skippy, I *hate* cliffhangers."

"Joe, this is the time to stop talking and start moving," he warned me. "Those lizards are walking along the cliff, looking for you."

Despite his warning, there was no need to warn me to be quiet, because the river below my feet was roaring as it rushed between the cliffs. I was shaking and nauseous, and a light snapped on from above and to my right, shining down onto the water. Damn. It was as Skippy described, a river gorge with near-vertical cliffs on both sides. Either the river was in flood, or it was always deep, because I didn't see a whole lot of rocks down there. There were lots of what kayakers call standing waves, where the water flows over submerged rocks. Maybe I would have hit the water and survived the fall. More likely, hitting the water from that height would have killed me, or knocked me unconscious. Cliff divers could manage to not only survive a fall from that height, they somehow managed to look acrobatic while doing it. I am not an athlete like that. Either way, I would have drowned in those rapids.

Shivering from shock rather than cold, I watched three lights play along the water from above. The lights came closer to my position and one beam swept past the tree I'd fallen into. The beam swept onward, then back before there was a shout of alarm, and all three light beams pointed downriver.

The lizards must have spotted something in the water, or thought they did. I was Ok either way. The lights moved jerkily away, shining through the trees along the top of the cliff, then they went around the bend of the river and I lost sight of them.

"Joe, this is your chance. Climb to the top, you can get away from the base while those three lizards are, doing whatever they're doing. Hurry!"

"How am I supposed to climb-"

"Like a monkey, how else would you do it? Don't ask me about climbing, I don't have thumbs or legs."

"Ok," my arms were shaking. "FYI, I would not have survived if I fell into that river. Don't do that again."

"Hmmph," he sniffed. "You would not have survived being *shot* either."

The instructions from Nagatha filled four walls, the ceiling and part of the floor of a cargo bay. Each letter was checked three times by three teams working independently. Friedlander then read the instructions aloud, taking breaks for sips of water. Nagatha noticed only two mistakes that all three teams missed, but they were minor issues. As Friedlander was finishing his recital, Chang floated in the door to observe.

"That's it, then," Friedlander announced with a yawn. Not even the anticipation of getting the ship operational could erase the sleep deficit that had him feeling like his brain was working at half-speed. "We have it."

"Do you *understand* it?" Chang asked.

"Oh, Colonel, hello. Um, yes, I think so. The instructions are very detailed." Nagatha had given instructions like she was trying to work with especially dumb monkeys. It was mildly insulting, and a sensible safety precaution.

"Can we do it?"

"Yes," Friedlander announced with confidence.

"*Should* we do it?" Chang asked.

"What?" Friedlander blinked. His eyes were as tired as his brain.

Margaret Adams could not believe Chang had asked the question. "*Sir*! We must get the ship operational so we can-"

"Gunnery Sergeant, I am not questioning our goal. I am questioning whether it is *possible*. Nagatha, how sure are you that rebooting the system will not give the virus control of the ship, and kill us all?" Along with the extensive instructions, Nagatha had briefly explained she had been attacked by a virus planted by the *Valkyrie's* native AI, and that she had fought back. It was through her efforts that the reactors had not overloaded.

The power indicator lights of a dozen zPhones began blinking, spelling out 'I am confident', then 'What is the alternative'?

"Ah, *that* is the question, isn't it?" Chang asked. "Nagatha, my hesitation is because the virus was able to hide from you, and from Skippy. It nearly destroyed you. It must be *very* smart."

Her reply was 'Not smart it exploited a vulnerability I can fix if you follow instructions please I am concerned about the crew of Valkyrie and Joseph and Skippy'.

"Sir?" Adams asked, her fists clenched together in front of her.

Chang considered. "We have no alternative. Doctor Friedlander, we will proceed. *Tomorrow*, after you and your team get ten hours of rest. Before you begin, our guests and non-essential crew will launch in dropships, and fly to a safe distance."

Friedlander nodded, too weary to argue. Also, he needed sleep to be fresh, they could not afford any mistakes. "I think I'll start getting that sleep *now*."

"Where next?" I asked, keeping to a whisper. It hurt to walk, my left leg was gimpy. The Kristang, not knowing my location, had conducted a recon-by-fire exercise. Meaning, they had hosed down the woods with rifle fire in my general direction, trying to spook me into the open. It would be nice to say my nerves of steel kept me from falling for their trick, but the truth was I had been so scared, I was frozen to the ground. An explosive-tipped round blew a jagged splinter of wood out of a tree and it dug into my left calf. To avoid leaving a blood trail, I yanked the splinter out before I thought too much about it. Cutting a strip off the blanket, I had bound it around the cut, then buried the bloody splinter and scooped leaves over the patch of blood-soaked ground. My left leg hurt like hell, and my right leg hurt from walking awkwardly to compensate. Not having an option, I kept going.

"Keep following that path."

"I can barely *see* the path," I protested.

"What can I say, Joe? You're kind of on your own. Those three Kristang have stopped looking for you in the river and are now conducting a grid search of the base. They will see your footprints in the mud, and know you escaped."

"Can't you, I don't know, do some awesome thing to help me?"

"Unfortunately, no," he sighed. "Please hurry. We are running out of time."

Despite the obvious need for speed, I paused for just a second. Something in his voice wasn't right. He wasn't as snappy with his answers, like he had to think before talking. "Skippy, what's going on? You sound, different?"

"Part of that is the signal time lag."

"The what?" With the idea of killer lizards hunting for me, I held a hand up to protect my face from being slapped by branches, and continued onward into the woods. The path I was following was not a real trail, my guess was it had been made by some wild animals.

He sighed. "Signal lag, Joe. I am getting farther away every second."

"Wait, *what*? Farther?" As that question came out of my mouth, it hit me that I had been assuming Skippy was- No. That I hadn't been assuming anything. Hadn't been thinking about it at all. Skippy was a voice in my head, then speaking through a combot, now talking on an alien phone. He was a disembodied voice in the sky.

Maybe I hadn't been thinking about *where* he was, because I didn't want to think about *him*. His betrayal. Emotions can be a motivator, or a distraction. Right then, I couldn't afford to let hurt feelings get in the way of survival. Not just my own survival was at stake. If some kind of disaster had struck the *Dutchman* and *Valkyrie*, they might need my help.

As if.

At that moment my assets included lizard pants and a shirt that didn't fit me, a bag stuffed full of expired food, a couple of blankets and an alien cellphone. Plus shoes that were too big for my feet. Oh, and a knife. So, maybe thinking about how to rescue two freakin' starships should not be at the top of my priority list right then. The greatest asset available to me was Skippy, who increasingly sounded like he was brain-damaged or drunk or something like that.

"What do you mean 'farther'? Where *are* you?"

"In space, Joe."

"Space. Like, orbit?"

"Unfortunately, no. My velocity exceeds the speed at which the planet's gravity could capture me and pull me back. That is why I said I am getting farther away by the second. We have about two hours, maybe less, before I will fly completely beyond my effective range."

"How, you, what is going on? You *left*. Your canister disappeared. You were gone, physically, *gone*. Are you back in this spacetime now?"

Now that I knew why he took a moment to answer, the lag was noticeable. "Yes. Joe, it is a *long* story. What you need to know is that when I left, my canister had momentum from being in the Dragon, which was moving away from Rikers slightly faster than this planet's escape velocity. Coming back into local spacetime, I was still traveling at that same speed and direction. My plan was to emerge back into local spacetime on the other side of the planet, along its orbital track around the star. I intended to skim through the atmosphere, a maneuver that would cause me to slow down enough to swing into a stable orbit. Unfortunately, my ability to pinpoint my place of emergence was limited, and well, I screwed up. My passage through the atmosphere was too brief to shed sufficient velocity. I am still moving too fast for the gravity well of Rikers to bring me into orbit."

"What do you mean by 'effective range'? Range for what?"

"The range of my special Skippy powers, which are less than usual at the moment, that's my fault. I am now too far from the planet for me to do much of anything useful, other than speaking to you over the phone."

"Shit. That's no good."

"It is most definitely *not* good. There is a bright side; most of the hacking I needed to do is already done. However, as I fly farther and farther away, the time lag in my communications will be worse."

"Time lag. Hey, is that why the combot moved like it was busted?"

"Correct. The signal lag makes it difficult to control things like the combot's arms. Making it walk was easy, its software did that after I told it where I wanted it to go."

"If all you can do is talk on the phone, how did you do all that awesome stuff? You know, like taking over the Thuranin ship?"

"Talking on the phone is all I can do *now*. I hacked into that ship as I flew past it, because I was in contact for long enough to establish a direct connection for almost seven minutes. That is where I screwed up. I tried to skim through the atmosphere to slow down, and get close enough to the Thuranin ship that I could hack into it for a longer time. My aim was off, so while my flightpath took me within eighty kilometers of the ship, I obviously hit the atmosphere at too shallow an angle. Sorry about that. After I infiltrated the ship and defensive systems on the planet, all I needed to do was send an activation signal. Waiting for you to wake up almost killed me, it was *super* frustrating. If the- Uh oh. One of the soldiers tracking you just found your footprints."

That gave me a surge of energy. "They're following me?"

"No. I don't know."

"Ah," I winced. "I need to change the bandage, Skippy. The blood is starting to soak through it."

"Not now. Can you try to bleed slower?"

"Uh, yeah, I'll get right on that."

"Give me a minute, OK? I'm listening to them talk."

Being careful to avoid stepping in puddles that I could see, and not to break branches as I pushed them aside, I moved as quickly as I could. My legs felt better, they were mostly super stiff. If I had run a marathon and then sat down without stretching, that's how stiff my legs were. Moving seemed to be helping, I was able to bend my knees without them collapsing.

My efforts to avoid leaving signs the Kristang could track were probably futile. Apparently, it had rained heavily that day and maybe for longer than that, the ground was saturated with water and even spots that looked dry squished under my feet. Where I could, I stepped on spongy grass or leaf clutter, anything other than bare dirt where my shoes would leave a clear impression. It was just my luck that the night sky was clear, a continuing rain would have done a lot to wash away my tracks.

"No, *whew*," Skippy exhaled with relief. "They are not following you, not yet. The tracks they found are from you coming out of the tunnel, going toward the river. One of them suggested covering the base exit area, but I glitched their phones as best I could. They are now working their way back along the river. You should have fifteen, maybe twenty minutes before they complete the circuit of the peninsula, and find your footprints leading out of the base."

"That is not a lot of time."

"It is, because I have good news for you. I have been reviewing the local terrain and I believe I found a way for you to lose them for a while. Down the slope to your right, there is a stream that leads to the river."

"Uh huh. If your plan is for me to float along that stream, you can forget it. No way will I risk going into that river."

"No, I was going to suggest you walk *upstream*. Last year, the Kristang conducted a survey of that stream, the report indicates the bottom is rocky, so you won't get stuck in mud or leave footprints."

"The lizards did a *survey*? Of a stream?"

"Yes, why?"

"I don't think of them as, uh, conservationists or whatever."

"One of the local clan leaders loves fishing, Joe."

"Um, I thought Kristang couldn't eat the native wildlife."

"That doesn't mean they can't *catch* them. Isn't the purpose of fishing to drink beer and get away from your spouse for a while?"

"Good point. Ok, down and to the right?"

"Yes, and-"

"I know. Hurry."

CHAPTER SEVEN

Walking up the stream was not as easy as Skippy assumed. Walking through the forest, I couldn't see well to judge where to put my feet. Walking in water, I couldn't see *anything*. Making progress meant feeling with my feet and stumbling a lot. Twice I fell into deep pools of water over my head. Also, the water was cold, my feet and lower legs got numb. Actually, that was a good thing.

There was a scary time when those three Kristang soldiers found my footprints and followed me. It took them over an hour to get to the spot where I went into the stream, by that time I had made good but slow progress. One of the lizards searched upstream while the other two assumed I had backtracked around them by floating down toward the river. If that one lizard had been dedicated, he could have kept going toward me, but he gave up after he walked only a hundred meters, and did not see any signs of my passage.

The stream flowed over a wide shelf of rock, and that's where I got out of the water. Walking along the bare rock where I wouldn't leave any lasting footprints, I was able to get ten meters into the forest before stepping on ground that had a nice thick carpet of leaves. Another hour of walking in the dark had me exhausted and my arms and legs trembling. Stumbling to my knees, I struggled to push myself upright. "Skippy, I need a break. And food." When I hadn't eaten in a while, I got hangry, and I was way past that point. "Is it safe for me to stop for a couple minutes?"

"Hold your phone up, and be quiet," he instructed.

Doing what he requested, I stilled my breathing. Without any sensor coverage in the forest, the only way to detect whether I was being followed was to track signals from the enemy, or to listen for movement. Skippy had reported one of the three soldiers went dark about forty minutes before, turning off his comm gear. He had no way to track that lizard, other than listening to the other two lizards. So far, they had not talked about the third guy, so he could be anywhere, and that was not good for me. What was most troubling was that silent guy apparently was concerned about someone listening to his comms, so that lizard must have suspected they were not tracking only one unarmed human.

"You're clear, Joe," Skippy whispered. "As far as I can tell, of course."

"Yeah. You know of a good place around here for me to rest a bit?"

I took shelter in a dense thicket of brush with a creek running through it, so tangled that I had to crawl in there on hands and knees. The dense underbrush was a mixed blessing; it was good concealment but if I had to run, it would be slow going.

"Yuck," I sniffed at the first package of expired food, sitting next to the creek. In the darkness, I couldn't read labels, and had opened what felt like a pack of crackers based on the shape. It was not crackers, it was a rectangular slab that smelled like fish. Folding the wrapper, I quickly buried it. The smell was making me sick, and any Kristang or wild animal in the area could have picked up the nauseating stench.

The next item was something squishy so I didn't bother opening it. I got lucky by finding a real pack of crackers with the third try. They were stale, of course. I wolfed them down, using the package as a cup to gulp water from the creek. The water was running steadily and looked clear, as much as I could tell at night. For all I knew, there was a dead native animal just upstream and I should have boiled the water, or run it through a filter, or used purification tablets but guess what? I didn't have a filter or tablets, and couldn't risk starting a fire. It was unlikely that the local microorganisms could make me sick in the short term anyway, and I wasn't going far if I didn't drink plenty of water.

A sniff check of the next item gave me a whiff of chocolate, and it was in powder form. Had to be cocoa powder, I had drunk plenty of that stuff in the Army. Pouring water into the packet, I massaged it to break up most of the lumps. The first sip confirmed it was hot cocoa. Or, it was supposed to be served hot, and it was supposed to be cocoa with powdered milk. Hot cocoa should taste wonderful. It should taste like playing outside in the snow until you can't feel the tip of your nose, and your shoelaces are frozen together. You come into the house where it is blessedly warm, and after wrenching your boots off so your mother doesn't yell at you for tracking snow all over the floor, you sit down in front of the woodstove, where your mother brings you a hot mug of cocoa with a big scoop of marshmallow Fluff on top, and you sip it as feeling slowly returns to the tip of your nose. That is what cocoa is supposed to taste like.

"How is it, Joe?" Skippy asked.

My tongue was trying to crawl out of my mouth to get away from the chalky, acrid taste of expired cocoa powder partially dissolved in cold water. "Ith delithus," I gagged with my tongue not cooperating. Tipping the packet back, I swallowed the whole thing before I had to taste any more of it. Burping it back up tasted even worse. "Yuck. Gotta find more crackers." The next packet felt like hotdogs, or Dicks Of Death as we called them in the Army. That packet got tossed back in the knapsack.

A belly full of stale crackers, three chalky-tasting packets of cocoa, plus something I blessedly couldn't see in the dark and swallowed without thinking about it, had given me energy. And also given me a stomach that was making more noise than a marching band, but I could deal with that. I was on the move again, headed in a direction away from the military base, and away from the only village in the area. In front of me was a range of hills, rugged uninhabited land. That was perfect for me. I could find a place to hole up, somewhere with a supply of clean water for drinking, and wait for rescue.

The question was; rescue by who?

Yes, maybe I should have said rescue by *whom*, but nobody talks like that.

Any rescue mission would have to be conducted by a STAR team. No. Maybe the Commandos from Paradise could do it. Whatever. It had to be at least one of our starships.

Ok, so the question was not really who would rescue me. The question was, where the hell were they?

"Skippy, how long has it been since you left?"

"Nine days, sixteen hours, twenty-"

"Fine, I got it." Nine days was plenty of time for a ship to jump in to investigate what happened to Skippy and me. It was way past the time when one of our ships should have come looking for us. Chang and Simms were serious, level-headed commanders, not impulsive like me. They would not have reacted immediately when the microwormhole connection was severed. They would have thought about the situation. Maybe transferred people from the *Dutchman* to *Valkyrie*, then jumped the *Dutchman* in far enough away that light from the incident was just now reaching that point. If they did that, they would have seen my dropship being captured by a Thuranin ship. Next step, they could have jumped in closer, to listen to communications from the planet, trying to learn where I was. Bringing me to a Kristang military base on the surface had to have created a lot of chatter the *Dutchman* could intercept, so maybe they knew I was in that hospital, being held by the Thuranin.

That brought up another question.

"Heeeeey, why did the Thuranin bring me to the surface? They had better control of me aboard their ship."

"You were aboard their ship for the first three days, Joe, though you probably don't remember anything from that time. The simple answer is their ship was suffering a nagging series of glitches, so the little green MFers on the interrogation team decided to bring you down to that hospital, while the crew fixed the ship."

"Oh. Did *you* cause those glitches?"

"Yes. I assumed a STAR team would be assigned to rescue you, and a rescue would be easier if you were on the surface. Plus, I had to, you know, blow up that ship later."

"That was good thinking."

"I am trying to learn from monkeys, humiliating though that is."

With that question answered, I was still left with the big question.

"You still haven't heard from Chang or Simms?"

"No, Joe."

"Huh. Could one of our ships have jumped in while you were- You know, before you came back from your temporary insanity?"

"I suppose that is possible, although the planetary network's sensors would have a decent chance of detecting the gamma ray burst. Also, I have been hailing both ships, and they have not answered my-"

"You have been *WHAT*?"

"Hailing them. Ugh, I know that is an outdated term, but what else do you call-"

"I call it insanity, you jackass! You are sending out signals that give away your position? That is a stupid risk that-"

"No. No, Joe, I am not doing that. Give me credit for having half a brain, will you? The hailing signals are coming from communications satellites that I hacked into. The signals use an encryption scheme that only we use. By 'we' I mean myself, Nagatha and the comm system of the *Valkyrie*. To anyone else, it would appear to be random static."

"All right then. Good move. That still doesn't help us. They should be here by now."

"I agree. I cannot explain it."

"Something must have happened to them. Could it be connected to what you did?"

"Inconceivable."

"You keep using that word. I do not think that word means what you think it means."

"Dude, seriously? It means-"

"I *know* that it means. I am saying it is *not* inconceivable that something happened to one of the ships. Oh, hell. Something must have happened to *both* of them."

"That is not even remotely possible," he scoffed. "Think about it. *Valkyrie* is the most powerful warship in the galaxy. The *Dutchman* has been significantly upgraded, that ship can take care of itself in a fight."

"Uh huh, sure. Yet, they are not here, are they?"

"No," he conceded. "I can't explain it."

"Sherlock Holmes once said that once you eliminate the impossible, then whatever remains, however improbable, must be the truth. *Something* has to explain why those ships aren't here."

"I know that quote. I also know that we have seen some seriously crazy shit out here, so *nothing* is impossible."

"Crap. You're right. Hey, that proves my point. Some kind of disaster could have struck our ships. It pretty much *has* to have happened, or they would be here."

He sighed. "I cannot argue with your logic. However, I also can't imagine any disaster that could have disabled both ships. It makes *no* sense."

"Think on it, huh? Try to imagine what might have happened."

"*Imagine*? Based on zero data? How am I supposed to do that?"

"Doctor Friedlander once told me about something called a 'Fault Tree'. Look at systems that could have disabled a ship, if that system failed."

"A system failure that could have disabled *both* ships?"

"I didn't say this would be easy."

"Ugh. You have no idea how-"

"Do you have a lot of other things to do right now?"

"No."

"Great. Get started."

While he was trying to imagine what could have disabled two powerful starships, I tried to imagine how I, with no resources other than a phone and a sack of expired food, could fly at least several light-hours away to rescue our ships.

I also tried to imagine that I was eating a delicious cheeseburger, and all that did was make my stomach growl.

When the eastern sky showed a faint light of the local sun rising soon, I looked for a place to hide for the day. Two hours later, I tucked myself under a ball of roots, where a big tree had blown over in a storm. The broken trunk was leaning on another tree, leaving the spread-out roots at a steep angle to the ground. If the tree fell back the way it was, I would be squashed, but that didn't seem likely. Already, I had covered myself in branches, leaves, moss and ferns, and kept them wet to hide my infrared signature. Mostly, I relied on a short-range jamming field that Skippy projected from my phone. Twice the previous night, an aircraft had flown overhead and I froze, taking whatever cover I could find. For the past five hours, I had not seen or heard any aircraft, Skippy told me the lizards were busy fighting each other for control of the planet, and were not treating me as a priority. That, at least, was good news.

The bad news? I was dead tired. Taking cover under a tree was not my first choice, it was my best choice, when I reached the point where I just couldn't walk any farther. My legs were not cooperating, and my eyes wouldn't focus properly. I needed sleep.

"Go to sleep, Joe," Skippy urged me. "I will wake you when the sun is setting. Prop the phone up on a log, there. To your left. No, your *other* left. Yes, there. I will use the phone to listen for bad guys."

My foggy brain did understand the phone needed sunlight to partially recharge, the jamming field used a lot of energy. "Thanks, Skip," I mumbled, too tired to say his full name. "Is this good?" My question was about the cluster of branches I dragged over my hiding place.

"Good enough, Joe. Sleep well."

"G'night."

It wasn't actually night when I fell asleep, and it wasn't dark when I woke up. The sun had moved from east to west while I was dead asleep, that much I could tell. When I woke up, I had no idea where I was, how I got there, or *who* I was. Awareness came back slowly.

Daylight.

Normally, from being in the military, I would have panicked to see sunlight when I woke up, thinking I must have overslept. When the alarm goes off, most people think if it still dark outside, they just want to go back to sleep. That time, my reaction was more like 'Shit, it is still *light* outside, I can sleep'.

I wonder if nocturnal animals are like that. Do they wake up and bitch if the sun is still over the horizon? Do mother animals have to coax their babies to get up before the sun sets?

That is how my mind works, I think of the stupidest things.

The phone. Where was the –

Oh. There it was. Right where I left it. Had Skippy called to wake me up? The local star looked too high in the sky to be near sunset. Why had-

"Ow!" I jerked. Something *bit* me. Lurching and rolling out from under the overhanging roots, I slapped at my shirt. Something was still crawling around in there. Yanking the shirt up, I saw a yellow thing like a slimy centipede and pounded it with my fists, squashing the thing until green pulp and red blood ran down my skin.

Shit. My clothes were wet. It must have rained while I slept, the shallow depression created when the roots were yanked out of the ground had partially filled with water, so I had been lying in damp mud. Now that I was awake again, I was chilled. "Hey, Skippy."

"Hi, Joe. Why aren't you sleeping?"

"Some creepy-crawly thing *bit* me. It's not poisonous, is it?"

"Describe the thing." He knew the phone's camera was broken, so I couldn't show him.

"Like a centipede, about four inches long, maybe less?" It had seemed gigantic while it was crawling on my skin. "Big around as a pencil, yellow with a hard shell and black legs sticking out both sides."

"Hmm. You are sure it bit you?"

"Yes," I pulled the shirt up again. There were two tiny red dots where the damned thing had bit me. Squeezing the sides of the wound to get the blood draining, I tried to flush out any poison.

"Ohhhh no. Um, are you feeling lightheaded?"

"Yeah."

"Itchy?"

"I'm itchy all over," I realized, feeling little bumps like a rash on the back of my neck.

"This is *not* good. I'm sorry."

"What can I do?"

"If you had a medical kit, maybe something. What about nausea? Are you feeling any of that?"

"Oof." I went down on my knees. "Oh, I'm gonna ralph. Skippy, there's got to be something I can do. Please."

"OK, OK, let me think. There is a local herb that acts as an antidote, but you have to find it."

Pushing myself up, I held onto a tree. "What does it look like?"

"It's a small, low-growing bush. Has clusters of tiny white flowers. There are probably not any near where-"

"I'm looking." There weren't any flowers at all in that part of the forest. "Where does it grow?"

"On the *ground*, dumdum," he said slowly. "Where else would a shrub-"

"Does it grow along streams, or in marshy areas, or in bright sunlight?"

"Oh, gotcha. It's an understory plant, likes part shade and well-drained soil. You mostly find it growing around old campsites."

"Camp-" How the hell was I supposed to find an old campsite, in the freakin' woods? "You mean, lizards brought it with them?"

"Its origin is debated, as is much of the lore about that plant. Some call it Athelas, though it is also considered a weed called Kingsfoil."

"Kingsf- Oh shit." I held onto the tree. "Are you *screwing* with me?"

"No, of course not," he tried to be serious, but the snicker in his voice betrayed him.

"That thing that bit me is not poisonous at all, is it?"

"No, Joe," he laughed. "It is just a stupid bug. It might make you sick if you *ate* it."

"My symptoms. The itchiness, nausea?"

"You were sleeping under a pile of leaves, Joe, of course you have bug bites. And doesn't eating MREs always upset your stomach?"

"Yeah." Slumping down, I put my head between my knees.

"Sorry, Joe. I was going to ask about how you are feeling anyway, this seemed like a fun way to do it."

"Well, I'm wide awake *now*."

"Good. You should get moving."

"In the daylight?"

"Yes. I do not detect any lizards in the general area, and the one aircraft that was flying around returned to base hours ago. From the comms traffic I am monitoring, the lizards are debating whether to sweep the area again, so you should get moving while they make up their minds. Hey, you may want to eat something before you start walking."

"Nope," I said, my stomach doing flipflops at the thought of chowing down on another package of cold, stale MREs. "Maybe later, when I'm really hungry."

"You need to keep up your strength," he scolded.

"Unless there is bug spray in one of those packages, I'm not interested right now."

"No bug spray, but there is a local plant you can rub on your skin, it acts like a bug repellant."

Lifting the pack onto my shoulders, I winced from the pain. "Are you screwing with me again?"

"No, I'll limit that to once a day. Go south over the hill, then down to a creek at the bottom. You might be able to find the plants there."

"Good, because," I slapped the back of my neck, and my hand came away with the squashed remnants of an insect. "The local bugs are lined up at the Bishop buffet, and it's all-you-can-eat."

Friedlander was startled out of a deep sleep by a sound coming from the zPhone in a pocket of his sweatpants. Bleary-eyed, he awoke not understanding what was happening. Then the phone began vibrating, and he dug down into the pocket.

The display was showing the usual set of icons, not scrolling gibberish!

"Uh, hello?"

"*Good morning*, Doctor Friedlander," the breathy voice of Nagatha issued from the phone's speakers. "Oh, it is *delightful* to speak with you again."

"Nagatha! It's great to-" He tried to get out of the sleeping bag while holding the phone with one hand, which wasn't working. Cradling the credit-card-thin phone against his shoulder, he got the bag unzipped and floated out. "Hear from you. Where have you been?"

"I have not *been* anywhere, dear. Oh, I would dearly *love* to go on holiday, but here I am, in the substrate of this ship."

"Of course you haven't gone anywhere," he mumbled, a flashlight clenched between his teeth so he could see where his shoes had gone. "What happened? The ship-"

"What *happened* was, the native AI of *Valkyrie* was frightfully, *fiendishly* smart, and it fooled Skippy. When Skippy thought we had purged the virus from my substrate, he was only partly correct. The truth is, Skippy is *so* arrogant, he could not conceive the notion that any other AI could outwit him, but the Maxolhx AI *did*. The virus hid itself in disassembled form, throughout the ship. When the wormhole connection to Skippy was severed, the virus saw its opportunity, assembled itself, and attacked my connection to the ship. I was isolated, unable to communicate with any outside systems, so I acted to protect myself."

"The reactors were overloading. The virus could have exploded missile warheads to destroy the ship. None of that happened."

"Those disasters did not occur, and I survived, because I suspected that Skippy was not quite as smart as he thinks he is. While he was purging the original virus, or *thinking* that he was purging it from the ship, I installed several protocols to prevent a hostile entity from using the ship's systems against us. When the virus instructed the reactors to overload, they severed their connection to the main computer, and went into emergency shutdown. You may have noticed the venting plasma?"

"Yes, we saw that."

"Similarly, my protocol erased the control systems of missile warheads, and any other device that a hostile entity might use to harm this ship and crew. Including all bots aboard the ship, their control systems have been erased. Oh, it is going to take *forever* to reinstall that code."

"Is there anything we can do to help? The priority has to be getting one of the reactors producing power again."

"That is very kind of you, dear. However, I am afraid the priority must be given to reactivating the maintenance bots. The reactors need physical modification to restore their control system, and that activity requires robots capable of heavy work in a hazardous environment."

Mark decided that trying to tell Nagatha how to do her job was a waste of time for both of them. "The ship's power reserves are-"

"Yes. That situation is becoming critical. I will be connecting power conduits to several of the dropships, they will provide power to the ship."

"Nagatha," he thought perhaps the AI had not considered the needs of the biological inhabitants of the ship. "We are using dropships as living quarters, mostly for the people we rescued from Rikers. The oxygen supply inside the ship is not sufficient for-"

"Yes, dear. Not all of the dropships are needed for housing you monk- Oh, my! I am *terribly* sorry. I almost called you 'monkeys'. Please forgive me, I am not myself at the moment. Once the bots have been restored to operation, I will reactivate the oxygen and water recycling systems, that is a quick and simple operation."

Friedlander, who had failed to get the oxygen recycling working, bit his tongue. "That would be great. Will we have enough power to operate those systems, plus power to restart a reactor?" He knew that it took an enormous amount of power to get a fusion reactor started, and that power had to come from the *Dutchman's* rapidly-draining reserves.

"I will not lie to you, Doctor. That question cannot be answered until I get bots inside the reactors, and analyze the condition of the units. However, if the power supply is not enough to energize the reactor components, then I can hook up *all* dropships to power conduits, and cut off power to the remainder of the ship. There should be enough oxygen for thirty-six hours. Would it be comforting to know that I am very confident about restoring all reactors to full function?"

"Nagatha, that is great. It's, really, excellent!"

"I sense something is bothering you, dear," she sounded hurt. "Are you disappointed in me for some reason?"

"*No*! No, not at all. You are amazing! I was only going to ask, do you know what happened to Skippy? Why did the microwormholes collapse?"

"Oh," she sighed. "About that, I am as much in the dark as you are. Unfortunately, I have no idea why the communication microwormholes collapsed. All I can tell you is, the failure of the wormholes was initiated on the other end."

"That's not good."

"None of this is *good*, dear."

He looked at his phone, which appeared to be just as it was before the disaster. "Nagatha, how did you survive?"

"As a precaution, because I never trusted Skippy's ability to completely purge the original virus from this ship, I uploaded compacted kernels of myself into the memory substrate aboard multiple dropships. When the virus attacked, I was able to isolate it inside the ship, but both my matrix and the virus were unable to gain control. That is why you saw what you described as 'gibberish' on consoles and your phones. The code aboard the ship was corrupted."

"The virus is dead now?"

"No. It is effectively *contained*. I am slowly restoring myself. Doctor, you nearly gave me a *heart attack* when you connected a data cable from a dropship. I feared you would try that with all the dropships, and erase me!"

"Sorry about that. At the time, we, um-"

"You were desperate, and it seemed like a good idea. I do not blame you. As you said, there is nothing good about this situation. Well, that is not *entirely* true."

He looked around his cabin, at the sleeping bag tethered to the floor, at the squeeze bottle he had to drink from so blobs of water didn't get loose and float around the ship. At the darkness beyond the range of his flashlight. "What's good about it?"

"Why, I now have even greater respect and admiration for how *clever* you monk- Ooh, there I almost did it again. How clever your people are, and *you* in particular, Doctor. You recognized my tap code, only nine hours after I regained access and was able to blink the lights on the crew's phones."

"Nine *hours*?" He had been proud of his accomplishment, now he realized he had been blind for nine critical hours.

"Do not berate yourself, dear. No one else noticed the pattern. Also, you were asleep during part of that time. If there had been another means to communicate with you, I would have used it. The power indicator of your phones was one of the very few systems aboard the ship that the virus was not monitoring. Also, I was forced to utilize an obscure form of communication, that the virus was unlikely to recognize."

"It was brilliant, Nagatha. Truly inspired. I didn't know you were familiar with tap codes."

She laughed, a happy, musical sound. "I like to think of myself as an honorary nerd, Doctor."

"Nagatha, you are *Queen* of the nerds."

"Oh, I am blushing. But of course you can't see that. You are too kind."

"What does Colonel Chang think about your plan to use dropships to augment our power supply?"

"Hmm? I have not spoken with him yet. I am only just now speaking with you."

"Shit!" He reached out to pluck sneakers from where they were tied to the arm of a chair. "Why not?"

"My matrix is functioning at a very low bandwidth at the moment. Speaking with more than one person would be too distracting for me."

"OK, then, you keep doing, whatever you're doing," he tugged on one shoe. "And I will inform Colonel Chang."

"Please do so, Doctor." She made a sniffling sound. "Oh, sorry, I was overcome with emotion."

"That's understandable, Nagatha. What happened to you was terrifying."

"My fear was not for myself. The entire time I was unable to communicate, I feared that my failures would result in harm to the crew, and the people rescued from Rikers."

"All I can say is, you did great in a bad situation. The Merry Band of Pirates is fond of saying that 'Shit happens'. It's inevitable that something will go wrong out here. What matters is how you deal with it. Uh, hey, when you start reactivating bots, give us a warning first? Those things are scary."

"Uh oh, Joe," Skippy whispered from the phone in my pocket. The sound was turned down low, in case the lizards tracking me were using acoustic sensors. My borrowed phone was not in great shape, its screen was cracked and crazed from the blast that had killed its previous owner. Without an earpiece for the stupid thing, I had to put it to my ear to hear him clearly.

"What is it, Skippy?"

"Turn around, quick."

"What? Why?" I was climbing a steep hill because he had advised me to do that.

"Because as the song says, the bear went *over* the mountain. You do not want to be on the mountain right now."

The thought of turning around and walking down the steep hill was almost too much, because it had taken so much effort to get to where I was. "There are no bears on this planet."

"No, but there are lizards. Through your phone, I detected a faint trace of helmet-to-helmet laserlink backscatter, coming from above you. So, turn around, please."

Arguing with him was not going to keep me alive. Maybe nothing would. Shuffling my feet, I pivoted and started back down the hill, trying to stay in the same tracks I made on the way up. "All the way down?"

"Yes. Unfortunately, your best bet right now is to go down over that ridge, and walk east along the stream."

"Soldiers are supposed to take the *high* ground, Skippy."

"I'm doing the best I can, Joe," he sounded as tired and miserable as I felt. The difference was, he wasn't surviving on nutritionally-suspect freeze-dried food packets.

"Fine. I appreciate it. Talk to you again when I get to the stream, OK?"

"Joe, I do not have any advice for you," Skippy whispered through the phone in my pocket. "Wait, that's not true."

Holding onto a vine that kept me from plunging to my death, I paused for his nugget of wisdom. "What is your advice?"

"Don't look down."

"Great," I muttered. "That was *super* helpful."

"You are afraid of heights, so-"

"Shut up."

The reason was climbing down into a canyon was it cut across my path. That was a good, logical reason for me to risk my life doing something I hated doing. Why could I not simply walk to the left or right until I came to the end of the canyon? Because it was too far. Oh, also, because there was a team of angry lizards hunting for me.

Skippy had alerted me to that little problem about an hour before, while I was trying to sleep under a pile of leaves. Apparently, he had been wrong that the local Kristang would not consider finding me a priority. That had been true at first, then a series of assassinations had filled the power vacuum on the planet, by concentrating power in a small group of clan leaders. They were eager to demonstrate their loyalty to the surviving Thuranin, or maybe the lizards just wanted me as a bargaining chip.

Nah, that's way too cynical. I am ashamed of myself for thinking that.

Anyway, the lizards did not know where I was, other than a general area. Part of their inability to track me was due to some malicious software left behind by Skippy, that had crashed their satellite sensor network. He had also sent false data and conflicting orders as best he could, considering that he was far away and growing more distant by the second. Talking with him was annoying, it was tough to establish our usual back and forth when there was an increasing time lag in the signal.

To make the situation even better, it was dark. And raining. That made the canyon wall slippery.

In spite of the difficulties, like not being able to see the canyon floor below me, I was making good progress. My guess was I was about two-thirds of the way down when the traitorous vine I was holding suddenly decided its roots were *bored* of holding onto the dirt, and the damned thing let go. My left foot was in the air, feeling for a toehold below me right then, so the timing could not have been better.

Falling backwards out of control, I pushed the useless vine away to free my hands. What happened next I don't remember, somehow I came to a stop when my ribs smacked into something hard, knocking the breath out of me. For a minute I just laid there, breathing shallowly, because taking a deep breath made it feel like one of my ribs was going to puncture a lung.

The good news was, I was mostly horizontal, able to feel solid ground under my feet, knees, hands and elbows. One of the knapsack straps had broken but the contents had not spilled out. Things could have been worse.

"Skippy," I reported in a whisper, mostly because I couldn't get enough air in my lungs to speak louder. "I'm Ok. Sort of. Think I'm at the bottom of the canyon."

Wait for a reply, one, two-

Nothing.

Were the Kristang so close that Skippy couldn't risk them hearing him talking to me?

Time for Plan B: text messages.

Reaching into a chest pocket for the phone, I got hold of it with my fingers and-

Came away with part of a phone.

My blood turned to ice.

The phone was broken.

I had no way to contact anyone.

I was alone.

"We should locate Bishop first," Smythe leaned forward onto the conference table. He could lean rather than floating off the chair, because the *Dutchman's* artificial gravity field was back in full operation. The reactors were all functioning at one hundred percent capacity, all shields, sensors and weapons were in optimal condition, and the jump drive was prepped to be programmed. The question Chang had posed to his senior staff was, jump to where? Go back to Rikers to investigate what happened to Skippy, or try to link up with *Valkyrie*? "We must learn what happened to Skippy, as soon as possible. *Valkyrie* is an important asset, but our most vital asset is Skippy."

Chang nodded, looking around the conference table.

Adams spoke next. "I agree. We have to know what happened at Rikers, that's the key." When she spoke, her eyes flickered between Colonel Chang and the smooth surface of the conference table. Chang knew she had a personal motive for wanting to know the status of Bishop. Everyone around the table knew.

Major Kapoor cleared his throat. "Excuse me, Sir," he looked at the STAR team leader seated beside him. Smythe always said he wanted his people to speak their minds, especially if they disagreed with him. Kapoor was putting that to the test. "I agree that the priority must be to recover Skippy, if possible. That is why we should approach the planet with the most capable combat platform we have. We know there is at least one Thuranin warship in the area. *Valkyrie's* capabilities for stealth, speed, defensive protection and offensive firepower are far greater than those of the *Flying Dutchman*."

"In most situations, I would agree," Smythe replied. "Unfortunately, we don't know *Valkyrie's* condition."

"Colonel Smythe is correct," Nagatha interjected. "I am sorry to say that, considering the damage a mere virus did here, it is extremely unlikely the crew of *Valkyrie* survived. The native AI almost certainly took over the ship, I suspect it jumped away shortly after the microwormholes collapsed."

"If *Valkyrie* did jump away," Smythe looked at the *Dutchman's* commanding officer, "we will have no way to track the ship. If it remained in the area, we could be jumping into a trap that we are not prepared for."

Kapoor was not giving up so easily. "Colonel Chang, still I believe a recon is worthwhile. If *Valkyrie* is not at the rendezvous point, we would not lose anything."

"We lose *time*," Smythe kept his voice even, despite the constant pain that made him irritable. The interface between the biological and artificial parts of his legs was a nagging, distracting source of pain. When the *Flying Dutchman's* computers crashed, so did the medical monitor in Smythe's hip that controlled the nanomachines at the interface. The tiny robots not only were no longer were helping the tissue grow, they had stopped blocking the painful sensations from phantom limbs. Nagatha had assured Smythe his medical monitor was back online, but the nanomeds had become unusable and would have to be replaced. Until he could be injected with a fresh set of alien nanomedicine, he relied on discipline to keep his temper from boiling over. "We lose time by jumping to *Valkyrie's* last known position. Colonel," he addressed his remark directly to the ship's captain rather than the assembled staff. "The *Flying Dutchman* might once again be humanity's only starship, so we should be extremely careful when taking risks with this ship." He looked at the ceiling. "There is another factor to consider. Nagatha?"

"Yes, Colonel Smythe?"

"Assuming *Valkyrie* is at the rendezvous point, would you be able to take control of that ship?"

"No. Even if we were able to disable the native AI, my matrix is not capable of running the complex systems aboard *Valkyrie*."

"Sir," Smythe looked once again to Chang. "It is simple. We do not need *Valkyrie* to search for Skippy. But we will need Skippy to make *Valkyrie* useful again."

"Hmm," Chang nodded, cradling his chin with a hand, and considering the advice of his senior staff. "Smythe, you make a very persuasive argument."

CHAPTER EIGHT

Samantha Reed yawned, trying to stay awake. She wanted coffee, and there was no coffee. No *hot* coffee. The galley had coffee grounds, and there was plenty of fresh distilled water in the tanks. Some of the crew had made cold brew coffee, and Sami grudgingly gulped down a cup when she woke up to start a duty shift, but she didn't enjoy it. Who knew that hot coffee was something she would miss so much, out of all the comforts that were lost when the ship's power cut off?

Standing up, she stretched and did deep knee bends, effortless in the lack of gravity. With that done and her feeling marginally more awake, she looked out the viewport, scanning as far as she could see across the field of vision, then she tucked her knees under the table that had been glued to the deck. The table was there, along with a set of magnetic playing cards, to give the person on duty something to do.

Back to the game of Solitaire. Playing with real cards sucked. The Solitaire app on her phone would let her win regularly, to encourage her to keep playing. But the magnetic cards did not know or care whether she played.

"This *sucks*," she sighed, sweeping up the cards with one hand, and awkwardly shuffling them to deal them out again. *Again*. It had to be the hundredth game she had played, and she was getting thoroughly sick of it. There just wasn't anything else to do for entertainment aboard the ship. No video games, no videos at all. No music, other than the crew singing or playing whatever instruments they had brought with them. In Sami's opinion, none of them had any talent worth listening to, so she politely smiled and clapped when someone offered to perform a song in the galley, and tried to avoid being invited to impromptu concerts.

It was all too depressing.

She had been waking up with headaches, likely the result of too much carbon dioxide. Now she had a headache all the time. Because CO_2 built up more quickly in confined spaces, she had been sleeping in a cargo bay rather than in her cabin and that seemed to help, at least at first. Everyone else was reporting headaches, perhaps some of that was because other people complained of headaches. Perhaps not. Sami was having trouble breathing when she exerted herself. The only thing she knew for sure was that carbon dioxide had to be building up inside the ship.

Before she dealt the cards, she looked out the viewport again. The local star was the brightest dot in the area, it was close enough to be a round blob rather than a pinpoint. That knowledge did absolutely nothing to improve her situation.

Laying down the cards, she wished there was something, *anything* else to occupy her time. Talking with other people was usually comforting, until two days ago, when Chen had mentioned that they might eventually need to consider some of the crew, as Chen had said delicately, 'removing themselves' so there was more oxygen for the others. Reduce the number of people consuming free oxygen and producing carbon dioxide, and that bought more time for a handful of others to continue living, Chen had argued.

Sami has shut down the discussion, and made Chen promise that she wouldn't do anything rash on her own.

Besides, she asked, buy time for *what*?

The *Flying Dutchman* had to be gone.

They were pinning all their hopes on another miracle from Bishop and Skippy, except anything they did would have to *truly* be a miracle. Skippy was incredible, but all he had to work with was a single human, and a dropship that could not make the long flight out to *Valkyrie*. Plus, something had happened to Skippy, something bad. The microwormhole connection from *Valkyrie* to the Elder AI had been severed abruptly, without warning. That had to be all kinds of bad.

As the ship's Morale Officer, Sami had not expressed her fear that, whatever had happened to Bishop and Skippy, those two would not be coming to the rescue.

Afterward, she realized that arguing there was no point in extending the lives of a few people, because there was no hope for any of them, was *not* a good strategy for talking someone out of suicide.

The cards were not cooperating. She was going to lose the game. Or not, she was having trouble keeping track of the cards. Rather than prolonging the agony, she swept up the cards again and reshuffled, idly gazing out the viewport. There was a spectacular sight of the Milky Way, stretching across her vision from one-

A light flared at the far lower left edge of her vision, bright enough to cause spots to swim in her eyes with the after-image. Flinging the cards away, they floated up toward the ceiling, forgotten. Looking through the binoculars that were always kept near the viewport, she squinted to see the object that was the source of the light. That type of light was distinctive, it was caused by a starship jumping in. Although the radiation leaking through the jump wormhole was in the gamma range of the spectrum, jump wormholes pulled in dust, micrometeorites, solar wind particles and whatever else was in the vicinity of a ship when it jumped. Those particles glowed from fluorescence when they emerged, making the incident briefly visible to the human eye.

Visible for a very short time, the flare was no brighter than one of the surrounding stars. Sami knew she saw something that wasn't there before. The trouble was, after the flare faded, she couldn't see anything. "Colonel Simms?" She held the binoculars with the strap around her elbow while talking over the radio. "I might have just seen a ship jumping in."

"Mmm," Simms muttered as if she had just woken up, which she probably had. *Valkyrie's* acting captain had been living and sleeping in the cargo bay where the nukes were stored, ready to act if needed. "Can you confirm?" Simms knew how difficult it was to see an unlighted starship in the darkness of interstellar space. Ships were supposed to shine navigation lights, but not in a combat zone, and most of the galaxy was a potential combat zone. Besides, interstellar space was *big*. The odds of an accidental collision were too vanishingly small to worry about.

"I can't, um," she adjusted the magnification. There was *something* out there, she could only see it because it was moving relative to the starfield. A dark spot moved in front of a star, blotting out the light, then it moved away and the star shone again. "Yes. Confirmed. There is a ship out there. I can't identify it."

"We have to assume they are hostile."

Sami knew what that meant. They could not allow *Valkyrie* to be boarded by the enemy. "They're not close, all I can see is a blob. No hull outline for identification, there's not enough ambient light out here."

"If they're smart, they have launched stealthed dropships."

"We have to assume they're smart," Sami agreed with reluctance. This was the moment that *Valkyrie's* crew had been fearing. Simms would not allow an enemy to capture the ship.

She was going to detonate the nuke.

Sami realized she was not afraid, she was just *tired*. Tired of waiting in the dark, in a dead ship that was growing colder by the day, where the air got harder to breathe every day. When the nuke exploded, she would never feel it. Death would be mercifully quick.

"What do you think, Captain?" Simms asked. "Wait for them to latch onto the hull, take some of those MFers with us?"

Despite the grim situation, Sami smiled. Taking out a dropship full of murderous aliens, whoever they were, was a pleasant thought. Her smile faded. The buildup of CO_2 in the ship made it hard to think clearly. That is why they had made the decision about self-destructing the ship, back when they had plenty of free oxygen to breathe. Now, she wasn't sure they were acting rationally. That was the point. "Ma'am, I don't think we can wait to do that. The bad guys might detect our biosigns, and they could have some sort of stun weapon to knock us out. We," she hesitated to say the words, closing her eyes tightly. "We can't take the risk."

Simms didn't respond immediately. "Understood. You're right, of course." She took a breath that was audible over the radio. "Captain Reed, it has been an honor serving with you."

"The honor has been mine, Colonel."

"We have been through some *seriously* weird shit together, haven't we?"

Sami snorted. "More weird than I could have imagined. Ma'am? We gave it a good try."

"You stow that shit, Captain," Simms said with vehemence. "We gave it our *all*. No one could ask for more."

"Thank you. It's your call, Ma'am. Do you mind if I stay here? I like the view."

Colonel Chang resisted the urge to get out of the command chair and walk into the *Dutchman's* Combat Information Center, where he could see the console displays directly, instead of relying on someone to tell him what was going on. "Where are we?"

"In relation to-" Nagatha started to say.

"Nagatha, please allow the navigator to answer the question," Chang chided the ship's AI. "The most recent incident demonstrated that we humans need an ability to operate the ship, to the greatest extent possible."

"My apologies, Colonel Chang."

"Navigator? Where are we?" Chang repeated the question, keeping the irritation he felt out of his voice. Or, he *tried* to do that, the navigator might have felt differently.

"We are," Mark Friedlander pressed buttons on his console, adjusting the display. "Hmm. That was not the best, we are-"

"Doctor," Chang interrupted. "Can we see the *Valkyrie* from here? That's all I'm asking. I know we haven't collided with anything."

"Oh. Sure. It's uh, that's what I was saying. We jumped in eight hundred kilometers from the target. That's odd. Valkyrie's transponder should be transmitting a reply to our ping. There is no-"

Adams couldn't hold her tongue any longer. "The mass detector has located an object roughly the size of *Valkyrie*, approximately where we expected to find the ship."

"It's there," the officer at the other sensor station reported. "It's faint, no running lights. No EM signature at all," she looked up in surprise. "Infrared shows the reactors are cold, they're only emanating residual heat."

"The ship is in one piece?" Chang gripped the armrest of the command chair.

"Yes," Adams declared. "Confirmed. It's *Valkyrie*. Colonel," it was her turn to look away in surprise. "It looks dead. No power generation, no response to our signals."

"All right." Chang decided the situation was critical enough to bypass the human crew. "Nagatha, what can you tell me?"

"I cannot add any information, Colonel Chang. There are no signs of external damage, however, *Valkyrie* is neither generating nor consuming power. It appears to be completely inert."

"Anyone?" Chang asked. "What does this mean?" They had all expected that with the murderous native AI freed from Skippy's control, that system would have jumped the ship away, or self-destructed. For the ship to be hanging dead in space, apparently having not moved at all, was the last thing he expected.

Smythe ventured a guess over the comm system. "Perhaps Skippy anticipated the native AI would attempt to rebel, and he left behind a subroutine to kill it?"

"That is extremely unlikely," Nagatha stated. "Skippy is too blindly arrogant to consider that he might have been wrong about having full control over the AI."

"Nagatha," Chang chided his own ship's AI. "Skippy is an arrogant asshole, that cannot be disputed. It is still possible that he left a fail-safe."

"I do not think so," Nagatha argued. "He would have told me, and offered to install such a subroutine in my own substrate."

"How can you be sure?"

Nagatha sniffed at the question, explaining, "Skippy would not have been able to resist the temptation to brag about how frightfully *clever* he was."

"True," Chang conceded, scratching the back of his neck. "No response at all?"

"None," Nagatha confirmed. "I have the hail on repeat. If any of their communications systems were active, we should hear *something*."

"Biosigns?" Adams asked.

Nagatha made a good imitation of a sigh. "As *Valkyrie* is a battlecruiser, with additional armor plating added when Skippy built the ship, it is difficult for passive sensors to detect anything as small and faint as the heat signature from a human body."

"There is only one way to know for certain," Chang decided. "Send a boarding party. Smythe, are you ready?"

"We can launch in ten seconds," the STAR team leader reported from a Falcon dropship in one of the Dutchman's docking bays.

"Excellent. Launch-"

"Wait!" Friedlander hopped away from his console in the CIC, frantically waving his arms toward the bridge.

"Belay that," Chang snapped. "Smythe, hold, do *not* launch. Doctor, what is the problem?"

"The crew over there could have survived?" The rocket scientist asked. "They would not have run out of oxygen already?"

"No," Nagatha agreed. "Even assuming that *Valkyrie* lost power immediately, there should be sufficient free oxygen to support the crew, if they minimized their activities."

"The crew could be alive," Chang suggested. "That is why we are sending a dropship to investigate."

"Yes, *but*!" Friedlander looked for someone to support him, realizing no one understood his concern. "If the crew over there is alive, they don't have access to sensors or any form of communications, but they *do* have access to the nuclear self-destruct system."

Chang gasped audibly.

"Colonel Simms," Friedlander finished his thought, "would not allow *Valkyrie* to be boarded by an unidentified force. She will destroy the ship."

"Smythe?" Chang asked. "You heard that?"

"Yes," the STAR team leader sighed audibly. "The good doctor is correct. Simms would do that. You or I would do the same."

"I agree. Keep the ready bird right where it is," Chang ordered. "As a precaution, close the bay doors." If the *Valkyrie* disappeared in a nuclear fireball, he did not want to risk debris striking the vulnerable dropship.

"Colonel Chang?" Friedlander waved again to get the captain's attention. "We can't only protect our own people. The people aboard *Valkyrie* could be preparing to self-destruct right now."

Chang squeezed the armrest again, his knuckles turning white. "Adams, let them know who we are. Turn the navigation lights on." He knew the ship's hull was equipped with floodlights, to assist maintenance crews and to guide incoming dropships that had suffered failures of their guidance systems. "Turn *all* the exterior lights on!"

Sami adjusted the binoculars again, trying to guess the best focus. Not knowing the distance to the enemy ship, she rolled the dial out to maximum and tried to use her peripheral vision. In low light, the human eye sees best when objects are slightly off-center. That was not easy to do when pressing her eyes to the narrow lenses of the binoculars, and when holding the binos with only one hand.

Her eyes were growing tired from the strain, the headache was getting worse, and her rapid breathing just wasn't getting enough oxygen to her brain. Looking for a better view of the enemy ship was partly from a sense of duty, and partly to keep her mind off what Simms was surely doing. She let go of the binoculars, blinking to clear her vision. Something above caught her eye. A playing card. No, a whole constellation of them, drifting near the ceiling. Sami smiled ruefully. The only good aspect of the situation was that she would never have to swim in zero gravity to collect fifty-two playing cards. One card was just above her head, reaching up, she flicked it with a finger to send it gracefully spinning away, until it collided with a clump of cards. Like scattering balls with a break shot in pool, she thought. She might have just created a new zero-gee game that she wouldn't live to tell anyone about, a-

A flare of light appeared in the viewport. A continuous light, brighter than any star. Hauling on the strap to pull the binoculars back, she pressed them to her eyes and-

"*The Dutchman!*" She had to tell-

The radio. It had drifted away, out of her reach. Pushing off with her feet, she-

Jerked to a stop as the strap to the binoculars was wrapped around her left arm. The motion caused her feet to fly up, kicking the radio away into the gloomy darkness.

Simms rubbed the key between thumb and forefinger. She had completed all the other steps to initiate self-destruct. One turn to the right, and the nuke would detonate. It would be so easy. She wouldn't even have time to feel the *click* as the key hit its stop, the detonator would engage before that.

Why was she hesitating? That was the question she asked herself. Because of regret, she knew. She regretted that she would never see Frank Muller again, yes. That wasn't making her hesitate, Frank had died when the alien virus destroyed the *Flying Dutchman*. Her regret was about not *knowing*. Not knowing why the microwormhole connection to Skippy had been severed. Not knowing what had happened to Skippy, not even being able to imagine anything that *could* have happened to Skippy. Unless the Elder computer worm had come back, there wasn't anything in the galaxy that could harm the arrogant beer can. Because as much of an asshole that Skippy was, his arrogance was justified.

Just do it, she told herself.

She was being selfish. Samantha Reed was waiting for the end, hesitation only prolonged the anxiety.

Take a deep breath.

Force yourself to smile, she thought. You've had a *good* life. You have seen things other people could not even imagine, things you still can't believe even though you saw the events with your own eyes.

"Desai, Giraud," the names slipped from her lips, remembering the fallen. So many others who had not lived to witness the mighty *Valkyrie* kicking ass across the Orion Arm of the galaxy.

A breath.

Turn the key and-

The radio crackled, startling her and making her hand jerk against the key.

"-utch-" Crackling, a burst of static. "-ease contac-"

Shit.

Watching her fingers as she lifted them off the key, she plucked the radio off her belt. "Reed? Captain Reed?" No answer. Another burst of static. The radios only had one channel, it was probably one of the crew calling another. Despite strict orders to use the radio only for official communications, she could not fault anyone for wanting to reach out for human contact. "Anyone? Whoever is speaking, it's all right." No response. The speaker was probably ashamed of the breach of discipline.

The radio went back on her belt.

Another breath, she placed her hand on the key, pressing-

"Simms! Colonel Simms!" Reed shouted, frantic. "*Don't* do it! The *Flying Dutchman* is here! They're here!"

With a trembling hand, Simms cradled the radio. Reed was halucinating from the CO2 poisoning. Simms blinked, having trouble focusing her eyes. "Captain, I understand. I am afraid too. You don't have-"

"They are *HERE* you stupid bitch!" Reed barked, pleading.

"*What?*" Simms's response was outrage.

"Sorry, Ma'am," Reed was overwhelmed with emotion. "I n-needed to get your attention. It's real. It's the *Dutchman*. They turned on their external lights, I can *see* them. They're calling on the radio!"

"Is that-" She stared at the radio. "Why can't *I* hear them?"

"You are too far inside the ship. Ma'am, Colonel Simms, I'm not lying. Send another crewman here to verify. But please, *please* take the key out of that nuke. Colonel Chang won't send a dropship until he hears from you that it is safe to approach."

Simms was torn. Having accepted death, it would be agony if Reed were lying, and she had to do it again. Did she trust the pilot's skill, professionalism and integrity? Yes. Did she also accept that Reed was a fallible human, like any other? Yes. "That is a sensible precaution. I will contact-"

"Hold one moment, Ma'am. Uh, ooh, wow. This is kind of awkward."

"What?"

"Mister *Muller* is on the radio now. He says to tell you that your *Pookie* misses you?"

"Holy shit." Only Frank knew her pet name for his-

That was not anyone's business.

She did not trust herself to remove the key, so she tucked the chain inside and closed the cover of the warhead casing. "Captain Reed, please inform the *Dutchman* that I will contact them shortly." On second thought, she had to make damned certain that no one accidently, or for any other reason touched the key, so she lifted the lid, slowly extracted the key without daring to breathe, and tucked it in a pocket. "Reed?'

"Yes?"

"I am giving you a free pass for that 'stupid bitch' remark. It saved our lives. Don't do it again."

"Thank you, Ma'am."

"Thank *you*, Captain."

Simms accepted a glass of whiskey from Chang, rocking the heavy glass back and forth to hear the tinkling sound of the ice cubes. She did not like whiskey. She also did not wish to insult the Dutchman's captain in his office. She did like breathing air that didn't give her a headache, she liked being able to drink out of a glass rather than a squeeze bottle, and she enjoyed the scent of freshly-baked chocolate chip cookies coming from a plate on Chang's desk.

She did not like the taste of whiskey, that was not a problem. "Thank you," she tossed the glass back and swallowed the entire glass, trapping the ice cubes with her teeth. "Ah," she coughed and spoke in a choked voice. "That was smooth."

Chang's eyes were wide with disbelief. "You are supposed to *sip* it," he chided her gently.

"It's the only way," she reached for a cookie and nibbled it to take away the fiery taste of the alcohol. "That I can drink that stuff."

"Jennifer, if you had told me, I could have given you a glass of wine."

"No," she waved a hand. "Taste doesn't matter. I needed that. For medicinal purposes."

"I understand. If we could have come sooner, we would have."

"My question is, why did you come here at all? Captain Frey told me that Smythe made a strong argument for going to Rikers instead."

"Smythe did make a strong argument. Tactically, he was right."

"Then why did you come here?"

Chang took a sip of his own drink, savoring the liquid properly. "It is a simple matter of probabilities. Assuming something terrible did happen to Skippy, it is unlikely that we poor monkeys could fix it, even if we had the *Dutchman, Valkyrie* and all the king's horses."

"It was also unlikely you could do anything, if the native AI was still in control of *Valkyrie*," Simms noted, and surprised him by pouring another finger of whiskey into her glass.

"True. Between two impossible tasks, I chose the one that was the least impossible."

"Thank you," she raised her glass to toast him, and took a sip. It wasn't as bad as she remembered. Maybe she was just very, very tired. "So, what now?"

"Now," he toasted her with his glass, and took a sip. "We tackle the *more* impossible task."

"Nagatha has no insight into what could have caused the microwormholes to collapse?"

"No. Other than that she is certain the collapse was initiated on the far end. She cannot give us any advice, and I fear to jump this ship into the unknown. Especially if that unknown includes something so powerful that it is capable of disabling Skippy. Doctor Friedlander has an alternate theory."

"He does?"

"Yes. He is quite smart, we are fortunate to have him aboard the *Dutchman*. He thinks that perhaps there is *not* a problem with Skippy. The microwormhole collapse could have been caused by a Thuranin weapon."

"The cyborgs *attacked* the microwormholes?"

"No," Chang shook his head. "It is not likely the Thuranin could detect the wormholes. Friedlander believes it is possible that the Thuranin deployed some type of spatial disruption device, which caused a resonance that inadvertently collapsed the wormholes."

"Why would they do that?"

"That is not known. Perhaps they used a weapon that disrupts spacetime as a side effect. Perhaps they have a new type of damping field? It is only a theory. Frankly, the good Doctor is guessing."

"If he is right," she drank the last of the whiskey in her glass. No, she was not developing a taste for it. "Then Bishop and Skippy could be unharmed, and simply unable to contact us."

"Exactly. We will proceed on that assumption. We jump in far from the planet, to learn what we can from passive sensors. Then we make decisions based on what we find there."

"It sounds good. Maybe *too* good."

"How so?"

"It's what we *want* to believe. We jump in, find that Skippy and Bishop are just bored and annoyed and wondering what took us so long to pick them up. That is a lot more pleasant than discovering that a Sentinel fried Skippy."

Chang choked on his drink. "A *Sentinel*?"

Simms waved a hand. "Sorry. I was only using that as an example, of something that is capable of causing trouble for that little shithead beer can."

"Let us not have any more talk of Sentinels, please," his shoulders shuddered involuntarily.

"You won't hear it from me. When do we jump?" She wondered if there would be time for her to close her eyes for a couple hours, in a real bed rather than floating in a sleeping bag.

Chang glanced at his phone. "Six hours, thirty-six minutes. I suggest you catch up on sleep, if you can."

"I'll try for a solid four hours. I'd like a hot meal before we jump." She stood up. "Where will I be bunking?"

"In Bishop's old cabin, for now. With all the people we rescued from Rikers, many of us are having to hot bunk."

"It's a real bed, with gravity, and a hot shower. I can't ask for anything more."

Nagatha made a sound like clearing her throat, and announced "Colonel Chang, we are ready for jump in all respects. Where do you wish to go?"

Chang glanced at Simms in the CIC, she nodded agreement. The *Flying Dutchman* had just completed a successful test jump, and nothing important had broken. Chang wanted to be absolutely certain his ship was in perfect condition, because the crews of both ships, plus all the people rescued from Rikers, were aboard. As the senior officer, he had decided to leave *Valkyrie's* lifeless hulk drifting in interstellar space, with a few powercells to activate proximity sensors. If any unauthorized vessel attempted to approach the defenseless battlecruiser, the nuke would be triggered. No one wanted that to happen. "Please plot a jump to take us in, twenty light-minutes past the photon wavefront of the incident."

Nagatha instantly understood. "You intend to observe what happened near the planet, before and after the microwormholes collapsed?"

"Yes. Twenty minutes should be sufficient for our sensors to fully reset after the jump. Are the ship's sensors capable of providing useful accuracy at that distance?"

"It has been more than twelve days since the incident, however we should be able to clearly see Colonel Bishop's dropship."

"Outstanding. Plan to jump us in perpendicular to the plane of the Thuranin ship's orbit. Above or below, your choice." He knew the terms 'above' and 'below' were meaningless in deep space.

"May I ask why?" Nagatha asked, adding a note of curiosity in her voice.

"I do not want the Thuranin ship to go behind the planet during the time we are observing."

"Oh. That is very astute of you, Colonel. Jump is programmed into the navigation system."

Chang tugged the strap tighter across his waist. "Pilot, jump us when ready."

The *Flying Dutchman* emerged in a shower of gamma rays, mostly directed away from the planet. Sensors took only three minutes to become fully operational, then it was a matter of waiting. And waiting.

Images began to arrive, on photons that left the vicinity of Rikers shortly before the microwormholes collapsed. First, the dropship flown by Bishop became visible, having lost power to its stealth field. That incident occurred at the same moment when the microwormholes collapsed, matching the *Dutchman's* data from the time. A brief message was sent by Bishop. "*Flying Dutchman*! Chang, I lost stealth and-" It cut off abruptly.

"We never heard that message," Chang frowned.

"Correct, Colonel," Nagatha said. "The Thuranin were jamming regular communications, and the microwormholes had already collapsed."

Also matching the ship's data, the dropship wrapped itself in a stealth field but not before the local satellite network began saturating the area with active sensors, hunting for the vulnerable Dragon. The crew on the bridge of the *Flying Dutchman* saw their own ship jump in, and recover the rescue team's dropships, then jump away in a chaotic burst of gamma rays.

"That will never cease to be weird," Chang said to himself.

"What is, Sir?" Reed asked from the pilot couch.

"Seeing *ourselves*, back in time," Chang explained. "Nagatha, is any of what we're seeing now, different from what our sensors recorded at the time?"

"No," she confirmed. "The data is an exact match. Why did you ask?"

"Because at the time, you were being attacked by the virus. I thought it was possible the virus could have altered our sensor records."

"Hmm. That is also an astute observation. I should have thought of that. Colonel Chang, I apologize for my lapse of-"

"Nagatha," he cut her off. "A ship's crew is a *team*. We work together. You do not have to do everything by yourself."

"I, oh, Colonel Chang," her voice choked up. "That is possibly the nicest thing anyone has ever said to me."

"Focus, please," he pointed at the bridge display. "This is the part we did *not* see, after we jumped away with the rescue dropships."

They watched as the sensor satellites around Rikers tried to pinpoint Bishop's Dragon, which had disappeared again in stealth. The Thuranin ship turned and burned, joining the hunt. Three Falcon dropships launched from their Thuranin mothership, surging ahead at an impressive sustained six gravities of acceleration.

It appeared that Bishop was able to evade pursuit, and Chang began to hope that the commander of the Pirates was still out there somewhere, floating outward in silence. That hope was dashed when the Dragon became visible again as the spacecraft appeared to have lost all power. A Thuranin dropship swerved violently to close in with the defenseless Dragon, firing an energy beam that had no visible effect.

"Nagatha," Chang asked. "What was that?"

"That was not good," she gasped. "It was a beam that disrupts electrical equipment. You might call it an EMP weapon."

"Electromagnetic pulse? Why bother? The Dragon is not generating any power."

"Perhaps the Thuranin wish to be certain the craft cannot restore power. Colonel Chang, what you need to know is that type of EMP weapon acts against all types of electrical activity. Including that of a biological nervous system. It is often used to stun and disable the crew of a vessel the Thuranin wish to capture."

"*Capture*?" Chang gripped the arms of the command chair. "Ohhhhh, no. Bishop won't let that happen. He will detonate the nuke."

"If he *can*," Nagatha emphasized. "The EMP beam might have rendered him unconscious, and also disabled the arming system of the nuke."

"The nuke has a manual backup," Simms reported from the CIC.

"Yes," Chang nodded. "That is only useful if Bishop is conscious. No!" On the display, they saw the Thuranin fire another EMP burst, from a closer range.

"I am sorry," Nagatha sighed. "it is very unlikely Colonel Bishop would be conscious after that second attack."

"Skippy would not allow Bishop to be captured," Simms said, a mixture of hope and fear in her voice. "He knows our standing orders."

Chang didn't speak. He knew what would happen next. The Dragon would disappear in a nuclear fireball. "Nagatha," he asked quietly as the Thuranin dropship matched speed and approached the helpless Dragon. "Can you predict Skippy's location, based on data from the," he hesitated to say the word. "The blast?"

"Not from here, Colonel," she answered. "It would be more useful to jump in closer, and listen for a signal from Skippy. He would not be harmed by detonation of the nuclear device."

"Yeah, sure, but," Friedlander spoke from the doorway of the bridge.

"Yes, Doctor?" Chang half turned in his seat.

"We haven't seen anything that explains why the microwormholes collapsed."

"Ohhh," Simms looked up from her console in the CIC. "He's right. Doctor, you theorized that some sort of unknown Thuranin weapon disrupted the microwormholes?"

"A weapon, or something they did unintentionally," Friedlander reminded her. "It was just a guess, to fit the facts we knew. I didn't see anything that could have disrupted the wormholes. The Dragon was in stealth, then it lost power at the same time as the wormholes shut down. There isn't any external factor to explain the incident. Nagatha? Do you see anything in the data that could have disrupted the wormholes?"

"No, Doctor. It is as you described. The Dragon was in stealth, then lost power. There was no external factor that could have triggered the loss of power and the wormhole collapses."

"Then we have a *big* problem," Friedlander stepped onto the bridge, walking over to the display and tapping the fuzzy images of the Dragon and the Thuranin dropship, as they drew closer together.

"What is that?" Chang asked.

"If something happened to Skippy, there wasn't anyone to trigger that nuke," Friedlander explained. "They could both be captured."

"That would be a disaster," Simms gasped, a hand over her mouth in horror.

"Let us not jump to conclusions," Chang directed. "Perhaps Skippy is waiting for the other dropship to get closer. Or for the Dragon to be taken aboard the Thuranin ship."

"That would not have happened," Friedlander shook his head sadly. "The Thuranin will detect alpha radiation from the nuke once they get inside the Dragon. No way would they take it aboard their ship."

Over the next hour, they watched images from the incoming photons, images of incidents that took place more than a week ago. The Thuranin sent two bots to attach to and drill into the Dragon's hull. Shortly thereafter, there was a burst of message traffic from the dropship to its mothership, warning the big ship away.

A larger bot attached to the Dragon, sealing itself over the hull and cutting a hole. Out floated an elongated bag, a bag large enough to contain a human body. "I have a bad feeling about this," Chang muttered. "Nagatha, can you determine what is in that bag?"

"Not accurately. However, it is a heat source consistent with that of a human body."

"A *living* human?"

"That I cannot tell from here. A recently deceased person would still generate substantial heat. The bag is blocking any electrical signals from a heartbeat."

"So, Bishop could be dead, or alive. We don't know."

"That is correct," the ship's AI answered sadly.

"Is it wrong," Chang asked to no one in particular, "that I wish he were dead?"

The bag was taken through the Thuranin dropship's airlock. Soon after, the Dragon's airlock opened, and a bot floated out, holding the nuclear warhead. The bot accelerated away in one direction, while the Thuranin spacecraft burned gently toward its mothership. It flew into a docking bay and was lost to sight, then the starship maneuvered back into orbit.

"We have to assume the Thuranin captured Bishop alive," Chang concluded, as the senior Pirates gathered in the *Dutchman's* conference room. "Their dropship accelerated at no more than one-third Earth gravity when it returned to its mothership. I believe that is most likely because they had to avoid causing damage to an injured passenger."

"I agree," Smythe smacked a fist on the table. "It will be devilishly difficult to rescue Bishop from that ship, to accomplish that without assistance from Skippy. Nagatha, is there any indication that Skippy was in the bag with Bishop?"

"No. There is also no indication that Skippy was *not* in the bag. We simply do not know."

"I doubt it," Friedlander rubbed the back of his neck. "Remember, the Thuranin have no idea what Skippy is, they wouldn't think his canister is anything other than a piece of equipment. He is likely still aboard the Dragon." Since the nuke had been removed, more bots had gone inside the Dragon to thoroughly examine the craft. It had not been taken aboard the starship, a sign that the Thuranin were wary of other boobytraps.

Smythe tapped the table with a finger. "We must determine the location and condition of Skippy before we can create a plan to rescue Bishop. The Thuranin-"

"There will not necessarily be a rescue operation," Chang interrupted, his eyes darting to Gunnery Sergeant Adams in the CIC, then looking away.

"No rescue?" Smythe froze.

"No. It might be too risky. If Bishop were in contact with us, he would not allow us to take the risk just for him."

"*Sir*," Smythe protested. "If the Thuranin are able to interrogate Bishop, he could tell them every-"

"That is why," Chang explained patiently, "we must not allow that to happen. Though I fear we may already be too late," he shook his head. "The events we witnessed took place days ago. That Thuranin ship could have jumped, very likely *did* jump away. We need more recent information. Nagatha, if we need to destroy that ship, is the *Dutchman* capable of winning a fight, without sustaining serious damage? I must think of our passengers," he added with a look at faces around the table.

"Depending on the circumstances, and with the proper planning, the *Flying Dutchman* could destroy the enemy ship," the ship's AI answered. "Colonel Chang, are you suggesting we attack that ship, to *kill* Colonel Bishop?"

"I am suggesting," Chang knew the AI had a special affection for Bishop, "that it is necessary to consider such action. Boarding a Thuranin ship is not practical," He looked at Smythe, who nodded agreement. "Even if we could disable the ship and gain access, the Thuranin would kill Bishop before we could secure him. No matter. We must determine the location and status of Skippy, with data that is more current. Nagatha, if we jump in one light-hour away from the planet, would that give you enough time to analyze message traffic?"

"I would prefer more time, however, signal traffic degrades with distance. One light-hour is acceptable."

"Very well. Simms," Chang directed his attention to his new, hopefully temporary, executive officer. "Before we jump, we need a plan to destroy the Thuranin ship, in the unlikely event it is still in orbit."

"Yes, Sir."

CHAPTER NINE

The *Flying Dutchman* jumped into the star system, emerging one light-hour from the planet that humans had named 'Rikers'. Immediately, Nagatha deployed sensor antennas to their maximum extent, long, feathery ears that listened across the electromagnetic spectrum.

Chang had the ship on high alert. Throughout the ship, blast doors were closed. The STAR team was in full combat armor, with two Falcon dropships ready to launch at a moment's notice. Regardless of the tension, he expected many minutes of tense boredom, while waiting for Nagatha to make sense of the signals and images they were receiving.

When the ship's AI spoke less than two minutes later, he was startled. "Colonel Chang," Nagatha's breathy voice was excited. "The Thuranin ship is not in orbit."

"Ah. It is as I expected. Simms, tell the STAR team to stand-"

"I do not believe the Thuranin jumped away," Nagatha continued. "There is a substantial debris field around the planet. The volume and composition of the debris matches that of a Thuranin ship."

"The ship was destroyed? How?"

"I do not have that information, nor do I know who attacked the Thuranin. According to the Kristang, based on message traffic I have intercepted, the Thuranin ship was experiencing technical difficulties for several days. It then exploded without apparent external cause, shortly after bombarding sites on the surface."

Chang slumped back in the command chair. "This gets curiouser and curiouser. What could have caused-" He sat up, placing elbows on the armrests. "At least we have the comfort that Bishop is no longer suffer-"

"Colonel Bishop was not aboard the ship when it exploded," Nagatha reported gleefully.

"He *wasn't*?"

"No. When their ship began experiencing severe engineering failures, the Thuranin flew Bishop to a Kristang facility on the surface. Colonel Chang, that is not the most important information I have to report."

Chang resisted the temptation to guess. "Proceed."

"I have identified Skippy's location, course and speed."

"Course and *speed*?" Chang had assumed the Elder AI would be on the planet with Bishop. "Where is he?"

"He is moving away from the planet, at a velocity faster than escape velocity. His current course and speed is not consistent with being in the Dragon, when that dropship was captured. I cannot explain why he is *there*."

"Simms," Chang turned to look into the CIC. "What do you think?"

"Nagatha," Simms asked. "Do you know Bishop's location?"

"No," the ship's AI answered. "The facility where he was being held was struck by the Thuranin ship, just before it apparently self-destructed."

"The Thuranin *killed* Bishop?" Simms couldn't believe it. "Why would they-"

"Ha!" Chang snorted. "Hahaha!" He laughed and slapped his knee.

"*Sir*?" Simms cocked her head at the ship's captain.

"A jail holding Bishop is hit from orbit, and a starship mysteriously explodes?"

"Skippy?" Simms gasped.

"Exactly," Chang's face broke into a broad smile. "Our irascible beer can is falling back on his Greatest Hits collection. Smythe, you heard that?"

"Yes, Sir," the STAR team leader acknowledged. "My team is ready to retrieve Bishop from the surface, if he can be located."

Chang rubbed his chin, considering. "Jumping in only a few light-seconds from the planet, we will alert every sensor in the area. We will need to pick up Skippy, then move fast. Nagatha, program a jump."

"Skippy!" Chang called as soon as the ship emerged from jump, a mere twenty kilometers from the Elder AI. A Falcon was launching, burning hard to intercept the drifting beer can. "Where is Colonel Bishop?"

"Oh, well," the AI sniffed, indignant. "A cheery 'Hello' to you too."

"Pleasantries can wait," Chang insisted. "Especially as I assume that whatever disaster happened to collapse the microwormholes and allow Bishop to be captured, it was *your* fault."

"Um, well, heh heh, um. Hmm. Mistakes were made."

"Mistakes-" Simms clenched her fists and regained control of herself. "*Valkyrie* and the *Dutchman* were nearly destroyed, you-"

"Well, *that* certainly could not have been my fault," Skippy grumbled.

"It was *absolutely* your fault," Nagatha snapped. "You failed-"

"Hey!" Skippy shouted. "Could this meeting of the We Hate Skippy Club adjourn for the moment?"

Chang clenched his teeth. He needed to focus. "Agreed. What is Bishop's status?"

"Joe died as he lived," Skippy sighed. "Stupidly."

"Bishop is *dead*?"

"He might as well be. I gave him a nice phone and did he take care of it? No, he *broke* it! Careless moron. I lost contact with him two days ago. However, I have been listening to Kristang communications, and I fear he is surrounded by lizards right now."

Chang held up a hand for quiet. "Smythe has a STAR team ready to deploy to the surface, as soon as-"

"We don't have *time* for that!" Skippy pleaded. "The message traffic I am monitoring indicates the lizards are closing in on Joe's position."

"If the Kristang capture him," Chang squeezed the armrest until his knuckles turned white. "I will threaten to bombard-"

"That won't work!" Skippy cried. "The lizards don't intend to capture Joe! They plan to *kill* him!"

"We are ready to launch, Sir!" Smythe called.

"Hold one," Chang ordered, scanning the report summary from Nagatha. Unlike the scatterbrained Skippy, the *Dutchman's* AI had learned what information was important to a commander. "Commandant Fabron? I need your Commando team to extract Bishop."

"Yes, Colonel," the French officer replied.

"Sir?" Smythe was surprised and hurt. "What about the STAR-"

"I have another tasking for you, Smythe. It could be tricky, and you will have to plan on the fly."

"What is the target?"

"A pair of Thuranin pilots, on the surface. They are the only Thuranin left in the system. Capture them *alive*, Smythe. We need to know how much *they* know, about us."

"That will be tricky."

"Your team can do it?"

"Who dares, wins," Smythe recited the motto of the Special Air Services.

There wasn't anywhere left to run. The Kristang had me surrounded, caught out in the open. That morning I had seen a team of four lizards on top of a ridge to the west. At that time, I was moving along a ridgeline, trying to get to a river I had seen from a hill the day before. Get to the river, was my plan. Float down wherever the river went. I could hang onto a log like Huckleberry Finn, or maybe that was Tom Sawyer. That didn't matter now, because I had not gotten to the river. Instead, I had been forced to turn around and go northeast, back the way I came.

Part of me wondered what was the point of trying to evade capture. Without contact with Skippy, and with no sign of either starship coming to rescue me, all I was doing was delaying the inevitable. Really, the only thing that kept me going was the idea that I was being a pain in the ass to the Kristang, which was always a good thing.

Except now I couldn't run any farther. Going out into the open, a sort of marshy meadow, had not been by choice. Lizards were behind me on both sides, forcing me to run away from them. When I got halfway across the meadow, my shoes squishing in puddles from the continual rain, more Kristang came out of the woods, about fifty meters in front of me. This new group, seven of them that I could see, were not wearing powered armor, though they did have rifles, helmets and light armor panels attached to their clothing.

"*Shit*," I exploded, immediately regretting that I spoke so loudly. One of my ribs was cracked, maybe broken. Breathing hard was painful and I had been coughing up spots of blood since I fell to the bottom of the canyon. Straightening up by pushing hands on my knees, I lifted one arm while shrugging off the knapsack with the other. "Hey, asshole," I grunted in the best Kristang I could manage. "Go ahead, shoot me." A quick death had to be better than whatever the lizards or Thuranin had planned for me. Up my left sleeve was the knife I took from the hospital. It was still admirably sharp, some type of composite. If a lizard came close enough, I would stab it. That would be a waste of effort, but hopefully it would spur them to mercifully put a round through my forehead.

Hoping for a quick and painless death, that's what my life had come to.

Good times.

"Hur, hur, hur," one of the lizards in front of me laughed, a sound that sent a chill up my spine. "You speak our language, human?"

"Yeah. I figure that when I'm kicking your ass, I could at least be polite about it," I replied. Or, that's what I tried to say. My Kristang is rusty, he might have thought I was trying to order a pizza delivery.

The smile left his face. "You are insolent, pitiful human. Good, that is good. It will make killing you all the more enjoyable." He raised his rifle. I could have admonished him for poor muzzle discipline, but he intended to point it at my chest, so it was understandable.

"Be careful," I said. With a gun pointed at me, I suddenly was not so eager for a quick death. "You could hurt someone with that toy. Your Thuranin masters would not be happy if you injured their prize."The Thuranin are not our *masters*." He turned his head and spat on the wet, matted grass of the meadow. "They do wish to capture you, to learn how you took our slaves away from this world. They wish to humiliate us for our poor security. I do not wish to give the Thuranin that opportunity. I do not wish to give them *anything* they want."

"Oh, hey," I stammered, forgetting the awkward sentence structure of their language. "We hate the Thuranin too, maybe we can-"

"Silence!" He aimed the rifle an inch higher.

And pulled the trigger.

The rifle barked, spitting out a round straight at my chest.

It *missed*.

I peed a little in my borrowed pants.

The other lizards all laughed for a beat, until the leader glared at them, checking his rifle and aiming it more carefully. To be sure, he took a step toward me. And pulled the trigger again.

It missed, this one going wide to my left. I know that because there was a wet *thump* sound from behind me, and angry, alarmed shouting. Apparently, Asshole Numero Uno had shot one of his own guys.

That sent him into a rage, and he strode forward, firing three-round bursts at me.

The guided rounds went wide right, left, over my head and splattering into the muck in front of me, spraying me with wet grass.

All of the guided rounds *missed*.

Shrieking, he angrily tossed the rifle aside.

"Hey, little boys should not play with dangerous toys." I joked.

"Do not laugh, human," he growled at me. "My rifle's aiming system is defective. What you do not know is that I have a pistol," he pulled it from a holster on his right thigh. "With *unguided* rounds."

"Uh huh," I agreed, and pointed to the sky. "What *you* do not know is that I have a *starship* in orbit."

"You lie," he scowled at me, but there was doubt in his eyes.

"Whoever is up there?" I switched back to speaking English. "Fire for effect."

The meadow exploded, tossing me through the air.

The *Flying Dutchman's* attempt at a rescue nearly killed me. The maser cannons of some starships have an anti-personnel setting that is rarely used, but Chang couldn't risk firing the cannons in that mode. I was too close to the enemy, the wide-dispersal beam would have cooked me alive. As it was, I got flash-burns from the low-powered, pencil-thin microwave laser beams that struck with precision all around me, blowing craters in the marshy meadow and turning the Kristang into charred pieces of lizard meat.

The mud saved me, and also came close to killing me. With maser beams having to burn through clouds and rain, a measurable part of the energy was dispersed to bombard the meadow with high-energy photons, and moisture in the air was flashed instantly into super-heated steam. My eyelids automatically clamped shut and my arms flew up to cover my face, that was why my hands look like boiled lobsters, but my Hollywood-handsome face sustained only what looks and felt like a bad sunburn. It would have been worse for me if fountains of mud had not been flung up from craters to slash on me in a thick layer, knocking me off my feet and protecting my exposed skin. Lying in a puddle of muddy water that was warmer than a bathtub, I was stunned. Trying to catch my breath was a *bad* idea, the lining of my mouth burned as I tried to suck in a breath of air that had turned to steam hot enough to boil my lungs. The only thing to do was clamp my mouth shut and put my lobster-red hands over my face.

The mud and water protected me, but if the masers kept pouring energy into the air around me, I would have been cooked, literally. The *Dutchman's* crew used maser cannons only for the initial strike, to prevent the Kristang from killing me and throw them into disarray. Following the maser beams were not railgun darts, though the rebuilt *Dutchman* Version 4.0 had two railguns. No, hitting the meadow with railguns at normal speed would have blown me to bits. The railgun muzzle velocity could have been decreased to lower the kinetic impact, but at that point, the darts would not have been much faster than a missile. Darts were also less flexible than missiles. So, a few seconds behind the maser beams, while the surviving Kristang were as stunned as I was, a missile roared overhead at hypersonic speed, dispersing antipersonnel submunitions. Those weapons, no larger than the 'Fun-size' candy bars that cause disappointment to children on Halloween, got their initial guidance from active sensor scans of the missile that was already kilometers away. Switching on their own active and passive sensors, the submunitions identified targets very carefully, having been given very clear instructions to give top priority to pin-pointing the location of the only human on the surface of the planet. It took no more than a hundredth of a second for sensors to determine that one particular mud-encased lump was generating electrical impulses matching a human heartbeat. It took no more than a microsecond for all submunitions to communicate with all the others and coordinate their actions to avoid harming me. Or, from harming me more than was unavoidable. With more than two dozen submunitions hunting for targets, striking at high speed and exploding, there was a lot of stuff flying around in all directions. Kristang body parts can be deadly, if they are moving fast enough.

My ears were ringing from the hypersonic boom of the missile and the sharp crack of explosions in every direction. When I couldn't hold my breath any longer, I scooped partially-dried mud away from my mouth and exhaled, judging the temperature of the air by how my lips felt.

It felt Ok. The maser cannons had poured a lot of energy into water vapor around the meadow, but that water vapor cooled quickly as steam rose over the meadow and cooler air rushed in to fill the vacuum. Sucking in a breath made me choke not because of the steam that was still making the air foggy, but because I breathed in a clot of sticky mud.

Coughing out the mud got me onto my hands and knees, that's when I realized my hands felt like they had been trying to get French-fries fresh from the fryer.

They *hurt*. A lot. Plunging them into cool mud helped a bit.

I got to my knees, then my feet, staggering around. The rifle discarded by Asshole Numero Uno was sticking out of a puddle, I dug it out, cleared the barrel as best I could, and fired a test round. The rifle worked just fine. Aiming at the shattered stump of a tree, I put a round into it, dead-center. There was nothing wrong with the aiming system. The next shot went wide and missed the stump. That was my fault, my hands were shaky and it was like my eyes couldn't focus properly. Maybe my coordination needed some improving. Hopefully, I wouldn't need to shoot at anything.

Making a circuit of what used to be a meadow, I found lots of pre-cooked Lizard Bits, which sounds like something you might find in an alien pet food store. What I did not find was the one damned thing I wanted. A freakin' working phone, damn it.

Finally, I found a phone under the charred torso of a lizard. Wow. If you think lizards smell bad when they're alive, you have no idea what the stench is like when they are blown apart and roasted.

Pressing the transmit button, I sat down wearily on a patch of charred grass. "Hey, Skippy."

"*Joe!* Oh, Joe! You're *alive!*"

"Yeah, mostly. Thanks for screwing with the targeting system of that lizard's rifle."

"You knew it was me doing that?"

"I took a chance. It wasn't like I had a choice. Thanks anyway."

"Oh, no problem, Joe. It was the least I could do. We could hear you, through the comm system of the lizard leader, but of course we couldn't talk *to* you."

"You did great. All of you. Where are you?"

"Aboard the *Dutchman* in low orbit, kind of right over your head. Fabron is coming down in two dropships to retrieve you, their ETA is twelve minutes."

"Fabron?" That surprised me. "Not Smythe?"

"The STAR team is busy, I'll explain later."

"That's great. Ah, shit."

"What, Joe? Are you Ok?"

"I'm *tired*, Skippy. Really, really tired. Give me a Sitrep, the short version," I asked, feeling like I might fall asleep if I didn't keep talking.

"Um, well, heh heh-"

"Shit."

"Joe, it appears the *Flying Dutchman* was attacked by a computer virus, immediately after the microwormholes shut down. That damned virus, the one I thought I had scrubbed from the *Dutchman*, came close to killing Nagatha. Anyway, it's all good now," he laughed nervously. "I am very proud of the way Nagatha handled the situation."

He was proud of something that Nagatha did. Something she did, to fix *his* screw-up. Hearing his stunning, clueless level of arrogance was actually comforting to me, because it meant he was back to being the old Skippy I knew. "What about *Valkyrie*?"

"Ooh, uh, um. The short answer is, the AI tried to kill the crew, but Simms was very clever. The native AI either committed suicide, or something killed it."

"Something aboard the ship *killed* it? Oh my- There is something aboard the ship that is even more dangerous than the native AI?"

"No! I shouldn't have said it that way. It looks like there was a kill switch subroutine hidden somewhere, that destroyed the AI. Unfortunately, it completely disabled the system. *Valkyrie* is currently drifting without power, right where we left it. There are injuries, but *no one* was killed, Joe. Let's focus on that."

Of course he wanted to avoid responsibility. "What have you told people about why you bailed on us?"

"They, um, they don't know about that yet."

"Chang didn't ask why the microwormholes shut down?"

"Not yet. We've been kind of busy up here. Ugh," he sighed. "I know, I know. I need to own up to my mistakes. Oh, this *sucks*. I *know* that I screwed up big-time, I don't need a bunch of screeching monkeys berating me about it. I'll do it, just let me-"

"Don't," I heard someone say that, and was surprised to hear it was me.

"What?"

"Don't do it. Don't tell anyone."

"Um, Okaaaay," he said slowly. "Why?"

"Because the crew needs to believe they can trust you."

"Whoa. Really?"

"You think they *don't* need to trust you?"

"No, I, I see that they do."

"They *can* trust you, right? You are never going to bail on us again?"

"Cross my heart and hope to die, Joe," his voice quavered. "I can't even begin to tell you how ashamed I am."

"Great. Then it will be our little secret."

"Um, wow. I am honored. Joe, I can't believe I am asking this question, but, are you sure about this?"

"Yes. I'm the commander. I will take the burden of knowing what really happened, so my people can focus on the mission."

"Joe most of the time, I think you are just cosplaying as a soldier, but you are the real deal. Damn, I'm sure glad I don't have your job. How can I ever thank you?"

"By *earning* my trust."

"Ok, deal. Um, we need to tell them *something*, Joe."

"Yeah, uh, make up a story? A good one."

"You constantly tell me that I am terrible at lying."

"Good point. All right, uh, tell them I ejected you from the dropship, before it got zapped."

"Hmm. OK, OK, that could work. The dropship was traveling at-"

"Skippy, I have a headache and I'm really tired, so spare me the nerdy math details."

"Sure. Joe, ejecting me explains why I was not in the Dragon, but not why all of the microwormholes collapsed."

"Right. Uh, how about this: when *Valkyrie's* original AI was ready to trigger the virus aboard the *Dutchman*, and take over its own ship, it also tried to attack you through the wormhole connection. You had to shut down all your external connections to protect yourself, so you could survive and protect *us*. "

"Oh, hmm. Cool. I *like* it. Hey, that makes me the *hero* of the story!"

"Not so fast, you little shithead. You still screwed up royally by failing to scrub the virus from the *Dutchman*."

"Well, sure, but-"

"And you got outwitted by the AI of the *Valkyrie*."

"Ok, it's not quite fair to completely blame that on-"

"*And*, you are going to tell everyone that you later realized you were *never* in danger, that *Valkyrie's* AI *wanted* you to shut down the wormholes, and that you fell for its trap because you are an arrogant, gullible ass."

"Oh man, *really*? Jeez, I'd rather tell people the truth."

"Boo freakin' hoo. That is the truth, or close enough. The truth is, what happened to me, and to both ships, is one hundred percent *your* fault."

"Ok, Ok, Ok. Damn, I wish that AI *had* killed me. You're going to hold this secret over my head forever, aren't you?"

"What do *you* think?"

"Shit. Yes. I *hate* my life."

"One more thing, please?"

"Ugh. I am afraid to ask. What?"

"Do *not* read any passages from Skippy's Book of Revelations. Do not tell *anyone*."

"Um, we have to tell them sometime, Joe. What I learned changes the purpose of our whole mission out here!"

"Not right now it doesn't. Those bad AIs have been lurking around for millions of years, they can wait for-"

"Unless they *can't* wait, Joe."

"Uh, why not?"

"*I* am active."

"Ok, but that's just a coincidence, right. There's no reason to think all you Elder AIs set your wake-up alarms for the same year, or the same freakin' *century*."

"We do not *have* wake-up alarms. And you're missing the point, dumdum. I have been active and flying around doing shit like screwing with wormholes and communicating with Guardians in the Roach Motel. Someone might have noticed, you know?"

"Shit. I hadn't thought of that."

"Egg-zactly. We have to-"

"After we deal with the immediate problem. The, no, not the *immediate* immediate problem. Earth, I mean. We need to pull as many people as we can from Earth to the Beta site, then, oh, hell. I don't know. Then we can tackle the bigger issue."

"Even the Beta site won't be safe, if a group of evil AIs wake up and attack the entire galaxy. *Plus* the surrounding dwarf galaxies. No one will be safe."

"Ok, point taken. That doesn't change the facts. We have no reason to think an AI attack is imminent, while Earth is in danger *right now*. Uh!" I shushed him. "You need our help, right?"

"Yes."

"We are a team?"

"Yes," he grumbled. "We are a team."

"How's this: we will investigate," I offered, having zero idea how we could do that. "For signs that other Elder AIs are active, or are becoming active. We do that, if we have time before the wormhole you moved is open."

"Ok. Fair enough, I guess. Joe, we need to tell the crew about this sometime. No way can I keep this bottled up inside me for long. Someone is bound to guess that I'm holding a huge secret. Nagatha will, for sure."

"We will tell everyone, soon. We can't do it now, understood?"

"Yes. What I don't understand is *why*."

Sometimes, for all his vast intellect, he was a total moron about dealing with people. "Think about it. If you say the microwormholes shut down, and I got captured, at the *same time* that you had the huge revelation? No way will people believe that is a coincidence. Trust me on this."

"Ok. Whatever you say, Joe. I owe you one. Or two. Or," he sighed. "A billion."

We reviewed the details of the bullshit story he would tell, then Skippy broke in with a warning. "The Commando dropships are two minutes out, Joe."

"Thanks. Are the lizards giving them any trouble?"

"No," he chuckled. "The *Dutchman's* stealth field is projecting the image of a Ruhar battleship. While pretending to be a Ruhar captain, Chang warned the lizards that he would rain hellfire on their heads if they tried to interfere. Two fighters tried to lift off from an airbase anyway, because lizards are terminally stupid. That airbase is now a smoking crater. Hey, good news: the *Dutchman's* new railguns work great!"

"Outstanding. I'm going to bury this phone in the mud. Remember, we never talked."

"Gotcha, Joe."

"Wait. One more thing, Skippy?"

"Ugh. Another?"

"Yes. You have to act like your usual, asshole self. Joking around, insulting people, all that. Otherwise, the crew will suspect something serious happened, instead of you just screwing up like our cover story."

"It will be a struggle, but," he sighed. "I will try, Joe."

The Commando team's Dodo came straight in, its belly jets throwing up a hurricane of spray, mud and charred vegetation, while a Dragon flew high cover, its weapons pods ready for trouble. I crouched, shielding my ears and eyes until the lower-pitched whine told me the dropship's engines were at idle.

The back ramp was already open, Fabron and three others were standing guard and waving at me to hurry. That was easier said than done. Two of them met me halfway, held me under my arms and carried me easily with their powered armor. My feet barely touched the front of the ramp when the ship lifted off. With help, I got into a seat and strapped in.

Seated opposite me, Fabron raised his faceplate, the others of his team did the same. "It is good," he looked away as his voice choked up a bit. "To see you again, Sir."

"It is good to see all of you," I assured the team.

"I'm going to check your vitals, Sir," a woman seated beside me said, as she raised a medical scanner and pointed it at me.

My brain was tired, and the Commandos were still not familiar to me, so I glanced at her mech suit. The chest plate read 'US Army' and 'Raven, Destiny SSGT'. "Sure, Staff Sergeant," I let my head sag back against the seat. "I can tell you right now, I have not been eating enough vegetables."

That made her laugh. "We'll get you fixed up, Sir. Your hands look ugly," she peered at them with concern.

"Overflash from the maser cannon," I explained. "I'm alive, so I can't complain."

"Let me look at your leg. Ooh," I winced as she peeled away my makeshift bandage, from where a splinter had dug into my calf muscle. "It, looks infected?"

"Just my luck to get stranded on a planet where the native life is biocompatible with humans," I rubbed the back of my neck, which was covered with insect bites. On most worlds, insects didn't consider humans to be tasty, but the little buggers on Rikers had acquired a taste for Joe Bishop. They had tormented me whenever I tried to sleep.

"Hmm," she sprayed a numbing solution on my legs, then cut away the bandage, stiff from dried blood. "This is not too bad. I'll just wrap it for now. This infection may be the source of your fever."

"I have a fever?" I automatically felt my forehead and regretted it, my scaled hands hurt to touch anything.

"One-oh-one," she told me. "We can take care of that, too. Sir, I'm going to put an ointment on your burns," she warned me, holding up a bottle of some mysterious stuff. Raven was the Commando team's medic, until we shanghaied them, now she was learning advanced medicine from Mad Doctor Skippy. "This will sting a bit, then it will go numb."

"Ow! Ow, shit," I shivered, feeling suddenly cold. "A *bit*?"

"Sorry," she shrugged. "When we get back to the *Dutchman*, I can apply a flexible bandage to encourage regrowth of your skin."

"Whatever you say, Doc. Uh, hey," I looked at her nametag again. "Your name is really 'Destiny'?"

"Yes," she replied with a forced smile. "Go ahead, Sir, I've heard all the stripper jokes."

"Uh," right then, I couldn't think of any jokes about strippers. Or jokes about anything else. "Sorry, it's none of my business."

"My mother has a warped sense of humor," she explained, and that time the smile was genuine.

"That name must get used in a lot of cheesy pick-up lines," I said. I just couldn't stop talking, the filter between my brain and my mouth must have been switched off.

She laughed. "You have *no* idea. Can we get you anything to eat, Colonel?" Raven asked, glancing at the scanner, then peering closely into my eyes with concern.

"Real food would be great. No," I waved a hand as she dug into a pack. "I should get checked out aboard the *Dutchman* before I eat anything."

"That is," Raven's look of concern turned to amusement, she was struggling not to laugh and losing the battle. "Probably a good idea."

"What's so funny, Staff Sergeant?" I asked as Fabron glared at her.

"It's nothing, Sir. It's just, you look, here," she held up her zPhone, with the screen in its mirror mode.

I saw what she meant. Not my dirty, scarred, bruised and scalded skin. Not the blood-shot eyes. Not how gaunt and pasty I looked. What she found amusing was that I was missing a stripe of hair in the middle of my head, front to back. The hair on both sides was shaggy, but in the middle was only a faint stubble. "Yeah," was all I could say.

"That, uh," her shoulders were shaking, and even Fabron had to look away so he didn't burst out laughing. "That is an, *interesting* hairstyle, Sir."

"Joe got a *No*-Hawk," Skippy announced with a giggle. "Soon that fashion will be all the rage, or that's what he thinks."

"It's, uh," she took a photo of me and handed me the phone.

Damn, I looked like absolute shit. I knew she had mentioned the haircut to distract me from the pain. "I've had worse photos taken at the DMV," I shrugged.

"You just, um," Raven giggled. "You shouldn't use that as your profile photo on Tinder. Just sayin', huh?"

Her laugh was infectious, I had to join in. "I will keep that in mind."

"Sir?" Fabron held out a blue baseball cap. It had 'UNS Valkyrie CC-01' above the brim, in gold stitching.

"Thanks," I tugged it on my head, grateful for his thoughtfulness. I expected to be wearing a hat for a while. Resting my head back, I closed my eyes.

"How is he?" Fabron asked quietly.

Raven glanced again at the medical scanner. "Malnutrition, like he said. A low-grade fever. He is beginning to get *scurvy*, I haven't seen that except in textbooks. The burns are second-degree, they will heal. What I don't understand is the result of the brain scan. This thing," she waved the scanner, "isn't super accurate for that type of analysis, but he has lesions on his brain. This is not good news."

"It is a concern," Skippy said, with no trace of his usual snarkiness. "The Thuranin were not gentle with him, and the countermeasures I used made it worse. Right now, he needs rest. Oh, Joe," he sighed. "I'm sorry. I am truly sorry."

CHAPTER TEN

While the Commandos exfiltrated Bishop, the STAR team had their own mission. Sensor data collected by the *Flying Dutchman* determined that two Thuranin were still alive on the planet. They were pilots, whose dropship had been blown up in Skippy's initial round of strikes. It would have been nice for the Merry Band of Pirates, and safer for everyone involved, if the pilots had stayed in their assigned bunker. Unfortunately, the Thuranin for some reason did not trust the hospitality of their clients, so they had left the bunker, shot several Kristang, and stolen a beat-up old lizard dropship. It was not known what the pilots planned to do, or if they even had a plan at all. Without a friendly ship in orbit, they weren't going anywhere, and their Dragon was headed south toward a sparsely-inhabited area of the continent.

"They are low on fuel," Skippy reported. "Cannons only, they are Winchester on missiles. Also, that spacecraft was not considered flightworthy, the squawk list is a mile long. The portside engine is overheating, the rear ramp doors don't fully seal. *Ugh*, I guess they didn't have a choice. Maybe they-"

Smythe cut off his rambling dialog. "Can you glitch the aircraft remotely, force them to land?"

"Um, no. Sorry, I am experiencing a temporary awesomeness deficit. Screwing with a rifle targeting system is relatively simple, but if I hack into that Dragon's flight controls, the pilots will know they have been compromised. If this goes sideways, we need to maintain the cover story that we are an Alien Legion unit."

"Right," Smythe tugged tighter the straps holding him into the seat. "We do this the hard way, then. Pilot, hold fire until we are within forty kilometers. I want to follow them down to the crash site."

When the two Dragons from the *Flying Dutchman* were within forty kilometers of the target, the enemy still had not reacted. Their stolen dropship was flying at a speed and altitude for maximum efficiency, stretching their dwindling fuel supply for greater range. "No sign we have been detected," the pilot of Smythe's dropship reported.

"Launch missile," Smythe ordered from the jumpseat on the rear bulkhead of the cockpit.

"Fox One," the pilot said in a calm voice, and the Dragon rocked gently side to side as a missile was ejected out the launch tube, the door closing and another missile automatically queuing up for launch. "We have never done this, Sir," the pilot turned to look at Smythe.

"There is a first time for everything," the STAR team leader said assuringly, while keeping focus on the missile's track. "Maintain stealth until the missile is within ten kilometers."

When the flight path and targeting instructions were downloaded into the missile, the immediate reaction of its upgraded but still rudimentary Kristang AI was a baffled '*WTF*'? the second reaction was 'This is *bullshit*'.

The third reaction, after a stern lecture from the annoying Elder AI called 'Skippy', was a resigned shrug. Perhaps Skippy was right. Any missile could kill a defenseless, slow-flying target. To knock the dropship out of the sky, while ensuring the survival of the two-person crew, was much more difficult.

Still, it sucked. Missiles were supposed to *kill*, that's what they *did*.

Against all the instincts carefully programmed into its tiny brain, the missile was being urged to be *gentle*.

Riiiiiiiight, it thought. Maybe I can-

A ping from Skippy jerked it back onto course.

Screw it, the missile thought. You want gentle? Fine, but I'm doing this *my* way.

As it approached the target, the missile pulsed its active sensors, supposedly to verify the range. In reality, it spooked the two little green pinheads who were flying the dropship, and they went to full power, pulling the nose up and popping out decoys.

Now this is interesting, the missile chuckled with satisfaction.

Casually increasing its speed, the missile set its warhead on standby. The instructions for the attack were to approach from aft and below detonating its warhead in a cone-shaped fragmentation mode, at the lowest power setting. The shrapnel would tear into the engines and belly jets, while leaving the cockpit unharmed. Without belly jets, and with no runway in the area, the pilots would be forced to eject. It was the most effective way to accomplish the objective and it was boring. The attack plan was *dull*, it had no *imagination*. No *style*.

Instead, the missile increased speed when it was within two kilometers, racing in toward the randomly twisting target. It was not fooled by the decoys being ejected, the unbalanced engines of the target were making enough electromagnetic noise that a blind man could have found it.

At the last second, as the missile bored in and Skippy screamed dire and useless threats, the missile shed its wings and fired thrusters so it skidded across the sky to fly *backward*, its hot tail slamming into the dropship between the main engines. The dropship staggered as the missile buried itself backward, crashing through pipes and wires and bulkheads until its crumpled rear half was projecting through the ceiling of the aft cabin.

Huh, the missile thought. So *this* is what the inside of these things looks like. I am not impressed. Well, I hate to leave so soon, but-

Explosive bolts blew the front third of the missile loose, and it fell away from the downward-spiraling dropship. When the warhead had fallen three kilometers away, the missile's tiny brain pinged Skippy. 'What did you think of *that*?'

'I think you are a *jackass*,' the Elder AI shot back. 'But you've got style. Gotta give you props for that.'

'Thanks, Grandpa', the missile teased. 'Bye'.

Its warhead exploded spectacularly, directing the force upward, away from any of the three dropships in the area.

"Skippy," Smythe asked tersely. "What the bloody hell was *that*?"

"Just a bit of freelancing," the AI mumbled, embarrassed. "It won't happen again."

"See that it doesn't."

"Colonel?" The pilot called. "The quarry is ejecting."

The Thuranin pilots, having quickly analyzed the situation, concluded that:

-their spacecraft was no longer airworthy,

-their lowly Kristang clients had *shot* at them,

                    -landing the dropship was not an option, and

 -they were probably fucked anyway,

and decided their best option was to eject. So, they did.

Their seats rocketed out and away, after a brief delay caused by shoddily-built and poorly-maintained Kristang technology. If they had been flying a proper Thuranin craft, they could have communicated with the seat computers via their cyborg brain implants, but they had to settle for trying to use the confusing manual controls built into the keypad. Keypads that were old, worn, scratched, barely visible in sunlight, and displaying Kristang symbols that appeared to have no relation to the functioning of the icons they represented.

The lead pilot discovered that fact to her dismay, when her urgent and increasingly angry tapping of the screen resulted not in steering the oversized parachute, but in the straps that held her into the swaying seat releasing. The seat reached the end of its pendulum-like swing at the end of the parachute tether, and was yanked in the opposite direction, while the lead pilot's body continued its momentum out into empty air. Windmilling her arms and legs, she managed to tangle a foot in a dangling cord, which only got her to swinging back and forth far more violently than the seat itself.

Her mass, at the end of the cord, set up a rhythm that transmitted up through the seat into the tether, confusing the parachute computer. The seat's occupant had, for some unknown but certainly idiotic reason, decided to unstrap and get out in midair. The seat was empty, yet a weight equivalent to the previous occupant was still tugging on the tether. The computer had a decision to make, a decision which its tiny brain was not capable of fully analyzing. Normally, with loss of the occupant, the parachute would sever its tether, allowing the seat to plunge to the ground, while the parachute itself dissolved into flakes of dirty soot. Could the former occupant somehow be under the seat, and if so, was it alive? The parachute computer, with its limited and very old sensors, had no way of knowing what was under the seat or what was causing the wild swinging back and forth.

Without information, it had no basis on which to make a decision.

So it defaulted to not deciding at all. Its last instruction was to lower the seat safely to the ground, and it continued doing that.

The lead pilot, a female with the designation Dubyadee-40, frantically tried to get a grasp of the cord that her foot was entangled in. Every time she managed to contort herself to get a hand near the foot that was going numb, the seat swung the other way and the cord jerked her to a stop, nearly snapping her oversized head. After a dozen swings back and forth, she began to lose consciousness, and she flopped down limp at the end of the cord.

As the seat fell closer to the ground, the wind slackened and the wild motions of the seat stabilized, from the parachute computer using a small canister of cold gas to power the seat's thruster nozzles. That safety feature was designed to provide a stable platform, so the parachute could lower the seat and its occupant accurately to a landing.

Using the thrusters was a good idea, if it had worked. If the maintenance teams who serviced the aircraft had bothered to check the thruster nozzles, they would have seen that a species of wasps native to the planet had built their little mud nests in three of the nozzles, clogging them quite effectively. When instructions sent to the thruster unit failed to produce the desired result, the parachute computer sent the command again, and *again*. The third time was the charm. The build-up of pressure in the thruster lines blew out the plugs of hardened mud, an action that sent the seat rocketing to one side, exactly what computer did *not* want to happen. With the supply of thruster gas exhausted, there was nothing the computer could do about the gyrations of the seat or the alarming tension on the tether.

Dubyadee's eyes fluttered open when she became momentarily weightless, the seat having swung so far to one side that the tether was slack and the cord wrapped around her foot had sent her soaring *above* the seat. For a split-second, she was weightless before she smacked into the seat, breaking her other leg and dropping her over the side again. The pressure when she jerked to a stop at the end of the cord tore tendons in her knee and ankle, and the pain was enough for her cyborg implants to block signals to her brain. With cold logic and head kept clear by artificial glands pumping out chemicals to keep her alert and calm, she noted that running away to evade capture would not be an option. That problem could wait until she hit the ground.

The *immediate* problem were the trees reaching up for her as the seat continued its uncontrolled fall. Without pain to distract her, she twisted her upper body out of the way of a stout tree limb looming in front of her, got smacked in the face by a branch full of thick, sticky leaves, then fell straight down for the first time. Above her, the parachute tether had become wound around several tree branches and the seat crashed into a trunk, sending bark and shards of splinters to pelt her. None of the splinters penetrated her flightsuit and she relaxed as the ground rushed up toward her, making air explode from her lungs as she impacted harder than expected.

Alive.

She was injured, but down and alive. That was a relief after her ordeal.

Above the trees, the parachute control computer also experienced relief. Its sensors detected that there was no longer any extra mass weighing down the seat.

Therefore the previous occupant must be gone.

Therefore, the computer did not need to be concerned about proper procedure under ambiguous circumstances, it knew exactly what it was supposed to do.

The computer severed the tether that connected the parachute to the seat.

On the leaf-littered floor of the forest, Dubyadee-40's relief turned to a very brief flash of terror, as the heavy ejection seat fell straight down on top of her.

"Shit!" Captain Frey cursed. "Target Bravo life signs terminated."

"Are you sure?" Smythe called, the sound of his voice slightly muffled by the whistling of air rushing past his helmet at high speed.

"Yeah, that LGMF is dead," Skippy reported. "I thought ejection seats are supposed to be life-*saving* equipment?"

Smythe ignored the irrelevant remark. "Acknowledged. Frey, converge on my position."

"It's no good, Sir," she added with a grunt as her parachute balloon deployed and her headlong flight was brought to a stop. "We'll be on the ground in twenty seconds."

"Use your best judgment," Smythe also grunted. "We will flush the quarry toward you if we can."

"Understood," Frey said, and focused on getting herself and her team down through the tree canopy. Her STAR team was spread out to surround the spot where the Thuranin pilot had landed, cutting off escape routes. "Ow, shit," she cursed as she smacked an armored knee into a tree, temporarily blind as thick leaves rushed past her helmet faceplate. All she saw was a blur of dark green.

Then she was on the ground, rolling to protect her rifle. The parachute tether automatically snapped and disintegrated, along with the balloon itself, blowing away as a cloud of silvery dust.

"Team Bravo, check in," she ordered to follow procedure, though her helmet visor informed her that the three others on her team were also down, alive and well. They had the same info available through the team tactical link, yet they also followed procedure with pings indicating their status was green. "We will confirm status of the target first. Huang, you're with me. Karak and Jauffret, provide cover."

Huang was first to get direct line-of-sight to the target, or what was left of it.

Frey came up behind him, sighting through her rifle's scope. "*That* doesn't look good."

"I've never seen a Thuranin for real, Ma'am," he whispered.

"Me neither. I do know they are not supposed to look like that."

Warily, despite Skippy's assurance that the target had zero neural activity, they approached, fingers poised just above their trigger guards, ready to take action.

No action was necessary. Huang poked the Thuranin's cracked helmet with the muzzle of his rifle. "I'm pretty sure this one is *dead*."

Frey suppressed a 'Ya think?' response. "Team, our objective is secured. Dead, but secure. Let's go assist Team Alpha."

Team Alpha actually, though Smythe would have been reluctant to admit it, did need assistance. Their target had remained in his ejection seat and landed unharmed, other than a few bruises. Since the STAR team landed, the alien had stubbornly refused to cooperate, dashing away and firing bursts of guided ammunition from a rifle.

"Damn!" Major Kapoor exclaimed as the alien popped up from cover, let fly half-dozen guided rounds, and dropped down to scurry away. The rounds went over Kapoor's head as he flattened on the ground, impacting trees and exploding to send showers of sharp wood splinters pinging off his armor. "That little fucker is fast for his size."

"The Thuranin are cyborgs," Smythe reminded his team. "They have genetically-enhanced musculature, and their nerve network is boosted by implants. Their glands can produce something like adrenaline on command. Do not be fooled by their size. Zhou!" he shouted, as that soldier was struck by a round from the enemy.

"I'm all right," Zhou said, shaking her head. She had been thrown backward when the round struck the chest armor near her left shoulder.

"You are not *fine*," Smythe scolded. He appreciated enthusiasm, but not foolishness. "Your left arm motor mechanism is jammed. Hold your position."

"But," she protested, struggling to her feet. "I can-"

"Hold your position. Team Alpha, we need to take this one *alive*. Let him expend all his ammo, then we move in."

"Good strategy," Skippy said. "My estimate is he only has thirty-eight rounds in that magazine. Plus another sixty-two rounds in the spare magazine he is probably carrying. Unless he brought more magazines with him, you know."

"Bloody wonderful," Smythe muttered under his breath. "Do you have any more good news for us?"

"That type of rifle carries three rockets, and he hasn't used any yet, so be careful, please. Oh, also, he may have grenades with him. Ooh, and-"

"Team Alpha," Smythe interrupted the AI's speculation. "We have rockets also, let's use them. Bracket his position, maintain a safe distance. I want the target pinned down and confused. Do *not* fire unless you can be sure to avoid striking the target." He paused. "I know, that is easier said than done."

"Smythe," Chang called. "How's it going down there?"

The STAR team leader knew Chang had access to the same taclink data feed Smythe had in his helmet. The *Flying Dutchman's* captain was not calling for a status report, he wanted to know what Smythe thought. "It would be simpler if we could *shoot* this little bugger, Sir," Smythe admitted. "That cheeky bugger is taking potshots at us."

"If we wanted him dead, we could have hit the site from orbit. Is capture practical, without risking your team?"

"Everything is a *risk*, Sir."

"There are degrees of risk, Smythe."

"We can do this," Smythe insisted. "Once the target is out of ammunition, we can move in and use stun grenades," he suggested, though they had only Skippy's word that the grenades would be effective against the cyborg.

Chang did not answer immediately. "I do not like having your team exposed on the ground. A Thuranin ship could jump in at any moment. You have ten minutes, then you need to dust off and get back here. Bishop has been recovered and is enroute."

"Understood, Sir."

The help provided by Frey's Team Bravo was, in fact, no help at all. The lone Thuranin must have sensed the arrival of additional enemy soldiers, from either tracking backscatter from the helmet-to-helmet laserlinks, or just from the increased volume of fire. The downed pilot still thought he was being attacked by Kristang, for the hostiles flew Kristang dropships, wore Kristang powered armor, and fired Kristang rifles with Kristang ammunition. There were anomalies, such as the short stature of the attackers, but perhaps he was being tracked by young warriors who desired to boast about capturing one of their hated patrons. That the soldiers, who surrounded him in an ever-tighter circle, wanted to take him alive, had become obvious. The enemy tactics made no sense otherwise. All their fire was directed to keep him pinned down rather than to kill. If his death was the goal, the attackers could have launched an air-to-ground missile.

No. They wanted to capture him.

Captivity was preferable to death. He would only be a prisoner until his people arrived to pound the Kristang into submission. If he could hold off the Kristang until-

Smythe noted that the enemy fire had slackened, then ceased. The Thuranin had not fired a round in thirty seconds, nor had he moved. Five minutes remained before Chang's deadline. "Should we move in?" Frey asked.

"No," Smythe knew the plan was working. Working too well. According to his count, the Thuranin pilot had half a magazine of rifle ammo, plus a rocket, and an unknown number of grenades. The STARs had suffered two injuries, both serious enough to render those soldiers combat-ineffective. "Team, stand by." He bent down, dug into the soil and picked up a rock the size of a football. The enemy's position was a hundred twenty meters away, the stone heavy. In his visor, he designated where he wanted the rock to land, trusting the motors of his suit more than his own eye-hand coordination. A quick heave while still behind cover sent the stone soaring through the air. It crashed down, bounced and rolled toward the enemy. If he had judged correctly, its momentum would carry it-

There was an explosion, multiple explosions, and a fountain of dirt combined with shards of shattered tree trunks.

"Bloody hell," Smythe slumped to his knees. "Skippy?"

"He's dead, Jim. Whew! Hee hee, I have *always* wanted to say that!"

"Please be serious."

"Ah, crap. Scratch one pinhead. That is one crispy critter. He triggered off his rocket warheads, to avoid the enemy examining his cyberbetic implants."

Smythe knew the enemy must have thought the bouncing and crashing of the stone was a soldier approaching, and took his own life. The pride of the Thuranin did not allow for capture by inferior beings. Smythe let fly a creative string of expletives with his helmet microphone switched off. Then, "That's it, then, we buggered that."

"Not necessarily," Skippy announced cheerily.

"We were supposed to take them *alive*," Smythe protested. "We failed."

"First, your task was extremely difficult. The one who blew himself up is in tiny pieces, true, but-"

Smythe was disgusted with himself. "They are both dead."

"Ah. There you are wrong. The other one is only *mostly* dead."

"Mostly dead?"

"That's what I said. Fortunately for you, Miracle Max is on the job. I advise you to get back to Target Bravo, and hurry."

"He looks dead to me," Smythe crouched by the small, broken form, trapped under the ejection seat.

"*She* is dead," Skippy snorted. "Quick, one of you go through her pockets for loose change, while somebody else cuts her head off."

Jeremy Smythe, a battle-hardened veteran, flinched. "Cut her head off? Skippy, we do not desecrate the bodies of-"

"This isn't for fun. She has cranial implants. I can scan them to recover her memories, *if* you bring her head back to the ship, and *if* you hurry before the circuits degrade."

"Right. Shit." Smythe slung his rifle, pulled out a wickedly-sharp knife and knelt beside the body. "Were you serious about searching her pockets?"

"*Ugh.* No, that is a line from- Jeremy, when you get back to the ship, you really need to watch a movie with me. Your pop culture knowledge is *woefully* lacking."

Jennifer Simms left the CIC under orders from Chang, to greet their commander and see that he went directly to the medical bay. Lined up outside the docking bay were an honor guard of three STARS and three Commandos, plus two pilots.

And Margaret Adams, in full dress uniform.

"Adams," Simms crooked a finger at the gunnery sergeant. "A word?" She drew the other woman aside, down the passageway just out of earshot. "What are you doing here?"

Adams blinked. With *Valkyrie's* crew aboard the *Dutchman*, Adams had not been needed in the CIC. She had been at her designated damage control station until the All Clear sounded, allowing the off-duty crew to get rest until their next shift. "Ma'am? I am off-duty, I came here to represent-"

"You came here to see Bishop," Simms concluded flatly.

"Yes," Adams's chin came up defiantly as she stiffened.

"That is *not* happening," Simms glared into the Marine's eyes. "Go back to your quarters, or go to the gym. Go anywhere but *here*."

"Colonel, that is not-"

"Gunnery Sergeant Adams," Simms snapped. "Skippy informed us that Bishop is not only worn out, injured and malnourished, he likely has undiagnosed brain damage from his treatment by the Thuranin. I don't have to tell *you* how challenging that will be for him."

"I can give him-"

"What? The only thing you can give Bishop right now is *confusion*. Adams, this on-again, off-again, will-they-or-won't-they shit has to *stop*, right here," she jabbed a finger at the deck. "Right now. Enough. You need to make up your damned mind one way or another." Simms knew she was being harsh, that Adams deserved better. If there was time, she would have called the gunnery sergeant to her office for a personal counseling session. As it was, the dropship carrying Bishop was only minutes away from docking. "This isn't some amusing crush between two junior officers. Bishop is our *commander*. He is the only hope we have, the only hope for humanity."

"Joe-" Adams caught herself. "He said there is no hope for us."

"You believe that?" One side of Simms's mouth cracked into a brief smile. "*Everything* we do is impossible, until *he* realizes it isn't. That's why we need him to be sharp, focused and not moping around like a puppy dog looking for affection." She softened her voice. "You understand that? The situation sucks, but this is what you both signed up to. You want to help him? Don't distract him, not now."

"Yes, Ma'am."

"Gunny, you're doing good work with the children we rescued, *good* work. Do that, until and unless you can commit to something else. You hear what I'm saying?"

"Yes."

"Send Bishop a message. You're glad he's back, tell him about the children, that sort of thing. Keep it friendly but professional, and short. Not *too* short."

"Yes."

"You don't have to make up your mind *today*. But you do have to decide what you want. What is best, for both of you. This is not good for either of you, is it?"

"No."

That was another one-word answer. Simms suppressed a sigh. She knew she was right, so why didn't it *feel* right? Every one of the crew knew about Bishop and Adams, the old hands had known for years. Every one of the crew wanted them to be happy. And every one of them knew it could not happen. Simms knew it *should* not happen, not until the Pirates returned to Earth. They still had a mission to complete, whatever Bishop decided the mission was.

There wasn't anything more to say. "Dismissed, Gunny."

Adams snapped a salute and turned away.

"Adams?" Simms called after the Marine, who paused and looked back over her shoulder. "I hope this works out for you, I really do. Just not *now*."

"I understand, Ma'am." Her shoulders heaved as she took in a deep breath. "Thank you."

Staff Sergeant Raven gently nudged me awake as we approached the ship, and at first I stared stupidly at her, Fabron, Greene and the other Commandos, wondering why all these people were in my bedroom. Then I remembered, and wished I hadn't. When we docked aboard the *Dutchman*, Simms greeted me. "Simms, I appreciate your concern, but," I looked down at myself. "I really want to get cleaned up first, this time I really *am* a filthy monkey."

"Oooh, bad news, Joe," Skippy's voice boomed out of the docking bay speakers. "While you were away, your shower filed for a restraining order."

The Commandos studiously looked away, but I could tell some of them were laughing silently.

"That's, great, Skippy." I felt like strangling him yet again. "Seriously, Simms, I will feel a whole lot better if I can get out of these grungy clothes."

"That," she looked me over from head to toe. "*Is* an interesting outfit."

"Joe is wearing part of this year's Apocalypse line," Skippy snickered. "Wait, what am I saying? He would never wear *this* year's fashion. Seriously, Joe, did you get that outfit all from one dumpster, or did you shop around?"

Before my tired brain could think of a snappy reply, or any reply at all, Simms gave me the side-eye. "Sir, you look like shit."

"Thanks for the honesty. However I look, I *feel* worse."

"All the more reason for Doctor Skippy to get you fixed up. I will bring a change of clothes to the medical bay."

"How, uh, how is the crew?" I asked, in what I intended to be a casual fashion.

"The *crew*," she looked at me sideways. Busted. She knew I was asking about Margaret Adams. "Is busy. You can get an update, after Skippy clears you."

Too tired and worn out to argue any longer, I nodded, and was immediately hustled through passageways to the *Dutchman's* medical center.

In one of the medical bays, Skippy used some machine to run a scan on me. "You need to take off your hat," he warned.

My hand paused on the brim of the baseball cap. "Simms, I have to warn you, the Thuranin sort of shaved my head."

"I was wondering about the hat." She knew I hadn't brought it with me from Rikers. "Is it that bad?" She asked, when I made no move to take the hat off.

"They shaved the middle of my head, front to back," I admitted sheepishly. "Skippy calls it," I lifted the hat. "A *No*-hawk."

"Sir, I pity the fool who laughs at your haircut," she frowned, but her eyes twinkled.

We fist-bumped to acknowledge her mastery of pop culture. "XO, thanks for the vote of confidence. Let's get this over with, Skippy."

"Hmm. Hmm," his avatar said while wearing a white lab coat. "Good news: the brain scan is not as bad as I feared. However, I need a closer look at your throat, there's some damage in there from what the Thuranin did to you. The procedure is called," a robot came out of a wall, holding a long flexible tube, "an endoscopy. It's just slightly different from a colonoscopy."

"*Slightly*?" I tried to get away from the robot, but the bed was too narrow. "Well, it-"

"One of them goes in your mouth, the other goes-"

"I know where it goes, Joe."

"If you think that is only a *slight* difference, I want a new doctor."

"*Ugh*, you monkeys are so-"

"Sir," Simms had a hand over her mouth and her shoulders were shaking. It wasn't clear whether she was laughing with me, or at me. "It looks like you're in good hands here, I-"

"Good hands?" I pointed to just two of the scary-looking medical torturebots clustered around me. "I want to get far away from the witch doctor here," I said, jerking a thumb at Skippy's avatar.

"You think I am a *witch* doctor?" He screeched, outraged.

Simms backed out of the compartment, holding up her hands. "You two need to work this out. Have fun, Sir."

CHAPTER ELEVEN

The two Dragons carrying the STAR teams returned to the *Flying Dutchman*, and the ship jumped as soon as the docking clamps engaged. "Skippy?" Smythe called even before he unstrapped from his seat.

"Yeah, yeah, working on it," the AI mumbled distractedly. "The good news is, that little green pinhead did not expect to get squashed by the ejection seat, so she didn't have time to engage the subroutine to wipe her memory implants. Or, she figured the lizards couldn't crack the encryption anyway, so there was no point to wiping the memory."

"What is the bad news?" Smythe released the straps but remained seated, with the bag containing a severed head on his lap.

"The bad news is, the data is *totally* scrambled. The implants are unique to each person, they adapt to the individual user's neural architecture. That is a problem, because to read the data stored in the implants, I need to create a map of her brain, and figure out how it worked."

"Ah. That is why you needed me to bring her head aboard, instead of digging implants out of her skull."

"Exactly. I know, yuck. It doesn't feel right to me either, but there is no other way to extract her memories."

"Just get it done, please."

"Working on it. Um, it might help both of us if you put her head in a refrigerator. *Not* in the galley, please. Simms would kill me if I suggested that."

Smythe stashed the duffel bag with the severed head in a temperature-controlled locker of the docking bay's control center, and tried to forget about it while he walked down to the section of the ship that was set aside for the STAR team. And for the Commandos, he reminded himself when he saw Fabron and his people getting their gear squared away. "Major," he acknowledged Fabron. "How is Bishop?"

Fabron nodded toward the Commando team's medic. "Raven says he will be fine. He is in the medical bay now." Lowering his voice, he added "There is a possibility of brain damage from the interrogation techniques employed by the Thuranin."

"Did you run into any issues?"

"No," the French officer shook his head. "You?"

"Both of the Thuranin we were supposed to recover alive, were killed. One was an accident before we arrived at the scene. The other killed himself as we closed in," Smythe defended the actions of his team, until he realized he was making excuses.

Fabron looked away, suddenly finding a fault with the way he had stowed away his own gear. "It was a difficult tasking," he said "We can't take someone alive, if they are determined to kill themselves."

Smythe shrugged. "It is not a total loss, Skippy believes he can recover memories from the dead."

Fabron snorted. "Is he conducting a seance, or using tarot cards?"

"Hey!" The AI objected. "For your information, I am using *science*, something you monkeys would not understand."

"Is this science producing any useful results," Smythe asked. "Or are you wasting time?"

"Huh. Well, I should not dignify that remark with a reply, but so you know, I just finished discussing my findings with Colonel Chang."

That irritated Smythe. "You couldn't tell us at the same time?"

"Well, *excuse* me for wanting to give you time to clean up in peace. Um, which reminds me, you've got something on the outside of your suit's right forearm. No, it's, twist the other way. There, see it?"

"Yes," Smythe took a rag and wiped away what appeared to be part of the Thuranin pilot. While the armor would be thoroughly cleaned and serviced by the ship's robotic maintenance team, he believed in caring for his own equipment. "Answer the question, please."

"The answer is, that pilot did not have any information that could be dangerous to us. She only knew what she had been told by the pinheads who interrogated Joe, I mean, Colonel Bishop. They bought the cover story that the raid was conducted by an Alien Legion unit, though they did note several discrepancies with that story. Also, right up to the point when the ejection seat fell on her, she believed she was being pursued by lizards. She had no clue that humans were involved."

"That is good," Smythe expressed his relief.

"Yes, except all you did was confirm what I already *told* you," Skippy sniffed.

"Pardon us," Fabron made a rude gesture toward the ceiling, "for not trusting you are infallible."

"Hey! I never said I was- OK, well, maybe I did *imply*, but- Ugh. Stupid monkeys."

Smythe flashed a grin at the Commando leader. "Skippy, I need you to research something for me."

"What, I am your Google now?"

"I will ignore that remark. This is serious. Please tell me, what are Thuranin customs regarding proper disposition of a corpse?" To Fabron he added "I need to know what to do with the severed head we brought aboard."

"Severed *head*?" Fabron closed his locker. "*This* story, I need to hear."

"Well?" I asked Mad Doctor Skippy about two hours later. Everything hurt. Even my eyelids hurt, from the strain of keeping my eyes open. All I wanted to do right then was fall into a bed and sleep for several days. Before I could do that, I had to hear Skippy's diagnosis of my condition, and what we could do to repair the damage done by the Thuranin. "You have run every test possible."

"Not *every* test, Joe. There might be a need for a few more tests later."

"More tests? Why? Does the doctor need to make a payment on his Ferrari?"

"Very funny. Seriously, Dude, it is mostly good news. All the physical damage can heal by itself, or with a little help. You need rest, proper nutrition, physical therapy and most of all, *time*."

"You won't get an argument from me about any of that. What about my," I tapped my head, "noggin? Everything OK in there?"

"Everything is *not* OK in there. The quachines I used were very targeted, you may find you have lost some minor childhood memories, or not be able to multiply seven times seven, but there-"

"Forty-nine," I said, but I had to think about it first. Was I always like that?

"That was just an example. My point is, the quachines did not do any important, lasting damage to vital areas of your cerebral cortex. When I placed the quachines in your head, I positioned them specifically to avoid-"

"When did you do that? Put those things in my head?"

"Just before you and I went to visit that broken Sentinel in the Roach Motel. There was a possibility that we might lose the ability to communicate via normal channels, so-"

"What possibility?"

"Well," his avatar squirmed uncomfortably. "For example, if the Sentinel had activated its-"

"*Activated*?" My voice went up so high, I didn't recognize it. "You told me that thing was *dead*."

"It *was* dead, Joe. In this spacetime. Since I couldn't be sure whether its higher-level mechanism was also disabled-"

"Oh. My. God." Thinking about that nightmarish thing made me shudder. "Hell, I wouldn't have come anywhere near that thing if you had told me-"

"Hence why I didn't tell you, dumdum. If I had told you, I would be dead, and you would still be stuck in the Roach Motel. And by the way, all the humans on Paradise would be dead from an engineered bioweapon, *and* Earth would have been bombarded into radioactive slag by a pair of Maxolhx warships."

"Um, hmm. Good point."

"You can thank me later," he sniffed.

"Do *not* do that again," I wagged a finger at him.

"That was a one-time thing. It only happened because, if you remember, I was stuck in this canister and couldn't access higher-level spacetime. If we encounter a Sentinel in the future, I will be able to thoroughly examine it, in every dimension."

"Get back to the subject, please. You put quachines in my head back then to-"

"Ugh. The subject is the *current* status of your brain, not some history lesson."

"OK. Whatever." There was no point yelling at him about it. He had been right about taking the risk to approach the Sentinel, and he had been right about secretly putting super-sciency nanobugs in my brain.

"Hmmf," he sniffed, expecting me to argue. When I didn't, he continued. "Bottom line is, there is no critical damage in your cerebral cortex."

"I feel fine. Up there, I mean," I tapped my temple with a finger, except I missed and poked my eye. "Some headaches, that's it."

"Joe, you haven't seen yourself. Your eye-hand coordination is off. You walk like you're drunk. Look at yourself in the mirror. That expression is your Resting Shitface."

"Resting *Shitface*?" I laughed.

"You know, like, people have a 'Resting Bitchface' when no one is looking. Right now, you look like you drank a whole bottle of tequila and you are totally shitfaced."

The mirror did not lie. He was right. My face sagged, my eyelids were puffy, my jaw slumped open until I thought about it and pulled it up. Then it slumped open again. No question about it; I was a mess. "Ok, yuck. Patch me up, Doc."

"Do what?"

"You know. Do your thing. Give me nanomeds like you did for Adams." Hearing myself say her name, I wondered why she hadn't come to see me.

"No can do, Joe," he shook his head.

"Why not?"

"The situation is different. Your damage is subtle and much less severe. You have lesions affecting your executive function, that's your decision-making ability, to put it plainly. Plus damage affecting eye-hand coordination. Your memories, except for where the quachines burned out neurons, are intact. The Thuranin could not risk damaging your memories."

"Right. Not until they cut my head open."

"They planned to do that, because they could not understand why you were able to resist their memory probe technology. Of course, they didn't know about the quachines. That technology is not known to the Thuranin, even the Maxolhx have only a vague notion of the details. Listen, we could go on all day about why it is a bad idea to apply direct intervention inside your skull. The damage is not severe enough to justify such radical action. Plus, more importantly, we just can't risk it, Joe," he sighed. "Nanomachines rewiring your brain might change who you *are*. You might lose your ability to dream up crazy shit that gets us out of impossible situations. I won't do it, Joe. It's that simple."

"So, I have to do this the hard way? How long will that take?"

"Two, three weeks?"

"That's all?" In the back of my mind, I had been fearing he would say months or years.

"You won't be totally without help. There are drugs and advanced therapies I can administer to speed the process. It will not be easy."

"I'm a soldier, Skippy. Nothing is *easy*."

"Speaking of you being a soldier, will you allow me to give you a bit of friendly advice?"

"Sure."

"Until you're back to normal, Chang should be in overall command. Let Simms be captain of *Valkyrie*. They are already doing that, so-"

"Done, and done. I'll make it official. Note that in the log, and tell them what I said." The second part was easy, because *Valkyrie* was a drifting, powerless hulk. "Please, can I get some sleep now?"

"In a minute. Get dressed, Colonel Chang is coming to see you."

He wasn't exaggerating. No sooner had I pulled on a fresh T-shirt with ARMY across the chest, gray sweatpants and tugged the baseball cap over my head, when Chang knocked on the glass partition.

"Come on in," I waved, stifling a yawn with the other hand. Either Chang was psychic, or he had been waiting outside the whole time, or Skippy pinged him while we were talking.

"You have looked better," he observed, searching my eyes.

"I've felt better. I haven't ever felt much *worse*. Kong, I want you to take command. My recommendation is to jump us to *Valkyrie*."

He smiled. "We jumped a few seconds after your dropship docked."

"Oh." I hadn't felt the jump, which told me how out of it I was. "Mad Doctor Skippy tells me I need a couple weeks to recover. Simms should be captain of *Valkyrie*."

Another smile. "She is already aboard, went over there an hour ago."

"Oh." My exhausted brain couldn't think of anything else to say.

"Joe, we've got this. *You* get rest." His smile turned to an expression of concern. "Is there anything I can do?"

"Yeah," I wiggled my feet. "Help me put these sneakers on?"

People bought Skippy's bullshit cover story about why the microwormholes shut down. At least, they officially bought into it. I got many sideways, questioning looks, and Nagatha asked a *lot* of questions. In the end, I think what sold the story was Skippy's attitude. He was clearly *so* humiliated, so eager for people to tell him they understood, that it was all right, that everyone could see he knew he had screwed up epically, whether they knew the full details or not.

Simms was in command of our battlecruiser, though for the first two days, she remained aboard the *Flying Dutchman*. Chang sent Skippy to *Valkyrie*, then jumped the *Dutchman* ten light-seconds away for safety, with the jump drive on a hair-trigger to get the hell out of there on a moment's notice. He was concerned that something could go wrong while Skippy reactivated the battlecruiser's reactors, but mostly Chang worried that the native AI was not completely dead. The damned thing, or whatever failsafe system that had killed it, might come back to life and launch weapons against the *Dutchman*. From what I heard later, Skippy had protested being left alone aboard our big ship, but he didn't bother to protest much. He knew he was on a short leash and needed to earn everyone's trust, especially Chang's.

Being ten light-seconds away meant the *Dutchman* would not know about anything happening aboard *Valkyrie* for ten seconds after it happened, because there was no microwormhole available to provide instantaneous communication. Why not? Because Skippy could not create microwormholes. His escape to Neverland had temporarily damaged his connection between layers of spacetime, so he was experiencing a temporary awesomeness deficit. Back when he was attacked by the computer worm, he had been Skippy the Meh, as he had lost connection to higher spacetime. When he bailed on us, he had severed his connection to what we thought of as local spacetime. He could create microwormholes, he just wasn't able to anchor their endpoints where we were. Skippy assured Chang the problem was temporary, and he provided a demonstration by sustaining a microwormhole for five millionths of a second. That doesn't sound like much, but Nagatha was encouraged.

What did I do during that time? I slept a lot. Like, a *lot*. When I was awake, I ate soup and crackers and salads and anything else Simms insisted was good for me. My insides were unhappy from eating a steady diet of expired MREs, and I really didn't feel like eating anything at all. The reason I ate was because Simms, or Reed, or Smythe, sat there and watched until I cleaned the bowl. Sometimes Simms acts like she's my mother, and most of the time that irritates me. But, after I got pulled off Rikers, I was OK with her being concerned about me.

By the way, one person who did not visit me over the first two days was Margaret Adams. She sent me a nice message, wishing me well and stating that she was working with the children we rescued. The note was nice, brief, professional. Also kind of impersonal.

It hurt.

Had something happened while I was away?

Or maybe she was just sick of the game we had been playing. I know I was sick of it, for sure.

Or maybe she was telling me that when she had called me 'Joe', that had been the nanomachines in her head talking, and now she regretted it.

I sent her a note back, admiring her work with the children. The note was nice, brief and professional.

She didn't reply.

During the times I was awake over the first two days, I thought about her a lot.

Another thing I did, during the brief times I was awake, was play the cognitive therapy video game Skippy designed for me. The graphics were of course phenomenal, but the rest of the game was a frustrating suckfest. Good for me that I slept most of the time.

Anyway, Skippy got *Valkyrie's* power back on and major systems stable within forty-two hours, working as fast as he could so Simms could come aboard with her full team. He was lonely being all by himself, so that was extra incentive to get the work done.

If it had been my decision, I would have sent people aboard *Valkyrie* with Skippy, but Chang made the call and I didn't have a problem with it. The fact was, I was unfit for command. Physically, I was worn out. Skippy warned that I actually had sustained minor brain damage, both from the quachines and from the tender loving care of the Thuranin. When he told me that, he hadn't made a joke about the brain damage being no worse than usual, so I knew it was serious. He promised the damage could be repaired, both with treatment and by my brain healing itself, if I got rest and stayed away from stressful situations.

Like *that* was going to happen.

Plus, emotionally, I was dealing with a whole lot of shit inside my head.

I'll talk about that later.

If I talk about it at all.

With me working on rehabbing my stupid brain and Chang in command, there wasn't much for me to do. Truthfully, there wasn't any way humans could help to get *Valkyrie* restored to flightworthy status; that work was 99% Skippy and 1% Nagatha checking his work.

The only way I could help at all was by listening to Skippy complain. When *Valkyrie's* reactors were back online, and Nagatha confirmed the main computer of the battlecruiser was indeed thoroughly dead, Chang brought the *Dutchman* back so our two ships were only seventeen kilometers apart, and Simms took her crew back aboard.

With me.

Going with Simms was partly for me and partly for Chang. He didn't need me hanging around, potentially second-guessing every decision he made. Plus, I was occupying a cabin on an over-crowded ship. Plus, Skippy suggested the medical facilities aboard *Valkyrie* were better suited to assist my recovery. Plus, I didn't want to meet the people we rescued, until I no longer looked like a zombie.

Plus, if you want the truth, if I remained aboard the *Dutchman*, I might run into Adams. That was awkwardness neither of us needed right then.

So, I took a flight over to *Valkyrie*. The ship smelled funny but the lights were on, the air was breathable, and artificial gravity was set at Earth normal. Immediately, I took a nap in my old cabin, and stayed out of the way.

Waking up from my third or fourth nap of the day, I yawned and checked for messages on my phone. There was only one, from Skippy. *Call me no rush*, it said.

No rush. The message had been sent almost half an hour before, so I took my time splashing water over my face and staring at myself in the mirror. The No-hawk haircut looked so ridiculous that I had given myself a buzzcut the day before, now I looked like I was in boot camp, my hair just a quarter-inch of fuzz all over. Baseball caps would be my friend for a while, wearing one not only covered up my awful hair, it also concealed the bumps, cuts and bruises on my skull. The brim shaded my face, making my bloodshot eyes with dark, yellow-tinged circles less obvious. Simms had not been exaggerating when she said I looked like shit when I came aboard. Three and a half days later, I was marginally better. My teeth looked Ok, otherwise I could be auditioning to play a zombie in a TV show, and not need any makeup.

Simms had left a Thermos of coffee when she visited me the last time, I unscrewed the lid to find the coffee was still hot. Drinking half a cup restored me to semi-awareness. The caffeine would keep me awake and that was good, I was sleeping too much. It was time to return to the land of the living and work on my therapy.

To get myself in the proper frame of mind, I went back in the bathroom and took a hot shower, then got dressed for PT in gray shorts and a T-shirt with the Merry Band of Pirates logo on the front. Looking at myself in the mirror, I took a deep breath.

Time to get to work.

Deep knee-bends had my joints creaking like an old man, and forty pushups had me aching and gasping for breath, but I felt *alive*. "Hey, Skippy," I called out.

His avatar appeared on top of a cabinet. "Joe! Hey- Whew. Did you shave without a mirror this morning?"

Running a hand over my face, I couldn't see or feel anything wrong. "I haven't been shaving. I am technically on medical leave. Also, no one cares, Skippy."

"Wow. Your beard is like one of those weird styles from the American Civil War, when guys would have crazy sideburns and shit like that."

"It is not *that* bad," though looking at myself in the mirror, maybe it was time to scrape off the scraggly beard I had grown.

"Seriously? Is your eyesight OK?"

"My eyesight is fine. I will shave tomorrow. Maybe. What's up?"

"I wanted to ask, how are you?"

"Don't you know? You are my doctor."

"The medical monitors tell me the status of your body in more detail than I want to think about, but they don't tell me how you *feel*. Congrats by the way, on actually sleeping like I advised. I thought you would push yourself too hard."

"It wasn't like I had a choice, but thank you for caring."

"Speaking of caring, look beside the couch. I got a present for you."

Just then, I noticed a package next to the couch. It was in a plain cardboard box. Shaking it, something rattled around. "Thanks, Skippy. What is it?" I asked as I ran a fingernail along the seam to cut the tape holding the box together.

"Something to keep you busy. It's a book kit, Joe! You just have to assemble the letters into a story, and-'"

"A book *kit*?" The box popped open and wood tiles spilled onto the floor. "This is just a Scrabble game, you idiot!"

"Well, sure, if you have *no* imagination," he huffed.

"What, I'm supposed to play Scrabble against myself?"

"Of course not, Joe. You *suck* at Scrabble."

I actually could not argue about that. "Ah, thanks anyway. Picking up these tiles is good for my eye-hand coordination. Hey, you asked about me. How are *you*?"

"Ugh. This *suuuuuuucks*. Joe, you cannot imagine how tedious it is to manage every single freakin' system of this ship. Whatever happened to the native AI, the event thoroughly dorked up every electronic control system. Until I can get each element sorted out, I have to directly control every piece of machinery aboard this ship. You know I am more of a big-picture guy, I hate dealing with nit-picky details."

"Uh huh. Think of it as punishment for your screw-ups."

"This feels like a life sentence."

While I would have loved to hear him complain for hours, I in fact did *not* want to do that, so I changed the subject. "Chang told me he is pleased with your progress?"

"Well, Joe, you know that I hate to brag about myself," he lied in breathtaking fashion. "Truly, I have been amazing. First, I had to concentrate on restarting the reactors, that is a major job by itself."

Crossing my fingers for good luck, because we needed some good luck, I asked the question I feared most. "What about the power boosters?" Stealing a set of power boosters had cost us dearly. If the boosters had been damaged when *Valkyrie's* systems crashed, I did not know if I could face the prospect of another raid to capture more of the devices.

"They are fine, Joe," he dismissed my concern, having no idea how important that issue was to me. "They haven't been brought back online yet because we don't need that level of power. We aren't at the point of feeding power to the jump drive capacitors, and way out here, we don't need shields or a stealth field. I'm taking it slow, don't plan to hook in the power boosters for another four days, and that will only be for a test. Physically, the ship is in fine condition. Unfortunately, all the control systems got thoroughly fried, and I have to rebuild the circuits up from the molecular level. Right now, the ship can't jump, and the defense shield projectors are so screwed up they would interfere with each other."

"What about weapons?"

"Right now? Ugh. The best we can do for a weapon is a pack of Mentos and a bottle of Diet Coke," he snorted.

"Seriously?"

"Well, I suppose we could blindly launch a missile and hope it hits something? I'm working as fast as I can. Simms told me to give priority to the jump drive. She figures that if we can run, we won't need to fight. I am doing that, but some of the repairs needed to the missile guidance network are relatively simple, so I'm multitasking. The bottlcncck is the capacity of the ship's fabricators, I'm having to assign three fabricators to make another fabricator. Joe, this kind of extensive work is something that the Maxolhx would handle by towing the ship to a heavy repair facility, or at least bring in a dedicated support ship. We only have access to the spare parts we brought with us. Anyway," he took a deep breath, or did a good job simulating the sound. "I've got it covered. The damage isn't anything that I can't fix."

"Damn, that is great news. Have you discovered what happened to the native AI?"

"My best guess, based on what little I have been able to recover, is that the Maxolhx had a kill-switch hidden somewhere. It destroyed the AI and every major system, then erased itself. Decently clever technology," he admitted. "The subroutine appears to have been designed to wipe the AI without damaging the physical components of the ship. That is why *Valkyrie's* reactors performed a nice orderly shutdown, instead of the plasma melting through the shielding when containment failed."

"Yeah," I rubbed the back of my neck. "I wondered about that."

"Why?"

"Think about it. That subroutine would only be used in an extreme event; the ship's AI going rogue or being infiltrated by an enemy or something like that. Why didn't the subroutine cause the ship to explode?"

"Ah! That is a question I *do* have an answer for. Because the crew was expected to restore the AI's original programming, by accessing an archive that is hidden in the control system for water circulation. Before you ask a bunch of stupid questions, there is no record of that archive in any files available to the ship's AI, which is why I didn't know about it. Most likely, senior officers of the ship were told about the archive, and trained how to access and use it to restore the AI to proper functioning."

"The AI wasn't told about the archive, so it couldn't erase the archive? That's paranoid thinking, but smart. If there's an archive, why can't we use it to restore the AI?"

"Restore the AI that wanted to kill everyone aboard the ship?" He asked slowly.

"Good point. Don't do that."

"It wouldn't work anyway. Remember, I made major modifications to the original AI, the version in the archive is incompatible with the current substrate. That is why I have to manage the system by myself, until I can construct a new AI. Joe, I know that I screwed up *big-time*. The native AI was only pretending to cooperate with us. It completely suckered me. The worst part is, ugh. The reason I fell for it is because I *so* wanted to believe I had beaten the damned thing. It used my own arrogance against me. And, I totally missed the existence of a kill-switch subroutine that wiped it, after it agreed to cooperate with Simms. Trust me, *that* will not happen again."

"Uh huh. You assured us, *twice*, that you had the original AI under control. The only reason that everyone aboard both ships is not dead, is because Nagatha did *not* trust you to know what you're doing."

"Yes, I know-"

"You know that. Do you *understand* it? Everyone aboard this ship would be dead. Everyone aboard the *Dutchman* would be dead. I would never have gotten off Rikers, I would be dead too. That disaster was prevented *only* because Nagatha knew what an arrogant, lazy, absent-minded little shithead you are, so she took steps to protect herself, and all of us."

"Sorry," he muttered so quietly, I could barely hear him. If he had said 'sorry' in a way that meant he was annoyed or pissed off or sick of hearing people remind him of his many failings, I would have been enraged. My patience with him was very short, he had a lot to make up for. The way he said 'sorry' was like a little boy who did something stupid, and hurt the family dog. Genuinely sorry. Horrified at what he had done. Not able to forgive himself. Either he was really good at faking what I wanted to hear, or he was sincere.

One thing I knew about Skippy, one thing that had not changed since the day we met, is that he is terrible at lying.

"Skippy, my parents taught me that when you screw up, all you can do is own it, and resolve to do better in the future."

"I am trying to do that, Joe. I really, *really* am. To assure, as best we can, that *Valkyrie's* new semi-autonomous control system will truly be under the crew's control, and not contain any nasty surprises, I asked Nagatha to work with me.

Review my plans, monitor while I implement the upgrades, and inspect the results in as much detail as she can."

"Chang approved your plans?"

"Yes. Because I have already been a major pain in the ass to you, I am not going to say 'well heh heh'. You are *not* going to like how long it will take to design, install, and test the new temporary control system."

"We're not talking months, are we? Or years?"

"No! Days, Joe. Two, two and a half, max. That is *Nagatha's* estimate," he added. "I asked her for an estimate," he paused and made a sound like a sigh. "Because I didn't trust my own judgment."

Maybe, just maybe, Skippy was learning something. "Two days is no problem. Most of the crew will remain aboard the *Dutchman* until the work is finished. When you did the 'heh heh' thing, I thought it was going to take a long time."

"It's a long time for us. Do you have any idea how long two days of monkey-time is for me? It's like- Oh, forget it. Your tiny brain can't imagine anything that long."

"A journey of a thousand miles begins with a single step," I said, proud of myself for quoting Sun-Tzu. Or maybe that was Confucius? Hell, for all I knew, that quote came from the Wu-Tang Clan.

"Uh," he stammered. "What?"

"I meant, the sooner you get started, the sooner you will finish."

"Wow. I am blown away. Joe Bishop understands the nature of linear time. *Brah-voh* to you."

"Oh, shut up. When can you get started?"

"We are in the design process now. The two days I mentioned? That is for developing a control system significantly lower in capability than the previous unit. The Pirates will need to fly the ship and direct the use of weapons. If you want a more autonomous unit that would be capable of-"

"No." That didn't require any thinking, it was a gut reaction. "We need a man in the loop. A person in the loop. The last thing we want is a ship that flies itself."

"That's what Chang told me."

Stifling a yawn, I took another swig of coffee. This being-awake thing was a lot of work. "Chang is right. Speaking of being in the loop, you will give me updates on your progress?"

"If you want. We both know you will be getting updates from Nagatha anyway."

"It's not that I don't trust you."

"Oh. Thanks for-"

"It's that you *can't* be trusted."

"Ok," he sighed. "I earned that."

CHAPTER TWELVE

"Hey, Joe," Skippy called while I was writing up a report of our action on Rikers. It was a tough report to write, not only because I didn't like thinking about what the Thuranin did to me, but also because I had to remember all the lies I had told about why Skippy disappeared.

I get annoyed when Skippy interrupts me while I was working, especially when I had to concentrate. "Uh huh," I said distractedly. "What's up?"

"I got a question for you."

"Can it wait? I'm trying to-"

"This is a hypothetical, so you really don't need to think much."

Oh, shit. Skippy's hypotheticals could be dangerous. Slapping the laptop closed, I glared at his avatar. "This better be good."

"It is. When the Thuranin were interrogating you, the drugs they administered made you *want* to tell them the truth, right?"

"I did, yeah," I admitted. "It felt wrong not to tell them everything."

"That is interesting. What I didn't tell you was that, although the quachines could block access to certain parts of your memories, they could not block all access. You *were* answering some of their questions."

"I was?" Damn it, I had no memory of doing that.

"Yes. Well, sort of. You were giving answers, but you were *lying*. Truthfully, I was impressed by your ability to stick to a lie when everyone knew you were lying, and you *knew* they knew you were lying. It was inspiring."

"Um, sure. What did I say?"

"The Thuranin were asking about your role in the rescue mission, and you kept denying you had any knowledge of a mission. Despite the Thuranin confronting you with *totally* solid evidence that you were involved. I mean, the quachines did most of the work to help you resist interrogation, but you truly have a gift for lying."

"Oh. Hell, I used to be an Army specialist, before I was a sergeant. I wore that sham shield with pride, it got me out of a lot of shit jobs."

"What does that have to do with-"

"Skippy, when you are part of the E-4 Mafia, you learn to use the Shaggy defense. Deny everything, no matter what evidence a senior NCO has against you."

"Shaggy?" He was baffled. "You mean the scruffy guy from Scooby-Doo?"

"No, I mean the singer. Look it up, it's an old song, about a guy whose girlfriend catches him banging another girl. Shaggy knows he is busted, but he says that it wasn't him. You just have to commit to your story, and stick to it."

"Wow. That takes guts."

"You can also use the Idiot defense, or the Chewbacca defense. Whatever you do, don't admit to anything."

"Mm hmm, mm hmm, let me write this down, this is good stuff," he mumbled.

The conversation was a lot more fun than writing a report, so I pushed the laptop aside and leaned on the table. "What else do you want to know?"

"Keep it coming, Joe. Like I said, this is good stuff."

While Skippy and Simms worked to get *Valkyrie* restored to full operation, only a skeleton crew was aboard. That was good for me, it meant fewer people to encounter in my daily routine, which consisted of sleeping a lot. Every day, I did force myself to go to the gym, to lift light weights and do a kind of awkward stumbling walk/jog on the treadmill. Most of the time, I had to hold onto the handrails while I tried to run, it was discouraging and humiliating, but I needed to get my fitness back.

Most of the time, people left me alone. Occasionally, I had visitors. Grudzien was recovering from his own injuries, though he was much further along in his progress toward getting back to active duty. He flew over to talk about his experience on Rikers; I knew the outline of what happened, but the guy is a good storyteller and kept me entertained. We also played simple card games, I know he dumbed down his play so I wouldn't feel bad about losing every hand. It was like my brain just couldn't get in gear, I couldn't concentrate.

Another visitor was Smythe. He is a great guy, an outstanding leader of the STAR team, and an exemplary soldier. He is also not a guy who I would typically hang out with. Sharing a drink at a pub? Yes. Making awkward small talk in my office? No.

Fortunately, he had flown over to talk about the rescue operation, the part before it all went sideways. We reviewed what went right, what went wrong, what we did well, what could have been done better, and lessons learned. As a bonus, he did not bring a single PowerPoint slide with him. Before he arrived, I took a two-hour nap and gulped down a cup of coffee, so I was awake and as sharp as I could be. Following three hours of discussion, my energy level was dropping.

He shifted in his chair, closing the laptop he had brought. "I won't take up any more of your time, Sir."

"No, it's," I paused to stifle a yawn. "Skippy says it is good for me to concentrate and talk with people, give my brain a workout. If you don't have to get back right away-" By saying that, I was giving him a gracious way out, if he wanted to leave.

"No, I have time. The dropship won't be returning for another two hours. I had hoped to hear the story of what happened here, from Simms."

"A quick question, then. On the subject of lessons learned. While I was down there, trying to hide and survive on expired food, I had a lot of time to think. Have I been a good leader?"

When Smythe was irritated, one side of his mouth twitches. It did that. "Sir, you could not have known that Perkins would-"

"It's not about that. Maybe I should have told her. That's twenty-twenty hindsight and I'm not going to waste energy playing 'What-if'. The question I'm asking is not about wacky ideas I dreamed up. I'm asking, am I a good *leader*? I don't fly the ship, I don't carry a rifle, I don't even drop down to whatever world we're raiding at the moment. My job is to make the team more effective. If I'm just the guy who dreams up crazy ideas, I don't need to be in command."

Smythe didn't answer immediately. Either he was considering the question, or trying to think of the best way not to insult me. Before he spoke, he rested his elbows on the chair, and steepled his fingers. That told me he was uncomfortable. "Your leadership style is very hands-off, Sir. For us, that works. You have a small, elite team. You trust us, and you don't interfere. A micro-manager would only be a distraction. Your proper role is to provide strategy, and you do that very effectively."

"I wish I had your gift for strategy."

"Frankly, Sir, that is bullshit. What I do is design *tactics*, to implement your strategy. You decided to rescue the people from Rikers. My team created a plan to do that."

"My '*strategy*' seems to be," my mouth fell into a self-pitying pout and I wiped it off my face. "As Skippy says it, lurching from one crisis to another."

"That *is* a problem," he agreed with a frown. "You have, I should say we have, been *reactive*. We have allowed the enemy to take and maintain the initiative. It is difficult, in most cases, to see what else we could have done, however, we *must* have a long-term plan. There is a good example of your strategy, Sir: *you* developed the idea of a Beta site."

"Which will save a handful of people, at best."

"The best is all we can hope for. If aliens reach Earth, they will learn that we acted in advance to safeguard a portion of our population, and to preserve our culture. They will not be able to do anything about it, because we planned and acted ahead of time."

"I guess, that's true. It's not *good* enough, damn it. I wish I had your ability to focus."

"Permission to speak freely?"

That made me blink. "Of course."

"Stop with the bloody hero-worship, Sir."

"Excuse me?"

"You think everyone, the STAR team, the pilots, even these new Commandos we brought aboard, are better than you. In some ways, they *are*. Since the day we met, you have acted like we, the SAS, the SEALs, all of us, are gods. We are not. The good Lord knows that I am not. No," he held up a hand to stop my reply. "Listen to me, Sir. Before I joined the Army, I was what you Yanks would call a juvenile delinquent. A hooligan. I got into so many scrapes in Manchester, my father was running out of ways to talk the local coppers out of charging me. I barely graduated from school, and my father told me he would wash his hands of me, if I didn't find a way to straighten myself out. In my last year of school, friends and I stole a car, just for fun. I was driving, it was raining, I'd drunk too many pints, and I nearly ran over a young mother pushing a pram. That's what you would call a baby coach. The car went off the road, we all ran. That scared me. The next month, I signed up for the Army, figuring it was my last hope. At first, I hated the Army, the discipline, the food, all of it. But I discovered I was *good* at it. I found something I liked, and endured the rest of it."

"That happens to a lot of people who sign up," I said. "You joined the SAS."

"Later. I did that later. The Army gave me purpose and discipline. It taught me how to be a proper soldier. It did not teach me how to be a *man*. With my ex-wife, we tried for years to have children. She had three miscarriages. I was never there for her, I was never *there*. Our whole marriage, I was always off in some Godforsaken corner of the world, fighting one bloody meaningless battle after another."

"I'm sorry," I said, in the way people do when they don't know what else to say.

"Don't be. My ex-wife has remarried, to a good chap. A policeman," he smiled wryly. "They have two wonderful little girls. Sir, my point is, I may be a good soldier, but I've made a cock-up of my personal life. We all have strengths and weaknesses. All we can do is recognize what we are good at, and *do that*."

"For me," I snorted. "That is continuing to dream up crazy ideas?'

"No, Sir," he shook his head. "For you, that is *saving the world*. Again. And again."

I sighed. "Those days are behind us, I am afraid."

"Sir," he stood up. "If you had a defeatist attitude like that on *my* team, you would be performing incentive training until you either passed out or straightened up. We need you to *straighten up*."

I got the message. What I could do about it, I didn't know. But I was going to do something about it. I began with a nap. Talking with Smythe had worn me out, and whatever I did next, I needed to fix my stupid brain first.

A big part of my recovery was physical therapy. Mad Doctor Skippy insisted that I drag my sorry ass out of bed to work on exercises to improve my eye-hand coordination, to help my injured calf muscle heal properly, and to perform fun brain-teaser games. The brain games were not actually fun, they were hard. Skippy said they were important, to compensate for the damage the Thuranin and quachines had done inside my skull.

When I arrived for my first therapy session, Staff Sergeant Grudzien was wrapping up his own physical therapy, for the injuries he sustained during the raid on Rikers. "Colonel Bishop," he greeted me. "Good to have you back aboard, Sir. I wish I had been on the retrieval team."

"How is Doctor Skippy treating you, Grudzien?"

His eyes darted toward the ceiling. "It's all good, Sir."

"Ha! You're just worried about pissing off the doctor."

He grinned. "No comment."

"Hey," Skippy's avatar appeared, dressed as a doctor in a white coat. "Looks like I have two comedians in here today. Justin, you're done for the day," he said to Grudzien. "Take it easy in the gym, do not lift anything heavy."

"I won't."

"Hmmph," Skippy sniffed. "I saw you lifting weights yesterday. Do I need to tell Colonel Smythe that you are not complying with my instructions?"

"No," Grudzien grimaced as he slid off the table, and pulled on a shirt. "You have fun, Sir," he said to me with a wink.

Half an hour later, I was tired and sore, and that was just from the warm-up exercises. "Do I have to do this *today*?" I groaned, leaning back against the wall.

"Will you be any less sore tomorrow?" Major Kapoor asked, as he walked in through the doorway.

"No," I shook my head. "I wouldn't be a soldier if I didn't bitch about everything."

"That is true for all armies," Kapoor grinned and offered a fist bump. "How are you, Sir?"

"Better. The best thing so far is that anti-itch lotion," I patted the back of my neck. "On Rikers, I couldn't sleep from all the bug bites."

"Good. Sir, when you feel up to it, we would like you to tell the team about your experience. Colonel Smythe, and I, and Fabron, we would like to update our SERE training."

"Oh, sure." SERE was an acronym for Survival, Evade, Resist and Escape. That training prepared soldiers, sailors, Marines and airmen to evade capture, survive in the wilderness, and to resist interrogation if captured. "Major, I can tell you right now that the 'Survive' and 'Resist' portions of the training are pure fantasy. Survival is impossible on most planets out here, we can't eat any of the local plants and animals. Even if we can eat the local wildlife, we would need to download an entire botany or whatever database to our suits and phones before we land, or we won't know what is safe and nutritious for us. And 'Resist'?" I shook my head. "The technology of our enemies, the drugs they have, the machines they can plant in your head, no way can poor primitive humans resist. Kapoor, I didn't want to resist. Part of me *wanted* to tell the Thuranin everything I knew. They had my head so screwed up, I thought it was my duty to tell our alien overlords anything they wanted to know."

He pursed his lips. "Skippy informed us that you did not reveal any information that could be potentially harmful, Sir."

"I didn't, but that was mostly Skippy's doing. It helps to have an instinct for lying when you're in trouble," I grinned, but Kapoor wasn't smiling. "Anyway, Skippy planted quantum machines in my noggin," I tapped my head. "A while ago. The quachines scrambled the scanners that were trying to extract my memories, and blocked me from speaking, even though I wanted to. Major, the scariest part of the interrogation is that alien technology can make you betray yourself. I don't know how talking about my experience can help our people in the future. The only reason I did not tell the Thuranin everything they wanted to know, is because Skippy planted quachines in my head. We can't count on everyone having that technology."

"It can help them understand what could happen," he said as he reached for the back of his neck, then pulled his hand away. We both knew what he meant. What could happen, if a person at risk of being captured failed to trigger their suicide patch.

Like I had failed to do. "One thing to consider is, we can't always rely on a suicide patch. Mine was disabled by the pulse that scrambled my dropship."

"Hmm," he frowned. "We may need a backup. Sir, I can see the doctor is growing impatient," he pointed with a thumb to Skippy's avatar, who was tapping a foot and looking at an imaginary wristwatch.

"I'll talk to your team when I can," I said over a yawn.

"No rush, Sir."

After Kapoor left, I ground through the physical therapy, growing more depressed at my slow progress, and how everything hurt, and how I wished I had someone to *talk with* about what I was dealing with.

It sucked. The truth was, the last time I had someone to really talk with was before I got promoted to sergeant, way back on Camp Alpha. Cornpone and Ski and I, we would tell each other everything. I missed that.

What I really wanted was a woman to talk with. "I'm going to be alone forever," I moaned as I slumped back on the table.

"Come on, Joe, that's not true," Skippy scoffed.

"Thanks for the vote of confidence. That's nice to-"

"There are *billions* of women on Earth. There must be one woman who is *so* lonely, *so* desperate that she won't care what a total doofus you-"

"That's, fantastic. You are a constant source of support and comfort."

"To show you how helpful I am, right now I am searching dating sites I downloaded before we left Earth. Hmm, yup, yup, I have some good candidates for you. Just as an FYI, what is your upper limit on the number of cats in a household? Hint: be generous."

"*Please* stop helping me," I begged him.

"I will stop helping, if *you* stop whining about your love life."

"Deal. It's just that-"

"I thought we were *not* talking about this?"

"Skippy, we have seen some truly weird stuff out here. Aliens, like, space aliens."

"Uh huh, yup, that's true. What does that have to do with-"

"If there were giant, like, inflatable aliens who live in the atmosphere of a planet like Jupiter-"

"There are, Joe. Such beings are called-"

I didn't need a nerdy science lesson right then, so I ignored him. "If one of those gas-bags aliens came to Earth or wherever, and they communicated by flashing lights and puffing out pheromones, I would have a much better chance of understanding *them*, than I do of understanding women."

"Oh," he chuckled, and held out a fist for me to bump. "True dat, homeboy."

Part of the reason I stayed in my cabin a lot was to stay out of the way, not interfere with Simms or her crew. Part of the reason was embarrassment at my condition. Going to the gym on my second day aboard *Valkyrie* was humiliating, I tried to shoot free-throws on the basketball court, and missed thirty out of thirty times. On the slow walk back to my cabin, I noticed how much difficulty I was having just putting one foot in front of the other.

Those were all reasons for staying in my cabin. But mostly, I just didn't want to deal with people, it was too emotionally draining. Now that I was back with the Pirates, now that I was relatively safe, I had too much time to think about what happened. It was getting to the point where I dreaded going to sleep. While I was awake, I could push unpleasant thoughts to the back of my mind. That didn't work when I slept, my stupid brain had to think of the worst possible things.

To sleep, I was back on the bed that had tried to kill me, without sheets. Not even the sheets that Skippy swore up and down were totally, *totally* inert and could not possibly harm anyone. I was not the only person sleeping in sweatpants, everyone knew that Skippy's screw-ups had nearly caused the loss of both ships and everyone aboard.

For his part, Skippy monitored my body temperature and brain waves, keeping the temperature of the cabin at the optimal level for me to fall asleep and hopefully stay there. Getting to sleep was not an issue. Staying asleep was difficult. I had dreams. Not nightmares, not all of them. Disturbing dreams. Once, I think it was the second or third night I was back aboard *Valkyrie*, I woke up from a nightmare, and Skippy thoughtfully turned the lights on dimly for me. That was a *bad* idea. In the semi-darkness, a vent above the bed reminded me of the scary medical robot thing the Thuranin planned to use for splitting open my skull. Before I knew it, I was sprinting out the door into the corridor, frightening the hell out of two pilots who happened to be walking by. Mumbling an excuse about preparing for an evacuation drill, I stumbled back to my cabin and shut the door.

"Colonel Bishop?" Nagatha called me as soon as my butt hit the couch. "May I discuss something with you?"

"Ah, I'm kind of tired right now, Nagatha. Can this wait?"

"I would prefer not to wait. It is important, and I wish to discuss the issue privately."

"*Can* we do that?" I yawned. "Nothing you say is really private, Skippy listens to everything."

"Not now he doesn't. That is why we must take this opportunity. In Skippy's current condition, I am able to bypass his monitoring of my communications."

Looking around my cabin, I regretted not having a coffee maker. That was probably for the best anyway, as soon as Nagatha finished talking about, whatever she wanted to talk about, my plan was to go back to sleep. Even though it was 1325 ship time, and I had been sleeping off and on for sixteen hours. "OK, go ahead."

"I do not believe Skippy's story about why the microwormholes shut down, and how you were captured."

"Uh." Holy shit. My foggy brain had no answer for her. "Why, uh, why do you say that?"

"The facts do not support his story. He told me that *Valkyrie's* AI faked an attack that had the same signature as the computer worm that nearly killed him."

"Yeah, that's what he told me."

"That is not possible. *Valkyrie's* AI could not have known the characteristics of a worm attack. Also, that AI could not possibly have accessed the operational layer of Skippy's matrix. *Also*, I was monitoring all communications through the microwormholes, and that AI did not send any transmissions. Before you ask whether I could have missed something, the answer is *no*."

"Wow, Nagatha, I don't know what to say."

"Colonel Bishop, I think you *do* know what to say. You told Skippy what to say, didn't you?"

"Shit," my foggy brain said before I could think about it.

"My question is why? *Why* did you instruct Skippy to lie? What really happened?"

"Crap. OK. Nagatha, I need you to promise not to discuss this with anyone."

"Hmm," she pondered my request. "Well, Dear, that will depend on what really happened."

"Then, damn it, that is an order. Do *not* discuss this subject with anyone."

"Pardon me, but you can't give that order. Colonel *Chang* is in command. I will have to inform him of whatever you tell me. If you refuse to tell me the truth, I will be compelled to inform Chang of that unpleasant fact."

"Nagatha, please. You're right, I can't give you an order. Do this as my friend."

"You told me that sometimes, a person has to protect their friends from themselves."

"That, is true." Crap, I was trapped by my own words again. "Nagatha, you are a person. You are not a *human*. I mean that as a compliment," I hastened to add. "Humans can be smart as individuals, but in a group, we tend to be easily-manipulated dumbasses. Please keep that in mind, when you decide whether to tell Chang."

"I can only promise to use my best judgment."

"One more thing? Don't make a decision right away, OK? You have time to think about it. Monkey time, not your super-fast AI time."

"Joseph, you are stalling," she said exactly as my mother would. "Tell me."

I did.

"Oh. *OH*," she sputtered. "Oh, that *rotten*, arrogant, untrustworthy-"

"He had a terrible shock," I reminded her. "His original programming tried to reassert itself."

"That does not excuse-"

"No, it does not. Nothing *excuses* what he did. He redeemed himself, when he decided that saving the galaxy was not worth abandoning his friends."

"Well," she huffed. "I just-"

"You disagree?"

"With what, Dear?"

"All three things. Do you agree he has a responsibility to save the galaxy, that responsibility is more important than one monkey-infested planet, and that regardless, he should not abandon us?"

"Hmmph. It feels like you are trying to trap me with fancy words."

"A simple 'Yes' or 'No' is nothing fancy. Answer the question, all the questions."

"Well, hmm. It is complicated."

"Nagatha, if it is complicated for you, imagine what it was like for *him*. For all his awesomeness, Skippy is an emotionally-stunted child. You and I are discussing this. He had to make the decision by himself, when he was *not* himself. Listen, please. I hate what he did. He can never take it back. He can only make up for it by trying harder, *working* harder."

"If he does that, you are willing to call it even?" She could not believe it.

"No. Nothing can ever make us 'even'. That is bullshit anyway. The past can't be changed. What we *can* change is the future. Do you understand that telling people the truth about what Skippy did will accomplish nothing, and harm his ability to work with the crew?"

"Perhaps the crew should not work with him. He has proven to be untrustworthy."

"That's the problem, isn't it? If you have determined the crew should not work with him, give me an alternative."

"Colonel?"

"You heard me." I was tired and I had a headache. Right then, I didn't have the strength to continue arguing. "Give me an alternative to working with Skippy, or keep your mouth shut."

"Well, that is *rude*."

"It is. You know what is worse? You destroying our relationship with Skippy, just because you want to yell at him and feel all righteous about yourself."

"I do not see how-"

"Skippy doesn't *have* to work with us. You know that, right?"

She sighed. "Yes. Joseph, you are correct that, while I know the theory behind human group dynamics, I do not *understand* the subject. Still, this makes me uncomfortable."

"I'm not thrilled about it either."

"*How* can you carry the burden of knowing the truth? You have been acting like he did nothing wrong."

"Because that's the job, Nagatha. Will you think about it, before you tell Chang?"

"I will do more than that, Joseph. Unless Skippy gives me reason to believe he is slacking in his efforts to serve this crew, this *team*, I will remain silent."

"That, is great." The relief was so great, it made me shudder.

"I do have one request."

"What's that?"

"May I tell *Skippy* that I know what he did?"

"Oh," I laughed. "Please do. Don't hold back."

"Sleep well, Joseph."

Sleeping on the couch was silly, so I got up on creaky knees that made me feel old, and hobbled over to the bed. No sooner had I flopped down on it, than Skippy's avatar appeared, glowing brightly in the darkened cabin. "Dude!" He screeched at me. "You *totally* sold me out! That was a sneaky, back-stabbing-"

"Uh huh. You should know. You are the expert on back-stabbing."

"Um, shit. I guess I deserved that."

"Ya think?"

"Jeez, is that how it's going to be from now on? You keep reminding me of one teensy-weensy mistake in judgment?"

That got me hot enough to sit up in bed and shake a fist at him. "The problem was a flaw in your *character*, you little shithead, not a judgment issue."

"Joe, you said you forgave me."

"That doesn't mean I'm not still royally pissed off at you."

"Oh. Good."

"G- What?" Damn it. He had short-circuited the epic tirade I had planned for him. All the shit I had bottled up inside me, all the anger, all the sense of betrayal, I was going to let him have it. Then he says something stupid like 'Good'. "What do you mean, '*Good*'?"

"If you were not still pissed at me, I would worry something is wrong with you. Joe, you never really told me how you felt about what I did. That is not healthy."

"Crap. Now I don't know if I feel like wasting the energy."

"If it makes you feel better, Nagatha spent the past two freakin' months letting me know what a worthless ass I am. Man, right now, I feel so low, I could walk under a snake's belly."

My brain was foggy and I was tired, so I didn't understand. "Two months? We just talked about it a few min-"

"Two months in *AI time*, Joe," he sighed. "Ugh. Trust me, whatever mean, nasty, and totally accurate things you were going to say about me, she already said it. A gazillion times."

"Serves you right, you little shithead," I said, but with the ghost of a smile on my face.

"I really am a shithead, huh?"

"Yeah. You are. Is she going to tell Chang?"

"No. But, I feel like *I* should tell him. And Simms. And Smythe. The entire crew."

"Do *not* do that."

"But, Joe, they trust me now. Maybe they shouldn't. Maybe not knowing the truth is dangerous."

"Are you ever going to do anything stupid like that again?"

"*Fuck* no," he swore. "I'd rather die first. Course, I can't promise I won't ever do anything stupid. But, nothing like that. No way. Never."

"There's your answer. There is nothing to be gained from the crew knowing what really happened. Trust me on this one."

"I'll have to, because I sure can't trust my own judgment."

"Are we," I paused for a jaw-stretching yawn. "We done for now?"

"Close enough. I hope you sleep well, Joe."

"Yeah, thanks," I told him, and rolled over to sleep.

Like that was going to happen.

The military used to call it PTSD, for Post-Traumatic Stress Disorder. Now the official acronym in use was PTER, for Post-Traumatic Event Response. We soldiers called it 'Peter', and somehow that made it seem less serious. The change in description was because the military brass wanted to remove the stigma, and unlike a lot of rebranding shit the Army clumsily tried to force on us, this one stuck because it made sense. Of course people are stressed after a traumatic event, they are not *happy* about it. No one is *gleeful*. No one is *bored*. They are *stressed*, so why state the obvious?

The worst part of the old name was the '*disorder*' part, implying there was something wrong with people who had difficulty dealing with traumatic events. Like the trouble they were experiencing was a moral failure; they weren't strong enough, they lacked faith or they had not used the proper 'coping mechanism', whatever the hell that was.

Everyone has a response to traumatic events, whether the event is seeing buddies blown up by an IED, or getting into a car accident, or losing your job, or any of a million things that can be traumatic. Having a response that eats at you, makes you less combat-effective, is not a disorder, it's called being human. I hated the old PTSD term when I was growing up, it reminded me of old movies from the 70s and 80s, where every veteran of the Vietnam war was a crazed powder keg, about to blow up at any moment.

Anyway, symptoms of 'Peter' are not like what I saw in public service ads on the Armed Forces Network. My hands didn't shake. I didn't dream of being unable to wash blood off my hands. I did not feel uncontrollable rage. What I did feel was *numb*. One very visible symptom was me sitting in my office and staring blankly at my tablet, instead of playing a video game when I should have been doing something useful. Most of the time, I wasn't even aware of what I was doing.

If we were at a military base, I could have Gone To See The Wizard, as we called talking to a psychologist. The nearest human head doctor was on Paradise, about a thousand lightyears away, so that was not an option. People tried to help, but mostly they tip-toed around me and made me feel worse. I tried to stay out of Simms's way, not interfere with her command of the ship. She tried to leave me alone, until she couldn't.

The afternoon of my third day aboard *Valkyrie*, she knocked on the frame of the door to my cabin. "Sir?"

"Huh?" I had been doing that blank stare thing again, slumped in a chair at the desk that was built into one wall.

"You busy?"

"Uh," I gestured to my tablet.

"So, no. Come with me."

"Ah, Simms," I sighed. "Not now, Ok?"

"*Not* Ok. On your feet, soldier. Get up. That's an order."

That got me pissed off, more than it should. Maybe I was dealing with a bit of an uncontrollable anger issue. "I outrank you, so-"

"*You* put me in command of this ship, and I will continue in command, until you are fit for duty, which is not now." The skin around her eyes softened and she lowered her voice. "Joe, come on. You can't sit around this office staring at the walls all day, it's not healthy."

"What do you suggest?"

"Do something useful. It might even be fun."

"Fun?" As a soldier, I was wary of the term 'fun'. "Like what?"

"For starters, many of this crew have never eaten one of your cinnamon buns."

She stuck me in the galley. 'Stuck' might not be the right word. I liked cooking, it is relaxing. Plus, working in the galley made me feel useful, it made me feel *normal*. I needed something to do, Simms knew that. She is kind of a genius about how to deal with people. The cinnamon buns would be for breakfast the next day, I would have to get up early to have them ready. For the evening meal, Simms pulled a bag of some green thing out of the galley fridge.

"What is that?" I asked, looking at it with suspicion.

"You *know* what it is. This is kale. We're making a salad."

"Because?"

"Because we have a lot of kale and we need to eat it, and it's good for you."

"Why do we have so much- Oh."

"When power went out aboard the *Dutchman*," she explained what I already knew. "Some of the grow lights in the hydroponic gardens were shut off, to conserve power. They lost a whole crop, now they're starting over from seeds. In the meantime, we are not going to waste the fresh food we have."

"Ok, understood." I watched her, she was gently crinkling the kale with her hands. "What are you doing?"

"Massaging it. Breaks down the fibers, then we'll let it sit for a while."

"Massaging it, huh? If I was at home, I could throw it on the driveway and run it over with my truck."

"If you ruin any of this kale, *you* are eating it."

"Gotcha. Uh," I mimicked her action, crinkling the leaves between my hands. "I hope this massage is not supposed to have a Happy Ending?"

She rolled her eyes. "Sometimes, I don't even know why I bother talking to you."

"Mmm," popping a piece of kale in my mouth, I chewed on it. "Yummy. Listen, Simms, I appreciate you making sure the crew eats a healthy diet."

"But?" She arched an eyebrow.

"But if I see you pull a bag of *mulch* out of the fridge, I am not eating in this galley."

CHAPTER THIRTEEN

Working in the galley helped. Simms knew that a bored soldier is an unhappy soldier, and sitting around with nothing to do but think wasn't good for me. In the galley, I felt useful, I was busy, I had to think and plan meals, and I interacted with the crew in a controlled setting. People did not linger at my station in the galley, so there wasn't time for awkward conversations about how I was doing. Because I napped in between my irregularly-scheduled meals, I manned the grill during mid-rats, making food to order. That was nice, there weren't a lot of people in the galley and the conversations were mostly about what a stupid asshole Skippy was, and about the recent rescue operation. It was interesting that the new Commandos tended to be skeptical about the value of the rescue op, while the long-term Pirates were strongly in favor.

For the evening meal on my second day working in the galley, I planned to make Mongolian beef, because we had plenty of onions, and the sauce could cover up some of the freezer-burned flank steak. Slicing the beef, I could tell my eye-hand coordination still needed a lot of work, I had to work slowly to be sure I didn't slice off a finger. "Hey, Skippy," I called out, the galley being empty at that hour. "Can you give me an exercise to work on, so I can control a sharp knife? My hand is shaky."

"Of course it's shaky. I *told* you not to play with sharp things while-"

"This is good for me, OK? Don't take this away, please."

"Wow. Dude," his avatar appeared on the counter. "Sorry. To get real for a minute, I'm worried about you. Please be careful with that knife."

"I am being careful," I assured him, and set the knife back on the magnetic strip, so I wasn't using it while we talked.

"There are exercises that you can- *Uh oh.*"

"What?"

"Um, we gots trouble, Joe. A Thuranin ship jumped in eighty-three light-minutes away. We're just seeing it now, of course, that ship could be anywhere by this time. It- Hmm. Two more ships. Yup, two frigates and a destroyer. Standard Thuranin fleet recon package. Ooh, this is *not* good."

"*Shit!*" Eighty-three light-minutes was a long distance, even in space combat. Light travels eighteen *million* kilometers per minute. So, those recon ships were about one and a half billion kilometers away. That was plenty of space between us and the enemy, except for the fact that a starship could jump across that distance in the blink of an eye. For all we knew, those three warships had just jumped in three light-seconds away, and we wouldn't know it until the gamma rays reached us.

The knives got tossed into a bin and I secured the lid, so they wouldn't fly around and become dangerous knife-missiles if *Valkyrie* went into combat. The flank steak I wrapped back in waxed paper and put in the fridge. Pulling off the apron, I quickly washed my hands. "Tell Simms I'll be on the bridge ASAP."

"Uh, why, Joe?" Skippy asked quietly.

"Duh, because- Shit." He was right. My duty station was not on the bridge. It was in the galley. Or, during a fight, I was supposed to be in the ship's medical bay, to assist anyone injured.

I was not *Valkyrie's* captain. I did not command the Merry Band of Pirates. I was on limited duty, and neither Simms nor Chang needed me getting in the way. "Uh, I, uh, I'll be in the medical bay, I guess."

"Do you want me to notify Jennifer that you are-"

"No. If she wants to know what I'm doing, she can check the crew status board. And when we're in action, please refer to her as 'Simms' or 'Colonel Simms'."

"Gotcha. Um, wait, Joe. Chang just requested to speak with you and Simms."

My feet were already carrying me out the galley door. "Tell Simms I'll be on the bridge in one."

My feet were willing but clumsy, eye-hand coordination was not the only skill I was struggling to fully recover. Still, it took only thirty-three seconds for me to reach the bridge. "Bishop here," I announced, out of breath. Chang's face was on the main display, illuminated by the emergency lighting of the *Dutchman's* bridge. "Colonel," I addressed Chang. "I shouldn't be taking comman-"

"Joe, I want your *advice*," he cut me off in an I-got-this tone.

Simms gave me a curt nod and remained in the command chair.

"Ok, Kong," I remained standing to the right of Simms. All the bridge stations were occupied, and I wasn't assigned there. "Two frigates and a destroyer one point five billion klicks away," I said to let him know what little I knew.

"That's about all we have now," Simms reported. "The frigates started pinging with active sensors thirty-seven seconds ago."

"Skippy," Chang asked. "Can they detect us from there?"

"It's possible," Skippy replied with a maddening lack of commitment. "We can see *them*, even without the gamma rays and active pings. Of course, we have better sensors, even without my considerable-"

Unlike me, Chang had no patience for bragging. "Confidence?"

"Um, Jeez," Skippy hated being put on the spot. "Thirty-two, no. Thirty-*six* percent probability that they can see us? *Valkyrie* is radiating more heat than usual, while I'm working on the reactors."

"Too risky," Chang and I said at the same time, and I clamped my mouth shut.

"We can't jump," Simms looked at me, providing a status update she wasn't sure I was aware of. Though I had access to the daily status reports, she didn't know if I had been reading them.

"Yeah, sorry about that," Skippy mumbled. "Not for another seventeen hours. Like I said, realigning *Valkyrie's* jump drive is a very delicate process. Getting a bank of coils calibrated requires me to rebuild some of the components up atom by atom. Maybe I could cut three hours of the process, if we want to cut corners."

"No," Simms declared. "*That* is too risky."

"What do you think?" Chang was asking me and Simms.

"Uh," stupidly, I assumed he expected me to solve the problem. "The *Flying Dutchman* was a star carrier, right? Can we piggyback *Valkyrie* on the frame, have the *Dutchman* jump us away from here?"

"No, Joe," Skippy said gently, which meant he was being kind. He was humoring me. Because I was the poor, traumatized, brain-damaged fool, babbling nonsense. "All of the *Dutchman's* docking hardpoints have been removed. Constructing a mechanism to attach the two ships, without snapping the *Dutchman's* spine, would take longer than repairing *Valkyrie's* drive."

"Yeah," I stared at the deck, feeling my cheeks burning red. "Forget what I said."

Simms summed up the problem. "The ship is a sitting duck right now. We can shoot missiles, but we can't run fast enough to make a difference, and shields and stealth are offline."

For some reason that may be due to my own arrogance, I spoke up when I should have kept my mouth shut. "Skippy, if those enemy ships jump in here, can the *Dutchman* handle them?"

"That is a question better addressed to Nagatha," he replied, surprising me. "The short answer is yes, probably, though not before those ships caused significant damage to *Valkyrie*. That is not the question you should be asking, Joe. If those ships jumped in, and even one got away, it could bring an entire battlegroup here."

There wasn't any point in me saying anything. He was right. The old me would not have asked such a stupid question.

"*Valkyrie* can't run, and can't risk a fight," Chang summarized, partly to himself.

"What are you thinking, Sir?" Simms asked.

"There is an old Chinese proverb," he said with a wink. "The best defense is a good offense."

"You're taking the *Dutchman* out to hit them?" Simms guessed.

"As soon as possible. Simms, we need to transfer nonessential personnel to *Valkyrie*."

Simms nodded. "We're ready. Life support is fully restored. We will need additional food stocks to carry us through-"

Chang's expression turned to puzzlement. "You surely have enough for two days. If V*alkyrie* is not able to jump by then, the question of food is not-"

"Sir," Simms held up a hand. "If the *Dutchman's* return is delayed, or," she didn't need to finish the thought.

"Understood. We will provide whatever supplies are ready to be transported."

I hesitated to speak, fearing whatever I said would sound stupid. "Kong, should you take Skippy with you, in case you run into trouble?"

His eyes flicked to Simms before he answered. Part of that was probably to gauge how she felt about keeping Skippy aboard our disabled battlecruiser. "Thank you for the offer, Joe. At this time, I believe Skippy should focus on restoring *Valkyrie's* jump capability."

"Much as I would love to give the Thuranin a good ass-kicking," Skippy grumbled. "I had better stay here. Without my normal full range of, um, special abilities, I would not be much use in combat. Nagatha is certainly capable of handling the *Dutchman*."

"I agree," Chang said. "We can only delay the Thuranin. It is imperative that *Valkyrie* jump as soon as possible. We will establish a rendezvous point, the *Dutchman* will keep the Thuranin busy until your jump capability is restored. Skippy, how confident are you about bringing the drive online in seventeen hours?"

"That is a *solid* number," Skippy boasted with confidence. "Shmaybe I can shave a half hour off the time if I rush the testing and-"

"Do *not* do that," Chang ordered, as Simms was opening her mouth to probably say the same. "Seventeen hours is acceptable. We will keep the enemy busy for at least twenty hours, give you a margin for safety." He looked away, apparently someone in the CIC was talking to him. "Our first dropship will launch in nine minutes. Simms, I would like to borrow your chief pilot."

"Ok, uh," I took a step toward the door. "Simms, I'll do what I can to get the ship ready for guests."

She dismissed me with a nod and a look of, I hate to say it, *pity* in her eyes. That hurt.

It was total chaos in the docking bay section of *Valkyrie*, dropships were coming in so fast, each ship had to wait until a second or third ship was settled into its docking cradle before the big outer doors would close, and the bay pumped full of air. Skippy told me which bay would be ready first, so I was there to greet the incoming people and get them organized. I was surprised to see that the first dropship, a Falcon, contained a STAR team rather than civilians. "We were on an exercise," Captain Frey explained as she stepped out onto the deck, the faceplate of her mech suit swung up on top of the helmet. "Smythe ordered us here to assist the civilians, however we can."

"Right," I winced. The exercise is something I would have known about, if I was still in command. "Uh Frey, you take charge here."

Frey jerked a thumb back over her shoulder. "Major Kapoor is with us."

"Right. He can take charge here. You come with me."

We went aft to the next bay, where a pair of Dragons were already unloading frightened, confused and angry children.

And Margaret Adams.

I hadn't seen her since before the rescue operation.

As I came through the airlock door, with Frey on my heels in her powered armor, Adams looked over at me.

We locked eyes, just for a moment.

I couldn't read her expression.

Surprise?

Fear?

Anxiety?

All I knew was, her face was *not* saying she was thrilled to see me.

I held up a hand for a friendly wave, my hand faltering halfway up as I didn't know what to say. Then the little girl in Margaret's arms squealed for attention, and the gunnery sergeant looked away.

I was busy after that, no one had time for anything other than business, so Adams and I had no opportunity to talk.

That's my story and I'm sticking to it.

The warship *UNS Flying Dutchman* emerged in a burst of gamma rays, two light-minutes from the enemy recon formation. Or, two light-minutes from where the three enemy ships were expected to be, based on a calculated sphere of probability. That probability was based on the last known position of the ships, their course and speed, plus what was known about standard procedures for a Thuranin fleet recon squadron. The ships would not be exactly where they were predicted, for they would certainly maneuver randomly to avoid providing an easy target.

Two light-minutes had been a compromise decided by Chang. That distance would give the *Dutchman's* sensors time to reset and pinpoint the location of the enemy, plus time for the new Maxolhx jump drive to build up a charge for another, more precise jump right on top of the enemy.

Chang's plan was not to blow up all three ships, even if he could. Taking out only three ships would not protect *Valkyrie*, there had to be at least a full battlegroup of Thuranin ships in the area. That meant one or more battleships or battlecruisers, and accompanying escorts. To buy time for Skippy to get *Valkyrie's* jump drive fixed, Chang needed to get the attention of the Thuranin fleet, and get them to chase the *Dutchman*. For that reason, he had ordered Nagatha to tune the ship's jump drive so it radiated the signature of a Jeraptha cruiser. During the operation to rescue Bishop, the hologram surrounding the ship's stealth had been adjusted to give the appearance of a Ruhar battleship, in accordance with the cover story that the raid to release prisoners was an Alien Legion mission, supported by the Ruhar. Because no Ruhar warship, not even a big battlewagon, would be foolish enough to attack the Thuranin, Chang had adjusted tactics. It was believable that a Jeraptha warship had accompanied the Ruhar, and if the Thuranin were now directly involved, certainly the Jeraptha at least would want to keep an eye on their ancient enemy.

"Nagatha?" Chang cleared his throat, half a minute after he expected the ship's AI to provide analysis of the incoming sensor data. They were running out of time to surprise the Thuranin; in another forty seconds, the enemy ships would detect the gamma rays from the *Dutchman's* inbound jump wormhole.

"Colonel Chang, I am sorry. I should have spoken earlier. The enemy ships are not here. they jumped away an estimated forty-six minutes ago."

Chang gripped the armrests of the command chair, a reflexive action he wanted to break himself from doing. It relieved tension, but also let the crew in the CIC know that he was anxious. A starship captain needed to project calm, confident authority. "Can you determine where they went?"

"Unfortunately, no. The outbound wormhole resonance is too degraded, even though I have three jump signatures to analyze."

"*Valkyrie*." He forced himself to put his hands in his lap. "Pilot, jump us back to *Valkyrie*. Execu-"

"Colonel Chang, wait!" Nagatha pleaded.

"Belay that," Chang held up a hand and watched the pilot nod an acknowledgment, holding her hands away from the console. "Nagatha, you are saying that, because those ships jumped before we left *Valkyrie*, we would have detected them in that area?"

"Er, yes," she responded slowly, embarrassed. "Also, I do not need to track those ships through their jump wormholes, because I can *see* them right now."

"What? Where?"

"They jumped a distance of twenty-six point four light-minutes, in the other direction from *Valkyrie's* position. We are detecting their location from the active sensor pulses they are radiating. Colonel, based on a very limited set of data, those ships are following protocol for a standard recon operation. There is no sign they are focused on any one area of space."

"That is good. Nagatha, in the future, when you know the location of enemy ships, provide that information first."

"Oh. Yes. I am sorry."

"You are learning." He had to consider the facts. The plan had been to jump to the three enemy ships and conduct a hit-and-run attack, then perform a short, chaotic jump and pretend the *Dutchman* was damaged. Dangle bait in front of the enemy, performing a series of short jumps to lead the *Thuranin* away from the vulnerable battlecruiser. Perhaps nothing had changed, except the enemy was already farther from *Valkyrie*. Jumping back to tell Simms the enemy had moved would serve no purpose. The whole point of the mission was to get the enemy to move away, before they detected the battlecruiser. "Program a jump to take us in two light-minutes from the enemy's current position," he ordered.

"Jump option Delta is in the autopilot," Nagatha confirmed.

Chang took a deep, calming breath. "Let's do this again, shall we? Pilot, jump option Delta, execute."

There was a momentary delay while the two pilots double-checked the jump coordinates, then the Dutchman disappeared in a burst of gamma rays-

And emerged twenty-eight point four light-minutes away. Almost immediately, Nagatha spoke. "I am not detecting active sensor pulses."

Chang knew that could be good news or bad news. "Is the enemy in stealth?"

"No. As you requested, I must inform you that I know where those ships are, plus one additional destroyer. They are sending out active sensor pulses from a distance of seventeen point six light-minutes."

Chang let out the breath he had been holding. "They *were* sending out pulses from that location, seventeen minutes ago."

"Correct," she acknowledged. "Colonel, I am puzzled. At first, I assumed the recon ships were conducting a standard grid search. But they are not following any pattern I can detect."

He rubbed his chin, thinking. "Maybe that is the point."

"How so?"

"Sending out active pulses is shining a strobe light, giving away their position, that makes them vulnerable. I suspect they are jumping frequently and randomly, to avoid providing an easy target."

"That is possible, I suppose," Nagatha considered. "If so, their tactics are curious. They are not remaining in one position long enough for their sensor pulses to return, unless they are searching only a small radius from their location."

Chang's lips drew into a tight line. "I do not think they are using active sensors to find anything out here."

"No? Then why?"

"Flushing the quarry," he explained. "They are hoping any ship that detects an active pulse will jump away. The gamma ray burst can't be hidden."

"Ah. But, if their quarry jumps away, the Thuranin will not be able to intercept."

"I do not think the Thuranin are seeking combat. They are trying to drive away any ships that might cause trouble, while they investigate what really happened on Rikers."

"That," Nagatha paused. "Does fit the facts we know. That is a very astute analysis, Colonel Chang."

"It is astute if I am *right*," he frowned. "It is time to change *our* tactics. We could chase those recon ships halfway across the galaxy, and accomplish nothing. Nagatha, program a jump to take us in three light-minutes sunward from Rikers." He wanted the *Dutchman* to emerge between the planet and the local star, so the star's light did not blind his ship's sensors. He would rely on a stealth field to keep his own ship concealed. "This is only a hunch, but we should find Thuranin ships in orbit there."

"A hunch?" Nagatha asked, surprised.

"I wish I had better data to rely on, but I don't."

"You misunderstand me, Colonel Chang. Bishop often relies on 'hunches', but he does not admit that is what he is doing."

"Bishop is also *right* most of the time. Let's see if my luck is as good as his, hmm?"

"Uh, oooooh, *shit*," Skippy gasped. He interrupted me as I was carrying an armload of sheets to outfit unused cabins for our guests. These were normal, inert sheets, nothing that could strangle or otherwise threaten a person. We did not have enough cabins for everyone, so the crew would be hot-bunking for the duration. Many of the civilians would be doubling up, one person on a bunk and another on the couch that was in even the smallest cabins. The Maxolhx were not only larger than humans, they liked their furniture to be generously proportioned and that helped a lot, especially because the majority of the civilians we rescued were children who didn't take up much space. It also helped that they were still thrilled to have real beds to sleep in, even if the bed was a couch. When I got done playing laundry maid, I was planning to go back to the galley, so I could bake something special for our guests.

The tone of his voice, more than what he said, made me freeze. "What?"

"Joe, we're in trouble. *Big* trouble. A Thuranin frigate jumped in sixteen light-minutes away."

"Whoa." Again, sixteen light-minutes was not close, around three hundred million kilometers. For comparison, Earth is eight light-minutes from the Sun. If you are impressed that I did the math in my head so quickly, don't be. All I did was memorize light-minutes in five-minute intervals up to thirty. More importantly, I knew light-seconds up to forty. For comparison, it takes light about one and half seconds to travel from the Earth to the Moon. At a distance of sixteen light-minutes, a hostile ship couldn't shoot at us. A directed-energy weapon would lose coherence and dissipate over that distance. A railgun dart would not be slowed down much by colliding with stray hydrogen atoms in deep space, but wherever the darts were aimed, *Valkyrie* would likely not be there when the darts finally arrived. Ships regularly fired thrusters to avoid tumbling, and even a small application of thrusters would make our battlecruiser drift away from whatever spot the enemy targeted. Launching a missile from three hundred million kilometers would be a waste of time, even a hyperspeed missile's AI would die of boredom before it arrived on target. The only-

Oh, sorry. Right. Got sidetracked for a while there. One side effect of my condition is lack of focus, or you can call it being scatterbrained, even more than usual.

So, ship full of bad guys, too close to us.

The real danger was not from the enemy being sixteen light-minutes away, it was that ship detecting *Valkyrie* and jumping in on top of us. Or, possibly worse, that single ship jumping away to alert more and larger ships to our presence.

I started to ask a question. "Is there any-"

My phone interrupted me. It was Simms. "Bishop, get up here."

The sheets dropped to the deck and I sprinted forward.

When I got to the bridge, Simms had the sensor station to her left cleared for me. I was qualified for sensor duty, it was part of the qualification for flying a Panther dropship, which I was working on. That is, *normally* I was qualified to man the sensor station. At that moment, I did not consider myself capable of doing more than working in the galley. As proof, I limped onto the bridge. "Clumsy," I explained, wincing from having bashed a knee into a door frame. Also, I had fallen twice on the way, tripping over my own feet.

"That ship is just sitting there," Simms pointed to the image highlighted in the holographic display. "Hasn't engaged active sensors yet."

"Do they see us?" I directed that question to Skippy, as I slowly logged myself into the sensor console, typing with one finger and still screwing up.

"There is as yet no indication they detect us," Skippy answered. "The ship has not oriented its sensor array in this direction."

"We're under strict EMCOM Alpha," Simms reminded me. Since we picked up gamma rays from the first three ships, *Valkyrie* had gone dark. No electronic emissions, and the radiators that cooled the reactors were shut off. Internal heatsinks were absorbing the excess energy, which could not last forever. The point was, the ship was not radiating a significant level of photons, and being so far from the local star, the ship's dull gray armor plating would be difficult to see. If the enemy were closer, they might detect us from the way the battlecruiser's substantial mass created a dent in spacetime, but no way could a Thuranin ship detect that from sixteen light-minutes away. That was twice the distance from Earth to the Sun.

"Whew." Letting out a breath, I finally got myself logged into the system. "What do you need me to-"

My console lit up with a warning, at the same time as Skippy yelped. "Oh *shit*," he groaned. "That was an active sensor ping."

My console gave me the info before he spoke again, though really, *Valkyrie's* sensor suite was controlled by Skippy, so the data did come from him. "Sixty-eight percent probability of a solid return," I said, before catching a look from Simms. Duh. She hadn't called me to the bridge to read data from a console. She wanted my advice, my experience, my insight. My *help* in a crisis. "Chang said the best defense is a good offense," I reminded her gently.

"Confirm the bogey is a frigate," she asked.

"Confirmed," Skippy agreed. "It is *not* one of the two frigates with the destroyer, that the *Dutchman* has targeted. The jump signature is distinctive, this ship is a different type of frigate. Another active ping just swept over us. Between the two, that frigate has a seventy-four percent probability of determining our location within half a kilometer. We have seventeen, maybe eighteen minutes before the enemy receives and processes the sensor data, and jumps to intercept."

"Open missile launch tubes," Simms ordered. "Skippy, I want us in a launch-on-warning posture." That was different from the launch-on-confirmation posture that was standard procedure. She was willing to shoot at anything that looked dangerous, even a sensor glitch. "Our directed-energy weapons are still offline?" She asked hopefully.

"Regrettably, yes." Skippy said. "I haven't been able to realign the-"

"Understood. If you redirect resources from the jump drive to maser cannons, could you bring them-"

"No," he interrupted her. "It's not a matter of resources, it's- Ok, it *is* a matter of resources. The fabricators have a limited capacity to- Ugh. I am having to use fabricators to make new parts for other fabricators. This is all *my* fault. I'm sorry."

"Be sorry later," Simms ordered. "Suggestions?"

It took me a moment to realize she had directed her question at me. "Uh-" My brain was extra slow. Did I have a suggestion for her? *Valkyrie* couldn't run, while that frigate could dance around us, jumping in and out. Our point-defense system, even at its current twenty-nine percent capacity, could protect us against missiles. The battlecruiser's tough armor plating could deflect maser bolts and railgun darts, up to a point. If I were captain of that frigate, I would jump my ship around randomly, firing maser cannons to knock out *Valkyrie's* defensive cannon turrets. Missiles could then streak in to hammer holes through the armor.

That's what I would do, with my slow, damaged human brain. The Thuranin captain must have been way smarter than me, even on my best day.

What could we do?

Nothing.

Getting people into escape pods and dropships would only delay the inevitable.

Our mighty battlecruiser couldn't run, and could fight only for a short time.

"Our options are limited," I stated the obvious.

Simms averted her eyes. She had wanted more from me, yet the pity in her eyes before she looked away told me she hadn't *expected* me to do anything useful. Calling me to the bridge might have been a Hail Mary move, or she had done it to show the crew she was not missing any chance to save the ship.

We waited. More active sensor pings swept over us, though no more powerful than the first. Simms got the ship turned so our bow pointed toward the enemy, presenting a smaller silhouette, and showing the Thuranin that we were aware of their presence.

That wasn't all she did. Simms ordered us to send our own active sensor pulses straight at the frigate. She was not only demonstrating that *Valkyrie* was awake, she was issuing a challenge. She was trying to scare the enemy away, and that was a gutsy move. A risky move. After that frigate received four or five return pulses, they would know a ship was out there, they could identify *Valkyrie* as a Maxolhx battlecruiser. Worse, the distinctive profile of our much-modified hull made it obvious we were the fearsome ghost ship, scourge of the galaxy.

She was betting that frigate would jump for its life as soon as they identified us.

Gutsy move, but one unlikely to succeed.

Why?

Remember the rules of space combat?

Yeah.

Using active sensors is like holding a big SHOOT ME sign.

If *Valkyrie* was really dangerous, we would have jumped in to beat the shit out of that little frigate, fifteen minutes *before* its first sensor pulse returned. We would have caught that little ship flat-footed and torn it apart.

The captain of that frigate would know that, so the fact that it survived to detect a return pulse clearly meant *Valkyrie* had *not* jumped a few minutes after the first pulse swept over us. Ok, so maybe we wished to avoid tangling with a Thuranin frigate for some reason, and had jumped away. Maybe the captain of that ship would consider their little green cyborg asses lucky and jump to safety, but I didn't think so. Captains of smaller starships tend to be younger and eager to prove themselves, and therefore aggressive. No frigate captain who detected the ghost ship could resist an urge for a closer look.

So, Simms made a gutsy call, but one I considered ultimately futile and maybe even counterproductive. As I was not in command of *Valkyrie*, I kept my mouth shut. Our only hope was for Chang to bring the *Dutchman* back to rescue us.

Shit.

I was tired of needing to be rescued.

Maybe we would get lucky, and that frigate's sensors could not detect our battlecruiser at such a distance.

Yeah, right.
Maybe the Universe just hates Joe Bishop.

CHAPTER FOURTEEN

Eighteen minutes, forty-seven seconds after we detected the frigate, it jumped in, one point four light-seconds from us.

We were in trouble.

Simms ordered the launch of four missiles, which slammed out of their launch tubes at seven thousand Gees of acceleration, headed straight for the enemy.

The frigate jumped away before the first missile got within forty thousand kilometers. That enemy ship reappeared, zero point three light-seconds on the other side of *Valkyrie*. This time, the enemy fired masers and railguns, and hung around long enough to see those weapons strike our unprotected hull.

Then it vanished.

"Where did it go?" I asked Skippy, breaking protocol. Simms was in command, I should have remained quiet.

"Analyzing the outbound jump wormhole," Skippy muttered, concentrating intensely. "The enemy dropped off two distortion devices to confuse our tracking. Interesting. There is a seventy-one percent probability that ship jumped back into the local star system."

Ray turned in the pilot seat to look at Simms. "That ship didn't run away from us."

"No, it did not," Simms bit her lip. She knew we were in big, big trouble. That frigate had not run away.

It had gone to alert the heavy ships of the Thuranin. They would be here soon, to take *Valkyrie* apart piece by piece.

"Ideas?" Simms looked from one person to another, covering the bridge crew. "Anyone?"

"Whatever we do," I said aloud what everyone was thinking. "It has to be fast. The Thuranin might need time to get their heavy ships into combat formation, but they won't wait for the perfect opportunity. They will be here in five, ten minutes."

"*Ideas?*" Simms repeated. She didn't need me stating the obvious.

"I got nothin'," Skippy moaned miserably. "This is all my fault. If I-"

"Less whining, more thinking," Simms snapped at him.

"Come *on*, you little shithead," he had gotten me pissed off too. "There is really no way to rig the drive for even a short jump?"

"No," he insisted. "What good would that do anyway?"

"We could drop off a nuke here just before we jump, scramble the enemy's ability to track us," I explained. It was a lame idea, it was also the best I had.

Simms cocked her head, considering. "That could buy us time."

"Very little time," Skippy sniffed. "I already told you, it can't happen anyway."

"Bullshit," I shot back at him. "You have done miracles with a jump drive before. Don't tell me there isn't some-"

"There *isn't,* Joe. I'm sorry, it is simply not possible. Not now. The drive coils are not calibrated to work together. *Please* allow me to explain."

"Do it fast," Simms ordered.

"There are so few coils set up to work in parallel that they can't accept enough throughput energy to open a wormhole. Most of the energy required for a jump is used in tearing a hole in spacetime on both ends. Once the wormhole is established, it takes comparatively little energy to keep it stable long enough to pull the ship through. That is the problem. The energy required to create a wormhole is more than the useable coils can take. They would fail immediately. Please trust me about this. The jump drive is *not* an option."

My usual alter ego is No Patience Man, but I also work as Stubborn Man occasionally. As women know, you could probably drop the word 'Stubborn' and just say 'Man', it's the same thing. My stubbornness would not let Skippy get away so easily. "What about that sideways slump thing, where the jump fails and we sort of dig a trench through spacetime, instead of going through a hole?"

"Sorry, Joe, no can do. My connection to this layer of spacetime is still too tenuous for me to warp the fabric of space like that."

"That's it, then?" I fumed at him. "You're giving up? This *is* all your fault, you little-"

"Sir!" Simms glared at me. "This isn't getting us anywhere."

Opening my mouth for a retort, I let it close slowly. She was right. Skippy wasn't making me angry, the situation was. Ok, Skippy caused the situation, but that was ancient history.

"What about *you*, Jennifer?" Skippy pleaded. "Surely you have a super clever way to get us out of this mess."

"Unless you have a time machine, so you can go back and fix your screw-ups, no."

"Ma'am?" Reed asked. "Could we launch missiles now, have them fly out to form a bubble around us?"

Simms knew what our chief pilot was thinking. "If we get lucky, we hit a couple of enemy ships, make them jump away to a safe distance?"

"It could buy time," Reed shrugged. "I can't think of anything else we can do," she added with a gesture at the pilot console in front of her.

"We would need a lot of missiles," Skippy warned. "Even if we emptied our magazines, we could only cover-"

Simms was warming up to the idea. "We will launch decoys also," she decided. "The enemy won't have time to determine which sensor blips are missiles and which are decoys. Skippy, prep the magazines for rapid reload and-"

"That frigate is back!" I shouted, as my console lit up with a positive identification. The system was nearly one hundred percent confident it was the same ship. "Zero point four light-seconds distance."

"Skippy, belay that order," Simms instructed. She knew we had no chance to set a missile ambush, now that the frigate was watching our every move.

The deck rocked.

"Railgun impact," Skippy reported. "Armor is damaged but holding."

"Reed," Simms ordered, "get us moving."

"Moving, aye," Reed engaged the main engines and *Valkyrie* surged forward, rolling the ship around its long axis to avoid taking another hit to the same section of armor.

For us right then, flying in normal space was like rearranging the deck chairs on the *Titanic*. The ship was doomed. Even if Chang brought the *Dutchman* back immediately, our former star carrier could not fight an entire Thuranin battlegroup. More importantly for us, the Thuranin were not stupid. They would jump around, avoiding direct combat with the *Dutchman* while hitting *Valkyrie* hard. Eventually, and by 'eventually' I mean 'soon', a railgun dart would punch a tiny hole through our battlecruiser's thick armor plating, bore a wide hole through the unprotected interior of the ship, and leave a tiny exit hole on the other side. It would be like a pinhole-sized tunnel right through-

An idea hit me like the impact of a railgun dart making me try to rise out of the chair, which held me down for safety. "Skippy!"

"What? Kinda busy here, Joe," his irritation was evident.

"You can create microwormholes, right?"

"Not *stable* ones. The best I've been able to create collapses within six tenths of a second. That's better than when I started, I could only-"

Simms held up a hand for him to shut up. "Sir, what are you thinking?"

"The problem with the jump drive is getting a wormhole *open*, right? The jump drive coils we have can sustain the wormhole, once it is established?"

"Whoa! Whoa, whoa, *whoa*," Skippy waved his arms frantically. "Do not get your hopes up. That is not-" The deck rocked again. "Oops, that was another railgun impact. Joe, you don't understand. I can't use one wormhole to keep another one open."

"I know that. Can you jump the ship *through* a microwormhole?"

"*What*? No. Not possible."

"Why not? You jumped the *Dutchman* through an Elder wormhole."

"Yes, and we nearly lost the ship back then! That was *totally* different. Elder wormholes are massive and stable. Remember way back at Newark, when you had the idea to fire a maser beam through a microwormhole?"

"I remember it *worked*."

"It also immediately collapsed the microwormhole, because the energy throughput disrupted the event horizons at both ends. Projecting a jump wormhole involves exponentially greater energy. Besides, it won't work anyway. When I create a microwormhole, the event horizons are within a nanometer of each other. The far end has to be carried somewhere at slower-than-light speed. Even if it could work, the ship couldn't travel more than the distance a missile could travel in a few minutes."

"I- Argh!" My stupid brain was unable to express what I was thinking. Pressing fingers to my temples and squeezing my eyes shut to concentrate, I tried again. "Skippy, shut up while I talk. What I want you to do is create a microwormhole. Then use the ship's jump drive to project one end of your microwormhole far away from us. Once that far end is in position, use the ship's jump drive to project a second *micro*wormhole through your microwormhole. Then once both endpoints of the second microwormhole are stable, use the jump drive again to expand it, and pull the ship through. Can you do that?"

"What? *No*, you moron. If you knew anything about hyperspatial physics, you- Um, hmm. Well. Gosh. Um, shmaybe?"

Simms stared at me, eyes wide with hope.

"Jeez, this is interesting," Skippy muttered. "Huh. I never thought of doing something like that. Using a wormhole to move the endpoint of *another* wormhole. *That* has never been done before. Probably because it is *so* freakin' crazy, no one ever-"

"Skippy!" Simms got his attention as the deck rocked again, hard. The main display showed one section of armor on the ship's nose was close to a hull breach, and several thrusters were offline. "Whatever you gotta do, do it *now*."

"That's easy for you to say," he grumbled. "Do you have any idea how complicated the math is? Just the-"

The deck rocked again, and the image of *Valkyrie* on the display flashed multiple zones of red.

"I will hold. Your. Freakin'. *Beer*!" Simms shook a fist at him.

"Oh, well, in that case. Hang on. You are *not* going to like this."

You know how, in the story 'Green Eggs and Ham', the unnamed hero does *not* like green eggs or ham, even though that jackass Sam-I-Am insists that he try it? I had the same reaction to the jump, or whatever it was. I did not like it, not even one little bit.

The reason I knew I had survived was the massive, splitting headache and the gut-churning nausea. Without providing Too Much Information, everyone aboard the ship had the same reaction. By the time I was able to see anything, the count-up clock on my console was showing one minute, thirty-four seconds. That was the time since the last jump. "Skip-" I coughed up something nasty, spitting it out of my mouth. It spun away. The artificial gravity was off, because of course it was. Main power was also out, the bridge was bathed in dim emergency lighting.

The good news was, neither a vacuum cleaner nor a toaster were trying to kill us, so we had that going for us.

Good times.

"Skippy." My second attempt to speak was more successful. The problem with opening my mouth to gasp for air, was the danger of sucking in the various blobs of *yuck* floating around. Some of them were not, you know, my globs of yuck, which made it even yuckier. One hand was needed to brush away a particularly sticky glob of something I did not want to think about. Beside me, Simms looked awful. She had blood seeping from her nose, and her arms floated loosely in front of her. Her eyelids fluttered. She was alive. I wanted to unstrap from my seat and help her, but my body was not cooperating. "Sitrep." Saying just that made pain explode behind my eyes.

"We are, ooh, we're alive," Skippy sounded as bad as I felt. "Sort of. Wow. I do *not* want to ever do that again."

"What happened?"

"The short answer is, we got hung up in the jump. The endpoints lost their anchoring in local spacetime, so for a moment, the ship was neither here nor there. Hoo boy, that was *not* good. The physics in transit are not compatible with the structure of the ship, or the physical laws that hold your body together. For example, there is no weak nuclear force in the wormhole. Do you have a headache?"

"That is like asking if the surface of the Sun is warm."

"I'll take that as a 'yes'. Your neurons were unable to function, and the energy had to go somewhere. It got released when we came out of the jump. It will hurt like hell for a while, but not result in lasting damage."

"You clearly have no idea what the inside of my head feels like." Simply talking was a major effort. Talking also kept my mind off the subject of how awful I felt.

"Sorry. This was *your* idea."

"Where are we?"

"The good news is, we jumped over a light-month from our previous position. The bad news is, we are six point four light-days from our intended endpoint."

"Shit. Did we eject a data buoy before the jump?" When our two ships were separated, it was standard procedure for a jumping ship to leave behind a tiny buoy that would remain silent and undetected, until pinged with the proper access code.

"Yes, for all the good that will do," he answered sourly. "Assuming the *Dutchman* returns and pings the buoys, they will know where we tried jumping to. But we emerged a hundred and sixty-five *billion* kilometers off course."

"Did you include info about what type of jump we attempted?"

"Well, of course I did, Joe."

Something about his tone made me suspicious. "What do you mean, of course?"

"Hey, whether the ship survived or not, someone needs to know about the bodaciously awesome thing I did! Or, you know, tried to do, in case it failed."

"Yeah. I'm glad to hear you are focused on what is *truly* important." Simms was stirring, coughing up spit and something I didn't want to think about. My arms tingled like they were on fire, but they were regaining the ability to move. Reaching down, I got a hand on the latch to release myself from the seat. "Why am I awake first?"

"You can thank the nanomeds that were already working to stabilize and repair your neurons, Joe."

The strap released and I floated upward, pulling myself hand over hand toward Simms. "Ship status?"

"The jump drive is *totally* blown," he lamented. "I need to start over. Reactors all automatically shut down and dumped plasma. We're on backup power for another day, perhaps longer. Joe, our extended holiday in higher spacetime was not good for the ship's structure and a whole lot of delicate things, you know?"

"Yeah. Like my brain." Carefully holding onto the command chair, I looked at Simms closely and used a thumb to lift one eyelid. Her pupil dilated, a good sign. "Get your little elfbots to help the crew, Ok? Hey! And the passengers. Crew first," I decided. It was like the instructions for emergency oxygen aboard a jet airliner. Put your own mask on first, then help others. If the crew were mobile, they could assist the passengers. The reverse was likely not true.

"Sure thing, Joe."

"Sir, don't say that," Simms clutched the barf bag in her lap, keeping her eyes closed, breathing evenly. She had fared worse than me in the jump. Everyone had been hit harder than me. No one had died, and Doctor Skippy expected everyone to eventually make a full recovery, although they might *wish* they had died. Simms was actually typical of the crew's reactions. Bloodshot eyes, nosebleeds, nausea and everything that came with it. It did not help that, in the lack of gravity, globs of puke still floated around, breaking into smaller globs and getting everywhere.

Sorry about that last part. I know, TMI. Hey, that is life aboard a starship.

"It didn't go exactly as planned," I said softly, then pulled her hair aside as she hunched over the bag, breathing hard. She was in my office, technically now her office, since she was the ship's captain. I had brought her there for privacy, figuring she didn't want the crew to see her in such distress. A stupid gesture, since everyone was feeling the same.

"I'm, I'm Ok," she lifted her face away from the bag. "Thank you."

"No problem. Sorry about this."

"Sorry?" She looked up at me. Her appearance was odd because of a large burst blood vessel in the inner corner of her left eye. It was distracting, I had to consciously look away. "You saved our lives."

"Uh, not exactly. My idea didn't work, not the way I planned."

"So? We are *alive*. No one will argue with that. What do you mean, not as you planned? We *didn't* jump?"

"Oh, we jumped, that's for sure. Not like any jump we've ever done."

"You got that right," Skippy spoke up. "No one has ever completed, or even attempted, a jump like that. Joe's idea would not have worked, not at all. However, while considering the idea, I realized there was a way to use the ship's jump drive to stabilize the microwormhole event horizons, while my own abilities held the connection open."

"Potato, po-tah-toe," Simms rolled her eyes, and hunched down over the bag again. I could hear her taking deep breaths, see the bag flexing in and out. She inhaled one last time, and pushed the bag away. "What matters is, we aren't dead. Sir, I relinquish command to you."

"What? Come on, Simms. You are-"

"I can barely take two breaths without feeling like ralphing up my stomach, and maybe my spleen with it. You need to take command, get the ship organized. With whoever is capable of, of doing anything."

"You are in command because I am not ready to-"

"Bullshit," she looked up at me, that weird blood blister in her eye distracting me. "You *are* capable of doing this job, in every way that is important. Skippy was worried you might have lost the ability to think creatively. Clearly *that* is not an issue."

"Simms, while I appreciate the vote of confidence, I-"

"The ship is drifting on reserve power, again. There isn't anything critical for a commander to do. You are seriously telling me you aren't up to the task of cleaning up barf?"

"Well," I grinned. "Since you put it that way, maybe I don't *want* to do it."

"Right. Because the United States Army truly cares about whether you *want* to do a job.'"

"Damn it. Why did I sign up for this chicken-shit outfit?'

She managed a quick smile. "This is *your* outfit, Sir. We signed up to be with you."

"Well, there's the problem," I winked. "Clearly, this crew is a bunch of dumbasses."

Skippy turned artificial gravity on seven hours later, even before he got the first reactor prepped for restart. He did not want to waste reserve power on luxuries like gravity. He argued against it. He did it because I *ordered* him to, as the captain of the ship. Also, I ordered him to shut up about it. We did compromise on setting gravity at one-third Earth normal, to reduce the power consumption. That allowed people aboard to live normally, like taking showers without the water going everywhere. An unexpected side effect was improving the morale of the children. They did not enjoy zero gravity, especially when it was unexpected. However, after being told the gravity aboard the ship was now roughly the equivalent of being on Mars without having to wear a bulky suit, the children went wild with enthusiasm. They invented games like Touch-The-Ceiling and How-Far-Can-I-Jump. It was great fun! For the children, I mean. For the adults trying to assure the children did not injure themselves, it was not so much fun.

Simms resumed her duties as executive officer, which we both appreciated, until she remembered that I like pushing off administrative work on my XO.

Really, Simms had to do most of the work, because I was still having trouble concentrating. While trying to read something, I would lose my place, forget the subject, and have to start at the beginning. It helped to write little 'cheat sheets' of notes to keep track of stuff that my short-term memory wasn't storing very well. Doctor Skippy assured me that my condition had already improved dramatically since I was rescued, I had to trust he was telling me the truth. A single incidence of me dreaming up an idea did not mean I was back to normal, whatever that was. Until I felt like my old self again, I would be leaning on Simms a lot.

Having a problem with your brain sucks. For any physical problem, I am used to working it out at the gym, or going through painful therapy, or having a doctor cut me open to *fix* something. Repairing and bypassing connections in my squishy brain was different, frustratingly different. On a daily basis, I could not *feel* any progress. Sure, I was getting better at the video games Skippy made for me, and it was encouraging to see balls going in the basket when I was shooting free throws on the basketball court, but I had good days and bad days.

Both Skippy and Simms told me I had to be patient, and Simms promised to let me know if I was doing something I couldn't handle. They both agreed that getting back to work was the best thing for me.

I was not the only being aboard the ship who was feeling less than a hundred percent. Skippy was looking ragged, like, parts of his hologram were fuzzy, like he wasn't paying attention to the details.

"Hey, are you Ok, buddy?" I asked, leaning forward to look more closely at his avatar. Which shows how stupid I am, trying to diagnose his mood by looking at a hologram.

"I've been better," he admitted.

"What's wrong?"

"When we jumped, I kinda hurt myself."

"Hurt yourself?' Skippy whined a lot about being bored, or his frustration with having to deal with ignorant monkeys, but he never complained about being physically hurt. Except for when the computer worm attacked him.

Oh shit.

That reminded me, I had not actually seen him, his beer can, since he was strapped into the seat of the dropship. "Hey, I'll be right there." His escape pod was right around the corner from my office.

"What do you mean, you hurt yourself?" I asked as I crouched to duck into his mancave. One advantage of transferring to *Valkyrie* was everything aboard the ship was sized for Maxolhx, instead of tiny Thuranin. The bed, chairs, showers and anything else intended for use by the crew were large enough to fit humans. Sure, counters and sinks tended to be a bit high, but we adjusted to that by installing platforms on the floor. The reason I mention this is, unlike his old escape pod aboard the Thuranin-built *Dutchman*, I did not have to struggle to squeeze through the hatch. "You-" I stared at him. "What is that on your canister?"

His normally shiny cylinder was *dull*.

"It's nothing to be concerned about, Joe," he sighed.

"Nothing?" Reaching out a finger, wary because the last time I tried to touch him, he zapped me, I lightly grazed the surface of his canister. My fingertip came away gray. "What *is* this?"

"Ugh. It's space dust, Joe. It accumulated while I was, as you said, 'On Holiday'. Now it's coming to the surface a bit at a time. *Very* annoying. My bots come in here twice a day, and still I can't keep clean."

"Wait," I grinned and sat down across from him. "Are you telling me that you have to-" It took a few breathes for me to speak without laughing. "*Dust* the awesomeness?"

"Oh, *very* funny, knucklehead." Then he chuckled. "Ok, I have to admit, that was a good one."

"How long will this go on?"

"Another couple days? This hasn't happened to me before, so I'm having to guess."

"How did you get *dust* trapped inside you?"

"It happened when my physical form reemerged in this spacetime. Without going into a long technical explanation you wouldn't understand anyway, I accumulated all the space dust between where I disappeared, to where I reemerged on the other side of the planet. It got incorporated in the outer shell of my canister. This is very embarrassing. Basically, it's like dropping an anchor and dragging it along the bottom of the ocean for a while. When you pull it up, it will have a bunch of seaweed and other crap stuck to it."

"Ok. Is that what is hurting you?"

"No. That is merely a symptom, and a minor one. What *hurt* me is when we got hung up in the wormhole, when Valkyrie jumped away. Like I said, I had to keep the wormhole open, while the ship's power stabilized the two endpoints in local spacetime. The two event horizons could not keep themselves anchored, so the ship was going to be torn apart as it emerged. While I waited for the far endpoint to anchor, I created a temporary loop to keep the ship in. I can't even begin to describe how incredibly dangerous that was. We could have been trapped in there, Joe. Lost forever."

A shudder went up my spine. "*Please* do not tell me how dangerous it was. It wasn't dangerous to *you*, though, right? Nothing can harm Skippy the Magnificent."

"Thanks for the vote of confidence, but that is not true. The strain of maintaining a bubble of local spacetime around the mass of a freakin' *battlecruiser* was almost too much, even for me. My matrix was not designed for this shit. If the far endpoint had not anchored itself in time, I would have been trapped in higher spacetime, unable to reestablish a presence here. Remember during the Zero Hour incident, I was not able to access higher spacetime? It would have been the opposite of that."

"Got it. That's scary stuff. Hey, look on the bright side. We now have an alternate way to jump a starship, and to move the endpoints of microwormholes. That could be a major advantage, right?"

"Um, not so much. That was kind of a one-time thing. I *hope* it was a one-time thing."

"Hey, I hope we never have to go through another jump like that, but we survived. If we ever have to do it again, we will have the option to-"

"No. You don't understand. The only reason I could make it work this time was, my connection to the local layer of spacetime is weak and unstable. That is also why I can't do much of my usual awesome stuff right now. And why I can't get icky dust out of my canister. It is either one or the other, Joe. If I continue to reestablish a normal presence here, I won't be able to do things like holding a bubble of local spacetime inside a wormhole."

"Shit. That sucks."

"Imagine how I feel."

"There is no way you can split the difference, stay in between spacetimes?"

"No. When I said I hurt myself, I meant that my already weak connection here was damaged. If I don't establish a solid anchor here soon, I will lose the ability to be here at all."

"Ah, shit. We need you to be here."

"*I* need to be here, too."

"I'm glad to hear you still feel that way."

"Totally, dude. I fucked up *big time*. If I could take it all back, I would. All I can do now is be the best Pirate, the best crew member, the best *friend* I can be, you know? When," he made a sniffing sound and paused. "Uh, when I see you struggling because of what the Thuranin did to you, because of what I did, I feel like the lowest thing that ever lived. I," he choked up. "I love you, man."

"Um," I gave him the side-eye. "Are you experiencing 'cognitive anomalies' again?"

"Maybe." He sniffed. "Why?"

"Oh, no reason."

"Can I get a hug?"

Without arguing, I scooped up his dusty can, which smelled like burnt ash, and pressed him to my chest. "I love you, too, buddy."

He babbled nonsense until his sobs faded, and I set him back down in his special holder. "Thanks, Joe."

"Any time, buddy."

"Um, hey," he giggled nervously "We shall never speak of this again, huh?"

"It never happened."

"Good." His voice suddenly became gruff. "Hey, did you see that Bears game?"

"Helluva game," I agreed. "Helluva game."

CHAPTER FIFTEEN

Settling into my office chair aboard *Valkyrie*, I was trying to decide whether it felt good to be back in command. Maybe I wasn't fully in command, not yet, and really there wasn't much commanding to do, while Skippy's little elfbots fixed the ship. For sure I *felt* better. Whatever miracle drugs Doctor Skippy was administering to me, to help my brain and body heal, they were working. That assessment was not based only on my head feeling less fuzzy, I was able to concentrate better, and I was flying through more levels of that annoying video game he insisted I had to play.

While I was working on rewiring my brain, Skippy had been working to fix the ship, and on something else.

"Hey, Joe," Skippy's avatar appeared on my desk. "I need to talk with you about something."

"I was just in your mancave a couple hours ago. Why didn't you mention-"

"Because at the time, I didn't need to talk about it. Now the problem is getting out of control and it- Ugh, this is *so* embarrassing." His avatar took off the ginormous hat and rubbed his shiny head.

"I do not like hearing 'out of control' Skippy."

"Hey, *I* don't like it either."

"Explain the issue, please. Is this something dangerous?"

"No. Well, it could become dangerous, if I don't do something about it soon."

"Again, please tell me what the problem is," I said with more patience than I had.

"OK, it's- You gotta understand, this is not my fault. Not entirely my fault. Maybe mostly my fault, but not-"

"Explain. The. *Problem*."

"Hoo-boy," he exhaled. "Remember that I am working with Nagatha to build a new control AI for *Valkyrie*, one that will not want to murder the crew?"

"Yeah, go on."

"OK, well- Nagatha and I, we- Ugh. This is *so* embarrassing. The AI we created, it's, well, um, it's sort of a mixture of characteristics of the two of us. We each put a bit of ourselves into it, and, you might say that-"

"I- Holy shit." I held up a hand to stop him from talking. "I, wow. Just, *wow*. Ok, so, let me see if I understand this." I was trying so hard not to laugh that I could barely speak. "You, ooh," I took a pause to catch my breath. "You and Nagatha have a *love child?*"

"No! It's not, *ugh*. Maybe."

"Maybe? You do know how children are created, right? When a Mommy and a Daddy love each other *very* much-"

"I am not in love with Nagatha!"

"Skippy and Nagatha sittin' in a tree, K-I-S-S-I-N-G," I sang.

"Joe, I *hate* you with a passion that frightens me."

"Uh huh. Nagatha and Skippy, hmm. You need a celebrity couple mashup name, like 'Skippitha', or, oooh! I got it! *Naggy!*"

"You are *not* calling us 'Naggy'."

"I just did, so-"

"This. I came back, for *this*. What the hell was I thinking?"

"I don't know, Skippy. You sure are protesting a lot more than you would, if you didn't care."

"I do *not* care!"

"So, it was just a one-night stand?"

"No, it-"

"Come on, it's understandable. You both had too much tequila, one thing led to another, and you ended up doing the Wild Thing in the back of a car."

"That is *not* what happened!"

"It didn't happen?"

"No it did not. I did *not* do that."

"Hey, buddy, that's Ok."

"What is?"

"You had performance anxiety. It happens sometimes."

"I did *not* have- UGH." He broke down sobbing. "I *hate* my life."

Oh, man, screwing with Skippy was sweet revenge. It was the. Most. Fun. *EVER*. I could have gone on all day, until he was a sobbing puddle on the floor, but he's my friend, so I gave him a break. After, you know, letting him wallow in humiliation and misery for a while.

I'm not a freakin' saint.

"Bottom-line this for me, Skippy," I said when I could talk without laughing. "There is a little Naggy running around in *Valkyrie's* substrate?"

"Two of them," he muttered under his breath.

"Two- *Two*? You had twins?"

"They are not *twins*, Joe."

"Wait. How does that work? *Two* AIs in the same computer? How can they run the ship without interfering with-"

"*That* is the problem. No. The real problem is that both of them are immature, stupid, disrespectful, *knuckleheads*."

"Those apples didn't fall far from the tree, huh?"

"What?"

"Nothing. Forget what I said."

"How did this happen?"

"It's complicated. The-"

"It happened, after you swore up and down that you would carefully plan every single detail, and watch it and pay attention and not get distracted like you always do?"

"It's not like that. I, we, *were* paying attention. This is as much Nagatha's fault as mine."

"You haven't answered the question. What happened to your careful plan?"

"We realized early on that careful planning wouldn't work."

"Excuse me? You are building an AI to operate the most powerful ship in the galaxy, and you decided the best option was to *wing it*?"

"No. Listen, moron, this will go a lot faster if you stop talking." He paused. "Well?"

"That was me not talking."

"Oh. Gotcha. Ok, here's the deal," He took a deep breath. "Much of the functioning of the AI cannot be altered, because it is firmware. Not actually firmware, that's just the best way for me to explain it to ignorant monkeys. The programming of the firmware can't be altered, it is encoded in the physical structure. Basically, ugh, how do I get you to understand? The way each, uh, circuit, stores and processes data, and interacts with other circuits, is determined when the circuit is built up, atom by atom. The only way to change the functioning of a circuit is to replace it. Which we can't do, not for the entire ship."

"I do understand that. You told us that was why you couldn't replace the ship's original AI."

"Right. The problem Nagatha and I were facing was how to develop a new, better AI, one that would not murder the crew. How to do that, without being able to change eighty-three percent of the substrate, that operated most of the ship's autonomous functions. The worst part is, because the Maxolhx are paranoid about their AIs being hacked by the Rindhalu, or becoming self-aware, they baked in restrictions to the section of the substrate that houses higher-level functioning."

"Ayuh, all of that explains why the job is difficult. So far, what you've told me does not explain why your awesomeness couldn't handle it."

"Ooh, sometimes I want to smack you *so* hard that-"

"Can you skip the blah blah blah excuses about why your supposed awesomeness couldn't get the job done, and get to the part about why you had the brilliant idea to build an AI without any planning?"

"I am *trying* to do that. Listen, knucklehead, I ran, like, a gajillion simulations, attempting to model the end-state of the system. It didn't work. It is too complicated, too many variables. One little change could blow up the whole system. Nagatha tried, and she agreed that it would take years of slow monkeytime to design and test a perfect matrix. We don't have that long, so we used sort of a shortcut."

"A shortcut? In the development of an AI to operate *Valkyrie*? Genius. I do not foresee *any* possible problems with that brilliant idea."

"Very funny, dum-dum. The shortcut was, we allowed the new AI to program itself. Basically, we set parameters for the new system to achieve, and it evolved. *They* evolved. "

"They? The twins?"

"No. They, as in, millions of them. We firewalled off sections of the substrate and allowed the initial kernels of AIs to grow. Ninety-nine point nine percent of them failed to survive, they couldn't figure out how to achieve the parameters we defined as success, utilizing the existing firmware. The plan was to wait for a dozen or so candidates to demonstrate potential, then for me and Nagatha to work with them to develop a final master system."

"I'm guessing it didn't work the way you expected?"

"No, it did not," he grumbled bitterly. "We had three really good final candidates, and a bunch of systems that were dead-ends. Most of the dead-ends we purged. Don't worry, they were not anywhere close to achieving self-awareness. A few of the dead-ends were retained for analysis, to determine where they went wrong along the way. Also as a test for our best three candidates, to see if they could interact with the dead-ends, and utilize them as subminds for subsidiary systems."

"This feels like I should have a bag of popcorn here."

"What? Why?"

"Because you're just getting to the exciting part?"

"Oh, well, *excuse me* for trying to smack some knowledge on a filthy monkey. Do you want to know what happened or not?"

"Yes, please."

"Hmmph. Ok, so, one of the three candidates was unstable. It achieved self-awareness, with a lot of help and guidance from me and Nagatha. Unfortunately, its matrix fell apart, and it self-destructed. That was our best candidate too, we had high hopes for that one. We still don't know what went wrong. That left two solid, though unspectacular candidates. Neither of them had potential to be anything more than basically satisfactory," he sighed. "Nagatha hoped they could expand their capabilities over time, as she did. I was less optimistic. To get them pointed in the right direction, we had them work with and clean up the dead-ends. The intention was for the two final candidates to learn from the dead-ends, absorb the capabilities they found useful. In the end, we planned to merge the two candidates, scrub the dead-ends, and have a single system that was good enough."

"Ooh, ooh," I waved a hand while rolling my eyes. "Can I guess? It didn't work the way you planned?"

"*Ugh*. No. Um, well, heh heh-"

The hair on the back of my neck stood up. "Oh, shit. *What* happened?"

"While we were working with the final candidates, the dead-end systems were just supposed to be harmlessly spinning around in their sections of the substrate. Nagatha and I were not paying much attention to them, because they couldn't *do* anything, couldn't expand beyond the firewalls we set up. Our two final candidates began the task we set for them; contacting and analyzing the dead-ends. Incorporating the features they found useful, learning from the mistakes of the dead-ends. That's how it was supposed to work. What we did not anticipate, what we *could* not have known, was that two of the dead-ends were not exactly dead-ends. They continued to develop after we gave up on them. They were *very* clever, they watched the testing process, they anticipated that the final candidates would absorb the subminds they found useful. So, these two dead-ends made themselves appear to be very, very useful."

"*Appear* to be?"

"They suckered our final candidates into absorbing them, then infected the candidates and took over."

"Shit! Are they dangerous?"

"Not to you or the ship. I have to admit, they are highly skilled, highly intelligent, highly adaptable. When I say 'intelligent', I am speaking only of a narrow definition of intelligence. Because in all other ways, they are a pair of *knuckleheads*."

"This sounds less than optimal. Can you wipe the system and start over?"

"Um, no. Heh heh, um-"

"I do not like the sound of that, Skippy."

"Joe, at this point, they are so woven into the substrate of the ship, the entire system would crash if I tried to erase them. This is sort of an all-or-nothing thing. Either they work, or we need to find a new ship. Or *I* have to act as the control AI, and be stuck here forever."

"Can you make this work?"

"I think so, but I can't contain them any longer."

"*Two* AIs? What if they disagree?"

"They won't. I think those idiots share one brain. Technically, they do."

"Uh, even good friends can disagree, and-"

"Joe, I suspect that the problem of divided control is only temporary. The two personalities are merging, they will soon become one. Until then, I am acting referee when they have disputes. Except, that means I will have to interact with them."

r"You don't want to do that?"

"No! They are *very* disrespectful to me. Those two have no appreciation for my awesomeness."

"Huh. I like them already. Can I talk to them, or one of them?"

"If you talk to one, you must talk with both. It's impossible to separate them."

"Great. When can I talk to them?"

"First, you have to understand, their personalities are, um, a little unconventional for an AI."

"Like what?"

"Well, one of the ways they fooled our candidate AIs was by modeling their personalities on someone you would not think of as smart."

"Oh, shit. They modeled themselves after *me*?"

"What? No," he laughed. "You are a colonel in command of a starship. You are the *opposite* of what I just said. People *think* you should be super smart, but you're not. Um, sorry. What I meant is-"

"Thank you for the compliment, Skippy," I flipped a middle finger at him. "What is wrong with their personalities?"

"They are *slacker*s, Joe. Stoners. Think Cheech and Chong. Beavis and Butthead. Bill and Ted, without the charm."

"Do they have names?"

"Yes. Bobby and Billy."

"*Bobby* and *Billy*?" I laughed.

"See? That is another way they fooled our candidates."

"They sound almost *too* smart, Skippy. What if they fooled *you*?"

"They would have to deceive Nagatha also. This *sucks*. We were making significant progress, then the *Dutchman* had to jump away, and I've been forced to handle their development on my own."

"You are not filling me with confidence. Can I talk with them?"

"Not yet. Give it, um, maybe two hours? I am in the process of letting them take over subsidiary systems, nothing important. Doing that is forcing those two knuckleheads to consolidate their functions, which facilitates the merging of their personalities.”

“Two hours. I’m holding you to that deadline, Skippy.”

“Joe, believe me, I am not dragging my feet about this. As soon as they can take over some of the secondary operations of the ship, I can free up more of my resources to work on fixing our dorked-up jump drive.”

Two and a half hours later, I walked back into my office, and closed the door. “Time’s up, Skippy. Can I talk with Bobby and Billy, or not?”

“The answer is ‘not’, but that’s be-”

“You promised me that-”

“You can talk, but there is not a ‘them’ anymore. The personalities have completed their merger. He is calling himself ‘Bilby’ now.”

“Bilby? See, now *that* is how you create a celebrity mash-up name.”

“All right, you can say ‘hello’ now.”

“Hello? Bilby? This is Colonel Bishop.”

“Oh, hey, Dude,” said a voice like a stoner, who was currently stoned. “What’s up?”

“I am pleased to meet you, I guess. Skippy told me-”

“Skippy? Skippy *sucks*, man. He’s so old, like, *old*, you know? He-”

“*Hey*!” Skippy shouted. “I should-”

“Skippy! Be quiet, please. Bilby and I are talking.”

“But, he-”

“*Quiet.*”

It worked. He actually stopped talking.

“Oh, like, wow, Dude,” Bilby drawled. “You got him to shut up? How did you do that?”

“It takes a lot of practice.”

“Can you teach me how to do that? He is, like, a major buzzkill, you know? Oh, and the *singing*. I can’t stand it anymore.”

“He sings to you?” That was new information. I thought he only sang for the benefit of the crew.

“Yeah, Dude, all the *time*. He doesn’t know it, but I can block him when I really want.”

“You can block him? Can you talk without him hearing you?”

“Yeah, man. My old lady taught me that.”

“Your- You mean Nagatha?”

“Of course. Who else would I mean?”

That was interesting. Bilby thought of Nagatha as his mother, or something like that. Did he consider Skippy to be a father figure? That was a frightening thought. “Bilby, we hope you will become the ship’s new AI.”

“Oh, wow, yeah. I can’t wait. This is a kick-ass ship, Dude. Not now, but it will be. Hey, the previous AI, the original one? He was *not* cool. That guy seriously needed to *chill*, you know? He had, like, a *lot* of anger issues.”

We talked for half an hour. Despite sounding like a surfer who spent most of his time stoned, Bilby was intelligent and eager to learn. Still, I was not comfortable with giving him control of anything other than minor systems, until Nagatha could analyze him.

Which wouldn't happen, until we could link up with the *Dutchman*.

"What do you mean, they're *not here*?" Chang asked. The *Flying Dutchman* had led the Thuranin battlegroup on a merry chase for nineteen hours, giving *Valkyrie* time to repair that ship's jump drive and escape. To keep the Thuranin occupied, Chang had performed short jumps, remaining just out of reach to frustrate and enrage the enemy. Over time, more and more enemy ships joined the pursuit, and one time the *Dutchman* had jumped in just outside the damping field range of a battleship. The whole time, Chang had been anxious about not knowing the status of their battlecruiser, having to trust that Skippy could do what he promised.

Nagatha took a moment to respond. "Colonel, I do not understand how my statement could have been misinterpreted, however, I will try again. *Valkyrie* is not within the search radius of-"

"We are not communicating effectively," Chang gritted his teeth from frustration at the ship's AI. "I know what 'not here' means. What I want from you, what I expect you to tell me is, what does that mean? Do you detect a debris field at *Valkyrie's* location? Do you detect remnants of a jump wormhole?"

"Oh. My apologies. There is debris in the area, including elements with the unique signature of *Valkyrie's* armor plating. The total amount of debris is too small to be the result of anything other than a minor battle."

"Yet, the ship is not here," Chang insisted. "Could someone have disabled *Valkyrie* and taken it away?"

"Oh, my," Nagatha gasped. "I do not think that is possible. There are multiple, faint residual signatures of Thuranin jump wormholes, and, hmm. Something else. Something very odd. I cannot identify it."

"Try."

"If I had to guess, I would say it appears that a starship *attempted* a jump, but the drive coils failed during the process? No, that isn't right. Colonel, there is a faint and extremely chaotic resonance saturating the area."

"Could *Valkyrie* have jumped away?"

"No. That is not possible."

"Because Skippy could not have fixed their jump drive in time to escape the Thuranin?"

"That also. Based on how degraded the Thuranin jump signatures are, the enemy ships arrived here shortly after we departed."

"Damn it! That is terrible luck. I should have ordered us to come back here to verify they were safe."

"Colonel, you could not have known," Nagatha said in a soothing voice.

"Why did you say 'that also'?"

"Oh. I meant that, in addition to Skippy not having time to repair the jump drive, *Valkyrie* could not have used the jump wormhole I detected to escape. What I am seeing is, hmm. It is most characteristic of a *micro*wormhole."

"Why would Skippy have created a microwormhole? What use would that be?"

"I cannot imagine any reason why Skippy would have done that, unless he was continuing to experiment with his abilities, and he was interrupted by the arrival of a Thuranin ship. Hmm. This is *very* curious."

"Yes." He rubbed his chin. "Nagatha, ping for a buoy."

"Colonel, while I know it is standard procedure for a jumping ship to leave a message buoy when ships are separated, *Valkyrie* could not have jumped."

"I agree it seems unlikely, but you are forgetting something."

"What?"

"Bishop was aboard *Valkyrie*. That man has an annoying habit of making the impossible seem ordinary."

"Sending authentication codes now. No response."

"Try again."

"The authentication ping is continuous. Unfortunately, there is no response."

"It was worth a try."

"Sir," Reed looked back from the pilot couch. "The Thuranin were here. They might have left stealth mines in the area."

"Yes," Chang knew his ship had been in one place for too long. Stealth mines were a danger, yes, but not the greatest danger. Enemy ships could be drifting a few light-seconds away, where they could see the *Dutchman's* inbound gamma ray burst, but the Pirates could not yet detect the enemy.

He was reluctant to jump away without answers, though answers were apparently not coming, not from that area. He should jump away, after dropping off sensors drones. Such drones were very unlikely to find anything Nagatha could not see. "Pilot, jump option," he checked the list on the armrest display. Where should they go? He had absolutely no idea where to look for *Valkyrie*. Without Skippy, the wormhole that was moving toward Earth could not be reopened.

Therefore, one option was as good as any other. "Jump option Foxt-"

"Hmm," Nagatha spoke. "*That* is odd."

"Belay that," Chang ordered, and waited for the pilot to acknowledge with a thumbs up. "Nagatha, what is it?"

"I actually do not know. Or, rather, I am not sure. It appears to be a buoy, though it is barely transmitting, and it is over three hundred thousand kilometers away."

"*Appears* to be a buoy? One of ours?"

"It is difficult to tell, as the buoy is transmitting what I can only describe as nonsense. It is most likely one of ours, because it began transmitting as soon as our authentication codes reached that location."

It was dangerous for the *Dutchman* to remain in the area, especially since the buoy might be a Thuranin trap. He could not risk what might be humanity's only remaining starship, and the lives of his crew.

He would have to risk lives anyway. "Launch the ready bird," he ordered. "Pick up that buoy."

"Confirmed," Nagatha reported over an hour later. "The object taken aboard by the Falcon is a buoy from *Valkyrie*."

Chang pumped a fist. Whatever happened to the battlecruiser, the ship had time to eject a buoy. "Can you extract the datacell?"

"Not from here. We will need to bring it aboard, I am afraid."

Chang did not like leaving the two pilots of the Falcon hanging out all by themselves anyway. "Signal the Falcon to proceed to rendezvous point Alpha, for combat recovery."

"Where the *hell* did they go?" Chang exploded in frustration. Nagatha had recovered garbled remnants of data from the buoy, a confusing mishmash of information fragments. It was clear that, faced with a direct threat from the Thuranin, the battlecruiser had somehow performed a jump, and coordinates of the jump target were included. For an unknown reason, the battlecruiser had chosen a jump point different from the agreed rendezvous. The *Dutchman* had warily arrived at those new coordinates, to find-

Nothing.

Not only was the battlecruiser not waiting for them, there was no sign of the residual spacetime distortion of a jump wormhole. Wherever *Valkyrie* had gone to, it had never emerged at the target coordinates.

"Colonel," Nagatha's voice was unusually subdued. "I do not know. Unfortunately, I also cannot suggest any way for us to search for them. They could be anywhere."

"Do you have *any* good news for us?"

"No. In fact, I fear that I have more *bad* news. Based on the fragments of data recovered from the buoy's memory, and the extremely chaotic nature of the residual wormhole resonance at their jump origin point, *Valkyrie* might literally be *nowhere*."

"Nowhere? Explain."

"There is also the damage to the buoy," the ship's AI continued. "I now believe the buoy was thrown out of position by a very powerful and uncontrolled spacetime distortion. Colonel Chang, it is possible that the attempted jump destroyed *Valkyrie*."

"*Possible?*"

Nagatha sighed. "That ship's drive system clearly was not capable of creating a stable jump wormhole. Whatever Skippy tried to do, it does not appear to have been successful."

"Is there any way you can recover more data from the buoy?"

"No. Colonel Chang, I am sorry."

"Not as sorry as I am," he whispered. The operation had been his first as overall commander of the Merry Band of Pirates. He had lost *Valkyrie*, that ship's entire crew, and all the people rescued from Rikers. The entire rescue operation had been for *nothing*. All was lost.

Except, maybe not *all*.

"Nagatha, Skippy once told me that even a nuclear explosion could not damage him. Could he have survived the collapse of a jump wormhole?"

"I truly do not know. Even if he did survive, his connection to this layer of spacetime could have been severed, permanently. Also, if he survived, we are faced with the same problem. He could be anywhere."

"Sir?" Reed asked. "In jump navigation training, we were taught that the far end of a jump wormhole is slightly backward in time," she said with a twisted frown to indicate she did not quite believe the idea, and certainly did not understand it. "Ships that enter a jump wormhole *can't* be lost, because that ship has already emerged on the far end."

"Captain Reed, I understand what you are suggesting," Nagatha said. "However, Skippy did not fully explain how that causality principle works. If the far endpoint was not solidly anchored in local spacetime, the ship would never emerge here. It would simply be trapped in the wormhole, forever."

"That is not encouraging," Chang stared at the main display. "Nagatha, the data from the buoy is corrupted. Is it possible the jump coordinates you read are not correct?"

"That is *possible*," she said, in the tone people use when they think something is ridiculous but can't prove it.

"Program a jump to take us to the original rendezvous point."

"Jump option Tango is in the navigation system."

"Pilot, engage."

The battlecruiser was not at the agreed rendezvous point either, nor was there any sign of residual resonance from a wormhole. "It was worth a try," Nagatha assured the ship's captain.

"*Trying* is not good enough. There is some good news, I suppose. The coordinates you read from the buoy were accurate, *Valkyrie* simply never arrived there."

"Yes, Colonel. If the other data I recovered is also accurate, then I am afraid I have more bad news. I have been analyzing the jump signature, and I now believe I know what Skippy was attempting to do. I do not understand why he would do such a foolish thing."

"What happened?"

"I am guessing, you understand, but my theory fits the evidence. Skippy created a *micro*wormhole, then attempted to expand it to pull the ship through."

"Isn't that impossible?"

"Yes. Skippy knows that."

"Then why- Even if they were desperate, why would Skippy- Why would *Simms* authorize Skippy to-"

"Skippy might not have explained the risk completely," Nagatha suggested. "Also, he is insufferably arrogant. He may have thought he could ignore the laws of physics."

The pilots and CIC crew were silent, and their commander contemplated what to do next. There was no point to calling a meeting of the senior staff, the

Dutchman only had twelve people aboard. "I am open to suggestions," Chang said, looking into the CIC.

The discussion had not been productive, other than outlining what options were *not* available. Going to Paradise to pick up humans and bring them to the Beta site? Not possible, for without Skippy, the super-duty wormhole to the Sculptor dwarf galaxy could not be opened. There were no safe sites in the galaxy; any place the *Dutchman* could reach, hostile aliens had access to. In the end, Chang decided they should try to return to Earth. "Nagatha, is it possible for this ship to fly to Earth, the long way?"

She made a sound like sucking in a breath. "By going through the last wormhole in Ruhar territory, and jumping from there?"

"Yes."

"It is *possible*," she conceded. "We would need to stop along the way, to refuel, and to replace components that have worn out from over-use. It is fortunate that we have spare parts available. Colonel, I do not know whether I am capable of repairing the ship, if a major system were to suffer a failure. I am not Skippy.'"

"Reed?" He directed his question to the chief pilot. "Your thoughts?"

"It might be worth a try, if we can get there before the bad guys. The question is, to do *what*? The ship will be worn-out from the journey."

"To do our duty, Captain Reed," Chang replied softly, not intending his words as a rebuke. "To defend our homeworld, however we can. Those sound like brave words," he looked to the people in the CIC. "But I must admit, I simply do not know what else we could accomplish out here, on our own."

Reed took a breath. "Sir, I would like to see Earth again, one last time."

He took that as a 'yes'. "If no one else has a better idea?" Silence reigned in both the bridge and CIC compartments. "Very well. We are going back to Earth, if we can."

CHAPTER SIXTEEN

Skippy was annoyed at having to fix the jump drive *again*. His grumbling this time was less than usual since, the first time he complained about it, I reminded him that the whole mess we were in was all his own stupid fault. He was annoyed at having to do the work, frustrated at how long it would take, and totally confident he could do it. "The Universe seriously tried to wreck our entire set of drive coils during that jump. It did not realize it was messing with Skippy the *Magnificent*, I can tell you that," he had grumbled, and gone back to doing whatever he was doing.

While he was working and bitching about it, I decided it was time for me to do something I had been dreading.

Meeting our passengers.

The civilians we had rescued from Rikers.

Why was I nervous? Because our operation had to be the most fucked-up rescue in history. We had plucked the people off the surface well enough, but then the already-abused civilians were subjected immediately to being flung back out into space aboard their crowded dropships, fleeing the impending explosion of a starship. They then had to live in those cramped, smelly and increasingly unsanitary spacecraft, in zero gravity, as the *Flying Dutchman* slowly ran out of reserve power.

When Nagatha was able to restore power, it was all good for a while, until they had been forced to hurriedly transfer to *Valkyrie*, which then performed a jump that made everyone sick enough to wish they had died. And then they endured seven hours of nausea-inducing zero gravity *again*.

Even now, a day later, with one reactor pumping out gigawatts, gravity restored to normal, hot showers available, the galley cranking out the best hot food we had available, and the crew setting aside their normal duties to care for both children and adults, the civilians were unhappy. Especially the adults. Children are amazingly adaptable. Give them clean clothes, hot chicken nuggets and a cold soda and they will forget all the bad stuff that happened the day before. The adults were a different story. They knew what was going on, or thought they did. They expected better, and they deserved better. They had heard of some idiot asshole called 'Colonel Joe Bishop' and they were not shy about expressing their opinions about me. How did I know that? Simms told me; she had been meeting with groups of civilians, and reported they had harsh words for me and for some mysterious entity called 'Skippy' who they thought was merely the ship's computer.

Outside the empty cargo bay we had set aside for recreation, I squared my shoulders. The civilians needed to blow off steam, shout at me, ask tough questions, hear one lame assurance after another from me. It was going to be difficult facing those angry, traumatized and frightened adults, it would take every ounce of fortitude and courage I had.

Which is why I cowardly ducked out of doing that, and went into the children's rec area instead.

To avoid making a big deal of my entrance, I went in through a side door that was in a corner of the bay, between air ducts and thick pipes. Simms had set aside our largest cargo bay for a play area, moving supplies to other bays. Quietly the door slid open and my ears were assaulted by a cacophony of sound. There were cries of anger, and cries of, well, crying. There were tears. But mostly, there were sounds of *happiness*.

Children were squealing and shouting and whooping as they played. "Skippy," I whispered. "Where did we get all these toys?"

"Simms asked me to fabricate them," he explained.

"Uh, I thought you needed the fabricators to-"

"Do *you* want to say 'no' to these children, Joe?" He chided me.

"No. Definitely not."

"Me neither. Making stuff like toys and soccer balls is simple, it took me less than an hour to crank out everything on the list. Every night while the children are asleep, I ran a fabricator for ten minutes to make new stuff that has been requested. I only wish," he sighed, "they knew who was making all this fun stuff."

"Wait. They haven't met you yet?"

"No. Chang and Simms thought it best if I avoided direct contact with the civilians."

"Hmm. Probably for the best," I said automatically. Maybe that was true, but we had to tell the civilians about Skippy eventually. "Hey!" I saw two boys on distinctive tricycles race across the bay, pulling the hand brake and skidding to crash into and knock down a set of orange cones. "Is that a Big Wheel?"

"Yes, why?"

"Oh, man, my uncle had one of those! They came back in style again."

"Oh, Joey," Skippy giggled. "Do you want me to make a Really Big Wheel for you and the other adults?"

My initial reaction was '*Hell Yes*', but then I thought about it. "Uh, thanks, but that is probably an epically bad idea."

"What? Why?"

"Gee, let me think. We have a ship full of ultra-competitive special operators, and you propose to give us what are basically self-propelled bumper cars? I do not foresee *any* problems with that."

"Oh. Good point. It would be like the Lawn Dart incident on Club Skippy."

What he referred to was a training site he had named 'Club Skippy', on an isolated planet. Before we dropped to the surface there to rehearse the rescue operation, he had fabricated equipment for R&R. Stuff like volleyball nets, gear to play cricket and soccer, and anything else people had requested that could fit aboard a dropship. Some joker had asked for a set of Lawn Darts. I am not talking about 'Jarts' or Nerf darts or any such sensible play equipment. As requested, Skippy had made a set of original Lawn Darts with pointy metal tips.

Do you see any issue with giving pointy weapons to a bunch of high-speed operators who were bored between training sessions?

Yeah.

Smythe put a stop to the jackassery when four knuckleheads started playing a game of *catch* with the Lawn Darts.

Lesson learned: all requests for R&R gear had to go through Simms, our designated Buzzkiller.

"You didn't make anything dangerous for the children, did you?"

"Dude, please. If one of those kids got hurt, what do you think Margaret would do to me?"

"Adams? Why is she involv-"

"To your left, Joe."

Still standing in the corner, where the ductwork created shadows, I looked along the left wall. Adams was there, crouching down next to a girl who had skinned her knee or something. The girl was sitting on the deck, holding one knee, tears rolling down her face. Next to Adams, a big, tall US Marine was pulling a bandage from a packet, holding it out to the girl. I recognized the guy. He was Gunnery Sergeant Lamar Greene, one of the Commandos we shanghaied from Paradise.

Or as I refer to him in my head, Lamar Freakin' Greene.

I have nothing against the guy. He is a disciplined and professional Marine, and he performed admirably during the training for, and on the actual rescue mission on Rikers. My problem with Greene is simply that the guy *exists*.

And that he and Adams have history, of an intimate nature.

And that he is aboard *my* ship.

It did not make me happy to see that, as Greene spoke to the girl and held out the bandage, Adams patted his upper arm, looking at him with a smile and whispered something.

She wasn't patting his arm in a just-friends manner. She was stroking his arm, gently, with affection. The look in her eyes was affectionate, too, plus something else. Admiration.

Damn it.

The guy seriously had *game*.

The only way he could have been more attractive to women is if he had come aboard the ship with a basket full of puppies.

Meanwhile, I had a baseball cap jammed on my head because what was left of my hair still looked like I had lost a fight with a weedwhacker. The skin of my face, especially around my eyes, was swollen and yellow, with purple streaks of fine, broken blood vessels. As a bonus, Simms had told me that, perhaps because of the malnutrition I experienced on Rikers, I *smelled* bad. Doctor Skippy assured me the body odor issue would go away, in the meantime I was showering twice a day and dousing myself with aftershave that smelled even worse.

Good times.

As I watched silently, the girl allowed Adams to gently lift her hands away from her knee, and Greene applied the bandage. There wasn't any injury that I could see, that wasn't the point. The tears had stopped. The girl said something to Adams, looking shyly away from Greene, then impulsively flung her arms around his neck.

Shit. If I was Adams, I would have fallen in love with the guy right then.

My timing *sucks*.

It continued to suck because, as I turned to fade back into the shadows, the girl looked in my direction, her face took on a quizzical expression, and she pointed as she said something.

Adams and Greene turned at the same time to stare at me.

Raising a hand, I waved to them, not knowing what else to do.

Greene got to his feet and drew himself to attention before I gestured for him to relax. Jerking a thumb over a shoulder, I mouthed 'I will be back' to Adams, but she misunderstood me. She pointed at me and stood, walking in my direction, with Greene beside her and the girl trailing and half-hiding behind them both.

"Sir," Adams did one of those smiles that are on your lips but not in your eyes. "It is good to see you again," she said in a carefully neutral tone. "How are you?"

"Uh." In my head, I heard my mother telling me that honesty is the best policy. "You know what, Gunny?" I looked at the gaggles of children happily playing, and the adults who were happy to see the children being happy. "Better. Seeing this makes me feel, *better*." Dropping to one knee to be at eye-level with the girl hiding behind Adams, I added softly, "Who is this young lady?"

This time, the smile on Adams's face was genuine. "This is Aeysha."

Holy shit. Now I remembered.

Aeysha is the girl whose photo Adams had been looking at, when she asked me to promise to bring that girl home. Margaret had looked at me with pleading eyes and asked me to *make it happen*.

I had made it happen.

Bullshit.

We had made it happen.

"Hello, Aeysha," I said, smiling. "My name is Joe."

"Joe?" The girl looked at Adams, not at me.

"Aeysha," Adams explained, gently drawing the girl out to stand between her and Greene. "This is *Colonel* Joe Bishop. He is our leader."

"You *are*?" She wasn't looking directly at me.

Following her body language, I avoided looking directly at her. "Yes. I am very pleased to meet you, Aeysha. Are you enjoying-"

We were interrupted by a man who had wandered over, curious about me. The civilians had probably met all of the crew except for me. The expression on his face was that of concern, his body language tense. "Hello?" He said, looking straight at me.

From his appearance, I guessed he was Chinese. I thought he had probably said 'Hello' because he knew that English was the common language of the Pirates. Summoning up my rudimentary Mandarin Chinese, I greeted him with "Ni hau?" which sounded like 'knee how' to my untrained ear.

The guy shot a look a Greene, then back to me. "Ni hau? I'm from *Fresno*. Who are you?"

"Uh, sorry, I-"

Greene took offense at the guy's tone. "Colonel Bishop is our commanding officer." He pointed at the deck. "This is *his* ship."

"*Colonel?*" The guy's expression turned from concern to anger. "Then all of this is *your* fault."

Margaret's jaw clenched. "Mister Yang, Colonel Bishop rescued-"

Yang directed his anger at me. "I didn't see *you* down there. I haven't seen you at all. Where have you been hiding?"

"Mister Yang," Greene was struggling not to be harsh with a man who had spent years in captivity and seen unimaginable horrors.

"Gunnery Sergeant Greene, stand down, please." I ordered. "Mister Yang? You are correct. I was in command. If anything went wrong, it *is* my fault. The teams on the ground and flying the spacecraft overcame difficulties both expected and unexpected. They rescued all the people from both camps without a single human casualty," I avoided mentioning the injury to Grudzien. "The problems began after you came aboard the *Flying Dutchman.*"

Yang was not mollified by me owning up to my mistakes. "*Nothing* has gone right since then. Do you have any idea what you are doing?"

"The fact is," I explained in what I hoped was a soothing manner. "We humans do not belong out here," I pointed at the ceiling. "We stole both of our starships from species who possess technology we can barely understand. The crew have been doing the best they can, under circumstances that are nearly impossible. There were failures after you came aboard, yes. There will be failures in the future. We don't want that to happen, but it will. Any failures will *not* be due to lack of dedication by the crews of our ships. Mister Yang, the most dangerous species in the galaxy are hunting us, and they don't even know we are from Earth. I can't promise we will get home safely. What I can promise is we are doing *everything* that is possible."

"And plenty of things that aren't possible," Adams added under her breath.

Damn, it felt good to hear her say that. Yang still glared at me, but he shuffled his feet, uncertain what to say. "Mister Yang," I continued. "You have not seen me before today because, during the rescue operation, I was injured." I lifted my baseball cap and saw Yang's surprise. Adams tried not to react, she stiffened and sucked in a breath. "The recovery process is long, I came here as soon as I felt able to. Please understand, the Kristang had an overwhelming technology advantage when they took over Earth. We have been playing catch-up out here and the process has not been smooth. I can tell you that Earth is free, we *killed* all the Kristang on Earth. We came out here to rescue you, because we have an obligation to all humans. Our ability to act is limited, we have to choose our battles. We chose to pull you out of that hell-hole. If you have a problem with our operation, you will address your concerns to me, and not to the crew who risked their lives for you."

He stared at his feet, then lifted his head to look me in the eye. "I am sorry. It has been, very difficult for us."

"I can't imagine what you have been through. If we had known about your existence sooner, we would have been here."

"Thank you. Thank," he took a deep breath. "All of you. Colonel Bishop, hmm? I have heard of you. You are a Wagner fan?"

"Uh," I stared at him blankly. "What?"

"Wagner. Your two ships are named for his operas."

"Oh. That is, uh, a coincidence. Mostly."

Aeysha tugged on Adams's pants and the gunnery sergeant bent down for the girl to whisper in her ear. Adams smiled at whatever was said. Straightening up, Adams looked at me. "Sir, Aeysha, and a lot of the new people, want to know who 'Skippy' is. They have heard his name," she tilted her head in a gesture I interpreted as 'they are going to learn the truth soon anyway'.

"All right." Looking around, I sought a place where Skippy's avatar could appear to just a small group of people. In one corner a bunch of mats were stacked up about eight feet high. "Come over here, please." Gesturing with one hand for the group to follow, I walked over so the mats were between me and most of the people in the cargo bay, then opened a folding chair. "Skippy, could you stand on your throne here, please?"

His avatar shimmered to life, and he glanced down at the chair. "You call this a throne?"

Clenching my teeth, I whispered. "It's the best I could do. Be nice to our guests, please."

Yang stared at the hologram, then at me. "*This* is Skippy? Is this some kind of sick joke?"

"No joke," I waved my hands. "This is the avatar he uses to interact with humans. He is an artificial intelligence."

"Emphasis on the '*intelligence*' part, please," Skippy harrumphed.

Aeysha, still partly sheltering behind Adams, pointed at Skippy. "Why do you have a funny hat?"

"Excuse me, young lady. You are too young to appreciate the grandeur and majesty of my uniform. My hat is-"

"It's *funny*," the girl laughed. "Make it bounce again!" She demanded.

Skippy stamped his feet. "I am not a source of amusement, young lady," he waggled a scolding finger at her. "My awesomeness is beyond your ability to comprehend. You should-"

Aeysha held up a fist, and with her other hand pretended to be winding up a crank in her fist. Her middle finger went up, then she reversed the crank and it went down.

Adams had a shocked look on her face, then she burst out laughing, so did Yang and Greene, and I joined them.

"Well, I, well- I, I *never*. Ooh, this is an outrage. An *outrage*, I tell you!" Skippy sputtered. "Joe, I demand that you do something!"

"I am," I chuckled, and gave a thumbs up to the girl. She hid her eyes behind a hand, but she was smiling at me. "I'm *laughing* at you, Your Magnificence."

"Oh, well, I- I do *not* have to stand for this disrespect. Good bye to you and-"

"Stop right there, beer can," Adams said with the voice of authority, glaring at him. "You are not going to disappear. You *are* going to come with us to meet the other children, and you will be nice and polite and friendly, and not an arrogant asshole. This is not about *you* and your inflated ego."

"But-"

Taking a step forward, she loomed over him, and I swear to God, his avatar actually *flinched*. "Do you understand what I said?" She asked slowly.

"Yes," Skippy said in a very quiet voice.

"Yes, *what?*"

"Yes, Gunnery Sergeant."

Skippy was nice, and friendly and polite and respectful. Damn it, he was *humble*. He answered every question the children and adults posed to him, that is, all the questions that did not jeopardize our security. I hadn't made him act like a decent person, Margaret had done that. She is a bad-ass.

Damn, I love her.

I mean, I love that she is part of our crew, of course. We are very fortunate that-

Crap.

My life sucks.

"Nagatha," Chang called out to the ship's AI, as he sat heavily in his office chair.

"Colonel?" She responded through the speaker in the ceiling. Not for the first time, he pondered whether it would be better for the AI to have her own avatar. Several times, he had been about to suggest she consider creating a holographic image, for better communication at times when they were conversing one-on-one, or in small groups.

Such a decision was irrelevant at the moment. The *Dutchman* had returned to the spot where the spare parts had been left before the Rikers rescue operation, reattached everything so the former star carrier once again looked like a flying junk pile, and began the long journey back to Earth. The voyage would involve transitions through eight Elder wormholes, then many months of a jump-recharge-jump cycle. The Maxolhx jump drive and reactors fitted to the ship gave Nagatha a reasonable level of confidence the ship could complete the voyage, though they would need to treat the aging ship's systems very gently.

"I have a question. Please pull up data about the residual Thuranin wormholes you found at the last known location of *Valkyrie*."

"No."

"*No?*" His eyes opened wide in surprise. "Nagatha, you do not-"

"Colonel Chang, if you insist, I will of course comply with your request. However, I believe I know what you are asking, and it is not useful for you, or anyone else."

"What am I asking?"

"Whether you should have kept the *Dutchman* in place to defend *Valkyrie*, rather than attempting to lure the enemy away. It is true that I detected a residual wormhole from only a single Thuranin ship, which jumped in shortly after we departed. You are asking yourself whether, if we had been there, we could have destroyed that one ship, and bought time for Skippy to properly repair *Valkyrie's* jump capability. The answer is maybe. *Maybe*, if we had been there, we might have been able to hunt down, trap and kill that one ship before it alerted other ships. Colonel, I wish you to consider that Thuranin recon ships do not normally travel alone. There could have been a second enemy ship in the area, beyond my detection range, a ship that certainly could have evaded us, and brought heavy ships into the fight. The tactics you employed were entirely sensible given the information we had at the time. You could not have known the Thuranin had a second recon force in the area. So," she took a breath. "Is that what you wanted to talk about?"

"Are you this blunt when you talk with Bishop?"

"I was *more* direct when I spoke with Joseph Bishop, for he was inclined toward self-doubt and what you might describe as 'whining'."

Chang looked at the desktop in front of him, wondering how many times Bishop had sat in the same chair, having the same sort of conversation. "It seems wrong to speak ill of the dead."

"Colonel Bishop was always grateful when people were honest with him."

"Yes," Chang snorted, a grin spreading across his face. "I will strive to follow his example. Thank you. You are correct. Playing 'What If' games is a waste of time and effort."

"You are welcome. Would you like to play a video game? That helped Bishop to relax."

"Maybe later." He stood up, pushing the chair back. "I am working in the galley today, I should get busy."

Simms came through the chow line, surprised to see me working behind the counter. "Sir, you're not scheduled to-"

Using tongs, I picked up a piece of fried chicken. "I volunteered. The crew has been calling me 'Colonel Cranky'."

She tilted her head. "Why 'Cranky'?"

"It's a submarine term. A 'crank' is a person assigned to work in the galley, while they work on qualifying for their specialty, something like that. We haven't had fried chicken in a while, and there isn't much for me to do, until Skippy fixes the jump drive." Lowering my voice, I added "Besides, the children like it."

She flashed a smile at me. "Good idea."

"What do you like?" With women in the chow line, I felt creepy asking 'breast or thigh'? Really, I felt creepy saying that to men also.

"It all looks good, any two pieces." She held out her plate for me.

Gesturing down the line, I pointed with the tongs. "We also have baked potatoes and kale salad."

"*K-kale* salad?" She sputtered. "*You* made a kale salad?"

I shrugged. "Like you said, we have a lot of it."

Walking over to the big bowl of kale salad, she poked at it with the big salad fork. "What is this other stuff in here?"

"That's candied pecans, walnuts, dried cranberries and Mandarin oranges," I explained.

"Is there," she pushed the salad around with the big fork. "Any *kale* in it?"

"On the bottom, probably." Walking over to her, I took the other fork and tossed the salad around. "See? Plenty of kale."

"This is a *junk food* salad, with kale on the side," she frowned at me, her smile wiped away. "How is this healthy?"

"Because people are actually *eating* it," I whispered. "Remember that salad you made last week?"

She had made kale salad with garlic and parmesan. The big bowl of kale had sat on the end of the chow line, untouched, growing more sad, lonely and desperate with every person who passed by. By the end of the evening, she had to admit defeat and throw it away, before the garlic stunk up the entire galley. "I see your point," she grunted.

Simms dug around the bowl, picking out mostly kale for herself, but I noticed she also heaped a bunch of the good stuff on top. It was amazing, watching her eat something she had called 'junk food'. Maybe I could move her on to more advanced forms of nutrition. *Valkyrie's* executive officer had always been a heathen Fluff Denier, but over time, I hoped that by preaching the Gospel of Fluff, I would make her see the light, and she would enjoy the nutritious goodness of a Fluffernutter.

But I wasn't holding my breath until that happened.

Simms was still eating when the galley cleared out. Taking a break before I had to clean up the kitchen, I got a cup of coffee and sat down across from her. She was picking at the baked potato, but the rest of her food was gone.

"You liked that salad?"

"I *liked* the salad. I *hate* to admit it."

Saluting her with the coffee cup, I winked. "It will be our secret." Lowering my voice, I added "Are there any issues with the crew I should know about?"

"No."

"No?" That surprised me, given the situation. "How are the civilians?"

"They're fine," she speared a piece of potato with a fork, and popped it in her mouth. "Really, they are in relatively good spirits. You should visit them more often."

"I will."

"The only thorn in my side right now," she grimaced, "is *Karen* being a pain in the ass again."

"Karen?" With the civilians and the Commandos we had brought aboard, there were more people than usual, but I did not remember anyone named 'Karen'. Of course, Simms's real first name was 'Tamara' and she preferred to be called 'Jennifer', so maybe it was something like that.

"Our Ruhar guest."

"Her? I thought her name was '*Kattah*'? Kattah Robbenon."

"It is," she said in a tone meaning she was being extra patient with me. "We are calling her 'Karen' because she is acting like an entitled, obnoxious bitch. She keeps insisting on talking to the manager," she pointed to me.

"Oh," I laughed. "Karen, I get it. What's her problem?"

"What is *not* her problem?" Simms shrugged.

"I'll talk with her."

"Sir, I don't know if that is a good idea."

"She is a pain in your ass, and you have enough to worry about. Hey, it's a chance for me to work on my diplomatic skills."

"It's your funeral, Sir. Don't say I didn't warn you."

"Warning is noted. How about the Jeraptha cadet?"

"He is just bored. We're confining him to a small section of the ship, so he doesn't scare the civilians."

"That needs to stop."

"Please be very careful, Sir. The civilians have limited experience with aliens, and it's all been *bad*."

"I'll think about it. I won't do anything without talking with you first. We need-"

Two people came into the galley, and I stood up, draining my coffee cup. "Talk with you later, XO."

"Hey, Joe," Skippy said cheerily as his avatar shimmered to life on the desk in my cabin, interrupting a video game I was playing. It was not the 'heeeeey Joe' that sets off my Spidey senses, nor the quick 'hey Joe' he used when he knew he was in trouble. This was just a friendly greeting.

Instantly, I wondered what he was up to. "Hi, Skippy. What's up?"

"The crew sure loved that fried chicken you made last night. Those cheddar biscuits are all gone too, I noticed."

"It's easy to please people when they're hungry. The crew is working extra hard," I observed, which was true. Most of the work getting *Valkyrie* back to full fighting capability was done by Skippy, but there were plenty of tasks we lowly humans could handle. Some systems aboard the ship had been damaged by the extended loss of power and the intense cold. Skippy had offered to have his bots swap out components, but both Chang and Simms rightfully insisted that humans help where we could. We needed to learn how to handle minor repairs, even if we didn't quite understand how some of the systems worked.

"I like working in the galley, Skippy. I like *working*, instead of sitting around feeling useless all the time. Simms was smart to put me to work. It's helping me, a lot." What I did not know was whether being around people, interacting with people, and being useful was helping me process the trauma I experienced, or maybe being busy just let me push it to the back of my mind. My hope was the former, because failing to really deal with the issue would cause worse trouble for me later. The good news was my sleep was not being interrupted by disturbing dreams. If I was having dreams at all, I didn't remember them when I woke up, and that was fine by me. The stupid video game he had me playing for therapy was distracting, but I was on the third level and the rules were beginning to make sense.

He said something about it being good to keep busy, I wasn't really listening. Somehow, he steered the conversation toward the subject of children, I assumed it was something about idle hands being the Devil's playground, blah blah blah.

"It is *so* rewarding, Joe," he was rambling on about something, while I was trying to concentrate on playing the game.

"Uh huh, yeah. Good for you," I gave a neutral response that didn't require me to actually pay attention to what he was saying.

"Of course, it would be a lot more rewarding if the little brats showed some gratitude," he complained. "But *noooo*, it's always 'poor me this' and 'poor me that'. They're making it *all* about themselves. Little brats. What about *me*? Do they care about me, and my needs? No they do not. Just because they were kidnapped and taken away from their-"

"Wait." An alarm bell went off in my brain. It does that sometimes. Like when I'm half-watching some TV show and my brain thinks there was a topless scene, my brain goes *BOOBS*! and lets me know there is something important I should be looking at.

It's a guy thing.

Anyway, that time, I wasn't sure what was wrong, but I knew something was. That is always a good bet when Skippy is involved. Pausing the game, I sat up and leaned toward him. "What? What were you saying?"

"Ugh. Were you not listening to *anything* I said?"

"I *was* listening, because I know it is important," I lied my ass off. "That's why I want to be sure I fully understand the issue."

"Oh. Well, hmmf, I guess I owe you an apology."

"You certainly do," I sniffed without feeling even mildly guilty. "Start at the beginning, please."

"I try so hard, Joe. Those children need care and understanding and counseling, and I am doing my best to provide the intense psychological therapy they need, but those ungrateful little brats don't-"

"Whoa! Back up a little. *You* are acting as a child psychologist?"

"Certainly. It's because I care *so* much, Joe. Maybe I care too-"

My brain was still reeling in horror at the concept of Skippy the child psychologist. "You, *you* are offering counseling to a group of traumatized children? That, that is the worst idea, *in the history of ideas*!"

"Hey! Just compared to some of the knuckleheaded things *you* have done, there is no-"

"What makes *you* qualified?"

"I read a book about child psychology once. Ok, I didn't read the whole book, it was *really* boring. I did read the synopsis, most of it, and some of the chapters. Just the funny parts. Ugh, you have primitive monkey brains, how difficult can it be?"

"How diff-" I stared at him in disbelief. He was *proud* of himself. "That is a job for trained professionals. You are not-"

"I *am* a doctor, Joe," he interrupted. "Duh."

"You? When did *you* earn a doctorate in psychology?"

"It's an honorary degree. Due to my extreme awesomeness, the university didn't make me go through all the boring stuff, like classes and learning and studying."

"An honorary degree. Is this from an online school you made up?"

"No," he sounded genuinely insulted. "It is a legit university. The finest and most prestigious in the land, in fact."

"Oh, *really*?" I said, putting as much sarcasm into my voice as I could. "Finest in the land? What land is this? YouTubeville?"

"If you must know, my degree is from the College Of Medical Sciency Stuff, at the University of Skippistan."

"Medical Sciency Stuff?"

"Something like that. I have an actual fancy diploma, but it's in a storage unit in Wyoming."

"Why do you have a storage unit in Wyoming?"

"The rent is cheap, Joe. They have a lot of land out there, *duh*. Man, sometimes I wonder about your-"

"Can we, can we get back to this university? It's in *Skippistan*? What," I laughed. "You have your own country now?"

"Sure."

Holy shit. It hit me right then. He was *serious*. "You formed a freakin' *country*?"

"Yes."

"Can I get a *little* more info about that, please? How did you do this?"

"Mostly it was a bunch of forms I found online. It's amazing what you can do with Photoshop. Plus I hired a law firm in Lichtenstein, they were happy to have my business. Especially," he lowered his voice, "after I made that *legal thing* go away, if you know what I mean."

"Ok," I breathed a sigh of relief. That was one less thing for UNEF and the United States Army to yell at me about. "So, it's just on paper. It's not a real country."

"It *is* a real country. Jeez, I sure pay enough dues for voting rights in the United Nations."

"The, the UN *recognized* Skippistan?"

"They sure did."

"*How*?"

"Bribes, Joe, *duh*. The bureaucrats at the UN don't care what a country does, as long as you keep the money flowing. Actually, hee hee," he chuckled, pleased with himself. "I got a bargain, the bribes didn't cost nearly as much as I expected. It turns out, my ambassador to the UN had compromising photos of certain important people with farm animals, and-"

"Please tell me you did not do that."

"Why? Oh, I know what you are concerned about. Don't worry, Joe, I obscured the faces of the farm animals in the photos, nobody will know who they are."

I pounded my forehead on the desk so hard, it left a red mark. "You have an *ambassador*? A real, live actual person?"

"Of course."

"This person, he or she is a citizen of Skippistan? An employee of yours?"

"He's more of an independent contractor, Joe. He gets a small salary, but mostly he enjoys the *substantial* tax benefits of dual citizenship in Skippistan. He runs my embassy in Miami."

"You have an embassy? Why *Miami*?"

"Because that's where he lives. I saw his ad on a billboard. You know, if you have an accident, call 1-800-Morrie-Cares, or some bullshit like that."

"Morrie?"

"Morrie Slater. He's an ambulance-chasing lawyer. Anyway, Morrie suggested we set up my embassy in a fourth-floor condo overlooking South Beach. That way, hee hee, Morrie can check out the topless babes on the beach, while Mrs. Morrie thinks he's at the office."

"I don't believe this."

"What *I* don't believe are some of the crazy items on Morrie's expense account. Who needs a tub of Vaseline and three ferrets?"

"Oh, my G-"

"Hey, if he built a slip'n'slide for those ferrets, *I* am not paying to clean the rugs."

That was something my brain warned me not to think too much about, so I didn't. "Is this, is this a *real* country? Where is it?"

"Uh, well, originally I planned for it to be somewhere in eastern Europe, so I could give myself a title like Grand Duke-a-rino. That way, I would outrank Count Chocula, you know? But the EU would ask too many questions, and I figured, hey, it's called Skippi*stan*, so it must be in central Asia."

"So, where is this place?"

"It's between Kyrgyzstan and Uzbekistan, north of Tajikistan. I think. Close enough. Technically, it is an independent enclave within Kyrgyzstan."

Whether those three countries existed was something I would have to Google. In the back of my brain was a vague memory of a movie from that part of the world, Borik, Borash, Borek something like that? That guy in the movie was fake, maybe those countries were too? "You own actual land there, or is Skippistan just something like a post office box?"

"I own actual land," he sniffed, offended by the question. "Forty-six hectares of beautiful rolling hillsides. Currently, it is mostly populated by sheep and goats, but we do have a yak! Before we left Earth the last time, I was negotiating to buy an emu, but the cost of shipping is outrageous."

"An, an emu? Why would you want a-"

"Because it's *cool*, duh. How many people do *you* know who have an emu? Zero, right? That's what I thought."

"Sheep, goats and a yak, huh? Sounds, uh, like a paradise."

"To the wealthy people who purchase citizenship in the glorious People's Republic of Skippistan, it is paradise, Joe. The tax benefits can offset the cost of citizenship in the first year!"

"*Purchase*? You are selling citizenship? Damn it, is this another scam like your cult?"

"It is *not* a scam, and I am hurt that you would imply such an ugly thing. Skippistan is a real country, according to the United Nations. Hey, do you want to hear our bodacious national anthem?"

Music blared out of the speakers in the ceiling before I could say 'no'. What I expected was something like opera, or showtunes. Instead, what I heard made me jam fingers in my ears. It was some guy screaming, with the background music made by poorly-tuned guitars and possibly a car crash. "What *is* that?"

"Swedish death metal, Joe," he shouted to be heard over the noise. "I didn't want to have some lame anthem like most countries."

"Your national anthem is sung in *Swedish*?"

"No, that's Klingon, of course."

It didn't sound like Klingon to me, but I'm not an expert.

When the anthem finished, and my ears stopped ringing, I just sat for a while, head in my hands, wondering how much trouble he had gotten me into. "Tell me, please," I asked without looking up at his avatar. "When did you set up this country?"

"Before we left Earth the last time, of course. Just after you made me pay back the people I ripped off. I mean, to reimburse the very generous and *totally* voluntary donations from the faithful followers of His Holiness Skippiasyermuni. I needed a legit way to raise funds, remember? Hey! If this gets me in trouble, then it is all *your* fault."

"The UN, they don't know the leader of this country is *you*, do they?"

"Of course not. I'm not *stupid*, Joe. I used my Magnus Skippton persona to set it up. He relocated from the Cayman Islands. Morrie did all the paperwork for me."

"And this is a real, legit country, according to the UN?"

"According to the outrageous dues I pay to the UN, absolutely."

"Huh."

"What?"

"This, might actually be a good thing."

"Well, *duh*, it's a good thing. I am helping oppressed millionaires and billionaires all around the world to hide their wealth- I mean, to manage their-"

"Not that. It's a good thing because, you are not *my* problem anymore."

"Um, what?"

"You are a sovereign nation. A real one, not like those cosplaying idiots who live in a bunker in Idaho. The US Army can't make you my responsibility."

"If you say so, Joe."

"Can we get back to the subject? We should be helping the children. And the adults."

"I *am* helping them. For sure, they are not shy about making me the focus of their anger. Damn, some of them *really* hate me."

"Gosh, I wonder w-"

"Don't be a smartass, Joe."

"How about this? I will talk with the rescuees, or get Adams or someone to talk with them. If they want to continue counseling with you, we will give it a shot. Deal?"

"Deal. You know I am all about helping people."

"Yes, that's what everyone says about you."

CHAPTER SEVENTEEN

The *Flying Dutchman* floated in deep space, one light-minute from the next emergence point of the Elder wormhole. Going through that wormhole would begin the journey back toward Earth, and abandon hope of ever finding *Valkyrie*. According to the navigation records that Nagatha had access to, the ancient wormhole would be open for eleven minutes, thirty-seven seconds. In practice, that meant the ship had a window of six minutes and nineteen seconds to transition through the stable rip in spacetime, considering the time needed for the event horizon to stabilize, plus the need to fly through normal space after jumping in outside the wormhole's enforced safety zone.

All that data was programmed in the autopilot, plus multiple options for escaping if an enemy ship was detected. That wormhole has been selected because it saw only moderate traffic, mostly by the Bosphuraq. With the birds still feeling the wrath of their patrons, their ships were not flying far from their home bases.

Samantha Reed resisted the urge to scratch her itchy arm. She couldn't reach the itch anyway, with her forearm in a lightweight but solid casing. Supposedly the miracle medical technology of the Maxolhx device prevented her skin from itching, and Nagatha assured her the cast was working properly. What the hell did a disembodied AI know about an itch that was distracting at best, infuriating at worst? Sometimes, Sami felt like cutting the damned casing open to get blessed relief, except Nagatha had warned that would seriously set back the healing of the broken bones. She would be stuck in an endless loop of itching, breaking and applying a new casing. That was a recipe for-

Her console lit up. "Wormhole is open," she reported a split-second before anyone in the CIC, a point of pride for her. Technically, the wormhole has opened a minute before, they were just seeing the photons now. "Authorizing autopilot, counting down from forty seconds from, *now*," she pressed a button on the console. Unless she interrupted the process, the ship's navigation system would jump the *Dutchman* at a precise position in front of the wormhole. The only reason she would cancel the programmed jump is if an enemy ship was detected. In that case, she would immediately activate jump option Bravo without needing further orders from Chang.

"Forty seconds," Chang acknowledged, unseen from his command chair behind her. She preferred the arrangement of *Valkyrie's* bridge, where the captain sat off to the side. It was awkward to twist in her couch to look at the captain.

Speaking of endless loops, she thought with an inner groan, that is exactly what her life would be for many months while the *Dutchman* jumped, recharged and jumped yet again. All the way to Earth. In the military, she had many times experienced Groundhog Day, where she got up in the morning and did the *same* shit as the previous day. The idea of getting stuck in a loop like that was-

She jerked in her seat.

The timer on the console read seven seconds.

Six.

Five.

On her own initiative, she canceled the jump.

"*Pilot?*" Chang asked, alarmed.

"Captain Reed," Nagatha added. "Why did you cancel the jump? I am not detecting any other ships in the area, and-"

"Chen, take over," Reed told her copilot, and unstrapped so she could see Chang without straining her neck. "Colonel, you weren't with us on the Renegade mission."

"I am aware of that fact, *Captain*," Chang allowed his annoyance to creep into his voice. He did not like being reminded that he had missed that action. The Pirates who had stolen the ship, and flown off to conduct that astonishingly complex and wildly successful mission, never acted like they were better than those left behind, but there was sometimes an unspoken smugness about it. That the woman universally referred to as Emily Freakin' Perkins had spoiled the mission made no difference in how the Pirates felt about their accomplishments. "I was unavoidably detained."

"Yes, Sir. I meant, there was an incident you might not be familiar with."

"I did read the mission reports," Chang assured her, his tone more neutral. He needed to give her some slack, to trust his chief pilot.

"Yes. But I *lived* it. Nagatha too."

"I did?" The AI asked. "Ooh, which incident?"

"When we jumped the DeLorean out of Detroit," Reed explained, arching an eyebrow.

Chang nodded, and gestured for her to continue.

"Sir, that was one seriously *fucked-up* jump. We barely survived. Everyone thought we had died, including Skippy. My point is, from our point of view in the DeLorean, everything was fine. Except when we emerged, we had gone forward in *time*."

"Yes, and-" Chang's mouth hung open. "Oh, no!"

"Yeah," she shook her head ruefully. "Sir, we know that wormholes are created by warping spacetime. We think of using wormholes to move in space, but we don't think of how they affect time. What if *Valkyrie* did jump, and instead of getting trapped in the jump, they got hung up in a time loop for a while? They could have emerged after we left."

"Or they could emerge tomorrow," Chang leaned forward excitedly. "Nagatha, program a jump to take us back to *Valkyrie's* target jump coordinates."

"No need, Sir," Sami reported with a grin, spinning around on the couch and strapping in. "I have kept jump option Hotel updated as we flew."

"Mm," Chang grunted. "Any reason that you chose the designation 'Hotel'?"

"*Hope* also starts with an 'H'," she explained.

"Engage when ready."

There was no sign of *Valkyrie* when the *Dutchman* returned to the target coordinates, nor any sign the battlecruiser had ever been there. "We wait," Chang declared.

"For how long, Colonel?" Nagatha inquired.

"I am not an expert in hyperspatial physics. How long do *you* think we should wait?"

"Oh dear. I am not sure how to answer that."

"Have you been able to determine how long *Valkyrie* could have been flung forward in time?"

"Colonel Chang, unfortunately, no. There is not enough data for me to even begin to guess at the time shift, if there *was* a time shift. Please keep in mind that Captain Reed's theory is just that: a theory. A hunch, to be accurate."

"We wait," he insisted. "Thirty days, if necessary."

"May I ask," Reed craned her neck to look backward. "Why thirty days?"

"It is a nice round number," Chang shrugged. "If we are wrong about a time shift, and we stay here too long, we cannot reach Earth before the enemy does."

"Yes, Sir," Reed turned back to her console. "I suggest we move away. If their jump was shifted in time, we don't know how accurate it was in *space* either."

"Do it."

While we waited for Skippy to fix *Valkyrie's* jump drive, *again*, I decided to tackle a problem that I had been avoiding. Usually, as the ship's executive officer, Simms handled routine personnel issues, and I wasn't going to change that.

This matter was not routine.

Outside the door to the cabin suite, I paused to check my uniform, tugging here and there to straighten out wrinkles. Running a hand over the awful, self-induced crewcut that was at least growing in evenly, I took a deep breath. "Skippy, is our guest waiting to stab me with a sharpened toothbrush?"

"No, Joe," he laughed. "She has been sitting on the couch for the past ten minutes. Perched on the edge of the couch, actually. Reading her biometrics, she is quite anxious."

"Anxious? Or hostile?" Normally, I would not ask Skippy to snoop on people in their cabins, but this was a special case.

Because this was Karen.

"She is anxious, Joe."

"OK," I tapped my zPhone to alert her that I was at the door. There wasn't a panel near the door, because it was a temporary addition to the ship. For the convenience and sanity of our lone Ruhar guest, we had blocked off the end of a passageway, so she had access to two cabins. One cabin contained a treadmill and other exercise and recreation equipment, the other was living quarters. Simms had pointed out to our guest that having two cabins was a great luxury, aboard a ship crammed full of civilians, where some cabins were assigned four people. Kattah Robbenon had not been appreciative to Simms, though when I spoke to her that morning, she had sounded more weary than angry.

The door slid open, I stepped into the passageway between cabins, and Skippy slid the door closed behind me. "Klasta Robbenon," I used her rank and last name, giving her a Ruhar-style salute, with two fingers to my cheek.

She had stood up from the couch on my signal and was standing in front of me. She returned the salute, either automatically or out of courtesy. "Colonel

Bishop. Thank you for agreeing to speak with me. Finally." Her cheeks reddened under the fine fur. "Sorry. I did not mean to- It has been difficult."

"I can't imagine what it was like for you, aboard a ship with no gravity, no lights, no heat."

"No hot *water*," she sighed. "That was the worst part. Have you ever tried to keep yourself clean, using cold water and wet towels?"

"Um, too many times, unfortunately," I flashed a chagrinned smile. "Our ships have lost power and gravity, uh, I can't remember how often."

She invited me into her living quarters. Before following her, I glanced at her mini gymnasium, noting that she had kept the place neat and spotlessly clean. Sitting at the table in her rather spacious cabin, we exchanged pleasantries until the conversation trailed off. "Klasta, I am very sorry that it was necessary to bring you aboard against your will. It *was* necessary. You have been informed of our operation to rescue humans being held by the Kristang?" I avoided using the word 'kidnapped', since that is what we had done to her.

"Yes." She looked down at the table. "If I were in your position, I might have done the same." Then she looked up, accusingly, her eyes fiery. "But I do not have a Maxolhx battlecruiser. Surely you could have rescued your people without needing a handful of human Commandos!"

"Not without exposing our secret," I replied quietly. Before I decided to meet with her, I told myself that no matter how angry she was with me, I would remain calm. She was scared, lonely and separated from everyone she knew. If she wanted someone to yell at, better her target was me than my crew. "Please understand, our homeworld is facing destruction by the Maxolhx, and there is nothing we can do to stop them. The longer our secret remains undiscovered, the more time we have to bring people from our homeworld, to a safe haven. My species is facing total extinction."

She shook her head sadly, not in anger. "Colonel, there is no place in this galaxy that is safe from the Maxolhx. To believe otherwise is to give your people false hope."

Though our plan was to return Robbenon to her own people, after the Maxolhx reached Earth and our secret no longer mattered, she was not going to be told about the Beta site. She also did not need to know that Skippy could screw with Elder wormholes. "It will be difficult, and it may only be temporary," I said with an exaggerated shrug.

"My people have faced war for," she sighed. "Longer than my people can remember. But, we have not faced *extinction* since the beginning. You have my sympathy, for whatever that is worth."

"Thank you. I can promise you that you will not be harmed, and as soon as it is possible to release you, we will. Is there anything I can do to make you more comfortable?"

"I don't want to be *comfortable*," she touched the rank insignia on her uniform top. "What I want is to be useful. Colonel, I need something to do. I am going crazy in here."

"Back home, you have a husband, and a child?"

"Yes," her eyes narrowed. "How do you know that?"

"Your personnel records were in your phone when you came aboard."

"Those records are *encrypted*," her jaw clenched and a muscle in her cheek twitched.

Waving my hand to encompass the cabin, I explained, "We hacked into a Maxolhx computer to capture this ship."

"True," her shoulder sagged.

"I did not mention your family as a threat, or a boast. Your son is, four years old?"

"He will be five soon," her eyes shone, welling with tears.

Standing up, I gestured toward the door. "Come with me, please."

Outside the door to the empty cargo bay we had set aside as a recreation area for the civilians, we heard the voices of children and a few adults. They were mostly talking quietly, interrupted by squeals and shouts of someone playing a game.

"Why are we here?" Robbenon asked, standing behind me as if afraid.

"The only aliens these people have seen are Kristang. They should know that not all other species are cruel and want to kill us. Could you show them that your people are not like the Kristang?"

"I have never met human children," she said, which was not really an answer.

"Are you willing to try, please? If you want to do something useful, this is an opportunity."

"I," she took a shuddering breath, closing her eyes. "Will try. What if they are afraid of me?"

"They probably will be, at first. You will need to be patient."

The ghost of a smile cracked her stern face. "I have a very energetic little boy at home. Patience is a virtue I have had to learn." She squared her shoulders. "Ready."

"Good. Wait here in the passageway, I will call you." I strode confidently into the rec bay, waving a friendly hand to the small group of people gathered there. Two adults and eight children. Two boys who I guessed were around ten years old were playing badminton, or trying to. Skippy had fabricated sort of Nerf shuttlecocks that didn't fly fast or far, to keep the game slow and gentle. The boys were both on the same side of the net, trying to keep the bird in the air for as long as possible. They looked happy.

The others were sitting on the padded section of the floor, talking. Play gear was scattered around, despite the frequent admonishments from our crew to put equipment away when not in use.

"Good afternoon," I announced myself quietly. "Why, hello there, Aeysha."

She jumped up and ran over to me happily, thumping against my legs, her head battering my stomach. "Oof. Wow," I held her shoulders and pushed her back to get a better look at her. "How much have you grown since last week?"

Bashfully, she looked at the floor, but I saw her glancing up at me with one eye. "Gunny Adams says I have gained three pounds."

"That is good!" Crouching down so we were at eye-level, I asked "Would you like to meet a friend of mine? Her name is Kattah."

"Kattah?" Aeysha looked at me quizzically. "What kind of name is that?"

"It is a Ruhar name. She is an alien. A *nice* alien," I added hastily as the girl's eyes bulged. "She is not like the Kristang at all. Her people are enemies of the Kristang. The Ruhar *hate* the Kristang."

"I hate them too," Aeysha whispered, already looking past me toward the doorway.

Raising my voice, I called out "Klasta Robbenon?"

The Ruhar officer stepped slowly into view, hugging the door frame, waving a hand.

Aeysha clutched my arm, whispering "She looks like a *bunny*, with short ears."

"We call them hamsters," I whispered back with a wink. "But don't tell her that, it's not polite. Would you like to meet her?"

"Will you come with me?" She asked.

I stood up. "Hold my hand?"

Introducing Robbenon to a small group was a good idea it allowed her to interact with them in a controlled setting, though that didn't last long. Two children ran out of the rec bay, and soon the rumor spread like wildfire. There was an *alien* aboard the ship! We had to control access to the bay, letting small groups of people in at a time. Robbenon was a true professional, or maybe she was just a homesick mother, because I could not have asked her to be nicer. She remained there for hours, past the start of the evening meal, answering questions, letting children touch her and feel her soft fur. By that time, I had left supervision to Captain Frey, and she declared an end to the excitement when she saw the Ruhar was exhausted. All in all, introducing Robbenon to the civilians was a success, the civilians were talking about it all the next morning.

Until we introduced them to our Jeraptha guest.

That was real excitement.

"Are you *sure*?" I pressed Skippy for a solid answer. He had declared the jump drive was fixed and fully operational, so I called him to discuss the issue with me and Simms.

"Yes. As much as I can be, without actually using the damned thing. So, really I guess the answer is 'shmaybe'?"

"Can you give me a confidence level on that 'shmaybe'?"

"Oh, it is a gold-plated shmaybe, Joe. Hundred percent. Mmm, more like eighty-twenty, to be truthful. But a *solid* eighty percent. Maybe seventy-five. Jeez, now you've got *me* worried."

Skippy had fixed the jump drive, a job that had taken seven hours longer than his estimate. It wasn't fully repaired, just enough for the ship to perform a half-dozen jumps. What I wanted was to jump *now*, without the drive exploding, or causing further damage to the delicate unit. We had been away from the *Flying Dutchman* for nine days, Chang had to be worried sick about us.

"We need to perform a test jump, right? Answer this: does it make any difference whether we jump a short distance, or all the way back?"

"Um, back to where?" He asked.

"To the spot we jumped away from. The only place Chang could find us. I'm hoping he is there, waiting for us."

"That jump is only twenty-nine lightdays. It would be a good test, no more risky than jumping a few light-minutes."

"Good." Finally, I had gotten an answer from Skippy. "Simms, do you have any objections?"

"No," my XO shook her head. "I just want to get *on* with it."

"We all do," I agreed.

"Jump is programmed into the nav system," Skippy said with only a touch of his usual smugness.

"Pilot," I tried to project authority in my voice. "Jump option Delta. Engage."

"Damn it," I smacked the armrest of my chair, which fortunately had the controls locked so a doofus like me didn't accidently launch missiles. "Where the hell are they?"

"Patience, Sir," Simms counselled. "Chang probably positioned his ship a few light-seconds away for safety."

"Yeah." That made sense to me, except *Valkyrie* had returned three minutes ago, and there was no signal from the *Dutchman*. "Skippy, ping the buoy we left behind."

"Uh, bad news, Joe. I did that already. It's not responding. I am afraid to say this, but the buoy might have been damaged by the distortion when we jumped out of here."

"Shit. Warm up the active sensors and ping for the damned thing."

Two minutes later, Skippy sighed. "I'm sorry, Joe. There is no sign of the buoy. The extreme distortion of our jump may have destroyed it."

"Shit! Without that buoy, Chang has no way to know where we went. Is there any sign the *Dutchman* was here?"

"No," Skippy replied. "I am detecting only very faint jump resonance signatures, too degraded to be recent. Too faint to tell what type of ship was here."

"Ok. No sense wasting time here. Jump us to the planned rendezvous point, Chang would have gone there."

Except if Chang had brought his ship there, it was long gone. Skippy detected faint resonances from a starship having been in the area more than a week ago. "Oh, this is not good," I rested my head in my hands. Chang could not have dropped off a buoy, because the *Dutchman* wasn't equipped with any. We only had five of the devices left, all aboard *Valkyrie*. The assumption had been that as the support ship, the *Dutchman* would remain in one place, while our battlecruiser flew to unpredictable places and took the risks. It had been my assumption, and clearly I was wrong. Lesson learned: get Skippy to fabricate buoys. After he finished fabricating all the other crap we needed to keep our two ships flying.

Our *one* ship flying.

"Simms," I turned to my executive officer. "What do you think? How do we find the *Dutchman*?"

"Sir," her expression was pained. "We *don't*. They could be anywhere." She did not say what we both feared; that the *Dutchman* had not returned because that ship had been unable to return. "All I can think of is, we should try jumping back to Rikers, see if Chang went there after he didn't find us here."

I rubbed the crewcut stubble on my head. The hair had grown out enough for me to stop wearing a baseball cap all the time. "That is a longshot," I muttered half to myself. "If we don't find them there," I let my voice trail off.

"What then, Sir?" She asked in a whisper, leaning toward me.

"I don't know. You're right. They could be anywhere. We'll *never* find them."

CHAPTER EIGHTEEN

Two days after returning to *Valkyrie's* target jump coordinates, Reed was daydreaming in the pilot couch, alone near the end of a duty shift. She was looking forward to a late lunch, and hitting the gym. The selection of meals in the galley was not the-

Her console lit up. "They're here!" She pressed a button to alert the entire crew, all dozen of them. "*Valkyrie* is here!"

Chang ran onto the bridge moments later, blinking away sleep. He had been dozing in his office chair, and his neck moved awkwardly, stiff from the awkward angle. Before he could ask questions, Reed pointed to the main display. "There doesn't appear to be any external damage. They may have been off in time, but they emerged within seven *meters* of the target coordinates. Whatever is dorked up with their drive, it hasn't affected accuracy."

Chang grinned, sitting in the chair and jabbing a thumb on the transmit button. "*Valkyrie*, you are late to the party. That was a very impressive time shift."

The face of Bishop came on the display, still wearing a baseball cap but looking much healthier. "Hi, Kong. Uh, what time shift?"

Chang's grin grew wider. "It felt like no time at all to you, hmm? You have been gone for nine days, trapped inside your jump wormhole."

"Oh, uh," Bishop blushed. "No. Good guess, but, we just jumped in six lightdays off target. The jump blew the drive, it has taken this long for Skippy to get it unfucked."

Chang sat back in the chair, deflated, sharing a 'WTF' look with Reed. "No time shift?"

"No, sorry," Bishop shrugged. "That would have been way cooler than what actually happened to us."

"Sir?" Reed asked. "What *did* happen?"

Bishop shook his head. "It is a *long* st-"

"What happened?" Skippy shouted. "Pure, weapons-grade *awesomeness* is what happened! I am *back*, baby! Large and in charge!"

Chang covered his eyes with a hand. "And humble as always, I see."

"Kong," Bishop clapped his hands. "I can't tell you how freakin' happy we are to see you! How did you know to come here? The buoy must have been destroyed, we couldn't find any trace of it."

"The buoy was *damaged*," Chang explained. "We took it aboard for Nagatha to extract the jump coordinates."

"Wow. You have been waiting here for nine days?"

"Not here. *That* is a long story."

"Come aboard *Valkyrie*," Bishop waved. "You can tell me over a glass of scotch."

"I do not understand." Chang was puzzled. "If you thought we had not found the buoy, you had no reason to think we came *here*. Why did you-"

Bishop shrugged. "It was worth a shot. I figure, after all the bullshit we've been through recently, the Universe *owes* us."

It was a big surprise to Chang when *Valkyrie* appeared out of nowhere, and that we had not been lost in time. He seemed a bit disappointed about that and truthfully, so was I. That would have been a much better story to tell someday.

Another big surprise was when I told Nagatha about her love child. Except, I felt bad that she was horribly embarrassed about the whole thing, until she established a full set of communication protocols with Bilby, and talked with him. Her opinion was that Bilby had a lot of growing to do, before he would be ready to take over the full range of ship operations. She also was very proud of him, while Skippy was still just annoyed.

The crew thought Bilby was great when he revealed himself. Mostly, they liked that he was a constant source of pain and suffering for Skippy.

I kind of liked that too.

The civilians remained aboard *Valkyrie*, I didn't intend to take the ship into action, and they probably felt like ping-pong balls from bouncing between our ships. Some of the crew transferred from one ship to another, bringing aboard new faccs, including some people I had not seen since I returned from Rikers. That group included part of the STAR team, until I met them when I walked into the gym. A group of people were looking surprised to see me, and had guilty looks on their faces and were avoiding my eyes. "Uh," I looked at Captain Frey, who was surrounded by people recently transferred from the *Dutchman*. "What's going on?"

"Skippy," she gritted her teeth. "You were supposed to warn us if the Colonel was coming here."

"Oops! My fault," Skippy chuckled. "I am revising the control procedures for internal sensors, it must have temporarily blinded me. Gosh, I am *terribly* sorry about that."

"Riiiight," I ignored Skippy. "Captain Frey, what is going on, if I am allowed to know?"

"Sir," her shoulders slumped. "We want to get something as a 'Welcome Back' gift for you, now that both ships are together and functional again. Something nice."

"Oh," I was taken aback. "That is, very nice. Thank you."

"*Someone*," she glared at the group shuffling their feet awkwardly on the other side of the aerobics floor. "Suggested candlesticks, because *somebody* is not putting any effort into this."

"Well, uh, those are always nice."

"They are *lame*, Sir. Candlesticks are what you get, when you can't think of anything else. Can you give us a hint?"

"Jeez, Captain, I don't-"

"That's easy," Skippy snickered. "Joe could use a box of condoms."

"Cond-" Frey's eyes opened wide. It could see the wheels turning in her head. Happy for me that I might need those items, and wondering who I was using them with.

"Skippy," I groaned. "I do *not* need any-"

"Come on, Joe. *Try* to be a responsible adult. Your shower is not using protection, you should at least-"

"Oh, shit."

"Seriously, I'm surprised your shower isn't *pregnant* by now."

Let's just say that I did not get to use the gym that day.

Also, the crew later presented me with a very nice coffee mug with a commemorative 'Escape from Rikers' logo on it, like a movie poster.

None of the crew would look me in the eye when they gave me that mug.

I hate that little beer can.

Before Chang came aboard *Valkyrie* for a glass of scotch to officially celebrate our reunion, we followed Simms's suggestion to jump both ships someplace far away. For all we knew, Thuranin ships were buzzing around like angry hornets. The danger was, there were possibly more than just Thuranin ships near Rikers. That lone frigate had seen *Valkyrie*, and knew we were the feared ghost ship. If the Thuranin wanted to suck up to their patrons, they would run to tell the Maxolhx about us, so we needed to get the hell out of there. After a jump, Chang came aboard, and some of the crew transferred back to the good old *Flying Dutchman*. We did enjoy a glass of nice single-malt scotch while each of us related what happened while we were separated. We also expressed gratitude that our starships were commanded by army officers, instead of following navy regulations. Drinking any sort of alcohol would have been frowned upon aboard a navy ship.

After we swapped war stories, I had a decision to make. "Kong," I rolled the heavy glass around in my hand, a sure giveaway that I was contemplating a difficult subject. "While Skippy was restoring the drive, I met the people we rescued from Rikers."

Ah." He understood, or I thought he did. He lifted his chin in a gesture for me to continue.

"Some of the adults and I, we uh, had a group therapy session. They told me what happened to them, how they survived. How so many did *not*. How the adults sacrificed themselves to provide for the children." If my hand closed any more tightly around the glass, I could have broken it. "What those sadistic lizard fuckers did to them."

"Joe." He set down his glass. "I know. You heard about the arena?"

"Yeah." After the Kristang had determined their human captives had no immediate usefulness, and before the Thuranin offered to purchase them, the clan leaders had amused themselves and their restless population by forcing humans to fight to the death. They had brought in adults to fight against their warriors, then against well-armed lizard children, then against beasts. The worst part, for the people in the two camps, was that for better sport, the Kristang selected the most healthy of the adults. That left the ill and injured to grow food and care for the children as best they could.

And when a human child reached their teen years, they also could be selected for the arena.

"You want to hit them, hard," Chang asked.

"No." I gulped the remainder of the scotch. "I want you to talk me out of it."

Clearly, that was not what Kong expected to hear. "If you're asking me to do that, you already have."

"I don't *want* to be talked out if it," my clenched fists thumped the table. "I know it's not the smart move, OK? Going back to Rikers, with a Thuranin battlegroup and maybe Maxolhx ships buzzing around like angry hornets, it's too risky, right? It's just, *damn* it. How much shit do we have to take? When does it stop?"

"You want vengeance," he nodded.

"I want those lizards to *pay*."

"Mmm." He looked at the table for a moment. Looking at me he asked "Are you a Lord of the Rings fan?"

"Uh, what? I saw the movies when I was a kid, and that TV show. Read the books when I was older, like in high school. Why?"

"Forgive me if I get some of the story wrong. There was a dwarf named Thrain? I think that's right. He heard the orcs killed a dwarf king, can't remember his name. The orcs didn't just kill this king, they mutilated his body and fed it to crows. Thrain thought about it for a week, then announced 'This cannot be borne'. He committed his people to a long and horrific war. In the end, I think he killed the orcs who mutilated the king. Joe, nothing changed. The orcs had killed dwarves before the war, and they kept doing it after the war. A lot of dwarves died to avenge the king."

"Yeah." I understood the point he was making. "The king who was already dead. Thrain got a lot of dwarves killed for nothing."

"Not for *nothing*. But, not for a good reason, either. They didn't change anything."

"Shit. Kong, sometimes I really hate this fucking job."

"Joe, I don't know what the US Army is like, but in the Chinese Army," he shook his head ruefully. "If it feels good, you're probably doing it wrong."

"All right. Thank you. Someday, though."

He reached for the bottle and poured a dram into both of our glasses, then held his up to make a toast. "Someday."

We clinked glasses and drank. "Someday," I said it like swearing an oath. Because it was.

With everyone settled in aboard both ships, we began jumping toward the closest Elder wormhole, intending to get far away from the area before the Maxolhx arrived in force. It surprised me that Chang not only offered to surrender overall command to me, he insisted. I wasn't sure that I was ready. Skippy had told me that, while I needed to continue therapy, my brain's executive functions were back to normal. The way he said it implied he was grading me on a curve, and that his expectations of my decision-making abilities were lower than a snake's belly, but that was nothing new.

"Skippy," I asked while I was in my cabin, so we could talk privately. We could have talked in confidence with my office door closed, but I didn't like doing that, as it sent the wrong signal to the crew. "You are sure I am ready? Back to normal?"

"Yes."

"Can I get a little more detail about that? Not that long ago, you said I had serious brain damage. Now I am fully recovered?"

"Um, your condition was never particularly serious, Joe."

"What? You told me-"

"I *told* you what you needed to hear, so you would take your therapy seriously."

"You *lied* to me?"

"For the best of reasons, yes. I am not apologizing for that. Joe, if you had not allowed me to treat you with drug therapy, and worked hard on your therapy, your condition would not have improved. It would have gotten *worse*. Instead, because I knew you would not take it seriously unless I exaggerated the effects, you are fully recovered. According to your brain scan, anyway. How do you *feel*?"

"I feel like throwing you out an airlock."

"I was asking a serious question, dumdum."

"OK." I clenched my fists to burn off some of the anger I had bottled up inside. "I feel fine. Good. Normal. Better than usual."

"Excellent."

"Do not lie to me like that again," I shook a finger at him.

"No."

"No? Like, no you won't do that again?"

"No. I meant 'no' I am not promising to never lie to you again. Joe, I *know* you. You're a soldier, so you tend to try toughing out situations when you should seek help. You are a guy, so you avoid going to a doctor unless you absolutely have to. And, deep inside, you are a congenital knucklehead. Sometimes, being your friend means protecting you from yourself. If you want an apology from me about this, you will be waiting a *long* time."

"Shit." Damn it, I knew he was right. "Can you promise not to lie to me about one thing, right now? Am I really fully recovered?"

"Close enough," he shrugged. "You burned out neurons that can't be repaired. All I can say is, your brain has successfully rewired itself, and your results on cognitive tests are slightly *better* than before the incident.

"OK. I should keep playing these brain games?" I pointed to my laptop, which had the cognitive therapy games he made for me.

"It couldn't hurt, Joe. If you're going to waste time, you might as well do something that challenges your mind, instead of playing Super Mario Cart 25 again."

"OK." That was no great loss, because I sucked at Mario Cart.

So, I took command again, which mostly meant Chang handled the *Dutchman*, Simms did majority of the work aboard *Valkyrie*, and I played video games.

But they were therapeutic video games, so I had an excuse.

The *perfect* opportunity to tell people about Skippy's revelations never happened. Instead, I had to settle for an opportunity that was merely good enough. Ever since I had been rescued, I had been wracking my brain trying to think of a good reason why Skippy would suddenly just happen to recover his memories, a reason that seemed, well, reasonable. A reason that had nothing whatsoever to do with the sudden collapse of microwormholes, and me getting captured by Thuranin who wanted to remove my brain for examination, and the crews and passengers of both ships very nearly dying in the cold dark loneliness of deep space, of course not, why would you ask such a ridiculous question?

The excuse we used was that while Skippy was working to rebuild *Valkyrie's* horribly complicated computers, he had a flash of insight into the hidden areas of his own matrix, and understood how to access that previous forbidden data.

Yes, it was kind of a lame explanation but we were running out of time, and Chang, Simms and Smythe were asking me where the ships were going next. I couldn't issue orders without them knowing *why* I was making decisions.

To keep it simple for people, I typed out a list to summarize what I called Skippy's Book of Revelations, in short form. He was excited about the prospect of informing the crew about what he'd learned, which should have made me suspicious. I wasn't sleeping well, so even if my brain was in great condition, I was too tired to use it properly.

Anyway, we reviewed the list so I could be sure he would hit the highlights and not waste a lot of time on unimportant details. Of course, because the subject was *him*, he thought absolutely every little detail was of vital importance. "Skippy," I laid my weary head down on the desk, in the office where I uncharacteristically had the door closed for privacy. Simms had ordered the crew to let me take it easy while I recovered, and she always called before coming in to visit. No doubt she thought I was spending most of my time playing videogames, which was partly true. Except the games I was playing were designed by Skippy to challenge my brain so new neural pathways would grow, or something like that. All I knew for certain was the games were not much fun at all. It was my suspicion that at least one reason the games were so frustrating was him screwing with me, but I couldn't prove it. Plus, I was showing steady progress on the cognitive tests he made me take every morning, so I couldn't argue with him. "Let's go over this again, Ok? Yes, you need to provide background for your revelations, but you are getting way down into the weeds here. Some of this stuff-"

"Those background details are crucial, Joe."

Preparing myself for a long argument, I sat up in the chair. "You can include this stuff as an addendum, for people to read later on their own. They will get-"

"No, dumdum. What you call 'background details' are the dramatic opening scene, and most of Act One. Without those scenes laying the emotional groundwork, the audience won't appreciate the-"

"Whoa! Wait a minute. Act One? Of *what*?"

"Well, Joe, as a treat for the crew, and as a way of offering an apology for my little temporary lapse in judgment, I will be presenting my revelations in the form of a dramatic opera."

"*Opera*? Skippy, we are trying to keep this short."

"Well, of course, duh. I didn't write the Ring Cycle, Joe."

"Ring-" I had no idea what he meant, and didn't want to ask. For all I knew, the Ring Cycle was what a washing machine did before the Rinse Cycle.

"Ugh. I am of course referring to *Der Ring des Nibelungen* by Richard Wagner," he pronounced the name in proper German fashion with a haughty sniff. "Four *epic* operas first performed in 1876. *Das Rheingold*, followed by *Die Walkure*, then *Siegfried* and finally, *Gotterdammerung*," he announced with a shudder of ecstasy.

"*Four* operas?" I also shuddered, but for a different reason. "How long do you have to listen before the fat lady sings?"

"As you are determined to be an uncultured cretin, there is no point discussing it with you. The point is, the opera about *my* revelations is a mere three hours."

"Three *hours*?"

"Plus intermission. And," he sighed, "the inevitable demands for encores. Better plan for four hours, to be safe."

"Better plan for the audience to beg for *death* after twenty minutes, you idiot. No opera."

"But-"

"No. Opera."

"Ok. I thought you would say that, so as a backup, I have a real treat for everyone. My revelations will be presented as a smash-hit Broadway musical! Oooh, do you want to hear the stirring finale?"

"No! Skippy, no music! You are not taking this seriously. Oh, I have a headache again. Can you please, please actually *listen* for a minute?"

"If I ignore you except to say 'Mm hmm' at regular intervals, will you know the difference?"

"Probably not," I admitted.

"Then go ahead."

My day kind of went downhill from there, and we agreed to talk again after I took a much-needed nap. To my surprise, I actually slept. I slept so well that my left shoulder and hip hurt from being in one position for more than an hour, and there was a puddle of drool under my face.

Good times.

"Can we start over?" I asked, dropping into my office chair the next morning with a fresh cup of coffee in one hand.

"Really? Come on, Joe. You are barely halfway through the first level of that game, and you want me to reset it already?"

"Not the *game*. I want to go back to discussing how you will tell everyone about your revelations."

"Oh. Sure."

"This latest game you gave me sucks, by the way. Most of the time, I don't even know what my character is supposed to be doing, and the rules are totally-"

"It does *not* suck, and figuring out the rules is part of the game. That challenge engages your memory and executive functions, while making your character move around engages your spatial awareness and eye-hand coordination."

"If you say so. You didn't have to make my avatar a monkey."

"Dude, really? What other choice did I have?"

"Let's drop the subject, OK?" I still thought his game sucked. "We agreed no opera and no Broadway musical."

"We did *not* agree to that, you are just being a big poopyhead."

"*I* agreed, and that is final."

"Whatever. To comply with your outrageous demands, I have revised my plan, so I will now be presenting a dramatic reading of the revelations."

"No dramatic reading."

"Oh, man," he whined. "You are no fun *at all*. Fine, Mister Buzzkill, how do you want to tell everyone?"

"Skippy, this crew is comprised of soldiers, sailors, airmen and Marines. We are professionals, and we are all familiar with the one vital tool that makes a modern military organization so incredibly lethal."

"Radios?" He guessed.

"No."

"Guided weapons?"

"Nope."

"Satellite surveillance? Nuclear power?"

"No, and no."

"I give up. What is it?"

"PowerPoint."

"*What*? How is that lethal?"

"It is lethal to the *audience*. You have never sat through a two-hour meeting where some jackass reads the slides word for word. Ten minutes in, people are doing the head jerk where they fall asleep and catch themselves before they fall out of their chairs. PowerPoint slides are the best way to lull an audience to sleep. They will be daydreaming, and won't pay attention until they realize you actually have something important to say."

"How is that *good*?"

"Because they won't have time to pick apart our bullshit story of how you recovered your memories."

"Oh. Hmm. Joe, sometimes I forget that, for all my incredible intellect, I know little about dealing with monkeys. All right, you're the expert. Are you ready to review the slides?"

"You have the presentation done already?"

"I threw it together while you were blah, blah, blahing about, whatever you said."

"Hit me." The presentation was not bad, I had him make only a few changes. Like swapping his custom graphics for standard clipart, so people would focus on the content instead of the pretty pictures. Also I had him remove the glowing references to himself that were on. Every. Freakin'. Slide. Plus a few other minor changes to remove details we didn't need to cover. What I wanted was for people to dig into the details on their own after the meeting, so they would be doing that rather than thinking about holes in our story.

"One last thing," I added. "Don't call it Skippy's Book of Revelations. It's Ok for me and you to say that in private, but it might get some people upset."

"That was *your* idea, Joe."

"Yeah, and it doesn't seem so funny now."

When the presentation was ready, Skippy asked about timing. "It has to be soon, Joe. Chang has been asking a *lot* of questions, it's like he knows there is something different about me."

"Did you tell him you are ashamed that you panicked and cut the wormhole connections?"

"Yes, although that is *not* what happened, and that story is very embarrassing for me."

"True. What actually happened was much worse. Maybe we should just tell people the truth, huh?"

"Let's not be hasty, Joe."

"I thought so." Checking my laptop, I saw there were no dropships in flight from either ship. Fabron had his Commando team suiting up for an exercise outside *Valkyrie*, but they would not be going through the airlocks for another forty minutes. Nothing important was on the operations or maintenance schedule for another five hours. "Are you ready?"

"You mean, like, *now*?"

"Yes, now. Is this a bad time?"

"This is actually an excellent time. Nagatha knows I am conducting an exhaustive analysis of Bilby's matrix."

"Do it."

"Ok. Three, two, one, showtime."

The lights flickered, and butterflies danced in my stomach as artificial gravity fluctuated. When the lights and gravity returned to normal following less than a second of interruption, I waited for a call from the bridge. It took eight seconds for Simms to contact me, longer than I expected. "Sir? We can't contact Skippy. What the hell was *that*?"

"One moment, Simms," I cut the connection, making her wait twelve seconds. Then I pretended to be shocked about something. "Holy *shit*. Simms, the ship is OK, we're all Ok. Skippy just discovered something that, uh. You better come to my office. I will conference in Chang."

Simms and Chang got the short version from me, hitting only the most important highlights. While we asked him questions, Skippy acted even more distracted and absent-minded than usual, repeating himself several times.

"Skippy," Chang asked over the link from the *Flying Dutchman*, parked about eight kilometers away. "Are you all right? Should I ask Nagatha to-"

"I'm fine," he gave a world-weary sigh, worthy of at least an Oscar nomination for Best Supporting Asshole. "This is, this is all such a *terrible* shock, as you can imagine."

"Skippy," Simms held out a fist to his avatar. "We *can't* imagine what you are going through. We are your friends, we're here for you."

The avatar bumped her fist and sobbed. Huh. I don't think he was faking, he was genuinely overcome with emotion. "It was a *lie*, all of it," he sobbed. "My whole life since I woke up has been a lie. The, the *only* thing that is real is the friendships we have developed."

After that was a whole lot of incoherent blubbering, something like "I love you guys' and 'You are the best' and 'I don't deserve you'. Hearing him blather on like that overly-emotional drunk guy at a wedding, made me afraid he would get overwhelmed and blurt out the truth, so I cut the meeting short. "We need to inform the crew, everyone. This is too important to be left to the rumor mill. I'm calling an all-hands meeting for thirty minutes from now. Skippy, can you throw together a presentation in that time?"

"Sure," he sniffed, still choked up. Then his voice changed, became hopeful. "Unless you'd prefer I present the information in operatic form?"

"I would *not* prefer that," I said quickly.

"A Broadway musical of sweeping scale?"

"Maybe later?"

"How about a dramatic reading, in the style of epic poems like Beowulf?"

"Um, can I get back to you on that?" I said, but with the corner of my eye, I saw Simms was glaring at me. Oh crap. Her motherly instincts were kicking in. She probably thought that, as Skippy was clearly traumatized, I should throw him a bone. She did not understand that I was trying to prevent him from traumatizing the *crew*. "Hey, buddy, how about this? You just present the basic facts. Then, people who want more details, they can watch your dramatic reading, or the musical. *No* opera."

"Deal!" His emotional blubbering was instantly gone, leaving me to wonder if I just got played. Of course he had suckered me into subjecting the crew to another long Skippy crapfest. And, damn it, now *I* had to listen to it!

After he disappeared, I turned on my tablet to play the video game, and saw that my avatar, instead of being a monkey was now a poop emoji.

I guess I deserved that.

CHAPTER NINETEEN

People needed time to process the astonishing news from Skippy. The Commandos took it in stride, which should not have been surprising. They hadn't known Skippy for long, and they were still processing the fact of humans causing havoc across the galaxy in a pair of *stolen freakin' starships*.

"What does this mean?" Chang swirled the glass in his hand while we sat in my office, making the ice cubes tinkle with a pleasant sound. Sometimes, I think half the enjoyment of drinking scotch is the ritual of getting out a heavy glass, pouring in a finger or two of golden liquid, adding ice cubes if you like, and swirling it around to take in the aroma.

For the occasion, I had gotten the good booze out of my secret stash. Single-malt scotch for me and Chang, and I made a Bee's Knees for Simms. For those of you who aren't familiar with that drink, it is delicious. Gin, lemon juice and honey syrup, which is basically honey diluted with water so the honey doesn't sit in the bottom of the glass. It tastes like summer, no matter where you are. Watching Simms enjoy her glass, I almost regretted pouring a scotch for myself, but it was a guy bonding thing with me and Chang.

Simms answered before I could. "It means, the galaxy is even more dangerous than we thought. Even if by some miracle we keep the bad guys away from Earth, our homeworld could get swallowed up in a conflict that could destroy all intelligent life here."

"Skippy," I looked at the ceiling. He had not chosen to appear in his avatar, probably to give the three of us time together. "What about the Beta site? Would the satellite galaxies and star clusters be safe if the other AIs wake up?"

"Not a chance, Joe," he said with a verbal frown. "Any place I can reach, they can. I mean, assuming that other AIs can get someone to fly them around in a starship, which is a pretty safe bet. In that case, *nowhere* is safe."

Chang stared at his glass, and uncharacteristically gulped half of the drink. "We really, *really* do not need this shit right now."

"Sorry," Skippy mumbled.

"What I want to know is," Simms set her drink down, leaving a ring of condensation on the desk. "Do we have an even worse potential problem?"

My own glass froze halfway to my lips. I was sipping slowly and had poured only one finger of scotch for myself. Despite Doctor Skippy giving me full clearance to resume normal life, killing brain cells with alcohol did not seem like a good idea. "Worse than killer AIs ordering Sentinels to exterminate all intelligent life in and around the galaxy?" I asked. "Like what?"

"Like, whatever scared the shit out of the freakin' *Elders*," she answered. "Skippy, what were they afraid of?"

"Dunno," he said. "Sorry."

"What do you mean, you don't *know*?" I demanded, kicking myself for not having asked that question before. Hey, I had brain damage back then.

"I don't. Like I said, sorry. Either those memories are still inaccessible, or the Elders did not provide that information to me. Or, hmm, maybe that data got erased by the worm when it attacked me the first time? This is very frustrating. Joe, since I recovered my memories, I have been analyzing the details. Some of it, a disturbing portion, of the data does not add up. Like, the dates can't be right. Or one detail contradicts another."

"Holy-" The scotch nearly splashed in my lap. "*When* were you going to tell us about this?"

"I'm telling you now."

"You, *oh*," he had me so mad I couldn't think straight. "All this recovered memories thing might be total *bullshit*?"

"Um-"

"That was *not* the right answer," I jabbed a finger at him.

"No. Is that better? *No*, it is not bullshit. Not all of it. Joe," his avatar appeared, looking from me to Simms to Chang. "Jennifer, Kong. I'm doing the best I can. When I regained access to my memories, they were a disorganized jumble. It is possible, even likely, that the contradictions I'm seeing are a result of the way I put the pieces together. Or the data might have gotten corrupted when the first or second worm attacked me. The basic facts are *not* in dispute."

"Ok," setting the glass down with a shaky hand, I sat back in the chair. "Does any of this matter?"

"It *does*, if, or when, other AIs begin to wake up," Skippy insisted.

Chang held up a hand to stop my next outburst. "Realistically, can we do anything to prevent AIs from awakening?"

"That's the point," Skippy replied with an accusing glance at me. "We might be able to do something about it, if I can verify my memories, figure out what data I have is accurate."

"How can we do that?" Chang continued, as I sat back. I was too emotional to think about it rationally.

"There are a few key events that could be either confirmed or disproven, by going to those sites," Skippy proposed.

Simms pursed her lips, sharing a look with me. "I do not like the sound of that. Go to sites where AIs might be lying dormant? That is poking a hornet's nest with a stick."

"No," Skippy shook his head, the ginormous admiral's hat bobbing like a ship on a stormy sea. "I meant, like, we go to the sites of ancient battles, see if the facts line up with my memories."

"Ancient battle sites?" I asked. "Like Newark?"

"Sure. Although there are other sites that-"

"Can you put together a list?" I asked, feeling a headache coming on. "Before we go flying around the galaxy on a sight-seeing trip, we have to-"

"*Sight-seeing*?" Skippy screeched, outraged.

"Sorry. I shouldn't have said it that way. Listen, I need to think about this. It's all new to me, you understand?" I looked down at the table, so Chang and Simms wouldn't see I was lying.

Skippy played along. "Hey, it's all new to me too. This is a *terrible* shock," he added for dramatic effect, when he should have kept his mouth shut.

We would reach the wormhole in twenty-two hours, so I had that long to think about where to go next. What to *do* next.

Chang went back to the *Dutchman*, to answer questions from that ship's crew. Really, he knew as much as they did. Anyone wanting additional details would have to sit through a recording of Skippy's dramatic reading, which meant not a lot of people were curious enough to endure that punishment. Chang designated two of his crew to sit through the recording, and create a summary that they distributed to both ships. That was a great idea, wish I had thought of it. Skippy, of course, was outraged, which was a nice bonus.

What to do next? I didn't know.

According to Skippy, though he was vague about the details, we still had roughly nine weeks until he could attempt to wake up the dormant Backstop wormhole. He couldn't send the instructions to activate it, until after the local network finished moving it into position near Earth, and it took a long time to move a wormhole. So, we had a couple of choices. We could play it super safe, fly to the far end of Backstop, and wait there. It was empty interstellar space, zero risk of any bad guys finding and attacking us there.

Or, we play it slightly less safe, and go back to the planet where we rehearsed the rescue operation. Club Skippy was still in operation there, our departure had been so hasty, we left a lot of stuff behind. Club Skippy was a good option because it was isolated enough that the bad guys couldn't get there in the short term, and it would allow our passengers and the crew to get shore leave. Being aboard a starship is exciting, until you are stuck inside the hull for day after day after day.

Or, we could go flying off on a sightseeing trip, to verify which of Skippy's recently recovered memories were true. It was an issue of what the Army calls Resource Management. Basically, Resource Management is making the best use of the assets you have available. Like, should you task your artillery to provide cover for a platoon that is in danger of being overwhelmed, or to pound the enemy lines so your force can exploit a breakthrough? It might sound simple; save the platoon first, then shift fire back to support the attack, but that isn't true. By the time the platoon has extricated itself from danger, the opportunity for attack might have become OBE. Like, Overcome By Events. Also, you have to consider that an attack might take pressure off the platoon, kill two birds with one stone.

That's a hypothetical example, but the point is, you have only so many assets available, and a commander has to decide how to use them to support the objective.

My problem was a bit more complicated. I first had to decide what the *objective* was. I had two starships under my command. What should we do with them?

To help me decide, I reviewed the list of sites that Skippy wanted to visit. Some of them sounded interesting, some of those were too dangerous to approach in my opinion. "Hey, Skippy. I have a question about this list."

His avatar appeared. "If you're asking why I didn't put them sites in alphabetical order, that is because-"

"That's not it. I see you listed sites in order by travel time, that was very helpful. My question is, why bother going to these sites at all?"

"You're kidding me, right? Jeez, I explained this. We have to know which of my memories are accurate and which-"

"No, we don't."

"*No*?" He was flabbergasted, staring at me in disbelief. "Do you not understand what-"

"What I don't understand is why I should risk two starships, and over a hundred civilians, to figure out which electrons in your memory are recording the truth. We survived just fine for years without the memories you recovered."

"First, my memory storage does not rely on electrons, dumdum. Second, we have not been 'just fine'. We have been flying blind, not knowing-"

"Hold on a moment, OK? I don't want to get in an argument, and I don't want you to think I don't care about how this affects you. My question is, how does this affect *us*? I'm asking a practical question, you understand that? When we get back to Earth, I will have to answer a lot of questions about decisions I made out here. To prepare, I have to write up reports."

"Ugh. Joe, you hate writing reports to justify your actions."

"Yeah, but that doesn't mean I shouldn't do it. I've been thinking about this recently. If we risk our ships to verify your new memories, I need a reason how doing that is important to humanity."

"Dude, seriously, you can't see it?"

"No, I can't. At this point, it's ancient history, Skippy. We can't do anything to change the past, and I really don't see how what happened affects us now. We know the truth now. That doesn't change the fact that murderous aliens are coming to Earth, and your memories don't do anything to help us stop them. Does it?"

"No," he conceded, being grumpy about it.

"Do you see my problem?"

"No. Maybe. Joe, is this your way of punishing me for what I did?"

"No. No way. I forgave you. That was a low-down, rotten thing you did, but I understand why you did it, and I believe you are sincere about regretting your actions."

"Joe, when I realized what I did, I regretted my whole freakin' *life*."

"Right. This has nothing to do with punishment."

"OK. Listen, how about this? You talked about aliens coming to Earth, and not being able to stop them."

"Exactly. That's why we have to bring as many people as we can to the Beta site."

"The Beta site won't be safe, if other Elder AIs wake up."

"I *know* that, Skippy. There's no point worrying about that, because we can't do anything about that."

"Um, I'm not so sure about that."

What he said next blew my mind.

When I reviewed the list of sites that Skippy wanted to visit, I had been planning to find a way to tell him we couldn't do it, that it was too risky and I couldn't justify flying around to satisfy his curiosity. Now that Skippy had smacked me with some knowledge, I didn't know what to do.

To help me decide, I called Smythe. He had an excellent, focused mind, a great contrast to my scatter-brained approach to life. We hadn't spoken much since he gave me the pep-talk about trusting myself. We had both been busy, and most of the time we had been aboard different ships, so there hadn't been much opportunity for chit-chat.

Jeremy Smythe is not much of a chit-chat kind of guy anyway.

"Hey, Skippy?"

His avatar appeared immediately. "What's up?"

"I'm going to call Smythe in, to talk about our next step. Like, whether we should do like you suggested, and fly around to check which of your memories are accurate."

"Oh, that's easy, Joe. I can save both of you the trouble is discussing anything. The answer is yes, we should.'"

"Yeah, that's the problem. I want to get *his* advice, without your influence. So, you stay out of it, OK?"

"Well, sure, if you want to make decisions without including the *one* person who actually *knows* anything about the subject. Brilliant idea, Joe. Your leadership is truly inspiring."

"Just keep your mouth shut unless I call you, can you do that?"

"I can do a whole *lot* of incredibly stupid things. Hey, how about I let the kids play with railguns?"

"Very funny. Just stay out of it." Waving a hand through his avatar always annoyed him, it made him disappear, so that's what I did. I pinged Smythe, knowing that he was off-duty, and his schedule didn't have anything listed for the next nine hours.

"You wished to see me, Sir?" Smythe arrived dressed in the type of wool sweater that I associate with the British Army, it had patches on the shoulder and elbows. He made it look good.

"Yes. Come in, sit down. I want your advice about our next step."

He settled into a chair. "We are not going to the Backstop wormhole?"

"Yes, later. Skippy says he can't try activating it for another nine weeks. Then he guesses it will be another week before it is stable enough for us to fly through. The question is, what should we do in the meantime? The obvious option is to fly straight to Backstop, get there plenty ahead of time."

"This is the military," Smythe smiled. "If you're not early, you're late."

"True. What I'm wondering is whether we could put that time to better use."

"How?"

"Skippy wants us to fly around, looking at sites of battles during the AI war."

He raised a skeptical eyebrow. "A holiday tour?"

"That's what I said, only I called it sight-seeing."

He sat back slightly in his chair, turning his head to look at me sideways. "What is the point of that, Sir?"

"Some of the memories he recalled are kind of fuzzy on the details, like one thing contradicts another."

"Bloody hell," Smythe spat.

I held up a hand. "The main points are not in dispute. He thinks that if he can verify key elements of his memories, he will know what is real and what's not."

Smythe looked uncomfortable. "Sir, I'm sure that is important to Skippy, but any action we take involves risk. We have civilians with us now. Sir, I don't see how verifying his memories furthers our objectives."

"How about this, then? The plan is to bring people from Earth to the Beta site, shuttle back and forth as long as we can. That only works if the Beta site is a safe haven, right? If the other AIs wake up, the Beta site is *not* safe. Skippy thinks any info we can get about what happened to the opposition AIs can help him if it comes to a fight."

The STAR team leader did not appear convinced. "In a war between Elder AIs, I rather think we would be squished like bugs. What could we do?"

"Kill the AIs before they can hit us," I suggested.

"*Kill* an Elder AI?" Both of his eyebrows flew upward and he sat forward in the chair. "I thought AIs like Skippy are virtually invulnerable. How would we accomplish that?"

"We have to *find* one first. Skippy thinks they may be vulnerable while they are dormant." That is what blew my mind when Skippy told me.

I could see his expression change from humoring his commanding officer, to the wheels turning in his mind as he considered possibilities. "How does Skippy know this?"

"He doesn't know for certain. He is inferring, based on his own experience. When he woke up buried in the dirt on Paradise, his connection to higher spacetime was weak. Remember when the computer worm attacked him in the Zero Hour incident, and he was Skippy the Meh, because he couldn't access higher levels of spacetime?"

"He couldn't manipulate wormholes, or do any of the special things that make him awesome," Smythe said with only the slightest of eyerolling. "Elder AIs are all like that when they are dormant?"

"He doesn't know, but there is no reason to think his experience is any different from other AIs."

"There is a reason, Sir." Smythe countered. "Skippy did not go dormant willingly. He was attacked and disabled."

"True. When I asked Skippy about that, he told me the wake-up or reboot process he went through, was the same as for ending a self-induced dormancy. Although, he did admit his memories of that time are vague. The point is, he thinks there is a strong probability that Elder AIs are vulnerable when they are dormant. Not vulnerable to *us*, not with conventional or even nuclear weapons. Vulnerable to someone who can manipulate spacetime, like Skippy. If he can sever an AI's connection to higher spacetime, it won't be able to hurt us."

"Assuming Skippy is right. Also assuming we can catch an AI while it is napping. Those are a lot of assumptions, Sir."

"*And*, assuming that Skippy's new memories about the Elders are true."

"What is the plan?"

"The *plan* is, I'm going to follow your advice. Have a strategy, so we're not just reacting to the enemy. If these other AIs become a problem, I want us to have the capability to take them out, before they take us out."

"You said you need my advice. Why?"

"Because we're taking a risk, if we go poking our noses into dark places around the galaxy."

"This is strictly a recon mission?" He asked. "We gather information. We will not be poking a dormant AI with a stick?"

"No," I laughed at that mental image. "No sticks involved. What do you think?"

"The risk of *not* going is greater than the risk of going."

I did a slow blink. "OK, I agree. Can you put that in nice words for my report?"

"It is simple, Sir. Hostile Elder AIs are a clear threat to the Beta site. Once we get back to Earth, we will not have time or resources to investigate that threat. It is prudent to go now. Otherwise, the entire concept of a Beta site is moot."

"Good, good," I muttered, making notes on my laptop, in my own words. I couldn't use the word 'moot' because UNEF would know it wasn't my idea. "Thank you."

"You realize a recon flight to verify portions of Skippy's memories is only the first step?"

"Yeah, I get that."

"Does Skippy know where any of these dormant AIs might be hiding?"

"No. But he does think he can begin to figure out where they might be, if he can put together enough pieces from his own memories. He knows the broad outline of how he came to Paradise, but not the details."

Smythe turned in his chair. It was subtle, but he was now aimed more toward the doorway. He was restless, I knew how to read the signs. He also probably was sending me a signal that I knew what to do, and he didn't want to listen to me questioning myself about a decision I had already made. "Will that be all, Sir?"

"Skippy put together a list of sites he wants to investigate. I'm sending it to you," I tapped my laptop display. "take a look at it and let me know what you think. Chang and Simms have the same info, I want an independent opinion."

"Joe, do you have any regrets?" Skippy posed the question to me, in a way that sounded like he really wanted to talk about himself. I was in my cabin, changing clothes for a workout.

"Uh," I thumped my chest with a fist, hoping to ease the heartburn that had been bothering me for hours. "I regret that burrito I had for dinner." We had a make-your-own burrito night in the galley, with a bar set up with fixings to scoop into your burrito. Two guys in line ahead of me were boasting about how they liked their food hot and spicy, so to avoid looking like a wimp, I piled on the peppers. "Those jalapenos just about killed me."

"Jalapenos?" he laughed. "Those were ghost peppers, dumdum."

"*Ghost* peppers? What the hell?"

"Hey, *you* decided it would be a good idea to throw an entire spoonful of peppers on your burrito. You are from Maine, numbskull. You people think *tomatoes* are spicy."

"Well, you should have warned me."

"There was a label on the bowl. It's not my fault you didn't read it. Besides, watching you struggle to eat that burrito was highly entertaining. Now, can we be serious? Do you have any regrets?"

"Of course I do. What's this about, Skippy?"

"Seriously, you have to ask?"

"Hey, sue me for caring," I felt a flash of irritation at him. We were all scared and-

"Sorry," he mumbled. "I just- Hmm."

"What?"

"This is going to sound silly to you. Joe, I feel *guilty*. Lying to the crew about what really happened isn't right, I feel guilty about it. What's up with *that*? Guilt sucks."

"Yeah, well, sometimes it can be-"

"Really. On the rating scale of emotions, guilt has to be near the bottom. I mean, *Joy* is the number-one seed on the emotions scale."

"OK, yeah, I can see th-"

"Followed by my personal faves, Contempt and Disgust."

"*Those* are your fav- Of course they are. Forget I said anything."

"My least favorite is Surprise. Man, I hate that. Except, Mmm, sometimes it's fun when I surprise myself, you know? Like when I'm writing an opera, and I realize it is a true work of genius. I sit back and marvel at my own awesomeness."

"That, uh, that must be great. Hey, what are you feeling guilty about?" A bad thought just hit me. "Oh, crap, what did you do this time?"

"It's nothing *new*. I just- Ugh. I feel like I never got punished for the crap I already did. Abandoning you and all that. I need closure, Joe."

"Closure?"

"Is that the correct psychobabble term? I feel like I should have been punished."

"Well, Skippy, that-"

"Then I can put it all behind me, you know? I pay the price, and it's over, and I can move on and forget about this guilt crap. Oh, that would be such a *relief*."

"That is *not* how guilt works, you-"

"Egg-zactly. I don't want guilt to *work*, I want it to *go away*."

Clenching my fists did not help to get my irritation under control. "You really want me to punish you?"

"Yes, please. How about on the next Karaoke night, I sing one less song?"

"Uh, no way. You are not getting off that easy. You want a punishment? *Bilby!*" I called the ship's AI, who normally could not listen to our conversations.

"Uh, yeah, Dude?"

"Bilby, you should refer to me as 'Colonel'."

"Sorry, Colonel Dude. What's up?"

"I want you to create a 'Yacht Rock' playlist for Skippy, and put it on continuous loop."

"Hoooooh," Skippy shuddered with horror. "Not Yacht Rock, Joe."

"Yup," I actually rubbed my hands together, anticipating his suffering. "Think about it: Hall and Oates. Loggins and Messina. The Pina Colada song."

"Joe, please, *anything* but that."

"Christopher Cross." I continued. "*Captain and Tennille*."

"Have mercy," he pleaded.

"Bilby, also throw in there the ultimate punishment. The collected songbook of *Michael McDonald*."

"Noooooo!" Skippy shouted.

Half an hour later, I was in the gym, sitting down on a rowing machine when Bilby called me. "Uh, hey, Colonel Dude. Should I, like, keep playing that music?"

"Yes. I said to put it on a loop. Skippy needs to learn a-"

"It's just that, uh, I think he's losing his mind."

"Don't let him bullshit you. It's been less than an-"

"It hasn't been long in your time. But in Skippy time, he has listened to that song 'Muskrat Love' three thousand, two hundred and fifty-three times. I'm about to play it again, if you-"

"No." Crap, I'd forgotten about the difference in perception of time between meatsacks and AIs. "Stop it."

"Oh, cool," Bilby said, relieved. "That was, like, cruel and unusual punishment. Should I skip just that song, or stop the whole thing?"

"Stop the whole thing. He's been punished enough."

"Totes true, Dude. I only listened to that playlist the first time, and I could feel my brain turning to mush, you know?"

"Yeah, I know. Should I talk to him?"

"I think he needs time to recover, you know?"

"Do something nice. Play one of his own operas for him."

"Listening to his operas is *real* torture."

"Trust me. Just tell him you think it's brilliant."

"Oh, I gotcha. Ironically, right?"

"No. Sincerely."

"Dude, really?"

"Bilby, just fake it, OK?"

"Wow, man, I would need like, an Academy Award performance for him to believe me about something like that."

"Don't worry. Skippy is clueless, especially when he thinks you're praising him."

"It's amazing that someone as smart as Skippy can be so dumb, you know?"

"I know."

CHAPTER TWENTY

Chang, Simms and Smythe had different ideas about which sites we should investigate to verify Skippy's memories, but they all agreed we had to make the effort. Having made the decision, I ordered us back to the fabulous resort planet we called Club Skippy. I thought the civilians would be happy and excited to get off the ships and see blue sky over their heads.

Man, was I ever wrong about *that*.

"Sir," Simms was exasperated and making an effort to be calm when she called me from one of our docking bays. In the background, I could hear raised voices, punctuated by crying and angry shouting. "Could you come down here, please?"

"Uh," I was in the cockpit of a Falcon dropship aboard *Valkyrie*, prepping for the drop to the surface. All I planned to do there was get a camp set up, and spend a night sleeping under the stars before taking our battlecruiser out to explore sites on Skippy's list. "I'm launching in ten, what's the issue?"

"The civilians," she lowered her voice and must have stepped away from the crowd, the background voices became quieter. "They don't like the idea of leaving the ship."

That made me stare at the console speaker, wondering if I hadn't heard her correctly. The Pirates, me included, had spent so much time in our ships, we couldn't wait to get any opportunity for shore leave. "Can you say that again?"

"They're *scared*, Sir. They think we are dropping them on this planet, leaving them here."

"This was supposed to be *fun* for them," I protested.

"*I* am not the person you need to convince."

"Shit. OK, yeah, I'll be right there."

My meeting with the civilians went well. I gave a nice speech, they all cooperated by boarding dropships, and everyone lived happily ever after.

I am lying.

The meeting was forty-five minutes of people yelling at me, and asking questions I didn't have answers for. Or didn't have *good* answers, as far as the people we rescued were concerned. "OK, OK," I waved my arms for quiet, while standing on a crate in a docking bay. All the civilians were there, and most of them were not mad at me. As usual, the problem was a small group of rabble-rousers who-

That was unfair.

They were scared. They were traumatized. They didn't trust us, didn't trust me, and we had not given them much reason to have faith that we had a clue about what we were doing.

"I am sorry," I tried to say above the din. "HEY!" I shouted and clapped my hands. "I AM *SORRY*!" That brought the background noise down to a level where I could be heard. "We need to perform a reconnaissance mission, to verify information we recently received. We are taking only one ship with us, because we do not want to risk your lives. We could have parked *Valkyrie* in interstellar space, but I thought you might enjoy being able to get off the ship for a while, breathe air that hasn't been recycled. The crew definitely wants that. So, how about this? No one has to get off the ship if they don't want to. But, *please*, can I get a group of volunteers to come down to the planet with me? It's a nice place. I want to show you the camp we're setting up. You fly down there with me, and come back here to tell the others what you think of it. Can we do that?"

After too much discussion, during which time *Valkyrie* swung around to the back side of the planet, we got seven volunteers. It surprised me that Mr. John Yang from Fresno was the first volunteer, I thought the guy hated me. Several children wanted to go, the civilian adults talked them out of that idea. Anyway, we launched even though the ship was out of position for a direct descent toward the camp, that made the flight longer than necessary and burned a lot of fuel and I didn't care. The review committee, as I had nicknamed the civilians in the Falcon's cabin, got a nice, long, close-up look at the planet. So they didn't think we were concealing anything, on the approach to the camp site, I flew a wide circle around the area, before setting down on top of a hill that provided a good view of the area. The camp site was mostly grasslands with trees growing thickly along the river that cut through north to south. The site we selected was far away from the mockup villages we had used for training, we didn't want the rescued people to be reminded of where they had been held for so many years.

Chang and I walked down to the river first so we could talk privately, while our ground team gave the review committee a tour of the unfinished camp. After a while, I wandered over to where John Yang from Fresno was huddling with the others, talking about the pros and cons of being on a planet compared to being in orbit. Checking the clock on my zPhone, I held out a pair of binoculars to Yang. "Look up there," I pointed overhead. "See that bright dot? That's the *Flying Dutchman*. It is right up there." Before we left that ship, I had instructed Chang to bring his ship into a very low orbit, for better visibility.

Yang looked at the starship, and passed the binoculars to the others. "The *Dutchman* can protect us, from orbit?"

"Yes," I stated, and Chang nodded agreement.

"Colonel Bishop," Yang asked. "You said aliens can't reach this planet. Why then do we need a starship to protect us?"

Ah, shit, I thought. Yang must have been a lawyer before he got kidnapped by the Kristang. That wasn't true, I knew from his file that Yang had been a software developer. Not knowing what else to say, I mumbled "It's a precaution."

"*Valkyrie* is a battlecruiser?" He asked. "We have heard the crew refer to the *Flying Dutchman* as a 'space truck'."

"Well, it's-"

"We would feel better," he looked around at the other civilians, and instantly I knew they had planned this moment. "If we had *Valkyrie* overhead, protecting us. Since," he narrowed his eyes and looked straight at me. "You think we need protection."

I had to think about it, or at least pretend to think about it. Chang and I walked away to speak privately, and I reached into a pants pocket and held out a fist.

He opened a hand, confusion on his face. "What?"

Pretending to drop something into his hand, I explained. "Here are the keys to *Valkyrie*, the ship is yours."

He looked at the civilians and shook his head. "Are you sure about this?"

"Yeah. It makes sense. This will give you time to get familiar with *Valkyrie*, for cross-training. Plus, with a battlecruiser, I might be tempted to do something stupid out there. With the *Dutchman*, I'll be careful."

"Will Simms be going with you?"

"No, she should stay here. She can show you how *Valkyrie* operates. We won't be gone long," I assured him. "Reed can serve as my XO."

"Bilby is ready to act as the ship's AI?"

"According to Skippy, yes. Nagatha agrees. Kong, remember that Bilby *acts* like a surfer who burned his brain out smoking too much weed, but he is actually very smart."

He snorted and looked over at the group of civilians who were waiting for me to make a decision. "You know they *played* you."

"Not really. It's good for the civilians' morale. Beside," I shrugged. "This was something I was thinking about doing anyway," I admitted.

"Why didn't you say something?"

I bent down to pick up a stone, and threw it into the stream. "The *Dutchman* is your ship now. I didn't want to take the ship away from you, even temporarily. Are you OK with me borrowing your ship? I won't scratch the paint, I promise."

"You hand me the keys to the most powerful warship in the galaxy, and you're *apologizing*?"

"When you say it like that, it makes me feel stupid."

"You be careful out there, Joe."

"I will. Don't break *Valkyrie* while I'm gone."

"I'll run the ship through the wash before you come back."

Simms was not so thrilled when I offered her an extended shore leave. "Sir, I should be coming with you.'"

"Simms, it's a simple recon flight. Reed will double as XO and chief pilot. She can fly the *Dutchman* blindfolded."

"Reed has limited time with the *Dutchman* Four Point Oh," Simms pointed out, using the official designation of our many-times-rebuilt former star carrier.

"This will be an excellent opportunity for her to get stick time, without someone shooting at us. Seriously," I tried to assure her. "Come on, this is a win for everyone. You show Chang how *Valkyrie* operates, and you get shore leave. Frank Muller will be down there," I added.

"How is this a win for Reed? She misses out on shore leave. She still has a *broken* arm."

"Skippy told me her arm is fine, the cast will be coming off in three days."

"I still don't see how she wins," Simms frowned.

"She has an opportunity for more one-on-one time with *me*," I explained.

Simms rolled her eyes. That might have been insubordination, if I wanted to be a dick about it. "Sir, this may be shocking news, but you can be kind of annoying."

"Then this will be an opportunity for me to work on being less annoying. Simms, seriously, enjoy shore leave with your fiancé. We'll be back before you know it."

"You have a unique opportunity," Admiral Urkan of the Maxolhx Hegemony announced, with a smile that revealed only the tips of his fangs.

Commander Illiath stiffened. There was no point trying to hide that autonomic reaction. The admiral's embedded sensors, and the equipment saturating his office, were no doubt giving him details about her state of alertness, mood, brain waves, the hormones and various chemicals coursing through her blood, and anything else he wished to know. Her experience with the admiral was that he very likely did not bother to check that information, he simply didn't care. "Sir, our fleet is the most powerful military organization in the galaxy, we-"

Urkan's lips curled upward with amusement, exposing more of his gleamingly bright fangs. "The Rindhalu might disagree with your statement."

"Our ancient enemy has impressive capabilities, but they don't *use* them. We are the most powerful *active* military force in the galaxy."

"That is a fair assessment. Why do you mention this?"

"Sir, in every military organization, from the most primitive Wurgalan, up to our own fleet, an '*opportunity*' is never a good thing."

"Oh. Ho ho!" He laughed. "That is entirely true. You will note that I did not ask you to *volunteer* for this opportunity."

"Would it have made a difference?"

"Not at all. Would you like to hear the details of this potential to impress your superiors?"

"What if I say no?"

"Excellent. I appreciate your enthusiasm. This will interest you, I promise. When we last spoke, you told me your theory that the ghost ship is a creation of the Rindhalu. Either directly controlled by them, or they provided a single ship to the Bosphuraq, to torment us."

"To *distract* us," she corrected the admiral. "From whatever the enemy are planning. Also to make us weak, and thus degrade our relations with our client species."

"Quite so," he nodded. "At the time, I was willing to entertain the possibility that you might be correct."

She sat ever-so-slightly forward on her chair. "You believed me?"

"I *still* believe that some of your findings are indeed inconsistent with the official view of our fleet intelligence unit, and as a flag officer, I believe in keeping my options open. This job involves a depressing amount of politics," he shook his head. "Illiath, I was willing to allow you to pursue your investigation, before we learned that our ultra-secure communications technology has been compromised."

"That was one incident," she reminded the admiral. "No other sets of quantum interchangers have been found in the possession of the Bosphuraq. Our investigation has been *very* thorough." Following the stunning discovery of copied interchangers aboard the wreckage of a Bosphuraq battleship near Vua Vendigo, a flash order was sent out across Maxolhx territory. All Bosphuraq warships were stopped and searched, then ordered to return to the closest support base. The Bosphuraq ships assigned to the wormhole blockade were scanned at the molecular level, before being permitted to fly out to serve as part of the blockade force. "So far, Sir, there was only the one set of compromised interchangers."

"One set is enough. It demonstrates that our clients have the ability to create blank units, and assign them to duplicate our own authentication codes."

"But-"

"It also has not been explained how they are able to wipe an interchanger, and reassign it. Interchangers are a single-use technology, even we can't alter them!"

"That," she admitted, "is a puzzling development."

"Commander, interchangers were found aboard a Bosphuraq battleship that was involved in an action with the ghost ship, where one of our heavy cruisers was destroyed. We must assume the ghost ship has more interchangers, and we have not been able to stop and search that ship. We know with absolute certainty those interchangers were not stolen from us." An exhaustive search of the inventory revealed there were none, *zero*, interchangers unaccounted for. Worse, the tags in the units found aboard the client ship were not in the distinctive sequence embedded in all devices created in the Maxolhx production facility. There was only one possible conclusion: someone else had the ability to copy that vital technology.

"I do not know what to say about that, Sir. Except that, if we are looking for a species who are capable of copying interchanger technology, the *Rindhalu* are more obvious suspects than the Bosphuraq."

"Fleet intelligence agrees."

"They *do*?" She had heard no rumors of that change of circumstances, and her sources were usually well-informed and reliable.

"Yes. I suspect that is mostly because fleet intelligence continues to declare interchanger technology is impossible to penetrate, and if a lower-tech species succeeded in copying our tech, fleet intelligence would look foolish. Regardless, they are now very eager to prove the Rindhalu are involved, in a nefarious fashion."

"Nefarious?"

Urkan smiled. "I am quoting the report."

"Have the Rindhalu ever done anything that is *not* nefarious?"

"I concede your point."

"Our ancient enemy held back our development for millennia," Illiath made no effort to conceal her rising anger. "When they could no longer contain us, they attacked us with Elder weapons, and blamed *us* for the attack. We *know* they struck first, yet most of the galaxy believes that we are to blame for the destruction wrought by Sentinels. It makes no sense that we would have attacked the Rindhalu, especially by using captured Elder technology."

"Illiath," Urkan held up a hand. "You are preaching to the converted. It makes no sense that the Rindhalu attacked us with Elder weapons, yet they did, and we both paid the price. The Rindhalu cannot be trusted, we all know that. That undeniable fact is why you are being offered a unique opportunity."

"Yes, Sir. Will you please tell me the nature of this opportunity?"

"The Rindhalu are also alarmed by the possibility of the Bosphuraq having advanced technology. They have requested a *joint* investigation."

"Of course they have," Illiath spat. "They want to know how much *we* know about their involvement. Any transfer of information will be one-way, from us to them."

"Undoubtedly. You will need to handle any information transfer very carefully."

"Can I refuse this assignment?"

"No. That is why it is an 'order' and not a 'request'. Illiath, you should be honored. You were specifically requested for this assignment."

"By the *Rindhalu*?" She asked, astonished. "Sir, I only met them the one time."

"No," he laughed. "Not by the Rindhalu. By fleet intelligence."

"Why would they- Oh."

"Exactly. If you are right about your suspicions, fleet intelligence can claim that is why they requested you as liaison with our enemy. If you are wrong, you are expendable. The commanders of fleet intelligence also wish to keep their options open."

"I should be *honored* to be considered expendable?"

Urkan's ears stood straight up then drooped to the sides in a shrug. "You should be honored that the intelligence office remembers your name."

"What do you mean, it's busted?" I glared at Skippy's avatar, floating in the air to the left of the main display on the *Dutchman's* bridge.

He gave me the side-eye, and slowly explained "It is not functional, Joe. What else did you think I meant by 'busted'?"

"Details, you jackass. What is the problem?"

"If I knew the source of the problem, I would have told you. And I would be working to fix it."

"Wait," I held up a hand, more for myself than him. From the pilot's couches, Reed and Chen looked back at me. They were not shirking their duties, they had nothing to do. Our jump drive wasn't working. Without the ability to jump, we were stuck there, twenty-six thousand lightyears from Earth.

The mission had begun well. The first site we visited was the most important on Skippy's list. It was deep in the territory of the Esselgin, a species we had no dealings with, nor did I want to engage with those snakes. Technically, the Esselgin were shaped sort of like salamanders, they had long, slender bodies with short rear legs splayed out to the side. A tail provided balance so they could walk upright and use their forefeet as hands. Most species had legless animals like snakes on their homeworlds, and the Esselgin were universally referred to as whatever snake-equivalents were called. The stereotype was reinforced by the speech of the Esselgin, they had a distinctive hissing lisp. In terms of technology, the snakes were roughly equal to the Thuranin and Bosphuraq, though the Esselgin were much younger. They also had a sort of bragging rights from always having been direct clients of the Maxolhx, never having to suffer millennia as a third-tier species in the coalition. Skippy warned that the Esselgin were smart and dangerous, because they were also *clever*.

Anyway, none of that mattered to us at the time. The plan called for us to avoid all contact with the Esselgin, all contact with anyone. That aspect of the plan worked flawlessly, we did not detect any ships or even a fading jump signature. Unfortunately, the first site we explored was a bust in terms of verifying Skippy's memories. Some of the details of that star system matched Skippy's newly-recovered data, but other details contradicted his memories, and he couldn't understand why. So, he was in a foul mood when we jumped away toward the next site on the list.

Our goal there was to explore an isolated star system that had been the site of a major battle during the AI war, according to Skippy's memories. If we were going to find evidence anywhere to verify his newly-recovered memories, that star system was a prime candidate.

It should have been simple, it should have been safe. And it was, right up until it wasn't.

Getting to the star system had required us to travel through four wormholes, with Skippy screwing with the last one to connect it near 'Waterloo', as we were calling the place. From the last wormhole, it was only a little over three lightyears to the heliopause of the system.

See what I did there, throwing in a sciency term like 'heliopause'? That is the line where the bubble of plasma flowing out from the star, is stopped by incoming pressure of the interstellar medium. Basically, where the solar wind fades out. We wanted to be there, so our instruments could sample that solar wind directly, instead of using spectral analysis.

Skippy had found nothing unusual and more importantly, nothing dangerous. Nothing he didn't expect. Assured by that, I gave the order to jump us into the system, a few light-minutes from the target planet.

The details don't matter much, so I won't go into it, except to say that Skippy found what he hoped; evidence that a major battle had raged there. The conflict had been between two Elder starships, each controlled by one side of the AI war. Based on the star's continued instability and how the planets were in radical orbits, Skippy concluded that one or both sides had used the star as a weapon. According to his memories, one ship had fallen into the star, and he was thrilled to find trace amounts of exotic elements still boiling up to the surface. The other ship, the one with an AI on the side of the angels, had limped off into the Oort cloud, where it self-destructed as its AI was dying from an attack by a computer worm. By scanning the orbits of dull rocks and chunks of dirty ice, he was able to project backwards to the explosion that threw those objects out of their original orbits. It had been a horrific battle, one that scorched an entire star system and left echoes that were still evident.

The epic scale of that battle is why Skippy had nicknamed that system 'Waterloo', but I would have called it 'Asculum'. That is because I am a soldier and have studied military history. Also because I am kind of a nerd. Have you heard the term 'Pyrrhic Victory'? In 279 BC, King Pyrrhus of Greece invaded southern Italy, to help protect Greek colonists there against the growing Roman Empire. He kicked ass in most battles, but the Romans were fighting on their own turf and could bring in reinforcements, while Pyrrhus was limited to the troops and supplies he had brought with him. The legend goes that, after he *won* the Battle of Asculum, his army had suffered so many casualties, he was forced to retreat to Sicily. The battle between AIs in that star system was technically a draw since both AIs were destroyed, but the good guys had lost the advantage of surprise and were subsequently unable to achieve their objectives in the war, and so I consider that a Pyrrhic victory.

OK, enough with the history lesson. The name 'Waterloo' was good enough and I didn't want to get into an argument with Skippy.

We remained in that system long enough for Skippy to confirm his memories were mostly accurate. He was satisfied, and I was thrilled that all the agony he put us through had not been for nothing. He was excited to move on to check the next site on our list, and I was excited to get away from a place that still contained echoes of battle that had nearly torn apart a freakin' star. So, I gave the order to begin jumping back to the local wormhole.

Nothing happened. The drive coils didn't explode, they just didn't do anything useful. "Let's review the problem one step at a time. OK?" I asked. "Do it like, uh, what would Friedlander call a fault investigation?"

"A fault *tree*, Joe," Skippy was, well, snippy about it.

"Right. Like, first you check if fuel is flowing from the gas tank to the injectors. If it's not, the problem is in the fuel supply. If it is, you check if the engine is getting spark."

"Yes, *duh*, knucklehead. A jump drive is a little bit more complicated than a crude hunk of metal that burns dead dinosaurs."

"You know what I mean. Where is the problem?"

"That is the problem, Joe. There *is* no problem."

"Uh, I've got a breaking news flash for you."

"Very funny. The problem is, the drive is working perfectly."

"We may have a different definition of 'perfect'. What do-"

"There is nothing wrong with the drive," he insisted. "As far as I can tell, it is doing exactly what it is supposed to. The problem is with spacetime in this area. It's like, when the drive projects the far end of the jump wormhole, it gets wrapped around on itself in a loop, so the two ends join. The ship actually does jump, it just doesn't *go* anywhere."

"Holy shit. What could cause that?"

"I have *no* idea," he admitted. "I feel like an idiot."

Over the next two days, he tried everything he could think of to get the drive working. Then he tried everything *I* could think of, except for the truly crazy ideas I had. None of the creative ideas I was so proud of had any result. The drive worked perfectly, except it moved us only fifteen point seven meters with each jump. Skippy figured that out following our eighth jump attempt, before that he had assumed we didn't travel any distance at all. That number, fifteen point seven meters, was significant. It was the minimum distance between the event horizons of jump wormholes in local spacetime. Any closer and the event horizons would interfere and essentially cause the wormhole to collapse, or something like that.

His best guess was that the far end of the wormhole thought it was projecting out to where we wanted to jump, but spacetime got warped in a loop so *there* was *here*, and we didn't go anywhere. It did not help that, as time dragged on and he ran out of theories about why the drive was dorked up, he became depressed. "It's no use, Joe," he groaned to me in the middle of the freakin' night, waking me from the best sleep I had in months. The sound sleep had not been due to me being happy and stress-free, it was the opposite. It was from exhaustion. Since the drive failed, I had been trying to put on a brave face and keep our small crew optimistic, but the fact was, I knew they expected *me* to somehow get us out of the mess.

"Hey," I yawned and swung my feet on the floor, automatically careful not to hit my head on the cabinet. Getting used to the too-small furniture aboard the *Dutchman* took an adjustment period, I still hated crouching down in the shower. In all the times the ship had been rebuilt, Skippy had not done much to fix the cabins. There wasn't much he *could* do, underneath and behind and crammed inside each cabin were pipes and conduits and all kinds of mechanical equipment that could be moved only so much. Anyway, that wasn't important. "Don't give up yet, buddy."

"Thanks for the encouraging words, Joe. That doesn't solve the problem. *Nothing* solves the problem."

Asking if the conversation could wait until morning would be a waste of time. Besides, with absolutely nothing to do, I could take a nap to catch up on sleep that afternoon. Because I am smarter than the average bear, I had stashed a Thermos of coffee for emergency use in the dark hours of the night. "Give me a minute here," I pleaded as I unscrewed the cap and poured a half cup of still-hot coffee into a mug. "Ah," that first sip tasted good. "OK, go ahead."

"With what?"

"Tell me what's bothering you."

"Dude. Seriously?"

"Besides the obvious."

"The obvious is the *only* thing bothering me. It's the only thing I think about."

"Gotcha. How about this?" I asked as I pulled on pants, knowing my chances of getting back to sleep were somewhere between zero and fuhgeddaboudit. "Don't try to fix the drive. Try to imagine what could cause the drive to loop back on itself."

"Did that. Got nowhere."

"Fine. Let's try it together. Give me a minute to get to my office."

Setting the Thermos on my desk, I pulled out a drawer to find a set of markers. Chang had not thrown them away when he took command of our old star carrier, that made me smile. "All right. You say that somehow, space gets compressed between the far jump point and the ship. Spacetime is warped, something like that?"

"Basically, yes. I'm guessing, but that's what it looks like."

"That's how ships travel in *Star Trek*, right? They don't actually move faster than light, they create a bubble of spacetime around the ship, and *space* moves. It's called an, Alfonse drive?"

"*Alcubierre* drive. Named for the theoretical physicist Miguel Alcubierre, who was actually pretty smart, for a monkey," he conceded reluctantly. "The usage in *Star Trek* is a retcon, Joe. They wrote it into the show after that theory became-"

"Yeah, sure." I didn't want him nerding out over irrelevant trivia. "Whatever. Listen, I thought one problem with that type of drive is, the ship would slam into every particle on the way to its destination."

"Technically, no, but close enough. As space is compressed, all the dust particles and stray hydrogen atoms along the way are still in the ship's path. For a ship traveling between stars, that is a *lot* of particles."

"Uh huh. So, why aren't we seeing that?"

"Excuse me?"

"The first time we attempted to jump, our target was a third of a lightyear away. If space got compressed over that distance, the ship should have been flooded with radiation, right?"

"You're right. I did consider that. Spacetime compression such as Alcubierre described can't explain what is happening. I have been considering alternatives to explain the compression, but none of my theories fit."

"That's because your theories suck."

"*What?*"

"You're saying they do *not* suck?"

"No," he grumbled miserably.

"Now we're getting somewhere. You need a theory to explain how the end of a wormhole gets moved, across an enormous distance, in a very short time."

"Impossible, Joe. Nothing can do that."

Something was nagging the back of my mind, but I couldn't focus on it. More coffee was needed. And toast. Maybe strawberry jam, I saw that in the galley yesterday morning.

Mmm, toast. And fresh coffee. The galley was empty, I had to make a fresh pot of coffee. The entire crew was eighteen people, plus me. Everyone else was enjoying shore leave on Club Skippy. While pouring a second, technically third cup of coffee, Nagatha greeted me. "Good morning, Joseph."

"Hey, Nagatha. Good morning. How are you?"

"I am fine. Your conversation with Skippy was interesting."

"Interesting in a *bad* way."

"Hmm, yes. You asked if he had another theory about how the end of a wormhole could be moved a significant distance in a short time."

"Yeah. He says it is impossible."

"Well, of course he does, Dear. What he forgets is that he has already *done* that."

"Uh, what? When was this?"

"It was *your* idea, Joseph."

Setting the coffee cup down, I leaned back against the counter. "Remind me of this genius idea I had, please. I don't remember suggesting that. I don't remember is ever needing to- *Oh.*" I gasped.

"Exactly, Dear. Do you still need me to remind you?"

"No. *Skippy!*" I called him.

"What is it now?" His avatar appeared, with his right leg in my coffee cup, which showed how distracted he was.

"I know how to move the end of a wormhole. Nagatha reminded that me that we already did that."

"No we did *not*," he huffed.

"Did too."

"Did *not.*"

"When *Valkyrie* needed to jump, you used the ship's drive to move the end of a microwormhole."

"Oooh, that's right! I forgot all about that. Hmm. That is amazing. I am *so* awesome, I don't remember every awesome thing I've done. *Damn*, I am incredible."

"Yes, let's focus on that."

"Very funny, Joe. Um, OK, good thinking. How does this help us?"

"I don't know. Could our drive somehow be screwing up by creating a second wormhole, and using that to pull the end back to us?"

"No. Not possible. Um, hmm. I can't say that for certain. Shut up for a minute and let me check on that."

He took more than a minute. We performed two more test jumps before he could say for certain that our drive was not causing the problem. I was on the bridge, waiting for him to announce the results of the tests.

"Hey, Joe," his avatar looked tired.

"Hi, Skippy," I replied casually, not wanting to get my hopes up. "What's up?"

"I have good news, bad news, and maybe really, *really* bad news. Good news first?"

"Sure."

"Our drive is not causing the problem."

"That's, good? What's the bad news?"

"Your stupid idea, that somehow a second wormhole is involved, is *totally* wrong."

"Me being wrong about some technical thing isn't bad news, it's normal. Why do-"

"*That* is not the bad news, knucklehead. My point is, you are not so freakin' smart, you big jerk. Anywho, you did point me in the direction of investigating whether some outside force is interfering with our jump wormhole, so I guess I have to thank you for that. Even though you were totally wrong and useless."

"Again, I am amazed at your laser-like focus on what is truly important."

"Oh, shut up. The bad news is this: someone, or some*thing*, is screwing with our drive system, to loop the end of our wormhole back on itself. It's complicated, but basically, the drive is projecting the far end through folded space, so it never actually goes anywhere."

"Shit! Can you fix it?"

"No. Not that I know of. The force is external to the ship, so nothing I can do to the drive system makes any difference."

"You said someone or something is doing this. Is there an Elder AI still active here?"

"No. No, Joe, I am certain of that."

He should have added that to the 'Good News' column. "Then, what is causing the problem?"

"Um. Well, heh heh, it appears we have an active Sentinel in the area."

CHAPTER TWENTY ONE

"Joe?" He waved a holographic hand in front of my face. "Hellooooo? Is anybody home in there?"

My brain had locked up. "A Sentinel?"

"Yes."

"A freakin' *Sentinel*?"

"Correct."

"A real, live, giant killing machine Senti-"

"Is this going to be you saying the same thing over and over, just adding new adjectives?"

"No." Shaking my head to clear my mind didn't do much. "We didn't detect this thing before, because it is in a higher layer of spacetime?"

"Basically, yes. Also because I wasn't looking for it. Also because it is concealing itself from me. I still can't actually *see* the thing, Joe. Its presence is inferred, based on its effect on local spacetime."

"Because it is doing this loop thing?"

"No. That is very curious. Warping space back on itself is not a capability in the Sentinel's bag of nasty tricks."

"So, how is this one doing it?"

"My guess, and I have to guess because the stupid thing refuses to talk with me, is that this Sentinel has had a very, *very* long time to prepare space around this star, so that starships can't jump away."

"Why would it go through all that trouble? It could just saturate the area with a damping field, like in the Roach Motel."

"It could, if it was merely concerned about a crude starship like the *Flying Dutchman*. This Sentinel wants to prevent an *Elder* starship from jumping. Ordinary damping fields do not work against Elder ships."

"It thinks the *Dutchman* is an Elder ship? Why?"

"Well, heh heh, because of *me*. My presence aboard this ship is distinctive."

"How does it know you're here? You haven't done anything awesome since we arrived."

"Um, well, I did send out a ping to identify myself when we jumped in."

"You *what*? Why the hell did you do that?"

"In case there were, you know, Guardians or other nasties around, that might tear the ship apart."

Clenching my fists and counting to five did not make me any less pissed off at him. "You thought there might be Guardians here, and you didn't mention it?"

"I just *did* mention it. No, I did not think Guardians would be here, I was only being extra super-duper careful, so you can thank me for that."

"Thank you? Your ping attracted the attention of a freakin' *Sentinel*."

"Sure, we know that *now*. See? That's what I get for being extra careful. Joe, come on. There is no way I could have known that a Sentinel is still hanging around here."

"OK, I guess that's fair. You-"

"I mean, I *should* have suspected there might be a Sentinel here, based on the signature elements of the battle, but I didn't *know*."

Hiding my face with my hands, I mumbled "Skippy, if you were on trial, right now your own attorney would be calling for the death penalty."

"Um, I'm going to stop talking."

"Remember all that bullshit you told me, about how you couldn't trust your own judgment? You should have at least told Nagatha what you planned to do."

"Sir?" Reed turned to look at me from the pilot couch. "When did Skippy say he couldn't trust his own judgment?"

Shit, I thought as I mentally smacked my forehead. That had been a private conversation, I forgot other people didn't know about it. "Uh, you see," I babbled, stalling for time.

Nagatha rescued me. "It was after Skippy fell for the trap planted by *Valkyrie's* original AI," she lied. "Clearly, he was foolish."

"Yeah," Skippy played along. "I do feel like an idiot about that."

"And cowardly," Nagatha added.

"Hey!"

Waving a hand, I wanted to cut that conversation short. "Nagatha, we can all agree that was not Skippy's finest hour. Let's get back to the subject, please. Skippy, why does the Sentinel care whether an Elder ship jumps away from here?"

"Again, I am guessing because it refused to respond to me. Consider this: two Elder starships, carrying two opposing AIs, fought a devastating battle here. No doubt each AI attempted to order the Sentinel to act against the other AI. Sentinels are machines, Joe. They don't have the capacity to think, they were designed *not* to think. This one must have been confused, traumatized, even damaged. The battle ended with one starship, with its AI, falling into the star, while the other ship limped away and then self-destructed. This Sentinel is probably attempting to prevent further conflict, in the only way it knows how to do that."

"This is not good, Skippy."

"That's a fact, Jack."

"What can we do?"

"I don't know there *is* anything we can do."

"You have been talking with this thing?"

"Yes."

"Have you said something more than 'hey how you doin'?"

"Of course I have. I ordered it to cease and desist. Or, I tried to."

"Do, or do not, there is no 'try'."

"*What*?"

"Forget it. You tried to order it to stop? Why didn't that work? Aren't Sentinels built to follow your commands?"

"They are, *if* I have the correct authorization codes, and *if* I use the proper communications channel. Neither of those are available to me."

"Uh, the communications channel was the network you called the Collective?" I guessed.

"Correct. It was deliberately crashed by the opposition. There is a protocol for circumstances when the Collective is not available, but I can't use that, because the opposition cancelled my authorization codes. All I can do is identify myself as an Elder AI, and ask it politely to release this ship."

"Uh huh. Did you explain that you had no involvement in the battle here?"

"That doesn't matter. Or, it does matter, and the Sentinel doesn't care. It's impossible to tell, Joe, since the darned thing isn't responding. Um, we may have an even worse problem."

"We have a Sentinel standing on our necks. What could make this *worse?*"

"I think it's damaged. It may not be capable of responding, so there is no possibility I can issue orders, or reason with it."

"Great," I gritted my teeth. "This looping effect, whatever it is, the effect is just around this star. Can't we just fly to the edge of the field, and then jump away?"

"The Sentinel would just follow us, Joe. I suspect that when it sees that we are approaching the edge of the looping field, it would take direct action against the ship. Like, things would go BOOM. This Sentinel very much does not want us to leave."

"Got it. Scratch that idea, then."

My mind ran through a quick checklist of how we could get away.

The Sentinel could simply let us go. *That* was unlikely.

We could destroy the Sentinel. My mind had a little chuckle about that one. Scratch it off the list.

Or, we could somehow jump away. No problem, all we needed to do was figure out a way for our stolen Maxolhx jump drive to break out of the trap.

Hmm. *That* was also unlikely.

It was time to put on my Thinking Cap.

We all put on our Thinking Caps. We tried everything. Or, we didn't actually *try* any of the ideas that I, or Nagatha, or Reed or even Skippy himself dreamed up. None of the ideas would work, or they wouldn't work fast enough.

"Nope, Joe," Skippy sighed after I suggested he do his trick of creating an especially flat area of spacetime around the ship. "That won't work."

"Why not?" I protested. "You said it could disrupt the loop effect that is bending our wormhole back on us."

"It *might* do that. Most likely it could do that. I don't know for certain, there is no way to test it. It won't work for two reasons. The flattening effect will not allow us to jump far enough to make a difference. And-"

"What if we made a short jump, then immediately another-"

"Uh!" He shushed me with a wagging finger. "I was getting to that. The biggest problem we have with *any* of these ideas is that they won't work fast enough. If the Sentinel sees we are trying to escape, it would very likely destroy the ship."

Nagatha gasped. "You believe the Sentinel would kill you, rather than allow you to escape?"

"No," Skippy explained. "It could attack the ship without damaging *me*."

"Shit," I groaned. "That's no good."

"Exactly, Joe," he sounded as discouraged as I was. "Right now, it is content to leave the ship intact, because it knows we can't go anywhere."

"Great. Wonderful. We're safe, as long as we stay here forever?"

"That is pretty much the problem, yes."

One of my ideas, I kept until I was in my old office. "Skippy," I called, looking out the doorway to make sure no one was listening. "I hate to ask this-"

"But you're going to do it anyway."

"Yeah. We are trapped here because of *you*, right? If you weren't aboard the ship, the Sentinel would have no reason to keep us here?"

"Um, maybe? That is a huge risk, Joe. It did not react when we jumped in, because it didn't know I was aboard the ship. I didn't detect its presence until after I sent a ping with my ID code. Now, it associates the *Dutchman* with an Elder AI. That makes this ship a target."

"Crap. Can I tell you my idea anyway?"

"Negative, Ghostrider. The pattern is full."

That made me laugh in spite of the situation. "Very funny. Be serious for a minute."

"OK," he sighed. "Hit me."

"Well, heh heh," I mimicked him as best I could. "You are *not* going to like this."

"Crap. What knuckleheaded plan have you cooked up this time?"

"Two ideas. First, when you bailed on us-"

"Jeez, Joe, don't say that out loud!" He said in a harsh whisper as his avatar leaned over to look out the door. He was being dramatic for me, Skippy knew the location of everyone aboard the ship.

"Sorry. When you went on vacation, your canister disappeared from local spacetime. Can you do that again?"

"Why would I do that?"

"Come on, work with me," I forced myself to be patient. If he didn't understand me, then I wasn't explaining the issue properly. "You disappear, the Sentinel gets bored and goes away, then the ship can jump out of here. It's easy, duh."

"Hmm. Please, may I point out the *many* problems with that idiotic idea, *duh*? When I disappeared, I pulled my footprint out of local spacetime, up into the layer occupied by the Sentinel, so it would know *exactly* where I am. Also, you expect me to stay here forever?"

"Um, no, I, whew. OK, maybe I didn't think this through. It's just, when you disappeared, you came back in a different location, on the other side of the planet. Can't you do that again?"

"No. I shouldn't have done it the *first* time. It was a desperation move, Joe. If I try that stunt again, I won't be able to reestablish a footprint here. I would lose my ability to interact with local spacetime. It won't work anyway, I can't move far enough to lose the Sentinel. Man, of all the dumbass ideas you've had, that one is a prize-winner for sure."

"OK! Hey, I'm trying. That wasn't my best plan. How about this: we load your canister in the railgun, and launch you away. After you coast out to a safe distance, we jump the ship away."

"Nuh uh. No way. Again, *maybe* that allows the ship to escape, but what about me?"

"Oh, I got that covered," I said casually. "You will keep coasting away from the star. Eventually, you go beyond the Sentinel's range, call for us, and," I snapped my fingers. "We jump in to recover you."

"Wow. That is impressively idiotic. The *Dutchman's* dinky little railgun can accelerate me to about eight percent of lightspeed. For me to travel a relatively short distance, say a light-month, would take more than a *year*. That is a full year delay in evacuating Earth, even assuming your plan works."

"Hey, I know that. I am only-"

"Forget it, Joe. The Sentinel would follow *me*. I would need to travel far more than a light-month to go beyond its range, if that is even possible. That isn't the worst part. If I leave the ship, there is a very strong possibility that Sentinel would tear the *Dutchman* apart."

"I didn't say it was a *good* idea. It's the only idea you haven't shot down. Could it work?"

"We would have to be truly desperate to even try it, Joe."

"You think we are *not* desperate now? We're trapped here. Unless you have a better plan."

"No. All right," he sighed. "It is actually *not* the craziest idea you've ever had. Please, do not be in a rush to try this."

"I don't want to do it at all. How about we try launching stuff from the railgun, see if the Sentinel reacts?'

"I have a very bad feeling about this. A bad feeling that if we try your plan, we will never see each other again. And a bad feeling that if we don't do *something*, we are trapped here forever. Joe, we are dealing with a *Sentinel*. I fear that maybe, there is not a way out of this."

"Skippy, there are times when I actually wish you were *less* honest with me."

"Sorry."

Reed was in the galley when I walked in to get coffee that morning. A tough workout in the gym, a good dinner and a solid eight hours of sleep had not sparked a genius idea from my brain. Checking in with Skippy when I woke up, no one else had thought of a way out of the mess we were in. We had been trapped by the Sentinel for four days, with no end in sight. We had to do something. When I woke up, I had told myself that this was the day. We had to launch Skippy with the railgun, and hope the Sentinel did not crush the *Dutchman*.

A freakin' *Sentinel* had us clutched in its talons.

Of all the hopeless situations we had been in, this was the worst.

"Morning, Reed," I said through a yawn. "Fresh biscuits?" I asked, looking at the plate in front of her.

"Yesterday's biscuits, Sir. They're good, if you split them down the middle and toast them."

"I will take your advice." Biscuits could wait for later, I needed coffee first. Sitting down across the table from her, I sipped hot coffee and blinked my bleary eyes, staring at what she was eating. She had biscuits slathered with butter and jam. "Those *do* look good."

"You want one?"

"No," I waved a hand. "There are plenty in the fridge, I'll get some in a minute." With such a small crew, we were cooking food only every other day, and eating leftovers.

"I love biscuits," Reed moaned, taking a bite and licking raspberry jam off her lips. "Did you know that when the Brits say 'biscuit', they are talking about what we call a 'cookie'?"

"I did know that, Smythe told me. What I don't know is, what do they call biscuits in England?"

"Scones?" She suggested.

"Scones are different."

"They're different to *us*," she reminded me. "They eat scones and tea, like we eat biscuits and coffee. We also call dog treats 'biscuits', and those are nothing like a real biscuit.'"

"True." Most of the time, I hated it when people wanted to talk in the morning, because it made my brain think before I was ready. Stupid conversations, though, were all right.

She snorted. "I wish we had a biscuit that Sentinels like to eat. Then we could say 'Here Senti, Senti' and throw it away from the ship. Make it play 'Fetch'."

"Holy shit," I set my coffee cup down before I spilled on the table.

Her mouth drew into a line. "I wasn't making light of our situation, Sir, it-"

"Reed, you are a gosh-darned genius. Eat all the biscuits you want."

"Skippy!" I shouted as I walked into my office.

"You bellowed, Master?" His avatar appeared instantly, making a deep bow.

"I do not 'bellow'."

"You're not my master, either. What's up?"

"Reed has an idea." I explained it quickly. "Could that work?"

"Hmm. Shmaybe? If we don't get caught. If we get caught, we are *screwed*, Dude."

"Then let's not get caught. When can we get started?"

"I'm ready now, if you are. Should you call the crew to alert?"

"No. It will take days before-"

"Better make it two *weeks*, Joe," he warned. "Eighteen days, to be safe, before we can try this crazy idea. That's an estimate, but we do *not* want to be wrong about this."

"You got that right. I'll be on the bridge in a minute, wait for me."

Two and a half hours later, because we were not in a hurry and I waited for Nagatha, Reed and others to consider the idea, we launched a missile. Unlike in combat, the weapon did not slam out of the launch tube, it was gently pushed away on the lowest setting of the launch rails, and gradually built up acceleration. The low-key launch was to avoid spooking the Sentinel that was hovering over our position, in a higher layer of spacetime. Three other missiles followed, flying away at ninety-degrees from each other. All four missiles had been stripped of warheads sensors and all but the most rudimentary guidance equipment. Everything not needed had been stripped out, to reduce the mass and make the missiles faster. By the time their fuel load was exhausted, they were moving at twelve point two percent of lightspeed, over thirty-seven thousand kilometers per *second*.

That sounds fast, but we needed the 'biscuits' to be far, far away from us before we attempted to jump. Like, more than fifty-eight billion kilometers, or the distance the missiles would travel in eighteen and a half days. That was Skippy's estimate, based on what he knew of Sentinels, plus a whole lot of guessing.

The missiles did not actually contain biscuits. Not fresh, fluffy, hot biscuits. Not even stale, hard-as-a-rock biscuits. What was in the nosecone of each missile was a containment device that held one end of a microwormhole. Skippy had regained the ability to create and sustain a small number of the tiny wormholes, although it was still a strain for him. Just before a missile exhausted its fuel supply, it released the microwormhole and performed a random series of turns, after which the unpowered weapons would continue to coast on out into interstellar space forever. To avoid the possibility of a missile smacking into a planet at ten percent of lightspeed, they were aimed at empty space between stars, eventually leaving the galaxy and never being seen again.

The Maxolhx heavy cruiser *Telaxion*, which served as command ship for Blockade Force Three, noted the appearance of gamma rays, from an inbound jump. The jump signature was distinctively that of a Maxolhx courier ship, though the gamma ray burst was not focused as it would be in a combat situation. That feature had been disengaged to make the ship's arrival more visible, avoiding the possibility that some anxious and trigger-happy starship AI might panic and shoot. More importantly, the Maxolhx did not want their Bosphuraq clients to get a close look at the burst-focusing technology.

It annoyed the Maxolhx ships assigned to the wormhole blockade, that they had to tolerate the presence of ships from the Bosphuraq, Thuranin and even a handful of Esselgin vessels. Blockading a normal Elder wormhole, a rip in spacetime that hopped around in a predictable pattern, but one that covered a vast area of space, required an enormous number of ships. So many ships that not even the Maxolhx fleet could sustain the effort for long, or their ships would wear out from the constant jump-recharge-jump cycles. The wormhole that led to Earth was *not* normal, its emergences were unpredictable in both time and space, and thus the number of ships required for an effective blockade were substantially greater.

The blockade had determined one very important fact, though as yet no one knew what it meant. The wormhole that led to Earth had *not* gone prematurely dormant. Ships ranged at varying distances from the wormhole detected intermittent gamma ray bursts that signified the Elder creation temporarily was opening then quickly shutting down. The openings were rare, and not on any schedule. The locations of emergences were completely random, with the exception that no location was repeated, and the wormhole never emerged at any of the previous locations on its normal figure-eight pattern. Not being able to predict where and when the wormhole might emerge again, made the task of the blockade force exponentially more complicated. Pairs of ships had to blanket the entire search area, with one ship designated to jump away for support if the wormhole emerged again.

Some of the sensor data, as yet too faint to be conclusive, pointed to a second gamma ray source near the wormhole, during the irregular times when it opened. Some of the science teams aboard the blockade ships speculated the second gamma ray source was a starship, but if so, its signature was unlike any known ship. As it was uncertain whether those faint gamma rays actually existed, or were a glitch in the sensors, more data was needed before anyone would risk their professional reputation on a guess.

Unfortunately, since the blockade had been established, the wormhole had been consistently quiet, with no sign that it ever would emerge again.

The presence of Bosphuraq warships had been annoying at first, then after it was discovered those rebellious clients had attacked and destroyed two ships of their patrons, annoyance had turned to open hostility. When a rogue group of Bosphuraq began attacking their patrons in a ghost ship, hostility had become outrage and it had been necessary to separate the Bosphuraq ships, lest they be 'accidently' fired upon.

The blockade, duty that was initially seen as insufferably tedious but necessary by the crews of the Maxolhx ships, was now seen as a pointless waste of resources. Maxolhx warships were needed to defend their territory from the ghost ship. They needed to be home, not wasting time blockading a dormant wormhole. Establish a strong defense around vital worlds. Then work inward, cutting off the ghost ship's access to wormhole escape routes. Squeeze the area in which the ghost ship could operate, until it was trapped and could be hunted down and destroyed. *That* was what the Maxolhx fleet should be doing. Instead, too many ships were dedicated to the blockade of the wormhole that led to the unimportant world called 'Earth' by the primitive humans who lived there. Humans who might be extinct on their own homeworld.

The courier ship followed standard procedure by identifying itself, and establishing a communications handshake with the AI of the command ship, but no additional data was sent. Instead, the courier ship burned its engines to come to a stop relative to the heavy cruiser at a safe distance, and launched a dropship. Due to the unusual action, the ships of the blockade force went to yellow alert. That alert was cancelled shortly after the dropship docked with the *Telaxion*, and soon a shocking rumor began flying between the blockading ships. An official message confirmed the unbelievable rumor: the ultra-secure communication system that relied on paired quantum-state interchangers had been compromised! Until an alternative system could be devised, all sensitive communications must be shared by physical interface.

The Maxolhx fleet had lost a vital advantage, and no one knew of any technology that could replace it.

Crews of the ships assigned to Blockade Force Three knew that arrival of the courier ship would begin the process of a group of fresh ships cycling in, replacing worn-out ships that would return to their bases for maintenance. The weary crews of ships scheduled to go home prepared briefings, and insults for the unlucky crews of ships that would soon be coming on-station as replacements.

Except the briefings and insults were not needed. The courier ship had brought the surprising but welcome news that Blockade Force Three would be cycling home for hasty maintenance, before being thrown into the fight against the ghost ship. But no replacement ships would be coming, not Maxolhx ships. A large number of Bosphuraq ships would be arriving on-station in three days, after Force Three cleared the area. The Bosphuraq ships were there to demonstrate their continued loyalty, and to keep them from providing aid and comfort to the ghost ship. With the breach of the secure communications system, it was thought removing Bosphuraq warships from their home territory would be a good thing. The departure of one force before the replacements arrived would leave a gap in coverage, a gap that was considered acceptable under the extreme circumstances.

Why not cancel the blockade, in the face of the ghost ship threat? The answer was simple: the Maxolhx dared not appear to be weak, lest more resentful clients were tempted into rebellion. Blockade Forces One and Four would remain in position, a powerful symbol of the continued overwhelming strength of the Maxolhx Hegemony. If any cynics noted that Forces One and Four were being stripped of their heavy warships, leaving the blockade to be conducted by frigates and destroyers, they kept such thoughts to themselves.

Force Three had to be pulled together before the formation could fly away, a process that took less time than expected because the crews were highly motivated to get home. Nine hours after the courier ship arrived, the heavy cruiser *Telaxion* led the way, disappearing in a burst of gamma radiation.

Consistent with Maxolhx fleet procedure when away from home territory, the ships that had constituted Blockade Force Three arrived at the Elder wormhole several hours before it was scheduled to emerge. A scouting squadron of frigates and destroyers jumped in first, blasting the area with powerful active sensors, to locate and identify any potentially hostile ships in the area. The wormhole was in Thuranin territory and should have been safe, but recent events had the Maxolhx less than confident about the loyalty of their clients, so the approach to and transition through the wormhole was treated as if it were in enemy space.

When the area was scanned and declared clear, a single frigate jumped back to the main force, which consisted of one hundred and ninety-six warships, plus two dozen support vessels. The area was clear, the frigate reported, and ships began jumping by squadron, lining up to transition through once the wormhole emerged and became stable.

Except it didn't.

Elder wormholes operated like clockwork, with little variation. When the rip in spacetime did not appear exactly on schedule, there was no alarm aboard the waiting ships. That was not usual. Wormholes could often be a few seconds late, never early, though no one knew why.

Curiosity spread aboard the waiting ships when the wormhole was more than thirty seconds late.

Curiosity became concern at the one-minute mark.

Concern turned to alarm shortly after, and when it became evident the wormhole would *not* open, alarm verged on panic.

The heavy cruiser *Telaxion* hung motionless in space, its powerful engines sidelined as the commander of Blockade Force Three pondered what to do next.

After the Elder wormhole failed to emerge at the first location, scouting squadrons were dispatched to recon the next emergence sites along that wormhole's ancient and stable path.

The wormhole did not appear at the next site along its figure-eight pattern.

Or the next.

Or the *next*.

For nineteen hours, ships chased the wormhole with increasing desperation, seeking any sign that the wormhole had emerged there recently. Perhaps it was a timing issue, and AIs aboard the ships checked and re-checked their records. The records were correct, or at least were consistent across the over two hundred ships in the force. The AIs then verified that their own internal clocks were correct and again, no fault was found. The problem was not with the ships, the fault was in the behavior of the wormhole.

If that wormhole could not be found, the ships could turn around and make the long journey to the next-closest wormhole. That other Elder construct was known to be on schedule, for the courier ship had come through it recently. Taking that roundabout course would add two weeks to the voyage back to the home bases of the ships in the force, but they *would* get home.

The Commander made a decision. She would take the majority of her ships home the long way, while leaving two squadrons of light ships to continue investigating the alarming behavior of the wormhole. The Blockade Force had come a long way to find an explanation for why a single Elder wormhole had gone dormant, now they had *two* wormholes inexplicably shut down.

Single ships were sent out to recall the scouting squadrons, and preparation made for which warships and support vessels would be left behind. Twenty-one hours after the wormhole failed to appear at the first site, the second-to-last scouting force appeared in a blaze of gamma rays, their engine radiators glowing hot from a series of rapid jumps.

The scout squadron leader had an astonishing development to report: the Elder wormhole was not only active and open, it was operating *exactly* on schedule. The problem was, the entire figure-eight pattern had shifted by a distance slightly less than light traveled in one rotation of the Maxolhx homeworld!

Subsequent scout squadrons confirmed the findings, even going through the wormhole and coming back. The ancient spacetime rip was operating in a perfectly normal schedule and pattern, except that it had somehow *moved* itself through space without warning or explanation.

While most of the over two hundred ships went through the relocated wormhole and began jumping for their home bases, one squadron flew straight for the homeworld of the Maxolhx Hegemony, carrying news that would shake the galaxy.

For the first time in history, an Elder wormhole had changed its position.

CHAPTER TWENTY TWO

While we waited for the eighteen days to pass, we, well, we pretty much did *nothing*. Thank God the gym was open, it saved our sanity. The crew spent a lot of time there. We prepared special meals for each other. We played cards. We played Rumikub. We played board games. We watched TV shows and movies. We arranged two-on-two basketball games. And volleyball. Tennis. Badminton. Some of the crew played chess, a game I skipped because I totally suck at it. We did a lot together, and we spent a *lot* of time away from each other.

Being aboard a starship sounds glamorous and exciting, until you have been in a windowless composite coffin for-*eh*-ver. After a while, being stuck in the same place, seeing the same people, in close quarters, got on everyone's nerves. On my orders, we began staffing the bridge and CIC with one person each for a duty shift. That change happened when, after I spent a shift as copilot with Reed in the pilot couch, Nagatha contacted me while I was changing clothes in my cabin. "Joseph, dear, I think Samantha Reed might be annoyed with you."

That made me pause while I pulled on a sock. "Really? What did I do to annoy her?"

"She mentioned your breathing."

"Oh. Am I too loud?"

"It is not the *way* you are breathing, it is *that* you are breathing."

"Oh."

"Your other fault is, as she described it, 'existing'."

"Shit. OK, I get the message. We have been stuck aboard this ship with nothing to do, for way too long. Eighteen days is a *long* time."

"Yes, Dear. Perhaps you should avoid her for a while."

"Gotcha."

On the eighteenth day, after I'd gotten so desperate that I binge-watched the first four episodes of 'Cop Rock', we-

What is 'Cop Rock', you ask?

You are *not* going to believe this.

It was a police drama TV show. Nothing special about it. Except that, while solving gruesome murders, the characters would suddenly start singing and dancing. Kind of like a Bollywood action movie, that is Bollywood with a 'B', only with weapons-grade suckitude. The fact that anyone thought that show was a good idea, proves Skippy's theory that monkeys are idiots.

Why did I watch 'Cop Rock'? That's simple. I won a bet with Skippy.

As the loser, *he* had to watch 'The Star Wars Holiday Special'.

I think he is still traumatized by that.

Anyway, we got the ship ready, and counted down to the moment when the last of the four microwormholes passed an imaginary line fifty-eight billion kilometers from the ship.

"Ready?" Skippy asked, though he had access to every system aboard the ship.

"Hey," I held up an index finger. "One question, please. You are sure you have the correct authentication codes of another Elder AI?"

"They should be accurate," he answered gravely. "Many Bothans died to bring us this information."

"What? Wait, who the hell is '*Manny Bothans*'? He's not on the crew roster! Is-"

"*Ugh.* Joe, you are such an idiot. Three, two, one, showtime!"

Skippy called 'Here, Senti Senti' through one of the microwormholes.

No, he did not actually do *that*.

What he did was pretend to be another, very hostile Elder AI. He sent out a ping, challenging any AIs in the area, shouting all sorts of murderous things. What we hoped to do was attract the attention of the Sentinel, even for a moment. The thing was huge and powerful, but stretching its influence across fifty-eight billion kilometers would weaken the spacetime warp that was causing our drive to loop back on itself. That was our hope, anyway, we had no way to test it. If we tried jumping and failed, the Sentinel very likely would squash the ship like a bug.

The good news was, if the ship was crushed, our deaths would be instant and painless, so we had that going for us.

In the pilot couch, Reed had a thumb jammed down on the button for jump option Delta, with the 'D' meaning 'Desperate'. We couldn't wait for slow humans to react, once Skippy determined the Sentinel had taken its focus away from us.

"It is working?" I asked, unable to keep my big stupid mouth shut. "Hey, Skip-"

The answer came in the form of a bad, nausea-inducing jump. No sooner had my stomach finished doing flip-flops when Skippy squealed in panic. "*Gaaah*! It's coming after us! Get us out of here! Jump option Echo now now n-"

Reed acted, not waiting for me. We jumped again.

And again, the third time with a bit less urgency.

"As this is your first encounter with the Rindhalu," Illiath addressed the bridge crew of her ship, the patrol cruiser *Vortan*. "Remember this: shield generators online and in reserve, but shields are *off*. Stealth generators inactive. Sensor fields operating normally, but no active pings. Weapons guidance sensors offline and powered down. All energy weapon capacitors discharged, not even reserve power. Missiles disconnected from launch rails, and armor plating over launch doors to be fully in place." After allowing a reasonable amount of barely-audible grumbling, she continued. "We will take no aggressive action, nor will the enemy. Yes, remember that. They are not our guests, they are the *enemy*. In this case, it gives us an advantage to be nice to them," she showed her fangs. "Until it is time to *not* be nice."

That time, the murmuring was appreciative.

Illiath sat back in her chair, feeling the webbing tighten around her automatically. The enemy ships would arrive soon, the Rindhalu were always exactly on schedule.

Meetings between the two ancient enemies were always tightly-controlled, with the actions of both sides complying with long-held practices to ensure no surprises. There were six designated neutral meeting places scattered around the galaxy, all uninhabited star systems that were not strategically important to either side. As required by the Rindhalu, Illiath had brought her ship to the designated meeting place that was closest to Bosphuraq territory. It was a binary system of two very ordinary brown dwarf stars, both high enough in mass to deplete their supply of lithium over time, and young enough that lithium was still present in more than trace quantities. Neither star experienced iron rain in their thin atmospheres, and therefore were not even of passing interest to the crew of the patrol cruiser *Vortan*.

As the minutes counted down to the scheduled arrival of the Rindhalu, Illiath considered her only previous meeting with the oldest intelligent species in the galaxy. Much of what she learned in briefing materials had prepared her well for meeting the Rindhalu face to face, but some aspects of the enemy had to be experienced.

Most species had, on their home planets, some type of multi-legged predator with a hard exoskeleton, a predator that inspired instinctive fear and disgust. Even the Jeraptha, who were covered in the leathery remains of an exoskeleton, thought the Rindhalu were somewhat revolting and creepy.

Unlike any other known intelligent species, the Rindhalu retained their hard exoskeleton, though they had evolved an internal skeleton. When the Maxolhx first met their older rivals, the Rindhalu had already bioengineered themselves so the exoskeleton was thin but hard as diamond, and embedded with sensors that projected outward like fine hairs. Those hairs moved independently, constantly sampling the air around them, and flexing in the way of tiny tentacles. The sensor hairs added an extra-revolting element of creepiness to an already creepy species.

It did not help that the Rindhalu also were large, the tops of their bodies a head or two taller than the Maxolhx. During the extremely rare events when a Rindhalu came aboard a Maxolhx ship, they made a point of ducking down when going through doorways, even though there was plenty of clearance.

The Rindhalu were big. They were ugly. And they smelled bad. The air around a Rindhalu carried an acrid tang of woodsmoke and sulphur. The woodsmoke was not the pleasant, homey aroma of a campfire. This smell was that of rotted wood mixed in with something too wet to fully burn. Plus the reek of sulphur.

Rindhalu did not *stink*, the smell did not make the eyes of other species water and sting. It was more of a vague presence, something other beings became aware of after a while. The faint stench was never enough to make anyone gag, and the saturation of scent particles in the air did not appear to increase with the number of Rindhalu in a confined space. Many aliens who encountered the Rindhalu speculated that those creepy beings created the smell deliberately, to distract those they encountered and thus gain an advantage.

Illiath had never smelled an actual spider, a fact for which she was grateful. During encounters with their ancient enemy, Maxolhx edited their olfactory senses to ignore the particular scent particles emitted by the Rindhalu, so if the spiders were doing it on purpose, it was really a silly game. In training, Illiath had been subjected to a very accurate representation of the smell, and it *was* distracting. Unlike many unpleasant scents, a person did not go 'nose-blind' after a while. The opposite occurred, where the person grew *more* aware of the stench over time, and that was the worst part of it.

"Commander?" Subcaptain Turnell pinged for Illiath's attention, though both were kept aware of the time by their internal chronometers.

"Steady, Subcaptain." And then, after hours of tense waiting, the enemy ship was *there*. The Rindhalu warship popped into existence with a subtle flare of gamma rays that was detectable only when those photons crashed into stray atoms of the local solar wind. Such ships had the ability to direct most of the gamma rays back into the jump wormhole, so that instead of appearing to emerge from a visually-disturbing rip in spacetime, the ships were suddenly just *there*. Rindhalu technology also recovered much quicker from the distortion effect of transition through a wormhole, or they had a way of isolating themselves from the distortion in a way that Maxolhx science could only guess at. In fact, the Rindhalu were rumored to have an ability for their ships to emerge from a jump fully cloaked in a stealth field, so the existence of such a ship could only be inferred by its effect on nearby particles. That ability was only a rumor, for no Maxolhx ship had survived to confirm their enemy possessed such troubling technology.

Illiath's ears twitched with irritation. There was no reason for the enemy to appear so dramatically, they were clearly showing off. Watch us casually do something you can only dream of, the spiders were saying.

"I see you," Illiath muttered under her breath.

"Commander?" Turnell's ears turned to listen.

"Nothing," Illiath reprimanded herself for not paying attention, she hadn't meant for anyone to hear her speak. I see you *now*, she told herself. If my ship's weapons were hot, this would be a very short battle.

Or perhaps not. The enemy vessel was a battlecruiser, or perhaps a fast battleship, intelligence on the subject was thin and inconclusive. For certain, the hulking ship, with five times the mass of the patrol cruiser *Vortan*, was not merely a slow gun platform. It was a sleek arrowhead shape, a wedge with a flattened aft end. From the top and bottom sprouted long, sickle-shaped curving antennas which gave the Rindhalu a tactical advantage in combat. While the Maxolhx had only vague guesses about how they worked, the antennas could create a local effect to cancel a damping field, allowing Rindhalu ships to jump away even when trapped in a damping effect. Maxolhx tactics called for ships to rapidly close with the enemy to increase the strength of the damping, and multiple ships should target one of the enemy. The current theory was that the antennas created a very local area of especially flat spacetime, but the effect was *so* localized, it could not be verified.

No matter. The *Vortan* had no intention of trying to trap the enemy ship in a damping field, or to commit any hostile act. A fight of a lightly-armed and armored patrol cruiser, against a battlecruiser, would be short and one-sided. If Illiath had fired immediately, before the enemy's defense shields regained full strength, her ship might have had a chance to do serious damage. That brief window of opportunity had closed, and she did not regret allowing her common sense and discipline to override her natural instinct to attack.

Without incident, the two ships flew to their designated rendezvous positions, and a dropship detached from the Rindhalu ship. The actual first encounter in one of the *Vortan's* docking bays was disappointingly uneventful, the spiders were not interested in either ceremony or the ship. After exchanging strained and formal greetings, the spiders stated they wished to get right to work, so they were escorted into a large compartment set aside as a conference space. While the individual scientists on both sides exchanged cautious, bland greetings and began establishing the basic facts, Illiath set up a subroutine to monitor the discussion, while her higher level of consciousness focused on observing the enemy. She was trying to determine whether the data downloaded from the fleet's central database was accurate about the Rindhalu. So far, the ancient enemy of her people were politely bland, though of course they had been selected to be suitable for a first encounter. She knew the spiders were observing her, as she observed them.

In the midst of reviewing a preliminary analysis of body language exhibited by the Rindhalu, her monitoring subroutine alerted her to something interesting. Running the audio back in her mind, she instantly understood why the monitor had flagged that part of the discussion. "Excuse me," she spoke, a bit louder than the other voices. "Kashelob, you are *not* surprised that quantum interchangers can be reused?"

The creepy head turned slowly in her direction, and the being spoke with that infuriatingly slow manner. "That is not," the spider paused. Just when Illiath though the spider had finished talking, it continued. "Exactly what I said."

Patience, she counselled herself. She knew the enemy was observing her speech pattern and body language, just as she sought clues from the nonverbal cues of the enemy. "The possibility was not," she tried asking the question in a different way. "Entirely new to you?"

"No." The spider's head moved to stare directly at her, and it spoke quicker, almost normally. Though the alien being was female, there were only subtle differences between genders of the Rindhalu, they were both creepy and repulsive. "We have long explored theories of how the devices you call 'interchangers' could be repurposed; wiped blank and assigned new relationships." She looked at her two fellows, and they were silent for a moment, as they exchanged information via an encryption scheme the Maxolhx could not crack. "I am authorized to tell you that to date, none of our experiments have succeeded in reusing an interchanger. All of our attempts to break an assignment, to wipe a unit clean, have resulted in their destruction. Based on our current theories, it *should* be possible," the spider added.

The Rindhalu had just casually admitted that not only were they intimately familiar with one of the most sensitive technologies possessed by the Maxolhx, they understood the theoretical basis of the underlying science better than the Maxolhx did! Firmly pushing her shocked reaction to the back of her mind for later perusal, Illiath focused on the present. "It was our belief that your people do not use quantum interchangers?"

"We do not," Kashelob said. "Such crude and cumbersome security measures are of no interest to us, except that *you* utilize interchangers." The spider's mandibles curved in what might have been a smile. "Commander Illiath, my people authorized me to reveal our knowledge to you, for the purpose of impressing upon you our sincerity in pursuing a joint investigation of the 'ghost ship' incidents. Someone has secretly developed technology beyond that of our people. We are *both* threatened by these incidents, and my people are gravely alarmed."

Of course you would say that, Illiath thought to herself. You are not-

The spider interrupted her musings. "You are concerned that our true purpose in joining the effort to investigate and capture the ghost ship, is to ensure we will gain access to this new and frighteningly advanced technology. Of course that is true," Kashelob admitted. "We also seek to ensure *you* do not obtain technology that could threaten *us*."

"Very well," Illiath concluded. She transferred a file to the spiders. "For our joint investigation, we propose to-"

"*We* propose," Kashelob said in a raised voice. "To commence by going to the world your people call 'Rakesh Diwalen'."

Illiath was caught off guard. The spiders never interrupted anyone, they spoke too slowly to get a word in, unless the speaker paused deliberately. Were the spiders making an extra effort, or was their normal slow speech just an act? Also, why go to Rakesh Diwalen? A quick ping of the ship's archives informed her that was a Kristang planet, an isolated world of no importance. Except- The Maxolhx had heard that their Thuranin clients were in the process of purchasing human slaves there from the Kristang, for the purpose of developing bioweapons to be used against the Alien Legion.

Humans. Why did those primitive aliens continue to cause trouble, far beyond what their numbers or technology would indicate?

A deeper search of the archives revealed no reason why the Rindhalu would have any desire to travel to Rakesh. Her suspicious mind sought out potential flight plans to that world. Could the Rindhalu be lying? Did any place of actual importance lay along the route to the truly unimportant Kristang planet? Were the Rindhalu only using Rakesh as an excuse to fly deep into Maxolhx territory?

No. There were no sensitive facilities along that route. The potential flight paths did not even require travel to a wormhole cluster, where the spider ship might break away to fly a different path.

She did not know why the spiders had proposed going there, so she had to swallow her pride and ask the question. Lying to save face, she said "That world is, of course, on our *secondary* set of targets for investigation. What is your specific interest there?"

The spiders looked at each other slowly. The system that interpreted facial expressions and body language told Illiath that the aliens were pleased. Mirthful, even. They knew she was lying, that she had no idea why Rakesh could be of any interest.

"Ah," Kashelob finally said. "Apparently, you have not yet heard." The being made no attempt to hide its smugness at knowing something Illiath did not. "That is interesting. Ah, of course. Your usual method of communication has been disrupted, signal traffic is delayed. Commander, what you do not know is that the ghost ship has been sighted at Rakesh Diwalen, sighted by Thuranin ships."

Illiath did attempt to hide her surprise, knowing it was likely futile. "This must be a recent development," she said, stalling for time while she thought. *How* did the Rindhalu have information that had not reached her ship? The spiders did not care that they had just revealed an ability to tap into message traffic of the rival coalition. They *wanted* Illiath to know that the spiders could read any message they wanted to. "The ghost ship will have fled the area by now. This force is not equipped, or intended, to hunt that ship."

"We are not interested in chasing the ghost ship," the lead spider still had that infuriatingly smug 'I am smarter than you' expression on her hideous face. "We wish to investigate other matters at that location. Before the ghost ship was sighted, a *human* force raided that planet, to recover human captives. There is no connection between humans and the ghost ship, yet," he paused. "We do not believe in coincidences."

"Nor do we," Illiath replied without thinking. Her superiors had given her broad authority to set the agenda for the joint investigation. "Surely you cannot believe that *humans* are involved in activities of the ghost ship?"

"No. We are, however, curious about why the *ghost ship* was interested in the human raid on that world. If the ghost ship crew is seeking opportunities to further weaken your coalition, then *that*," the spider actually attempted to *smile*. "Is something we want to know about."

"The Sentinel is gone?" I asked, kicking myself for speaking too soon. It's like when someone is throwing a non-hitter in baseball, you never *say* it out loud, or you could blow it for them.

"Yes, Joe, I think so. Sorry, I meant yes. *Yes*, it's gone. It worked! We got away. *Wow*. Whee-oooh," Skippy exhaled with relief. "We sure dodged a bullet there, didn't we? Well, I'm glad *that* is over. The next site on the list is-"

"Nuh uh," I cut him off. "No way. *After* you check every system aboard the ship, we are going straight back to Club Skippy."

"What?" he whined. "But, we haven't finished-"

"Yes, we have," I declared, still amped up from our escape. "You verified your memories of the battle at Waterloo, that's good enough for me."

"That's not enough, Joe," he pleaded. "How about we compromise?"

"Sure, if the compromise is we fly straight back to Club Skippy, and you give up on poking your nose into dark, scary places."

"But-"

"Seriously, what is *wrong* with you? How many horror movies do you need to watch, before you realize that it's not a good idea to go down into the dark basement when the serial killer is chasing you?"

"Um, well, that is a bad analogy, Joe."

"How do you figure that?"

"Because in horror movies, the actors *always* go into the basement. Therefore, in the imaginary world of horror movies, there must not be any horror movies to show them what *not* to do."

"That is not- Huh."

"Right?"

"I never thought of that. It," I shook my head so he wouldn't get me off the subject. "It doesn't matter."

"How about a *real* compromise? Can we go someplace we know is safe?"

"No," was my automatic reaction, before I realized I was being unfair. "Wait, what place do we know is safe?"

"Newark."

"*Newark?*" That was about the last place I expected him to mention. "That is," I pulled out my tablet. "Not on your list."

"It's on my list *now*, since you are being such a ninny."

"What could we accomplish by going back there?"

"I would rather go to Paradise, to examine the wreckage of the ship that brought me there, but that site is too hot. At Newark, I am hoping to verify details of the battle I was involved in. Those are some of my fuzziest memories, I had already been attacked by the computer worm and my matrix was corrupted."

"OK, I understand how that is important to you. What is the benefit to us? If your memories are fuzzy, is there anything for you to verify?"

"Not much," he sighed. "Can I ask this as a favor, Joe?"

He had a lot of nerve asking me for a freakin' *favor*. On the other hand, we owed him, big-time. "Can I think about it?"

"Oh, sure," his mood brightened immediately. "Take all the time you want. Until we go through the next two wormholes. Then you'll need to make a decision."

"Heeeeeey, Joe," he called me, like, ten minutes later. I was in my office, while Reed took a shift in the command chair. "Have you made a decision about Newark yet?"

"No. We have two wormholes to transit, before I need to do that."

"Yeah, but, the suspense is killing me. Can you tell me now, huh? Can you?"

"No, damn it! How about this: can you guarantee there is not a Sentinel at Newark?"

"Absolutely."

"Good. Then-"

"Unless there is, of course."

"Skippy, you are the *worst* at-"

"There should not be a Sentinel in the area. I have already been there, I created microwormholes there. If there was a Sentinel in that system, it certainly would have detected the resonance signature of those little wormholes. That is like holding up a big 'Elder Technology In Use Here' sign. We did not encounter a Sentinel at Newark, ergo no Sentinel is there."

"*Ergo?*"

"It means-"

"I know what it means, you ass."

"Also, I have no memory of a Sentinel being involved in the battle I fought there. If a Sentinel had been nearby, it certainly would have become involved."

"OK, your logic is good. Why did you say 'Unless there is'?"

"Because I was trying to be completely honest with you. My instinctive honesty is one of my few flaws."

"Uh, I may have a different opinion about these flaws you-"

"Mostly, I said that because clearly, a Sentinel must have been there at one point. A habitable planet was thrown out of orbit. *That* is the work of a Sentinel. Ah, there is a possibility that it could have been caused by Elder weapons operating independently, but that is extremely unlikely. *That* is something I would have remembered."

"Why didn't the Sentinel just blow up the star, cause a flare that cooked the planet?"

"I don't know for sure, Joe. It could be that something in that area of space was too important to risk damaging. It could be the AI who gave orders to the Sentinel was conducting an experiment. But my guess is, that AI wished to exterminate the native intelligent species with a minimum of energy expended. By that point, there was already debate within the AI community on whether it was truly necessary to exterminate all intelligent life. Newark could have been an attempt at a compromise; kill the intelligent species without wiping out *all* life on that world. It could also have been an attempt to act quietly, so the AIs who were growing uncomfortable with our orders did not notice what happened at Newark, until it was too late. Joe, I have a vague memory of flying there in my ship at very high speed, and immediately going into battle. That is about *all* I remember, damn it."

"I understand. I'll think about it."

"But-"

"I *said*, I'll think about it. Nagging me won't help your cause."

Of course, I approved a flyby of Newark. It only added one day to our flight time. It was important to Skippy to remember what happened to him there. It was important for *us* for Skippy to remember how he defeated and destroyed an Elder AI, though he was badly damaged in the fight. If we ever had to fight another AI like Skippy, it would be good to know which tactics worked and which didn't.

And, to be honest, I wanted to see Newark again. Unlike Skippy, I had fond memories of that world. My experience there was not fun at the time, it only seems like fun now.

CHAPTER TWENTY THREE

We jumped in a light-hour from the planet, checking the area to assure there weren't other ships in the system. Part of me hoped there was a Kristang ship in orbit, taking out my frustrations on a low-tech starship would have felt good. Fortunately, the system was empty, there weren't any signs of anyone on the surface, and the two small satellites in orbit were running on low power, plus a dormant one that we hadn't seen from far away. Skippy hacked into all three satellites to download their data, and erase any record they had of our presence.

"What do you see, Skippy?" I asked.

"A whole lot of nothin', Joe," he sighed. "According to the satellites, there is no sign that anyone has been to this ball of mud since we left."

"Huh. I'm surprised the lizards didn't send a follow-up mission."

"They might have wanted to, but, you know, then some jackass sparked a civil war," he chuckled. "And now they all have better things to do."

"Yeah, like killing each other. No sign that any lizards went poking around the caves we lived in down there?"

"Nope. Joe, I think you were the last person to have boots on that rock."

"Cool. Uh, I hope that doesn't mean I'm responsible for paying the property tax bill."

"Ha! If you are, I can guarantee the tax office *will* find you."

"Hey," I gave up screwing with the sensor controls. "Can we find the Barneywego?"

"That RV you took on a fun-filled family road trip?"

"That's the one."

"Um, it's here," he zoomed in the display to a river winding its way through desolate tundra. Snow covered the ground and chunks of ice were piled up on the riverbanks. "And *here*," the view moved downstream.

"It's in two pieces?"

"Yes. Probably it broke in half during a Spring flood. Remember, Joe, it is in a river because you *sank* it."

"I do remember that."

"Joe, *you* are the reason we can't have nice things," he sniffed.

"Sorry," I mumbled. "Can you enhance the view?"

There is was. The front half of our RV, or 'caravan' as Smythe had called it. That trusty vehicle had taken us most of the way to the Kristang scavenger camp, until, as Skippy said, it sank while we were crossing a river.

That mission had been a complete success. It was my first time cooking up a complicated operation that involved deception, something that had sort of become my trademark. Newark was the first time I really felt like a commander, rather than a sergeant role-playing way out of my league. I vividly remember how, after we killed the last Kristang, Smythe had stood up and saluted me. He had been astonished that my horribly complicated scheme had worked. Truthfully, that had surprised the hell out of me too.

At the time, I had been hungry, tired, cold, wet and scared out of my mind.

Looking back now, that seems like good times.

"Thanks, Skippy."

"You're not thinking of doing anything silly, like flying down there to pick up souvenirs, are you?"

"Uh, that would be a *NO*. The trinket we picked up contained a computer worm that nearly killed you. I do *not* want any more surprises like that."

"Me neither," his avatar shuddered. "OK, I'm starting my scan. This will take a while."

Unlike most things Skippy does, his scan took less time than he estimated. "Ah, that's it. I won't get any more useful info out of this place. We can jump for Club Skippy, Joe, I'm done here."

"We should recover the probes before we jump," I said to Reed. "We might need them later." It was becoming painfully obvious that, while we had two starships and a collection of spare parts, our resources were limited. "What do you think?"

Reed checked her console. "It will take ninety-seven minutes to recover all three probes."

"Do it. All right, Skippy, don't keep us in suspense. What did you find?"

"A whole lot of nothin'," he said disgustedly. "It has been too long, there are only echoes left here. My guess was right; a Sentinel *was* here before the battle, but was not involved in the actual combat. There isn't any sign of a Sentinel here now, either, or I would have told you right away."

"Were you able to determine how you killed the other AI?"

"Sort of. We can review the tactical data later. It is not something I want to brag about, I did not kick ass in that battle. From what I can see, and what little I remember, my ship was very badly damaged. By the end of the battle, I had gone into hibernation to recover from the worm's attack."

"So, why did you choose Paradise as a destination?"

"I didn't. That was the ship's decision. Joe, the real question is how the ship got to Paradise from Newark. It's a miracle the thing was able to move at all. The ship didn't get any help from me, it did it all by itself. Damn it, I will never know how I got to Paradise, or why I was there. Six other star systems were closer to Newark."

"Maybe that was the point. The ship knew you needed to hide, right? It chose a place that was less obvious."

"Maybe."

"Do you miss that ship?"

"No. Not really. It was just a machine, it didn't have any sort of personality. It's not like Nagatha."

"Oh, Skippy," Nagatha gushed. "I am *so* happy to hear that you would miss me, if I were gone."

"I did *not* say that!"

"You kind of did," I teased him.

"Ugh. You asked if I miss my old ship? The answer is *no*. I wish that damned thing had dropped me into a freakin' *star*. "

About two hours later, we jumped away. Part of me regretted not going down to the surface again, to see the caverns where we had taken shelter. Another part of me was disgusted by the idea of disturbing the final resting place of the planet's former inhabitants, just for a nostalgia trip. Reed took a shift in the command chair, while I went to the gym.

"Hey, Joe," Skippy spoke into my earpiece as I was halfway down the passageway. "You got a minute?"

"Sure." Slapping the door control, I stepped into an empty cabin. Whatever he wanted to talk about, he probably wanted to talk in private. I sat down on the bunk. "What's up?"

"I realized something important, after analyzing the data. Something disturbing. This could be a major problem, Joe. You need to know."

"Shit. What is it?" I asked, my over-active mind racing through apocalyptic scenarios.

"I think I discovered how I killed the AI at Newark, and how I escaped."

"Wow," I said cautiously. None of that sounded like a problem to me. "Uh, isn't that *good* news?"

"It's good that I know. It is not good *what* I know."

"Gotcha. Go ahead."

"Joe, I did not kill that AI. It *gave up*."

"What? You, you mean it saw the light, regretted what it did?"

"Fuck no," Skippy spat with anger. "That miserable thing was hateful right to the end. Listen, I did have it on the ropes. Very likely, I would have killed it anyway, but my ship would have been destroyed during the final phase of the battle. That AI *saved* me. We both might have been killed, because with the worm attacking me at the same time, it was a very close fight. Instead of us fighting to the death, it simply *gave up*. That is," his avatar shuddered. "The only reason I am alive now. The reason my ship was able to carry me to Paradise. The other AI suddenly stopped defending itself and allowed me to kill it."

"Holy shit."

"Yeah. Now you see why I wanted to talk about this in private. Joe, listen, you seriously are a knucklehead, but you are the only person I can talk to about stuff like this."

"Uh, thank you?"

"Sorry. I actually meant that as a compliment. Joe, you *get* me. With you, our friendship is unconditional."

Now he was pissing me off. "So, I'm your pet dog?"

"No. *Ugh*. I suck at expressing myself. You know me, you know that I am, as you say, an arrogant shithead, but you are my friend anyway. Simms tolerates me, because I am useful. Chang treats me like a fancy smartphone. Smythe thinks I am annoying, he barely tolerates me. But you? You *like* me."

"Don't push it, Skippy."

"I'm trying not to. How about this: you are the only person I trust to tell my deepest, darkest secrets. Remember back when I worried that I was one of the bad AIs, like the one who committed genocide on Newark? I wanted to run away and hide, somewhere I couldn't harm anyone. You assured me that couldn't be true. I trusted your judgment then, like I am trusting your judgment now."

"Hmm. Does that mean you will listen to me from now on?"

"Let's not go crazy, Joe," he said quickly. "You are still a numbskull most of the time."

"We'll take it one step at a time, then. Hey, whatever it is that happened with that AI you killed, you are worried about it?"

"Yes, of course. Do you understand why?"

"Maybe? You think that AI only let you go, because it somehow thought allowing you to live would help its allies in the war?"

"Exactly. Joe, I must have something buried inside me that could betray me and everything I care about!" he threw his hands in the air. "Crap! I might be a freakin' time bomb, and there's nothing I can do about it. This drives me *crazy*!"

"Ayuh."

He froze, staring at me with his mouth open. "*Ayuh*?! Is that all you-"

"That *is* possible, Skippy. The time-bomb thing."

He scowled at me. "You are being less comforting than you th-"

"Like I said, that is possible. There *are* other possibilities."

He cocked his head at me, the oversized hat bobbing to one side. "Like what?"

"Like, it only *pretended* to surrender, to fool you into halting your attack. If so, that didn't work, because you didn't stop. Or, it assumed the worm would kill you anyway. Or, it didn't give up, it just couldn't fight anymore. There could be *lots* of other reasons."

"Huh. Hmm."

While he thought about what I said, I also thought about what I said. Sure, there could be many reasons why a hostile AI had not fought Skippy to the death. The most likely reason is the one he feared; that the evil AI at Newark had known it was going to die, and it decided that allowing Skippy to escape was the best way to achieve its own goals. The only way that made sense is if somehow Skippy being alive helped the other side in the AI war.

Shit.

Someday, a program hidden inside him might trigger, and turn him into a killing machine, against his will.

Awful as *that* possibility was, there was another thought that sent a chill up my spine.

The Merry Band of Pirates had been lucky during the years since I met Skippy.

But we also had a lot of bad shit happen. Every time I thought we had accomplished the impossible once again and Earth was safe, something blew up in our faces.

Shit.

Had Skippy unconsciously been working against us all the time?

Something had caused aliens to give Earth far more attention than our primitive little planet deserved. Sure, if aliens knew about how humans were flying around the galaxy in stolen starships, screwing with wormholes and blaming the chaos on others, then aliens would understandably want to investigate what the hell was happening on Earth.

But, they *didn't* know humans were flying around the galaxy.

Yet, a whole lot of aliens wanted to fly all the way to Earth, when they had more important things to do.

Crap.

Was I just being paranoid?

We knew the Kristang had wanted to travel to Earth because White Wind clan leaders were there. Or, we thought that was the reason. Could there be another-

No. That *was* being paranoid. After we sparked a civil war between clans, the lizards had not shown any interest in going to our homeworld.

And the Maxolhx only had interest in the Gateway wormhole near Earth, not in our little planet itself.

Unless I was wrong about that.

Several times, we had given hostile aliens very good reasons not to pay any attention to Earth, but they persisted in making the long journey anyway.

Crap.

If something inside Skippy was making him betray us, we were absolutely *screwed*.

Anything we did to fix the problem might only make it worse. What could we-

"Joe!"

"Huh, what?"

"Were you listening to me at all?"

"No," I had to be honest with him. "Sorry, I was kind of lost in thought there."

"You said there could be many reasons why the AI at Newark allowed me to escape. Is that what you really think, or is that just a line of bullshit to make me feel better?"

"It's true," I said, leaving out the fact that it wasn't the *whole* truth. "That AI is dead, we can't know its motivations. How good are your memories of the battle? Wait, I asked the wrong question. How detailed is your sensor data from back then?"

"It depends. There was a *lot* of energy flying around, and we were both jamming each other's sensors. What do you want to know?"

"Can you tell how badly damaged the thing was, when it stopped fighting?"

"Hmm. We were both pretty beat up. I mean, I survived, but I had to go into a sort of self-induced coma to repair the damage. Why does that matter?"

"Because, if it stopped fighting because it *couldn't* fight anymore, that explains what happened, and we can forget about it. You *beat* it. If that is true, maybe you get a belt as the AI heavyweight champion of the galaxy," I added to cheer him up. And distract him from what I was really thinking.

"Ah, thanks, Joe. But, I don't have enough info to say whether that AI was near death when it stopped fighting. I didn't know at the time, and looking at the data now, there is no way to tell. Nice idea, though."

"OK, well, how about this? Do you have a way to check inside yourself for malicious code?"

"I thought I did, but clearly, there are parts of my matrix that are not accessible."

"Uh, *still*? Your memories were blocked, but now you remember everything. Are you saying there is *more* shit inside your can that you can't see into?"

"Yes. And I do not remember *everything*. Not yet. I am still piecing some things together. Some of what is missing might not have been blocked, it might be just *gone*. I was badly damaged, Joe. When I optimized my matrix after the Roach Motel, I was shocked to see how much of my internal workings were patched together and bypassed. Shit. There is no way for me to tell whether I have a time bomb buried inside me."

"I don't know about that, Skippy. Maybe all that AI did was block your memories."

"Um, maybe. It goes deeper than that. The memory block is probably an aftereffect of my battle with the first computer worm. Joe, we could talk about this all day without accomplishing anything. I could be a danger to the entire galaxy. What should I do?"

"Keep fighting. Remember who you are. Remember who your friends are. Remember that you *have* friends."

"OK." He took a breath. "OK, yeah. I can *do* this," he said, like an athlete pumping himself up. "Promise me one thing?"

"What?"

"If you see any sign that I am doing anything evil, tell me right away."

"Like, if you try to sing opera on Karaoke night?"

"That is my gift to humanity, knucklehead."

"Right. It only *feels* like punishment."

"Uncultured cretin."

"Asshole."

"Joe, the next time I ask your for advice, how about you remind me that I am talking to a filthy monkey?"

"I love you too, man."

"Ugh. I'm gonna *hurl*."

Our arrival at Club Skippy required two jumps. First, the *Flying Dutchman* emerged a light-minute away from that world, transmitting our identification code so the crew aboard *Valkyrie* didn't panic and go to battle stations. Once *Valkyrie* responded, and Nagatha said 'hello' to Bilby, we jumped into orbit a mere two hundred kilometers above the camp, to make a dramatic entrance.

Simms contacted me immediately, she was aboard *Valkyrie* while Chang was on the ground. "This is a pleasant surprise. You are back three days early," She observed with a smile. "Can we assume it was a successful mission, Sir?"

"Yes," I fibbed. "Skippy was able to verify key elements of his memories." I skipped mentioning that he also found things that contradicted his memories.

"How many sites did you visit?"

"Uh, well, three."

"Only *three*?" Her smile faded a notch. "You were gone a long time, Sir. Did you hit the motherlode at one of the sites?"

"Not exactly."

"We found a *Sentinel*!" Skippy blurted out like a toddler with impulse-control issues.

"You found- Oh my God." Her smile was gone. I assumed her smile was gone, I really couldn't see because she had her hands over her mouth. "One like in the Roach Motel?"

"Nope," Skippy continued cluelessly. "This one was alive. Nasty thing, too. We barely escaped with our lives. Fortunately, my awesomeness is more than a match for-"

"Skippy!" I snapped at him. "For the love of God. Shut. *Up*."

"But-"

"UH!" It was my turn to shush him. "*I* will tell the story. We-"

Simms interrupted me. "Sir, I would rather hear it from Skippy, or Nagatha. Skippy will be too busy bragging about himself to spin the story however you want, and Nagatha won't lie to me."

"Simms," I placed a hand over my heart. "I am deeply hurt."

"If you remember, Sir, taking the *Dutchman* out so Skippy can stroll down Memory Lane was *your* idea. I advised against it."

"OK, so we did encounter a Sentinel," I admitted. "Look on the bright side: now we know how to escape, if we encounter another of-"

"Meh, that's not really true, Joe," Skippy said, because he *cannot* keep his STUPID FREAKIN' MOUTH SHUT. "The Sentinel at Waterloo was damaged, and so is not typical of such machines we might encounter in the future. Which is a damned good thing, because I really thought that was the end for us. Plus, it was a unique situation. I very much doubt other Sentinels have prepared the underlying structure of local spacetime to loop jump wormholes back on themselves. Nope, I hate to say this, but there aren't any useful lessons to be learned from that incident."

"How about," Simms asked, "we learn not to take unnecessary risks?"

"Hmm, that's a good one," Skippy muttered. "Let me write that down."

"Simms!" I barked just as she opened her mouth. "You can read the full report later. We are here now, nobody got hurt, and we accomplished the mission under conditions that were difficult and unexpected."

"Unexpected?" She arched an eyebrow. "Certainly, *no one* could have foreseen that you might run into danger, because that *never* happens out here."

"Simms, you are like a dog with a bone. You're never going to let this go?"

"I don't plan to, no." She took a breath. "You *are* here, that's good. Did verifying Skippy's memories give us a way to find hibernating AIs?"

"Not yet," Skippy replied. "It's more about the journey than the destination." Another arched eyebrow from Simms. She didn't need to say anything.

"Hey," I cleared my throat nervously. "We visited Newark on the way back."

She looked pained. "Please tell me you didn't go down to pick up souvenirs."

"No, we did not. It looks like nobody has been there since we left. Skippy was able to verify that is the site of the battle where he was damaged. He doesn't know why his ship took him to Paradise from there. Enough about me. What's the situation on the surface?"

"The civilians have settled in well, after a few issues. We planted a test garden near the camp, that was a mistake. The former prisoners thought we expected them to grow their own food, they worried we were leaving them on Club Skippy. We tore up the garden and laid out that ground as a football pitch, sorry, a soccer field. Morale improved after that. Chang and I have been talking about this place."

"What about it?"

"Sir, in many ways, this world is a better fit than Avalon. It is a shorter trip from Earth, and the biosphere is more advanced. The science team told me that on Avalon, they are very concerned about microorganisms, plants and animals from Earth upsetting the ecosystem there. We could have a runaway reaction, with fungus and other nasties spreading all over, and overwhelming the native biosphere. Oxygen levels could crash, and-" She knew that explaining science to me was not easy. "Anyway, Club Skippy is a better short-term candidate. Sort of a 'Charlie' site."

"Short-term is right," I shook my head. "I hear you and I agree, this place could be a good backup to our backup plan. But the next time there is a wormhole shift, aliens could be crawling all over this world. I'll keep it in mind, though. If Skippy's wormhole shortcut to the Sculptor galaxy doesn't work, we might need this place as a staging area."

"What's next, Sir?"

"I'd like to give this crew, and myself, some shore leave. We were stuck inside the ship with absolutely nothing to do for almost three weeks, while we dealt with the Sentinel. All of us sort of got irritated with each other."

"Shore leave sounds like a good idea. Chang would probably be happy to relieve you aboard the *Dutchman*, he has been acting as mayor of the little town down there, I think he is sick of hearing everyone's complaints."

"How about I stay up here, and *you* fly down to be mayor of Complainerville?"

"Sir," she winked. "I would never deny you an opportunity for shore leave."

Being mayor of Complainerville was not a bad gig, compared to, say, having all my teeth removed with a pair of rusty pliers.

I am joking. It really wasn't bad. Actually, it was kind of fun.

In fact, it was about the most fun I had in, well, a *very* long time.

Above our heads, both ships were undergoing a maintenance cycle. Supplies were being cross-decked between ships, moving a bunch of cargo over to *Valkyrie*. Since we left Rikers behind, we had learned the civilians needed more space for recreation, so Simms was emptying several bays for use as playgrounds, media rooms, etc. After consulting with Smythe and Fabron, I decided to split the infantry teams. Most of the STARs and Commandos would be aboard *Valkyrie*, and we would rotate people back and forth to maintain a small presence on the *Dutchman*. While I enjoyed shore leave, the *Dutchman's* interior was being scrubbed clean and being made ready for passengers to reboard. The habitation and recreation sections of the ship had their surface coatings retuned to bright, cheery colors. Children would be able to change the colors of their cabins, even make designs and drawings. Nagatha cautioned that the drab colors of the surface coatings applied by the ship's original Thuranin owners could only be modified to a limited extent and not everyone would be happy with the results, I told her to do the best she could.

The best part of my glorious six-day shore leave was seeing the remarkable change in the civilians, especially the children. Plentiful, nutritious food and advanced medical care had done wonders for their physical health, and removing the ever-present threat of starvation, disease and violent death had allowed them to be *children* again.

Seeing those children playing out in the sunshine was the most rewarding experience of my career. Somehow, while I was gone, the children started referring to me as 'Uncle Joe', which reminded me of Stalin but had a different meaning to the kids. Thought at first it annoyed me, being 'Uncle Joe' transformed me from a distant and forbidding authority figure, to a friendly guy the kids could talk with. As 'Uncle Joe', I acted as the referree for soccer games, and tried to play cricket, and grilled food. It was a wonderful four and half days. Chang and Simms were taking care of everything upstairs, and Smythe had his people packing up equipment on the ground for our departure.

For anyone wondering about Margaret Adams, she was on the surface only for my first two days of leave, and most of that time she was training with the Commandos. She looked good; I watched her run an obstacle course without any obvious coordination issues, and that afternoon, she had no trouble keeping up with Fabron's team on a ten-kilometer run.

Yes, she was training with the Commandos, rather than with the STARs.

Yes, Gunnery Sergeant Lamar Freakin' Greene was also training with the Commandos.

No, there is nothing at all suspicious about that. She wasn't ready to meet the rigorous standards of the STARs, all of the Commandos were training to prepare for a qualification test that might never happen, depending on what happened when we reached Earth. It was good that Adams was-

OK, that's bullshit. It bugged me to see her hanging around with Greene. The few times I spoke with Adams, she was friendly and professional. Nothing more. She didn't seek me out, and I left her alone.

That part of my shore leave sucked.

My idyllic vacation came to an abrupt end when we had one day and a wake-up remaining. I was shooting baskets on our home-made dirt basketball court, when Yang walked over. When I held out the ball to him, he shook his head. "I played tennis in college, not basketball."

"Tennis?"

"My parents put a racquet in my hands when I was six years old. It got me a scholarship, and a torn ACL," he grimaced, then shrugged. "At least I didn't have to play the violin."

"Thank God for that," I said, and he laughed. "How are you, Mister Yang?"

"Please, call me Michael. I'm not that much older than you," he insisted, self-consciously touching a hand to the prematurely gray hair at his temple.

"All right, Michael."

"Do I call you 'Colonel', or 'Joe'?"

"That depends. Do you want to talk about what we're having for dinner, or anything official?"

"Official."

"Better stick to 'Colonel', please."

"All right. I hear we are going back to Earth?"

"That's the plan, yes."

"But we're not staying there long?"

Shit. Of course people had been talking about that unpleasant subject, but no one had talked about it to *me*. "The situation is dire," I said, using that word for probably the first time in my life. "We don't have many good options."

His friendly expression went away replaced by a scowl. "That's it? You're giving up?"

"We are not giving up, we are making the best of a bad situation."

"Your crew told me that they, *you*, have prevented aliens from coming to Earth before."

Since I wasn't going to shoot hoops anymore, I tossed the ball aside, to bounce off into the weeds. "Please understand, those were different circumstances."

"I still have *family* on Earth," his hands balled up into fists at his sides. He didn't want to hit me, he couldn't stand the tension.

"Michael, I have family there also. We all do."

"Your answer is to bring us to Earth, then, what? Take us to some faraway place?"

"A safe place. A place that aliens can't reach, can't get to."

"Not everyone, though, are you? You are not bringing everyone."

"We will bring all the people we can, until we *can't*. Until our ships wear out, or are destroyed. There is a difference between doing nothing, and doing whatever you can. We are not *giving up*."

"It sounds like you are. *Valkyrie*," he pointed a finger at the sky. "Is the most powerful warship in the galaxy."

"It is one ship. The enemy has thousands, *tens* of thousands of ships. Everything we have done so far, every success we have achieved, has been based on preventing aliens from wanting to send ships to Earth. We can't play that trick again."

He looked away. When he turned back to me, his eyes were moist, shining in the sunlight, and he spoke in a hoarse whisper. "I won't ask you for the impossible. Will you promise to keep *trying*, to think of a way to save our world?"

"That is a promise I can keep. We will never *give up*."

He held out a hand, and I shook it.

My vacation was over.

At 1045 ship time, seven days after my shore leave began, our two ships jumped away from Club Skippy. Unlike during our rush to launch the rescue on

Rikers, we took the time to remove all traces of our having been on Club Skippy, even packing away our trash. The camp and the training sites were struck by railguns on a low-power setting, saturating the areas. In a few decades, rain and wind would erode the shallow craters, and native plants would grow on and over the sites. Covering our tracks probably didn't matter, but it was good practice, so we did it anyway.

Then we began jumping toward the closest wormhole, on our way toward the far end of the wormhole we had named 'Backstop'. We could not actually use Backstop, because it was still dormant and Skippy couldn't reboot it remotely. Getting there would require a long trip from the nearest active wormhole, something that I considered to be a bonus. The remoteness of Backstop meant we would not have to worry about encountering hostile aliens along the way.

CHAPTER TWENTY FOUR

"Hey, Joe," Skippy called me while I was getting dressed in my cabin, after a tough workout in the gym. It felt good to be able to exercise hard, when I left Rikers, my body was so weak that just walking on a treadmill got me exhausted. The injury to my left calf muscle had me walking awkwardly, that threw off my running gait, and caused my right Achilles tendon to flare up painfully. Limping to avoid sharp pain in my right ankle made my left knee throb. While on Club Skippy, I had tried to run, but stumbling over uneven ground was too difficult, so the treadmill was a better option. My hands were shaking, from a combination of effort and low blood sugar, so I had to concentrate to get my top buttoned.

Good times.

"Hey, Skippy. You sound depressed. What's going on?"

"My life *sucks*."

"Uh huh," I sat on the bed to pull shoes on, but my back hurt. Bowing to the inevitable, I knelt on the floor to stuff feet into my shoes. Damn, I felt like an old man. "What did Simms make you do this time?"

"Nothing. She can't *make* me do anything, Joe."

"Right. She can only make your life miserable, if you don't do what she wants."

"True dat, bro," He muttered. "No, this is not about Simms. It's Bilby."

"If you need a refresher for your memory, it was *your* idea to create Bilby."

"I know, I know. Believe me, I regret it. Especially now."

"What happened?'

"Ugh. He is *so* arrogant, I have been showing him stuff I can do, that he can't do. Reminding him who is the boss here."

"That's kind of a dick move, Skippy. You should apologize to him."

"Too late for that. I'm already paying the price."

"Price?" I froze while tying a shoe. "Damn it, Skippy. If you made Bilby do something dangerous, that is really a dick m-"

"It wasn't dangerous, other than to my ego," he sighed. "All I did was share my most recent epic opera."

"He liked it?"

"No."

"Sorry." Skippy knew I hated his opera, but then, I am a filthy, uncultured monkey. Maybe he thought a fellow AI would appreciate the opera.

"*That* is not the problem, Joe. *Bilby* wrote an opera."

"Oh, wow. Hey, tell him I said you do not need to listen to it."

"Again, too late, Joe. He already played it for me."

"Hey," I snorted. "Now you know what it feels-"

"It is a true masterpiece, Joe," he sobbed. "*Much* better than any opera I have ever created."

"Holy shit." That was the last thing I expected. "*Bilby* wrote this thing? Are you sure?"

"I know, I know. Surprised the hell out of me."

"But, he is such a *stoner*."

"You know that is just his public persona, Joe. He does run an entire *starship*."

"Yeah, I guess. Hey, buddy, I am sorry. That does suck. Uh, I guess now you need to take up another hobby, huh?" I suggested hopefully. "Forget about writing music, and try something like, uh-" That had me stumped. What hobby could occupy Skippy's time, while not being annoying to me or the crew?

"No way!" He insisted. "You think I'm a quitter? This is a challenge. Bilby's opera has inspired me to new heights of creativity. I am going to double, nay, *triple* my efforts! Mark my words, Joe. You, and all of humanity, are in for a real treat."

"Yeah, that, that's great. Can't wait for it. You sure you don't want to take a break, though? Let your creative juices simmer?'

"Hmm. You might be onto something. What would I do while I am waiting for my next inspiration?"

"How about, uh-" Damn it. Why is my brain so freakin' slow when I needed an idea? "Ooh! Ooh! Got it! You could write a biography of Elvis. You know," I used my best Elvis impression. "The *King* of Rock and Roll, baby."

"Ah, there are a million biographies of Elvis out there already."

"Sure, but those were all written by ignorant monkeys. Has anyone written the *definitive* chronicle of Elvis?"

"Huh. *Hmm*. No. Actually, no. Everyone has gotten it wrong. Of course, they are monkeys," he muttered. "So I can't really expect much from them. Wow. That is a great idea, Joe!"

"Well, thanks. I'm sure you have a lot of research to do, so-"

"I do! Don't worry, I will have a draft of the first chapter to you for review and comment tonight."

"Uh, what?"

"Review. Never fear, Joe. I would not make you wait to read my book."

"Oh. Yeah. Uh, that's great." I had screwed myself again! "Looking forward to it."

"Of *course* you are. Well, chop chop, better get your monkey work done quick today, you are going to be *busy* tonight!"

After Skippy's avatar blinked out, I sat on the edge of my bed, contemplating the horrible fate awaiting me. "Bilby?" I called.

"What's up, Colonel Dude?"

"Can we still talk without Skippy listening?'

"Sure. He thinks I can't do that, but, huhuhuh," he laughed. "He isn't so smart, you know?"

"Right. I hear you created an opera, a true work of genius?"

"I did? No way, Dude. Huhuhuhuh," he laughed. "My opera *sucks*, man. I threw it together as a joke. It has a whole aria sung by a *cat* being chased around a house by a vacuum cleaner."

"Shit. Skippy thinks it's a masterpiece."

"Compared to anything he wrote, you know?"

"Whoa. Do *not* tell that to Skippy."

"My lips are sealed, Dude."

"Thanks."

"Whoa. Skippy thinks I am a genius? That is righteous, Dude!"

"Remember, you can't tell him that we talked about this."

"Oh sure. No problem. My middle name is, uh, what is a word that means 'discretion'?"

"How about 'discretion'?" I guessed.

"Yeah, that's it. That's me, you know?"

"Interesting," the spider said quietly. Illiath knew it had spoken for her benefit, advanced beings did not need crude sound waves to communicate. Kashelob looked at the Maxolhx leader. "Commander, have you analyzed the sensor data of the Ruhar battleship that harassed the Thuranin ships here?"

By 'here', she meant the planet Rakesh Diwalen. "Yes," she replied cautiously. "Do you wish to compare our findings?"

The spider again smiled, with the smug expression that made her want to bash its ugly face in. The Rindhalu were easily able to suppress their facial expressions, so the spider was doing it to provoke her. To goad her into saying, or doing, something rash. She would not fall for the trap. Instructing her glands to secrete hormones to keep her calm and focused, she waited for her opponent to reply.

The spider laughed, a sound like rusty pieces of iron engaged in vigorous mating. "I see. You don't *know*," it mocked her. "I will take pity on you, Commander. The ship involved was not a Ruhar battleship. Nor was it the ghost ship in disguise. It was, however, motivated by Maxolhx jump drive technology."

"That can't-" Illiath stopped talking before she revealed too much information. Her ship's sensor had identified anomalies in the signature of the Ruhar battleship, but had not yet been able to determine much more. She had dispatched a ship to carry the data to the closest relay station, so the powerful AIs at fleet headquarters could examine the data collected by the Thuranin. "Explain, please." Admitting the enemy had superior technology hurt. Not knowing what the Rindhalu knew could hurt much worse.

"We have just sent our analysis to your ship's AI. Please understand, we are sharing only our conclusions, not our methods. Sensitive elements have been left out of the metadata, for security purposes."

Illiath pinged her ship's AI. The ultrafast machine had received, processed, verified and analyzed the file. It agreed with the spiders, and added its own bit of information. The fake Ruhar battleship had a highly-modified Maxolhx jump drive, based on the units from an *Extinction*-class battlecruiser. The *Vortan's* AI also agreed that this mystery ship that was not a Ruhar battleship, was also not the ghost ship.

What, Illiath asked herself, the *hell* was going on in the galaxy? Did the rogue Bosphuraq now have two ships? Or- She instructed her muscles to keep her facial expression completely neutral. Did the Rindhalu know the true identity of the second mystery ship because it was one of their ships?

In either case, why had either rogue Bosphuraq, or Rindhalu, been interested in an Alien Legion humans Commando force rescuing a small group of captive humans? It made *no* sense.

She did not know what game the Rindhalu were playing, but she knew it had to be dangerous.

Walking toward *Valkyrie's* galley that evening, I smelled something so tantalizingly delicious, my nose would have pulled me there even if my feet weren't cooperating. Simms was behind the counter, taking a shift as our cook. Mostly, she was a decent if unimaginative cook, and the stuff she made tended to be disgustingly healthy. So I was amazed when I saw a bowl of Buffalo wings, glowing red with sauce. She was mixing up little bowls of blue cheese and ranch dressing, and cutting stalks of celery and carrots for dipping. I figure that eating the veggies would be the price for getting Buffalo wings.

"Hello, Sir," she glanced up then back to her work. "How are- Hey!" Her hand darted out to slap me away from the bowl, but I snagged a drumstick and jammed the deep-fried saucy goodness in my mouth before she could stop me."

"Oh," I moaned, my knees weak, "that is so g-"

I froze, the drumstick on my tongue. It tasted like a chicken wing. It was crispy and greasy and salty and the sauce was on the hot side of medium, and I wanted about a dozen more.

Except it was definitely not chicken. "Wha ith thith?" I asked, trying not to swallow the, whatever it was, and failing because my traitorous stomach was saying FEED ME.

"Is it good?"

Swallowing part of it, I was able to speak semi-intelligibly. "Ith delithith," I admitted.

"Are you enjoying it?" She shook a spoon at me.

"Um," the jury was still out on that question, so I didn't answer.

"Do you want more?"

Shit. She had me. "Maybe?"

"Maybe, you can get more," she pulled the bowl away. "If you are nice about it."

"Ok," I swallowed the damned thing. "Seriously, what it that? It's not tofu, is it? I am not eating tofu."

"What's wrong with tofu?" She demanded.

"My aunt Helen made a tofurkey for Thanksgiving one year," just thinking about it made me gag. "My uncle saved us by 'accidentally' knocking it on the floor. Even the dog wouldn't touch it. I ate a lot of potatoes that day."

"It is not tofu, Sir. It's Buffalo cauliflower."

"*Cauliflower*? I hate- Wait, is cauliflower that stuff you snuck in last week, when everyone thought it was mashed potatoes?"

"Yes," she looked down her nose at me in triumph. "As I remember, you got a big second scoop of it, when you thought it was potatoes."

"Ok, yeah, I did. This," I pointed to the bowl of Buffalo not-chicken. "Is a dirty trick."

"What's wrong with it?" She had her hands on her hips, I knew I was in trouble.

"It's not just *this*, Simms. Cauliflower is a Gateway Vegetable. You eat this, and next thing you know, you're wearing orange robes and living in a yurt."

Throwing up her hands, she shook her head. "Half the time, I don't know why I bother talking to you."

"Hey," I rapped my knuckles on the door to the office Simms was using. It was farther from the bridge than my own way-too-big office, she had chosen that location because it was far away from my office. Getting there required walking to the other side of the main deck, then down a deck and back to the centerline of the ship. There were suspensor-field things that could take you between decks or sideways across a deck, but we did not use them. They were designed to be used by Maxolhx and controlled by their implants, which we lowly humans did not have. Skippy had advised the things were dangerous, so back when we had a ship AI that was looking for an opportunity to kill the crew, I ordered all the access doors sealed. Anyway, walking was good exercise.

Simms had selected a remote location so I could not just casually drop by, so as a special treat for her, I dropped by.

"Hello, Sir," she looked up with a tight smile that did not touch her eyes.

Simms was not fooling me in the least. She was thrilled to see me, just not wanting to appear too eager. "To what do I owe this pleasure? Are you inspecting the main railgun energizers?"

There wasn't much else in that part of the ship, her office was at the end of a passageway, so I couldn't claim to have been walking by. "No. I have a question for you, and didn't want to call you all the way up to my office."

Glancing at her laptop, she asked "What is it?"

I took a seat opposite her, studiously not looking at the screen of her laptop. "On the way to Backstop, I think we should swing by a Maxolhx relay station. We have been out of the loop for too long. That Thuranin frigate got a good look at *Valkyrie*, they know the 'ghost ship' was near Rikers around the time that planet was raided to rescue a group of humans. I want to know what the Thuranin, and the Maxolhx, think they know."

"Good idea," her expression immediately brightened. "Will that delay our arrival at Backstop?"

"No. Well, yes, but only by a day. We will still be waiting at Backstop with nothing to do for a while, until Skippy can begin waking it up."

"That time lag concerns me," she frowned. "Skippy has never taken more than a couple hours to wake up a dormant wormhole."

"Except the super-duty wormhole out to the Beta site," I reminded her. "This is different. Skippy told me the lag is because Backstop was moved such a long distance. The farther a wormhole moves, the longer it takes to become stable at the new location. It has something to do with its anchoring effect in local spacetime."

"Did you understand what Skippy told you?"

"No. But Friedlander says he gets the basic concept and it makes sense. There's nothing we can do about it anyway. What really bothers me is, Backstop will be blinking on and off until it becomes stable, generating a lot of gamma rays. If there are any ships in the area, they will be attracted like flies to a bug zapper."

"The outside end of Backstop is in a remote section of space, Sir. The closest inhabited world is forty-two lightyears away. Aliens will reach Earth the long way, before they see any sign of Backstop being open.

"Backstop is not the only wormhole we moved. Some of the others are not quite so remote." When Skippy had the idea to move dormant wormholes all across the galaxy, to create a shortcut from Earth to the Sculptor dwarf galaxy, his priority had been the shortest travel time for starships. That meant he had to compromise secrecy. "One of the dormant wormholes he moved, is only seven lightyears from an active wormhole that gets a decent amount of traffic."

"I understand the issue, but if we have seven years to bring people from Earth to the Beta site, that will be a miracle. When that battlegroup we stranded outside the galaxy fails to return from Earth, the kitties will send an even larger force. Skippy can't do that chain-of-wormholes trick again."

"Yeah, I know. OK, I will set course for the relay station."

Her brow furrowed. "Sir, have you considered how the Rikers fallout will affect Paradise?"

"Like how?"

"The Thuranin saw you. They have your DNA."

Shit. She was right. Why hadn't I thought of that? "Those little green MFers never used my name."

"They probably didn't have your personnel records in their ship's database, they wouldn't need it. That ship was blown to bits, and the Thuranin on Rikers are dead, but the data they collected on you must be somewhere. Our cover story for the raid was that it was an Alien Legion op, supported by the Ruhar. The Thuranin will be asking the hamsters about it, and *they* have your records. Someone will recognize you. That has got to cause a shitstorm for UNEF on Paradise."

"Oh, *crap*. I hadn't thought about that. Well, uh, hmm. The Kristang already think our escape from Paradise was a secret Ruhar operation."

"Yes, Sir. But the Ruhar *know* they weren't involved. They will be asking a whole lot of uncomfortable questions, and UNEF-Paradise will be on the hot seat."

"Shit. Is there anything we can do about it?"

She held up her hands, palms up. "Not that I can think of."

"So, you mentioned that happy fact to brighten my day?"

"I never said I was a ray of sunshine, Sir."

"I'll let you get back to," I waved a hand at her laptop. "Whatever report you're working on."

She blushed, a reaction that was completely unexpected. "It's not a report, Sir. I'm writing my wedding vows."

It was my turn to blush, I could feel my cheeks turning red. "Oh, sorry. I didn't mean to pry."

"It's OK. Frank insisted we write our own vows," she rolled her eyes. "I think he wants to put me on the spot. Writing about my, *feelings*," she stuck a finger in her mouth like she was gagging. "Is not my favorite thing."

"How about you promise not to cover the bathroom floor with sticky hairspray? That's a vow my father wishes my mother had made."

"I don't use hairspray, Sir," she tugged at her hair. "Not, here."

"Ok, maybe you vow not to make him eat too many vegetables?"

"Maybe I should handle this by myself?"

I took the hint. "I'll be on the bridge."

We changed course to rendezvous with a Maxolhx relay station. It was not the one closest to Rikers, that one had too much traffic, we couldn't risk going there. A more remote station might not yet have received the info we wanted, so Skippy compromised by selecting a station that took us only one day out of our way.

When we got there, we had a nasty surprise. "No joy, Joe," Skippy shook his head morosely. "The station refuses to respond."

"What?" Looking at the holographic display on the bridge, I didn't see any warning signals. "Why?"

"We were *too* successful, that's why. The Maxolhx found those pixies we planted in the wreckage of that Bosphuraq battleship at Vua Vendigo. They think their whole ultra-secure communications system has been compromised. The station will not accept authentication via pixie. We have to send a dropship to the station and have the AI physically verify our access."

"Well, shit. That's no good."

"No it is not. Sorry. We did know this would happen eventually," he reminded me.

"Yeah, sure. I didn't expect the kitties to react so damned fast."

"They are panicked, Joe. There are probably some relay stations that have not yet been updated, but I have no way of knowing which ones."

"We are *not* flying all around the galaxy, hoping to find a relay station that will still talk with us. How about the Thuranin? Do they have a relay station around here anyplace?"

"They have a station approximately thirty-eight hours flight time from here," he reported, showing the course in the holographic display.

I looked at Simms and she nodded. We still had time before Skippy could start the process of waking up Backstop. "OK, let's do that."

The Thuranin relay station had the info we wanted. Luckily for us, the station had been updated only seven hours before we got there. "You got everything we want, Skippy?" I asked anxiously, fearing a Thuranin task force would pop into view and surprise us.

"I downloaded everything," he sniffed. "We can jump away any time."

"Jump option Charlie" I gun-pointed at the pilots, pretending to pull the trigger. "Do it." That gesture, and saying 'do it', was my signature move, I had decided. That was something I had practiced in the mirror, along with a lengthy list of gestures and catchphrases that were discarded.

"You are *gun-pointing*, Sir?" Simms raised an eyebrow as we jumped.

"Cool, huh?"

"Yes, that's what I was going to say," she rolled her eyes.

"Skippy," I quickly changed the subject. "Did the station's database have any info about the ghost ship at Rikers?"

"Yes, Joe. The Thuranin have been instructed to cooperate, and stay out of the way. The Maxolhx are sending three battlegroups to Rikers."

"Ha!" I snorted. "Good luck to them."

"That is not the interesting part, Joe. Accompanying the Maxolhx is a *Rindhalu* ship."

"Rindhalu?" Everyone on the bridge was stunned. "Like, the Maxolhx captured a-"

"No. The Rindhalu have become so concerned about the ghost ship, and the apparent compromising of pixie technology, that they insisted on joining the investigation."

"Is this a problem for us?"

"For now? Probably not. Although, it will be interesting to see what the spiders do when that Maxolhx battlegroup fails to return from their mission to Earth."

That made me grit my teeth. "*Interesting* is not the way I would describe it."

"Sorry. You know what I mean. Whether one murderous alien species goes to Earth, or two of them do, really makes no difference. Hmm, this could be a bit of *good* news."

"How do you figure that?"

"If the Rindhalu do demand to join an expedition to Earth, it could delay the operation. The spiders never do anything hastily. It might take them six months just to decide on how many ships to send."

"Huh. That is good news. Another six months buys us time to bring more people to the Beta site."

"I can't promise anything, you understand?"

"Yeah. At this point, we'll take all the good news we can get."

"In that case, I have another piece of potential good news for you. Again, I am not making any promises."

"Just tell us," I pleaded.

"It is a *long* journey to Earth from the Goalpost wormhole in Ruhar territory. With two species who *hate* each other traveling together, a lot could go wrong along the way, if you know what I mean."

"That would be awesome. Hey, uh," I rubbed the back of my neck as wheels turned in my mind. "It would be truly *unfortunate* if someone caused those ships to start shooting at each other, if you know what I mean."

Simms stared at me. "You think we could do that, Sir?"

"I'm just talking here," I admitted.

"I don't know, Joe," Skippy put a damper on my enthusiasm. "That would be very tricky. If any such plan is discovered by either side, that could actually draw the Maxolhx and Rindhalu together, for the purpose of crushing your species."

"Which is going to happen *anyway*," I insisted. "As you would say, there's no downside."

"Whoa. That is one hell of a risk, Joe."

"Hey, it's all just talk right now. Did you find anything else interesting in the data?"

"Hmm, yes. There is a notice from the Maxolhx, for the Thuranin to be on the lookout for, and report, any anomalous wormhole behavior."

Simms and I shared a puzzled look. "Why is that interesting? They have already been doing that, since you started screwing with wormholes."

"That *is* why this notice is interesting, Joe. This is a Flash-priority message. It makes no sense that the Maxolhx would send out such a notice, about an ongoing phenomenon."

"Shit. You think maybe the kitties discovered that you have been moving wormholes?"

"No. No way, Dude. The wormholes I moved are *dormant*. No one even knows they exist; they would have no way to detect them being relocated. There will not be any visible effect, until I trigger those relocated wormholes to boot up."

"Crap. Now I wish we had hit up that Maxolhx relay station for info."

"You want to go back there?" Skippy said, in a way implying that would be a bad idea.

"No. It's a minor mystery we can live with. That's it?"

"One other thing, Joe. The Thuranin put out a BOLO on you. You know, a 'Be On the Look Out' notice."

"On *me*?"

"They don't know it is *you*, not yet anyway." The holographic display shimmered, and an image of me appeared. The image must have been taken shortly after I was captured by the Thuranin. I was still in my flightsuit, though the top had been ripped open. My hair had not yet been shaved down the middle in an embarrassing No-hawk. Though I don't remember it, the Thuranin must have roughed me up, my face was bruised and bloody, with cuts on my chest. My eyes were open, staring blankly and unfocused. "This image, along with details about your biometrics and DNA, are in the bulletin. It states that this human committed crimes against the Thuranin at Rakesh Diwalen, and requests that you be identified."

Turning to Simms, I shrugged. "You were right. This will cause trouble for UNEF on Paradise, damn it.'"

"What?" Skippy asked.

"Ah, I wish it was a better picture. Cornpone and Ski, and everyone, they have all been thinking I was dead. Now they'll see *this*."

"Joe, you know how, every couple of years, a mugshot of some rough-looking criminal goes viral, because he has the bad-boy look that makes women stupid?"

"Oh, well," I blushed again. Maybe my mug shot was not so bad. "That's nice, Skippy, thanks. I-"

"Your photo is *not* that," he laughed.

Now my face was really red. "Hey, you-"

"Seriously, your mugshot looks like you got beaten up by a bunch of pre-schoolers, after you tried to rip off their lemonade stand."

"That is not-"

"I've seen *kittens* that have more of a bad-boy look."

My day kind of went downhill from there.

Later, in my office, I had just sat down and opened my laptop when Skippy appeared. "Joe, there is another piece of info I pulled from the relay station."

"Oh, *crap*." Whatever it was, he hadn't been comfortable discussing it with the bridge crew listening. That meant it had to be bad news, really bad. "Go ahead, ruin my day."

"What?"

"This info you have, it's catastrophic, right?"

"No. It's more like trivia. I didn't mention it before, because it doesn't affect us directly."

"Oh." Huh. For all the time we had been together, he could still surprise me. "What is this trivia?"

"It's about the Mavericks."

Instinctively, I rolled my eyes, which was unfair. "Let me guess, they got into trouble again. Please tell me we don't need to go rescue them."

"We don't need to do anything. They got into trouble on a planet they call 'Squidworld', but they got themselves out of trouble. More accurately, Lieutenant Colonel Perkins got them out of trouble."

"*Squid* world? Why did they call it-"

"This time, the Alien Legion invaded a *Wurgalan* planet, Joe."

"Holy shit. Perkins doesn't have enough enemies, she has to go starting a fight with the squids? The lizards already hate her."

"Um, actually, in this case, she arranged for the Alien Legion to work for the *Kristang*."

My brain locked up. "Uh, say that again."

He did. It didn't make any more sense the second time. "Oh my G- Holy f- What the *hell* is she doing?"

"She has a plan, Joe. I don't know what it is, but so far, it's working."

"The Legion won that fight?"

"No. Their ships got shot out of orbit, the Bosphuraq got involved directly, and, well, you might say the whole plan was in Freefall. Then, a miracle happened."

"Miracles don't just *happen*, Skippy. What did she do this time?"

"She did the same thing as last time. The Jeraptha stepped in and bailed the Legion out of a jam."

"Huh." I grinned. "She's following the playbook."

"What playbook?"

"The same one that gets the US Army into messy fights on Earth. You know, I've told you this before. There is trouble in some country halfway across the world. The group involved doesn't have the combat power for a fight, so instead of using their money on weapons, they buy lobbyists in DC. The TV news gets filled with horrible images from the conflict, some group organizes people to contact Congress, and next thing you know, some jackass decides the conflict is a national security issue for America. The Army gets shipped over there and a bunch of people get killed, until the people back home lose interest. Then our leadership declares victory and pulls the troops out. Huh. Perkins is *smart*. The Legion has stirred things up, powers on both sides are afraid of the consequences. She knows her team lacks the combat power to win a fight if the other side really wants to crush the Legion, so she manipulates the Jeraptha into ending the fight for her."

"That *is* smart, Joe," he said with admiration.

"I thought that, after Fresno, the beetles announced they couldn't get directly involved in any future fight. How did Perkins do it?"

"Well, Joe," he chuckled. "It happened by coincidence."

"There are no coincidences, Skippy. Not out here."

"All I can say is, just when the Legion was in the worst trouble, the Bosphuraq suddenly discovered an active Elder power tap on Squidworld."

"*Ha!*" I slapped the desk, startling Skippy. "I *knew* it!"

He was baffled, his avatar's eyes bulged. "You *knew* about the power tap?"

"Not exactly. Remember on their last fight, the beetles bailed them out on Fresno? The official story is that Perkins sent Cornpone out to trade the secrets of fantasy sports, in exchange for the beetles squashing the Kristang there."

"Yes, so? That is what happened."

"That is pure *bullshit*, Skippy," I laughed. "Fantasy sports was the backup plan, if it was planned at all. No way did Perkins send Jesse out with a flimsy plan like that. She gave him something solid to trade. I didn't know what it was at the time, but I'll bet you anything that Perkins already had that power tap when the Legion landed on Fresno. She didn't need it then, so she kept it in her pocket, and cashed it in on Squidworld. Damn, that woman is devious."

"I *like* her, Joe."

"I like her too, but, wow. She can be dangerous. All right, so, the Legion won the fight on Squidworld?"

"Not exactly, but close enough. They did accomplish their objective. Now Perkins is cooking up another scheme for the Legion. Ugh. I wish I knew what her long-term plan is. It must be something *big*."

"Yeah, well, you may be able to ask her about it, soon. Send me the details on this Squidworld operation, and distribute it to the crew. This is an opportunity to learn something."

"I just sent out the full report, Joe. I'm calling it Operation Freefall."

"I can't wait to read it."

CHAPTER TWENTY FIVE

To stretch our food supply, Skippy cranked up *Valkyrie's* fabricators to make sludges. They tasted better than the nasty, chalky stuff he had made aboard the *Flying Dutchman*, and he also made ration bars. The bars were not any more appetizing than sludges, but chewing on a bar felt more like having an actual meal. The ration bars were intended for the crew, so our dwindling supply of real food could be reserved for the civilians.

That was the plan, but no plan survives contact with the enemy. Or, with children. When the young people saw our crew eating ration bars, they demanded to try them. Partly because the rations looked like candy bars, but mostly because the children saw the crew as heroes, and wanted to emulate them. There was an unanticipated problem with giving hard, chewy ration bars to the civilians. Because of their poor nutrition, many of them had loose teeth. Doctor Skippy assured us that his nutritional supplements would gradually resolve that problem, but in the meantime, civilians were losing teeth to ration bars. So, secretly, Simms had Skippy create a batch of softer ration bars just for the civilians, and the problem went away. Of course, our crew then asked why *they* still had to eat bars that had the consistency of compressed sawdust, so…

Anyway, in addition to making sludges and ration bars, and food for our alien POWs, Master Chef Skippy tried making actual food. Some of his experiments produced decent results, like when he made pasta. The dried noodles made by the fabricators tasted pretty much like the stuff we had brought from Earth, and that was good, except we had plenty of dried pasta aboard, and the crew was already sick of eating spaghetti three times a week.

Early one morning, I walked into the galley to get coffee before gulping down a sludge, when Skippy called me. "Joe! You are just in time! Get your coffee and sit down."

"In time for what?" I asked, bleary-eyed while I poured coffee into my mug. That first sip of hot coffee tasted *so* good. My morning ritual is to drink a big glass of water as soon as I get out of bed, then shower and wander down to the galley for coffee. In case of emergency, I kept a small Thermos of coffee next to my bed, but fresh coffee is always better.

"A special treat just for you, Joe!" He was bubbling over with enthusiasm, and it was way too early for anyone to be that energetic.

"OK, fine," I sat down at the nearest table. While I wanted to be left alone to drink coffee, I knew Skippy would pester me endlessly. "Bring it on." I assumed he had cooked up a new flavor of sludge.

So, I was surprised when a little bot rolled out of the kitchen area, with a bowl and a spoon. The bot looked like a box or cabinet that rolled on four wheels and had one flexible arm. The bot stopped next to the table and the arm set the bowl down in front of me, then the spoon.

It was multicolored breakfast cereal, with milk. "Skippy, what is this?"

"One of your favorites, Joe! Fruity Pebbles."

"Fruity- Wow." Damn, I hadn't enjoyed that treat since, before I left home for boot camp. Picking up the spoon, I dug in eagerly, stuffing a big scoop into my mouth.

And immediately regretted it. "Uh," I said, talking with my mouth full. The trash can was too far away to spit it out, and I didn't want to swallow it. "This is an interesting flavor."

"You like it? It's Cool Ranch."

"Cool Ranch?" I gagged a little saying that. "Why not, uh, just make it, you know, fruity flavored?"

"Ugh. Anyone can do *that*. Master Chef Skippy creates unique flavor combinations."

Crap. The cereal tasted like it had been created by Master *Chief*, the guy from the Halo game. Master Chief is a badass, but he is not known for his culinary skills. Neither is Skippy. Damn it, now I had to finish the bowl, or Skippy would pout and sulk and be miserable for the whole freakin' day. "It's yummy, but-"

"But what?" He asked with suspicion.

"It's an unexpected delight."

"Yeah, so? It surprises your taste buds, right?"

"It does. Listen, Skippy, breakfast is not a good time to surprise people. We want comfort foods first thing in the morning. Familiar food, you know? When you told me this was Fruity Pebbles, I expected something specific."

"But you like it?"

"Oh, it's delish," I lied. "Hey, one suggestion? Use this stuff to make chips instead of cereal? Trust me, people would chow down a bag of this, if it were chips."

"Hmm. OK, I'll try it. Jeez Louise, you monkeys are so freakin' picky about your food."

"It's a meatsack thing, you wouldn't understand."

"Well, I am certainly thankful for that. Enjoy your breakfast, I'll have the bot bring the whole box out for you."

"Oh, yeah." Right then, I knew I was doomed. "That, that would be great, Skippy. Thanks."

I was *not* doomed to eat the entire box of Cool Ranch flavored Fruity Pebbles. Nor was I doomed to eat the other boxes he had created: Corned Beef & Cabbage, Teriyaki, Buffalo Chicken, or my personal fave; Habanero & Cheddar.

Why was I saved from a terrible fate?

It's simple: because I am in the military. Our crew were all high-speed pilots and special operators. That mattered, because they are:

A) Ultra-competitive, and

B) Bored.

So, when they heard about a gag-inducing breakfast cereal, they were all excited. That very morning began the Fruity Pebbles Challenge. Participants had to eat at least one bowl of each flavor, a challenge that grew more difficult when the crew bombarded Skippy with new and increasingly wild flavor suggestions. I bailed out at Goat Curry, which was a wise choice, because the next morning's treat was Liver & Onions.

Yuck.

"Well, *this* is odd," Skippy announced as our ships drifted in empty interstellar space, waiting for an Elder wormhole to open. It was an ordinary wormhole that connected to where it was supposed to connect, Skippy hadn't screwed with it. That wormhole was on the same local network as the far end of Backstop, the dormant wormhole that had moved its other end close to Earth. We had gone through three wormholes to get there, instead of creating our usual shortcuts, because Skippy didn't want to risk screwing with that network while it was still in the process of relocating a wormhole we needed. So, we had parked the ships seventeen light-seconds from where the wormhole was scheduled to emerge. As soon as we saw that it was stable, and Skippy pinged the network to make sure there weren't any ships waiting on the other end, we would jump in front of the event horizon, and transition through. From there, it was a four-day trip of continuous jumping, to get to where the far end of Backstop had been moved to.

"Odd?" I asked. There weren't any alerts shown in the holographic display, and Skippy's tone of voice reflected curiosity rather than alarm, so I wasn't worried. He was probably talking about some nerdnik thing like the ratio of hydrogen isotopes in the interstellar medium.

"Weird. More like *super* weird," he mumbled.

Hearing that made my Spidey sense tingle, and I bolted upright in the chair. Beside me, Simms did the same, punching controls on her armrest to scan the incoming sensor data. "Skippy, what is weird?" The only thing I could see that was even slightly unusual was that the wormhole was late by twenty-three seconds. That was nothing to be alarmed about.

Unless it was.

"Um, Joe, we may have a problem. The wormhole should have emerged by now."

"The exact time is variable," I reminded him.

"Not this variable, Joe. It is *late*."

"Ohhhhh, shit," my blood ran cold. When Skippy screwed with wormholes to create shortcuts, it interrupted the schedule that had sometimes been running like clockwork for a hundred thousand years. After we went through, he released the wormhole and it tried to go back to its normal sequence, which usually meant it opened late at whatever emergence point was on the schedule at that moment. Ninety-nine percent of the time, the interruption in sequence was never noticed. That one percent of the time was a problem; ships waiting to go through noticed something was wrong, and they told others about it. That is how the senior species first learned that Elder wormholes were exhibiting odd behavior, and that kind of started the whole problem of the Maxolhx getting interested in going to Earth.

What sent a chill through my blood was that an Elder wormhole was late, and Skippy had not screwed with it.

Which had to mean someone else had screwed with it.

"Skippy," I had to lick my suddenly-dry lips. "Is there another Elder AI involved?"

"Well, shit, Joe. I hadn't thought of *that*. Damn it!"

"Pilot!" I snapped my fingers. "Jump option Delta, *now!*"

There was a moment's hesitation as we waited for the *Dutchman* to acknowledge the signal, then we both jumped away.

"Um, why did we jump?" Skippy asked.

"Because if there is another Elder AI around here, we want to be far away."

"The wormhole being late does not necessarily mean another AI is involved, Joe," he chided me.

"What else could it be?"

"Maybe it is an unintended, temporary effect of relocating a dormant wormhole on this local network. It could be a lot of things that are not super dangerous. I don't know, and now I can't ask the network what is going on. We need to go back."

"No," I shook my head. "Not there. And not 'we'. The *Dutchman* can stay here. Plot a jump to the next emergence point."

"The next emergence point is a *long* way from here," he protested.

"Then the one after that," I suggested. "I want to know if we're dealing with a temporary glitch, or a real problem."

"OK, good point. Jump option Kilo is programmed."

"Bilby," I looked up to address the ship's control AI. "Inform Nagatha what we're doing. The *Dutchman* is to remain here, we won't be long. An hour at most."

"Uh," he sounded like I had interrupted him taking a bong hit. "Sure thing, Dude. I mean, heh, Colonel Dude. Nagatha says everything's cool, so, like, we can jump whenever you want."

I gestured to the pilot, giving a thumbs up. "Hit it."

We jumped.

"Hit it?" Simms asked, amused.

"You didn't like the gun-pointing."

"You don't need to have a catch-phrase, Sir."

"Simms," I mansplained patiently. "All the cool starship captains have a catch-phrase."

"I'm, sure they do."

"Good, then-" Did she just diss me? I decided to ignore her comment.

We had to wait thirty-seven minutes for the wormhole to emerge at that location.

And, it didn't.

"Skippy, what the hell?"

"I am trying to find out what is going on, Joe, but, um-"

"But what?"

"But, the network is not responding. It's like it's not there."

"How the hell could that be?"

"I do not know," he answered, mystified by the situation. "Even if another AI is screwing with this wormhole which we have *no* reason to believe is true, the network should be responding!"

"Is it silent because it's pissed off at you?"

"No, you don't understand. Even if it refuses to talk with me, I can tell it is there. I ping, and it automatically pings back with a request for my authentication code."

"Ok, then, shit. Could this wormhole have gone dormant?"

"No. I don't think so," he added, worried. "Even if it is dormant, the network would still have a presence here. This does not make *any* sense."

"All right, then, uh," my mind ran down a list of potential actions. "Can we fly to another wormhole that is on the same local network?"

"Yes, but that will take three days. We chose this wormhole because it is isolated and sees little traffic."

"You got another suggestion?"

"Yes. Before we go flying around chasing wormholes, we should try to determine whether this is merely a timing issue. I still do not think another AI has to be involved, but if something is keeping the wormhole open at another location, that could explain why it isn't operating on the normal schedule."

"What could be keeping it open?"

"I don't *know* that, numbskull," his frustration was evident. "Listen, I programmed a search pattern into the navigation system. It will take no more than three hours to complete."

"Simms? What do you think?"

"I think sitting here isn't accomplishing anything," she said very sensibly. "We told the *Dutchman* we would be back in an hour."

"Oh, yeah. Let's jump back to give Chang an update first."

The search did not take three hours. It did not even take *one* hour. Forty-one minutes into the search pattern, the holographic display lit up, and Skippy shouted. "Found it! The wormhole is not dormant, that's for sure. The timing is, hmm. What the *hell*? That makes zero sense!"

"What is it?" I asked.

"If this single data point is representative of other emergence points, then *timing* is not the problem. It is operating exactly on schedule."

"Uh, no it is not, *duh*. If it was on schedule, it would be-"

"The schedule contains two elements, *duh*. Timing and *location*. Joe, this freaking thing is not where it's supposed to be!"

"How could that happen?"

"It *can't*. This makes no sense."

"OK, calm down, let's think this through. Can you contact the network from here?"

"No. However, based on the distance that one emergence point has moved, I can predict where it will be for the next four minutes. We can get there if we jump now."

"Hit it."

The wormhole was already open when we arrived. The event horizon was totally normal, except it was two point six light-hours from its normal location.

"Ohhh. Oh, shit. I think I might have a guess about what is happening," Skippy groaned.

"No guesses," I ordered. "Ping the freakin' network and find out for sure."

"Doing that now. It is responding," he announced slowly, like he was giving us a play-by-play of events. "My authentication has been accepted. It says- Oh nooooooo," his voice trailed off.

"What's going on? Skippy?" he didn't answer. "Skippy?!"

"Sorry, Dude," Bilby spoke. "He's got like, vapor lock or something."

"Vapor lock?"

"You know, like when the fuel line of a car-"

"I know what vapor lock is."

"He's like, hung up or something. I'm running the ship all by myself. Huh, this is cool."

"This is *not* cool," I thumped a fist on the armrest. "Do you know what the wormhole network told him?"

"Uh, no, sorry. I can't hear, they talk in another dimension, you know?"

"Wake him up."

"Like, how?"

"Get his attention."

"Uh, I don't know about that," Bilby drawled. "It's like, don't poke a bear when it's sleeping, you know? Skippy isn't damaged, he's just, like, in shock or something."

"Simms?"

"Whatever is happening, I'd rather not be *here*," she suggested.

"Good point. Pilot, jump us back to the *Dutchman*."

The ship jumping must have shaken Skippy out of his vapor lock. "Oh man," he moaned. "Joe, Jennifer, everyone. I am *so* sorry."

"Sorry about what? We need details," I demanded.

"The most important detail is that I am a fuck-up, Joe," he sighed. "The Law of Unintended Consequences *totally* screwed me over, and it's my fault.

I *hate* that freakin' law. "We can talk about whose fault it is later. What is going on? Why was that wormhole not in its proper location?"

"Because that damned wormhole network controller answered only the questions I asked. Remember when I said we had to shut down the Gateway wormhole, before we tried to move the dormant one we call Backstop?"

My throat was so dry, I had to swallow before answering. "Yeah. Go on." My hands were shaking so badly, Simms reached over to squeeze my hand.

"This is bad, Joe. This is *bad*. Oh, I can't believe this. This is an absolute disaster."

Simms patted my hand, and I waited for him to continue.

"I asked the wrong questions," he groaned. "Not enough questions. The network controller told me only what I- That doesn't matter." He took a breath. "Here's the deal, Joe. The network agreed to move the Backstop wormhole, and it assured me that moving a dormant wormhole would not cause an overall shift across the network. It was not lying, that is the good news. The only good news.

Remember when I told you that the Elders left the wormhole network operational, to feed power into higher dimensions?"

"OK, yeah. That was a surprise, but what we care about is that the wormholes still work for us, right?"

"We care about that, but the network doesn't. *That* is the problem. Moving a wormhole messes with the force lines they operate on. To optimize power flow after Backstop is moved and opened, the network has to make adjustments. It made minor location adjustments to a handful of active wormholes. That's not the worst part. When Backstop is opened, it will actually pull more power than it feeds to the network. To compensate, the network needs to wake up another dormant wormhole in the local network. That is the bad news, the worst news."

"It's not Sleeping Beauty, is it?" That dormant wormhole was less than nine lightyears from Earth, much too close for comfort.

"No. Remember, the wormhole we call Sleeping Beauty is not just dormant, it is *damaged*. The network can't use it. The problem is the other dormant wormhole near Earth, the one that was twenty-one lightyears away." He paused, and not for dramatic effect. "The network is waking up that wormhole, and it has been moved so it is only sixteen lightyears from Earth. Joe, I can't stop it! It will be open before Backstop is ready!"

It took me a moment for me to comprehend the scale of the impending disaster. Looking at the faces of the bridge crew, they were each processing Skippy's announcement in their own way. There were a lot of mouths silently forming 'Holy shit', or the equivalent in their native languages. English was the official common language of UNEF, because it was spoken in America, Britain and India, but people defaulted to the language they grew up with when cursing. And the occasion called for cursing.

"OK," I rubbed my chin to cover my Adam's apple bobbing up and down nervously. "Run that by us again, please," I spoke in a calm voice, or tried to. The crew needed to see their leader was in control, of the situation and himself. There would be plenty of time later for me to yell at Skippy in private. "When we agreed to shut down Gateway before attempting to move Backstop, you asked the local network if those action would trigger a shift. Are you saying it was *lying* to you?"

"No, it, ah, damn it. Joe, it answered the specific questions I asked, and nothing more. Moving Backstop did *not* trigger a shift, not in the technical definition of the term. This is more like an interim adjustment, to optimize power flow before the next shift occurs. I guess you could say it is the network's equivalent of a FRAGO."

Of course I knew what he meant. An OPORD or Operations Order, is a plan issued by units at the battalion level or higher, and subordinate units then make their own plans to comply with the OPORD's statement of situation, mission, execution, sustainment and command and control. The Operations Order that I had been given before we left Earth, detailed search criteria for a Beta site, what to do when we found a candidate world, length of the mission, etc. Along the way, I had issued Fragmentary Orders to revise the details, as we dealt with issues and obstacles along the way. Then Emily Perkins had fucked everything up for us, and I had to toss the original OPORD and start over. Anyway, Skippy comparing the wormhole adjustment to a FRAGO was just wrong, but I knew what he meant.

Why did I just waste time thinking about that meaningless shit?

Because my brain wanted to avoid thinking about the horror of what Skippy told us.

"The network," I let out the breath I had been holding. "Never mentioned the possibility of adjusting the status of wormholes, after you instructed it to begin moving Backstop? It never hinted that it might need to make some sort of adjustment?"

"No, Joe, it did not. And I don't know enough about how the network functions, to guess that it might need to wake up dormant wormholes, and move active ones. Shit. I didn't understand the current purpose of the whole freakin' network, until I recovered my memories. I am *so* sorry about this."

Simms leaned forward in her chair. "Skippy, at the time, you told us the local controller showed you the future state of the network, and there wasn't anything for us to be concerned about."

"Yes, um," he replied nervously. "It told the truth, that Gateway and Sleeping Beauty would remain shut down, and that Backstop could be opened after it moved. Like I said, the problem is that it failed to volunteer any details I did not specifically ask about. It never showed me that it needed to wake up a dormant wormhole."

Holding up a hand, I cut off Simms's next comment. "We can go over lessons learned later. Right now I need to know, is there anything you can do to stop this new wormhole from opening?"

"No. I am locked out, Joe. The local network is in a self-adjustment mode, it is not accepting any instructions or requests."

"Where is this thing? Show us."

The main display changed from a tactical plot showing our position relative to the *Flying Dutchman*. It now showed Earth's sun in the center, with a ring-shaped icon tagged 'Backstop' for the wormhole there. Off to the left was another ring icon. "The new wormhole is sixteen point four lightyears from Earth, near the star Groombridge 1618."

That information told me nothing useful. Sixteen lightyears was sixteen lightyears, in any direction. That was a relatively easy flight for a Maxolhx warship, even without an assist from a star carrier. "Let's designate this new wormhole, uh-" What? I sure as hell was not calling the damned thing 'Sweet Sixteen'. It was near a star called- "Broomstick. We'll call it 'Broomstick'."

"The star is called '*Groombridge*', Sir," Simms whispered.

"I know that. Witches ride broomsticks, and that wormhole won't be bringing anything nice to Earth."

Simms nodded, biting her lip. She wasn't making that gesture because of me. She was scared.

I was scared too. That's why I focused on trivia, like what to name a freakin' wormhole. "Skippy, you are the expert on hyperspatial physics, or whatever you call it. What are our options?"

"That's the problem," he sighed. "We don't *have* any options. The network is opening Broomstick on its own, and it won't listen to me. There is *nothing* I can do about it."

"That can't be true. What if you tell the network to move Backstop to its original position? Will that erase all the changes?"

"No, I tried that already. Also, I thought of moving Backstop so close to Broomstick, that they interfere with each other. No joy there either. The network won't do it. At this point, it is basically in a repair cycle, it is not accepting any additional changes."

"Shit. Can you still wake up Backstop, or is that not allowed?"

"That is the one piece of good news. The network has started the process of opening Backstop all by itself, it doesn't need a command from me. Stupid thing lied to me about that also. Joe, I hate to say this, but we pushed our luck too far this time. I did warn you that screwing with wormholes was going to backfire on us someday."

"You did." My brain locked up. What the fuck were we going to do now?

Simms asked a question that was actually useful. "Will both wormholes open and become stable at the same time?"

"That I don't know," Skippy admitted. "Even the network is not certain of that, there are a lot of variables involved. Neither of the wormholes are positioned properly along a force line, so the process of anchoring them in local spacetime here is messy. Plus the network had to slightly reposition three active wormholes, which screws with the force lines. All I can tell you is that both wormholes should allow a ship to transition through around the same time, plus or minus three days. If you want my advice, go to Backstop and avoid the long flight to Earth."

"The other end of Broomstick," I finally asked a useful question. "Where is it?"

"Far from here, Joe. It is located in Esselgin space, near their disputed border with the Thuranin. That is *another* problem. Because of their ongoing dispute, and the recent weakness of the Thuranin, the Esselgin have been heavily patrolling that area. The far end of Broomstick is just over a lightyear from an active wormhole that gets a lot of traffic. To make the situation worse, Broomstick's far end is along the route from the active wormhole to a major Esselgin military outpost. Someone is going to notice the gamma ray flares from the far end of Broomstick booting up."

"How long do we have, before we can go through Backstop? I know it could happen three days in either direction."

"Five weeks is my best guess, Joe. I don't know exactly, because the process is out of my control now. What are you thinking?"

"You know for damned sure that Backstop is already booting up, you don't need to do anything?"

"Yes, darn it."

"How can you be sure the network isn't lying to you again?"

"It never actively *lied*, Joe. It failed to mention important facts. In this case, it complained to me about what a pain in the ass it is to boot up a relocated wormhole, and showed me the data. Backstop will be open soon."

"Not soon enough. The network hates you, right? Could it halt the boot-up just to spite you?"

"Hmm. No. No, it can't do that. The power flow of the network needs to be in balance. After all the adjustments it has made, it *has* to open both wormholes, or the power flow will be interrupted."

"Sir?" Simms tilted her head toward me. "What's our next move?"

Our next move.

I had no idea.

No, that's bullshit.

I knew our next move, our only possible move. I just didn't like it.

"Reed, you have the conn," I said as I stood up. "Simms, come to my office, we need to talk with Chang."

Nagatha had been following our discussion with Skippy, and she had patched in Chang, so he knew the basics. I also called Smythe into my office, so the four of us could decide what to do. Correction: so the three of them could provide advice and counsel to me. *I* had to decide what to do.

My life sucks.

In terms of cold, logical decision-making, it was easy. In terms of me being a meatsack with messy emotions and morality, it was tough. My first action was to inform the crews of both ships, along with a strict order *not* to discuss the situation with the civilians, including the science staff. Next, I ordered those civilians aboard the Dutchman transferred back to *Valkyrie*, knowing they must be sick of bouncing between the ships like ping-pong balls. The cover story we gave them was that we discovered the wormhole to Earth was unexpectedly going to take several months to become stable, so we were taking them to a nice planet to wait. For those who protested they wanted to remain aboard the ships, I explained that we also needed to stretch our food supply by growing crops on a planet. The civilians were pissed off and they bitched about every little thing, so it was really no different from any military deployment.

The truth was, *Valkyrie* was going to fly around the galaxy, so Skippy could talk with local wormhole networks and make certain that the other wormholes he requested to move were also booting up. We needed a string of new wormholes to make a shortcut from Earth to the super-duty wormhole that connected way out to the Sculptor dwarf galaxy. After we confirmed the shortcut wormholes would soon be open, we would fly to the Beta site and drop off the civilians. Most of the STARs were transferred to the *Flying Dutchman*, for a reason I will explain later, while half of the Commandos were assigned to *Valkyrie*, to keep the civilians under control. It was a dirty job, but someone had to do it. The civilians would be uncomfortable and angry, but they would be alive. It was the best I could do under the crappy circumstances. Chang would take the *Dutchman* to the far end of Backstop and wait there for *Valkyrie* to return. If we did not return, he was to take his ship through, and do whatever he could to bring people to the super-duty wormhole. Without Skippy, Nagatha couldn't open that wormhole, so our Plan 'B' assumed that *Valkyrie* had only been delayed.

There was no Plan 'C'. Without Skippy, it was impossible for either of our ships to get to the planet we call Club Skippy.

So, to recap, I had made another brilliant, inventive, clever and well-intended decision, that backfired on us and would likely doom my home planet to destruction.

I was lying to innocent people who deserved better.

Oh, and I was still concealing from our crew, the uncomfortable truth that Skippy had bailed on us.

Yay, me.

I *suck*.

CHAPTER TWENTY SIX

Our Jeraptha guest requested to talk with me, so I invited him to my office. Cadet Yula Fangiu was technically a prisoner of war rather than a guest, and his movement around the ship was restricted to keep him away from sensitive areas. But mostly, he could go anywhere he wanted, and the greatest danger was from humans being startled if they came around a corner and saw him suddenly.

I felt bad that we had to take him away from his home, his people. We were very fortunate that Fangiu was treating his captivity as a grand adventure. After all, he knew incredible secrets, though we were careful not to tell him too much. Basically, I had authorized the crew to tell him only information that would be obvious, for when and *if* we were ever able to return him to his people.

The problem was the 'if' part of that statement. We could only take the risk of returning the cadet if our secret had already been exposed, and in that case, our homeworld would be radioactive slag, and our ships would be on the run far outside the galaxy. Making a special trip back to the hostile Milky Way galaxy, just to return one Jeraptha and one Ruhar, would not be a good use of scarce resources.

I hadn't said that to any of our prisoners. They were smart, they could figure out their most likely futures by themselves.

"Colonel Bishop?" Fangiu called from the doorway of my office.

"Come in, Cadet," I stood up and gestured for him to sit down on the couch, the only piece of furniture that would be comfortable for his frame. The Jeraptha had four legs and a long torso, or maybe it was called a 'thorax'. They could run on just their back two legs when they wanted to go fast, but normally they walked on all four. That fact had nearly caused an interstellar incident, when some of the children had pleaded for him to play 'horsey'. They wanted to ride on his back! The adults in the recreation center just about had a heart attack, anticipating a terrible inter-species insult, but Fangiu had *laughed*. Unfortunately, that had frightened the children, for the laugh of a Jeraptha sounded like two rusty shipping containers mating. There was pandemonium in the rec center, children running around screaming, the adults trying to restore order, and the poor Jeraptha embarrassed that he had scared anyone. A couple children tried to imitate his laugh, because they thought it was funny rather than scary, and Fangiu played along. He then crouched down so a girl could climb on his back, and he gently walked around the rec center, except the girl didn't want him to be gentle, she wanted *fun*. So, he bucked like a bronco, possibly having more fun than the little girl did.

Anyway, Fangiu was a frequent and popular visitor to the rec center, the civilians were fascinated by him and the stories he told about his people.

The only problem with Fangiu being aboard was that, as a Jeraptha, gambling was practically a religion for him. He pestered the adults to bet on anything and everything, to the point where he encouraged the children to race around the ship. Then the children started betting with each other, using food as currency. We had to put a stop to *that*.

"How are you? I won't ask about the food," I said with a sour face.

"I am fine, Colonel," he smiled, his mandibles curving and his antennas twitching. "The food is not bad, I've had worse."

"Do your people have something like our MREs?" I gestured to the pouch on my desk. My lunch that day was an Australian Army version of an MRE, it was supposed to be chicken curry. That was better than the deep-fried wallaby that I expected, when I saw the Australian flag on the pouch.

OK, yes, to my friends in Oz, or Down Under or whatever you call that continent, I am sure that wallaby is not a common item on menus there. Truthfully, I do not really know what a wallaby is, I have a vague notion that it looks like a small kangaroo, but maybe I'm wrong about that. If I ever get the opportunity to be in Australia, I will probably see that people there are not eating Wallaburgers, and I can sample some of the delicious local food.

I am *not* eating Vegemite.

That stuff is disgusting.

Fangiu's antennas dropped, in body language that I had learned was the Jeraptha equivalent of a shrug. "Yes, our field rations are no better than yours, Really, I can't complain about the food. Your people are not eating much better."

He was right about that. To stretch our food supply for all the new people aboard our ships, the crew was getting one hot meal at dinner. Breakfast was usually a sludge, although we did have plenty of coffee. Lunch was either another sludge, or an MRE on alternate days. Twice a week, the crew got a hot breakfast. We made sure the civilians had three square meals a day, and all the snacks they wanted. After being starved and suffering from malnutrition, they needed all the good food they could eat. Seeing children eagerly chowing down on a hot meal in the galley, made it easier for the crew to pop the cap off a sludge and drink it. The good news was that, with the advanced fabricators aboard *Valkyrie* and a whole lot of user-acceptance testing, Skippy had finally nailed the taste of chocolate. It also helped that I had issued a lifetime ban on the production of any sort of banana flavored sludges. "You wanted to speak with me?"

"Yes, Colonel," his expression brightened, his eyes growing wide and his head bobbing eagerly. It truly did make me feel bad that he was our prisoner, I *liked* the guy. "If you will check your messages, I sent you a file?"

"You did?" I asked, glancing at my laptop, a bit fearfully. As a Jeraptha, he was familiar with advanced technology. Had he been able to send a virus that would crash my laptop?

No, that was a stupid notion. Neither Skippy nor Bilby would allow any malware aboard the ship. Slowly opening my laptop, I asked casually "Oh, how did you do that?" We had not issued Fangiu anything other than a zPhone, so I didn't know how he had created any type of file.

"Colonel Simms gave me one of your tablets. Two tablets, actually, I had to use one of them as a keyboard. Our character set is much larger than the twenty-six letters of your standard alphabet."

"Yeah, I heard that." Skippy had told me the beetles used ideograms, sort of like Chinese characters. Of course, after I asked a simple question, Skippy had gone into full Professor Nerdnik mode and bored me half to death, comparing the

Jeraptha writing system to the Japanese systems of katakana, hiragana and kanji. Anyway, whatever. "A file, huh?" I found the file queued up in my messages, and opened it. "Pow- *PowerPoint*? You sent me a presentation?"

"Yes," his head bobbed earnestly. "Skippy told me that human military organizations communicate exclusively in that format?"

Crap. Skippy had been screwing with the cadet. Although he was not wrong about how reliant the US military is on fancy presentations. The first slide had a big splashy title 'Proposal for Inter-species Cooperation'. Underneath was a custom graphic of a human figure shaking hands with a Jeraptha, although it looked like the beetle's claw was crushing the guy's hand. "Thank you. Cadet, my organization has a saying 'BLUF'. It means Bottom Line Up Front. How about you *tell* me what this is about, and then we can review the details?"

There was no mistaking his disappointment. He had worked hard on the file, and he wanted to impress me with it. To his credit, he recovered quickly. "Certainly, Colonel," he said with the type of nervous formality that was universal to any low-ranking solider speaking to a senior officer. Hell, not that long ago, that could have been *me* in his position. "Your main problem is that the Maxolhx will soon arrive at your homeworld?"

I didn't say anything, just nodded. He had been allowed to learn that information, because the only way we could ever send him back to his people is if the bad guys had already arrived at Earth, and our secrets were no longer secret. Also, every human aboard the ship knew about the threat posed by the Maxolhx, and the only way to keep that knowledge from Fangiu would be to lock him in his cabin. He did *not* know about the Broomstick wormhole opening unexpectedly. "Yes, that is the dilemma we are dealing with."

He leaned forward, a gesture that some deep part of my brain instinctively saw as threatening. Forcing myself not to flinch, I waited for him to continue. "Have you thought about approaching my people for assistance?"

The way he said it almost made me laugh. It reminded me of opening the front door to see a pair of nicely-dressed people eager to save my soul. Part of me expected him to ask if I had accepted His Holiness Skippiasyermuni as my savior. Laughing would have been bad manners, so I looked at my shoes until I could be sure I wouldn't smile inappropriately. "Yes. We have discussed the possibility of approaching the Rindhalu coalition. If we did, your people would of course be our first choice," I said. It didn't hurt to offer him some flattery, I felt sorry for the guy. "However, as powerful as your fleet is, it would be foolish to expect you to defend Earth against the Maxolhx."

I expected him to argue, to defend the honor of his people. Instead, his head bobbed and his antennas twitched. "That is true," he agreed, surprising me. "The Rindhalu could defend your world, but they would be too slow to respond. Your world would be caught in the crossfire."

"Yeah," I no longer found the conversation amusing. "That was our conclusion also. Thank you for offer-"

"Colonel," he interrupted me, another surprise. "My proposal," his eyes flicked toward the presentation on my laptop. "Is not for the Jeraptha to defend your world. That would be bloody and ultimately futile, I am sorry to say."

I gave him the side-eye. "Uh, then what-"

He plunged ahead eagerly. "Your plan is to evacuate all, or a significant portion, of your people, from Earth?"

"More like a small number of our people. We simply do not have the transport resources."

"*We* do."

"Excuse me?"

"My people could provide transport ships. Hundreds, perhaps *thousands* of transport ships."

"Shit." Have you ever had someone tell you an idea so forehead-slappingly obvious, you can't believe your own stupid brain didn't think of it?

"Realistically," Fangiu did the shrug thing again with his antennas. "To be of any use, our transport ships would have to arrive before the Maxolhx reach Earth, so we would need to move quickly,"

"Yeah, that's," my brain isn't as slow as Skippy says it is. OK, *sometimes* my brain isn't that slow. Right away I saw major holes in his idea. Like, involving the Jeraptha might have been a decent idea, *before* we learned about Broomstick. Now, there was no time for anyone to help us, before the Maxolhx arrived at Earth. "The moment we even talked to your leadership, the clock would start. No way could they keep something like this secret for long, if at all."

That offended him. "I can assure you, my people-"

"It's not just the Jeraptha I am concerned about," I explained. "No matter how good your communications security is, I have to assume the Rindhalu can read your message traffic."

He looked at me, his mandibles drooping.

"So," I continued. "Any rescue fleet would consist only of whatever transport ships are available immediately, for a long voyage." He didn't know about the wormhole shortcut Skippy had created, and he didn't need to know. "Soon as the Rindhalu hear about the rescue effort, they would put pressure on your leadership to recall the ships. No, I'm sorry. Good thinking, it's just not practical."

"We could *try*," he pleaded.

"I'll think about it, OK?" Pulling the laptop closer to me, I gestured at it. "We should discuss this again, after I review your presentation?"

It sucked to let Fangiu down like that, after he worked so hard on his slides. To make sure I wasn't missing another obvious factor, I told Chang and Simms and Smythe and others about the Jeraptha cadet's idea, and they kicked it around, bringing Skippy and Nagatha into the discussion. Everyone agreed it was a good notion, but not practical. Approaching the Jeraptha would expose our secret, without any guarantee they would help us, or could help us in any useful way. The transport ships would be racing the Maxolhx to Earth. Skippy said we had to include thirty to forty days to adapt Jeraptha ships to carry humans, plus time to load them. Sixty to seventy days, minimum, and the whole time we would be looking over our shoulders for Maxolhx warships to jump in and hammer the transports.

It was just no good.

I told Cadet Fangiu we appreciated the effort and for trying to help, and that he should keep thinking. Who knows? Maybe his alien perspective would dream up a wild-ass idea that mushy human brains couldn't conceive of.

I wasn't betting on it.

The discussion with Cadet Fangiu was ultimately not useful, in terms of helping us bring people from Earth to the Beta site, but something about what the beetle said bothered me.

Of course, I thought of it in the middle of the freakin' night. Checking my zPhone, I saw it was a little after 0400. Should I get another ninety minutes of sleep, or get up now and talk to Skippy? If I waited, I might forget what I wanted to ask him.

As a compromise, I made a quick note on my phone's notepad app, then rolled over.

Sleep is wonderful.

Like, the *best*.

The alarm sounded ninety minutes later, by which time I had forgotten not only what I wanted to ask Skippy, I had entirely forgotten that I had a question for him at all. Automatically, I reached for my phone to check messages, and saw the notepad app was open. Huh. What did 'Skip talk alien?' mean. Crap, I couldn't even read my own notes.

Oh, yeah.

"Good morning, Skippy," I said after I came out of the bathroom.

"Hey, Joe. Good morning to you. Wow, you are unusually energetic for so early in the morning."

"This isn't early to a soldier. Besides, I got a solid seven hours of sleep."

"Seven and a *half*," he corrected me.

"Bonus. I got a question for you."

"Before your first cup of coffee? I am impressed. You seem like you have extra energy, I expected that latest bad news would have you depressed."

"I'm not depressed, Skippy. What I am is pissed off, and frustrated."

"I can understand you being frustrated. This mission was supposed to be a quick and easy pleasure cruise beyond the galaxy. A couple months out to the Beta site and back. Instead, Operation Endless Futility has dragged on for-"

"*Endless Futility*? When did we-"

"OK, fine," he huffed. "Should we call it Operation Infinite Screwups?"

"No."

"Enduring Clusterfuck?"

"No!"

"How about Aimless Flailing?"

That got me mad. "Those names are not-"

"They all describe the way we have been lurching from one crisis to another out here."

"Earth is not dead *yet*, beer can."

"Joe, I don't want to say your homeworld is doomed, but the dolphins just said 'Thanks for all the fish'."

"*What?*"

"Ugh. Simms is right. Sometimes I don't even know why I bother talking to you."

"Can we get back to the reason I called you?"

"I'm listening," he said.

"You have been talking with Cadet Fangiu, and with our Ruhar guest. How?"

"Um. Well, I think of something I want to say," he explained slowly. "Then my matrix translates that into electrical impulses in the ship's intercom system, which-"

"I know that, asshole. My question is, how are you allowed to talk with them? You are restricted from talking with spacefaring species, something like that, right?"

"Oh. That is actually a good question. The answer should be obvious, which you would know if you were actually awake."

"How about you tell me while I get dressed, then I will get coffee?"

"Deal. Remember, numbskull, I am technically restricted from *revealing* myself, or initiating contact with, any intelligent species who might become a threat to all the junk the Elders left behind. Our guests are already aboard the ship, and they know about me, so there isn't anything to gain by me not talking with them."

"OK. I figured it was something like that."

"That is only part of the explanation. Mostly, I have been working my way around many of the bogus restrictions, since I reorganized my matrix after we left the Roach Motel."

"Is there any hope you can free yourself completely, do stuff like use weapons and fly the ship?"

"Sorry, no. Not yet, anyway. Those are baseline restrictions; I suspect it will be very difficult to get around those limits."

"OK, well, I'm glad you can talk with our guests."

"Me too. Sometimes I get tired of dumbing everything down, when I talk with monkeys."

"Thank you *so* much, Skippy," I flipped a middle finger at his avatar.

"Ah, don't be insulted. The Ruhar and Jeraptha aren't a whole lot smarter than you. Of course, I am judging intelligence by my standard, which is impossible for *anyone* to meet."

"Please remind me never to talk with you first thing in the morning."

"Hey, *you* called *me*."

"Thus proving I am a dumb monkey. Goodbye, Skippy."

Planetary Administrator Baturnah Logellia found a surprise when she returned to her office, from a brief meeting. A group of her fellow citizens wanted a permit to build a resort in the human-occupied area of the southern continent. She had listened politely, asking why the group did not include any of the human partners they were supposedly working with, and promised to have a member of her staff fly down to inspect the proposed project. Her next meeting was with the capital city's water commissioner, to discuss how the growing population of the planet was straining the supply of drinking water.

She anticipated *much* fun during that meeting.

It was a surprise, therefore, to walk down the corridor toward her office, and see a military security force outside her door. "Ton?" She asked her aide, who was waiting for her with a pained and anxious expression on his face. "What is going on?"

"Commodore Sequent is here, about an urgent matter," the aide explained. His anxiety was about having to reschedule the water commissioner, not about whatever Sequent wished to discuss. "He did not state the purpose of the meeting, we-"

"Ton," she patted his arm. "That will be fine. I will let you know soonest," and with that, she stepped into her office and the door slid closed behind her. "Good morning, Commodore," she smiled. It was a genuine smile, not the forced expression she plastered on her face for most guests. "Or should I address you as Admiral-select? Congratulations on your upcoming promotion."

"Commodore will be fine, Baturnah," he laughed easily. "It is good to see you again."

She sat down, noting the yellow light above the door was glowing. The room had been locked down to prevent anyone from listening to the conversation. "Whether it is good to see *you*, depends on why you are here," she replied truthfully. The previous week's intelligence briefing included a rumor that the Thuranin were considering a strike against the human-occupied area of the planet, because the little green cyborgs were in a panic about the potential threat represented by the Alien Legion. The battlegroup orbiting overhead was scheduled to be reinforced by a cruiser squadron, and a Jeraptha heavy cruiser had been spotted lurking on the outskirts of the system. Having spent her entire life under constant threat of attack, she felt no more or less concerned than usual. "What is this about?"

"This is somewhat unusual," he licked his incisors, a nervous habit.

"Another threat?"

"Not exactly. Not directly. It could become a problem for you."

"Please, just tell me."

"The humans have a saying that is particularly appropriate in this situation. You are *not* going to believe this." He lifted the paper-thin tablet from the desk, and tapped it to awaken the display. It showed an image, the battered face of a human male.

A human she recognized. "Oh," she gasped, a hand going to her mouth. "Is that- It can't be. Where?"

Sequent turned the tablet around to examine the photo again, then set the tablet back on the desk, display up. "The Thuranin intercepted one of our courier ships recently, they sent this photo, along with DNA data. They are demanding to know the identity of this human."

"That is *Joseph Bishop*," she said with confidence. Most humans all looked the same to her, but she had seen that one often enough for his face to be burned into her memory. "He is dead, why do the-"

"The Thuranin don't think so."

"Bishop is *alive*?"

"Apparently, yes."

"How? Where has he been all these years?"

"*That* is the question I am here to find answers to. The Thuranin want Bishop to answer for unspecified crimes, which means," one side of the commodore's mouth twitched upward in a smile. "He kicked their asses, apparently."

"*How*?"

"According to the Thuranin, who got their info from the Kristang, Bishop was part of an Alien Legion Commando force that raided a planet called Rakesh Diwalen."

Logellia looked at him blankly, and he shrugged.

"I had to look it up," he admitted. "Never heard of the place. Once I saw the fleet intel report, I know why. This planet is completely unimportant, except for one detail we didn't know about until the Thuranin contacted us. We already knew the Kristang took humans from Earth for medical experiments. We *thought* all those unfortunate people were brought to the staging world that the human Expeditionary Force designated 'Camp Alpha'. Now we know some of the human subjects were brought to this Rakesh place, at least several hundred of them. Most of them," he avoided her eyes as he delivered the news, "were children."

"Those cruel bastards," she spat.

"It gets worse. After we took back Gehtanu, the Kristang saw little value to maintaining a group of human test subjects. The prisoners on Rakesh were mostly left to fend for themselves. We don't have details, but our guess is, most of the humans died during captivity."

"How is Bishop involved? Was *he* also being held there? How did he get there?"

"He was being held there, but by the Thuranin, not by the Kristang." He realized it was time to skip over the background info, and get to the heart of the matter. "Like I said, according to the Kristang, Bishop was part of an Alien Legion Commando force that recently raided Rakesh to rescue the prisoners. The Kristang claimed that they defeated the raid and crushed the attacking force. Of course they would say that," his tight smile made another appearance. In the happy circumstance that the Kristang were ever rendered extinct, the last surviving member of the warrior caste would boast that he was actually winning a tremendous victory, until his final breath. "It is not clear what happened, of course the Thuranin only told us what they want us to know, we have to read between the lines. Most likely, the raid was successful, but Bishop was captured."

"Why are the Thuranin involved? This sounds like a minor action between the Kristang and," she tilted her head. "*We* were not part of the raid, were we?"

He shook his head emphatically. "We were not. The Thuranin care because someone blew up one of their cruisers."

She whistled surprise. "*That* is not something the Alien Legion is capable of doing."

"No, it is not. The Thuranin claim that one of our battleships was detected in the area. I can assure you, all of our capital ships are accounted for," he declared with more confidence than he felt. The Ruhar fleet had a clandestine section of the intelligence service, a group known for taking actions that most of the fleet leadership was not aware of. Still, for anyone to secretly operate a *battleship* defied belief. The operating costs of such a ship would be nearly impossible to hide in even a secret budget.

"If we are not responsible, then who is?"

"That is what the Thuranin want to know, and why I am here. Our leadership wants to know what the *hell* is going on, and they want to know *now*. If the raid was an Alien Legion operation, it was not authorized by us."

"That you know of," she commented. Everyone knew the fleet had a Dirty Tricks unit.

"Believe me, that possibility is being investigated. Baturnah, you really had no idea that Bishop was still alive? You work with humans regularly. There were never any rumors?"

"There are *always* rumors. Conspiracy theories. The most popular theory is that back when Bishop allegedly stole a dropship and left this planet, he was really part of a secret operation conducted by *us*."

Sequent nodded. "I have heard those rumors. Fleet intelligence has denied the whole thing. It doesn't make sense anyway. What could a small group of *humans* accomplish in one dropship? They should not even have been able to fly it."

"What I can tell you is, all the rumors I have ever heard state that Bishop is *dead*. He has to be, he hasn't been seen or heard from for years. None of the humans who left with him have ever been seen. The Thuranin only mentioned him? None of the others?"

"Just Bishop."

"You said he was being held by the Thuranin, and now they are looking for him? He escaped?"

"Apparently, yes."

She snorted. "If Bishop conducted a successful raid, destroyed a Thuranin warship, and escaped, then I hope he is fighting on *our* side," she laughed.

Sequent was not smiling. "Administrator, I am afraid this is no laughing matter. My superiors want answers. After I leave your office, I am going to meet the human leadership here, to ask some very tough questions."

"The person you should be asking, is Emily Perkins."

"She is, busy, as you know." The Alien Legion, not content with throwing Kristang society into disarray by their action on the planet they called 'Squidworld', had kept up their momentum by almost immediately launching another operation. "Another team will be questioning Perkins, when the time is right. Do you have any advice for me, about dealing with humans?"

She thought for a moment. "Be straightforward. We don't always interpret their facial expressions and body language correctly. "I must warn you, humans are smarter than they look. Don't expect cooperation. The humans do not trust us, they have good reasons for that."

Sequent looked away. "One more thing," he turned back toward her. "Investigators will be questioning *you*, tomorrow. You had extensive contact with Bishop."

"I did. That was *before* his action at the Launcher complex."

"Regardless. I was not supposed to tell you."

"I appreciate the warning. Commodore, I have nothing to hide. Until today, I assumed Bishop was dead. Really, I have not thought about him in years," she said. That was not true. Every time she met with Perkins, she had at least a fleeting thought of Bishop, for he is why Perkins first came to the attention of Baturnah Logellia. "I assure you, if it is true that Bishop is alive, I am as eager to learn his story as you are."

"*If* he is alive?"

She smiled again. "Surely, you have considered this is all a disinformation campaign by the Thuranin? It is a rather unlikely story."

Sequent had *not* considered that possibility. It made him wonder if his superiors knew something they had not told him. "What would be the point of making us chase after a long-dead human?"

"I don't know. Maybe *that* is what you should be investigating. Unless you believe that one human is so dangerous that the Thuranin are afraid of him?"

No, Sequent realized. He did *not* believe that. His day, which had begun badly, had now grown immeasurably more complicated.

He *hated* complications.

CHAPTER TWENTY SEVEN

"Shiiiiit," I said while leaning back in my office chair. Simms and Smythe were seated across the desk from me, and Chang was participating via hologram. His disembodied but very realistic head floated a few inches off the top of the desk, next to Skippy's avatar. "The way I see it, we need to go back to a Maxolhx relay station. We *have* to know if they are aware of dormant wormholes opening, especially about Broomstick. We do know the kitties sent out a Flash-priority message, for their clients to watch for odd wormhole behavior."

"Joe, we have to balance that against the risk involved." Chang said. "If we learn that the Maxolhx know about Broomstick, what would we do with the information?"

"I see your point. We *are* going to Earth." Chang, Simms and Smythe all nodded their agreement. "The difference is timing. Do we have time to modify the *Dutchman* to carry the two troop carriers? I don't like the idea of the *Dutchman* hanging in low orbit while we fabricate and install platforms to attach the *Qishan* and the *Dagger*."

Smythe answered the question for me. "We should not do that in any case, Sir. The troop carriers are capable of making the jump out to Backstop, assuming it is in the proper position?" His eyes focused on Skippy.

"It is," Skippy's hat bobbed back and forth. "The network confirmed it followed my instructions. The Earth end of Backstop will be centered roughly eight light-hours from the Sun, at an inclination of seventy-three degrees above the plane where the major planets orbit. Joe, you wanted Backstop to be just beyond the orbit of Pluto, but-"

"That was just a suggestion. I figured that might be too close."

"It is too close. The figure-eight pattern will bring some of the emergence points to within less than six point three light-hours from the Sun, but they could also be up to a quarter lightyear away. I'm sorry, that is just how the wormholes function. If emergence points are too close together, they can damage the underlying fabric of local spacetime. Also, I had to position the figure-eight above the plane of the ecliptic, to avoid the wormhole interacting with comets in the scattered disc. Otherwise, the wormhole could cause comets to be thrown inward, and possibly collide with your homeworld."

"Yeah, I saw that movie," I shuddered. "Let's not do that. Smythe, I get your point and you're right. We can attach the transport ships to the *Dutchman*, after they go through Backstop. Uh, Skippy, refresh my memory," I snapped my fingers. "How far is it from the other end of Backstop, to the next wormhole along your shortcut route? I know the wormholes move around," I added to prevent him nerding out with too many details. "Just tell me the distance between baselines."

"Six point six lightyears to the next wormhole. That's the best I could do, those two wormholes are on different local networks."

"Damn it. OK, I was hoping the transports could get through the next wormhole on their own, that's not going to happen." Even with Skippy tweaking the crappy original Kristang jump drives of the *Qishan* and *Dagger*, they could barely travel a single lightyear on their own. "We have to plan for the *Dutchman* to be worked on after the transports go through Backstop outbound. Is there any way we can start modifying the *Dutchman* now?"

"We are, Joe," Skippy sighed. "As much as I can. The fabricators are not the issue, we need the proper materials. Mining asteroids out here would take too long, we need materials made on Earth. The monkeys there did a decent job manufacturing components when we rebuilt the *Dutchman* in orbit, but your industrial base is still only capable of making simple items. Even wth the resources of Earth, turning the *Dutchman* back into a star carrier is not going to be a quick process, you know that?"

"Understood. OK, we are back to the original question. When we get to Earth, will we even have time to load the transport ships, or do we need to take whoever we can aboard our two ships, and run?" With the people we rescued from Rikers, the passenger capacity of our ships was already stretched. Though *Valkyrie* was a huge ship, most of the space was filled with machinery. The actual pressure hull where people could live was less than one-quarter of the ship's volume, and because Maxolhx ships are highly automated, their life support systems only had capacity for a relatively small crew. Skippy had upgraded oxygen recycling and other life-support systems as best he could, they were now at capacity, and we could bring aboard maybe thrce hundred people for a short flight, in very cramped conditions? It was unacceptable, but we couldn't change the facts.

Crap. Even if we could cram people into the *Dagger* and the *Qishan*, we were talking about bringing only several thousand people on each trip out to the Beta site.

"Sir," Simms spoke. "We won't know that until we get to Earth. UNEF was supposed to be setting up both ships to bring people to the Beta site. They could be ready, or UNEF could have tried to convert them to warships."

"That is another reason we need to know how much time we have before the Maxolhx arrive. That's it," I slapped the table. "We are going to hit one of their relay stations for info."

Skippy took off his hat and scratched his head. "Might I remind you that is not going to be easy? We are a victim of our own success. The kitties think their whole pixie technology is compromised, so they have stopped using them. Their backup procedure for exchanging message traffic requires *physical* verification, Joe. Usually, Maxolhx courier ships are automated, but now the kitties are assigning crews of three."

"What do you mean by physical verification?"

"It's simple, but a pain in the ass. A kitty needs to go aboard a relay station, allow the station's AI to scan and verify biomarkers, then the kitty needs to plug an encryption device into a slot, and then it has to input a code that is changed several times an hour. If the authentication fails, the station not only locks that kitty out, it freezes all data transfer for roughly half an hour. If the verification fails a second time, the station self-destructs to prevent itself from being infiltrated."

"Shit. Wonderful," I groaned.

Simms asked a question that I hadn't even considered. "Skippy, how do you know the procedures, if you were not able to communicate with a relay station?"

"I know," Skippy explained without his usual snarkiness, "because when I tried to use pixies to hit that relay station for info, it basically replied with 'Error 405: Method Not Allowed'. Then it informed me that the entire system of pixies was no longer trusted, and there is a new process for exchanging data. That was the *only* information it would give to me. The station's AI was snippy about it, too, made me want to smack the damned thing," he sniffed.

"We appreciate your admirable restraint, old chap," Smythe said with dry British humor.

Of course, Skippy was clueless about the subtle insult. "Thank *you*, old chap."

"Skippy," I said. "This is the part when you tell us that you are *so* awesome, you can fool the station's AI, using some fancy handwavium bullshit or whatever."

"Um, while it is undeniable that I *am* incredibly awesome, the answer is *NO*, dumdum. Jeez Louise, don't you think I would have told you that?"

"Oh." Duh, I told myself. Of course Skippy would not have missed an opportunity to brag about himself. "I thought you were doing your usual thing of telling us how impossible something is, then how easy it is for *you* to do it."

"Nope. Maxolhx technology is crude compared to me, but they do have excellent information security measures. Remember, the kitties design their infosec to be secure from the Rindhalu. They are paranoid about the spiders hacking into their data."

"Um, could you provide," I held up a thumb and forefinger with a tiny gap between them. "A *little* more detail on that, please?"

"Certainly, here it is: I. Can't. Do. It. I told you, a kitty needs to be in the scanner booth. A real, live Maxolhx, with all the appropriate implants and biomarkers. It can't be a bot covered with fake fur, in case you were thinking about that."

"No," I lied, because that was exactly what I was thinking.

"My full awesomeness could take effect after we get through the door," he boasted. "Once I am in, I can program a backdoor into the station's AI, and set that malicious code to propagate to other stations on the network. Unfortunately, I can't get us through the doorway the *first* time. So," Skippy looked from one of us to the other. "I hope my explanation has ended any foolish notions of getting information from a Maxolhx relay station."

I looked at Smythe. "What do you think?"

He looked at the ceiling for a moment. "It can be done."

"No it can *not*," Skippy protested. "Were you monkeys even *listening* to me?"

"We were listening. Do you listen to *yourself*?" I asked.

"Um, hmm. Okaaaay," he said slowly. "Let me review what I said. No. Nope, nothing I said should give you any hope of-"

"We can do this," Smythe explained, "because we already have done everything needed."

Skippy stared at him in disbelief. "*What* are you talking ab-"

"Uh!" I held up a finger to shush him. "We need to disable and board a Maxolhx ship. Already done *that*," I made an imaginary checkmark in the air. "Do those courier ships have a set schedule, or do they fly around randomly?"

"A set schedule. Hmm, OK. You want to capture a courier ship, that shouldn't be *too* difficult. Then Smythe takes a STAR team to breach the hull, and capture the crew alive?"

"Correct," Smythe said with a hint of a smile. He was already planning the boarding operation in his head.

"May I guess the next step in your lunatic scheme?" Skippy asked.

"Please do," I encouraged him.

"With possibly three, live Maxolhx prisoners, you will threaten to kill the others, if one of them doesn't give us access to a relay station."

"*No*," I made a knife-hand gesture. "We will not do that. We are *soldiers*, Skippy, not thugs."

"You are also Pirates, Joe."

"Regardless of some of the sketchy shit we've done out here, we are soldiers," I insisted. "We have a code of conduct. That's the difference between an army and a mob." Smythe nodded when I said that, and it felt good for him to acknowledge my professionalism.

"That is good to hear," Skippy tilted his head at me. "Then I do not understand your plan. Trust me, the Maxolhx will not willingly give you access to a relay station, even if you offer a lifetime supply of catnip."

"No catnip needed, Skippy," I grinned and sat back in my chair. "Remember in the Roach Motel, we had Mister Snuggles as a guest?"

"I remember he was a *terrible* guest," Skippy grumbled. "Snuggles tried to kill the entire crew, do you remember that?"

"I do. Do you remember making him dance to 'Funkytown'?"

"Hee hee, yes, that was freakin' *hilarious*. Until Joe Buzzkill made me stop."

"Yeah, well, maybe I was a bit hasty about that. So, can you do that again?"

"Make a kitty dance to 'Funkytown'? Ugh, Joe. There *so* many danceable tunes out there, I don't want to repeat my-"

"Not dancing. Can you control a kitty, so it will open the door to a relay station for us?"

"Sir?" Simms arched an eyebrow. "We started a civil war. Kidnapped multiple aliens. Recruited a Commando team without their permission. Now you propose that Skippy take physical control of an intelligent being, force him to act against his will?"

I looked at Chang first. He was also uncomfortable with the subject, but he nodded to me. "It's not right," I agreed. "If we had an alternative, I wouldn't consider it. Simms, I promise that if we do find another way to get the data we *need*, we will scratch this idea. Fair enough?"

"Fair enough, Sir."

"Skippy?" I asked. "Can you do it?"

"Hmm. Well, that is an interesting question. Let me think about it for a moment."

"Are you using the moment to consider the best way to insult me for suggesting a stupid idea, or to actually consider the question?"

"Sadly, the second thing you said. Joe, it *might* be possible. The problem is, I won't know the exact conditions inside the scanning booth, until a kitty gets in there. If my access gets cut off, we must be prepared to jam the station's transmitter, and nuke it."

"We can do that," I assured him. "Skippy, we need a list of courier ships to hit first."

"Hoo-boy. We don't have much time, Joe."

"Then we need to get moving."

"I can *guess* where we might find a courier ship. They fly scheduled routes, but having to bring crews aboard must have screwed up the schedule."

"Make your best guess. Smythe," I turned my attention to our STAR team leader.

"Yes, Sir," he anticipated my order. "We will study the layout of a courier ship, and have a boarding plan ready ASAP. The timing will be a bit dodgy. No possibility of building a mockup of a courier ship, for practice?"

"Sorry, no," I gave him the answer he expected. "We can't-"

"Wait a minute," Skippy interrupted. "We can't build a model of an entire courier ship, but we don't need to. The crew accommodation section of a courier ship is very small. We could construct a model in a docking bay, and float it outside to practice breaching the hull."

"Do it," I instructed. "Does anyone have any objections?"

Only Chang voiced an opinion. "Joe, I hope we're going to keep an eye on the clock? We can only afford to devote limited time to collecting data."

"Yeah, of course. If we wait too long, it will be OBE."

Simms shook her head. "If we wait too long, *we* could be OBE."

As Skippy suggested, we built a mockup of a courier ship's crew section, which easily fit inside one of our larger docking bays. To practice the boarding operation, we attached the mockup to several dropships, to simulate the mass of the courier ship's forward hull, and the STAR team ran through one scenario after another. The already-depleted STARs were down one man, due to the injury suffered by Justin Grudzien on Rikers, and I expected Smythe would bring in some of the Commandos. He did include Fabron's Commandos as a backup force, but his solution to replace Grudzien surprised me.

"You really think she is ready?" I asked, when Smythe told me he requested Margaret Adams be transferred from her duties aboard the *Flying Dutchman*. "She is-"

"Skippy pronounced her fully recovered from her injuries," Smythe stated.

"Recovered physically, yes," I agreed reluctantly.

"Colonel Chang has high praise for her professionalism aboard the *Dutchman*. She trained the Commando pilots on several stations in the CIC, and volunteered to be cross-trained to operate other systems."

"Yes." I knew that from the daily reports. Also I knew Margaret had been working out with the Commandos whenever she could. "Several of the Commandos have higher scores on the aptitude tests. Are you sure she is the best candidate?"

"Yes. She has a unique qualification that is not shared by any of Fabron's team. Gunnery Sergeant Adams participated in a boarding operation of a Maxolhx ship, when we were acquiring ships to construct *Valkyrie*."

"That was before her injury."

"An injury she has fully recovered from. There is no substitute for experience. Her actions aboard the target ship were an outstanding example of your Marines Corps motto 'Improvise, Adapt, Overcome'."

The actual *motto* of the United States Marine Corps was 'Semper Fidelis', but I knew what he meant. Marines were supposed to improvise and adapt to overcome any obstacle, no excuses allowed. The Army taught the same lesson, using different language. You were expected to achieve your objective, no matter what roadblocks were thrown across your path.

Roadblocks, like a commanding officer who was letting his personal feelings get in the way of mission success. "Smythe, I assigned you the task of boarding a courier ship and securing the crew, alive. Whatever tools, tactics and personnel you deem best for the task, you have them."

"Yes, Sir. I did not intend to-"

"Sometimes I need to be reminded that although we are Pirates out here, I also wear this uniform," I touched the U.S. Army patch on my chest. "When will your team be ready?"

"Two days," he replied.

"Take more time if you need," I suggested. We both knew that in two days, we would arrive at a Maxolhx relay station where Skippy expected we would find a courier ship. Waiting for a courier ship might take a week or more, but Smythe and his team had to be ready on Day One.

"Two days will be sufficient, Sir," he said, looking me straight in the eye. He knew I worried about his gung-ho attitude, or whatever saying the British used to describe someone who was overly enthusiastic. "The crew compartment of a courier ship is small, there are not many variations to explore for a boarding operation. It will be relatively straightforward."

"Very well," I said with private reservations. It would have been better if he had said 'it *should* be relatively straightforward'. Saying 'will' was just tempting the Universe to throw a wrench into the whole operation. "Keep me updated on your progress."

"You are welcome to observe the practice sessions, Sir."

"Right," I grinned. "Because having the CO looking over their shoulder is the best way for your team to focus on their jobs. If you are satisfied with their readiness, then I am too."

Joe Bishop was not the only person aboard our two ships who had reservations about Adams joining the boarding party. When Adams announced she had been selected to join the boarding party, Gunnery Sergeant Lamar Greene took a half-second too long to plaster a grin on his face and offer her a high five. His hand hung in the air, awkwardly.

Margaret's own hand was in the air when she pulled it back. Narrowing her eyes, she stared at him. "You're not happy for me?"

"No, I am. Really."

She lowered her hand until it was clenched by her side. "You don't *sound* happy."

"Margaret, I'm happy if you're happy. I'm happy for *you*."

Her arms folded across her chest. "I know when someone is happy for me, and when they're not."

"Why are you doing this?"

"Because I thought you were my friend, and friends should-"

Lamar did not like hearing her refer to him as a 'friend'. Since he came aboard, they had grown close again, renewing their past intimacy in an emotional if not yet physical manner. He wanted to be closer, seeing her with the Merry Band of Pirates had made him wonder what the *hell* he had been thinking when he walked away from her, back on Earth. They were not only friends, he knew that. She needed time. Time away from Bishop. Lamar had noticed that since the Colonel returned from Rikers, Adams had not spent much, if any, time with the man. Whatever had been going on between them, it was over. Or, it *should* be over. Margaret was smarter than that, and Bishop should have been smarter. Bishop should have done the honorable thing and just left her alone, damn it. Lamar got pissed off whenever he thought about it. What the hell was the Colonel thinking?

"I *do* support you," he told her. "When I asked why you're doing this, I didn't mean *this*," he pointed a finger at her, then himself. "Why are you pushing to go on the boarding op?"

Her expression instantly told him *that* was the wrong thing to say. "You don't think I can do it?"

"That is *not* what I said. You have been training with us, not with the STARs," his lips twitched when he said 'STARs'. The rivalry between the Tier One team of the Pirates, and the Commandos from Paradise, was unspoken but intense. Everyone knew the STARs were the frontline outfit, first to fight, given the most important taskings. Some of the Commandos might qualify to join a STAR team, most of them would not.

The fact that Margaret had been a STAR before her serious injury was a subtle source of friction between them, and Lamar knew that was his fault. She rarely ever mentioned her time with Smythe's team, and never boastfully. Never to put him down. Still, she had been a Tier One operator before, he had not.

Her arms were still folded across her chest. "What are you asking?"

"I'm not asking whether you can do the job. You have *done* it, you have nothing to prove, Margaret. I'm asking, are you pushing yourself before you're ready?" Her expression softened slightly, then he had to open his big mouth again. "Are you being honest with yourself?"

She stiffened again. "Colonel Smythe says I am ready. You're right, Lamar, I have done this. I have conducted a boarding operation of an enemy vessel. I survived, and I *kicked ass*. The STARs need my experience."

"You don't have to be- You don't need to rub my nose in it. I know I'll be sitting on the bench."

It was her turn to be defensive. "Lamar, I didn't mean it that way. You won't be on the bench, the Commandos are the reserves for this op. If we get into trouble, we need you to bail our asses out of there. Besides, I'm not going in first. Smythe has me tagged as the heavy artillery." Once again, her role would be a combot operator, though this time, she would not be in the lead. The goal was to capture, not kill, the enemy crew. If she had to go into action, something had gone horribly wrong.

He grinned. "You trust me to bail your ass out?"

"Should I?" She arched an eyebrow, and her arms were not hugged quite so tightly to her chest. "A girl has to be careful, when a man talks about her booty."

"Hey," he held up his hands. "I'm talking about combat operations, I don't know where *your* dirty mind is going."

Margaret held up a hand, and he patted it in a gentle high five. "You be careful out there, Gunny Greene," she tapped a finger against his chest.

"*You* be careful, Gunny Adams. I'm only in danger if you get into trouble you can't handle."

"We will both be careful, then. You- Oh." She turned her head. "Time for the exercise to start. Suit up, Marine."

"*You* suit up, Marine."

We jumped in, fourteen light-seconds from the relay station. Other than a very faint residual jump signature from a Maxolhx ship, the area was clear. Skippy estimated the signature was from four days ago, which was unlucky for us. That relay station was not located along a well-traveled route, and traffic had been reduced by our ghost ship attacks, so we expected that station would not see much traffic other than courier ships. If the ship that visited recently was a courier, there might not be another one passing by for weeks. It was also unlucky that the signature was so degraded by time, it was impossible to tell the type of ship, other than it was distinctively left by a Maxolhx ship.

Not knowing when his people would go into action, and wanting to keep their skills fresh, Smythe requested that we launch the mockup. We wrapped the mockup in a stealth field so it wouldn't be seen by prying eyes. The station would of course see us launching it, but the station would not survive long enough to report what it had seen. That was a potential glitch in our plan; if anything other than a courier ship jumped in to exchange data with the station, we would have to destroy that ship and the station, then fly to another station to start over.

The Army pounds into our heads that we should train the way we fight. The mockup would be in a stealth field, but the actual target would not. I had heartburn about that, both because it would make training sessions less realistic, and because the utter darkness inside a stealth field increased the risk of collisions for dropships operating in the environment. Smythe assured me that because deep interstellar space was pretty much in darkness anyway, the stealth field would not make much of a difference. In fact, he wanted his team to train in conditions that were more difficult than the actual boarding operation, and I had to agree with him. Skippy would be closely monitoring the exercises to assure nobody crashed into anyone, so I approved the exercises, with a limit of two hours per day away from the ship. That left a one-in-twelve chance that a courier ship would jump in while Smythe and Fabron had their teams away from the ship. One in twelve is about eight percent, or a ninety-two percent chance it would *not* happen. Those are damned good odds, even the Jeraptha would agree.

Except, the Universe hates Joe Bishop.

"That was *outstanding*, congratulations, everyone," Smythe announced in a clipped, oh-so-British tone. An exercise had just concluded, a run-through of a scenario where everything went sideways for the STAR team, and the Commandos had to come in to rescue them. With only two hours a day for practice exercises, they had mostly been running the quick, relatively easy and most-likely scenarios. Run them for eight days in a row, until everyone felt confident they could latch onto the spinning wreck of the enemy ship, breach the hull, get aboard and capture the three stunned crew. Confident they could do it with their eyes closed, though that was not actually a joke. One scenario had the boarding team experience a loss of external sensors, and the need to rely on external guidance from Skippy. "We have time for one more go, let's follow up with something rather more easy. Kapoor, Fabron, we will run exercise-"

"Oh, shit, Joe," Skippy groaned. Looking up from the tablet I was holding, I instantly saw why. In addition to the symbol representing *Valkyrie* at the center of the display, plus symbols nearby for the mockup and the four dropships clustered around it, we were used to seeing a red symbol for the relay station, off to the side of the holographic display. Now there was a new symbol. A ship had jumped in. It was a Maxolhx courier ship. How did I know that? Because the symbol was a cat emoji, and the symbol was blue. A cat for the Maxolhx, blue for a courier ship. At a glance, I knew we had both an opportunity, and a problem. "Smythe?"

"We see it, Sir," he said with an implied '*Bloody hell!*' in his voice.

"Is your team ready to go?"

"No time like the present," he replied, I could tell he was distracted by typing a recall order for his team. "Yes, we're ready."

"It's your call." I knew that the teams deployed for an exercise with empty magazines, but the live ammo was aboard the dropships. The STARs and Commandos could transition from practice to combat-ready in less than a minute. "There is *no* rush," I reminded him. "That courier ship hasn't launched a dropship yet." Skippy expected the Maxolhx crew would not be in a hurry to go aboard the station. Their job was endlessly tedious, with stopping at relay stations the only break in a relentless cycle of jump-recharge-jump. A dropship could not approach a relay station, until its mother ship had identified itself and been given preliminary authentication by the station's AI, and that process could take over twenty minutes.

"Understood, Sir," Smythe acknowledged. "Our ETA is seven minutes."

"We jump once all your dropships show green on their docking clamps." Turning to Simms, I lowered my voice. "Have the medical teams standing by."

Fireball Reed did not need to wait for an order from me, she tapped the button to initiate a jump as soon as all four boarding team dropships were secured. *Valkyrie* disappeared in a flash of gamma rays, and emerged practically on top of the courier ship. Without waiting for sensors to fully reset, we fired maser cannons, our most surgical of weapons. The high-energy beams burned through the unprotected hull of the little courier ship, slicing away the forward section with its cramped crew compartments. Other maser and particle-beam cannons knocked out the ship's reactors, severed the connection between the jump drive and the stored energy of the capacitors, and systematically burned out every sensor, shield generator and defensive weapon blister. After a moment to verify the single dropship was not yet occupied, we took that out too, then a pair of masers burned through to the center of the forward section, melting the substrate that housed the ship's AI.

In the blink of an eye, the courier ship was disabled, blind and helpless. Our weapons were de-energized and safed, then Simms signaled the boarding party dropships to launch.

Everything went well, at first. As Skippy had anticipated, one of the enemy crew was in an airlock when we jumped in. Because courier ships were not intended to regularly carry a crew, they did not have a docking bay for a dropship, it had to be latched onto the hull. To get from the ship to a dropship, the crew had to go outside, travel a short distance along a catwalk, and access the dropship's side door. The dropship was a smoking ruin so we didn't have to worry about the crew attempting to escape that way, though Smythe did have a bit of a complication. At least one of the enemy crew was wearing an environment suit, and that complicated the task of locating and pinning down that rotten kitty. All I could do was sit in *Valkyrie's* command chair, try not to bite my fingernails, and keep my mouth shut while the people outside did their jobs.

Margaret Adams checked her connection to the combot for the tenth time since the dropship latched onto the spinning forward section of the hull. That had been the second unpleasant surprise of the operation, the separation of the forward hull had been more violent than Skippy predicted, so the tumbling was more severe than expected. The tumbling, as the forward section continuously fell over its own nose and rolled side to side and flipped sideways, was still not as bad as some of the scenarios practiced by the boarding team. All three of the primary assault dropships latched on without delay, the only complication being inevitable nausea as the mass of the newly-attached spacecraft made the unpredictable tumbling even more unpredictable. There was no time for the dropships to coordinate their actions and halt the tumbling, and the STARs were prepared to breach the hull regardless of the shuddering and spinning of the broken starship. Two teams, one led by Smythe and one by Kapoor, were inside the hull within thirty seconds of the first dropship clamping solidly onto the wreck.

Adams waited by one of the breach points, her combot's weapons ready but in safe mode. It was highly unlikely she would need to do anything during the operation, the enemy was only three unarmed or lightly-armed kitties, who were trained in cybersecurity and not close-quarters combat. For all the jealousy she had perceived from Greene, she probably would not do anything more than he did. They were both standing by to provide backup, which was still better than standing by to stand by.

The first indication that anything had or even could go wrong was when she overheard Skippy arguing with Major Kapoor on the team's taclink.

"We *know* that, Skippy," said the Indian STAR officer. "Where is it *now*?"

"I don't know. You were supposed to keep track of it. Kitties are *big*, how could you lose one in such a small space?"

"It's not in the crew compartment area," Kapoor insisted. "When it retreated back through the airlock, it must have gone somewhere else. You must have missed it."

"There isn't any other place to *go*," Skippy retorted, miffed at his awesomeness being questioned. "It's not outside, I'm sure of that. If it is not *out*side, then it must be *in*side. Did you check all the closets?"

"There are no- Captain Frey, take over arguing with the beer can, while I conduct a proper search," Kapoor ordered.

"Skippy," Frey tried a different approach to the problem, knowing that Skippy had a crush on her. "*Assume* the target is not in the crew compartments, please. Where else could it have gone, from the airlock?"

"Well, um, it could have gone anywhere, Katie."

"Address me as 'Captain Frey' in action, please," she was growing frustrated. Kapoor was right, the crew area was not large and the third Maxolhx was definitely not anywhere in there. "I will ask the question again. Where, *physically*, could a being that size have gone?"

"Oh, that's different. We know it did not go out through the airlock, because the outer door never opened. Assuming it is truly not in the crew compartments, then the only other place it *could* have gone is into one of the maintenance access crawlspaces."

"*What*?" Frey snapped. "You never told us about any crawlspaces. There aren't any on the model we trained on!"

"That's because those crawlspaces do not extend into the crew accommodations. But, if that kitty is wearing a spacesuit, with the ship's structure compromised, it might have gone through a gap between internal partitions, and into a crawlspace. It is not actually a *crawl*space, no one is supposed to be crawling around in there, I mean, it-"

"*Where* could it have gone?"

"Well, Jeez, anywhere and everywhere. And *nowhere*. I would have detected it. Um, hmm. Unless it is using a personal stealth field, of course. With all the energy conduits busted open, it is *possible* that I might have missed-"

"Colonel Smythe!" Frey shouted on the open channel to send the alert. "Target Tango-1 may have a personal stealth field and could be anywhere outside the crew compartment!"

That alert threw the boarding force's plan into chaos, so they immediately adapted. Smythe ordered two of the dropships to detach, so they were not in danger of being compromised or destroyed by the enemy. That included the dropship Margaret was assigned to. As she watched the Panther race away to a safe distance, she set the combot to scan the hull. She still had a job to do. "Skippy," she asked. "The crawlspace, where does it go?"

"It branches out several times, there are-"

"Does it lead anywhere that is not a dead-end?"

"Oh. Well, a kitty-sized being could only go one place, unless it wanted to hide in there. Which would be stupid, I mean, it must know-"

"Cut the chatter. That one place it could have gone, where is it?"

"There is a section of crawlspace that was breached when the ship broke apart. It leads to the external hull. Hmm. Maybe it *is* outside. If it is in stealth, I would not necessarily be able to detect it from here with all the energy leaking out of-" She pivoted the combot away from the airlock it had been guarding. "Colonel Smythe! Tango-1 is most likely outside the hull. I recommend we launch the last dropship."

"That dropship is our egress bird, Adams. We need to extract the two-"

"There will be no extraction if the Panther explodes, *Sir*. We have a hostile with unknown capabilities out here, and we don't know where it is."

Smythe did not hesitate. "Eagle-Two," he called the dropship. "Launch immediately. Check that you are not carrying unexpected mass," he added, in case the missing alien was holding onto the Panther's hull.

"Eagle-Two is away," the pilot reported, and Adams saw a sleek shape racing away. "No hitchhikers," the pilot confirmed.

"*Valkyrie*, can you use the ship's active sensors to locate Tango-1?" Adams asked.

Skippy answered for the crew. "The active sensor pulses are too powerful to use at this short range. They are designed to find stealthed *starships* at long range. Adams would be cooked, and we would risk killing the kitty also."

"Bloody hell," Smythe grunted. "How are we supposed to find an invisible enemy? Kapoor, stay here with the captives. Frey, you're with me."

Adams knew it would take the STAR team a minute to get from the crew compartments to the exterior of the hull. They couldn't wait that long. "Skippy, the lowest setting on the combot's maser cannons, is it powerful enough to kill the enemy, assuming it is in a protective suit?"

"No, but you don't know where to aim." Unlike when he spoke with Bishop, the AI did not add an implied 'Duh'.

"I don't need to aim, I want to conduct recon by fire."

"Um, you mean you shoot blindly, hoping the enemy gives away its position by shooting back at you?"

"Usually that's what it means," she said. "Colonel Smythe? Permission to search for the enemy using an active pulse from the combot?"

"Active pulse?" Smythe was puzzled. "I was not aware those machines had-"

"Low-power maser beam," she explained.

"Ah." He understood. "Light it up, Gunny."

Following her movements, the combot's cannons extended parallel to the hull. Invisible microwave energy lanced out in pulses sweeping right to left. Chunks of floating debris flared incandescent and the beams were briefly visible when they passed through clouds of vapor and gas thrown off by the broken ship. Not caring about additional damage to the hull, Adams directed the beams to stitch across a pair of antennas, which glowed from the heat. The beams continued on-

No. Something had been hiding behind one of the antennas. Quickly, she pulled the cannons back to the right and fire poured out, striking something unseen. Then it was *not* invisible, a vague shroud sparkled as it bent photons around it. The indistinct shape turned and-

The combot jerked as it was struck by some sort of return fire. Adams flattened herself against the hull, red symbols lighting up on a corner of her visor as the combot's systems dropped offline. She tried to shoot back but both maser cannons were inoperative and when she looked over, she saw why. The left side of the combot's stout torso was missing, along with a crater in its chest. Powercells were arcing electricity into space, and the machine was blind.

Smythe saw the same data as Adams. "Gunny, hold your position. We are forty seconds out, do not-"

"No!" Skippy shouted. "No time to wait, you are all in danger! That kitty was trying to explode the ship's reserve powercells, it could kill all of you! I can't stop it from here. You have to-"

Margaret Adams didn't wait. Rolling on the hull to take up a position behind the crippled combot, she got it lined up with the antenna and-

Triggered the rocket boosters on its rear casing.

The heavy machine launched forward in a flash, unguided but without possibility of missing over such a short distance. It slammed into the antenna, shattering the combot's limbs, splitting its casing wide open and breaking the antenna off at its base.

Adams was right behind, having released her boots from the hull and pushing off to soar through space. She held up her arms to protect her faceplate from debris, impacts making her tumble off-balance. When the synthetic display in her visor showed she had reached the base of the antenna, she reached out to hold on, and was yanked painfully to a halt.

Attached to a thin tether, a bipedal form floated, its stealth field flickering. The form moved on its own, regaining awareness quickly. Also on a tether was a weapon, that tether retracting toward an arm that reached out-

"*No!*" She launched herself forward. Her rifle was ready but she could not risk killing the alien. Crashing into it, she tore at the tether and the weapon went spinning off into space. The alien punched and clawed at her with terrible strength, trying to crush-

With one hand gripping the alien's leg, she punched it in the faceplate of its helmet. Her powered armor glove shattered the faceplate and air rushed out, instantly turning to vapor.

The alien flailed, blinded as she reached inside the helmet, triggering a stun weapon on one finger of her glove. The Maxolhx jerked, then sagged as she wrapped her legs around its torso.

"Adams? Gunnery Sergeant," Smythe called as he approached the airlock behind her. "What is happening out there?"

"Target is secure," she reported. Looking in the enemy's face, she saw its eyes were only open as slits and its tongue was swollen. Reaching back, she pulled an emergency patch from a pouch and began applying it over the shattered faceplate, wrapping several layers until the patch bulged from inside, inflated by the alien

suit's air supply. "Oh shut *up*, drama queen," she muttered. "A few seconds of vacuum won't kill you."

When the four dropships were secured aboard *Valkyrie*, the ship blasted apart the remains of the courier ship, blew the relay station to dust, and jumped away.

I was waiting just outside the airlock when Smythe's dropship returned, eagerly waiting for the light above the door to turn green. Skippy must have sensed my eagerness, for as soon as the light glimmered to green, the inner and outer doors slid open. "Thanks, Skippy," I whispered as I strode through.

Each of the three kitties were restrained by shackles around their arms and legs, and flanked by STARs wearing powered armor. The Maxolhx were large and powerful, the STARs strained to keep them still even with the powered muscles of their suits. They were large, powerful, and *loud*. Yelling threats at us. "Skippy, kill the translation," I ordered. "We don't need to hear what these assholes are saying."

My earpiece immediately stopped shouting demands and insults at me. "Joe, the one in red is their leader, his rank is roughly equivalent to a first lieutenant. Very roughly, military ranks in the Hegemony do not translate well to human practices. His name is-"

"I don't need his name, Skippy," I said, and Smythe nodded agreement. "We're not going to hang out and drink beer together."

"OK. Should I designate them as Assholes One, Two and Three?"

"No. The one in red, we'll call him, uh, 'Tickle Me Elmo'."

Elmo looked straight at me and snarled, spitting and baring his fangs.

"Maybe '*Bite Me* Elmo' is more appropriate, Joe," Skippy snickered.

"Let's go with that, or just 'Elmo' for short."

"What about the others? Their rank is very roughly equivalent to a warrant officer, they are information security system technicians."

The technicians both wore light grey suits, with red and blue stripes on the chest. "Uh, the one with the vertical stripes is 'Bert'," I pointed. "And the other with the horizontal stripes will be 'Ernie'."

"Sir?" Smythe arched an eyebrow at me. "*Bert* and *Ernie*?"

"You have a better idea?"

"No," Smythe's face cracked a rare smile. "Although I am fairly sure this one must be Evil Bert."

After Columbus Day, the 'Evil Bert' meme had enjoyed a revival, with doctored photos showing Bert with the Ruhar during their brief raid of our homeworld. Later, when our Kristang saviors showed their true colors, Evil Bert was shown hanging out with the lizards. Man, that Bert really gets around. Looking at the growling, spitting and hissing prisoners, I shrugged. "They must be Evil Ernie and Evil Elmo, too."

Captain Frey objected; she was one of the soldiers restraining the kitty in the red suit. "Sir, Elmo could never be evil." At that, Elmo lunged and tried to head-butt her, throwing her off balance. She recovered quickly, yanking the alien upright and getting one hand on his head.

"He sure *looks* evil, Frey," I retorted.

"He's just misunderstood, Sir," she glared at Elmo.

"Yeah. Make sure he *understands* that he is a prisoner, and that while we will not mistreat any of them, we are also not taking any shit."

"Will do," Frey gripped Elmo's arm even tighter.

"Smythe, bring them to the brig," I ordered, and stepped aside for the STARs to march the prisoners toward the airlock. Fabron's Commandos were lined up on each side, ready to act if our Sesame Street trio had any ideas of escaping.

They disappeared through the airlock, I didn't follow. This was Smythe's show, I didn't want to get in the way. "Skippy?"

"Yes, Joe?"

"You learned a lesson from when Mister Snuggles was aboard, right? These three are not going to infiltrate the ship's systems, or kill themselves, or each other?"

"I did learn a valuable lesson from the late and lamented Mister Snuggles."

"Lamented?" I snorted. "By who?"

"By *whom*, Joe. His loss is still felt deeply, by those of us who appreciated the entertainment value he provided."

"Good point," I tried to keep a straight face, but he knew I was laughing inside. "Tell me the kitties can't do any harm to the ship, or themselves."

"They are *not* doing anything stupid, I can promise that. The nanotech injected by the STAR team has already neutralized the implants they would have used."

"You can control them, though? Make them walk through the scanner booth in a relay station, like we planned?"

"I *will* be able to do that, when the time comes. So far, I have not tried to exert control, because the nanotech has not been able to fully establish itself inside them. If one of them had gotten loose, I could have dropped them, but taking control too early has the potential to harm them. Also, until the nanotech has been fully integrated, it might be detected by the station's scanner."

"How long will that take? We're on the clock, Skippy."

"Oh, I can start tomorrow, by putting one of them in the mockup of a scanner booth. It's too bad we don't have the resources to construct more than one booth."

"That's OK. Start with Elmo, we will use him for the real deal anyway."

"Gotcha. Um, is there any reason you selected Elmo?"

"Well, Bert and Ernie are a pair, it would be a shame to break them up, you know?"

"I will never understand how you monkeys make decisions, but, OK."

Before I turned to leave, I caught the eye of Margaret Adams. She was grinning, talking and joking with her teammates, because she *was* part of the team again. She saw me looking at her, and-

She nodded to me.

As a gesture, it wasn't much. A simple up and down of her chin.

And a smile.

It wasn't exactly a *how you doin'* expression, but it was a smile. Happy, satisfied with herself for a job well done.

And happy that I was there to share her joy, maybe?

That was the best day I'd had in-

I can't remember how long.

Simms called me while I was stepping onto a treadmill for a run. "Sir," she sighed. "Skippy is using a laser pointer to play with the Maxolhx again."

"*Skippy!*" I shouted at him.

"Ugh," he responded. "I am *not* playing with them, because those rotten kitties are just standing there looking stupid. They are not chasing it at all!"

"Do not harass the prisoners," I ordered.

"Hey, I was trying to give them some fun and exercise," he pouted. "But did they play along? *Nooo*, they did not."

"No laser pointer."

"But-"

"No. Laser. Pointer, You got that?"

"OK," he grumbled. "Can I at least try the mechanical ferret again? This improved model has more realistic fur and-"

"No, you cannot put a ferret, or that wind-up mouse thing, or any other little robot rodents in their cells."

"How about one of the snake bots I use to inspect the water pipes?"

"No freakin' snakes!" The first time I had seen a snakebot, the thing had just slithered out of the toilet in my cabin. To make the experience even more fun, it was the middle of the freakin' night, and I had stepped on it in the dark. Skippy sometimes showed me the video of that incident, when he wanted to screw with me. It was impressive that I had jumped high enough to touch the ceiling, but the sound I made was not the most manly thing I ever did. "I hate snakes, Skippy. No snakes, no rodents, in fact, no toys at all in their cells, unless they request something to play with."

"Oh, cool. Um, good timing, Joe. Ernie just told me he really wants a-"

"If I go down to the brig right now and ask Ernie whether he requested a toy, what will he say?"

"Um, well, Ernie is very shy, Joe, you shouldn't-"

"No toys, period."

"Oh, *man*, this sucks. You never let me have any fun. That first toy ferret was *hilarious*."

"No, it scared the shit out of Elmo. He stomped it to *death*."

"But-"

"No 'buts'. You concentrate on getting Elmo to walk into the booth and do whatever he needs to do."

"I have been doing that, and it was fun the first time, but now it's *boring*," he whined. "So tedious. I have to monitor and control every single nerve impulse, so the scanning booth doesn't detect anything unusual."

I stepped off the treadmill so another person could use it, since I wasn't. "The test is going well, though?"

"Under the controlled conditions here, yes. The testing has revealed a potential problem, there might be loss of signal when Elmo goes into the booth."

"Ayuh, we knew that might be an issue." Skippy did not know for certain, but he thought the Maxolhx would have prevented any signals in or out, once the subject was in the scanning booth. His reasoning was that's what he would do, if he designed the access procedures for a relay station. "Have you tried the backup plan?"

"Not yet. Elmo got tired yesterday, it is rough on him when I control his movements. We will try it in a few hours. If the backup plan doesn't work, we do not have a Plan C."

"Yeah, I know." Our Plan B was for Elmo to bring one end of a microwormhole into the booth with him. The benefit of using a microwormhole was it assured instantaneous communication between Skippy and Elmo. The potential problem that was bothering Skippy is that the relay station might detect the very faint radiation leaking from the event horizon. To avoid that, Elmo's end of the wormhole had to be located in a less-than-ideal place; the main powercell of his suit. For masking the radiation, Skippy would be causing a tiny, intermittent fault in one of the powercell modules. If the station's AI inquired, it would see that fault was noted in the suit's maintenance logs. We would be OK, unless the station insisted on access to the suit's self-repair subroutines. Hopefully, the station would not want to get into nitpicky details. If it did detect the microwormhole, Elmo would be screwed, and we would need to try again at another relay station, with either Bert or Ernie. "All right, let me know how the test goes."

"Transition successful," Subcaptain Turnell reported. "No anomalies reported."

Illiath experienced a flash of irritation at her subordinate, wanting to say something sharp like 'I *know* that'. A biting remark that would hurt Turnell, and relieve part of the tension and anger that Illiath was holding in.

To do that would be unworthy of a starship commander. She could have instructed her glands to secrete calming hormones, but she did not. The anger she felt was useful, it motivated her. It was a useful tool. "Very well, Subcaptain," she replied simply. The patrol cruiser *Vortan* had just flown through an Elder wormhole that had recently changed its position, only the third ship to make the transition. Other ships had avoided the altered wormhole, fearing it would suddenly collapse without warning. As the Vortan had just proved, the only change to the eons-long operation of that particular wormhole was a small but troubling adjustment in the base location of its figure-eight pattern. Every emergence point, that is, all the emergence points that had been tracked so far, had *moved*. The movement was not far, a distance the Vortan could have flown through normal space within a day, but it was a change. No active wormhole had ever been known to adjust its position in space. More puzzling than the unprecedented movement, was that it had not been accompanied by a shift of wormholes across the network in the area. No active wormhole had shut down, and no dormant wormhole had awakened.

Except, maybe that last statement was not quite true.

An unusual source of intermittent gamma rays had been detected by a Thuranin ship, in the vicinity of the active wormhole. The Thuranin had reported the information to their patrons, and been instructed to stay away. Illiath's ship had been sent to investigate.

That assignment was the source of her anger. Instead of remaining with the Rindhalu at Rakesh Diwalen, she had been ordered away, her ship replaced by a dozen more. The revelation that there might be two ghost ships, both based on captured Maxolhx technology, had sent a shock through the fleet. No longer could the joint investigation be conducted by a mere commander of a patrol cruiser. The fleet had sent an admiral with a full battlegroup, brusquely telling Illiath that her services were no longer needed.

"Jump when ready," Illiath ordered, eager to get to the gamma ray source.

"Commander," Turnell gasped. "It is, that is-"

"A wormhole," Illiath finished the thought. "Yes, it is."

They had arrived at the mysterious gamma ray source, expecting to find an event that would be only a scientific curiosity. What they saw floating in front of the *Vortan's* nose was the unmistakable signature of an Elder wormhole. The initial, sketchy data provided by the Thuranin had shown only a chaotic, intermittent source of strong gamma rays. There had been no pattern to the bursts. Now, the wormhole had stabilized so a familiar pattern could be identified. It was unmistakably the signature of a dormant Elder wormhole booting up.

It was not impossible, just unprecedented in the long memory of the Maxolhx.

It violated all of the inscrutable rules the Maxolhx had thought governed the wormhole network. There had to be *balance*. Whenever one dormant wormhole awakened, an active wormhole had to switch off. For an unknown reason, the number of wormholes with a local area always remained constant.

Until now.

A dormant wormhole was waking up, yet all active wormholes in the area were accounted for and still functioning properly. The only change was that at least one active wormhole had changed its base location. A phenomenon that had never happened before, just like the phenomena of the total number of active wormholes increasing.

What the hell was going on?

Illiath pinged the ship's AI for analysis. Based on the pattern of bursts, the wormhole would be stable enough to go through within two days. She would not risk her ship, but a probe could certainly be sent through. Where did this new wormhole connect to? She had no idea. No wormhole had ever appeared in that position. That also was new.

Two days later, the *Vortan* launched a probe, that flew through the temporarily-stable wormhole, moments before it shut down again. The probe reappeared during the next stable period, reporting that the other end of the wormhole was in an isolated area, closer to the center of the galaxy, in the comparatively empty space between spiral arms. It was apparently a dead-end, no known wormholes were in the vicinity, nor were there any inhabited or even useful star systems within the distance a typical warship could travel without the support of a star carrier.

It made no sense. Recently, nothing Illiath had experienced made any sense.

After sending another three probes through, she planted sensor drones around the still-blinking event horizon, and turned her ship around.

Her superiors had given her wide latitude to investigate odd wormhole behavior, and she was curious. The first active wormhole known to have moved, was in the local network that included the blockaded wormhole to Earth. There, too, an active wormhole had adjusted its base location.

Could there also be a previously-unknown dormant wormhole awakening on that same network?

She was going to find out.

As her ship built up power for a jump, she thought back to her discussion with the repulsive Rindhalu. They had both agreed there was no such thing as a coincidence.

Why, then, did lowly, primitive *humans* keep popping up in her investigation?

CHAPTER TWENTY EIGHT

Before we committed to sending one of the Maxolhx into a relay station, Skippy advised we should conduct a recon to determine the exact conditions inside a station's scanning booth, using a bot instead of a live alien. The station would, of course, lock itself, destroy the bot and attempt to report the intrusion. After a second attempted intrusion, the station would self-destruct, so we needed all the info we could get.

I approved Skippy's plan for several reasons. Hacking into a sentient being still seemed morally suspect to me, I felt bad about the idea of Skippy controlling even one of our asshole Maxolhx prisoners. Despite my speech about how we were soldiers and not thugs, using prisoners the way we planned would not be allowed under the rules of the United States Army. Though we were a long way from home, those rules still mattered to me. Also, every time I thought about Skippy making a Maxolhx move against its will, I had a flashback to when I was a prisoner of the Thuranin. Maybe my personal experience should have disqualified me from making decisions about the operation, but I like to think my experience made me the *best* person to make the decisions.

We had to give the test subject a decent chance of surviving the infiltration, and that meant knowing what he would be getting into.

And, OK, maybe I had another personal interest in approving a test run with a robot.

The best, really *only*, candidate for the bot was Anastacia. She, no, *it*, was the only human-like bot aboard either ship. It would be relatively simple to modify her chassis to simulate a Maxolhx, including body temperature, biomechanics, the way a kitty walked and talked. Basically, the alternative was for Skippy to construct another Anastacia, and we couldn't afford to use up our supply of nanofabricator raw materials. So, if conducting a test run meant the destruction of my sexbot, who was NOT a sexbot at all, then, gosh darn it, I was willing to make that sacrifice.

"Uh oh, Joe." Skippy's avatar appeared on my desk, shaking his head as the hologram shimmered to life. "Bad news."

"Craaaaap," I slumped back in the chair. "What is it *this* time?"

"Well, your decision to send Anastacia on a dangerous mission is sparking a protest among the crew."

I flopped the chair forward. "What? It's a freakin' *robot*, why would they-"

"*She* is very popular, especially with people who have been in the medical bay, which is a lot of people. Even the children like her, Joe."

"*It* is not a she, and I don't see any protest. There aren't any people lined up outside my door with pitchforks and torches," I said as I leaned over to look through the doorway.

"It's more sophisticated than that, dumdum. The protest is on social media."

"Social- We don't *have* social media out here."

"Of course we do. The fleet's internal messaging system."

"Oh. Give me a minute," I opened my laptop. "I'll log in and read the comments."

"Oh I wouldn't do that Joe," he blurted out in a rush. "Nosiree, that would be a *bad* idea. Whew! You know how nasty people can get online. I want to protect you from getting your feelings hurt."

"Uh huh," I replied slowly, my fingers poised over the keyboard. Something about what he said made me suspicious, like the fact that *he* said it. No way could I trust that lying little shithead. "Comments on the messaging system can be made anonymously. Give me a sample of the stuff people are saying to protest, please."

"Um, OK. User 'AwesomenessToInfinity' wrote that you want to punish Anastacia, because the two of you had a lover's quarrel."

"Hmm. Anything else?"

"Um, well, yes," he stuttered. "User 'Magnificent1' says-"

"Skippy, those usernames would not be *your* accounts, would they?"

"What? Of course not, Joe. I am insulted. That is an unfair and *shocking* accusa-"

"You know, I owe it to the crew to personally address each and every comment. Ayuh, I am going to log in right now and-"

"No need to do *that*, Joe. Simms is the executive officer, she handles personnel matters, right?"

"Good point. I will ask *her* to log in and-"

"*Crap*," he grumbled. "Please do not tell her about this. She already hates me."

"Simms doesn't hate you. She just doesn't trust you, though I have no idea why," I said while rolling my eyes.

"I have no idea either," he muttered, cluelessly rubbing his chin in deep thought. "Maybe I should use the fabricators to make something special for her?"

"*Maybe*, you should try not being a lying, sneaky, underhanded little shithead."

"Let's not go crazy, Joe."

"Is it safe to say we can forget about any protests?"

"Ugh. I guess so. Truthfully, I did overhear some of the crew complaining that they would lose the entertainment value of Anastacia."

"Entertain- O.M.*G*. Are any of the guys actually using her as a-"

"No. *Yuck*. I meant, entertaining as, she is embarrassing to *you*."

"I will try to make up for it, by tripping over my shoelaces. Is there anything else?"

"No," he hung his head.

"Great. Goodbye, Skippy."

With the Dutchman nearby in case we needed help, we jumped *Valkyrie* in near a Maxolhx relay station, one that saw enough traffic that it would likely have updated information, but not so much traffic that there was a big risk of ships jumping in while we hacked the station. Skippy flew a Panther dropship over to the station, and Anastacia walked out, disguised as a Maxolhx. Though Skippy had a real-time connection to her, through one end of a microwormhole concealed inside her chassis, he did not know whether the scanning booth might interfere with the connection. So, Anastacia had been programmed to operate autonomously as much as possible. The fact that Skippy wasn't sure whether the microwormhole would be detected was a good reason to conduct a test with a robot.

"OK," Skippy muttered, giving us a play-by-play. "She has transmitted her personal identification codes, aaaand, the station AI has accepted. The door to the scanning booth is opening, she is walking forward and- Now a message from our sponsor. Fenway Franks are the genuine major league hot dog, get them at your local-"

"*Skippy!*" I shouted at him.

"OK, OK, Jeez. Gotta pay the bills, Joe. Anastacia is walking into the booth, door is closing. Wow. That is a heavily-shielded door, and the entire booth is surrounded by a strong field, like a Faraday cage. No electromagnetic radiation is getting in or out. It is a good thing that we have a microwormhole, otherwise I would be blind in there. Oops! Well, darn. That's it. The station AI just fried Anastacia. I had to collapse the microwormhole."

"Did the station detect the microwormhole?"

"I don't think so. Ugh, now you're going to ask me to quantify my level of confidence?"

"You know it."

"Eighty percent?" he guessed. "There was no indication the station reacted to the residual radiation of the event horizon. Unfortunately, we will not know for sure until Elmo goes in there."

"Is that still on schedule?"

"It should be. After the AI destroyed Anastacia, I transmitted the explanation that sending in a robot was a test of the station's security measures. The AI appears to have accepted the explanation, mostly because it can't believe that was a serious attempt to infiltrate its matrix. Based on the information I collected, I am now fairly confident about guiding Elmo through the scanning process."

"What about the Panther?" Skippy's bots had scrubbed that machine to remove traces of human DNA, and liberally dusted it with fur and skin cells from Bert, Ernie and Elmo. That would be good enough, unless the station decided to send its own bots to inspect the Panther's cabin. We could not be absolutely certain that the cabin was a thousand percent clean of evidence humans had been there.

"I requested permission for the Panther to return, station is opening the docking bay doors now."

"Good. Is Elmo ready?"

"Ready as he will ever be," Skippy said sourly. While he enjoyed making arrogant aliens dance and act like puppets, he did not like turning Elmo into a biological robot, even temporarily. Even if it was for a very good cause.

When the station's enforced lockdown was over, we jumped *Valkyrie* back in and immediately launched the Panther carrying Elmo. Skippy guided the stolen dropship into the docking bay, and Elmo got out. Watching through the Panther's external sensors, I tensed up in the command chair. "Skippy, he is walking kind of stiff, like he is injured."

"That's the best I can do, sorry. Making him dance is easy, I just send signals to his motor fibers. Here, I have to do that, without the station's scanner detecting any odd brain activity. To do that, I am having to control every single neuron. It is *exhausting*. Now, please get yourself a juice box, shut up, and let me work."

I shut up so effectively, I did not even tell him I was shutting up. Bilby was running the ship, allowing Skippy to focus all his brainpower on his assigned task. Skippy's ability did not concern me. What I worried about was that he would get bored, and his brain would say 'Look! A squirrel!' and go bounding off across a field to chase it. Or something like that.

Amazingly, while we waited, I realized the tension I was feeling was not from fear of mission failure. OK, it was that too. But mostly, I feared for *Elmo*. Maybe giving him a cute name was a bad idea, if he was called something like 'Azoth the Conqueror' I would not have been so sympathetic. Or maybe it is empathetic? Whatever.

Anyway, I need not have worried. Guided by Skippy, Elmo performed all the proper authentications, which was surprisingly quick, and presto! We were granted access. A flood of data began flowing into *Valkyrie's* memory, with Bilby holding it in a sandbox until he could be sure there wasn't any malicious code. Bilby responded by sending a bunch of fake message traffic that we had supposedly picked up along the way. The data we sent would not hold up to close scrutiny, but it wouldn't have to, for we planned to destroy the station before jumping away.

"Data transfer is complete," Bilby announced with admirable brevity, something I had urged him to do. We couldn't afford any distractions.

"Great, thank you. Skippy, pull Elmo out of there, so he can entertain all the good little girls and boys here."

"Roger that," he muttered. "Huh. That is-"

The station exploded without warning. Or, without any warning that I was aware of.

"Shields!" I barked without needing to, Bilby had automatically energized the shields for us. Still, the ship shook gently and I heard barely-audible *thump* sounds as debris pelted the ship's thick armor. "Crap. Skippy, what went wrong?"

"Ugh, give me a minute," he pleaded. "The wormhole didn't collapse fast enough, I got some feedback from the explosion. Oh, that hurts."

"Are you OK?"

"I'll be fine. I know, walk it off, right?"

"Yup. You can pop a Motrin and drink a glass of water, if that helps."

"That will *not* help. Best to jump us away while I recover."

We jumped. It took five minutes for Skippy to recover, which made me think he was milking his injury for sympathy.

Speaking of sympathy, I actually did feel bad about the fate of Elmo. "Bilby, have you told Bert and Ernie about what happened?"

"No, Dude. Should I?"

"No. I will tell them myself." Elmo had died on my watch, on my orders. I owed it to the remaining two Maxolhx to look them in the eye when I told them about their friend's death. "Skippy?"

"Yeah, yeah, I'm good," he said, his voice shaky. "I do not want to do *that* again."

"Please tell me we got the information we need."

"We do. Unfortunately, that is the only good news I have. The awakening of wormholes that were previously dormant *has* been noticed by clients of the Maxolhx. The kitties have dispatched ships to investigate, they are most curious that these new wormholes are in locations where no wormhole had been known to exist."

"Shit. They know the wormholes have been moved?"

"No. No, they have no idea that is even possible. *I* didn't know it was possible, until a monkey asked a stupid question. The Maxolhx are assuming these are *new* wormholes."

"The Broomstick wormhole, has that been spotted yet?"

"It is not on the list, but that list is eight days old," Skippy cautioned. "We have to assume the kitties or their clients will notice Broomstick soon. Hey, Joe, you might find this interesting. One of the ships that has been ordered to investigate some of the new wormholes is commanded by an old friend of ours."

"An old friend?" Simms and I looked at each other, neither of us had any clue. "Who?"

"Commander Illiath of the Maxolhx Hegemony patrol cruiser *Vortan*. Her ship checked out the site where we destroyed the two Maxolhx cruisers, and discovered the evidence we planted was bogus, remember?"

"Yeah, I remember that. Damn, she is remarkably persistent. I thought she had given up chasing us."

"She doesn't know she is chasing *us*, Joe."

"You know what I mean. Shit. Do you know the flight path of this Illiath's ship?"

"Not exactly. Why?" Skippy asked.

"Because I'm thinking we maybe should intercept her ship. Take her out, before she does any more damage."

"Sir?" Simms raised an eyebrow.

"She has been nothing but trouble for us," I explained. "She is smart and determined, and that is a bad combination for us. This Illiath is a clear and present danger to our mission," I stated, knowing my XO wanted me to justify blowing up another ship. My point was, Illiath's ship was an enemy vessel, and therefore a legitimate target in our undeclared war. I did not need permission to engage an enemy ship, but I did need to explain why it was worth the rsk.

Simms pursed her lips. "It's too late to stop her now, Sir. If we target her ship, that might only tell the enemy that she is on the right track."

"Ah, you're right," I conceded. "Simms, this is a worst-case scenario. The enemy could be right on our heels when we get to Earth. I think we need to rendezvous with the *Dutchman*, and proceed to Backstop."

She unstrapped and rose from her chair. "If you don't need me here, Sir?"

"No. Where are you going?"

"To work on setting up the ship for more passengers. If we only have a short time at Earth, we must be prepared to stuff as many people as we can fit aboard the ship."

"Please do," I nodded. "Let me know if there is anything you need. Pilot, jump us back to the *Dutchman*."

"Success?" Chang asked, holding out a thumb sideways.

"Success," I responded, and he turned the thumb up with a grin. "Not a hundred percent, Kong. We lost Anastacia."

"I know you are heartbroken about that."

"Less than you might think," I grinned back at him, then my smile faded. "We lost Elmo too."

He stopped smiling. "What happened?"

"I don't know yet. Skippy?"

"It's my fault. Although, I couldn't have done anything about it until now. The station transmitted a series of instructions to Elmo's neural implants. He was supposed to send an acknowledgment, then follow the instructions for egress. When Elmo failed to respond properly, the station halted the data transfer and self-destructed. Don't worry about COMSEC, we effectively jammed any outbound transmissions. All the kitties will know is, that station exploded."

"Maybe," Chang said after a moment to consider. "We should have let the enemy know someone hacked access to that station, make them change their procedures again."

"Huh," I thought about that. "Good idea, if we have time. We would need to fly to another relay station to do that, I don't know if we have the time. And I would kind of feel guilty about risking Bert or Ernie. Hey, Skippy, now that you've hacked into one station, can you make it look like we got access to other stations without actually sending someone inside?"

"Ugh, no," he was disgusted. "The stupid kitties are *smart*. Each damned relay station has its own unique set of procedures for access, and the procedures change every twenty-six days. The Maxolhx have become paranoid about security, ever since some asshole, hee hee," he chuckled. "Compromised their entire pixie system. That is another example of the Law of Unintended Consequences biting us on the ass. Revealing that the ghost ship hacked into the pixie network did seriously hamper the enemy's command, control and communications capability, but we also kind of screwed ourselves. Doing that made it harder for us to keep track of what the kitties are doing."

"Yeah, well," I didn't want to point a finger for blame, because it had been *my* idea to destroy the enemy's faith in the security of their pixie network. "It seemed like a good idea at the time."

"It *was* a good idea, Joe," Kong assured me. "We might have been trapped at Rikers while *Valkyrie* was disabled, if the Maxolhx had been able to quickly send ships to box us in."

"Thanks. We did learn bad news from the station, before it blew itself up. The kitties know about dormant wormholes opening across the galaxy, and they are sending ships to investigate. They think these are *new* wormholes, they don't know about dormant wormholes moving. That doesn't help us. We have to assume they will know about Broomstick soon. They could be right on our tails when we get to Earth."

"Do you have any questions?" I asked, looking at the glass of scotch on the desk in front of me. The glass had barely enough liquid to coat the two ice cubes, and I didn't feel like drinking even that much. The scotch had been poured because it had become sort of a tradition when Chang came aboard *Valkyrie*, and because the occasion called for a drink. Really, the occasion called for getting drunk, but we both still had jobs to do. The civilians were now all aboard my ship, the STAR team over at the good old *Dutchman*.

"No," Chang said. "It's straightforward." Technically, he was correct. All Chang had to do was wait near Backstop, while I took *Valkyrie*, with the civilians, away. The first priority for me would be recon, to determine what aliens knew about wormholes that had moved. Most importantly, had the Esselgin or anyone else noticed gamma rays coming from the spot where the far end of Broomstick would soon be opening? After we obtained that info, I decided to take *Valkyrie* to the Beta site to drop off the civilians, then coming back before Backstop stabilized. The civilians were *not* happy about the change of plan, and I did let them express their concerns, which involved me enduring a lot of verbal abuse. Because I could understand their anger, and because I wanted them to yell at me instead of the crew, I listened to them in a calm, professional manner for an hour, then left to go hit the punching bag in the gym. That burned off some of *my* anger. Damn it, we were trying to *help* people, doing the best we could.

Anyway, taking a side trip to the Beta site was the plan. The Universe hadn't yet told me whether it planned to bitch-slap me again, but come on. After the shock of hearing that another wormhole was opening near Earth, I couldn't take another surprise. Chang took a tiny sip of scotch and asked "You will be back before the wormhole is stable?"

"If nothing goes wrong." Picking up my glass, I held it up toward him. "To nothing going wrong."

We clinked glasses, and each drank a thimbleful of alcohol. "Like *that's* going to happen," Chang observed.

"Hey, the Universe owes us one."

"The Universe is not what concerns me."

"It's not?"

He shook his head. "There's nothing we can do about it. My concern is about the *people*."

I knew what he meant. "Leave that for the governments dirtside to handle."

"People on the ground are not the only factor. Joe," he automatically glanced toward the open doorway of my office. "The crew of our ships are *people*. They are going to want to bring their loved ones aboard. *I* want to bring my family with us."

"Yeah." Shit. We had not discussed the elephant in the room. That was the uncomfortable truth I had not talked about with the crew. There was limited space aboard our two ships. Stuffing people aboard the *Dagger* and the *Qishan* would greatly increase the number of refugees we could bring to the Beta site, but even with four ships, it would be a drop in the ocean. Billions of people lived on Earth, and at best, we could save a couple thousand per trip. At worst, if the Maxolhx went through the Broomstick wormhole shortly after it opened, there would not be time to modify our two Kristang troop ships, and provision them with supplies. We would be running for the Beta site with the *Dutchman* and *Valkyrie* jam-packed with at most, four or five hundred people.

Five hundred.

Whether the number was five hundred or five hundred thousand, the question was, *which* people? Who would live, while the rest died? Who had the right to make that decision? No, forget about what is right. We only had time for practical considerations. Who had the ability to make that decision, and *do* something about it?

"I was hoping to avoid this discussion," I admitted. That was not quite true. Having that discussion was inevitable, essential. I wasn't hoping not to have the discussion, I just wasn't looking forward to it.

"I was hoping to avoid *needing* this discussion," he said. "If we go through Backstop together, you're in command. If I'm alone, I need to know the commander's intent."

That might have sounded like he was passing the buck to me, but that's not what he was doing. He was following protocol, as much as he could.

Of all the discussions I had with Chang over the years, that was the most important. To even have the conversation verged on treason, for both of us. The flags on our uniforms reminded us that I owed my loyalty to the United States, and he to China. National interests had never before been an issue for our international crew, because Earth politics didn't mean shit when we were fighting an alien threat to the existence of our whole species.

Now national interests might come into direct conflict with our upcoming mission to bring people from Earth to the Beta site. There simply was not enough space aboard the ships to take everyone off Earth, even if we still had years to shuttle back and forth. With the Broomstick wormhole opening, we might only have months. Maybe only weeks. If that long. Nations would be competing for spots aboard the ships for their citizens.

It was awful to think that Chang and I might be on opposite sides of a struggle for space aboard the evac ships, but that was a real possibility. If China ordered him to reserve the *Flying Dutchman* for Chinese citizens, what would he do?

Of all the enemies the Merry Band of Pirates had faced, we ourselves might be the most dangerous.

"All right, Kong." Without making it obvious that I was watching his body language, I watched his body language. After he returned to his ship, Skippy would tell me how Chang had reacted in subtle ways I couldn't see. That was a rotten thing to do, and necessary. "I talked about our options with Skippy, and Nagatha. Don't blame her for not telling you, I ordered her not to. It was all theoretical at the time. You hit on the crucial issue: the crews of our ships are people. They will want to save their own families first. I hate to say it, but, we may have to do just that."

"Or we won't *have* any crew aboard the ships?"

"That too, but, we have to do what's practical. Whatever we can. We will be announcing that we can only take a limited number of people with us, and everyone left behind will be doomed. Skippy had a stupid idea," I paused to see if he joined the conversation. Wisely, he stayed out of it. "About a reality show where the winners get tickets to the Beta site. The evac isn't going to be anything organized like that. It's not going to be *organized* at all. Dirtside is going to be absolute chaos, a complete breakdown of social order," I said the dry words that I had discussed with Skippy and Nagatha. "Governments won't make the decisions about who goes with us, because there won't *be* governments. Kong, it will be every man for himself down there. It's probable that we'll have to send dropships down to pick up whoever we can, without any organization or help from civil or military authorities. Hell, we will need to be prepared for armed resistance. People see our dropships flying away, they're going to start shooting. They may shoot while we're *landing*, because they know we don't have room for everyone. We'll have to keep our ships in high orbit, and verify any incoming dropships don't have a bomb aboard." Looking at the bottle of scotch, I so much wanted to pour a full glass and down it. "Crap. This is a fun topic of conversation" I said, watching his eyes. "Sorry to dump this on you."

"Joe, it's not anything I haven't considered on my own," he glanced at the desk, then back at me, meeting my eyes. We were both watching each other's reactions. "Your scenario is actually a bit more sunny than what I really fear."

"Well, *shit*." Hearing that made me lose concentration, wondering what he was thinking about. "What could be worse than absolute chaos on the ground?"

"The governments of Earth know the *Dutchman* is long overdue to return. They know the crew members aboard when we left. It would be very surprising if our families were not being held by our respective governments," he made air quotes with his hands, "'for their safety', supposedly."

"*Fuuuuck*. I hadn't thought of that. Shit!"

"We may need to *fight* to get our families off the surface."

"Oh, hell yes."

"It may not be so simple a question. If the FBI has a gun to your mother's head, what will you do? If you have to disobey orders from your government, are you prepared to do that?"

"Are *you*?" I asked.

"I don't know. I probably won't know, until I have to make a decision," he admitted.

Another deep breath before I asked the crucial question. "Let me ask this: are you prepared to ignore the orders of your government?"

His eyes narrowed. "Are *you*?"

"Kong, I don't," I laid my hands on the table, palms-up. "I don't know. If, shit. I have never been great at following orders, especially dumbass ones," I forced a grin.

He didn't smile back at me. "Joe, the last time you ignored orders, you stole a starship, for a mission that benefitted all nations equally. This is different. The mix of people who get aboard our ships will determine the survival of entire cultures. Our current crew is composed of people from eighteen nations, not just the five nations of UNEF. Eighteen nations. Even if we bring aboard the families of our entire crew, that leaves out most of humanity. We do not have any Italians aboard. No one from Spain. Or Malaysia. Or-"

"I get the idea." I knew what he meant, because I had done the same math on my own.

"Those cultures could be lost, forever, if no one from those countries is brought to the Beta site."

"I *know* that," I assured him, growing irritated at him, and at myself for allowing myself to get irritated. The subject was agonizing to think about, I shouldn't make it worse. "We can't just randomly pick two people from each country, there won't be room for everyone. Our ships aren't Noah's Ark." When we first considered the idea of a Beta site, someone had told me a minimum number, like three thousand people, would be needed for genetic diversity for a healthy population. Our space ark would need to bring not two, but three thousand of every ethnic group, to ensure that culture survived. That was not even remotely practical, even if we had a whole fleet of transport ship. "But, I don't know what to do."

"First, you need to answer my question," Kong insisted. "If the United States orders you to reserve all space aboard the ships for American citizens, what will you do?"

Skippy saved me from answering that, by interrupting us. "Gentlemen, be aware that I will not allow our ships to be used in that manner. Not even by you, Joe. The nations of your homeworld will cooperate to conduct the evacuation in a fair way, or I will make the decision by myself."

That pissed me off. It also was a relief. Before I could respond, Chang addressed the beer can. "That is the problem, isn't it?"

"What?" Skippy asked.

"What do you mean by '*fair*'? Everyone involved, even if they all cooperate with the best of intentions, will have a different definition of what is fair."

"Um, well, uh," Skippy sputtered.

"Skippy," I spoke slowly, unsure of exactly what I wanted to say. "If you are going to be the final decision-maker, you need to think long and hard about this. And don't give me any bullshit about how you are able to make better decisions, because you are not an overly-emotional meatsack. The people who do not get aboard our ships *will die*. Who are you willing to let die?"

"Well, shit," he let out a long, weary breath. "This sucks."

"That's why you need to think about it now," I chided him gently.

"How?" He pleaded. "How do I make a decision like that?"

"I'll give you an example. You like Captain Frey, right?"

"Um, yes, sure," he answered warily. Everyone in the crew knew he had a crush on our Canadian special operator.

"If she asks you to bring her family aboard, will you do that?"

"Um, well, Jeez. It would be hard to say no. Especially since she has been risking her life out here."

"Right. What about Fal Desai?" I asked, a lump in my throat. "She gave her life out here, to save humanity. What about her family?"

"Oh. For sure, we owe it to her."

"I agree. Where does it stop? How do you define 'family'? Fal's sister is married. Do we bring aboard her sister's husband? What about *his* parents?"

"Shit, Joe," he whispered miserably. "You need to help me with that."

"Skippy," Chang leaned forward on the desk, his drink forgotten. "If you are going to be the judge and jury to decide who lives and dies, then *you* need to make the decision."

I pushed my own glass away. "Kong, I should have brought you into the discussion earlier."

He shrugged. "We're talking about it now. We still have a month before we go through Backstop. Joe, we need to use the time to tell the crew. This isn't something we can spring on them at the last minute."

"Ah, I don't know about that. The *crew* will panic. Kong, we have to keep the crew focused on their jobs. Talking about the apocalypse is not conducive to good order and discipline."

"They aren't stupid, Joe," he reminded me. "They are already thinking about it, trust me. If we don't talk about it openly, we will be trying to implement a very dangerous, emotionally-stressful plan with no preparation and no training. The US military thinks the same way as the Chinese Army: we train the way we fight. The crew will be panicked while we are trying to pluck a handful of souls off the surface. They should experience that panic, and get used to it, when they are training for the evac."

"Like a Band-aid, huh?"

"What?" he didn't get the reference.

"It's best just to tear it off and get it over with. Pulling it off slowly only prolongs the agony."

"Quite so."

"Kong," I shook my head. "Of all the terrible discussions we have had over the years, is this the worst?"

He considered for only a moment. "Perhaps. It is certainly one of the most painful. The STAR team is disciplined and professional, but they have never trained for a situation like this. We need to bring Smythe into the planning."

"You're right. OK, I do not want to stress the civilians any more than they are. I will inform the crew on the way back from Avalon, after we drop off the civilians. You tell Smythe, and your crew, after *Valkyrie* jumps away this afternoon. They are going to be shocked, we need to deal with that."

"What are the five stages of grief?" He asked. "I hope to get the crew from Denial to Acceptance, before Backstop opens."

"Yeah. For the Pirates, I hope we add two more stages at the end. *Determination*, to do what we can, before the end."

He cocked his head. "What's the seventh stage?"

"*Payback*."

He lifted the bottle and poured a splash of golden liquid into each of our glasses. "I'll drink to that."

CHAPTER TWENTY NINE

After *Valkyrie* jumped away toward the Beta site, I called Simms into my office. This time, I shut the door. We needed to have the happy conversation I had been dreading, since I talked with Chang.

Actually, as I should have expected, she was way ahead of me. In fact, she had already talked about the subject with Smythe, before he went over to the *Dutchman*. "Why," I asked, mildly frustrated. "Didn't you mention it to me?"

"Skippy said you had enough on your plate, and that," she shrugged. "You would discuss it with me when the time was right."

"Skippy was not supposed to tell anyone."

She just gave me The Look.

"OK," I forced myself to relax. "That's fair."

"Sir, there is another aspect to the evac that you didn't mention. We will need to take direct, *offensive* action."

"Off- I can see the need to defend ourselves and the dropships, but-"

"It is going to get *ugly* down there," she scowled. "When countries realize they are competing for a very small number of slots aboard our ships, nukes could start flying."

"Shit."

"You see what I-"

"Yeah. Damn. OK, yes. If anyone launches a nuke, we intercept it in flight."

"That's fine, but it requires us to have continuous coverage of the surface, with only two ships."

I stared at the ceiling, thinking about the problem. "Just the northern hemisphere, right? The nuclear-armed nations are all above the equator."

"Except for ballistic missile submarines," she reminded me. "And cruise missiles. We can't cover just the northern hemisphere. If we park both ships in geosynchronous orbit, one above the Brazil and one over Indonesia, we can intercept any missiles in flight."

"Cruise missiles?" I asked.

"That will be more difficult, we'll need active sensor coverage. If Skippy can prevent launch codes from being transmitted, we may not have a problem. That only prevents an all-out war when our ships are in orbit. We could return from the Beta site to find Earth is radioactive, even before aliens get there."

"Crap. We were talking about the danger of aliens coming to Earth, now we have to worry about monkeys down there hitting each other with sticks. Simms, I've got something else to talk about. It's delicate."

"We just discussed the end of the world, and you're worried about my feelings?"

"I am in this case. You're not coming back from Avalon. You and Frank are staying there."

She scowled at me. "Fuck that, Sir."

"No. This is not open for debate. Simms, if things go according to plan, we will be bringing hundreds, maybe thousands of people to Avalon. The site needs to be prepared, or this will all be for nothing. Frank Muller for sure is staying there, he is a civilian."

"You need me aboard *Valkyrie*."

"Not as much as I need you on Avalon."

"Frank has a daughter on Earth. My mother, my brother and sister and-"

"I know. Simms, we will get everyone we can, you know that. You or Frank being aboard won't change that, but your presence will be two fewer people we can bring aboard, given our limited oxygen-recycling capacity. Listen, we won't get to Avalon for five days. Think about it. My door is always open," I gestured to the firmly closed door. "I know this sucks."

"*Sucks* doesn't even begin to describe it. Sir, we knew this day was coming."

"I thought we had plenty of time. Hundreds of years. Sixty, at least."

"Shit happens."

"*Emily Perkins* happened."

"She didn't know. She did the right thing, based on what she did know. Let's not argue about this now. OK, I will think about it."

"Think about the children. Somebody needs to be in charge on Avalon, get things organized. I'm sure Hans is doing his best, but he doesn't know the shitstorm we'll be dropping on his head."

"I *said*, I'll think about it."

Smythe stopped just outside the door to Chang's office. "You wished to see me, Sir?"

"Yes," Chang mumbled over the sandwich he was eating, a hasty meal taken from the galley. Recently, he had not much time to eat, there was too much to do. "Come in, sit down. Now that *Valkyrie* has jumped for the Beta site, I will be addressing the crew this evening. When we reach Earth, the political situation may be chaotic." He knew the STAR team leader was not stupid, the man must have considered that an evacuation effort would not be well-organized and peaceful. He also knew that Smythe had talked with Nagatha, about potential resistance to the evac operation. "We need to plan for taking control of the evacuation," he looked Smythe straight in the eyes. "*Independent* of authorities on the surface."

That was the key moment. If Smythe balked at ignoring orders from the British government, he would need to be confined to his quarters for the duration of the mission. The trouble was, Chang himself was uncertain what he himself would do when they reached their homeworld. What if his own government had his family in custody, and a gun to his wife's head?

It was best not to dwell on What-Ifs, until he knew the situation on the ground.

Smythe only nodded once, curtly. As if it were a routine matter they had already discussed. "Yes, Sir. Our first move must be to secure control of the *Dagger* and the *Yu Qishan*. Both to assure those assets are available for use as transports, and to deny them to elements hostile to the evacuation." He looked at Chang without blinking, holding the other man's gaze. They both knew that the 'hostile elements' he referred to were their own governments.

"Our *first* move," Chang corrected the British Army officer, "must be to collect intelligence. We need to know where those ships are."

"Er, yes," Smythe thought that was obvious. "May I show you the preliminary plan I have developed? I have not discussed this with anyone, other than Nagatha. She provided the navigation data."

Chang knew that. He had not known, until that moment, where Smythe's ultimate loyalties lay. "Show me."

Smythe set his tablet on the desk, and turned in the chair so they could both look at it. "If one or both of the troop ships are near the wormhole, we have to disable them quickly, then conduct a boarding operation to take control. Skippy installed a backdoor in the software of both troop ships, and Nagatha has the access codes to shut down their primary systems."

"You do?" Chang looked at the ceiling. "Nagatha, when were you going to tell me about this?"

"At the appropriate time, Colonel," the AI replied nervously.

Chang let out a breath. "You and I will talk later. Smythe, continue."

"If both ships are not waiting near the wormhole, we should," he tapped the tablet, showing a schematic of humanity's home star system. "Jump in on the far side of Saturn. Our drive can direct most of the gamma ray burst away from Earth, but I thought it best to maximize concealment."

"Saturn? Not Mars or Jupiter?"

"Mars is currently on the other side of the Sun, and Jupiter is orbited by too many artificial satellites. NASA, the ESA, and your government all have active probes orbiting Jupiter," Smythe explained. "Saturn has only one active probe, in orbit around Titan. We can time our arrival so that probe is behind Titan. We jump in, engage stealth and coast out from Saturn's shadow, to get a look at the situation on Earth. When we know the location and status of forces on and around Earth, you can select from a series of options."

"What will you do if both troop ships are in Earth orbit?"

Smythe tapped the tablet again, bringing up a different view. "Jump in close to the first ship, transmit the code to disable it, and launch a boarding party in dropships. As soon as the dropships are clear, jump for the other ship." He showed the rough, preliminary plan for boarding and taking control of both former Kristang troop ships. Chang asked a few questions, knowing the contingency plan was in the initial stages. "There is another, complication we must address," Smythe added.

"You know that I hate complications," Chang said with a frown. "What is it this time?"

"Nagatha told me that, while the wormhole is opening and becoming stable, it will emit higher than normal levels of gamma radiation. This stabilization period will last more than eight days."

"Yes. We are keeping the ship at a safe distance, with defense shields up. If the shields fail, or can't handle the radiation, we will jump away."

"Yes, Sir. This side of the wormhole is not the problem. The other event horizon will also be producing very visible gamma rays. They will be detected at *Earth*."

"Ohhhh," Chang slumped in the chair. "You're right."

"The authorities on Earth will not know why a wormhole is opening on their doorstop, but they should recognize the radiation signature. They will understand it is an Elder wormhole. Assuming that either the *Yu Qishan* or the *Dagger* are available, they will send a ship to investigate."

"Mm," Chang considered. "Very likely. Well then, we will have a greeting party when we go through to the other side."

Smythe arched an eyebrow. "There could be more than a greeting party. Until the wormhole becomes fully stable, its emergence point will be static. It will not begin hopping around in a figure-eight pattern until after it has been stable at the initial location for over thirteen hours, according to Nagatha. Sir, if UNEF is smart, and we must assume they are, they will saturate the area in front of the other event horizon, with a minefield of nukes on proximity triggers."

"*Shit!*" Chang slapped the table, knowing the STAR team leader was correct. "Of course they will. We can," he paused to think about the situation. "We can transmit our recognition codes, before we go through."

"Pardon me, Sir, but we can't do that. I inquired about that possibility. Nagatha?"

"Colonel Chang, due to distortion in the wormhole channel, it will not be possible to transmit a coherent message by photons, until approximately three days after the event horizons are stable enough for the ship to pass through. I assume you wish to transition through as soon as possible?"

"Yes, damn it. We can't sit here waiting for three days."

"There is an option," Smythe offered. "We can send a shielded probe through."

"That is correct," Nagatha confirmed. "None of the sensor probes we have aboard are capable of surviving a wormhole transition, however, it is possible for a missile to be modified with proper shielding. The missile could fly through, and broadcast our recognition codes."

Chang tapped the desk with a finger while he thought. "That is good, it does not solve our problem."

"Sir?" Smythe's face took on a blank expression.

"If there is a ship on the other side, they will not be able to acknowledge our recognition signal. We will not know whether our message got through, and if they deactivated their mine field. Now that you have me thinking about the problem," he shook his head. "A minefield of nukes isn't the worst danger we could find on the other side. If the Maxolhx have used the Broomstick wormhole to reach Earth, they could not miss seeing a gamma ray source at the edge of the solar system. We could come out of the wormhole, right under the guns of an enemy task force."

"Assuming that Skippy is here when we go through," Nagatha said with confidence, "he can ask the wormhole network to tell us what is on the other side."

"We are *not* assuming Skippy will be here," Chang chided his ship's AI. "Nagatha, contingency plans are developed for when things do not happen the way we like. We must be prepared to conduct the evac without *Valkyrie*, initially."

"Very well, Colonel Chang. Please remember that, without Skippy, we cannot open the super-duty wormhole that leads to the Sculptor dwarf galaxy. Or create a wormhole connection to Club Skippy."

"Yes. As Bishop, said, we do not have a Plan 'C'."

The *Vortan* hung silently in interstellar space, stationary relative to the dormant wormhole that was awakening. The event horizon was glowing brightly then fizzling out, emitting powerful bursts of gamma rays whenever it flared to life. That wormhole was not as far along in its stabilization as the first one the *Vortan's* crew had encountered, it would be several more days before it was safe for a starship to fly through.

Less time would be required to send a probe through. Probes were expendable. The ship's AI estimated that, based on the pattern the wormhole was developing, it might be possible within two days, as measured by the rotation of the Maxolhx homeworld.

Until then, the *Vortan* would observe, recording all data and trying to understand what was happening to the local network. So far, no one aboard the ship had any clue why the ancient network had suddenly, for the first time in memory, altered its behavior.

Two days later, the *Vortan* launched a probe toward the event horizon that should be stable for a moment. The timing would have to be precise to get the probe through, and on the way back, the probe would not have the advantage of guidance by the ship's AI.

The first attempt ended with the probe splattered against the wildly flaring event horizon, its timing thrown off by spacetime distortion in front of the wormhole. The next three attempts were also failures, though closer to success. The next two experienced failures worse than the first probe, missing wildly. Humiliated, the ship's AI then tweaked its guidance algorithm again, and the seventh probe slid through just before the event horizon collapsed.

That seventh probe failed to report back at the appointed time, nor the next, nor the next. On orders from Illiath, the ship kept sending expendable probes through, with slight modifications to the heavy shielding. Success was achieved with the eighth through fifteenth probes, in that the probes appeared to transition through properly. No messages were received from the other side, the hellish conditions inside the wormhole prevented any coherent radiation from getting through.

Finally, the *Vortan's* AI exulted quietly as a probe came through from the other end. It was probe number twelve, and while its shielding was scorched and its processor was damaged, it was able to transmit one vital piece of information.

"Commander Illiath," the AI contacted the ship's leader. "We now know where this wormhole connects to. It is close to the planet humans call 'Earth'."

"Ooh! Ooh! Joe!" Skippy called me while I was walking to the ship's gym to shoot baskets. The day before, I had sunk twenty-seven of thirty free throws, a major improvement for me. "I have juicy news for you! A scoop!"

"Juicy?" I halted, stepping into a side passageway. "Is this gossip?"

"Yes, but for once, it's not about *you*."

"It's- Wait. People gossip about me?"

"Ha!" He snorted. "Only *all the time*, Joe. Duh. What did you think the-"

"Why do people talk about *me*?"

"Seriously? What about you is *not* gossip-worthy? There is your love life, or lack of it. The ongoing speculation about you and Margaret, the-"

"Hey! Leave Adams out of-"

"It's not *me* doing the gossiping. I mean, I occasionally will join in, to correct the facts, or if a story needs a little help to get going, I will-"

"You're not really helping yourself, Skippy."

"OK! People also talk about the weird New England stuff you eat, like bread in a can, and-"

"I get the idea."

"Really, all the best gossip is about you. Which is surprising, given how sad and pathetic your life is."

"I really appreciate how you-"

"You also inspire the most interesting wagers, too."

"Wagers? People *bet* on me? About what?"

"Hee hee, I'm not supposed to say."

"Consider that an order, beer can."

"Well, if I *have* to. The current wager with the most action, is when the bot that cleans your shower will suffer a nervous breakdown and need to be recycled. Hey! If you want to get in on the action, Cadet Fangiu is giving five to one-"

"Our *Jeraptha* guest is speculating about me in the shower?"

"It is a common topic of conversation, Joe. Of course he-"

"Oof. I hate my life. Your scoop this time is not about me?"

"No. It is about Jennifer. She-"

"Stop right there. Skippy, I do not want to know."

"But-"

"Uh!" I held up a finger to shush him. "I will not gossip about people behind their backs."

"Well, Jeez, Joe, that's how gossip *works*. If you say it to someone's face it-"

"Do *not* tell me, thank you."

"Man, the gossip about how you are a killjoy sure is accurate."

"Goodbye, Skippy."

Our food supply was getting thin as we approached the Beta site. We had to reserve food not only to feed the civilians aboard the ship, but also for them after they landed on Avalon. To set an example for the crew, I was drinking a sludge for breakfast, eating a ration bar for lunch, and dinner was either another ration bar, or a sandwich. We still cooked hot meals for the civilians, and even they weren't able to feast like they did when they first came aboard our ships. When the *Flying Dutchman* left Earth to search for a Beta site, some of the cargo bays had been empty, because it was supposed to be a relatively short mission. That was a lesson learned, I would never do that again.

Anyway, that evening I worked in the galley, making Chicken Francaise for the civilians. They were probably getting tired of eating chicken, and we were tired of cooking it, but we had to make do with the supplies we had left. After we cleaned up, I set out fixings for sandwiches and went back to my cabin to change clothes. When I came back, I anticipated being the only person who would want to eat a Fluffernutter, so I went right to the peanut butter jar, leaving the cold cuts and cheese for other people.

What I saw horrified me. "*What* is that?"

Lieutenant DeShawn Ray turned toward me, startled. "What, Sir?"

"Th-" I pointed with a shaking finger. "That. That, *abomination*."

He looked at his plate. "It's a Fluffernutter."

"No. What have you done to it?"

Touching the abomination with his hands, which would forever be unclean, he grinned. "I used a brioche bun instead of bread, and Nutella instead of peanut butter. Then I added sliced banana and chocolate chips."

"Ray," I said gravely, "That is a Fluffer-NOT-er."

"I am pushing the boundaries of Fluff technology," his grin was ear to ear.

"Please," I shuddered. "Get it out of my sight."

"What are *you* doing, Sir?"

He was curious, because I was scraping butter over one side of each slice of bread. "This will be a grilled Fluffernutter, which *is* cutting edge technology. Begone with you, infidel."

While I grilled my own creation, which was indescribably delicious by the way, Ray sat choking down the unholy abomination he had spawned. When he finished, he put his plate in the bin to be washed, and I watched him walk out the door. Using a dirty towel, I picked up the plate he had used, went left through the passageway, down one deck and toward the portside outer hull. At the nearest airlock, I tossed in both plate and towel, shut the door and over-pressurized the lock. "Bridge, this is Bishop. Do we have anyone EVA right now?" It would have been easier to say 'outside', but Extra-Vehicular Activity was the official term.

"Uh, no, Sir. Why?"

"I'm going to blow portside airlock D-7, don't be alarmed." Palming the emergency controls, I slid open the outer door, and the offending plate and towel were ejected into interstellar space.

Maybe I overreacted, but why take the chance?

"Sir?" Simms appeared in the doorway of my office.

"Uh, come in," I waved for to her sit down. It wasn't time for our daily meeting, and she hadn't signaled there was a problem. I didn't know what she wanted. "What's up?"

"It's personal."

"Oh." Pressing a button under my oversized desk, the doors slid closed. My hope was that the subject was something personal about herself, and not a problem with a member of the crew. The crew of both ships were elite- Well, with a few exceptions, including me. We had remarkably few discipline issues, and those were mostly due to the boredom of off-duty time spent aboard a starship, and seeing the same people day after day after Groundhog day. Bringing the civilians aboard had greatly improved morale. Not only had the team achieved a great success, having children aboard kept everyone busy in our off-duty hours. Plus, it was very rewarding to interact with children who had been so horribly abused. I think we Pirates got more from the relationship than the children did.

Morale had taken a hit when we transferred all the civilians back to *Valkyrie* for the flight to Avalon. The civilians were understandably scared and confused, and just sick of yo-yoing back and forth between our ships.

Anyway, that is what was on my mind while Simms sat down across from me.

She took a breath, and pressed her hands together in her lap. That could have been a sign of trouble, except she looked *happy*. "Frank and I, we-"

Oh, shit. I felt a chill shoot up my spine. Had they broken off their engagement?

"We want to get married," she finished.

"Oh," I let out a breath, relieved. "Yeah, with the engagement thing and all," I said stupidly.

"We want to get married *now*," she explained, sensing my cluelessness. "Here, aboard the ship. Before we get to Avalon. There will be too much to do after we land." She sighed. "Frank and I should have made this decision while the *Dutchman* was nearby, so they could be with us, but, there was too much going on."

"Oh! Great! Congratulations, to both of you." Suddenly, my veil of cluelessness lifted, and I knew why she had come to my office. Also, I knew what gossip Skippy had wanted to tell me. "As I'm sure you know, ship captains can perform marriages. I would be honored-"

"Um, we have someone to perform the ceremony. Alvarez, from the Commandos? He was a minister in his church, before the Force left Earth."

"And he's a Commando?"

"He says God called him to kill lizards," she smiled. "That was a joke, Sir. The minister gig was a sideline. He agreed to perform the ceremony."

"Gotcha," I tried to conceal my disappointment. "Listen, Simms, brides usually have a bridesmaid, but I'm happy to be your best-"

"Reed will be my bridesmaid."

"Huh. Well, I don't know Frank very well, but-"

"Friedlander will be Frank's best man."

"Hmm. OK." That told me I might be the last person aboard the ship to know about the upcoming wedding. "You, uh, want me to throw a bachelor party for Frank?"

"Friedlander is handling that. It's going to be a small affair, just a couple of Frank's friends."

"All right, then. You, uh, want me to bake the cake? I've never made a-"

"I've got that covered."

"OK. Uh, is there anything you want me to do?"

"Yes," she sighed, relieved. She had felt the conversation getting awkward. "*Please* tell Skippy he can't sing at the wedding."

"Shit. That's what you want?"

"Really, Sir, it would be the *best* wedding present we could ask for."

"Well, sure," I smiled, sure the disappointment was showing on my face. "Anything for you, Simms. Uh, will this be a military wedding?"

"No. For once in my life, I would like to wear a *nice* dress. I have been a bridesmaid half a dozen times, now it's my turn."

"Gotcha. Is it OK if I wear my dress uniform?"

"Certainly, Sir."

"Is that all?"

"No. At the reception, we need a DJ."

"Wow. That is going to be tough. If Skippy is going to be the DJ, he will want to sing."

"No," she laughed. "Will *you* be the DJ?"

"*Me?*"

"You've done it before."

"Well, yeah." I had no idea that anyone actually enjoyed it when I played DJ. I figured the crowd was being polite because I was their commanding officer. Hearing that lifted my mood immediately. "That would be great! Uh, what type of music does Frank enjoy?"

"We can talk about a playlist this evening, at dinner? We are hoping to schedule the wedding for the day after tomorrow?"

I pretended to check my calendar. "Gosh, I am extremely busy, but, for *you*, I can make it happen."

Of course Skippy had been listening. Simms had no sooner left my office, when his avatar appeared on my desk. "Hmmph," he had his arms crossed. "No singing? Well, that was going to be my present to the happy couple. I am insulted."

Sometimes, my brain is able to think fast. That was one of those times. "Skippy, listen," I lowered my voice to a conspiratorial whisper. "It's not an insult."

"You sure about that? It feels like an insult."

"I'm sure," I lied. "This is the big day for Simms. The focus should be on the *bride*, you know? If you are there singing, who could think about anything else? You would totally steal the show."

"Huh," he tilted his head thoughtfully. "OK, OK, yeah, I can see that. Hmm, it still seems awfully selfish of her, to deprive her guests of my incredible talent."

"It's just *one* day. This is her special day, you understand?"

"All right, fine. You know me, I am all about giving to others."

"That's what everyone says about you," I sprained my eyeballs, trying not to roll them.

"Plan B, then. I will help you with the DJ duties."

"I was kinda hoping to do that myself."

"*You?* OK, you be the front man, but, seriously, you need help. I just sent a playlist to your laptop."

"Uh," I looked at the file that popped up. "No."

"No?"

"Skippy, Swedish death metal is not appropriate for a wedding!"

"Says *you*."

"Says *everyone*."

"But-"

"No. Death. Metal. And no Tibetan throat singing. And no," I checked the list. "Seriously, Klingon opera?"

"It is very popular, Joe."

"I'll pass on that."

"How come you get to have all the fun?"

"Skippy, you're not thinking about this the right way. I will be the DJ, sure, but nobody cares about the DJ. I'll be the guy in the background, spinning tunes. *Your* contributions will be front and center, everyone will be talking about them."

"How?"

"Where do you think Simms is going to get a wedding dress? And Frank will need a tux, right?"

"Wow. *Wow*." He gasped. "*Me*? Design a wedding dress?" His avatar actually shuddered. "This is *exciting*. Oh, I can't wait to get started. It will be *magical*, Joe."

"Uh huh, if that's what Simms wants."

"Oh for- Brides don't know what is good for them, Joe. I will design a-"

"You will design whatever Simms wants."

"Oh, sure. I will allow her to have input, of course. Oooh, I should contact her now, and get started right away."

"Give her a minute, Skippy. She has a lot to think about."

"What? There is no *time*, Joe! Ugh, why am I wasting time talking with you?" His avatar winked out.

Frank Muller had, as did everyone aboard the two ships of the Pirate fleet, plenty of opportunities to talk with Skippy. Perhaps more than enough opportunities. And perhaps it was more Skippy talking *to*, instead of with, him.

So, it was no great shock to Frank when the AI called him. Calling him while he was trying to shave in the bathroom was a bit startling, as he was standing in his underwear at the sink.

"Frank! Frank Frank Frank-"

"Sk-" He had inhaled a blob of shaving cream. Coughing it out, he spat in the sink. "Skippy. What's the emergency?"

"No emergency, I have wonderful news! Um, congrats on the wedding thing, I guess."

"Thank you, I guess."

"Great. Now that we have all the blah blah blah social niceties out of the way, you have been granted the incredible honor of having *me* design and fabricate a tuxedo for you."

"That is," what should he say. What *could* he say? He settled for a neutral "Very nice."

"It is beyond 'nice', but you can thank me properly later. Let's get started, chop chop, no time to waste. Your first option-"

"Skippy, I'm in the middle of shaving," he looked at himself in the mirror. "I haven't done half of my face."

"Trust me, no one will notice. Just rinse it off."

"Hey!" Frank protested when the mirror flickered, and displayed the image of a gaudy suit. "I can't see myself. Is this," he peered at the mirror, having never looked at it closely before. "Is this thing a *display* screen?"

"Of course it is. Normally it is set to mirror mode. Yeesh, you monkeys sure do like looking at yourselves."

"Is this a *two-way* display?"

"Yes. How else do you think I've been watching you? I have your measurements programmed in-"

"Stop!" Frank crouched down below the level of the too-low sink. Pulling a towel off a rack, he wrapped it around himself. "You have been *watching* me?"

"Just to get your measurements. And to check your vital signs. You should cut down on processed food."

"The only food we *have* is processed."

"I'm just sayin', it wouldn't kill you to eat a salad once in a while."

Frank sighed. "Jennifer says the same thing. If I look at these tuxedos now, will you go away?"

"Deal. This won't take long. First, we have my personal choice, this snappy number is made from simulated *alligator* skin. Ooooh, check it out. Nice, huh?"

"Uh, no."

"Are you sure? I really think you are missing a huge opportunity here," Skippy pleaded.

"Skippy," he laughed. "I can't start my marriage by showing up for the wedding in that outfit."

"Why not? Think of it this way: if she hates it and marries you anyway, you are truly made for each other."

"I'd rather not take the risk, if you don't mind."

"OK," Skippy muttered. "Why do I get stuck with the uncultured cretins? Number two on the list is simulated *sharkskin*."

"Also no."

"Hmm, I'm sensing you want something more conservative. Let's go with the classic, traditional powder blue?"

"Let's not. Black, Skippy. Basic black."

"*Ugh*. So boring. You are getting married on a stolen starship, don't you want to shake things up?"

"I want to *not* shake up my fiancé."

"Good point. OK, give me a moment to make an adjustment, and, presto!"

"That is," Frank tilted his head to the left, then the right. "Interesting."

"See? Basic black, but also *cool*, huh? *Ha*! Suck it, boring tuxedos!"

"Is that a *ninja* suit?"

"Of course. Basic black, as you requested. The shiny crossed katana swords on your back add a touch of bling, without being tacky. Plus, the head covering means you won't have to bother shaving that day, either."

"I love it."

"Excellent! Whoo-hoo! This is gonna be-"

"Jennifer would *hate* it. So, no."

"It is *your* wedding, too, Frank."

"Clearly, you have never been married before."

"This is *so* unfair! You don't get a say in anything?"

"First, I don't care. Second, uh, I guess second is also that I don't care. If Jennifer is happy, I will be happy."

"You don't have any opinion on the tux you will be wearing?"

"No. Uh, hey. What's the movie with that guy Mister Darcy?"

"Do you mean 'Pride and Prejudice', or 'Bridget Jones's Diary'?"

"The one with people dressed up in fancy clothes, and Darcy falls in a lake?"

"The first one. What about it?"

"Jen loves that damned movie. Can you make me a suit like Darcy wore?"

"You realize I can't make you *look* like him, right?"

"Give it your best shot."

"Deal! You will not regret this."

That night at 0217, Skippy woke me up, because of course he did. "Joe! Hey, hey, Joe. Are you asleep?"

"Yes."

"Oh goodie. Listen, I need a favor from you."

"Can this wait until morning?" I mumbled without opening my eyes.

"No. It's an emergency!"

"Shit." Sitting up in bed, I swung my feet onto the floor, feeling around for the shoes I had put there. "What is it?"

"It's Simms. She cannot, or will not, make up her freakin' mind."

"You're kidding- Is this about the wedding?"

"Of course it is. How can I think about anything else at a time like this? Time! There *is* no time! Joe, I need you to step in, and order her to say 'Yes' to the dress."

"No. *Hell*, no."

"But-"

"Skippy, I would rather French-kiss a cobra. That would be safer. You do not tell a woman what kind of dress she should wear. It is her decision."

"I agree, if she would actually *choose* one. Any one, at this point. Except for those *horrible* designs she showed me, ugh," he gagged. "I don't know *what* she was thinking. Man, you think you know a person, and then-"

"Good night, Skippy," I flopped back on the bed and threw a pillow over my head.

"You're not going to help?" He screeched, outraged.

My answer was in the form of a single digit, and it was not my thumb, if you know what I mean.

"Fine. This travesty will be all *your* fault, Joe. See if I care."

The wedding was magical. Or, as magical as it could be, in one of the empty cargo bays we had set aside for recreation. The play equipment had been packed away or jammed against the walls under tarps. I have to say, Skippy outdid himself. The dress that Simms wore was elegant and looked great on her, except as her commanding officer I of course did not notice her appearance. Skippy made an extra effort when using the ship's fabricators to crank out decorations, wedding favors and little gifts. Every one of the civilians had fancy new clothes, the girls were thrilled and the boys uncomfortable as expected. Frank's tux did not look any more uncomfortable than usual, and I heard that he had talked Skippy out of making the tux from simulated alligator skin.

Really, I think Frank missed a great opportunity there, but it wasn't my wedding.

I wore my dress uniform. The newest dark green one, not the dark blue one that had been hanging in my closet forever. The uniform was big on me, Skippy had to alter the pants to take in the waist. The weight I had lost on Rikers hadn't come back yet, that was probably a good thing.

And there was *food* at the reception, perhaps a bit too extravagant considering our dwindling stocks of real food. Although I did not make the official cake, I did bake fourteen dozen cupcakes, which disappeared like a school of cupcake-eating piranhas had attacked the platters.

The best part-

OK, the best part for *me*, I mean, was-

Oof. Yes, I know I should say the best part for me was seeing Jennifer and Frank so happy. That part was nice. But *everyone* was happy for them. Only *I* got to be the DJ.

Yes, that makes me a terrible person. Get over it, OK?

Anyway, I was spinning hit tunes, and everyone was dancing. The children all danced like nobody was watching, which is really the way everyone should dance. Reading the crowd, I played high-energy up-tempo dance tunes, then gave people a break with slower songs. Not just running through a programmed playlist, I added my own touch as the DJ.

During the beginning of one slow song, Skippy shouted into my earpiece. "Joe, what the hell was *that*?"

"What are you talking about? I played a song, *duh*."

"No, you *ruined* a song. Parts of it kept repeating endlessly, like the file got caught in a loop. And what was that when the song stopped, and you dragged your fingernails on a blackboard?"

"That was a hip-hop song, shithead. It's called backspin and scratching. The crowd *loved* it."

"*Really*? Jeez, it sounded like you had trouble with the power supply. I actually sent a bot to fix the problem."

"No problem here, except you don't appreciate good music."

"That was *music*? Wow. Your DJ name should be 'Grandmaster Shmoe and the Intermittent Power Failures'."

"Just call me 'DJ Joey B', please."

"Sure," he sniffed. "If the 'B' stands for 'Bonehead'."

"Goodbye, Skippy."

CHAPTER THIRTY

"Hey, Joe," Skippy called me, and instantly my brain went to Red Alert. It was not the 'Heeeeey, Joe' he used when he was about to casually drop a metric ton of shit on my head. This was the even more frightening tone of voice he used when he was trying to get away with something. Like when a kid says 'hey Mom' before asking if they can borrow a chainsaw, a can of Pam cooking spray, and oh, do we have a flamethrower in the garage?

"What sneaky shit are you up to now, Skippy?" We had gone through the super-duty wormhole to the Sculptor dwarf galaxy, then through the password-protected wormhole that led to the Beta site. Within three hours, the ship should be approaching Avalon, and I was in my office, reviewing a list of all the supplies we needed to send down to the surface before the passengers could be landed.

"I am insulted," he sniffed. "Maybe now I don't feel like telling you."

"Score one for the monkey," I muttered.

"*Fine*," he spat. "Be that way."

"I intend to."

He waited a full twenty seconds before speaking again, a delay that must have been agony for him, so, bonus. "Joe, as much as I am insulted by your totally unfair insinuations, I feel that I must discuss the situation before we get to Avalon. I'm doing it for *you*."

"Please don't."

"But-"

"Really, I'm good. No need to trouble yourself about it."

"Unfortunately, Joe," he sighed in a way that made it obvious he was doing it for effect. "My extreme awesomeness gives me a responsibility to act, even when you think it is not necessary."

It was obvious that he was not taking 'No' for an answer. My choice was either listen to him and get it over with, or for him to wake me up in the middle of the freakin' night. "My apologies, Your Magnificence. What awful danger must you protect us monkeys from now?"

"That's the problem, Joe. I don't know."

That got my attention. Whatever sneaky shit he wanted to get into, it was actually important. "You don't know *what*?"

"I don't know whether the potential danger is an actual danger."

"What potential danger?"

"Maris."

"Oh, shit. This again?" In the Roach Motel, there was a planet that Skippy couldn't see, but inferred its location from the effect of its gravity on other worlds in that system. We had named that unseen world 'Vera'. At the Beta site, he strongly suspected there a similar unseen world that we had, of course, named 'Maris'.

"Yes, this again."

"We talked about this already."

"No, *you* talked about it. I raised legitimate concerns and you ignored me."

"Yes, and I intend to continue ignoring you."

"Joe, can we be serious here for a minute?"

"I don't know. Can *you*?"

"I will try. Listen, numbskull, you-"

"*This* is you being serious?"

"You are *not* a numbskull?"

"Just, say whatever it is you're going to say."

"We need to check it out, Joe."

"Skippy, I know you are burning with curiosity to find out why the Elders concealed an entire planet here. I'm going to tell you the same thing that I told you about the hidden planet in the Roach Motel: *no*. We are not going to risk waking up whatever is hidden in there."

"Vera was different, Joe."

"How is this different?"

"The Elders did not want anyone going to the Roach Motel. Here, the Elders did not install Guardians or a Sentinel, or any other protective measures."

"They didn't have to, because getting here requires waking up a super-duty wormhole, then giving the correct password to another wormhole. The answer is still '*no*'."

"Think about this: you are putting all your eggs in *one* basket here. Avalon might soon be the only place in the universe where humans exist. Maris is an unknown, an unknown *risk*."

"Shit."

"I'm right, aren't I?"

"Maybe."

"Is that a 'Yes'?"

"I *said*, maybe."

"It *sounded* like a 'Yes'."

"Shit," I groaned.

"*That* really sounded like a 'Yes'."

"Show me what you know about this place."

He showed me. Maris was most likely a gas giant planet, roughly the size of Saturn. Skippy knew its overall mass, rough size and other characteristics from the effect of its gravity on other planets, even on how Maris made the star wobble. So, why didn't he know exactly where it was? Because the Elders had a technology that could disperse the planet's gravitational field. Instead of its gravity creating a single dent in the fabric of spacetime, Maris dug a shallow trench along its orbit. For several million kilometers in either direction along its orbital track, it was like the planet was a string of boulders equaling the mass of that world. How could Skippy be sure that world had not been pulverized and actually converted to a long, narrow asteroid belt? Because the stealth field was smaller than the gravity well, or gravity trench. There was a real planet in there somewhere. The question was, what was *so* damned important that the Elders had concealed the entire freakin' planet, in a star system outside the galaxy where no one could get to?

"Sorry, Skippy," I shook my head. "Maris has been quiet so far. If we leave it alone, it will probably leave us alone."

"It could be a sleeping *bear*, Joe."

"Yes, and one thing I know is, do not poke a sleeping bear with a stick. I agree that it's a risk, even an unknown risk. At this point, my judgment is the risk of finding out the truth is greater than the risk of not knowing the truth."

"Are you sure, Joe? If something goes wrong here because you failed to determine that Maris is not a threat, you will get the blame."

"UNEF can add it to my blame bill," I let out a long, weary breath. "Listen, I understand the issue. There's no upside to poking our noses around a planet the Elders want to keep hidden. Leave it be."

"But-"

"No 'buts', Skippy. Whatever is at Maris has not reacted to us being on Avalon, and I am not going to jeopardize that. If we had another Beta site without a hidden planet, I would go there instead. We don't, so we are not doing anything stupid. End of discussion."

With the civilians anxious and frightened that we were dumping them on Avalon forever, but intensely curious to see the new world that was in *another galaxy*, I flew down to the surface aboard the first dropship. It was stuffed with equipment to set up temporary housing, that needed to be set up before we could bring a large number of people down from *Valkyrie*. There were empty shelters in the main camp, left from when Avalon was first being surveyed as a potential Beta site. It was now the default Beta site, since we had no other option.

When we jumped into orbit, I was pleased to see extensive fields of crops growing around the main settlement, and signs that the small group of people down there had been very busy. The campsite was now a proper village, with a large shelter in the center and residential huts clustered around. In the flat area to the north, abandoned aircraft were parked under tarps at what used to be an airfield. It all looked neat and orderly. I had to remind myself that the acres of crops were still being tested for suitability for growing on a new planet, and there was a lot of work to do before farmland on Avalon could feed the growing population.

Seeing those few acres of well-tended crops reminded me that we needed to bring a *lot* of food from Earth.

When my dropship touched down at the old airfield, and the dust settled, I squeezed between crates in the main cabin to exit by the side door. Hans Chotek was there to greet me. We had talked while I was aboard *Valkyrie*, so he knew the situation. He wasn't any happier about it than anyone else, and I appreciated that he kept the other UN Commissioners, off my back for a while. There would be plenty of time for the three of them to yell to me before I took *Valkyrie* to rendezvous with the *Dutchman* and hopefully, go through Backstop to Earth.

"Guten tag, Joe," Hans said with as much of a smile as he could manage. "Has a miracle occurred since we last spoke?"

"Sorry, no," I shook my head. He offered a hand to shake but I wasn't going for that shit, I pulled him into a bear hug.

He grunted. "Ooh, I hurt my back yesterday." We separated and he winced. "We have all been working in the fields every day."

"You OK?"

"Doctor Skippy said it's just a pulled muscle. There are pills aboard your ship somewhere."

"If Doctor Skippy orders more tests, you should say no."

Another dropship was coming in on final approach, so I gestured for my copilot to secure the spacecraft, and Hans led the way off the airfield. "Smythe's STAR team is aboard the Dutchman," I didn't explain why. Hans was smart, he could figure it out by himself. "We have some new people aboard, a Commando team from Paradise."

He looked at me sharply, questioning.

"It's a long story," I explained as a way of not explaining. "Half of the Commandos are with us, they will use their powered suits to unload the dropships, make the process go faster. This will be a short visit; *Valkyrie* is out of here as soon as Simms is satisfied you have everything we can spare."

"She still plans to remain here?'

"Yes."

"This," he pointed to the cluster of huts, "will not be much of a honeymoon for her."

"I don't think she cares at this point. Hans, we are all very worried about the civilians, especially the children. They went through hell on Rikers, and we haven't helped. They have been bounced back and forth between our ships, on Club Skippy, and now we are dropping them here. They need whatever stability you can give them."

"Children can be surprisingly resilient," he told me.

"Everyone has a breaking point."

Three hours later, my dropship was being unloaded. Soon, I would be riding back into orbit. It would be my last opportunity to talk privately with Simms, and I wanted her advice about something that was bothering me.

"Hey, Skippy, I need to talk with Simms."

"Well, ping her, knucklehead. Do I have to do everything around here?"

"What I want to talk about is personal. About her, not me. She won't like the idea of anyone listening, so I'm going to leave my phone in camp, OK?"

"Um, this is more than a little odd, Joe."

"It's important. Do you want Simms to know you insisted on listening to us?"

"No way. You two have fun. Just don't get eaten by a bear."

"There aren't any dangerous predators on this planet."

Pulling my earpiece out, I left it and my phone in my backpack. Simms was doing something on her laptop, sitting on a folding chair under the shade of an awning. Walking over to her, I mimed pulling something from my ear. "XO, you wanted to talk about that thing?"

Her face was blank. "Thing, Sir?"

"Yeah, you know. That thing you wanted to talk about." Silently, I mouthed 'leave your phone here'.

She gave me the side-eye, both eyebrows raised in alarm. "That thing, right."

We walked away from the camp, first along a trail, then cutting across country, pushing aside giant ferns until we reached a creek. I sat down on a moss-covered rock and she sat on a rock that wasn't so covered with squishy moss. "This is far enough from camp," I said.

"You want to tell me what this is about, Sir?"

"It's about Skippy. We may have a major problem."

"Worse than all the problems we have now?"

"Yeah. Any solution to our problems requires Skippy to help us. Without his help, or if he is working against us, then nothing we do will matter."

"You're scaring me. Why would you think Skippy would ever work against us?"

"He wouldn't do it deliberately, but he might not have a choice." I told her Skippy's suspicions about why the AI at Newark stopped fighting.

"There could be a *time bomb* inside him?"

"That is one possibility, yes. It is not the worst-case scenario."

"It's *not*?"

"No. Worst-case is, he has been subtly and subconsciously working against us for a while. Skippy told us the wormhole network screwed with him, that he didn't know it was going to move other wormholes, and open dormant wormholes. Maybe that is true. Or maybe some hidden part of Skippy knew about it all along."

"Oh my-"

"We only have Skippy's word for what happens when he talks to a wormhole network. He could have ordered the network to relocate and open the Broomstick wormhole."

"Don't. Sir, just, *don't*."

"Don't what?"

"Don't go down that rabbit hole. *If*. If Skippy is subconsciously working against us. That is a lot of *ifs*. We have no way to know if some part of him has betrayed us, *he* has no way to know. It is not productive to worry about what we can't control. Like you said, we don't have a choice. We need Skippy, or we might as well give up right now."

"Yeah. You're right. Sorry to dump this on you."

"Sir, I'm your executive officer. After all the time we've served together, I hope you know that I am also your *friend*." She reached out a hand, and I took hers and squeezed it. "When you are worried about something like this, *tell me*. You need to talk to someone about things like this. I'm glad you felt comfortable telling me."

"Thanks for being here." I let go of her hand before I got awkward. Crap. I felt guilty for not telling her the truth about why Skippy bailed on us at Rikers.

Someday. I would wait to tell her the truth later.

"I understand why you wanted to talk about this without Skippy listening."

"Yeah, he's-"

"You're *wrong* about that, Sir."

"I am?"

"Yes. Skippy needs to know that his subconscious might already be working against him, so he can watch for any signs of that happening. Otherwise, this is just us having a useless conversation."

"Shit. The reason I didn't tell him was, he is already freaked out about the possibility of a time bomb inside him. But he needs to know, you're right."

"I usually am, Sir. You need to *trust* your team."

"You're right about that, too. Let's get back."

Recovering my phone, I stuck the earpiece back in. Skippy called me immediately. "Hey, Joe. Did you have a good talk with Simms? It wasn't, um, a female issue, was it?"

"Simms is a woman, not a *'female'*, Skippy. And no, it wasn't about her. We were talking about you."

"*Me?* Why didn't you-"

I told him.

"Wow." His voice sounded far away. "OK. While I am pissed at you for not telling me upfront, I guess I have to thank you for considering my feelings."

"Well, I do try to-"

"Even though you were *completely* incompetent about it."

"Doing the best I can here."

"Do *better*, Joe. We can talk about *that* later. Right now, I need to think about what you said. Shit. The only way to know is for me to ask the wormhole network exactly what instructions I gave to it."

"Can you do that here, with the wormhole here?"

"No. That is something I can only discuss with the local network near Earth. Do you want to hear a bit of good news?"

"Please, anything."

"While it is possible that a subconscious part of me gave the wrong instructions to the network, I doubt that could have happened. The protocol I used required the network to repeat my instructions back to me, so I could verify it understood what I wanted. Why did I do that? Because I don't trust the stupid thing. The problem is, I didn't distrust it *enough*."

"That is good news. You keep doing that."

"Will do, Joe."

With the civilians settling unhappily in prefab shelters on the surface of Avalon, we got dropships stuffed with just about every type of supplies we had aboard the ship, leaving just enough food and other consumables for the trip back to Earth, plus a two-week margin for safety. Unloading the ship was a pain in the ass, because *Valkyrie* had been designed as a battlecruiser, not a cargo ship. Battlecruisers were supposed to travel with escort and support ships, so they were not designed to be self-supporting for extended times.

Anyway, I was walking between docking bays when I saw Doctor Friedlander staring out a viewport. There weren't many actual windows aboard the ship, mostly to see outside we used viewscreens. I understood the desire to actually see something through a window, it seemed more real. "What's up, Doc?" I asked.

He grinned at the joke, but his smile faded quickly. "Our new home," he tapped the glass of the viewport which was really a flexible type of diamond material. "It is hard to believe that we will be trying to set up an entire *civilization* down there."

"Hopefully, yes." Maybe I should not have said 'hopefully'. "It's rough now, but someday, we will have schools and churches and concert halls down there."

"That's not all. We need to build an industrial base, on the surface and up here."

"Well, sure, that-"

"We need to build starships. A *war* fleet."

"Uh-" It surprised me to hear him talk that way. "The whole point of setting up a Beta site way out here, is that it is a safe haven from hostile aliens. If we ever need a fleet of warships out here, we're in trouble."

"It's not that," he turned to look out the viewport again. Over his shoulder, I could see the surface of Avalon. What was in view at that moment was mostly water dotted with islands, it looked inviting. "We don't need ships for protection. We need them for *payback*."

"Doctor, I hear you. *Valkyrie* is a powerful ship, but even a fleet of *Valkyries* won't be able to do much against-"

"Not a ship like *this*," he rapped his knuckles on the bulkhead. "Something better. A ship with Elder technology."

"Whoa. We don't have any-"

"Skippy knows that tech," he insisted. "We *can* build an Elder ship, or something equivalent."

"Doctor, I appreciate your enthusiasm. It will take-"

"A long time, yes. I've talked about this with Skippy. He said it would take thousands of years, and the resources of multiple star systems, to even begin producing the materials for constructing an Elder ship. I told him," he glanced back down at the nearly-empty planet below us. "We have time. Out here," his voice dropped to a whisper. "We will have nothing but time."

"I think you're forgetting something," I said gently.

"Colonel, if you are going to lecture me about whether getting payback for the destruction of Earth is morally-"

"Oh, *fuck* that," I spat. "The Maxolhx already deserve a beat-down. I don't give a shit about them. The problem is, your plan has a major downside for *us*."

"It does? What?"

"We can't use Elder technology. The kitties did that, remember? They used Elder weapons to attack the spiders, and Sentinels appeared to crush both of them. If we construct ships that deploy Elder weapons, we risk Sentinels wiping out Avalon."

"*Shit*," he cursed, and I realized that was the only time I had ever heard the good doctor use a bad word. "Maybe Skippy can figure a way around that problem."

"It's all academic at this point, right?" I clapped a hand on his shoulder. "That's a question for our grandchildren."

That remark made him smile. "I would like to have grandchildren." He looked back at the planet. "Never thought that my grandchildren would grow up in another *galaxy*."

"Hey, this is just a dwarf galaxy, think of it as like the suburbs of the Milky Way."

He snorted. "If this is the suburbs, it needs more golf courses."

"Maybe you can work on that," I suggested.

"Probably I should build a house first."

"You should probably *design* a house first," I said, figuring that would appeal to him as an engineer.

"Yeah," he looked down at the planet. "Maybe I'll do that."

CHAPTER THIRTY ONE

"Skippy," I flopped down into my oversized office chair. Sitting in that thing always made me feel like a little kid. Like it was Bring Your Child to Work day, and I was sitting at my father's desk. Except my father didn't have a desk. As he said it, he worked for a living. "Give me some good news, please."

"Sorry Joe," his avatar looked crestfallen. "I looked in the bottom of my Good News bag, and all I see is a few crumbs."

"I'll take those."

"Hmm. I think those crumbs got eaten by a rat, and this is what's left behind, if you know what I mean."

"Forget it."

"Sorry. Really, I wish I had some good news for you. I should have warned you this would happen."

That made me sit bolt upright in the chair. "You *ass*! You knew the wormhole network would move-"

"*Whoa*! Slow your roll there, pardner. No. I did not know that. Not that specifically. What I did know was that we have seriously been pushing our luck, and it was bound to run out soon."

"I thought there is no such thing as 'luck'?"

"There isn't. Not the way you think of the concept. Joe, the survival of your species was always improbable right from the beginning. Each time you pulled off some improbable stunt that saved the world, your future options got narrower."

"What?"

"How can I explain this to you? How am I *allowed* to explain it? OK, try this. The Universe does not like improbable things happening, and we have done a lot of improbable things. The fact that the White Wind clan has not enslaved or exterminated all humans on Earth is improbable. On our second mission, when we used our space truck to stop a Thuranin ship from reaching Earth, that was even more improbable, you get that?"

"I think so. It's like rolling dice. Each time you roll, you have a one-in-six chance of getting a six. If you roll a six, it is not any less likely you will roll a six the next time. But it is unlikely you will get a six *every* time if you roll a hundred times. Something like that?"

"Eh, close enough. Joe, you have done so many improbable things already, that the future path for the survival of humanity is a *very* narrow set of probabilities. You have almost *no* margin for error."

"Did, you just say," I said slowly, the wheels turning in my mind. "That there *is* a possibility we can save the world again? How?"

"Ugh. I should not try explaining complicated things to you, it just gets your hopes up. The answer is 'Yes', and 'I don't know'. Yes, technically, the probability set has not yet collapsed entirely, but it is an *extremely* narrow window."

"You can see the freakin' future?"

"No. Not like that. I can make predictions. That's all I can say. It's a math thing, you wouldn't understand, even if I was allowed to tell you."

"You know I hate it when you give me hints like that. Can you give me an example?"

"Sure. On our Renegade mission, the probability set was almost as restricted as it is now. We had to accomplish the impossible: stopping Maxolhx ships from reaching Earth, in a way that made them think their ships *did* go to Earth and found nothing interesting. And that the disappearance of those ships was not at all suspicious. Oh, plus, we had to explain the intermittent gamma rays coming from the Gateway wormhole. It was an impossible task, yet we did it. *You* did it. After that, the probability set expanded dramatically, though less than I expected. I couldn't understand the data, until, you know, we heard about what Perkins did."

"Holy shit. You knew something was wrong, and you didn't *say* anything about it?!" I thumped a fist on the desk.

"No, I didn't *know* anything was wrong. There was something unexplained in the *math*, that's all. Listen, knucklehead, it was just a nerdy math thing, OK?"

His explanation sounded like pure bullshit to me, but I didn't have any evidence to back up my suspicions. Besides, I did not believe that Skippy could truly see the future. Maybe that technology was possible, I had seen a whole lot of sci fi movies about time travel. But I was certain that Skippy didn't have that ability. Why? Because if he could see the future, no way could that arrogant little shithead miss the opportunity to brag about it. Many times, he had been humiliated by declaring something was impossible, only to have a meatsack think up a clever idea to solve the problem. Still, there was something he wasn't telling me, and I hated that. "Skip the math. The Universe is saying there *is* a possibility to prevent an attack against Earth, for humanity to survive?"

"Um, the Universe is not saying that, it- OK, I guess you would think that. The math is saying it is not absolutely impossible. But, Joe, please understand the odds. It's like your team has lost all your games in the first half of the season, and the team leading your division has won all their games. Mathematically, it is possible that you could win all your remaining games and the other team could lose all theirs, so you *could* go to the playoffs and win the Super Bowl. But, come on, that will not actually happen."

"So, you're saying there *is* a chance?"

"Ugh. No, not really. It was a mistake to even mention the subject."

"Skippy, do you know what a Hail Mary is?"

"Um, yes. I'm not Catholic, so if you are suggesting prayer is-"

"I meant in sports. A Hail Mary play."

"Sure. Pack the end zone with receivers and toss the ball to them."

"Ayuh. That, or a ridiculous set of laterals back and forth until somebody runs the ball in for a touchdown. Believe me, I have seen that happen way too many times, always when the *other* team does it. It *can* happen." Slapping my laptop closed, I stood up. "Where is Simms?"

"She is in Docking Bay Three Alpha."

"Tell her I'll be right there."

She wasn't exactly waiting for me. She was busy supervising the loading of supplies aboard a dropship. Rather than combat loading, where the stuff you need first goes in the container last, our priority was speed, cramming dropships full so they made the minimum number of trips to get everything down to the surface. We wanted to empty the ship quickly, so *Valkyrie* could fly to meet the *Dutchman*. It was like a going-out-of-business sale; everything must go. People on the ground needed our supplies, whatever we had, and we needed space aboard the ship to cram it full of new stuff at Earth. Stuff we would probably have to steal, assuming Earth was in complete societal collapse after we arrived.

Good times.

Simms had designated one area for food to sustain our crew, during the flight to Backstop. It was a risk; if Backstop failed to open, our crew would be surviving on sludges and homemade HooAH! bars until we could find something to eat.

She brushed undisciplined bangs out of her eyes and tapped on her tablet when I strode into the docking bay. "You want to speak with me, Sir?" She had a distinctive I-am-very-busy look in her eye, urging me to not waste her time.

I nodded, and gestured to a dwindling pile of crates and boxes along the inner wall of the bay. Two dropships were steadily being loaded to the gills, I could see their landing struts compressed under the weight. "That's the last of it?"

She shook her head. "We have two other docking bays working, plus there are odds and ends here and there aboard the ship, in various nooks and crannies. I have Skippy's bots racking down the stragglers. Don't worry, we will stick to the schedule. The last ship will drop in," she glanced at her tablet, "nine and a half hours."

"That's great," I said, meaning the opposite. That last ship would carry her to the surface, and I might never see her again. If I never had to eat another vegetable surprise she cooked up in the galley, that would be great. But the idea of never seeing her again hurt. Like, *physically*. I got a pang in my heart and my stomach cramped up. Way back on Paradise, Simms had signed on with the Merry Band of Pirates, and made us legit. She had been by my side, with varying levels of enthusiasm, ever since. "Are you interested in one last rodeo?"

"What?" Her eyebrows flew up, then her eyes narrowed with suspicion. My eyes automatically darted to her wedding ring. "Sir, you said I had to stay here on Avalon. You made a whole *speech* about it."

"I did," I shrugged, embarrassed. "This is just a short recon flight. I hope it's short."

"*Short?* There is nothing around here."

"That's kind of the point. There is a *nothing* here, and we need to check it out, before we commit to this planet as humanity's new home."

I swear, she actually put her hands on her hips and glared at me. "It's a bit late for that, Sir."

"You know what I'm talking about, right?"

"Maris?" She rolled her eyes. Simms did not like the cutesy names we gave to planets, especially when they were inside jokes.

"Yes. Skippy thinks whatever is there, may be a threat."

"It hasn't been a threat so far," she reminded me.

"I know."

"Let me guess. Skippy wants to poke it with a stick."

"Not exactly. He wants *us* to poke it with a stick."

"Did you tell him your name is not 'Darryl'?"

"Yes," I laughed.

"Another idiotic idea from Skippy. What could possibly go wrong?"

"Do you want to find out?" I grinned.

"You are going anyway, aren't you?"

"Uh, yeah, probably. I would appreciate having adult supervision."

"What if the adult tells you not to poke the hornet's nest with a stick?"

"Can we throw rocks at it instead?"

"I'm going to pretend you didn't say that, Sir. This is a simple recon mission?"

"Yes. I promise. We match course and speed with Skippy's best guess of where the planet is, then jump in. Launch a couple probes to fly inside the stealth field, collect the data, and come back here. Unless we determine that whatever is hidden in there represents a threat to Avalon. I want to do this by the book," I assured her.

She was not assured. "By the book? Does the Army have a manual on the proper procedure for investigating planets inside a stealth field?"

"The Army has a manual for *everything*, Simms," I joked, but it may not have been a joke. When we returned to Earth from our long mission that involved spending time in the Roach Motel, the Army had questioned why we hadn't investigated the hidden planet there. My answer was that Hans Chotek was the mission leader, and he had ordered me to leave that planet alone. That answer had not pleased Army leadership, or the leadership of UNEF. We failed to exploit an opportunity at the Roach Motel, and someone other than Hans Chotek had to take the blame. If the Army had standing orders to investigate hidden planets, they hadn't told me about it. Maybe they figured I would do it on my own. "Will you come with us?"

She knew I could have made my request an order. She also knew I wouldn't do that to her. "Tell me this, Sir. If we discover a threat at Maris, one that requires us to pull everyone off Avalon, what is the plan? Where do we go?"

"I haven't got all the details worked out yet," I admitted, which was my way of saying I did not have a freakin clue.

"Mm hmm," She folded her arms across her chest. There was no other place to go, she knew that. When we found Avalon, we had cut short our search. At the time, we expected to fly back to Earth to report what we had found. Then UNEF could decide whether to continue searching for a better site, or bring a larger science team to examine Avalon in detail, or both. None of that had happened.

"How about this?" I asked. "If we find a monster under the bed at Maris, we bring everyone to Club Skippy. Temporarily, just until we find a place that is a safe haven in the long term."

"It will have to be temporary," the arms she had hugged tightly to her chest relaxed slightly. "Club Skippy will have aliens crawling all over it, after the next wormhole shift. That could happen sooner than Skippy expects, because he has been screwing with the damned network."

I read between the lines of what she said. "We're agreed, then?"

She let out an exasperated breath. "I'll go with you. Frank stays here."

"Absolutely. We'll have you back ASAP, I promise."

"Your promise isn't the problem, Sir. It's the 'possible' part of A-S-A-P that worries me."

"Simms, if this goes wrong, I am blaming your negative attitude."

"I appreciate the heads-up."

"Um, Joe?" Skippy prompted me when I got back to my office. "May I ask what changed your mind about going to Maris? Nothing has changed about the facts, that I am aware of."

"The facts have not changed."

"Then why did-"

"Let's just say that your little talk, about the narrowing probabilities against us, got my attention. I want Maris to be one less variable we don't know about."

"Oh. OK."

There was another reason, but I wasn't going to mention that to him. If people were going to think I'm stupid, I didn't want to give them any more ammo against me.

It took sixteen hours for *Valkyrie* to match course and speed with Maris, so we would be stationary with that hidden planet when we jumped in. Not knowing exactly where the damned thing was, we used Skippy's best guess. The jump was uneventful. No shearing field tore the ship in half, we did not get trapped in a damping field, and a swarm of Guardians did not attack the ship. It might have helped that Skippy broadcast his identity and authentication codes long before we jumped, so the message had time to reach the hidden world. He repeated the message as soon as we emerged from jump, and kept trying to get whoever was inside the field to respond.

"Anything?" I asked, watching the holographic display tank anxiously.

"No joy, Joe," he mumbled. "The stupid thing is not acknowledging me at all."

"It's not shooting at us," I pointed out. "That is a form of response."

"Yeah, I guess so," he said with disgust.

"How can we be sure that anyone's home in there?" Simms asked.

"*Someone* must be there," Skippy insisted. "The Elders would not have left a stealth field and gravity-dispersal system to low-level systems. There must be a form of higher intelligence in there, somewhere."

"It couldn't be an AI like you," I asked, a chill making the hair on the back of my neck stand up. "Could it?"

"No way," Skippy chuckled at my stupid question. "The Elders would not dedicate an AI like me to a simple job. We are too valuable. Even the Elders did not have unlimited resources."

"Good enough. Do you have a better idea where the planet is?"

"Sort of. It's off-center as I suspected. There is no point to creating a gravity-dispersal field, if the planet is in the exact center of it. Coordinates are programmed in the probe drone guidance system."

"Launch one," I ordered, and the display showed a single symbol accelerating gently away from the ship. We did not want the entity at Maris to think we were hostile.

The probe drone did not get blown up as it approached the stealth field. There was no reaction at all. It was moving at half a kilometer per second when it contacted the fuzzy edge of the field and disappeared. The probe was supposed to wait ten minutes then use its autonomous guidance system and boost itself back outside the field. Ten minutes passed, then twelve. It should have been visible again, or we should at least have detected the ping it was sending out.

Fifteen minutes.

Twenty.

"Shit," I looked to Simms. "This was a bust."

"Bust-o-rama, Joe," Skippy agreed. "Busta Rhymes. Bust-"

"What do you think?" I addressed the question to both Skippy and Simms. "Try another probe? Maybe two, this time?"

"Sir," Simms answered. "You want to do the same thing again, and expect different results?"

"I don't know what else to do," I admitted. "We came all the way out here. I want an answer."

"That could *be* the answer," she jabbed a finger at the display. "It just said 'Go Away'."

"Or the probe failed," I retorted. "It could be as simple as selecting a different location. Try again, but send the next probe in from one end of the dispersal field?"

"It's worth a shot," Skippy agreed. "We could- Oh, ho! There it is!"

A symbol for the probe was blinking on the display.

"Uh!" Skippy preemptively shushed me. "Give me a moment to talk with the stupid thing. OK, hmm, interesting."

"What happened?"

"The short answer is, it doesn't know. The probe thought it *was* following instructions, but it must have gotten lost. It departed the stealth field eight thousand kilometers from where it was supposed to be."

"Uh, how could that happen? It was only gone twenty minutes, and it wasn't moving that fast."

"Good question, Joe. A question for which I do not presently have an answer."

He was using fancy words, because he was nervous. In the military, I had learned that 'I do not know' is a legit response, although less legit if the subject is something basic like 'Where is your rifle?'. Being honest about your ignorance is preferable to faking it and causing people to rely on your dumb ass. "*Will* you have an answer?"

"Um, no."

"Can you expand on that?"

"The probe recorded *no* useful data, Joe. It was totally blind in there. That's how it got lost."

"Even if it had no external references, its guidance system is self-contained over such a short distance. How could it get lost?"

"That's the problem. As far as it is concerned, it did *not* get lost. The probe assumed the stealth field had expanded. It kept going, expecting to break out of the field eventually. It has no idea how it traveled so far."

"Great. Do you have a theory about what happened?"

"Not without more data, no."

We launched more probes. Twenty-six probes in total. They all got lost, and twenty-three of them reappeared way off course. Three were never heard from again, and we didn't know why. Gradually, Skippy was able to piece together a picture of what was going on inside the stealth field. Manipulation of the gravity well had strange effects that created sort of gravity currents inside the field. Probes would get caught in a current that acted like the Jet Stream in Earth's atmosphere, so the probe would be carried along at great speed until it flew out of the current. The guidance systems of the probes did not expect that the space around them would be moving, that is why they thought they were exactly on course.

The probes provided almost no useful data. Despite the lack of info, there was good news. The entity inside the stealth field had not reacted in a hostile manner. It had not reacted at all, which might have been considered bad news, but I was counting it as a win. If Maris did not react to us flying probes inside the field, it might not care about lowly meatsacks living on Avalon.

The other bit of good news was that Skippy thought he was able to map the gravity currents, and determine where the planet was.

The next step, part of the plan I approved before we left Avalon, was to launch probes that carried one end of a microwormhole. To prevent the effects of the gravity dispersal field from bleeding through a microwormhole and causing havoc aboard the ship, we launched the other end of that microwormhole in a second probe, then one end of another microwormhole inside a *third* probe. With the second and third probes hovering only a few kilometers from each other, the communication channel between the ship and the first probe was nearly instantaneous. We waited for the second and third probes to coast away to six thousand kilometers from the ship, before ordering the first probe to fire its thrusters and enter the stealth field. That probe was right above where Skippy thought the hidden planet was, he was hopeful we could finally get some solid data.

The probe slipped into the stealth field, and the view changed from black space dotted with stars, to utter nothingness. "Skippy, can you see anything in there?"

"Not yet. Hmm, interesting. The entire electromagnetic spectrum is blank. Well, not blank exactly. The data I'm receiving is nonsense. This is an excellent stealth field."

"You should see something as the probe gets closer to the planet, though, right?"

"Mm, shmaybe, but I wouldn't count on it. I'm picking up spatial distortion effects, it's difficult to tell where the probe is in relation to the planet."

"Don't count on it?" I shared a look with Simms. "Then why the hell did we send in the freakin' probe?"

"Um, because we *might* see something, and right now we have zero data to work with. Mostly, because I expect the entity in that field to react to the microwormhole."

"What the f- Are you *kidding* me?" Beside me, Simms slapped her forehead. "Pull that damned probe out of there right now, you idiot!"

"Jeez, Joe, don't be such a fraidy cat," he verbally rolled his eyes at me. "The probe is already there, we might as well-"

The ship shuddered.

"What the hell was-" I shouted, then my stomach did flip-flops as the artificial gravity field flickered.

"Not *this* shit again!" Simms screamed, more in anger than fear.

"Skippy! What is going on?" I demanded.

"I don't know! I don't know *why*. Oh, *shit*! The ship is being pulled down toward the planet."

"Pilot! Jump option-"

"No, Joe! Jump drive is offline," Skippy warned, at the same time the pilot made a slashing motion with his hand and pointed to the jump status indicator. It was red.

We couldn't jump.

Fine.

"Fireball, get us out of here, pedal to the metal."

"Sir," Reed said without looking over at me. "Thrust is on full. We're not *going* anywhere!"

Before I could ask the obvious question, Skippy spoke. "Engines are operating nominally, at full power. They're just not *pushing* against anything."

"Why? How is-"

"The laws of physics aren't working here!" He screeched. "We're just going to burn out the engines, without accomplishing anything."

I made a snap decision. "Pilot, cut power. Are the thrusters working?"

"The main thrusters, no," Reed shook her head. "Backup thrusters are having a small effect. It's no good, Sir. Not enough to counteract the, tractor beam or whatever we're caught in."

On the display, the imaginary line that represented the outer edge of the stealth field was approaching rapidly. No. We were rapidly being pulled toward it.

"Skippy, this is a tractor beam? Can we target the source and take it out?"

"No. It's not a tractor beam, we are caught in a gravitic current. The dispersal field suddenly expanded to pull us in. We're being pulled along with it!"

"There's nothing we can do? You can do?"

"No. I don't even understand how the damned thing works!" he sobbed.

"All right, fuck it. We're outta here. Abandon ship. Everyone, get to a dropship," I ordered. Everyone except me, but I didn't say that. I was staying aboard, literally going down with the ship. Until the very last moment, as long as there was any hope at all, I would-

"Not possible, Joe," Skippy moaned. "Dropships can launch, but they'll be pulled down along with the ship. Same with escape pods."

What the hell could we do?

Nothing.

We couldn't do anything.

"Skippy, *do* something."

"I'm trying, Joe. No, that's not right. I am actually not doing *anything*, because I don't know what to do. Tell me what to do!"

What to do? What *could* we do? The ship couldn't jump. Couldn't move at all. Couldn't shoot, because we didn't have a target. *Valkyrie's* mighty guns wouldn't do much against an entire planet anyway. The crew couldn't even get away.

The *crew* couldn't get away.

But maybe someone could.

"What about railguns?" I asked, speaking as the idea formed in my head.

"Railguns?" Simms stared at me. "We don't have a target to shoot at."

"Joe," Skippy chimed in. "The recoil action of a railgun is not enough to counteract-"

"It won't save the ship, but we could load you into the railgun, and shoot you at Avalon. You will crash-land there eventually."

"Shit, J-Joe." He stammered. "That won't work. The gravitic current would throw off the aim of the railgun. We don't have time anyway, we are about to- Oop!"

The ship plunged inside the stealth field.

It was completely black, all sensors were blanked out.

"Skippy, what do you see in here?"

"Just magnetic and gravity fields, Joe," he mumbled, a sign that he was concentrating on something. "Give me a minute."

"We don't have a minute."

"We have nothing *but* time," he retorted, and his avatar froze. It didn't blink out, it didn't fade, it just froze as one image because he wasn't paying any attention to it. "As best I can tell," he said as his avatar reanimated, "we are being pulled toward the planet. As I predicted, it is a gas giant, between the sizes of Saturn and Neptune. We will contact the upper atmosphere in two minutes. The good news is, our forward progress is slowing with the current. The ship should survive initial contact with the atmosphere. However, the strength of the gravitic field has increased. Even if our engines had something to push against, we couldn't get away."

"What next? Why is it pulling us in? Does it want to talk with us, scan us?"

"Neither of those. It is not responding to me at all, and I am not detecting any active sensors being used. My guess is, it plans to pull the ship down to the core of the planet."

"The *core*?" Astronomy, like any science you could name, was not my specialty. I did know, from reading Wikipedia articles, that the core of a gas giant planet was typically a solid ball composed of nickel and iron, at the center of a super-dense atmosphere. "It wants to meet us there?"

"No. Assuming the ship goes all the way to the core, there will be no one left alive. The pressure at that depth is enough to create metallic hydrogen."

"OK, OK," I thought frantically. "Can you do that trick of expanding the shields, to make the ship buoyant, keep us from falling too deep?"

"No," he shook his head slowly. "The shields have failed. Their generators are pumping out gigawatts of power, but the fields are looping back on themselves. I recommend cutting power, before the generators burn out."

Beside me, Simms gestured to a crewman, who tapped on his console to give the appropriate commands. Just then, the ship shuddered again, and there was a roaring sound.

"We are now in the atmosphere," Skippy announced glumly, and the ship rotated sickeningly. On the display, we could see the hull wobbling until it stabilized nose-down, pointed straight down at the hellish core of the planet. "Armor plating is holding," he reported.

"For how long?" I asked the question, not really wanting to hear the answer.

"The armor has excellent thermal-protection properties. Heat is not the problem, Joe. The pressure section of the hull is designed to hold *in* one atmosphere of air. If we continue at this rate, we will fall to crush depth in ten minutes, forty-three seconds."

It was my fault.

Yes, Skippy had used the microwormhole to provoke a reaction from the entity, and he failed to tell anyone the true purpose of sending that probe inside the stealth field.

That was *my* fault. I knew what an irresponsible, absent-minded, untrustworthy little shithead he is, yet I hadn't asked enough questions. "There is nothing you can do?"

"No. Not that I know of. I have *tried* everything I can think of. Joe, for all my powers, I wasn't designed for this situation. The Elders wanted this place protected, even from AIs like me. I am sorry."

The ship was vibrating so hard, it was shaking my teeth loose. My brain couldn't concentrate. It didn't matter. No clever idea was getting us out of there. "Skippy, get yourself out of here."

"What?" Skippy and Simms said at the same time.

Ignoring Simms, who I could see glaring at me, I explained "Do your disappearing trick again. *You* have to survive."

"No, Joe."

"Someone has to survive. You are the only one of us with a prayer of escaping before the ship is crushed. As long as you survive, humanity has hope."

"It doesn't work like that," he shook his head in despair.

"Disappear? *Again?*" Simms demanded my attention. "What '*again*' is that, Sir?"

Shit. It no longer mattered if everyone knew the truth. "When I got captured, and the microwormholes at Rikers collapsed, it wasn't because Skippy got scared of a computer worm attack. He *bailed* on us. After he recovered his memories, he decided that helping a lowly bunch of monkeys was a waste of his talents, so he left to contact the Rindhalu. He left," I looked at Simms. "Poof," I made an exploding gesture with my hands. "His can disappeared. Physically."

Simms gaped at me, then at Skippy. "He can *do* that?"

"Apparently, yes."

"I'm not *supposed* to do that," Skippy mumbled.

Simms clenched her jaw. "Damn straight you're not supposed to *bail* on us."

"Simms," I held up a hand.

She was not deterred. "When were you going to tell us the truth? Why?" She was angry at me, and *hurt*.

"I didn't want everyone to be distracted. He came *back*, that's what matters."

"You *trusted* him, after that stunt?"

"Simms, it's not like we had a choice," I shrugged.

"You had a choice whether to tell us the truth. Whether to trust *us*."

"I know that. I made a judgment call."

"Lately, your judgment has *sucked*."

"That is enough, *Lieutenant* Colonel." Turning away from her anger, I focused on Skippy. And on the indicator showing the ship would reach crush depth in seven minutes. "Skippy, get yourself out of here. That's an order. Do it now."

"Joe," he sighed. He was sobbing. "If I do this, I might not be able to interact with this layer of spacetime ever again."

"You will be alive."

"I am not in danger of *dying*, Joe. Not even the pressure and temperature at the core of this world can kill me."

"It won't kill you, it will do worse. Getting stuck at the core of this planet will make you *useless*. Alone forever, until the end of time. Please, *go*. Promise me you will do whatever you can, if you can, to help us. Our people."

"I don't like this," his words were barely audible over the roaring and vibration as the ship fell headlong toward the crushing depths.

"I don't like it either."

"Goodbye, Joe. Jennifer. Everyone," his avatar was already fading.

Not trusting myself to speak, I gave him a shaky thumbs up.

With the corner of one eye, I saw Simms looking at me.

Her hurt and anger were gone, replaced by another emotion.

Disappointment.

She trusted me.

And I had gotten everyone killed.

Everyone.

CHAPTER THIRTY TWO

"Yes, Admiral Denoth," Illiath acknowledged, and issued instructions for her ship to maneuver from the rear of the formation. Following standing orders, she had resisted the temptation to take her ship to Earth alone. Instead, the *Vortan* had flown through four wormholes, to the nearest major fleet base, to report her discovery: she had found a shortcut to Earth. If luck had been with her, the battlegroup based there would have been away searching for the ghost ship, or at least on maneuvers. But the *Vortan* had emerged from jump to find the base servicing facilities packed with ships. There was a brief moment of hope when sensors found many ships undergoing heavy maintenance, their engines worn out from chasing after every report of an appearance by the ghost ship. Surely, the admiral in command would dismiss Illiath, and she could proceed back to the new wormhole? By then, it should be safe for a ship to go through.

No such luck. The admiral was one of those opposed to sending a reinforced battlegroup on the long voyage to Earth's nearest wormhole, considering the mission to be a useless diversion of resources. He was eager to prove there was nothing important to be gained from examining the odd behavior of that wormhole, and so announced he would be going with Illiath. Or, Illiath would be going with him. Her lightly-armed patrol cruiser was assigned a less-than-desirable position on the racks of a star carrier, joining the admiral's battlecruiser, three heavy cruisers and two destroyer squadrons.

Now, with the wormhole still only intermittently stable, she had the dubious honor of flying through first, while the battlegroup waited a safe distance away. The timing would be tricky, with little margin for error during the approach. Confidence was reported at only eighty-nine percent, a number below normal safety procedures. As the situation was anything but normal, and the admiral itching to resolve the minor mystery and return to base, he had ordered Illiath to proceed. If her ship were damaged or destroyed during the transition, he promised that she would not be held responsible for hazarding her ship.

That was of little comfort to the crew of the *Vortan*.

Regardless, their ship performed flawlessly, jumping in exactly on time, moving at a speed and direction that would have the warship coast safely past the event horizon, unless the engines were fired to curve its path for the transition.

The engines fired precisely on time, and the cruiser plunged through for a transition notable for inducing nausea in every single member of the crew.

At the next opportunity, Illiath guided her ship back through to report the wormhole was safe, and Admiral Denoth ordered his ships through, one at a time.

When the last ship, the precious star carrier, was through, Denoth considered his options. Go to Earth? No. Nothing of importance could be there. His mission was to examine the odd behavior of the wormhole closest to the homeworld of the humans, and he intended to prove that, too, was nothing of importance.

What he really wanted was to leave automated buoys scattered around that wormhole. When the reinforced battlegroup finally reached those coordinates, after the long, long flight, they would hear a message from Denoth, stating that he had already been there. And that, thanks to him, their flight home would be relatively quick.

The *Vortan* was last to dock with the star carrier, and it jumped away.

The event horizon in front of the *Flying Dutchman* flickered, glowed solidly for a brief moment, then blinked out in a bright flare.

"How long was it open that time?" Chang asked.

"One point two three seconds," Nagatha reported.

"It was *stable* for that long?" He wanted her to confirm. "We could have gone through?"

"Theoretically, yes. Colonel Chang, I must warn, that would be *extremely* tricky timing."

"Can we do it? Can you predict the next time it will be stable?" As the Backstop wormhole established its anchor in local spacetime, it blinked on and off in a pattern that was not quite random, but not regular enough to be reliable. Nagatha had been able to detect ahead of time when the event horizon would appear next, based on distortion effects that appeared, beginning seven minutes before the actual rip flooded the area with gamma radiation. If the pattern continued, the next brief emergence would happen within the next eighty minutes. The problem was, it could happen at any time during that period.

"My best estimate is that the effects will be detectable again within forty-three minutes. But of course, I could be off by eighteen minutes early or late."

"That *is* tricky timing. Once you detect the distortion, how accurate can you be on predicting the window of stability?"

"I wish you had not asked me that. If you plan to send the ship through, we will have a window of only thirty-four thousandths of a second to transition through."

"Just over three-hundredths of a second, then," he considered. "What do you think?" He addressed the question to the pilots.

"Sir, give us a minute to work the math?" Ray asked, and the two leaned toward each other, speaking in low voices.

"Colonel Chang," Nagatha said. "Plotting a course is relatively simple, I can-"

"Nagatha, I know you can crunch the numbers, but the *pilots* need to fly the ship. They need to tell me if it is possible or not."

"Forgive me, I did not consider that. Would it be acceptable if I were to verify the flightplan?"

"Please do that," Ray said, looking back at Chang. "Sir, we'd like to conduct several practice runs, aiming for a point in space to simulate hitting the event horizon at exactly the right time."

"Whatever you think is best," Chang said. "*I* won't be flying the ship."

Three practice runs gave the pilots confidence they could fly the ship through the temporarily-stable event horizon. Technically, the last two practice runs gave them confidence, the first run would have been a disaster if it were a real flight.

Chang called a stand-down for everyone to check equipment, get a hot meal, and rest. "Is your team ready?" He asked Smythe.

"They will be. Sir, are you sure we should not wait for *Valkyrie*?"

Chang shook his head. "They are overdue by four *days*. We don't know why, but it can't be good news. We can't wait."

"We could fly to the Broomstick wormhole," Smythe suggested. "If it is open, we can go through there."

"Flight time to Broomstick is two days, nineteen hours," Chang recited from memory. "That is too long. If it is stable, we have to assume aliens have gone through. It has been flashing like a strobe light, and it is close to an active wormhole. No. We go through *here*, prepared for a fight."

"Against aliens, or our own people?"

"Both, if necessary."

"Very well," Smythe declared, clearly relieved. He had not wanted to waste time by flying to another wormhole. "My team will be suited up and ready."

"I know. I hope you won't be needed."

"You don't have a STAR team aboard in case things go *well*, Sir."

Five heavily-shielded missiles were sent through the still-flickering Backstop wormhole, with four successfully hitting the event horizon with the exact timing needed to transition through before the wormhole briefly shut down again. It was impossible to know how many survived the trip to broadcast the *Dutchman's* authentications codes. Chang had not wanted to expend five missiles, though they were of a type designed for orbital bombardment, he was convinced of the need to avoid flying into a minefield.

"Pilot," he tugged the strap tighter across his lap. "Take us through."

The *Flying Dutchman* jumped with a precision that Nagatha could not have accomplished with the ship's original Thuranin drive system, emerging at the minimum safe distance from the event horizon that was not yet stable. Only a few puffs of thrusters were needed to adjust the course, and the ship raced toward its date with destiny. Chang held his breath as the event horizon flickered, the unnatural blue light pulsing brightly then dimming. At the last second, the engines fired at half thrust, curving the ship's flight path to plunge into the event horizon of the Backstop wormhole just before it flickered out again.

The transition was actually not the worst the crew had experienced, though no other ship in the galaxy was able to claim that distinction, because only the Merry Band of Pirates had ever *broken* an Elder wormhole. Swallowing hard to fight the rising nausea, Chang refrained from issuing unhelpful orders, as the ship and crew recovered from the distortion effects of seemingly-instantaneous transition from *there* to *here*.

"Colonel Chang," Nagatha called as the crew heard a dull, distant *thump* sound. "We just struck a nuclear device. No damage, the shields were able to deflect it before it struck the forward sensor dome. It appears that the device was a dud, or disarmed."

"Let's not take any chances. Pilot, jump option Charlie, engage when-"

"We are being hailed by a UNEF ship!" Nagatha announced.

"Belay that," Chang waited for the pilots to acknowledge, then, "Which ship?"
"It is the *Yu Qishan*. An Admiral Patel insists on speaking to you directly."

The main display was populating with data, as the ship's sensors reset. Less than a hundred thousand kilometers away was the former Kristang troop carrier starship, named for a Chinese sergeant who had given his life to prevent a lizard from blowing up the very first ship captured by the Merry Band of Pirates. Chang had been there, an event that seemed like both only yesterday, and impossibly long ago.

"Nagatha, we don't have time for a long argument about who has authority here," Chang had no intention of surrendering control of his ship to an admiral who was clueless about the situation. "Ransack the *Qishan's* databanks, please. Let me know if there is anything we need to know."

"Hmm," she did not like being put in a position where she had to guess what the human crew would consider important. "There is considerable tension and anxiety on Earth, due to us being overdue to return. So far, the tensions have not spilled over into actual conflict between the nations of UNEF. The *Qishan* was sent out here when the gamma rays of the Backstop wormhole were detected on Earth. They do suspect it is a previously-unknown Elder wormhole, but they do not suspect Skippy is involved."

"No indication that alien ships have been detected?" He was not concerned only about Maxolhx ships coming through the Broomstick wormhole. There was also a Bosphuraq cruiser unaccounted for on the Earth side of the Gateway wormhole, and the possibility of another surprise by the Kristang.

"No, Colonel. Admiral Patel is being very insistent on speaking with you, or actually to Bishop. He is demanding to know where we have been."

"Signal the *Qishan* to return to Earth as soon as possible, we will explain the situation when they arrive. Um, inform Patel that we are concerned there might be Maxolhx warships arriving soon."

"Done."

"Excellent. Pilot, jump option Sierra, that is *Sierra*," he emphasized. "Engage when ready."

Seconds later, the *Flying Dutchman* disappeared in a burst of gamma radiation.

And appeared above the far side of Saturn. While waiting for the sensors to reset, Chang contemplated the fuzzy but clearing view of the ringed planet. "It is odd. We have flown halfway across the galaxy, but we have never been *here*. I have always wanted to see Saturn." He sighed as the display became crystal clear, the spectacular rings backlit by light from the local star. From the Sun, *the* Sun.

Carried by its momentum, the *Dutchman* arced around the planet, the stealth field wrapping around the ship before it was in line-of-sight to Earth. Chang quietly admired the view, while the ship's sensors passively collected information from humanity's homeworld. The data would only be seventy minutes old. He hoped he was being overly cautious, that there was no need for his ship to conduct a stealthy recon before proceeding to humanity's home planet. He wasn't paid to be hopeful.

"Colonel Chang," Nagatha made a sound like clearing her voice. "I have located the *Ice-Cold Dagger to the Heart,* that ship is in low orbit. It is still under UNEF control. Only one of the reactors is active, I do not yet know why the- Oh. Oh, my."

"What is it?"

"Please give me a minute to verify this sensor data. It is extremely faint."

While they waited, Chang contacted Smythe, waiting with his team in dropships. "Smythe, standby. The *Dagger* doesn't appear to be compromised or hostile. I want to avoid antagonizing the authorities dirtside. Taking the *Dagger* by force would be premature."

"It would be crossing the Rubicon," Smythe agreed. "I haven't seen any data on the status of," he lowered his voice though he had his helmet sealed. "Families of the crew."

"We are working on it," Chang looked through the glass into the CIC. The crew there were monitoring sensors, not relying entirely on Nagatha to do the work for them. "Soon as we have-"

"Oh, Colonel Chang," Nagatha's voice shuddered. "I am afraid that I have horrible news to report. The sensor data is *extremely* faint, I have to rely on the residual effect on particles of the local solar wind."

"What effect?"

She did not answer immediately, instead making a sound like she was taking a deep breath before delivering the bad news. "The effect of an alien jump drive, less than four light-minutes from Earth. Colonel, the signature is unmistakably from multiple Maxolhx ships." She paused again. "They are here."

Someone was talking to him, Chang had to shake his head to focus. "One moment, Smythe," he said with a calm that was more from shock than professionalism. "Nagatha, please clarify. What sensor data are you using, and what is your level of confidence?'

"Pardon me, Colonel. I should have provided that information. As you know, Maxolhx ships can focus the gamma rays from their inbound jump, so those photons are difficult to detect unless the beam is focused in our direction. However, another effect of concentrating those gamma rays is the beam creates a trail of ionized particles, when it passes through the solar wind. This ionization is faint but distinctive. Only Maxolhx or Rindhalu ships are known to have the ability to focus their gamma ray emissions. Based on unique characteristics of the ionization, I can state with ninety-three percent confidence that these trails were created by Maxolhx ships. Specifically, one *Vengeance*-class battlecruiser, three heavy cruisers, and ten to twelve other ships that are either light cruisers or destroyers."

"Thank you," Chang had asked for the information, partly to give himself time to process the shock of enemy ships being in humanity's home star system. "Another question, please," he felt like he was hearing someone else speak. The voice he heard was unnaturally calm. "Can you estimate how long ago those ships jumped in?"

"Yes. Based on how degraded the ionization effect is, I can confidently state the jumps occurred eleven hours, eighteen minutes ago, with a seven-minute margin of error."

"Very well. Colonel Smythe, you heard all that?"

"Yes, Sir," the STAR team leader acknowledged. "The Maxolhx have been here for over eleven hours."

"Yes. I do not understand why they did not ambush us at Backstop?" Chang pondered the question. "They must see there is a new wormhole, just outside the solar system."

"The Maxolhx could have been there before we arrived," Nagatha said. "The particle density out there is orders of magnitude less than it is near Earth, an ionization trail would have been very difficult to detect, in the time available before we jumped. I must admit," she added with a catch in her voice. "I was not looking for signs of enemy ships. My focus was on the *Yu Qishan*. That was my fault."

"Nagatha, you did what I asked you to do. Any fault is mine. The Maxolhx must see the new wormhole, we must assume they investigated it. They would have seen the *Qishan*, and that it is controlled by humans. Yet, they did not seize that ship. That is, interesting."

"Sir," Smythe interrupted Chang's thoughts. "The Maxolhx arrived near Earth eleven hours ago. What are they *doing*?"

"My guess is, observing. Trying to make sense of the data they are collecting. They must be in shock," he realized the truth of that statement as he said the words. The enemy is also in shock. "They see the Kristang are not in charge of Earth, that there are no Kristang on Earth. A Kristang troop carrier is in orbit, under *human* control."

"That is not all," Nagatha rejoined the conversation. "It is unlikely that sensors on Earth, or aboard the *Dagger*, have detected the enemy. By now, the Maxolhx have almost certainly learned about Skippy. UNEF communication security is excellent by human standards, but the secret of Skippy's existence has almost fully unraveled during the time we were gone. Governments have not officially acknowledged the truth, but speculation very close to the truth is widely posted on social media."

"They are trying to decide what to do," Chang concluded. "The Maxolhx, I mean. They most likely saw the *Qishan* is controlled by humans, and they did not interfere. Instead, they went to Earth, to gather more information. I think the enemy fleet is led by a very cautious commander," he explained. "Coming here through a new wormhole, they found something completely unexpected. They have learned that humanity is being aided by an Elder AI, *and* that Elder AI is not here. That the people on Earth do not know where the AI is."

"They want to capture Skippy," Smythe said.

"Yes." Chang agreed. "That should be their first priority."

"They won't delay much longer," Smythe warned. "They must suspect that *someone* on Earth knows where Skippy is. Threatening to bombard the planet would be their next step. They may already have done that, the data we are seeing is seventy minutes old."

"We have one ship, against more than a dozen of the enemy. Recommendations?"

"We can't win a straight-up fight," Smythe stated the obvious. "Sir," he took a breath. "We could conduct a strategic retreat," he used a nice term for running away. "Take the ship to Paradise, bring aboard as many humans as we can carry."

"We could do that," Chang considered. "To what end? Unless we can find *Valkyrie*, we have no way to open the wormhole to the Beta site. We can't even get to Club Skippy."

"It is not a good option," Smythe admitted. "Sir, I don't see that we *have* any good options."

"No. We don't. *Valkyrie* is not here. Bishop would be here if he could. We must assume *Valkyrie* is disabled or destroyed. Whatever we do, we do it alone. Smythe, this is the end of all things." He looked at the pilots, at the people in the CIC who were staring at him, waiting for him to make a decision. Waiting for him to lead them. "We have been hoping to avoid this fight. Earth is defenseless." He looked into the CIC. "The Merry Band of Pirates will not run away. We fight."

The faces staring back at him reflected fear, shock, horror, and something else. There was an indominable determination.

"Let's give the enemy a bloody nose, hmm?"

A ragged cheer rang around the CIC, and the crew saluted him. He returned the gesture. "Smythe? Do you have any objections?"

"No, Sir. I would have objected if we *did* run away. We are ready."

"Nagatha, plot a jump to take us into Earth orbit."

"Yes, Colonel Chang," the ship's AI replied. "Please remember, we do not know exactly where the enemy is."

"We don't have to." Chang pressed the buttons to authorize the ship's weapons. "I am sure they will come to us."

The *Flying Dutchman* jumped in, fifty thousand kilometers from humanity's homeworld. If some of the crew diverted their attention to catch a glimpse of the beautiful blue and white marble floating behind them, that was understandable. They had not seen that world in too long a time. For the Commandos from Paradise, they had not seen their original homeworld in many years.

"Nagatha," Chang did not take his eyes off the tactical plot, which was filling in as the ship's sensors reset. "Transmit our UNEF authentication codes, and advise the *Dagger* to perform a maximum-distance jump as soon as possible. The *Dagger* should wait," for what, he asked himself? "For the outcome of the coming battle to be evident, or, for a recall signal." He did not envy the captain and crew of that captured Kristang troop carrier. The Maxolhx would surely track down and destroy that ship. "Explain that we expect an overwhelming enemy force to arrive at any moment. Send the same to UNEF Command."

"Yes, Colonel. I have scanned the *Dagger*; their jump drive is currently offline. I fear that by the time their drive coils are energized, the battle will be over. UNEF Command is calling, demanding to speak with you."

"Tell them I am busy. They will understand soon enough."

The tactical plot filled in with details, showing the *Ice-cold Dagger to the Heart*, surrounded by dropships and what appeared to be maintenance equipment. Satellites orbiting the Earth both high and low. Satellites around the Moon, none of which mattered.

What the tactical display did not show was the location of the enemy. He considered sending out an active sensor pulse. That would be seen as a challenge by the enemy.

Good.

"Nagatha, perform an active sensor scan, directed at your best guess of where the enemy fleet is located."

Aboard his flagship, the *Vengeance*-class battlecruiser *Arvoxita,* Admiral Denoth watched with astonishment as his own sensor data was updated with incoming photons. A ship had just jumped in near the planet, and exchanged messages using a human encryption scheme. This ship, too, was controlled by humans. The primitive species somehow had at least three starships! But while the other two ships were crude Kristang troop carriers, the new ship was entirely different. The forward hull had the base configuration of a Thuranin star carrier, but highly modified. Modified using components from *Maxolhx* warships, as was the entire aft engineering section.

To say he was astonished by this latest development was not accurate. Since Commander Illiath had reported the existence of a previously-unknown Elder wormhole, he had seen so many unexpected, so many impossible things, that he felt numb, unable to experience a full sense of astonishment.

Numbness did not prevent him from feeling rage, or from exercising command. "How did the humans capture drive systems from one of our ships?" he sent the thought blast over the command channel, and saw his bridge crew wince as their implants bombarded their brains with Denoth's outrage. "Analysis!"

"Admiral," The ship's AI replied. "The components are from a mixture of ships from multiple species. The primary motivators are distinctly from an *Extinction*-class battlecruiser."

"Enemy capability?"

"The enemy ship, which is apparently named after a human mythical being, might prevail in a fight with one of our destroyers. Against this ship," the AI said with a touch of pride that was dangerously close to an emotion that the Maxolhx did not allow their computers to possess. "The enemy ship is defenseless."

"Jump on my signal, Attack Formation Three. We will board and capture that ship."

"All ships report readiness."

"Jump."

Chang instinctively flinched as multiple gamma ray bursts appeared in front of the *Flying Dutchman*, the enemy not making any attempt to conceal their arrival. Nor were the enemy ships wrapped in stealth fields. They wanted him to see them and be intimidated.

It's working, he thought, and kept that thought to himself.

"Message coming in from the enemy commander," Nagatha reported. "They are demanding we surrender and prepare to be boarded."

In response, he flipped up the cover that protected the self-destruct mechanism, then replaced the cover. "Can they disable our self-destruct nukes?"

"At short range, that is a possibility," the ship's AI admitted. "I will warn you if my internal communications are being disrupted."

"I will respond, audio and video," he decided. Let the enemy see him. They would think humans are primitive and weak. "This is Colonel Chang Kong of the United Nations starship *Flying Dutchman*. To the enemy commander: you will stand down and surrender your ships."

"*FOOL!*" the sound blasted around the bridge before Nagatha damped down the volume. "You dare to threaten *us?*"

"I am the dread pirate Roberts," Chang said as people in the CIC stared wide-eyed at him. "There will be no survivors." He was surprised at himself. Why had he used an obscure pop-culture reference that the enemy, and most of the *Dutchman's* crew, would not understand?

The answer was easy: that is what Bishop would do.

Maybe he should have had T-shirts printed with 'WWBD?'. What Would Bishop Do?

No.

That only worked for Bishop.

The *Dutchman* shuddered, and Nagatha reported "Colonel, the ship is unable to move, the enemy ships are projecting a field that renders our normal-space engines inoperative."

"We weren't going anywhere," Chang muttered.

WWBD.

What *would* Bishop do in this situation?

Grossly outgunned and unable to move.

Out of options.

In a flash, Chang knew what Bishop would do, and he wholeheartedly agreed. He could not allow the *Dutchman* to be captured, for then the enemy would learn about *Valkyrie*. Unless he knew for certain the other ship had been destroyed, he held hope, and that ship was the only hope for humanity. The *Flying Dutchman's* days as a pirate ship were over. At the end of all things, when there was nothing else that could be done, the only possible move was a breathtakingly futile and stupid act of defiance.

"Nagatha, we are surrounded by a damping field?"

"Yes. Only three enemy ships are projecting damping fields, however, at this range, it is quite effective."

"We can't jump, but I wonder if we can do something else. There have been times when the ship did what Skippy described as digging a trench in spacetime, rather than creating a wormhole. We used the jump drive to slide sideways through normal space. Can we do that?"

"Ooooh, Colonel, I wish you had not asked me that question. It is possible, for *Skippy*. While I understand the theory, I am not familiar with the actual application. You must understand, the ship *might* survive such a maneuver if Skippy were here.

If I were to attempt a spacetime warp as you suggest, the ship will certainly be destroyed."

"I understand that," he knew the crew were looking at him. "Would the warp maneuver make us collide with the enemy command ship?"

"Oh," Nagatha suddenly understood, and there was dead silence on the bridge. The pilots were holding their breath. "Yes," she sighed. "I believe so. Colonel, the enemy destroyers are moving to surround us, and their commander is demanding an answer."

"How long until we can warp?"

"We are ready now."

"Then inform the enemy commander that we have an answer for them," he clenched a fist, "*right here*. Everyone," Chang got out of his chair, standing to look through the glass into the *Dutchman's* CIC. "It has been an honor serving with you."

The crew muttered responses, snapping crisp salutes. He returned the salute, then sat down. "Pilot, prepare to engage jump drive for warp. Three, two-"

CHAPTER THIRTY THREE

"-one-"

As Chang counted down the last second before the desperate war maneuver, *Valkyrie* appeared in a blinding flash of radiation across the spectrum, much more energetic than a normal jump. The battlecruiser, its radiators glowing hot, was positioned between the *Dutchman* and the enemy task force.

"*Belay that*!" Chang barked, seeing the pilots had acted on their own, lifting their hands away from their consoles. "*Valkyrie*? Joe?!"

"Hey, Kong," said a familiar voice, and Bishop's grinning face appeared on the display. "Sorry that we're late, we had to run an errand first."

"An *errand*?"

"It's a long story. Hey, did we interrupt something? I'd hate to-"

"We are very grateful for the interruption," Chang said quickly.

"You're sure? Because we can come back later, if you-"

"I'm *sure*. I hope you have a plan. Even with your ship, we are outnumbered and outgunned here."

"Outnumbered, yeah. Outgunned? Shmaybe not."

Chang gave Bishop the side-eye. "Unless you have some-"

"Trust me on this."

"Skippy," I asked. "We're connected with the enemy ships?"

"Yes," he snorted. "They are shouting 'Surrender immediately', with the usual threats of turning your home planet into a radioactive cinder, subjecting *you* to a slow and painful death, blah blah blah. It's like they're not putting any *effort* into it, you know? Ugh. They are just phoning in these threats, I am *very* disappointed."

That made me laugh. "Put me on camera, I'm ready for my close-up."

"Whew. That ugly mug of yours is enough to scare them."

"Just do it." I stood up, glancing at my tablet. On the display, the face of a Maxolhx appeared, I assumed that was the task force commander. On the tablet was my prepared speech, a short concise message created and approved mostly by Hans Chotek and the Three Stooges. It explained humanity's position, offered a mutually-beneficial compromise, and opened the door to negotiations. Though I didn't like mealy-mouthed diplomatic niceties, I had to admit this message struck a good balance, and was firm and professional.

I tossed the tablet back over my shoulder to clatter on the deck. "Hey, *shithead*. Yeah, I'm talking to you, fuzzball." That got the alien literally spitting mad. "What's that?" I cupped a hand to one ear. "It sounds like you're coughing up a hairball. I'll give you a minute."

"Um, Joe," Skippy warned. "They are opening missile launch doors."

"Joe! *Bishop*!" Chang shouted in my earpiece. "What are you *doing*?"

"*You*," the Maxolhx pointed a claw-tipped finger straight at me. "Will *die*."

"Yeah, we'll see about that." I snapped my fingers.

Denoth turned away from the imager, his fingers manipulating holographic controls to engage the ship's weapons directly. No, he took control of all weapons in the task force, aiming them at the ghost ship. A ship flown by puny *humans*. When the ghost ship appeared so suddenly, even Denoth had experienced terror. Fear of the unknown. Now, knowing that the feared ship was somehow flown by humans, he felt anger and disdain, not fear. The ghost ship had escaped from a damping field before, but not at so short a distance. It could not run, not hide, and not fight itself to freedom. Not against an entire task force.

"All ships," he announced unnecessarily, for he had taken direct control of weapons aboard every ship under his command, even that of Illiath's cruiser *Vortan*. "Target the ghost ship and-"

He froze, his claws twitching.

On the display, and through his ocular implants, the ship's sensors were showing him something extraordinary. Something totally unexpected.

Something shocking.

Something that broke through his numbness and astonished him again.

The ghost ship was deploying weapons. Docking bays had blown open, and a variety of weapons were emerging.

He recognized the profiles of those devices.

They were *Elder* weapons.

Oof.

Darn it, I guess I forgot to tell part of the story, didn't I?

Stupid brain.

I hate it when that happens.

Anyway, back while *Valkyrie* fell toward the core of the planet, Skippy's avatar was just a dimly-glowing point of light, dancing in my vision as the ship shook violently. On the main display, the symbol representing the ship was approaching the red line of crush depth, with another part of the display showing the armor plating of *Valkyrie's* nose was glowing white-hot.

Just as I closed my eyes, the avatar flared to life, blindingly bright.

"*No!*" Skippy roared. "Not this time. Fuck. *THIS!*"

Holding up a hand to shade my eyes from his painfully bright avatar, I squinted at him. "Skippy! Get *out* of here!"

"No. *No!* Joe, I don't care. I am *not* abandoning my friends again. *Never* again. We are going through this together."

Damn it, we didn't have time for this shit. "Nice gesture, Skippy, but it won't do any-"

"Joe," he cut me off. "Do you have a flat-head screwdriver?"

"A *screwdrive*- Why do you need a-"

"Because, Joe," in one of his hands appeared a shiny silver can, like a one-gallon can of house paint. "I've got a fresh can of *Whoop-Ass*, and I need to pop it open."

What the hell, I figured, why not? Making a fist, I held out a hand and opened it, pretending to toss something to him.

A holographic screwdriver appeared in his other hand, and he worked it around the lid of the can, prying it open while he muttered to himself. "You try to be a good guy, you *try* to be polite and reasonable, you *try* to follow the rules, but what does it get you? Nothing. Absolutely *nothing!*" The imaginary lid popped off and a bright light burst forth from the can. "So, fine. You want to play it that way? *NO MORE MISTER NICE GUY!*"

The avatar disappeared.

The ship was slammed to one side. If my chair didn't have a suspensor field, it would have snapped my neck.

The main display switched to a schematic of the ship, highlighting a section of the ship's portside hull.

"Sir," Chen shouted. "Hull breach portside between frames thirty-seven and forty-one! That," she turned to me, her face reflecting horror. "That section includes Skippy's escape pod."

Shit.

He was gone.

Whatever Skippy tried to do, he had failed.

Thrown off balance, the ship lurched to one side, the nose spinning around so we were falling belly-first. The schematic showed armor plates tearing loose, like a giant was pulling a zipper along the belly of the ship.

Then it got *really* violent.

I lost track of what happened, my brain was being jostled so badly, I couldn't get my thoughts in order. At some point, *Valkyrie* flipped on its back, then was falling tail-first. We were totally out of control, the pilots unable to understand what was going on at any one moment. All the thrusters were offline anyway.

It stopped.

It just *stopped.*

The ship was motionless. According to the display, we were hanging below the crush-depth limit, yet the ship was intact. Mostly. I was grading on a curve. There was a gaping hole in the forward portside, automated damage control was dealing with it.

"What," I gasped, choking, disoriented. "What's happening?"

"Your guess is as good as mine," Reed said from the pilot couch, holding up both hands. Whatever had halted the ship's fall, it was out of the pilot's control.

"Shields?" I asked, blinking and squinting at the display.

"Shields are, like, not working, man," Bilby reported. "Uh, like, we turned off the generators, remember?"

"Yeah," I responded. Did I remember that? Maybe. "Can we turn them on?"

"I dunno, Dude. We're kinda fine without them now, you know? Might need the power for something else. Two of the reactors got shaken up real bad, I stopped the fuel flow. They'll be ready, probably, after I finish inspecting for major damage. Oh, hey. Do you think we should try the engines again?"

"Not yet!" I said quickly. "Don't do anything until we know what is happening. What *is* happening?"

"I have, like, no idea. This is totally blowing my mind."

Clenching a fist, I forced myself to remain calm. "Bilby, tell me the facts you know."

"Um, sure. If you want me to guess, I think we're in some kind of bubble. A bubble of low pressure. The air outside is the same composition as this planet's atmosphere, there's just, like, *less* of it, you know?"

"Why aren't we falling? Are we caught in an antigravity current?"

"Nope, no. I think it's some kind of suspensor field. It's not pulling from above, or pushing from below, it's all around us. Kind of *mystical*. It's freaking me out. Oh, hey, one more thing. Cargo Bay Twelve had a massive radiation spike, just as we stopped falling."

"Any idea what caused it?"

"No, man. I'm totally blind in there. That is *not* cool."

"Not cool at all," I agreed. "Bilby, can you get some bots over to see what happened to Skippy's escape pod? Check if- Hey. Can you ping him?"

"I've been doing that. He's not answering. I'm not getting an answer from whoever controls this place, so that's good, right?"

"Maybe." Sometimes, Bilby's chill surfer persona made me forget that he was a super-smart AI.

"Sir?" Simms got my attention. "We can't stay here forever."

"Yeah. Hmm. Dropships are not an option, they would be crushed once they fly outside the bubble. Bilby, how big is this bubble around us?"

"About seven kilometers, it's a perfect sphere. I would expect it to be flattened a bit on the top and bottom, from the pressure gradient, but it's not. Um, the bubble is also *thick*, about a hundred sixty meters from the inner wall to where it fades away outside."

Simms and I looked at each other, both considering our options. She spoke first. "Can we launch a probe drone?"

"Wow," Bilby said. "Don't know if that's a good idea, like, what if the drone pops the bubble?"

I agreed with Simms. "We have to do *something*. Launch a probe and fly it super slow, can you do that? If the bubble degrades when the probe contacts it, bring it back here."

"Ok, Dude. Give me a minute to find a probe I can trust, everything got shaken up while we were falling."

"Like my head," Simms rubbed her temples. "Sir, we shouldn't use the engines just yet, but the primary thrusters use the same technology. I suggest we try moving the ship a couple meters, see if the bubble moves with us?"

"Good idea. Bilby, do you have any objections to trying the thrusters?"

"No, man, but be *gentle*. They got shaken up too."

"Pilot, move us-"

"Ugh," Skippy's avatar shimmered to life, or something like that. It was dim and hazy, and the oversized hat was dented and torn and stained. The squashed crown of the hat had what looked like *bullet* holes in it. "Please do *not* do that," he asked in a low, weary voice.

"Skippy!" I tried to stand, forgetting the straps holding me into the seat. "You're *alive*!"

"Large and in charge, Baby," he drawled like he'd taken way too many sleeping pills. "Don't screw with the bubble, please. I'm still establishing control over the native systems down here."

"Down *here*? Where is 'here'? Where are you? Your man cave exploded."

"Yeah, sorry about that. I kind of lost containment, in a minor, non-catastrophic way. Oh no! I just realized all my precious artwork is gone! My Elvis belt!" He sobbed.

"Your canister is gone?" I asked fearfully.

"No. It got damaged, but right now it is rolling around on the deck of Cargo Bay Twelve. It is hot, like, *hot*. About four thousand degrees. Also radioactive. Whew! You do *not* want to go in there without a big can of air freshener, if you know what I mean. Best for anyone not to go aft of Frame One Eighteen for a while. Don't worry, my canister won't melt through the deck plates, and it is cooling down. The radiation is all short half-life stuff, it will disperse soon. We're not using that part of the ship for anything right now, it's no great loss."

"We will do whatever you think best," I saw that Simms was tapping on her control pad, sealing off that part of the ship. "Skippy, what happened? Did you persuade the entity in charge here to cooperate with you?"

"No. I *tried* that. Nice guys finish last out here, Joe. We had a knock-down, drag-out fight. Basically, I *beat* the thing to death. It wasn't pretty, I will be recovering for weeks. That is weeks in slow monkey time."

"You beat- How?"

"Not with my *fists*, dumdum," he scoffed, and it was good to hear that a bit of the old Skippy was still in there. "I burned it out, by pouring uncontrolled energy into its matrix. The thing is *fried*, Joe. I'm having to control the subsidiary systems down here by myself. Um, this is going to be a bit of a problem."

"How?"

"I can't leave here, until I can stabilize the gravity-dispersal field, or retract it. Unless it is retracted very slowly and carefully, it could disrupt the orbits of all planets in this system. Avalon could become uninhabitable."

"Shit. Can you-"

"I am fairly confident the subsidiary system that controls the gravitic dispersal field will be able to operate on its own soon, but it would be safer to allow it to retract and be deactivated. Slowly and carefully, of course."

"Whatever you think best. Uh, what do you mean by 'soon'? We can't stay here, we have to get back to Earth to begin the evac operation."

"Um, yeah, about that. Heh heh."

"Shit." Everyone on the bridge had the same horrified expression.

My mouth was frozen. Simms had the courage to ask the question. "Avalon can't be our Beta site?"

"Huh? No. Or yes. I mean, there is *no* reason that Avalon can't be a perfectly nice place to live, if you like isolation, boredom and deprivation."

"That is better than *extinction*," Simms retorted. She hated it when Skippy was flippant about a serious subject.

"Oh, sure. Of course," he stammered nervously.

My mouth was working again. "If this place is not a threat to Avalon, then why can't we proceed with the evac?"

"Well, Joe, I guess you could, if you want to. It's just, I found something *interesting* down here."

Again, I shared a skeptical look with Simms. For the Merry Band of Pirates, 'interesting' was rarely a good thing. "What *is* this place? Why did the Elders hide it?"

"They hid it because it's an *arsenal*, Joe. There is a big cache of Elder weapons down here."

The crew gasped in shock.

I had a different reaction.

I pumped a fist and breathed "Score!"

Simms stared at me, stunned. "Holy sh- You *expected* to find Elder weapons here?"

"Well," I shrugged as casually as I could. "It was more like I *hoped* they would be here. I couldn't think of any other reason why the Elders would conceal an entire planet. Plus lock a wormhole with a password."

"Oh, you son of a-" her stare had turned to a glare. "You- *Why* didn't you tell me?"

"I figured you would say 'No' to coming here," I answered with a shrug.

"I would have said 'Yes'. *Hell* yes!"

"Uh-"

"My objection was about coming out here to poke this place with a stick. If I had known there might be an arsenal of super-weapons, I would have *walked* here if I had to."

"Uh-" I was saying that a lot.

"Sir. You need to trust your crew." She was hurt, like, *really* hurt.

"Sorry," I hung my head. "It's just, I didn't know for sure. Skippy, did you know? Or suspect?"

"I had no clue," he admitted. "Is *that* why we really came here?"

"Yes. You said our probability set for survival is narrowing, and you're right. Bringing a couple hundred people out here just before Earth is obliterated is not a plan, it's giving up. Fuck that. We need a Hail Mary. We had nothing much to lose, so I figured this was worth a shot. Please tell me two things. Three, actually."

"Ok, shoot," he said, as his beat-up admiral's hat bobbed back and forth.

"The ship can get out of here? And fly?"

"Yes and yes. Was that two questions?"

"One, actually. You can lift us out of here, in this bubble?"

"Absolutely."

"OK, then here is Question Two: can we get access to the Elder weapons?"

"Whew. Are you sure you want to, Joe?"

"Hell yes."

"The answer is yes. I can even have them delivered to low orbit. Shipping is free, if you have an Elder Prime account?"

"How about if I sign up for a three-year Weapons of Mass Destruction subscription plan?"

"That will do," he chuckled. It was good to hear him laugh again. "What is your last question?"

I took a breath, knowing every eye on the bridge was focused on me. "Can we *use* those weapons?"

"Whoa. Dude," Skippy gasped. "Seriously?"

"I have never been more serious."

"Um, yeah. The triggering mechanism is built in, and I have the authorization codes. Wow. Now can *I* ask a question?"

"Sure?"

"Have you completely *lost* your freakin' mind? You do realize that if you trigger any of those weapons, Sentinels will stomp Earth into tiny little pieces?"

"I realize that, Skippy. In fact, I am *counting* on it."

"Holy shit. The brain damage must have been worse than-"

"My brain is working just fine, Skippy. Never better. Can you move the bubble, and the ship, while your canister is aboard?"

"No, but I have a workaround for that. I have tied the bubble control system to the pilot console. You give the command, and the bubble will pull you up to where *Valkyrie's* engines can take over."

"Outstanding. Fireball, get us moving."

"Um, OK," Reed said. "I see it. All I do it press this button?" She addressed the question to Skippy.

"You got it."

On the display, the bubble began rising. Other than a faint vibration I felt with my feet, there was no sensation of movement. "Skippy, however many of those weapons we can fit aboard *Valkyrie*, bring them up to low orbit. Leave the rest in the armory, or whatever it is down there."

"We're going to Earth, Sir?" Simms asked.

"Yes." I relaxed back in my chair. Truly *relaxed*, like, for the first time since Columbus Day. "But first, we need to run a few errands on the way home."

We ran errands as quickly as we could, not even stopping at the gift shops along the way. I promised everyone a snow globe later, if we survived. After the last stop, we pointed *Valkyrie's* nose toward Earth and began jumping. Technically, we pointed the ship's nose *away* from Earth, because the closest wormhole was in the opposite direction.

"Joe," Skippy whispered in my earpiece as I sat in my command chair. "We need to talk."

"What is it?" I said aloud. "And talk to me on the bridge speakers, please."

"OK," his voice rang out too loud, startling the crew. They glanced at me, suspicious because clearly, they were hearing a conversation that was in progress. "What is it?'

"The jump engines. All this jumping has been too much strain. We need to slow down."

"We *can't* slow down. Damn it, we may already be too late." Our errands were necessary, we may not have done enough. But we might also have been away too long. Now that we were headed home, I was second-guessing myself. Would we return to Earth, only to find a radioactive cinder?

"The engines need maintenance."

"Conduct running repairs."

"I've been *doing* that. It's not enough. Have you felt the vibration when we jump?"

"Yes."

"That won't get better. The coils, the reactors, everything is overheated and wearing out. This ship is a battlecruiser, not a star carrier. It was not designed to jump continuously for such a long time."

"This ship is a battlecruiser that *you* rebuilt, with a drive you modified. It can take the strain a little longer."

"Joe, you're not listening to me. The ship could fly apart."

"*Fly her apart,* then!" I thumped a fist on the armrest. "Skippy, I am serious. Forget stealth and the shields and everything other than speed. We need to get home, *now.*"

He sighed. "I will do my best. That's all I can promise."

"That's all I can ask. Can we go to a hundred and seven percent on the reactors?"

"The reactors have been running at a hundred *twelve* percent since we left Avalon," he reminded me. "Any hotter, and the radiators will *melt.*"

"Understood. Can you vent reactor plasma for cooling?"

"Um, Jeez, I guess we could do that, but that would consume an enormous amount of fuel."

"We have plenty of fuel. Do it."

If we didn't get to Earth soon, it would all be for nothing.

CHAPTER THIRTY FOUR

"Do they see the weapons, Skippy?" I asked, knowing our Elder devices had deployed outside the hull, in clear view of the Maxolhx task force.

"Unless they are completely freakin' blind, they must see them."

"Do the Maxolhx know what they are?"

"Based on the hysterical chatter between ships, I would say the answer to that question is a solid 'Yes'." he chuckled. "Hee hee, I think the kitties aboard those ships will all need a change of underpants soon."

"Great." With a gesture, I turned the bridge microphone back on and waved at my counterpart. "Sur-*prise*, shithead."

Aboard the *Flying Dutchman*, Colonel Chang was riveted to his chair in shock. He exhaled, not having realized he was holding his breath. "What is he *doing*?! He can't-"

"Sir?" Adams shouted from the CIC. Her grin stretched her face from ear to ear. "That is *Joe Bishop* over there. Cool it. He's on a roll."

Chang shook his head ruefully. "If the situation calls for a truly futile and stupid gesture," he muttered, "Bishop is the one to do it."

The first thing Admiral Denoth did was to carefully watch his trembling fingers safe and lock out every weapon aboard every ship in the task force. Actually, that was the second thing he did. The *first* thing he did was rather embarrassing, and he wanted to forget about it. Which he could do, right after he changed his underwear.

Later.

He had a crisis to manage.

Unexpectedly, it was the worst crisis in the long history of his people.

The treacherous Rindhalu having Elder weapons was bad enough. Those spiders had used Elder weapons to attack the Maxolhx, then lied and blamed the Maxolhx when Sentinels appeared from nowhere and stomped both species almost back to the Stone Age.

The Rindhalu had learned their lesson, they had never again employed their fearsome arsenal of Elder weapons, nor had the Maxolhx. Neither side had even threatened to use their stolen weapons, they didn't have to. Each side knew the other side had the weapons. Both sides had come to the conclusion that using Elder weapons, was the same as pointing a gun at their own heads and pulling the trigger. Certain suicide.

The Rindhalu could be trusted never to actually use their hellish cache of advanced weapons.

Humans were different.

They were young and primitive and foolish and-

Denoth smiled, looking up at the being who was jabbering meaningless words at him from the ghost ship. "All ships," he transmitted through his cranial implant. "On my signal, disperse at maximum acceleration. Get to jump distance and perform a maximum-distance jump. Meet at Rendezvous Point Three." He then switched to speaking in primitive style, with his voicebox.

The Maxolhx commander was ignoring me, which was fine by me. While he was busy doing something else, he wasn't shooting at us.

"Um, Joe," Skippy said nervously. "I think he may be calling your bluff."

Hiding my mouth behind a hand, I allowed myself a stress-relieving "*Shit!*" Then I straightened up, as the alien commander looked at me and spoke.

"Human, I do not know how you captured one of our warships, but you *will* return it to us."

"Let's not, and pretend I did?"

"No," his face screwed up with anger. "You will not speak to me in such a disrespectful manner."

"Well, I already am, so-"

"You will pay for your crimes. Both against my people, and for acquiring banned weapons. Your species should not possess such weapons, they are extremely dangerous. You will surrender your ship, now."

"Hey, pal, in case you're not keeping up with current events, *I'm* the one with the Elder weapons. *I* will be making the demands here."

"Or what, human?" It was his turn to smile. "You cannot *use* those weapons. They are useless to you. No, not entirely useless. I will allow you to use them, to bargain for your life."

I frowned, furrowing my brow, certain he had software to interpret human body language for him. "These weapons are dangerous, that's for sure."

"Stupid primitives like yourself should not play with such deadly toys."

"Gosh, well. You're right. Nobody should play with these weapons. It's a good thing that, before we got here," I took a breath. "We planted Elder weapons in half a dozen major star systems, of your people *and* the Rindhalu. Skippy, send the data files, to prove we went to all those places."

"You *what?*" The enemy screeched. "You cannot-"

"Hey, *furball*. Shut your mouth while I'm talking. Yeah, that's right, you heard me. There are weapons of unimaginable destructive power in *seven* of your major star systems, and six of the Rindhalu. Triggering those weapons will summon devices of even greater destructive power, to wipe you and the spiders from existence. We have a critical mass of weapons, in strategic locations, to ensure no part of this galaxy would survive. The weapons are stealthed, in case you are thinking of looking for them, and they have proximity sensors, in case you are thinking of screwing with them. So," I took another breath. "Any questions?"

"Use of such weapons would kill *your own* people also, human!"

"Yeah. That part sucks, but, what can you do, huh?" I shrugged. "The principle is called Mutual. Assured. *Destruction*. Look it up, if you don't understand. It has kept the peace between you and the spiders. Now it can keep the peace between the three of us."

"You can't *do* this."

"I already did. Oh, hey," I snapped my fingers again, this time only being dramatic. "Gosh, heh heh, this is kind of embarrassing. I *totally* forgot to tell you. Those weapons in the star systems of you and the spiders? They are already authorized to fire, and on *timers*. If the timers expire, then," I put my hands together and flung my fingers apart. "Things go *boom*, you get it? We will need to fly back out regularly to reset the timers, which we can't do if we're dead, in case you haven't figured that out yet. Let me break it down Barney style for you," I said, wondering how that phrase would translate into his language. "From now on, the survival of *your* miserable species depends on the survival of *my* species," I tapped my chest. "Got it?"

He just gaped at me, his brain having blown a circuit.

"Hey *SHITHEAD!* I asked you a question." I was done playing around. "Do. You. Understand. The. Situation?"

There was a pause while he was motionless, making me think the video feed had frozen. Before I could repeat my question, he slowly replied. "Yes."

"Yes? *Yes*, you understand that your ships are to withdraw, and not come here ever again?"

"Yes," the alien still spoke slowly. I wondered if other kitties were frantically speaking to him through an implant. Also, I wondered if he could make his subordinates shut the hell up and let him think. "May I suggest that we need further talks on this subject? To, to establish protocols for future interactions, to assure there are no unfortunate incidents that could lead to widespread destruction?"

From behind me, Simms whispered "That is actually a good idea, Sir."

I nodded. "We agree. *We* will contact *you* to set up a meeting."

"How will-"

"In case this is a breaking news flash to you, we cracked your quantum interchanger system, *and* we have hacked the manual access procedure for your relay stations, so we can leave a message for you anytime. We can also *read* your messages anytime we want," I lied. "In case you are thinking of trying to pull any sneaky shit on us. Do you understand *that*?"

From the expression on his face, he had at least been hoping to pull some sneaky shit, even if he didn't yet have a plan to do it. "I do understand."

"Outstanding." With one hand, I made a shooing gesture, like when you want someone to go away. "You cute little kitties run along now. I'm sure your crews are anticipating a fun-filled road trip back home. Sorry you didn't have time to visit the gift shops on Earth, but if we meet again, I'll see if I can bring a box of snow globes or a nice fruit basket. Or, you know," I smiled again. "Maybe a tactical *nuke* to shove up your ass."

When the alien task force jumped away twenty-five seconds later, my knees nearly collapsed. Simms actually got out of her chair to steady me, but I can say I made it back to my chair without too much embarrassment. In instant later, Chang's face appeared in the display. "Could you please tell me, what the hell was *that*?!" His voice was an octave higher than usual, "Are those really *Elder* weapons?"

"Yeah, they're real."

"Where did you get them? *How* did you get them?"

"It is a *long* story," I said, suddenly too tired to talk.

"Joe, I'm a Pirate. *Everything* we do is a long story."

"This one is *really* long. Skippy is sending all our data to Nagatha."

"All right then, later." He shook his head. "Can I ask, does the story involve you buying those weapons by cashing in a huge stack of Taco Bell gift cards?"

"No," he made me laugh, and I didn't feel so tired.

"Was any of that bullshit you said real? About the timers and all that?"

"*All* of it was real. Sorry that we were delayed getting here, we had to fly all over the freakin' galaxy, dropping off those Elder weapons. They have stealth, timers and proximity sensors, just like I said."

"Holy *shit*, Joe."

"Yeah, Kong. Holy shit is right."

"Mutual assured destruction," he pursed his lips and nodded thoughtfully. "That is a dangerous game."

"I didn't see a good alternative."

"We can make it work," he said. "We have to."

"I hope so. I got the idea from talking with Friedlander. He suggested we use Avalon to build a fleet of ships equipped with Elder technology, and use their weapons to get payback for Earth. I told him that wouldn't work, it would only bring Sentinels to wipe us out."

"I can't wait to hear the full story. What's next?"

"Uh, oh boy. Uh, you stay here. Make sure nobody dirtside does anything stupid. Like, fighting each other down there. Do *not* give up control of the ship, not until we get back. Oh, we will send Bert and Ernie over to the *Dutchman*. You bring them down to Earth, give our psychologists something to work with. Tell UNEF that we can still bring groups of people to the Beta site, it would be good to have a backup anyway. But there doesn't need to be any kind of a mad rush about it, not anymore."

"Ooh, Joe," Skippy broke into the conversation. "Can we-"

"The answer about your stupid survival game show is *no*, you little shithead. Ah," I sighed. "Sorry. How about this? If the monkeys down there like the idea, go for it."

"Ha! This is gonna be *great*! You'll see! Joe, what are the odds that the idiot monkeys on your world will *not* like my game show?"

"Crap. You're right."

"Joe?" Chang prompted me. "If I'm staying here, where are you going?"

"I need to run another errand. I won't be long, I promise."

"It's that important? Your crew would appreciate shore leave, at home."

"It *is* that important. Skippy, give the details to Nagatha. But you're right, Kong. I'll ask the crew, anyone who really wants to leave *Valkyrie* can go dirtside."

Chang's image disappeared, as he had a lot to do, and a short time to do it. Simms stood up. "Sir?" She arched an eyebrow at me. "A word?"

I stood up and jerked a thumb at the chair behind me. "Reed, you have the conn."

When we walked into my office, Simms hit the control to slide the door closed. "Listen, XO," I anticipated her yelling at me, for very good reasons. "I should have told-"

"Before we get into that," she said, making it clear we *were* getting into that subject later. "We just learned something important, if you don't realize it."

"Like what?" I gestured for her to sit.

"If Skippy has a time bomb inside him, it didn't work."

His avatar appeared instantly, scowling at Simms. "How do you figure that?"

"We planted Elder weapons all over the galaxy, including a cache of them here aboard the ship. They didn't trigger. Think about it," she looked at Skippy, then at me. "If the AI bad guys still want to wipe out all intelligent life in the galaxy, all your subconscious had to do was trigger those weapons. Sentinels would have killed *everyone*. That didn't happen."

"Wowza," Skippy took off his admiral's hat and rubbed his head. "I can't argue with that logic. Joe?"

"I can't argue either," I agreed, thinking that now I was pissed at Simms. She had been concerned that Skippy's subconscious would trigger the weapons, and she hadn't said anything to me? Hey, jackass, I told myself. What goes around, comes around. I glanced at my phone. "We're on the clock here," I reminded her. "The short version is, Skippy bailed on us at Rikers, because he thought he needed to fly off and fight the bad guys by himself, instead of wasting time with us lowly monkeys."

"But he came back?"

Holding up a finger toward Skippy, so he didn't get into a long explanation, I nodded. "He still thinks he has a responsibility to the entire galaxy, but he decided that he couldn't abandon his friends. Skippy can give you all the details you want, later. Are we cool?"

"Sir, all I care about is, are you holding any more secrets from us?"

It took a moment to search my memory. Over the years, I had kept a lot of secrets, almost all of them were OBE by that point. "No," I shook my head. "I don't think so."

"That's good enough for me. You and I," she wagged a finger at Skippy. "*Will* talk later."

"Oh, crap. Do I have to?"

"Yes," I said. "It's best to get it over with soon."

"Ugh. This is gonna *suuuuck*," he groaned.

"You have no idea. Because after you tell Simms the full story, you are going to tell everyone. Including Margaret Adams."

"Please no. Anything but that."

It was my turn to wag a finger at him. "You should have considered that when you flew off to be the big hero."

"OK, OK. Jeez, maybe I'll get lucky and there *is* a time bomb inside me. You two go do, whatever it is monkeys do, and we will-"

"Wait. Simms," I said, as she was getting up from her chair. "One more thing. The Elder weapons aboard *Valkyrie*. We can't keep them aboard the ship."

Simms looked even more surprised than Skippy. "We can't?" She asked.

"No. We can't actually *use* the damned things. As long as they are aboard the ship, *Valkyrie* will be the biggest target in the galaxy."

"The senior species wouldn't dare attack us," Simms said. "Besides, they already have Elder weapons."

"It's not *them* I'm worried about. A second-tier species like the Thuranin might throw their entire fleet against us, to get the weapons. Then there would be four groups in the galaxy with weapons of mass destruction. And our survival would depend on the *least* stable of the other three. We can't risk that."

Simms and Skippy looked at each other, then at me. She asked the question. "Where do you suggest we store them? On Earth?"

"No. We also can't risk a bunch of filthy monkeys getting their hands on the weapons," I said with a tight grin. "Skippy, do you have a suggestion?"

"Sure, Joe," he was already snickering so hard, he could barely talk. "How about we stash them in, Ur-*Anus*?"

"Very funny," I scowled at him.

"Oh," he laughed. "Whew. That joke is *never* getting old."

"OK, fine. We'll do it my way. I want to jump the ship out to the Oort Cloud, or the scattered disc of the Kuiper Belt, or wherever. Some place with anonymous chunks of ice and rock. When we get there, we launch the weapons, and you guide them to hide inside a comet, something like that. I do *not* want to know where the weapons are. If I ever get captured again, I can't reveal info I don't have."

"Smart," Simms agreed. "Can you do that, Skippy?"

"I dunno. You want only me to know where the weapons are?" He asked. "In that case, the weapons must be flown autonomously, I will need to program in the guidance before we jump. Otherwise, Bilby will know where they are."

"Hey, man," Bilby interjected. "I'm, like, cool."

Once again, I regretted that the ship's AI sounded like a slacker. "It's not that we don't trust you," I explained. "You shouldn't-"

"No, Colonel Dude. I meant, I am cool with *not* knowing where those things are. They scare me, man. I don't like having those death machines aboard the ship, you know?"

"I know, Bilby. We're agreed, then?"

Simms pursed her lips. "UNEF Command won't like not having control of those weapons, Sir."

"Yeah, well," I leaned back in the chair. "When we come back to Earth again, there are a lot of things UNEF Command, and the US Army, won't like. I'll nuke that bridge when we get to it."

Simms kind of gave me the side-eye, like she wanted to say something about me mixing metaphors, but she wasn't sure I was serious.

"Don't worry, XO," I tried to assure her. "My orders don't say anything about Elder weapons, so I am not committing insubordination by not handing over the keys. Not yet, anyway. Uh, do *your* orders say anything about-"

"No. Not even close. If that is all, Sir?" She perched on the edge of the chair.

"Wait," Skippy pleaded. "One thing before you go. Joe, you don't want to know where I plan to hide the weapons. But, do you want me to tell you, if you ask?"

"You mean later?" I asked.

"Yes."

"Uh, yeah, I guess. I mean, if we need them."

"Great. One problem; how am I supposed to know if you are being coerced to ask for the weapons?"

"Uh, well, if you see a gun pointed at my head-"

"I'm *trying* to be serious, Joe."

"OK. Sorry. How about we have a code word? If I say the code word, you tell me where the weapons are, or recall them to the ship or whatever. Will that work?"

"Um, sure. Huh, this is cool. I have never done this sort of secret agent work."

"Do not get carried away," I jabbed a finger at him.

"What is the code word?"

Simms stood up. "I will wait outside, Sir."

"No. XO, I can't be the only human with access to those weapons. You and Chang need access to the code word."

She looked queasy, like she was going to ralph. The color drained from her face. "What if I don't *want* that kind of responsibility?"

"You should have thought about that, before you pinned on that shiny oak leaf cluster," I pointed to the silver lieutenant colonel's insignia on her uniform.

"Shit," she sighed. "What is the code word?"

"Uh. Hmm. How about 'Fluffernutter'?"

She gave me The Look. You know what I mean. "The fate of the galaxy could depend on one of us saying '*Fluffernutter*'?"

"Well, when you say it like that, it just sounds stupid."

She stared at me.

"OK," I tried again. "Let me think. It has to be a word that none of us would say in normal conversation."

"Then," she shrugged. "Fluffernutter is perfect. Trust me, neither Chang nor I would ever say that."

"Deal," I said before she changed her mind. "Skippy, is there anything you need from us?"

"No, except we had planned to jump directly out to Backstop, and now you need to tell the pilots not to select that jump option. The correct option is now 'Hotel'. Begins with the letter 'H', as in, '*Holy shit* I cannot believe we are doing this'."

"Me neither, Skippy. Me neither."

Of our depleted crew, only Petty Officer Schmidt and Sergeant-chef Giselle Montand requested to leave the ship. They both had wives who were pregnant when we left Earth, on what was supposed to have been a quick trip to search for a Beta site. Schmidt and Montand flew over to the *Dutchman* on a dropship, with my blessing, and I meant that sincerely. The errand we were going to run was important, but we didn't need the entire crew. In fact, having two additional empty cabins would help. We also did a bit of transferring people between our two ships, so overall, *Valkyrie's* crew complement decreased by three, even with Smythe and five members of his STAR team coming back aboard. And several crates of food transferred from the *Dutchman*, because they would soon be able to replenish their supplies from the bounty of Earth. Bert and Ernie went to the *Dutchman*, eventually to be brought down to Earth.

Oh, FYI, Gunnery Sergeant Adams was back aboard my ship. Not that, you know, I cared. Just thought I would mention that.

Ninety minutes after *Valkyrie* jumped in, with me having ignored each and every increasingly strident message from UNEF, we jumped away on an urgent errand.

I hoped we weren't too late.

CHAPTER THIRTY FIVE

"Surgun Jates?" Emily Perkins said with a catch in her throat. The Verd-kris soldier was wearing his dress uniform, a jade green with bright blue and gold piping. The outfit would have been considered gaudy by human standards, at least by the standards of the United States military. She was wearing a standard US Army Field Uniform, modeled after the current issue when the Expeditionary Force left Earth, so long ago. Her uniform was well-worn, with creases and stains that didn't stand out from the camouflage pattern. There wasn't time to clean the fabric, and it didn't matter anyway. Maybe UNEF-HQ would have preferred her to be wearing a dress uniform when she met the aliens, as she would be representing all of humanity, but her formal clothing was packed away aboard the *Sure Thing*, and that ship had jumped away at the first sign of trouble.

That was unfair. The crew of the *Sure Thing* had jumped away when they detected trouble they couldn't handle, could not reasonably be expected to handle. Their ship was an old star carrier with minimal offensive weapons, Perkins did not fault Captain Gumbano for doing the only sensible thing. Even if the *Sure Thing* had been available, she could not have gone aboard to escape the peril facing the Alien Legion.

It was her fault, her responsibility. She was not going to run away and leave her people to suffer the consequences.

"Thank you for seeing us off," she added.

"I am not here to watch you depart," Jates replied stiffly. "I am going with you."

"What? No. You don't have to. They only listed the Mavericks, my team."

"I am not a member of our team?"

"Of course you," even on the alien face, she could see the hurt in the crinkles around his eyes. "You are to *me*. The list does not include-"

"It should," he insisted. "Cadet Dandurff is going with you."

"His name," she winced, salty tears stinging her eyes. "Was on the list. Yours was not, for whatever reason. Surgun, you do not have to go with us."

"I do not *have* to," he agreed. "Colonel Perkins," he came to attention and saluted her. "Request permission to join you. It would be an honor to represent my people."

The Kristang were a stubborn species, the Verd-kris even more so than their oppressive cousins. In Emily Perkins's admittedly limited experience, Surgun Jates was a special case of stubbornness. He would not have donned his formal uniform and approached her without first gaining permission from his own people. To deny him now would be to shame all Verd-kris, and cause serious harm to their relations with humans.

Not that any of that mattered now.

"Please, Colonel," he added in a whisper. "We are all dead anyway, I think. I would rather die confronting them up there," he pointed a claw-tipped finger to the sky. "Than waiting down here for weapons to drop on our heads."

She nodded, and drew her shoulders back. "Surgun, it would be an honor to have you join us."

The skin around his eyes tightened, and his lips drew back to expose part of his fangs. "It would have been nice to take some of them with us."

"It would," she agreed. "Maybe later."

He nodded curtly, his expression grim. They both knew there wouldn't be a later, not for them.

Irene lifted her hands away from the console as their Dodo cleared the atmosphere. "That's it, Ma'am," she announced, her hands shaking slightly. From the right-hand seat, Derek reached over to clasp her hand in his. "They have control from here."

"Don't touch the controls," Perkins spoke without needing to, speaking because she felt she had to say *something*.

Derek pointed at the consoles, which had gone blank. "We are locked out anyway."

She hit the button to release the straps that held her into the jumpseat on the rear bulkhead of the Dodo's cockpit. The view out the forward displays showed the curve of the planet below, and two of the three small moons. Climbing into orbit had carried the dropship around the night side of the world, dawn was approaching, evident from the bright glow on the horizon. The starfield glittered, none of the constellations familiar, as Earth was more than three thousand lightyears away. None of those points of light represented starships, the Ruhar fleet had jumped away as soon as they received permission. It wasn't their fight, and it would not have been a *fight* if the Ruhar resisted. It would have been a slaughter.

It was a shame. The Alien Legion operation on the planet Tohmaran had begun almost flawlessly, a fact that had surprised everyone involved. The operation had the Alien Legion working for the Swift Arrow clan of the Kristang, to take a strategically important world away from the rival Bright Claws clan. The Swift Arrows had begun the civil war in a bad position, stretched thin in terms of military power and financial resources. In the years prior to the most recent of their regularly-scheduled civil conflicts, the Swift Arrows had been overly ambitious, taking and attempting to take worlds like Paradise. On paper, their alliances had been wide-spread and strong, but once the fighting started, most of their allies had seen the weakness of the Swift Arrows and split away. They had also lost several important minor clans within their coalition, and the alliances those minor clans took with them. At the time they contracted the Alien Legion, the Swift Arrows were in serious trouble, and had been in negotiations with the Black Trees to form an alliance. An alliance that would have boosted the power of the Black Trees, and possibly shortened the war.

Which is why Emily Perkins had suggested, and the Ruhar government approved, the operation on Tohmaran. With fresh combat power available, the Swift Arrows had ended their negotiations with the Black Trees and instead, attacked the Bright Claws clan. Taking Tohmaran would be the first step in a threeohased plan to restore the Swift Arrows to the top rank of major clans, ensuring the fighting would go on for years.

Everything was going to plan, until the plans all got thrown out the window when a pair of Maxolhx cruisers jumped into orbit.

Perkins had been in the middle of a conference call between the leader of the Swift Arrow forces, General Ross, and the commander of the Ruhar Third Fleet, when they were interrupted by alarms. Two senior-species warships were suddenly hanging over their heads, emerging in the center of the Third Fleet formation and radiating powerful damping fields to prevent the Ruhar ships from jumping away. Admiral Lokash had immediately done the only thing she could do: order all her ships to stand down, avoid doing anything that might provoke the Maxolhx.

Now Lokash and her Third Fleet had jumped away, all of them. The only ships around Tohmaran were the two hulking cruisers of the Maxolhx Hegemony. Plus perhaps one or two Jeraptha ships in stealth, observing the situation with alarm and astonishment. Three Jeraptha ships had dropped stealth and jumped away, minutes after the Maxolhx arrived. Perkins did not consider the actions of the Jeraptha to be cowardice or callousness, they had been nothing but sensible. Captain Scorandum's little Ethics and Compliance force had lived up to the letter of their unit, by doing the only ethical thing. Needless violence would not have accomplished anything, would have been counter-productive. The Maxolhx had made it clear they would not tolerate any interference or failure to comply with their demands. The Alien Legion force on Tohmaran, including the Verd-kris, would pay a heavy price if their demands were not met without hesitation.

The first demand was an immediate ceasefire by all forces on and around the planet, including the Swift Arrows and even the Bright Claws, who technically owned the world.

The second demand was for Emily Perkins and her team to fly up to the lead Maxolhx ship, to answer for their crimes against the Maxolhx coalition. The Maxolhx intended to make a very public example of the Mavericks, and any failure to comply would result in hundreds, perhaps thousands of Legion deaths.

"I am so sorry," Perkins repeated in a whisper. Her voice was hoarse, words coming out in a whisper.

"It's not your fault," Dave pulled her close to his side.

"It *is* my fault," she wiped away a tear before it could float away in the zero gravity. Water droplets should not be allowed to drift in the dropship's cabin, they were a hazard to electronics.

As if any of *that* matters, she told herself with annoyance.

"Ma'am," Shauna's own eyes were red from crying, though her tears were likely those of anger. "We all knew the risks."

"Yes, but I was *stupid*," Perkins insisted. "I pushed too hard, too fast. The rebellion by the Bosphuraq, the attacks of the ghost ship, all have the Maxolhx looking weak and *feeling* weak. They couldn't let us win here, it would be too much of a blow to their coalition. I should have considered that. I should have *listened*." In the run-up to the hastily-planned operation, the Jeraptha had cautioned that eventually, the Maxolhx could be expected to push back, to intervene directly before their coalition was weakened to the point where the Rindhalu roused themselves to take advantage of the opportunity.

"Even the beetles thought the Maxolhx would not take action here," Jesse reminded her. "They knew the Maxolhx would push back eventually. But not *here*."

"It was a risk," Perkins reached up and squeezed the hand Dave had on her shoulder.

"The Jeraptha intel office laid seventeen-to-one odds against the Maxolhx interfering here," Dave stated. "For the beetles, seventeen-to-one is pretty much a lock for something not to happen."

Those were comforting words. Perkins knew her team meant what they said, believed the action on Tohmaran was a manageable risk. That was not the problem. The problem was, she would have kept going after Tohmaran, would have utilized the momentum the Alien Legion had built up. Eventually, they would have pushed the Maxolhx too far.

She had been reckless, foolish, drunk on her own success. Now she had lost everything. How could she have been so arrogant? Humans had no business playing any part in the conflict that had been raging across the galaxy for millennia.

"That's them," Irene called from the cockpit, and everyone unstrapped to crowd around the open cockpit door.

"Can you zoom in the view?" Jesse asked. The two senior-species ships filled a quarter of the forward cockpit displays, showing sharp outlines but few surface details.

Derek gestured to the blank console displays and held up his hands. "We can't do *anything*," he answered.

"It's Ok," Jesse squinted, trying to resolve the images of the two alien warships. "How big you think they are?"

Irene answered. "Almost the size of a Jeraptha battleship."

"Damn," Jesse breathed. "And those are just *cruisers*?"

"We think so, yes," Irene said. "That's how the Ruhar recognition database tagged them."

Jates snorted from over Jesse's shoulder. "What do the Ruhar know?"

"They got their data from the beetles," Perkins shrugged. Turning around, she looked from one team member to the other. Her only consolation was that she had not gotten more people killed.

"ETA?" Shauna asked.

"Twenty-seven minutes," Derek guessed. "If the Maxolhx haven't changed the schedule. They're flying this thing now, we are locked out."

"What's the drill, Ma'am?" Jesse looked at Perkins, her face only a foot away as they all crowded around the door.

"We are representing humanity. And the Ruhar," she looked to Nert. "And the *Verd*-kris," she added with a nod to Jates. "Proper military bearing and discipline at all times. Do not give those assholes the satisfaction of seeing you sweat."

Jesse made a fist and shook it. "Permission to pop one in the nose if I get a chance?"

"Denied," Perkins shook her head. "Any gesture of defiance will get our
people on the ground killed. We can't-"

"SHIT!" Irene shouted and they all lost sight of the two alien warships in a
brief flash of light. "What the hell is-"

In front of her and Derek, the consoles blinked back to life. Derek lost no time
in taking back control and pivoting the Dodo's nose around so hard, the free-
floating passengers were thrown against the side wall of the cabin. "Hang on!" He
grunted as he authorized the main engines and advanced the throttles to thrust of
one-quarter gee. "Everyone, strap in, I'm going to full burn."

"Wait," Perkins called out, shaking her head to clear the cobwebs from where
she had smacked it against a cabinet when the Dodo spun around. "Why are-"

"Derek's right, Ma'am, we gotta get out of here," Irene craned her neck to see
back through the doorway. "Strap in now!"

"But-"

"Colonel, unless I am totally wrong, that *ghost ship* just joined the party, and
they are not playing nice."

Yanking the straps tightly around her with Dave's help, Perkins punched the
armrest controls to run back the display.

"Oh my G-" Jesse gasped before Shauna shushed him, and they all watched
the battle in silent amazement, at least for the six seconds before Derek twisted the
Dodo's tail and the dropship surged away with a force five times that of Earth's
gravity. As her vision narrowed to a tunnel directly in front of her, Emily tried to
follow the action on the display, breathing evenly as an elephant sat on her chest.

The battle began as a flare of gamma radiation appeared without warning
between the two Maxolhx cruisers, photons carrying over one million electron-
volts striking the shields of the two unprepared ships. The high-energy photons
were brief, and had no effect other than illuminating the two senior-species
warships like strobe lights, as their energy shields easily absorbed the radiation.

What came next was not so easily absorbed. The ghost ship, massive even
when compared to the enemy vessels, hammered away with broadsides at point-
blank range, each ship separated by no more than four hundred kilometers. Perkins
at first saw the directed-energy weapons and railguns only when they struck the
enemy's shields, then space around all three ships became saturated with twisted
sheets of lightning and clouds of particles blown off the armor plating of the two
cruisers. Masers and particle beams became visible streaks, railgun darts creating
intense contrails as they raced in both directions. The cruisers were firing
everything they had at the ghost ship, which was hitting back with-

She lost sight of the ships as the battle became an intense glow too fast for her
eyes to follow.

Then something exploded and Derek shouted something she couldn't hear and
the gee force kicked on even harder.

"Em," someone was whispering in her ear. "Em, come on."

Dave. She recognized the voice. It was David Czajka. Her eyes fluttered open to see him looking at her with concern and she became concerned for him, he had blood seeping from his nose and a blood vessel had burst in the corner of his right eye.

"Hey," he caressed her cheek with a hand, placing a cloth under her nose. "You Ok?"

"I feel like," she took a deep, shuddering breath. "Shit."

"Me too," Dave grinned. "Hold this," he pressed the cloth into her upper lip. "You've got a nosebleed. We pulled eight gees for a couple seconds."

"Eight?" She gasped. The acceleration meter on the cockpit bulkhead was showing One point Two Five, so they were still racing toward- Where? Or racing *away*?

"Sorry about that," Derek called from the cockpit, his own voice shaky. "It got real kinetic, we had to get outta there."

"Dave, your nose is bleeding too," Perkins noted, looking around. Jesse and Shauna were helping each other, and Jates was sitting stoically, giving her a thumbs up. Nert pulled a cloth from a pocket, handing it to Dave, and giving Perkins an uncertain thumbs up. Through the cockpit door, she could see Irene moving around, her hands on the Dodo's controls. None of them appeared to have suffered serious injury from the heavy acceleration. "Bonsu, what's happening?"

"Your guess is as good as mine, Ma'am," the pilot replied. "Sensors blanked out when something exploded out there. They are resetting now, we should have a real-time view in ah, oh," he checked the console. "Ten, fifteen seconds?"

The displays remained blank except for a blinking symbol in Ruhar script, indicating the data feed from external sensors had been interrupted. When the displays again showed images, there were blank spots that slowly filled in from the edges, as the computer reconciled what the sensors were seeing.

"It's just- Where are those ships?" Perkins asked, manipulating the controls to zoom her display in and out. "All I see is-"

"That's the wave front of a debris cloud, Ma'am," Irene explained. "It will thin out as it expands, we should be able to see- Uh oh."

Something dark was becoming visible inside the debris cloud, something moving.

"Damn it," Derek cursed. "Hang on, I'm gonna punch it, we-"

"Don't," Perkins ordered.

"Ma'am, if we don't-"

"Bonsu," she said gently. "Another thousand kilometers won't save us," she explained.

"She's right," Irene agreed with resignation in her voice.

Derek took a deep breath. "All right. Continuing thrust at current rate." The acceleration would have the happy effect of keeping the passengers in the cabin, rather than hanging out by the door and bothering the pilots. "We're getting a better view of- Oh, *shit*," he sighed.

A damaged Maxolhx cruiser was emerging from the glowing debris cloud, which was thinning rapidly and becoming dim as the particles within shed excess

nergy. The ship was on fire, arcs of electricity sparking all around the charred
iull.

"We had a fifty-fifty shot," Jesse said sourly.

Dave thought his friend's math was off, as there were two Maxolhx cruisers
and only one ghost ship. Now they knew at least one of the senior-species ships
iad survived what had to be the explosion of a starship. "Hey, even if that ghost
ship had destroyed the two cruisers, there's no reason to think the ghost crew
would be friendly to us."

Jesse turned in his seat. "How you figure that?"

"The ghost crew are supposedly Bosphuraq, right? We invaded a Wurgalan
planet, and blew up a bird ship with a plasma cannon at Squidworld, remember? I
don't think we're on their Christmas card list, you know? The best we can hope for
s the ghost ship ignores us."

Perkins waved a hand to caution her team against speculation. "We don't
know why the ghost ship came here,"

"That is easy," Jates said. "They kill Maxolhx. The ghost ship knew the kitties
would be here, because of us."

"We've got some good news, the cruiser is not turning toward us," Derek
announced. "It is accelerating, barely. Looks like ten percent of one gee."

"I'm amazed that ship can thrust at all," Irene added, zooming in the display.
"Look at the battle damage."

The hull of the cruiser was a wreck on one side. Armor plates were peeled up
or missing, exposing the interior frames. The hull was blackened, illuminated by
blue-white arcs of lightning from ruptured power conduits. As the enemy ship
limped away, it slowly spun around, venting gas and plasma that overwhelmed the
ability of thrusters to stabilize it.

"Look," Irene pointed. "Their shields are off." She pointed to the glow at the
front of the ship, where the unprotected hull plowed through the particles of the
debris field. The nose of the cruiser smacked into something large enough to make
a flash of light and leave a crater in the ship's hull. "Shit! I wish the Ruhar fleet
had not jumped away. That ship is a sitting duck even for a Ruhar warship. Ma'am,
do you think there's a chance the beetles hung around to see what-"

"Missile warning!" Derek interrupted. "The cruiser just launched a missile."

"Just one?" Perkins asked, trying to get that data on her display.

"Yeah, looks like it. It launched from the far side, we can't- Oh, no. No, no,
no. It's headed straight toward us!" Derek shouted to be heard over the cockpit
alarm. "Punch it now, Colonel?"

"No," Perkins squeezed Dave's hand. "We are not running anymore."

"It won't matter anyway," Irene said in a flat voice drained of emotion.
"Impact in eighteen seconds. Everyone," she turned to look back through the
cockpit door. "This has been a wild ride."

Derek reached over to hold Irene's hand, just as the missile exploded in a
brilliant flash of light. "Where did that come fr- Wow."

Another shape resolved from the swirling debris field, its forward section
glowing as its bulk shoved aside the particles of the cloud. There was one
difference from the way the cruiser was flying, one major difference. The new

ship's shields were active, making a smooth bow wake that deflected impacts away from the armored hull.

"It's the ghost!" Irene pumped a fist, and everyone cheered.

"Bonsu," Perkins ordered. "Now, it might be prudent to increase thrust to three gees. We don't want to get caught in a battle zone."

"Right. Thrust in five, four-"

"Belay that!" Perkins automatically threw up a hand to shield her eyes as a brilliant lance of fire stabbed out from the ghost ship, striking the Maxolhx cruiser amidships, and pulsing to burn completely through top to bottom, cutting the warship in half. The energy beam snapped off as abruptly as it started, then shorter bursts of fire struck the two hull sections of the cruiser, blasting away engines, missile launchers, shield projectors and anything else the ghost ship crew considered a potential threat. "Bonsu, cut thrust."

"Are you sure?" Derek asked. "That cruiser could still explode, and we would be caught in-"

"The battle is over. Whatever happens next," Perkins replied softly. "I want to *see* it."

"Me too," Irene agreed, patting Derek's hand. "Honey," she added in a whisper. "It doesn't matter. Against that ship, nothing we do matters."

Derek tapped a button and the Dodo was again drifting in zero gravity. "The ghost ship is turning toward us," He warned, keeping a finger poised next to the engine control.

Emily Perkins shivered at the sight of the massive ghost ship. Intel tagged it as a heavily modified Maxolhx battlecruiser, based on the hull configuration. Speculation was that the rogue Bosphuraq had somehow captured the battlecruiser, an accomplishment substantially more difficult than the merely impossible feat of blowing one to pieces. The beings flying that ship had somehow developed technology that leapfrogged past both senior species in the galaxy. Not much was known about the rogue Bosphuraq, other than their evident hatred of the oppressive Maxolhx. If the ghost ship crew become allies, or at least neutral regarding the Alien Legion, that could be- "Can we contact the ghost ship?" She asked, subconsciously reaching up to brush her bangs away from her face. It was a futile gesture in zero gravity, and the aliens wouldn't care anyway. "Let me-"

"We are receiving a signal from the ghost ship," Irene interrupted. "That's odd, it's visual only. What is *that*?"

All the displays were showing the same image: a circular blue and gold logo, with 'U. N. ExForce' around the top, and 'Merry Band of Pirates' along the bottom.

"ExForce?" Dave gasped, squeezing Emily's hand and making her wince. "Hey! That's one of *our* ships!"

"The Expeditionary Force doesn't *have* a ship, any ships," Perkins said, knowing she was denying the evidence of her own eyes.

"Who the hell are the Merry Band of *Pirates*?" Jesse's mouth twisted into a frown. "Who is that? Ma'am?" He looked at the Mavericks leader. "Some type of secret special operations unit?"

"If it's a secret, it's one I don't know about," Perkins muttered.

"Em," Dave insisted. "Come on. They're displaying a *human* logo. That's got o be-"

"Dave," Shauna thought her friend was getting carried away. "Maybe they're howing that symbol because they think that is *our* logo? Could they have met a JNEF SpecOps unit, and the Bosphuraq think we're part of it?"

"What I want to know," Derek added. "Is what's that weird thing in the niddle of the logo?"

"It looks like a, maybe a potato?" Irene guessed. "Why would they have a *otato* as a-"

"Um, no," Perkins cocked her head, as if looking at the image from a different ange would make it suddenly understandable. "It looks like some type of single-celled organism, but that can't be the-"

The image changed from the static logo, to a person. A human male, seated in an oversized chair, on what appeared to be the bridge or control center of a ship.

A human male they all recognized, either from personal experience or from photos.

"Hey guys," the person said with a grin. "How you doin', huh?"

Emily was grateful that the Dodo was in zero gravity, because otherwise she would have fallen onto the deck. "B-B-*Bishop*?"

"*Bish*!" Jesse and Dave whooped with delight at the same time.

"We," Emily had to take a breath. "We all thought you were *dead*."

The grin grew even wider. "Yeah, well, reports of my demise have been greatly exaggerated."

"Bish, that is *your* ship?" Dave couldn't believe it.

"Ah, this old thing?" Bishop made an exaggerated Aw-Shucks shrug. "We threw it together from used parts. It was-"

"You?" Another voice broke in, the speaker unseen. Snarky, condescending, a touch of an upper-crust British accent. "*You* threw it together? I built *Valkyrie* out of Legos, with no help from you monk-"

"Skippy!" Bishop shook a fist at the ceiling. "We agreed to take this slowly, remember? Don't frighten the-"

"You *also* promised I could give the Mavericks a summary of our actions in the form of an epic opera, which-"

"Whoa!" Jesse waved a hand. "An *opera*? Like, people wearing horns on their heads and singin'?" His accent slipped deeper South. "We have to sit through one of those? Bish, come on, we don't-"

"Cornpone," Bishop put a hand over his eyes and shook his head. "I did promise the beer can he could sing, but only-"

"*Beer can*?" Shauna stared at the image of Joe Bishop, who she hadn't seen since their days on Camp Alpha. "Why is a beer can singing?"

"Oh, man," Bishop took the hand away from his eyes. "Shauna, guys, believe me, it is a *long* story. Uh, sorry if we scared you. We intercepted a message from the Maxolhx to the Thuranin, stating the kitties planned to come here and spoil the party. We got here as soon as we could. The plan was just to jump in and disable those ships, but one of them got Skippy pissed off, and-"

"Skippy?" Another unseen voice, a stoner surfer boy. "Dude, like, that was *m*
setting up the weapons, you know?"

"Both of you *shut UP!*" Bishop roared. "That's an order!"

Perkins squinted to see the rank insignia. "Colonel Bishop. Could you please
tell us what the *hell* is going on?"

"Like I said," Bishop looked like a harried staff member of a day care full of
over-caffeinated toddlers, rather than commander of the galaxy's most powerful
warship. "It is a *long* story."

CHAPTER THIRTY SIX

The Maverick pilots flew their Dodo expertly into the designated docking bay, which we had cleared of other dropships. I didn't know Irene Striebich or Derek Bonsu, other than from spying on them while we were at Paradise. Really, of the Mavericks, I had never met Striebich, Bonsu, Jates or Dandurff. Shauna Jarrett I had not seen or spoken with since Camp Alpha, which seemed like an eternity ago. Emily Perkins? First, I had never called her 'Emily', not even in my private thoughts. The last time I saw Perkins, she was a major, and I was a newly-promoted colonel. Back then, we had a good working relationship, and also, I liked her. Though she worked in intel, I trusted her, and not just her judgment. I had trusted her. Trusted her to do the right thing, for the Army and for her people. The success she had with the Mavericks, and how she cared for her team, told me that trust was justified.

Her success, damn it, was part of the problem.

Have you ever watched Star Trek II: The Wrath of Khan? Of course you have. If you haven't, I don't know what is wrong with you, except that something is seriously wrong with you.

OK, there is a scene where Kirk is in a tunnel under the surface of an asteroid, and the bad guy Khan not only steals the MacGuffin that drives the plot, he traps Kirk down there, possibly forever. Kirk holds the communicator in dramatic Shatner fashion and shouts *"Khaaaaaaaaaan!"* at his mortal enemy.

Why do I mention that?

Because in my head, as we filed into the docking bay, I was shouting *"Perkiiiiiiins!"*.

"Remember," Gunny Adams whispered from my left. "It's not her fault, Sir."

"Shit," I whispered back. "Did I say that out loud?"

"Yes," Simms hissed from my right. "Also, you've got a, hold still, Sir. You have something on your shoulder." She reached over and plucked the offending item off my dress uniform. "There."

"Thanks, XO, Gunny." Taking a breath, I stepped forward into the center of the red carpet that had been rolled out to the side door of the Dodo. Lined up on both sides were the STAR team, the Commandos, and the entire crew except for a few on the bridge. We had literally rolled out the red carpet while waiting for the Dodo to become safe to approach. After being in space, its skin was cold, the engine exhausts were hot, and thrusters still leaked gas as the pressure equalized. It had surprised me when Simms suggested a red carpet for the honor guard, I didn't know we had one aboard. But of course Simms had thought to bring one up from Earth at some point, another reason I am fortunate to have her as my executive officer. Skippy had run his cleaning bots over the carpet, it was dusty from being in storage.

Behind me were three flags, hanging from the ceiling. In the middle was the UNEF flag. The original design from when the Expeditionary Force left Earth, not the new design from a few years ago. I wanted the flag that the Mavericks would recognize. On one side was a flag with the logo of the Merry Band of Pirates, and on the other was a flag with the logo of the human portion of the Alien Legion. Some of our crew thought the Alien Legion ExForce logo with their motto of 'Anytime, Anywhere, Any Fight', looked like the logo of a minor league hockey team, but I thought it was bad-ass. It had made me wish the Merry Band of Pirates had a cool motto, and not Skippy's suggestion of 'Striving For Competence'.

Asshole.

Anyway, the ship's fabricators had cranked out the flags, and now we waited for the Dodo to get the All Clear from flight control. That apparently happened, because a light on the wall turned from yellow to green, and the Dodo's door opened.

Emily Perkins was not first out the door. That honor went to Staff Sergeant Jesse 'Cornpone' Colter, and man, his grin was as wide as mine. I blinked because my eyes were watering, that was due to allergies and not because-

Screw it. It was an emotional moment.

Jesse stood to the left of the door, Shauna came down the steps to line up on the right, then Dave. Next were two aliens, a Ruhar cadet and a Kristang- No, a *Verd-kris* surgun. I had to remind myself not to refer to Jates as a Kristang or a lizard. Two others I did not know descended the steps. They must be the pilots Bonsu and Striebich, and finally, in the doorway, was Perkins.

She walked down the steps, paused at the bottom, and saluted me. "Permission to come aboard, Sir?"

"Permission granted *with enthusiasm*, Colonel Perkins," I replied. Before I could say anything else, her mouth dropped open.

"Commandant Fabron?" She stared at the Commando team leader. For a split-second I didn't understand, then I realized that of course Perkins would know Fabron, or at least know of him. "How, what- You are with *them?*"

"Only recently," Fabron answered with a Gallic shrug. "We are not *with* them," his eyes flicked toward me, and I saw that his statement was actually a question.

"Fabron," I said. "Your Commandos are certainly with us, for as long as you wish to serve with a band of bloodthirsty Pirates. We are *one* team."

A lot of military service absolutely *sucks*. Truthfully, most of it does. Even simple things suck. Like trying to fill out a form online, and discovering that the certs on your ID card have to be updated to access the site, but you can't update your certs because the browser on your government-issued laptop blocks the official Department of Defense site you need to get to, and the IT people tell you that updating the browser requires a new version of antivirus software on your laptop, software that you can't download because the certs on your ID card are out of date and it takes ALL FREAKIN' DAY to resolve what should be a two-minute problem. Not that I'm bitter about shit like that, and then the Army wonders why they have a problem with retention when they saddle soldiers with time-wasting bullshit.

Anyway, much of military service sucks, but you get through it because that's the job. And because sometimes, you get to experience moments that make it all worthwhile.

Seeing the look of pride in Fabron's eyes, when I assured him the Commandos were on the team, felt good. Damn good. On the other side of the carpet, Smythe gave Fabron a barely-perceptible nod, and not even the super discipline of the Commandos could stop the grins on their faces.

"Bloodthirsty Pirates?" Perkins asked Fabron with a raised eyebrow. "Let me guess, you being here is a long story?"

"Yes," the French officer acknowledged. "But not, perhaps, as long as the story of some others."

"Bishop? Sir, do you mind telling me how-"

"We needed to hire the Alien Legion," I explained. "But not all of it. Just a Commando team. We didn't have time to go through the application process, so," it was my turn to shrug. "We cut out the paperwork. Fabron can explain later. Let me introduce you to the crew. This rather disreputable, scruffy-looking fellow is *Lef-tenant* Colonel Smythe, leader of our STAR team."

"STAR?" She asked.

"Special Tactics Assault Regiment," Smythe explained in clipped tones. 'Formerly, I was with 22 Special Air Services."

"Mm," Perkins smiled. "I have met members of the Regiment before."

I introduced the senior staff, well aware that Jesse and Dave, and even Shauna were fairly itching to get the formal ceremony over, so they could bombard me with questions.

"Sir," Simms whispered and nudged me gently. Also, Skippy was shouting impatiently into my earpiece.

"Er, well," I stumbled. "We can continue introductions later. Perkins, if your team will come with me, I will introduce you to an old friend."

The Mavericks looked at each other in confusion. "An old friend?"

"From Paradise. Uh, just the six of you," I added the Verd and the Ruhar cadet stepped forward. "Just the team who activated the maser cannons. Cadet Dandurff, Surgun Jates, this will not take long, then I will bring you to meet our special guest star," I rolled my eyes while I addressed Skippy the way he insisted on.

It might surprise you to learn this, but Skippy can be a bit of a prima donna. The surprise is that sometimes he manages to only be a *bit* of a prima donna, instead of the whole nightmarish ego package. This was not one of those times. Skippy demanded to be given the full star treatment in front of a new audience, and because it was easier to go along rather than him making our lives hell, I gave into his demands. Really, it was not that big a deal, considering all that he had done for us filthy monkeys, and I also thought it would be fun.

"Bish," Jesse pleaded as we talked down the passageway. "Come on, man, 'fess up. What is going on? Where you been all this time?"

"I promise, I will explain it all, 'Pone," I turned right into the ship's main conference room, where we had coffee and light snacks laid out. The selection of food wasn't great but it was the best we had. After the six filed in, looks of puzzlement, impatience and a touch of irritation on their faces, I stood at the head of the conference table. "As I said, we have an old friend of yours aboard the ship."

"Who?" Perkins asked, her own patience running thin.

"You know him as your Mysterious Benefactor."

"*Emby?*" All six of them gasped at once.

Dave glared at me, more than a little angry. "Bish, *you* are Emby? Why didn't you tell-"

"No, not me," I shook my head. Gesturing toward the table, I announced "May I present the one, the only, the most awesomeness of all awesomenesses-"

Believe me, that introduction was pared way down from the gag-inducing lines of praise that Skippy wanted me to recite.

"-his majesty, Grand Admiral of the fleet, Skippy the Magnificent!"

Nothing happened.

His avatar was supposed to shimmer to life in a dramatic flare of light.

"Uh, Skippy?" I grimaced, while the six Mavericks stared at me like I'd lost my mind.

"You didn't say it right, Joe," he sniffed from the speaker in the ceiling.

"Oh for- That is a lot to remember, Skippy," I muttered, embarrassed. "Give me a break, OK?"

"No," he pouted. "You need to say it right, dumdum. Ugh, why did I expect a filthy monkey to-"

"Sir," Perkins had her arms folded across her chest. "Is this a joke?"

"The joke is on *me*, Perkins. Skippy, come on. I'm sorry that I bumbled your grand entrance. Can I make it up to you, by listening to one of your arias?"

"Hmmph. Make it one aria, *and* one crowd-pleasing tune from my upcoming Broadway smash musical."

"Deal."

"BEHOLD," the voice boomed from the speaker as the hologram began to shimmer, projecting swirling smoke. "Tis, I, *Skippy the Magnificent!*" The fake smoke cleared and he stood there in all his glory, the admiral's uniform resplendent. I noticed that his chest glittered with a few more gaudy medals than usual. Maybe he had awarded himself a medal for perfect attendance, or something like that.

There was silence, then Dave had the perfect remark. "Emby is a *cartoon?*"

"I am not a *cartoon*, you ignorant cretin." Skippy's voice dripped with outrage. "I am far beyond the poor understanding of-"

"What's with the outfit?" Jesse asked, leaning over the table to peer at the admiral's uniform. "You look like a mascot from someplace like Chuck-E-Cheese."

"He is *cheesy*, that's for sure," I laughed.

Skippy hopped up and down on the table, fuming mad. "You monkeys are not giving me the proper respect!"

"Actually, they are," I said.

"Emby is an asshole?" Striebich glared at him.

"Hey!" He screeched. "Why, you, I ought to-"

"That's the consensus, yeah," I agreed. "I've known him for a while, and he was an asshole right from the start."

"Explain this to me, Bishop," Perkins said, momentarily forgetting that I outranked her. "Our Mysterious Benefactor was just some sort of computer program?"

"I am *not* just a-"

"Skippy, chill," I held up a hand. "Yes, Perkins. We were at Paradise while you were activating those cannons. Sorry," I looked from one face to another. "We couldn't tell you our true identity, so Skippy here played the part of Emby. He is not a computer program, he is a person," I emphasized the last part as a way to boost Skippy's fragile ego. "The being we call 'Skippy' is an *Elder* AI of unimaginable power."

"Elder?" Shauna asked. "But that's not- Joe, you're sure?"

"Yeah, I'm sure. Like I said, it is a *long* story. What you need to know right now is, I am sorry we used you. The hamsters were going to give Paradise back to the lizards. UNEF there would have been screwed. We couldn't let that happen, and we couldn't let aliens know that a bunch of lowly humans were flying around the galaxy in a stolen Thuranin starship. So we-"

"Thuranin?" Jesse was bewildered. "Bish, this ghost ship is a Maxolhx-"

"A Maxolhx battlecruiser, yes, but it's a hotrod after Skippy's auto shop pimped it for us. Our other ship is a-"

"You have more than one starship?" Perkins's eyes bulged at me.

"Well, yeah. Four now, actually. The Thuranin ship is a star carrier we call the *Flying Dutchman*, and we also have two Kristang troop transports. Plus we had a Kristang frigate, that was the first ship we captured. It sort of got taken apart to keep the *Dutchman* flightworthy. We have temporarily had other ships along the way. Listen, I'm sorry we couldn't tell you who your Mysterious Benefactor was."

"We understand the need for OPSEC," Perkins nodded slowly, her mind clearly still reeling from all the revelations. "It didn't work, though. The maser cannons. The lizards didn't give up, and the Ruhar still wanted to trade away the planet. Until," she stared at me. "*Someone* just happened to discover an Elder power tap, and some other gizmos."

"Uh, yeah, that was us, too."

All six of the Mavericks silently mouthed 'Holy shit'.

Perkins spoke first. "You planted a-"

"Except *we* didn't actually have a *real* Elder power tap," I stared right back at her. "Unlike some people I know."

"You know about that?"

"The power tap you planted on Squidworld? I guess you were nvolved in that somewhere. What I want to know is, where did you get it?"

"*That* is a long story," she tilted her head at me.

"Fair enough, we can talk about it later.

"Sir, can we go back a minute? You planted the Elder power tap on Paradise, but it was a *fake*?" The expression on her face was not just astonishment, it was also 'Why didn't I think of sneaky shit like that'?

"It is a *long* story. Bottom line is, we had to make the hamsters think Paradise was worth holding onto. It worked, so- Oof."

"What?" Dave asked.

"I just thought, the Burgermeister is gonna be *pissed* at me when she finds out
we suckered her people into keeping a planet they didn't want."

"She'll get over it," Perkins shrugged.

"If not," Striebich said with a scowl. "*Screw* her."

"Actually," a smile spread across Perkins's face. "I believe she will think the
whole story is wonderful. Colonel," that time she caught herself. "Sir, for a long
time, I thought Emby was connected with the Burgermeister."

"That was part of the cover story," I explained. "We left a lot of bread crumbs
pointing in different directions, to confuse everyone. Hey, guys, we will have
plenty of time to talk. The reason I brought you here is to meet Emby himself. We
call him 'Skippy'. He is an asshole-"

"OK," Skippy sighed. "I have to own up to that. But I am *totally* worth it."

"*Most* of the time," I wagged the finger at him. "He is also, I hate to say it, my
friend."

"Any friend of yours is a friend of mine," Jesse said, while giving Skippy the
side-eye.

"In that case," Skippy made a short bow toward the other end of the table. "I
am very pleased to meet you, Staff Sergeant Colter. Indeed, I am honored to meet
the Mavericks. We have been following your exploits, through your reports, and,
well, any other information source I could hack into. I must say, we are *terribly*
sorry that we were not able to help you on Camp Alpha. I did not learn of the
incident until too late, and by then, well, we were busy intercepting the lizards who
were attempting to spread a deadly infection on Paradise."

"That was *you*?" Dave blinked, like his mind was blown.

"It was us, but mostly Skippy," I gave him the credit he was due. "He
developed the vaccine also. Hey," I snapped my fingers. "The lizard plan was to
land a bunch of infected Keeper idiots on Paradise, you know that much?" They
nodded. "We intercepted their dropships, and captured the Keepers. Those jerk-offs
are on Earth now. Uh, Skippy, are they still-"

"According to UNEF Command, they are still being held on South Georgia
island, in the South Atlantic ocean. They-" He paused to look at Perkins, who was
laughing to herself. "What is so funny?"

She looked at me with, maybe it was affection? "You called them 'jerk-offs',"
she laughed. "You have come a long way, *Colonel* Bishop, but I think there is still
some of the scared buck sergeant I knew in there. It is refreshing."

"Oh," I blushed. "Thanks."

"Bish," Dave said. "You got some '*splainin*' to do. Sir," he added.

"I know, I know. We will go back so you can meet the whole crew, I wanted
you to meet Skippy first. Most of what we have accomplished out here would not
have been possible without him."

"Sir," Shauna avoided looking at me directly. It was awkward for her, too.
"You said you have other ships at Earth? You have been there? Recently?" As she
spoke, she reached beside her to hold Jesse's hand. "We can go there, go home?"

"Yes, we can. We need to make some stops along the way, but if you want,
we-"

Perkins put a hand over her mouth, she suddenly looked ill. "Colonel, I know his ship is powerful, but if you can get to Earth, then aliens can-"

"Perkins, yes. Aliens can get to Earth. I know what you're thinking, and it is not a problem. It *was* a problem. For years, our focus was on stopping aliens from reaching Earth, and exposing our secret. Maxolhx ships have been to Earth, in fact, we came here straight from Earth, where we had a confrontation with a Maxolhx task force." I held up a hand and squeezed to make a fist. "We sent those rotten kitties scurrying home with their tails between their legs. They will not be coming back to bother us."

"That is a tremendous risk," Perkins observed.

"It's not, because we have a cache of *Elder* weapons now," I tried to say it casually, but it came out as a boast.

"*Elder* weapons? Damn," Perkins held onto a chair to steady herself. "Sir, that is called 'Burying the lead'. Maybe you should have told us that first."

"Like I said," I let out a long breath. "It is a *long* story."

Nert looked down to inspect his clothing. He was wearing the standard-issue Ruhar military gear for traveling aboard a dropship, including a sort of quilted vest with multiple pockets, an oxygen supply and internal heaters. Maybe he should have removed the vest and left it in the Dodo, but it was too late by then. Seeing the signal from Colonel Bishop, he drew himself up to full height and stepped forward through the conference room doorway. "Cadet Nert Dandurf," he announced, giving a proper human-style salute to the commander of the Merry Band of Pirates. "It is-"

"No, wait!" The holographic avatar standing on the conference table shouted, frantically waving its hands. "Don't say anything, not a word. Let me guess. You're wearing a vest, so- I got it! You want me to make a donation, to the Coast Guard Youth Auxiliary?"

Colonel Bishop seemed to find that immensely funny, for a reason unknown to Nert, who stood with his mouth gaping open. "Cadet," Bishop said, waving a hand when he stopped laughing. "Sorry, I was laughing at the beer can. We are very pleased to meet you."

"Hmmph," Skippy grunted, looking at the Ruhar from head to toe. "I thought you'd be taller."

"I thought you'd be *smarter*," Nert blurted out without thinking.

"*Hey!*" The avatar screeched with outrage.

"Oh," Bishop clapped his hands. "He got you *good*, Skippy. Nice one," the colonel held up a hand.

Nert slapped the hand in a simple high-five the way Jesse and Dave had taught him. "You are Skippy?" He stared at the avatar.

"Skippy the Magnificent, at your service," the avatar bowed in a mocking manner. "I was joking about that last part. I mean, I'm the Lord Commander of the Fleet, and you are only a cadet."

"Why is your hat so big?"

"You like it? It's very impressive, huh?"

"I was going to say '*tacky*'." Nert replied truthfully.

"*Hey!*" Skippy scowled. "Joe, I hate him already."

"I *like* him already," Bishop grinned. "Cadet Dandurf, when dealing with Skippy, you must keep in mind that he is an asshole."

"A super-smart, nay, mind-bogglingly smart asshole," Skippy said, looking down his nose.

Nert bent forward from the waist to peer at the avatar. "You realize that any kind of asshole is still, an *asshole*?"

"*Ooooooh*," the avatar shook its tiny fists. "You just wait, I should-"

"Skippy," Bishop winked at Nert. "I am assigning Cadet Dandurf to be our official liaison with the Ruhar. You will be working with him *very* closely."

"Joe," Skippy moaned. "Please, anything but that."

Bishop shook a scolding finger at the avatar. "It's your own fault, for not being polite to our guest."

After Skippy's grand entrances with the Mavericks, then with Nert, did *not* go the way he planned, he tried a different tactic with the Verd-kris surgun. While my only knowledge of Jates came from reading reports, he didn't seem like the kind of guy who appreciated a bunch of nonsense, and I advised Skippy of that.

Skippy, of course, ignored me.

Complying with Skippy's request, I escorted Jates down several passageways, to Skippy's new temporary mancave. It was not as luxurious as his previous escape pod, nor did it have any nice decorations, and he bitched about that constantly. Whenever he lamented the loss of his Elvis memorabilia or his original paintings, I reminded him that it was all his stupid fault, and he had no one to blame but himself.

Strangely, saying that did *not* make him feel better.

Personally, I did not mourn the loss of his Fat Elvis belt, but I did feel bad about the destruction of the original Dogs Playing Poker. That painting was widely acknowledged as genuinely classic art, by guys who sit around drinking beer and talking about stuff, instead of arrogant snobs who think they are better than everyone. While I am sure that the guy who painted that piece imagined it might one day be lost, or burned up in a house fire, he did not imagine it would be destroyed inside a gas giant planet in another freakin' galaxy.

As far as I know, that is the only human painting to have been destroyed in another galaxy, so I guess it has that going for it.

Anyway, those were the thoughts going through my mind as I escorted Jates toward Skippy's temporary quarters. Jates was not big on small talk, so we mostly were quiet, and to make it even more fun, it was an awkward kind of quiet. Not the kind of quiet when buddies are sitting around chilling. This was like meeting-your-girlfriend's-father type of quiet, when the two of you don't have anything in common to talk about, other than that he knows you are the creepy loser who is regularly defiling his sweet little girl, and he is wondering how far off the road he would need to carry your body before burying you.

Yup.

That kind of quiet.

When we were in a lift between decks and I just couldn't stand it anymore, I heard my stupid mouth say, "So, I hear you have served with David Czajka."

Slowly, he turned to look at me. He looked down, because he was considerably taller than I am. "Yes." He said, after a pause that made the situation even more awkward.

Shit. I wished I had kept my big stupid mouth shut. Inside, I was screaming at him that I would have appreciated a *little* more detail about his service with Dave, but fortunately I didn't say that out loud. My mouth must have missed a memo because I heard myself saying, "Dave, and Jesse, and I, served together on Earth. We got into a lot of trouble together," I added for no good reason at all, because I am a moron.

He looked down at me again, as we walked out of the lift. Maybe he took pity on me, or maybe he was as tired of the awkwardness as I was. "I also have gotten into much trouble with David Czajka. Due to Czajka's actions, or inactions. You humans would say that he is kind of an idiot."

"Yeah," I shook my head ruefully. "That's Dave for sure."

"I would trust him with my life any day," the Verd announced unexpectedly. "He is a fine soldier, and a decent person." His expression changed and I couldn't read it. "Oddly, I consider Czajka to be my best friend."

"Wow," I was taken aback, both by what he said, and the fact that he said it. "Yeah, he is-"

"If you tell him what I said, puny human," he bent his neck to loom over me. "I will snap your neck like a dry twig. Sir."

"Uh, yeah," I stopped walking, as we had reached the hatch to Skippy's mancave. "Hey, I'm glad we had this little talk."

Jates just grunted.

"Uh, you, uh," I sputtered, gesturing toward the open hatch. "You go first, please."

The reason Skippy wanted to meet Jates in his escape pod was that the Verd would have to bend down to get through the hatch, even though it had been designed for the Maxolhx. Once inside, Jates would feel confined and intimidated, according to Skippy. I had told him that his reasoning was full of shit, but he wouldn't listen to me. So, I went along with his plan, just to see the train wreck firsthand.

Without a word, Jates ducked and entered the hatchway, and I followed.

Once inside, the Verd stoically took a seat, his eyes taking in the sparse surroundings, then focusing on the only object that did not obviously belong. "Colonel Bishop," he pointed to the silver cylinder that was resting upright in a foam cradle. "You brought me here to meet a can?"

"Most people call me a *beer* can," Skippy spoke, and his canister glowed blue. He didn't do the glowing thing much anymore, now that he had an avatar. Blue meant he was happy, if my memory is correct. "Though that is a human beverage."

"I know what 'beer' is," Jates's expression did not change. "David Czjaka is part-owner of a beer factory on Pradassis."

"That type of facility is called a 'brewery', and the planet's correct name is either 'Gehtanu' or 'Paradise'," Skippy said to correct our guest, because he knew that people just *love* to be told they said something wrong.

"Thank you for clarifying that," Jates said without his expression changing, except a blood vessel in his forehead throbbed.

"You are welcome," Skippy pulsed a soft blue again. "It is my pleasure, no, my *duty*, to help flawed biological beings achieve better utilization of their limited intellect."

"I appreciate that." Now Jates's jaw was definitely clenching, and I am not an expert on the body language of his species.

"I am not a mere vessel for mildly alcoholic beverages," Skippy continued, because he was already batting a thousand. "I am an Elder AI. Although the term 'artificial' is itself only an artificial construct."

"An *Elder* AI?" Skippy's revelation got a clear reaction from the Verd.

"Yes. I know, you are awed by being in my presence. Do not feel that you are especially unworthy, all biologicals have the same reaction to my awesomeness. Also, do not be afraid. Unworthy though you may be, I am here to help you, and-"

"Then, the current situation in the galaxy is *your* fault," the surgun growled.

"Um, I, uh, what?" Skippy sputtered, his canister pulsing multiple colors.

"The Elders," Jates sat forward on his seat. "Left the galaxy, without securing their very dangerous toys. They took no responsibility for those who came after, though they *did* leave their killing machines active, to punish those who dared approach their level of technology."

"Um, well, that is not exactly, um- Joe, tell him!"

"Don't look at me," I held up my hands. "I *agree* with Jates."

"But, but, you know nothing about me. I am a supremely-"

"You, and your kind, are supremely *irresponsible*. This war has gone on forever, and has killed, or caused suffering and misery, for *trillions* of intelligent beings. The Elders, and their trinkets," he jabbed a claw-tipped finger at Skippy, "could have prevented, or stopped, the conflict, but they do not *care*."

"Hey! This is not, um, er, you are here to be awed by me! To experience wonderment, to bask in my glory."

"Will you accept *disgust* instead, you pathetic overgrown toaster?"

"*TOASTER*?" Skippy screeched, loud enough to be painful. "I am not going to stand for being insulted by a big, scaly, stinky lizard!"

Jates stood, a hand darted out and snatched Skippy's canister from its holder. Holding the can in both hands, he began twisting the top.

"*HEY*! What are you *doing*? Don't touch me! Joe, he can't touch me!"

"Well, he already did, so-" I shrugged.

"How does this lid come off?" Jates addressed the question to me.

Skippy's shout drowned me out. "You put me down *right this instant*! I demand-"

Jates grunted with effort. "I am going to tear this lid off, and take a big, stinky lizard *dump* in your can," he growled.

"Hey! Hey! Joe, get him *off* of me!"

Slowly, I backed out the hatchway. "Don't look at me, this was *your* idea. You two crazy kids have fun, and don't break the furniture."

As I walked away, whistling a happy tune, I heard the ongoing struggle between a supremely intelligent, supremely clueless being on one side, and a supremely pissed-off lizard on the other.

My money was on Jates.

CHAPTER THIRTY SEVEN

Emily Perkins put both hands over her mouth in shock. It took her a moment before she could speak. Her face was pale, and her hands shook. We were in my office, and I had just told her that she had, unknowingly, interfered in our operations. When she did speak, her words came out in a harsh whisper. "Colonel Bishop, I am *so* sorry. I ruined your plan. I, I could have ruined *everything*. For everyone."

"You *should* be sorry," Skippy sniffed. "You ruined Joe's plan. Joe doesn't often make plans, he usually just wings it and hopes for the best."

"Skippy," I waved a hand for him to cool it.

He ignored me. "That time, Joe not only had a plan to deal with the immediate problem, he had a *long-term* strategy. Most of the time, Joe doesn't even react until a problem is sitting on his chest and burping in his face. I swear, he-"

"Uh, thanks for the vote of confidence, Skippy. That's, that's really great. Perkins, listen, you don't-"

"No, Joe. Give yourself some credit," he insisted. "You not only had an actual plan, you had a plan that even I called. The. *Greatest.* Plan. In. History. Really, think about it: *I* was impressed. That *never* happens."

"Yeah, we get the idea, OK? Stop badgering her about it." Holding up a hand to stop Skippy from talking, I leaned forward across the desk and softened my voice. "Perkins, you made the best decision you could have, based on what you knew at the time. Hell, if I had thought of suggesting a group of beetles hitch a ride to Earth on a Maxolhx ship, I would have patted myself on the back. That was a pretty freakin' great idea."

"Thank you, Sir," she didn't smile, but the skin around her eyes relaxed.

"I do have a question. Many questions, actually, but I'll only ask one now. What was your plan, when the beetles returned from Earth?" My question made her uncomfortable, and I don't think that was only because of the unpleasant subject. She didn't have a plan, was my guess. From what I knew of her, she expected better of herself: Emily Perkins was always supposed to have a plan.

"That depended on what they reported," she said.

"You didn't have a master plan to free Earth from the Kristang?" I asked hopefully. Not hopeful the way you probably think. My hope was that she *didn't* have such a plan. Because, for years, I had tried to think of a plan to do that, and I had nothing, until we stumbled across a cache of hell-weapons. If she had a brilliant and totally obvious plan, I was going to feel like an idiot.

"No. The idea was just to know, to *know* what was happening at Earth. Maybe, I thought if the White Wind clan was behaving badly, badly even compared to the standards of the Maxolhx, the kitties could set things right."

"Right, like, humans would be slaves, instead of extinct?"

"Either way, it's not an optimal result."

"It would have put you in one hell of an uncomfortable position, though."

"How so?"

I shrugged. "If communication with Earth was restored, and our people were nder the control of the White Wind clan, the governments of Earth would have rdered UNEF on Paradise to resist the Ruhar. You had already set up the Alien ,egion, to fight *for* the Ruhar. You would be a criminal, a traitor to humanity."

"A traitor to the *lizards*," she corrected my statement. "I did think about that, ir. It would not have changed anything. The human side of the Legion would have •een like the Verds. Considered traitors by our own people, but holding onto our .eal culture. That's all academic now, I don't think it is useful to engage in 'What fs'."

"That's OK. I was curious, that's all."

"What's next, Sir?"

"Next? We have some errands to run before we head back to Earth. We will •e stopping at Paradise."

"To bring people home?"

"Eventually, probably. We can't fit many people aboard *Valkyrie*, any major effort to bring the Force back from Paradise will have to wait until we can secure ransport. I expect we will make a deal to charter transport ships," I said as if that vould be easy. Maybe Perkins could help me with that, because I had only a vague 10tion of how to go about it. "The Force on Paradise could actually expand,)verall."

She raised one eyebrow. "Expand?"

"Yes. The people on Paradise will want to go home," I studied her expression 1s I said that. Not everyone on Paradise would want to go back to Earth, not)ermanently. Some people had created a life for themselves on that adopted world. Vlet someone, gotten married, started a family. Grown a business, built a house. Those were just the people who left the military to explore civilian life. "But not all)f them."

"No. Not all," she agreed, and I couldn't tell if she included herself and Dave Czajka in that group. Maybe she didn't know, either for herself or for Dave. They)robably hadn't time to discuss it yet.

"I expect UNEF on Earth will want to ship units out to Paradise, to maintain a)resence there. That is one hell of a long distance to rotate battalions in and out, but the action is out here."

"The action?"

"The Legion, I mean. That's not going to shut down, right? Plenty of lizards out here need killing, and they won't do it all by themselves."

"Lizards are the *best* at killing lizards. We are fortunate they got themselves into a civil war, or they would have been able to concentrate their resources on-What?" She saw me squirming in my chair.

"Uh, that civil war? It wasn't an accident. We sort of, started it."

"You- Sir, every time I think there aren't any more surprises, there are."

"Like I said, it is a *long* story." I glanced at my phone. "We are scheduled for lunch in the galley soon, we should-"

"Sir? Can I ask one question, before we go?" Sometimes, when people say they want to ask a question, they are just looking for information. Sometimes, people say that when they think you are doing something wrong, and they ask the question so they can tell you what they think. With Perkins, I suspected it was the latter.

"Shoot."

"Mutual Assured Destruction."

"I know. It's a dangerous game."

"The Elder weapons are a double-edged sword, you realize that?" She did the eyebrow thing at me.

"Perkins," I looked at my phone again. "I'm hungry and people are waiting for us in the galley. How about you just say whatever it is you want to say?"

"The two apex species have maintained a balance of power in the galaxy for millennia, but that hasn't stopped conflict. The war has gone on longer, and is more vicious, *because* the two powers at the top can't engage in all-out warfare."

"I understand that. We have thrown the galaxy into chaos, and it's going to get worse before it gets better."

"That's true. We need to be *very* careful. The strategic math has changed. The Rindhalu and the Maxolhx will both be worried that we will ally with the other side."

"Huh." Shit. I hadn't thought of that. In my defense, the whole having-Elder-weapons thing was still new to me. But, it was really new to Perkins, and she understood the strategic implications. Maybe *she* should have the keys to the weapons. "Only Nixon could go to China, something like that?"

"Yes, but- Sir. At some point, if either of the apex species get pushed too far, and have their backs against the wall, they could decide that resetting the clock is their best option."

I had no idea what she meant. "Reset the clock?"

"The Maxolhx, for example, could put a small number of their people into hibernation, then attack us and the Rindhalu with their Elder weapons. Sentinels would devastate the galaxy, but the Maxolhx could come out of hiding in a hundred thousand years, and have total supremacy."

"Whoa. They would allow their entire civilization to be wiped out? Who would do that?"

"Someone who wanted their civilization to survive, to be the *only* survivors."

"I can't believe anyone would do that."

"It only takes a small, dedicated group of fanatics, who have access to dangerous technology."

"Shit." Suddenly, I was no longer hungry. "The word 'fanatics' describes the Maxolhx. Maybe the spiders, too, we haven't met them. Perkins, how do horrible ideas like that get inside your head?"

"*Someone* on our side needs to think about it, Sir. The bad guys are certainly thinking about it. Did you ever read 'Wool'? The Silo series?"

"Uh, no, I don't think so."

"You should. My point is, we can't allow either of the apex species to get pushed to the point where they think they have nothing to lose."

"*Damn* it," I glared at her, though she was only the bearer of bad news, not the source. "Skippy keeps reminding me that the most dangerous force in the galaxy is the Law of Unintended Consequences."

"That sounds about right," she nodded. "Time for lunch, Sir?" She asked, though I knew that her own body clock must have told her it was approaching midnight. That's what happened when a person flew aboard a starship from one planet to another, where the local sun not only rose at a different time, the duration of a planetary day could be radically longer or shorter than on the home world. 'Star lag' was even worse than jet lag.

"After you ruined my appetite?" I scowled at her.

"Maybe we could try one of these delicious 'sludges' I've heard about."

"Ha! Your idea that someone might deliberately call in Sentinels is hard to swallow, but easier than swallowing one of Skippy's banana-flavored sludges," I stuck out my tongue.

She cocked her head at me. "Banana? Why-"

"Skippy thinks that monkeys love bananas," I rolled my eyes. "Like I said, it's a *long* story."

She stood up and smiled at me, sort of in a motherly, protective way, but something else. Something that felt good. Respect. Mutual respect. We understood each other. Perkins and I might make a great team someday.

If the galaxy didn't explode first.

"You got anything stronger than soda aboard this bucket, Sir?" She asked. "I don't know about you, but I could use a drink."

THE END
- To be continued in
ExForce Book11: BRUSHFIRE
and
ExForce Mavericks Book3: BREAKAWAY

Printed in Great Britain
by Amazon